The Brethren

John Grisham

THE
BRETHREN

THE
SUMMONS

C

Published by Century in 2004

Copyright © 2004 by Belfry Holdings, Inc.

John Grisham has asserted his right under
the Copyright, Designs and Patents Act, 1988 to be identified
as the author of this work

The Brethren First published in the United Kingdom
in 2000 by Century
The Summons First published in the United Kingdom
in 2002 by Century

Century
The Random House Group Limited
20 Vauxhall Bridge Road, London, SW1V 2SA

Random House Australia (Pty) Limited
20 Alfred Street, Milsons Point, Sydney,
New South Wales 2061, Australia

Random House New Zealand Limited
18 Poland Road, Glenfield
Auckland 10, New Zealand

Random House (Pty) Limited
Endulini, 5a Jubilee Road, Parktown 2193, South Africa

The Random House Group Limited Reg. No. 954009

www.randomhouse.co.uk

A CIP catalogue record for this book
is available from the British Library

Papers used by Random House are natural, recyclable
products made from wood grown in sustainable forests. The
manufacturing processes conform to the environmental
regulations of the country of origin

ISBN 0 09 1904064

Typeset by Deltatype Ltd, Birkenhead, Merseyside
Printed and bound in Great Britain by
Mackays of Chatham, PLC

THE BRETHREN

ONE

For the weekly docket the court jester wore his standard garb of well-used and deeply faded maroon pajamas and lavender terry-cloth shower shoes with no socks. He wasn't the only inmate who went about his daily business in his pajamas, but no one else dared wear lavender shoes. His name was T. Karl, and he'd once owned banks in Boston.

The pajamas and shoes weren't nearly as troubling as the wig. It parted at the middle and rolled in layers downward, over his ears, with tight curls coiling off into three directions, and fell heavily onto his shoulders. It was a bright gray, almost white, and fashioned after the Old English magistrate's wigs from centuries earlier. A friend on the outside had found it at a secondhand costume store in Manhattan, in the Village.

T. Karl wore it to court with great pride, and, odd as it was, it had, with time, become part of the show. The other inmates kept their distance from T. Karl anyway, wig or not.

He stood behind his flimsy folding table in the prison cafeteria, tapped a plastic mallet that served

1

as a gavel, cleared his squeaky throat, and announced with great dignity: 'Hear ye, hear ye, hear ye. The Inferior Federal Court of North Florida is now in session. Please rise.'

No one moved, or at least no one made an effort to stand. Thirty inmates lounged in various stages of repose in plastic cafeteria chairs, some looking at the court jester, some chatting away as if he didn't exist.

T. Karl continued: 'Let all ye who search for justice draw nigh and get screwed.'

No laughs. It had been funny months earlier when T. Karl first tried it. Now it was just another part of the show. He sat down carefully, making sure the rows of curls bouncing upon his shoulders were given ample chance to be seen, then he opened a thick red leather book which served as the official record for the court. He took his work very seriously.

Three men entered the room from the kitchen. Two of them wore shoes. One was eating a saltine. The one with no shoes was also bare-legged up to his knees, so that below his robe his spindly legs could be seen. They were smooth and hairless and very brown from the sun. A large tattoo had been applied to his left calf. He was from California.

All three wore old church robes from the same choir, pale green with gold trim. They came from the same store as T. Karl's wig, and had been presented by him as gifts at Christmas. That was how he kept his job as the court's official clerk.

There were a few hisses and jeers from the spectators as the judges ambled across the tile floor, in full regalia, their robes flowing. They took

2

their places behind a long folding table, near T. Karl but not too near, and faced the weekly gathering. The short round one sat in the middle. Joe Roy Spicer was his name, and by default he acted as the Chief Justice of the tribunal. In his previous life, Judge Spicer had been a Justice of the Peace in Mississippi, duly elected by the people of his little county, and sent away when the feds caught him skimming bingo profits from a Shriners club.

'Please be seated,' he said. Not a soul was standing.

The judges adjusted their folding chairs and shook their robes until they fell properly around them. The assistant warden stood to the side, ignored by the inmates. A guard in uniform was with him. The Brethren met once a week with the prison's approval. They heard cases, mediated disputes, settled little fights among the boys, and had generally proved to be a stabilizing factor amid the population.

Spicer looked at the docket, a neat hand-printed sheet of paper prepared by T. Karl, and said, 'Court shall come to order.'

To his right was the Californian, the Honorable Finn Yarber, age sixty, in for two years now with five to go for income tax evasion. A vendetta, he still maintained to anyone who would listen. A crusade by a Republican governor who'd managed to rally the voters in a recall drive to remove Chief Justice Yarber from the California Supreme Court. The rallying point had been Yarber's opposition to the death penalty, and his high-handedness in delaying every execution. Folks wanted blood,

3

Yarber prevented it, the Republicans whipped up a frenzy, and the recall was a smashing success. They pitched him onto the street, where he floundered for a while until the IRS began asking questions. Educated at Stanford, indicted in Sacramento, sentenced in San Francisco, and now serving his time at a federal prison in Florida.

In for two years and Finn was still struggling with the bitterness. He still believed in his own innocence, still dreamed of conquering his enemies. But the dreams were fading. He spent a lot of time on the jogging track, alone, baking in the sun and dreaming of another life.

'First case is Schneiter versus Magruder,' Spicer announced as if a major antitrust trial was about to start.

'Schneiter's not here,' Beech said.

'Where is he?'

'Infirmary. Gallstones again. I just left there.'

Hatlee Beech was the third member of the tribunal. He spent most of his time in the infirmary because of hemorrhoids, or headaches, or swollen glands. Beech was fifty-six, the youngest of the three, and with nine years to go he was convinced he would die in prison. He'd been a federal judge in East Texas, a hardfisted conservative who knew lots of Scripture and liked to quote it during trials. He'd had political ambitions, a nice family, money from his wife's family's oil trust. He also had a drinking problem which no one knew about until he ran over two hikers in Yellowstone. Both died. The car Beech had been driving was owned by a young lady he was not married to. She was found naked in the front seat, too drunk to walk.

4

They sent him away for twelve years.

Joe Roy Spicer, Finn Yarber, Hatlee Beech. The Inferior Court of North Florida, better known as the Brethren around Trumble, a minimum security federal prison with no fences, no guard towers, no razor wire. If you had to do time, do it the federal way, and do it in a place like Trumble.

'Should we default him?' Spicer asked Beech.

'No, just continue it until next week.'

'Okay. I don't suppose he's going anywhere.'

'I object to a continuance,' Magruder said from the crowd.

'Too bad,' said Spicer. 'It's continued until next week.'

Magruder was on his feet. 'That's the third time it's been continued. I'm the plaintiff. I sued him. He runs to the infirmary every time we have a docket.'

'What're ya'll fightin over?' Spicer asked.

'Seventeen dollars and two magazines,' T. Karl said helpfully.

'That much, huh?' Spicer said. Seventeen dollars would get you sued every time at Trumble.

Finn Yarber was already bored. With one hand he stroked his shaggy gray beard, and with the other he raked his long fingernails across the table. Then he popped his toes, loudly, crunching them into the floor in an efficient little workout that grated on the nerves. In his other life, when he had titles – Mr. Chief Justice of the California Supreme Court – he often presided while wearing leather clogs, no socks, so that he could exercise his toes during the dull oral arguments. 'Continue it,' he said.

5

'Justice delayed is justice denied,' Magruder said solemnly.

'Now that's original,' said Beech. 'One more week, then we'll default Schneiter.'

'So ordered,' Spicer said, with great finality. T. Karl made a note in the docket book. Magruder sat down in a huff. He'd filed his complaint in the Inferior Court by handing to T. Karl a one-page summary of his allegations against Schneiter. Only one page. The Brethren didn't tolerate paperwork. One page and you got your day in court. Schneiter had replied with six pages of invective, all of which had been summarily stricken by T. Karl.

The rules were kept simple. Short pleadings. No discovery. Quick justice. Decisions on the spot, and all decisions were binding if both parties submitted to the jurisdiction of the court. No appeals; there was nowhere to take one. Witnesses were not given an oath to tell the truth. Lying was completely expected. It was, after all, a prison.

'What's next?' Spicer asked.

T. Karl hesitated for a second, then said, 'It's the Whiz case.'

Things were suddenly still for a moment, then the plastic cafeteria chairs rattled forward in one noisy offensive. The inmates scooted and shuffled until T. Karl announced, 'That's close enough!' They were less than twenty feet away from the bench.

'We shall maintain decorum!' he proclaimed.

The Whiz matter had been festering for months at Trumble. Whiz was a young Wall Street crook who'd bilked some rich clients. Four million dollars had never been accounted for, and legend held that Whiz had stashed it offshore and managed it from inside Trumble. He had six years left, and would be almost forty when paroled. It was widely assumed that he was quietly serving his time until one glorious day when he would walk free, still a young man, and fly off in a private jet to a beach where the money was waiting.

Inside, the legend only grew, partly because Whiz kept to himself and spent long hours every day studying financials and technical charts and reading impenetrable economic publications. Even the warden had tried to cajole him into sharing market tips.

An ex-lawyer known as Rook had somehow got next to Whiz, and had somehow convinced him to share a small morsel of advice with an investment club that met once a week in the prison chapel. On behalf of the club, Rook was now suing the Whiz for fraud.

Rook took the witness chair, and began his narrative. The usual rules of procedure and evidence were dispensed with so that the truth could be arrived at quickly, whatever form it might take.

'So I go to the Whiz and I ask him what he thinks about ValueNow, a new online company I read about in *Forbes*,' Rook explained. 'It was about to go public, and I liked the idea behind the company. Whiz said he'd check it out for me. I heard nothing. So I went back to him and said, "Hey, Whiz, what about ValueNow?" And he said he thought it was a solid company and the stock would go through the roof.'

'I did not say that,' the Whiz inserted quickly.

He was seated across the room, by himself, his arms folded over the chair in front.

'Yes you did.'

'I did not.'

'Anyway, I go back to the club and tell them that Whiz is high on the deal, so we decide we want to buy some stock in ValueNow. But little guys can't buy because the offering is closed. I go back to Whiz over there and I say, "Look, Whiz, you think you could pull some strings with your buddies on Wall Street and get us a few shares of ValueNow?" And Whiz said he thought he could do that.'

'That's a lie,' said Whiz.

'Quiet,' said Justice Spicer. 'You'll get your chance.'

'He's lying,' Whiz said, as if there was a rule against it.

If Whiz had money, you'd never know it, at least not on the inside. His eight-by-twelve cell was bare except for stacks of financial publications. No stereo, fan, books, cigarettes, none of the usual assets acquired by almost everyone else. This only added to the legend. He was considered a miser, a weird little man who saved every penny and was no doubt stashing everything offshore.

'Anyway,' Rook continued, 'we decided to gamble by taking a big position in ValueNow. Our strategy was to liquidate our holdings and consolidate.'

'Consolidate?' asked Justice Beech. Rook sounded like a portfolio manager who handled billions.

'Right, consolidate. We borrowed all we could

8

from friends and family, and had close to a thousand bucks.'

'A thousand bucks,' repeated Justice Spicer. Not bad for an inside job. 'Then what happened?'

'I told Whiz over there that we were ready to move. Could he get us the stock? This was on a Tuesday. The offering was on a Friday. Whiz said no problem. Said he had a buddy at Goldman Sux or some such place that could take care of us.'

'That's a lie,' Whiz shot from across the room.

'Anyway, on Wednesday I saw Whiz in the east yard, and I asked him about the stock. He said no problem.'

'That's a lie.'

'I got a witness.'

'Who?' asked Justice Spicer.

'Picasso.'

Picasso was sitting behind Rook, as were the other six members of the investment club. Picasso reluctantly waved his hand.

'Is that true?' Spicer asked.

'Yep,' Picasso answered. 'Rook asked about the stock. Whiz said he would get it. No problem.'

Picasso testified in a lot of cases, and had been caught lying more than most inmates.

'Continue,' Spicer said.

'Anyway, Thursday I couldn't find Whiz any-where. He was hiding from me.'

'I was not.'

'Friday, the stock goes public. It was offered at twenty a share, the price we could've bought it for if Mr. Wall Street over there had done what he promised. It opened at sixty, spent most of the day at eighty, then closed at seventy. Our plans were to

9

sell it as soon as possible. We could've bought fifty shares at twenty, sold them at eighty, and walked away from the deal with three thousand dollars in profits.'

Violence was very rare at Trumble. Three thousand dollars would not get you killed, but some bones might be broken. Whiz had been lucky so far. There'd been no ambush.

'And you think the Whiz owes you these lost profits?' asked ex-Chief Justice Finn Yarber, now plucking his eyebrows.

'Damned right we do. Look, what makes the deal stink even worse is that Whiz bought Value-Now for himself.'

'That's a damned lie,' Whiz said.

'Language, please,' Justice Beech said. If you wanted to lose a case before the Brethren, just offend Beech with your language.

The rumors that Whiz had bought the stock for himself had been started by Rook and his gang. There was no proof of it, but the story had proved irresistible and had been repeated by most inmates so often that it was now established as fact. It fit so nicely.

'Is that all?' Spicer asked Rook.

Rook had other points he wanted to elaborate on, but the Brethren had no patience with windy litigants. Especially ex-lawyers still reliving their glory days. There were at least five of them at Trumble, and they seemed to be on the docket all the time.

'I guess so,' Rook said.

'What do you have to say?' Spicer asked the Whiz.

10

Whiz stood and took a few steps toward their table. He glared at his accusers, Rook and his gang of losers. Then he addressed the court. 'What's the burden of proof here?'

Justice Spicer immediately lowered his eyes and waited for help. As a Justice of the Peace, he'd had no legal training. He'd never finished high school, then worked for twenty years in his father's country store. That's where the votes came from. Spicer relied on common sense, which was often at odds with the law. Any questions dealing with legal theory would be handled by his two colleagues.

'It's whatever we say it is,' Justice Beech said, relishing a debate with a stockbroker on the court's rules of procedure.

'Clear and convincing proof?' asked the Whiz.

'Could be, but not in this case.'

'Beyond a reasonable doubt?'

'Probably not.'

'Preponderance of the evidence?'

'Now you're getting close.'

'Then, they have no proof,' the Whiz said, waving his hands like a bad actor in a bad TV drama.

'Why don't you just tell us your side of the story?' said Beech.

'I'd love to. ValueNow was a typical online offering, lots of hype, lots of red ink on the books. Sure Rook came to me, but by the time I could make my calls, the offering was closed. I called a friend who told me you couldn't get near the stock. Even the big boys were shut out.'

'Now, how does that happen?' asked Justice Yarber.

11

The room was quiet. The Whiz was talking money, and everyone was listening.

'Happens all the time in IPOs. That's initial public offerings.'

'We know what an IPO is,' Beech said.

Spicer certainly did not. Didn't have many of those back in rural Mississippi.

The Whiz relaxed, just a little. He could dazzle them for a moment, win this nuisance of a case, then go back to his cave and ignore them.

'The ValueNow IPO was handled by the investment banking firm of Bakin-Kline, a small outfit in San Francisco. Five million shares were offered. Bakin-Kline basically presold the stock to its preferred customers and friends, so that most big investment firms never had a shot at the stock. Happens all the time.'

The judges and the inmates, even the court jester, hung on every word.

He continued. 'It's silly to think that some disbarred yahoo sitting in prison, reading an old copy of *Forbes*, can somehow buy a thousand dollars' worth of ValueNow.'

And at that very moment it did indeed seem very silly. Rook fumed while his club members began quietly blaming him.

'Did you buy any of it?' asked Beech.

'Of course not. I couldn't get near it. And besides, most of the high-tech and online companies are built with funny money. I stay away from them.'

'What do you prefer?' Beech asked quickly, his curiosity getting the better of him.

'Value. The long haul. I'm in no hurry. Look,

this is a bogus case brought by some boys looking for an easy buck.' He waved toward Rook, who was sinking in his chair. The Whiz sounded perfectly believable and legitimate.

Rook's case was built on hearsay, speculation, and the corroboration of Picasso, a notorious liar.

'You got any witnesses?' Spicer asked.

'I don't need any,' the Whiz said and took his seat.

Each of the three justices scribbled something on a slip of paper. Deliberations were quick, verdicts instantaneous. Yarber and Beech slid theirs to Spicer, who announced, 'By a vote of two to one, we find for the defendant. Case dismissed. Who's next?'

The vote was actually unanimous, but every verdict was officially two to one. That allowed each of the three a little wiggle room if later confronted.

But the Brethren were well regarded around Trumble. Their decisions were quick and as fair as they could make them. In fact, they were remarkably accurate in light of the shaky testimony they often heard. Spicer had presided over small cases for years, in the back of his family's country store. He could spot a liar at fifty feet. Beech and Yarber had spent their careers in courtrooms, and had no tolerance for lengthy arguments and delays, the usual tactics.

'That's all today,' T. Karl reported. 'End of docket.'

'Very well. Court is adjourned until next week.'

T. Karl jumped to his feet, his curls again vibrating across his shoulders, and declared, 'Court's adjourned. All rise.'

13

No one stood, no one moved as the Brethren left the room. Rook and his gang were huddled, no doubt planning their next lawsuit. The Whiz left quickly.

The assistant warden and the guard eased away without being seen. The weekly docket was one of the better shows at Trumble.

TWO

Though he'd served in Congress for fourteen years, Aaron Lake still drove his own car around Washington. He didn't need or want a chauffeur, or an aide, or a bodyguard. Sometimes an intern would ride with him and take notes, but for the most part Lake enjoyed the tranquillity of sitting in D.C. traffic while listening to classical guitar on the stereo. Many of his friends, especially those who'd achieved the status of a Mr. Chairman or a Mr. Vice Chairman, had larger cars with drivers. Some even had limos.

Not Lake. It was a waste of time and money and privacy. If he ever sought higher office, he certainly didn't want the baggage of a chauffeur wrapped around his neck. Besides, he enjoyed being alone. His office was a madhouse. He had fifteen people bouncing off the walls, answering phones, opening files, serving the folks back in Arizona who'd sent him to Washington. Two more did nothing but raise money. Three interns managed to further clog his narrow corridors and take up more time than they deserved.

He was single, a widower, with a quaint little

15

townhouse in Georgetown that he was very fond of. He lived quietly, occasionally stepping into the social scene that had attracted him and his late wife in the early years.

He followed the Beltway, the traffic slow and cautious because of a light snow. He was quickly cleared through CIA security at Langley, and was very pleased to see a preferred parking space waiting for him, along with two plainclothes security personnel.

'Mr. Maynard is waiting,' one of them said gravely, opening his car door while the other took his briefcase. Power did have its perks.

Lake had never met with the CIA director at Langley. They'd conferred twice on the Hill, years earlier, back when the poor guy could get around. Teddy Maynard was in a wheelchair and in constant pain, and even senators got themselves driven out to Langley anytime he needed them. He'd called Lake a half-dozen times in fourteen years, but Maynard was a busy man. His light-lifting was usually handled by associates.

Security barriers collapsed all around the congressman as he and his escorts worked their way into the depths of the CIA headquarters. By the time Lake arrived at Mr. Maynard's suite, he was walking a bit taller, with just a trace of a swagger. He couldn't help it. Power was intoxicating.

Teddy Maynard had sent for him.

Inside the room, a large, square, windowless place known unofficially as the bunker, the Director was sitting alone, looking blankly at a large screen upon which the face of Congressman Aaron Lake was

16

frozen. It was a recent photo, one taken at a black-tie fund-raiser three months earlier where Lake had half a glass of wine, ate baked chicken, no dessert, drove himself home, alone, and went to bed before eleven. The photo was appealing because Lake was so attractive – light red hair with almost no gray, hair that was not colored or tinted, a full hairline, dark blue eyes, square chin, really nice teeth. He was fifty-three years old and aging superbly. He did thirty minutes a day on a rowing machine and his cholesterol was 160. They hadn't found a single bad habit. He enjoyed the company of women, especially when it was important to be seen with one. His steady squeeze was a sixty-year-old widow in Bethesda whose late husband had made a fortune as a lobbyist.

Both his parents were dead. His only child was a schoolteacher in Santa Fe. His wife of twenty-nine years had died in 1996 of ovarian cancer. A year later, his thirteen-year-old spaniel died too, and Congressman Aaron Lake of Arizona truly lived alone. He was Catholic, not that that mattered anymore, and he attended Mass at least once a week. Teddy pushed the button and the face disappeared.

Lake was unknown outside the Beltway, primarily because he'd kept his ego in check. If he had aspirations to higher office, they were closely guarded. His name had been mentioned once as a potential candidate for governor of Arizona, but he enjoyed Washington too much. He loved George-town – the crowds, the anonymity, the city life – good restaurants and cramped bookstores and espresso bars. He liked theater and music, and he

17

and his late wife had never missed an event at the Kennedy Center.

On the Hill, Lake was known as a bright and hardworking congressman who was articulate, fiercely honest, and loyal, conscientious to a fault. Because his district was the home of four large defense contractors, he had become an expert on military hard-ware and readiness. He was Chairman of the House Committee on Armed Services, and it was in that capacity that he had come to know Teddy Maynard.

Teddy pushed the button again, and there was Lake's face. For a fifty-year veteran of intelligence wars, Teddy seldom had a knot in his stomach. He'd dodged bullets, hidden under bridges, frozen in mountains, poisoned two Czech spies, shot a traitor in Bonn, learned seven languages, fought the cold war, tried to prevent the next one, had more adventures than any ten agents combined, yet looking at the innocent face of Congressman Aaron Lake he felt a knot.

He – the CIA – was about to do something the agency had never done before.

They'd started with a hundred senators, fifty governors, four hundred and thirty-five congressmen, all the likely suspects, and now there was only one. Representative Aaron Lake of Arizona.

Teddy flicked a button and the wall went blank. His legs were covered with a quilt. He wore the same thing every day – a V-necked navy sweater, white shirt, subdued bow tie. He rolled his wheelchair to a spot near the door, and prepared to meet his candidate.

★

18

During the eight minutes Lake was kept waiting, he was served coffee and offered a pastry, which he declined. He was six feet tall, weighed one-seventy, was fastidious about his appearance, and had he taken the pastry Teddy would've been surprised. As far as they could tell, Lake never ate sugar. Never.

His coffee was strong, though, and as he sipped it he reviewed a little research of his own. The purpose of the meeting was to discuss the alarming flow of black market artillery into the Balkans. Lake had two memos, eighty pages of double-spaced data he'd crunched until two in the morning. He wasn't sure why Mr. Maynard wanted him to appear at Langley to discuss such a matter, but he was determined to be prepared.

A soft buzzer sounded, the door opened, and the Director of the CIA rolled out, wrapped in a quilt and looking every day of his seventy-four years. His handshake was firm, though, probably because of the strain of pushing himself around. Lake followed him back into the room, leaving the two college-educated pit bulls to guard the door.

They sat opposite each other, across a very long table that ran to the end of the room where a large white wall served as a screen. After brief preliminaries, Teddy pushed a button and another face appeared. Another button, and the lights grew dim. Lake loved it – push little buttons, high-tech images flash instantly. No doubt the room was wired with enough electronic junk to monitor his pulse from thirty feet.

'Recognize him?' Teddy asked.

'Maybe. I think I've seen the face before.'

'He's Natli Chenkov. A former general. Now a member of what's left of the Russian parliament.'

'Also known as Natty,' Lake said proudly.

'That's him. Hard-line Communist, close ties to the military, brilliant mind, huge ego, very ambitious, ruthless, and right now the most dangerous man in the world.'

'Didn't know that.'

A flick, another face, this one of stone under a gaudy military parade hat. 'This is Yuri Goltsin, second in command of what's left of the Russian army. Chenkov and Goltsin have big plans.' Another flick, a map of a section of Russia north of Moscow. 'They're stockpiling arms in this region,' Teddy said. 'They're actually stealing them from themselves, looting the Russian army, but, and more important, they're buying them on the black market.'

'Where's their money coming from?'

'Everywhere. They're swapping oil for Israeli radar. They're trafficking in drugs and buying Chinese tanks through Pakistan. Chenkov has close ties with some mobsters, one of whom recently bought a factory in Malaysia where they make nothing but assault rifles. It's very elaborate. Chenkov has a brain, a very high IQ. He's probably a genius.'

Teddy Maynard was a genius, and if he bestowed that title on another, then Congressman Lake certainly believed it. 'So who gets attacked?'

Teddy dismissed the question because he wasn't ready to answer it. 'See the town of Vologda. It's about five hundred miles east of Moscow. Last week we tracked sixty Vetrov to a warehouse there. As you know, the Vetrov –'

'Is equivalent to our Tomahawk Cruise, but two feet longer.'

'Exactly. That makes three hundred they've moved in during the last ninety days. See the town of Rybinsk, just southwest of Vologda?'

'Known for its plutonium.'

'Yes, tons of it. Enough to make ten thousand nuclear warheads. Chenkov and Goltsin and their people control the entire area.'

'Control?'

'Yes, through a web of regional mobsters and local army units. Chenkov has his people in place.'

'In place for what?'

Teddy squeezed a button and the wall was blank. But the lights stayed dim, so that when he spoke across the table he did so almost from the shadows. 'The coup is right around the corner, Mr. Lake. Our worst fears are coming true. Every aspect of Russian society and culture is cracking and crumbling. Democracy is a joke. Capitalism is a nightmare. We thought we could McDonaldize the damned place, and it's been a disaster. Workers are not getting paid, and they're the lucky ones because they have jobs. Twenty percent do not. Children are dying because there are no medicines. So are many adults. Ten percent of the population are homeless. Twenty percent are hungry. Each day things get worse. The country has been looted by the mobsters. We think at least five hundred billion dollars has been stolen and taken out of the country. There's no relief in sight. The time is perfect for a new strongman, a new

21

dictator who'll promise to lead the people back to stability. The country is crying for leadership, and Mr. Chenkov has decided it's up to him.'

'And he has the army.'

'He has the army, and that's all it takes. The coup will be bloodless because the people are ready for it. They'll embrace Chenkov. He'll lead the parade into Red Square and dare us, the United States, to stand in his way. We'll be the bad guys again.'

'So the cold war is back,' Lake said, his words fading at the end.

'There'll be nothing cold about it. Chenkov wants to expand, to recapture the old Soviet Union. He desperately needs cash, so he'll simply take it in the form of land, factories, oil, crops. He'll start little regional wars, which he'll easily win.' Another map appeared. Phase One of the new world order was presented to Lake. Teddy didn't miss a word. 'I suspect he'll roll through the Baltic States, toppling governments in Estonia, Latvia, Lithuania, etc. Then he'll go to the old Eastern bloc and strike a deal with some of the Communists there.'

The congressman was speechless as he watched Russia expand. Teddy's predictions were so certain, so precise.

'What about the Chinese?' Lake asked.

But Teddy wasn't finished with Eastern Europe. He flicked; the map changed. 'Here's where we get sucked in.'

'Poland?'

'Yep. Happens every time. Poland is now a member of NATO, for some damned reason.

22

Imagine that. Poland signing on to help protect us and Europe. Chenkov solidifies Russia's old turf, and casts a longing eye westward. Same as Hitler, except he was looking to the east.'

'Why would he want Poland?'

'Why did Hitler want Poland? It was between him and Russia. He hated the Poles, and he was ready to start a war. Chenkov doesn't give a damn about Poland, he just wants to control it. And he wants to destroy NATO.'

'He's willing to risk a third world war?'

Buttons were pushed; the screen became a wall again; lights came on. The audiovisuals were over and it was time for an even more serious conversation. Pain shot through Teddy's legs, and he couldn't keep from frowning.

'I can't answer that,' he said. 'We know a lot, but we don't know what the man's thinking. He's moving very quietly, putting people in place, setting things up. It's not completely unexpected, you know.'

'Of course not. We've had these scenarios for the last eight years, but there's always been hope that it wouldn't happen.'

'It's happening, Congressman. Chenkov and Goltsin are eliminating their opponents as we speak.'

'What's the timetable?'

Teddy shifted again under the quilt, tried another position to stop the pain. 'It's difficult to say. If he's smart, which he certainly is, he'll wait until there's rioting in the streets. I think that a year from now Natty Chenkov will be the most famous man in the world.'

23

'A year,' Lake said to himself, as if he'd just been given his own death sentence.

There was a long pause as he contemplated the end of the world. Teddy certainly let him. The knot in Teddy's stomach was significantly smaller now. He liked Lake a lot. He was indeed very handsome, and articulate, and smart. They'd made the right choice.

He was electable.

After a round of coffee and a phone call Teddy had to take – it was the Vice President – they reconvened their little conference and moved forward. The congressman was pleased that Teddy had so much time for him. The Russians were coming, yet Teddy seemed so calm.

'I don't have to tell you how unprepared our military is,' he said gravely.

'Unprepared for what? For war?'

'Perhaps. If we are unprepared, then we could well have a war. If we are strong, we avoid war. Right now the Pentagon could not do what it did in the Gulf War in 1991.'

'We're at seventy percent,' Lake said with authority. This was his turf.

'Seventy percent will get us a war, Mr. Lake. A war we cannot win. Chenkov is spending every dime he can steal on new hardware. We're cutting budgets and depleting our military. We want to push buttons and launch smart bombs so that no American blood is shed. Chenkov will have two million hungry soldiers, anxious to fight and die if necessary.'

For a brief moment Lake felt proud. He'd had

the guts to vote against the last budget deal because it decreased military spending. The folks back home were upset about it. 'Can't you expose Chenkov now?' he asked.

'No. Absolutely not. We have excellent intelligence. If we react to him, then he'll know that we know. It's the spy game, Mr. Lake. It's too early to make him a monster.'

'So what's your plan?' Lake asked boldly. It was quite presumptuous to ask Teddy about his plans. The meeting had accomplished its purpose. One more congressman had been sufficiently briefed. At any moment Lake could be asked to leave so that another committee chairman of some variety could be shown in.

But Teddy had big plans, and he was anxious to share them. 'The New Hampshire primary is two weeks away. We have four Republicans and three Democrats all saying the same thing. Not a single candidate wants to increase defense spending. We have a budget surplus, miracle of all miracles, and everyone has a hundred ideas about how to spend it. A bunch of imbeciles. Just a few years ago we had huge budget deficits, and Congress spent money faster than it could be printed. Now there's a surplus. They're gorging themselves on the pork.'

Congressman Lake looked away for a second, then decided to let it pass.

'Sorry about that,' Teddy said, catching himself. 'Congress as a whole is irresponsible, but we have many fine congressmen.'

'You don't have to tell me.'

'Anyway, the field is crowded with a bunch of

25

clones. Two weeks ago we had different front-runners. They're slinging mud and knifing each other, all for the benefit of the country's forty-fourth largest state. It's silly.' Teddy paused and grimaced and tried to reshift his useless legs. 'We need someone new, Mr. Lake, and we think that someone is you.'

Lake's first reaction was to suppress a laugh, which he did by smiling, then coughing. He tried to compose himself, and said, 'You must be kidding.'

'You know I'm not kidding, Mr. Lake,' Teddy said sternly, and there was no doubt that Aaron Lake had walked into a well-laid trap.

Lake cleared his throat and completed the job of composing himself. 'All right, I'm listening.'

'It's very simple. In fact, its simplicity makes it beautiful. You're too late to file for New Hampshire, and it doesn't matter anyway. Let the rest of the pack slug it out there. Wait until it's over, then startle everyone by announcing your candidacy for President. Many will ask, "Who the hell is Aaron Lake?" And that's fine. That's what we want. They'll find out soon enough.

'Initially, your platform will have only one plank. It's all about military spending. You're a doomsayer, with all sorts of dire predictions about how weak our military is becoming. You'll get everybody's attention when you call for doubling our military spending.'

'Doubling?'

'It works, doesn't it? It got your attention. Double it during your four-year term.'

'But why? We need more military spending, but a twofold increase would be excessive.'

'Not if we're facing another war, Mr. Lake. A war in which we push buttons and launch Tomahawk missiles by the thousands, at a million bucks a pop. Hell, we almost ran out of them last year in that Balkan mess. We can't find enough soldiers and sailors and pilots, Mr. Lake. You know this. The military needs tons of cash to recruit young men. We're low on everything – soldiers, missiles, tanks, planes, carriers. Chenkov is building now. We're not. We're still downsizing, and if we keep it up through another Administration, then we're dead.'

Teddy's voice rose, almost in anger, and when he stopped with 'we're dead,' Aaron Lake could almost feel the earth shake from the bombing.

'Where does the money come from?' he asked.

'Money for what?'

'The military.'

Teddy snorted in disgust, then said, 'Same place it always comes from. Need I remind you, sir, that we have a surplus?'

'We're busy spending the surplus.'

'Of course you are. Listen, Mr. Lake, don't worry about the money. Shortly after you announce, we'll scare the hell out of the American people. They'll think you're half-crazy at first, some kind of wacko from Arizona who wants to build even more bombs. But we'll jolt them. We'll create a crisis on the other side of the world, and suddenly Aaron Lake will be called a visionary. Timing is everything. You make a speech about how weak we are in Asia, few people listen. Then

27

we'll create a situation over there that stops the world, and suddenly everyone wants to talk to you. It will go on like that, throughout the campaign. We'll build the tension on this end. We'll release reports, create situations, manipulate the media, embarrass your opponents. Frankly, Mr. Lake, I don't expect it to be that difficult.'

'You sound like you've been here before.'

'No. We've done some unusual things, all in an effort to protect this country. But we've never tried to swing a presidential election.' Teddy said this with an air of regret.

Lake slowly pushed his chair back, stood, stretched his arms and legs, and walked along the table to the end of the room. His feet were heavier. His pulse was racing. The trap had been sprung; he'd been caught.

He returned to his seat. 'I don't have enough money,' he offered across the table. He knew it was received by someone who'd already thought about it.

Teddy smiled and nodded and pretended to give this some thought. Lake's Georgetown home was worth $400,000. He kept about half that much in mutual funds and another $100,000 in municipal bonds. There were no significant debts. He had $40,000 in his reelection account.

'A rich candidate would not be attractive,' Teddy said, then reached for yet another button. Images returned to the wall, sharp and in color. 'Money will not be a problem, Mr. Lake,' he said, his voice much lighter. 'We'll get the defense contractors to pay for it. Look at that,' he said, waving with his right hand as if Lake wasn't sure

28

what to look at. 'Last year the aerospace and defense industry did almost two hundred billion in business. We'll take just a fraction of that.'

'How much of a fraction?'

'As much as you need. We can realistically collect a hundred million dollars from them.'

'You also can't hide a hundred million dollars.'

'Don't bet on it, Mr. Lake. And don't worry about it. We'll take care of the money. You make the speeches, do the ads, run the campaign. The money will pour in. By the time November gets here, the American voters will be so terrified of Armageddon they won't care how much you've spent. It'll be a landslide.'

So Teddy Maynard was offering a landslide. Lake sat in a stunned but giddy silence and gawked at all that money up there on the wall – $194 billion, defense and aerospace. Last year's military budget was $270 billion. Double that to $540 billion in four years, and the contractors would get fat again. And the workers! Wages soaring through the roof! Jobs for everyone!

Candidate Lake would be embraced by executives with the cash and unions with the votes. The initial shock began to fade, and the simplicity of Teddy's plan became clear. Collect the cash from those who will profit. Scare the voters into racing to the polls. Win in a landslide. And in doing so save the world.

Teddy let him think for a moment, then said, 'We'll do most of it through PACs. The unions, engineers, executives, business coalitions – there's no shortage of political groups already on the books. And we'll form some others.'

29

Lake was already forming them. Hundreds of PACs, all flush with more cash than any election had ever seen. The shock was now completely gone, replaced by the sheer excitement of the idea. A thousand questions raced through his mind: Who'll be my Vice President? Who'll run the campaign? Chief of staff? Where to announce? 'It might work,' he said, under control.

'Oh yes. It'll work, Mr. Lake. Trust me. We've been planning this for some time.'

'How many people know about it?'

'Just a few. You've been carefully chosen, Mr. Lake. We examined many potential candidates, and your name kept rising to the top. We've checked your background.'

'Pretty dull, huh?'

'I suppose. Although your relationship with Ms. Valotti concerns me. She's been divorced twice and likes painkillers.'

'Didn't know I had a relationship with Ms. Valotti.'

'You've been seen with her recently.'

'You guys are watching, aren't you?'

'You expect something less?'

'I guess not.'

'You took her to a black-tie cry-a-thon for oppressed women in Afghanistan. Gimme a break.' Teddy's words were suddenly short and dripping with sarcasm.

'I didn't want to go.'

'Then don't. Stay away from that crap. Leave it for Hollywood. Valotti's nothing but trouble.'

'Anybody else?' Lake asked, more than a little defensive. His private life had been pretty dull

30

since he'd become a widower. He was suddenly proud of it.

'Not really,' Teddy said. 'Ms. Benchly seems to be quite stable and makes a lovely escort.'

'Oh, thank you very much.'

'You'll get hammered on abortion, but you won't be the first.'

'It's a tired issue,' Lake said. And he was tired of grappling with it. He'd been for abortions, against abortions, soft on reproductive rights, tough on reproductive rights, pro-choice, pro-child, anti-women, embraced by the feminists. In his fourteen years on Capitol Hill he'd been chased all over the abortion minefield, getting bloodied with each new strategic move.

Abortion didn't scare him anymore, at least not at the moment. He was much more concerned with the CIA sniffing through his background.

'What about GreenTree?' he asked.

Teddy waved his right hand as if it was nothing. 'Twenty-two years ago. Nobody got convicted. Your partner went bankrupt and got himself indicted, but the jury let him walk. It'll come up; everything will come up. But frankly, Mr. Lake, we'll keep the attention diverted elsewhere. There's an advantage in jumping in at the last minute. The press won't have too much time to dig up dirt.'

'I'm single. We've elected an unmarried president only once.'

'You're a widower, the husband of a very lovely lady who was well respected both here and back home. It won't be an issue. Trust me.'

'So what worries you?'

31

'Nothing, Mr. Lake. Not a thing. You're a solid candidate, very electable. We'll create the issues and the fear, and we'll raise the money.'

Lake stood again, walked around the room rubbing his hair, scratching his chin, trying to clear his head. 'I have a lot of questions,' he said.

'Maybe I can answer some of them. Let's talk again tomorrow, right here, same time. Sleep on it, Mr. Lake. Time is crucial, but I suppose a man should have twenty-four hours before making such a decision.' Teddy actually smiled when he said this.

'That's a wonderful idea. Let me think about it. I'll have an answer tomorrow.'

'No one knows we've had this little chat.'

'Of course not.'

THREE

In terms of space, the law library occupied exactly one fourth of the square footage of the entire Trumble library. It was in a corner, partitioned off by a wall of red brick and glass, tastefully done at taxpayer expense. Inside the law library, shelves of well-used books stood packed together with barely enough room for an inmate to squeeze between them. Around the walls were desks covered with typewriters and computers and sufficient research clutter to resemble any big-firm library.

The Brethren ruled the law library. All inmates were allowed to use it, of course, but there was an unwritten policy that one needed permission to stay there for any length of time. Maybe not permission, but at least notice.

Justice Joe Roy Spicer of Mississippi earned forty cents an hour sweeping the floors and straightening the desks and shelves. He also emptied the trash, and was generally considered to be a pig when it came to his menial tasks. Justice Hatlee Beech of Texas was the official law librarian, and at fifty cents an hour was the highest paid. He was fastidious about 'his volumes,' and often bickered with Spicer about their care. Justice Finn Yarber, once of the California Supreme Court, was paid twenty cents an hour as a computer technician. His pay was at the bottom of the scale because he knew so little about computers.

On a typical day, the three spent between six and eight hours in the law library. If a Trumble inmate had a legal problem, he simply made an appointment with one of the Brethren and visited their little suite. Hatlee Beech was an expert on sentencing and appeals. Finn Yarber did bankruptcies, divorces, and child support cases. Joe Roy Spicer, with no formal legal training, had no real specialty. Nor did he want one. He ran the scams.

Strict rules prohibited the Brethren from charging fees for their legal work, but the strict rules meant little. They were, after all, convicted felons, and if they could quietly pick up some cash on the outside then everyone would be happy. Sentencing was a moneymaker. About a fourth of the inmates who arrived at Trumble had been improperly sentenced. Beech could review the records overnight and find the loopholes. A month earlier, he had knocked four years off the sentence of a young man who'd been given fifteen. The family had agreed to pay, and the Brethren earned $5,000, their biggest fee to date. Spicer arranged the secret deposit through their lawyer in Neptune Beach.

There was a cramped conference room in the back of the law library, behind the shelves and barely visible from the main room. The door to it had a large glass window, but no one bothered to look in. The Brethren retired there for quiet business. They called it their chamber.

34

Spicer had just met with their lawyer and he had mail, some really good letters. He closed the door and removed an envelope from a file. He waved it for Beech and Yarber to see. 'It's yellow,' he said. 'Ain't that sweet? It's for Ricky.'

'Who's it from?' Yarber asked.

'Curtis from Dallas.'

'The banker?' Beech asked excitedly.

'No, Curtis owns the jewelry stores. Listen.' Spicer unfolded the letter, also on soft yellow stationery. He smiled and cleared his throat and began to read: ' "Dear Ricky: Your letter of January eighth made me cry. I read it three times before I put it down. You poor boy. Why are they keeping you there?" '

'Where is he?' asked Yarber.

'Ricky's locked down in a fancy drug rehab unit his rich uncle is paying for. He's been in for a year, is clean and fully rehabbed, but the terrible people who run the place won't release him until April because they've been collecting twenty thousand dollars a month from his rich uncle, who just wants him locked away and won't send any spending money. Do you remember any of this?'

'Now I do.'

'You helped with the fiction. May I proceed?'

'Please do.'

Spicer continued reading: ' "I'm tempted to fly down there and confront those evil people myself. And your uncle, what a loser! Rich people like him think they can just send money and not get involved. As I told you, my father was quite wealthy, and he was the most miserable person I've ever known. Sure he bought me things – objects

35

that were temporary and meant nothing when they were gone. But he never had time for me. He was a sick man, just like your uncle. I've enclosed a check for a thousand dollars if you need anything from the commissary.

' "Ricky, I can't wait to see you in April. I've already told my wife that there is an international diamond show in Orlando that month, and she has no interest in going with me." '

'April?' asked Beech.

'Yep. Ricky is certain he will be released in April.'

'Ain't that sweet,' Yarber said with a smile. 'And Curtis has a wife and kids?'

'Curtis is fifty-eight, three adult children, two grandchildren.'

'Where's the check?' asked Beech.

Spicer flipped the sheets of stationery and went to page two. ' "We have to make certain you can meet me in Orlando," ' he read. ' "Are you sure you'll finally be released in April? Please tell me you will. I think about you every hour. I keep your photo hidden in my desk drawer, and when I look into your eyes I know that we should be together." '

'Sick, sick, sick,' Beech said, still smiling. 'And he's from Texas.'

'I'm sure there are a lot of sweet boys in Texas,' Yarber said.

'And none in California?'

'The rest of it is just mush,' Spicer said, scanning quickly. There would be plenty of time to read it later. He held up the $1,000 check for his colleagues to see. In due course, it would be

36

smuggled out to their attorney and he would deposit it in their hidden account.

'When are we gonna bust him?' Yarber asked.

'Let's swap a few more letters. Ricky needs to share some more misery.'

'Maybe one of the guards could beat him up, or something like that,' Beech said.

'They don't have guards,' replied Spicer. 'It's a designer rehab clinic, remember? They have counselors.'

'But it's a lockdown facility, right? That means gates and fences, so surely there's a guard or two around. What if Ricky got attacked in the shower or the locker room by some goon who wanted his body?'

'It can't be a sexual attack,' Yarber said. 'That might scare Curtis. He might think Ricky caught a disease or something.'

And so the fiction went for a few minutes as they created more misery for poor Ricky. His picture had been lifted from the bulletin board of a fellow inmate, copied at a quick print by their lawyer, and had now been sent to more than a dozen pen pals across North America. The photo was of a smiling college grad, in a navy robe with a cap and gown, holding a diploma, a very handsome young man.

It was decided that Beech would work on the new story for a few days, then write a rough draft of the next letter to Curtis. Beech was Ricky, and at that moment their little tormented fictional boy was writing his tales of misery to eight different caring souls. Justice Yarber was Percy, also a young man locked away for drugs but now clean and nearing release and looking for an older sugar

37

daddy with whom to spend meaningful time. Percy had five hooks in the water, and was slowly reeling them in.

Joe Roy Spicer didn't write very well. He coordinated the scam, helped with the fiction, kept the stories straight, and met with the lawyer who brought the mail. And he handled the money.

He pulled out another letter and announced, 'This, Your Honors, is from Quince.'

Everything stopped as Beech and Yarber stared at the letter. Quince was a wealthy banker in a small town in Iowa, according to the six letters he and Ricky had swapped. Like the rest, they'd found him through the personals of a gay magazine now hidden in the law library. He'd been their second catch, the first having become suspicious and disappearing. Quince's photo of himself was a snapshot taken at a lake, with the shirt off, the potbelly, the skinny arms, the receding hairline of a fifty-one-year-old – his family all around him. It was a bad photo, no doubt selected by Quince because it might be difficult to identify him, if anyone ever tried.

'Would you like to read it, Ricky boy?' Spicer asked, handing the letter to Beech, who took it and looked at the envelope. Plain white, no return address, typed lettering.

'Have you read it?' Beech asked.

'No. Go ahead.'

Beech slowly removed the letter, a plain sheet of white paper with tight single-spaced paragraphs produced by an old typewriter. He cleared his voice, and read: ' "Dear Ricky: It's done. I can't believe I did it, but I pulled it off. I used a pay

38

phone and a money order so nothing could be traced – I think my trail is clean. The company you suggested in New York was superb, very discreet and helpful. I have to be honest, Ricky, it scared the hell out of me. Booking a gay cruise is something I never dreamed of doing. And you know what? It was exhilarating. I am so proud of myself. We have a cabin suite, a thousand bucks a night, and I can't wait." '

Beech stopped and glanced above his reading glasses halfway down his nose. Both of his colleagues were smiling, savoring the words.

He continued: ' "We set sail on March tenth, and I have a wonderful idea. I will arrive in Miami on the ninth, so we won't have much time to get together and introduce ourselves. Let's meet on the boat, in our suite. I'll get there first, check in, get the champagne on ice, then wait for you. Won't that be fun, Ricky? We'll have three days to ourselves. I say we don't leave the room." '

Beech couldn't help but smile, and he somehow managed to do so while shaking his head in disgust.

He continued: ' "I am so excited about our little trip. I have finally decided to discover who I really am, and you've given me the courage to take the first step. Though we haven't met, Ricky, I can never thank you enough.

' "Please write me back immediately and confirm. Take care, my Ricky. Love, Quince." '

'I think I'm gonna vomit,' Spicer said, but he wasn't convincing. There was too much to do.

'Let's bust him,' Beech said. The others quickly agreed.

39

'How much?' asked Yarber.

'At least a hundred thousand,' said Spicer. 'His family has owned banks for two generations. We know his father is still active in the business, so you have to figure the old man might go nuts if his boy gets outed. Quince can't afford to get booted from the family gravy train, so he'll pay whatever we demand. It's a perfect situation.'

Beech was already taking notes. So was Yarber. Spicer began pacing around the small room like a bear stalking prey. The ideas came slowly, the language, the opinions, the strategy, but before long the letter took shape.

In rough draft, Beech read it: '"Dear Quince: So nice to get your letter of January fourteenth. I'm so happy you got the gay cruise booked. It sounds delightful. One problem, though. I won't be able to make it, and there are a couple of reasons for this. One is that I won't be released for a few more years. I'm in a prison, not a drug treatment clinic. And I'm not gay, far from it. I have a wife and two kids, and right now they're having a difficult time financially because I'm sitting here in prison, unable to support them. That's where you come in, Quince. I need some of your money. I want a hundred thousand dollars. We can call it hush money. You send it, and I'll forget the Ricky business and the gay cruise and no one in Bakers, Iowa, will ever know anything about it. Your wife and your children and your father and the rest of your rich family will never know about Ricky. If you don't send the money, then I'll flood your little town with copies of our letters.

'"It's called extortion, Quince, and you're

40

caught. It's cruel and mean and criminal, and I don't care. I need money, and you have it." '

Beech stopped and looked around the room for approval.

'It's beautiful,' said Spicer, already spending the loot.

'It's nasty,' said Yarber. 'But what if he kills himself?'

'That's a long shot,' said Beech.

They read the letter again, then debated whether the timing was right. They did not mention the illegality of their scam, or the punishment if they got caught. Those discussions had been laid to rest months earlier when Joe Roy Spicer had convinced the other two to join him. The risks were insignificant when weighed against the potential returns. The Quinces who got themselves snared were not likely to run to the police and complain of extortion.

But they hadn't busted anyone yet. They were corresponding with a dozen or so potential victims, all middle-aged men who'd made the mistake of answering this simple ad:

> SWM in 20s looking for kind and
> discreet gentleman in 40s or 50s
> to pen pal with.

One little personal in small print in the back of a gay magazine had yielded sixty responses, and Spicer had the chore of sifting through the rubbish and identifying rich targets. At first he'd found the work disgusting, then he became amused by it. Now it was a business because they were about to

41

extort a hundred thousand bucks from a perfectly innocent man.

Their lawyer would take a third, the usual cut but a frustrating percentage nonetheless. They had no choice. He was a critical player in their crimes.

They worked on the letter to Quince for an hour, then agreed to sleep on it and do a final draft the next day. There was another letter from a man using the pseudonym of Hoover. It was his second, written to Percy, and rambled on for four paragraphs about bird-watching. Yarber would be forced to study birds before writing back as Percy and professing a great interest in the subject. Evidently, Hoover was afraid of his shadow. He revealed nothing personal, and there was no indication of money.

Give him some more rope, the Brethren decided. Talk about birds, then try to nudge him to the subject of physical companionship. If Hoover didn't take the hint, and if he didn't reveal something about his financial situation, then they'd drop him.

Within the Bureau of Prisons, Trumble was officially referred to as a camp. Such a designation meant there were no fences around the grounds, no razor wire, no watchtowers, no guards with rifles waiting to nail escapees. A camp meant minimum security, so that any inmate could simply walk away if he chose. There were a thousand at Trumble, but few walked away.

It was nicer than most public schools. Air-conditioned dorms, clean cafeteria serving three squares a day, a weight room, billiards, cards,

42

racquetball, basketball, volleyball, jogging track, library, chapel, ministers on duty, counselors, caseworkers, unlimited visiting hours.

Trumble was as good as it could get for prisoners, all of whom were classified as low risk. Eighty percent were there for drug crimes. About forty had robbed banks without hurting or really scaring anyone. The rest were white-collar types whose crimes ranged from small-time scams to Dr. Floyd, a surgeon whose office had bilked Medicare out of $6 million over two decades.

Violence was not tolerated at Trumble. Threats were rare. There were plenty of rules and the administration had little trouble enforcing them. If you screwed up, they sent you away, to a medium-security prison, one with razor wire and rough guards.

Trumble's prisoners were content to behave themselves and count their days, the federal way.

Pursuing serious criminal activity on the inside was unheard of, until the arrival of Joe Roy Spicer. Before his fall, Spicer had heard stories about the Angola scam, named for the infamous Louisiana state penitentiary. Some inmates there had perfected the gay-extortion scheme, and before they were caught they had fleeced their victims of $700,000.

Spicer was from a rural county near the Louisiana line, and the Angola scam was a notorious affair in his part of the state. He never dreamed he'd copy it. But he woke up one morning in a federal pen, and decided to shaft every living soul he could get close enough to.

He walked the track every day at 1 P.M., usually

43

alone, always with a pack of Marlboros. He hadn't smoked for ten years before his incarceration; now he was up to two packs a day. So he walked to negate the damage to his lungs. In thirty-four months he'd walked 1,242 miles. And he'd lost twenty pounds, though probably not from exercise, as he liked to claim. The prohibition against beer was more responsible for the weight loss.

Thirty-four months of walking and smoking, twenty-one months to go.

Ninety thousand dollars of the stolen bingo money was literally buried in his backyard, a half a mile behind his house next to a toolshed – entombed in a homemade concrete vault his wife knew nothing about. She'd helped him spend the rest of the loot, $180,000 altogether, though the feds had traced only half of it. They'd bought Cadillacs and flown to Las Vegas, first class out of New Orleans, and they'd been driven around by casino limos and put up in suites.

If he had any dreams left, one was to be a professional gambler, headquartered out of Vegas but known and feared by casinos everywhere. Blackjack was his game, and though he'd lost a ton, he was still convinced he could beat any house. There were casinos in the Caribbean he'd never seen. Asia was heating up. He'd travel the world, first class, with or without his wife, stay in fancy suites, order room service, and terrorize any blackjack dealer dumb enough to deal him cards.

He'd take the $90,000 from his backyard, add it to his share of the Angola scam, and move to Vegas. With or without her. She hadn't been to Trumble in four months, although she used to

44

come every three weeks. He had nightmares of her plowing up the backyard looking for his buried treasure. He was almost convinced she didn't know about the money, but there was room for doubt. He'd been drinking two nights before being shipped off to prison, and had said something about the $90,000. He couldn't remember his exact words. Try as he might, he simply could not recall what he'd told her.

He lit another Marlboro at mile one. Maybe she had a boyfriend now. Rita Spicer was an attractive woman, a little chunky in places but nothing $90,000 couldn't hide. What if she and a new squeeze had found the money and were already spending it? One of Joe Roy's worst recurring nightmares was a scene from a bad movie – Rita and some unknown male with shovels digging like idiots in the rain. Why the rain, he didn't know. But it was always at night, in the middle of a thunderstorm, and the lightning would flash and he would see them slogging their way through the backyard, each time getting nearer and nearer to the toolshed.

In one dream the new mystery boyfriend was on a bulldozer, pushing piles of dirt all over the Spicer farm while Rita stood nearby, pointing here and there with her shovel.

Joe Roy craved the money. He could feel the cash in his hands. He would steal and extort all he could while he counted his days at Trumble, then he would rescue his buried loot and head for Vegas. No one in his hometown would have the pleasure of pointing and whispering and saying,

45

'There's old Joe Roy. Guess he's out of the pen now.' No sir.

He'd be living the high life. With or without her.

FOUR

Teddy looked at his pill bottles lined along the edge of his table, like little executioners ready to take away his misery. York was seated across from him, reading from his notes.

York said, 'He was on the phone until three this morning, talking to friends in Arizona.'

'Who?'

'Bobby Lander, Jim Gallison, Richard Hassel, the usual gang. His money people.'

'Dale Winer?'

'Yes, him too,' York said, amazed at Teddy's recall. Teddy had his eyes closed now, and was rubbing his temples. Somewhere between them, somewhere deep in his brain, he knew the names of Lake's friends, his contributors, his confidants, his poll workers, and his old high school teachers. All of it neatly tucked away, ready to be used if necessary.

'Anything unusual?'

'No, not really. Just the typical questions you'd expect from a man contemplating such an unexpected move. His friends were surprised, even

47

shocked, and somewhat reluctant, but they'll come around.'

'Did they ask about money?'

'Of course. He was vague, said it would not be a problem, though. They are skeptical.'

'Did he keep our secrets?'

'He certainly did.'

'Was he worried about us listening?'

'I don't think so. He made eleven calls from his office and eight from his home. None from his cell phones.'

'Faxes? E-mail?'

'None. He spent two hours with Schiara, his –'

'Chief of staff.'

'Right. They basically planned the campaign. Schiara wants to run it. They like Nance of Michigan as VP.'

'Not a bad choice.'

'He looks fine. We're already checking him. Had a divorce when he was twenty-three, but that was thirty years ago.'

'Not a problem. Is Lake ready to commit?'

'Oh yes. He's a politician, isn't he? He's been promised the keys to the kingdom. He's already writing speeches.'

Teddy removed a pill from a bottle and swallowed it without the aid of anything liquid. He frowned as if it was bitter. He squeezed the wrinkles in his forehead and said, 'York, tell me we're not missing anything on this guy. No skeletons.'

'No skeletons, Chief. We've examined his dirty underwear for six months. There's nothing that can hurt us.'

48

'He's not going to marry some fool, is he?'

'No. He dates several women, but nothing serious.'

'No sex with his interns?'

'None. He's clean.'

They were repeating a dialogue they'd had many times. Once more wouldn't hurt.

'No shady financial deals from another lifetime?'

'This is his life, Chief. There's nothing back there.'

'Booze, drugs, prescription pills, gambling on the Internet?'

'No sir. He's very clean, sober, straight, bright, pretty remarkable.'

'Let's talk to him.'

Aaron Lake was once again escorted to the same room deep inside Langley, this time with three handsome young men guarding him as if danger lurked at every corner. He walked even quicker than the day before, his head even taller, his back without the slightest curve. His stature was rising by the hour.

Once again he said hello to Teddy and shook his calloused hand, then followed the quilt-laden wheelchair into the bunker and sat across the table. Pleasantries were exchanged. York watched from a room down the hall where three monitors hooked to hidden cameras relayed every word, every movement. Next to York were two men who spent their time studying tapes of people as they talked and breathed and moved their hands and eyes and heads and feet, in an effort to determine what the speakers really meant.

'Did you sleep much last night?' Teddy asked, managing a smile.

'Yes, actually,' Lake lied.

'Good. I take it you're willing to accept our deal.'

'Deal? I didn't know it was exactly a deal.'

'Oh yes, Mr. Lake, it's exactly a deal. We promise to get you elected, and you promise to double defense spending and get ready for the Russians.'

'Then you have a deal.'

'That's good, Mr. Lake. I'm very pleased. You'll make an excellent candidate and a fine President.'

The words rang through Lake's ears, and he couldn't believe them. President Lake. President Aaron Lake. He'd paced the floor until five that morning trying to convince himself that the White House was being offered to him. It seemed too easy.

And as hard as he tried, he couldn't ignore the trappings. The Oval Office. All those jets and helicopters. The world to be traveled. A hundred aides at his beck and call. State dinners with the most powerful people in the world.

And, above all, a place in history.

Oh yes, Teddy had himself a deal.

'Let's talk about the campaign itself,' Teddy said. 'I think you should announce two days after New Hampshire. Let the dust settle. Let the winners get their fifteen minutes and let the losers sling more mud, then announce.'

'That's pretty fast,' Lake said.

'We don't have a lot of time. We ignore New

50

Hampshire and get ready for Arizona and Michigan on February twenty-second. It's imperative that you win those two states. When you do, you establish yourself as a serious candidate, and you're set for the month of March.'

'I was thinking of announcing back home, somewhere in Phoenix.'

'Michigan's better. It's a bigger state, fifty-eight delegates, compared to twenty-four for Arizona. You'll be expected to win at home. If you win in Michigan on the same day, then you're a candidate to be reckoned with. Announce in Michigan first, then do it again hours later in your home district.'

'An excellent idea.'

'There's a helicopter plant in Flint, D-L Trilling. They have a large hangar, four thousand workers. The CEO is a man I can talk to.'

'Book it,' Lake said, certain that Teddy had already chatted with the CEO.

'Can you start filming ads day after tomorrow?'

'I can do anything,' Lake said, settling into the passenger's seat. It was becoming obvious who was driving the bus.

'With your approval, we'll hire an outside consulting group to front the ads and publicity. But we have better people here, and they won't cost you anything. Not that money will be a problem, you understand.'

'I think a hundred million should cover things.'

'It should. Anyway, we'll start working on the TV ads today. I think you'll like them. They're total gloom and doom – the miserable shape of our military, all sorts of threats from abroad. Armageddon, that sort of stuff. They'll scare the hell out of

51

people. We'll plug in your name and face and a few brief words, and in no time you'll be the most famous politician in the country.'

'Fame won't win the election.'

'No, it won't. But money will. Money buys television and polls, and that's all it takes.'

'I'd like to think the message is important.'

'Oh, it is, Mr. Lake, and our message is far more important than tax cuts and affirmative action and abortion and trust and family values and all the other silliness we're hearing. Our message is life and death. Our message will change the world and protect our affluence. That's all we really care about.'

Lake was nodding his agreement. Protect the economy, keep the peace, and American voters would elect anyone. 'I have a good man to run the campaign,' Lake said, anxious to offer something.

'Who?'

'Mike Schiara, my chief of staff. He's my closest adviser, a man I trust implicitly.'

'Any experience on the national level?' Teddy asked, knowing full well there was none.

'No, but he's quite capable.'

'That's fine. It's your campaign.'

Lake smiled and nodded at the same time. That was good to hear. He was beginning to wonder.

'What about Vice President?' Teddy asked.

'I have a couple of names. Senator Nance of Michigan is an old friend. There's also Governor Guyce from Texas.'

Teddy received the names with careful deliberation. Not bad selections, really, though Guyce would never work. He was a rich boy who'd skated through college and golfed through his thirties, then spent a fortune of his father's money to purchase the governor's mansion for four years. Besides, they wouldn't have to worry about Texas.

'I like Nance,' Teddy said.

Then Nance it would be, Lake almost said.

They talked about money for an hour, the first wave from the PACs and how to accept instant millions without creating too much suspicion. Then the second wave from the defense contractors. Then the third wave of cash and other untraceables.

There'd be a fourth wave Lake would never know about. Depending on the polls, Teddy Maynard and his organization would be prepared to literally haul boxes filled with cash into union halls and black churches and white VFWs in places like Chicago and Detroit and Memphis and throughout the Deep South. Working with locals they were already identifying, they would be prepared to buy every vote they could find.

The more Teddy pondered his plan, the more convinced he became that the election would be won by Mr. Aaron Lake.

Trevor's little law office was in Neptune Beach, several blocks from Atlantic Beach, though no one could tell where one beach stopped and the other started. Jacksonville was several miles to the west and creeping toward the sea every minute. The office was a converted summer rental, and from his sagging back porch Trevor could see the beach and the ocean and hear the seagulls. Hard to believe he'd been renting the place for twelve years now.

Early in the lease he'd enjoyed hiding on the porch, away from the phone and the clients, staring endlessly at the gentle waters of the Atlantic two blocks away.

He was from Scranton, and like all snowbirds, he'd finally grown weary of gazing at the sea, roaming the beaches barefoot, and throwing bread crumbs to the birds. Now he preferred to waste time locked in his office.

Trevor was terrified of courtrooms and judges. While this was unusual and even somewhat honorable, it made for a different style of lawyering. It relegated Trevor to paperwork – real estate closings, wills, leases, zoning – all the mundane, nondazzling, smalltime areas of the profession no one told him about in law school. Occasionally he handled a drug case, never one involving a trial, and it was one of his unfortunate clients at Trumble who'd connected him with the Honorable Joe Roy Spicer. In short order he'd become the official attorney for all three – Spicer, Beech, and Yarber. The Brethren, as even Trevor referred to them.

He was a courier, nothing more or less. He smuggled them letters disguised as official legal documents and thus protected by the lawyer-client privilege. And he sneaked their letters out. He gave them no advice, and they sought none. He ran their bank account offshore and handled phone calls from the families of their clients inside Trumble. He fronted their dirty little deals, and in doing so avoided courtrooms and judges and other lawyers, and this suited Trevor just fine.

He was also a member of their conspiracy, easily

indictable should they ever be exposed, but he wasn't worried. The Angola scam was absolutely brilliant because its victims couldn't complain. For an easy fee with potential rewards, he'd gamble with the Brethren.

He eased from his office without seeing his secretary, then sneaked away in his restored 1970 VW Beetle, no air-conditioning. He drove down First Street toward Atlantic Boulevard, the ocean visible through homes and cottages and rentals. He wore old khakis, a white cotton shirt, a yellow bow tie, a blue seersucker jacket, all of it heavily wrinkled. He passed Pete's Bar and Grill, the oldest watering hole along the beaches and his personal favorite even though the college kids had discovered the place. He had an outstanding and very past-due bar tab there of $361, almost all for Coors longnecks and lemon daiquiris, and he really wanted to clear the debt.

He turned west on Atlantic Boulevard, and began fighting the traffic into Jacksonville. He cursed the sprawl and the congestion and the cars with Canadian plates. Then he was on the bypass, north past the airport and soon deep into the flat Florida countryside.

Fifty minutes later he parked at Trumble. You gotta love the federal system, he told himself again. Lots of parking close to the front entrance, nicely landscaped grounds tended daily by the inmates, and modern, well-kept buildings.

He said, 'Hello, Mackey,' to the white guard at the door, and 'Hello, Vince,' to the black one. Rufus at the front desk X-rayed the briefcase while

Nadine did the paperwork for his visit. 'How're the bass?' he asked Rufus.

'Ain't biting,' Rufus said.

No lawyer in the brief history of Trumble had visited as much as Trevor. They took his picture again, stamped the back of his hand with invisible ink, and led him through two doors and a short hallway. 'Hello, Link,' he said to the next guard.

'Mornin, Trevor,' Link said. Link ran the visitors' area, a large open space with lots of padded chairs and vending machines against one wall, a playground for youngsters, and a small outdoor patio where two people could sit at a picnic table and share a moment. It was cleaned and shined and completely empty. It was a weekday. Traffic picked up on Saturdays and Sundays, but for the rest of the time Link observed an empty area.

They went to the lawyers' room, one of several private cubbyholes with doors that shut and windows through which Link could do his observing, if he were so inclined. Joe Roy Spicer was waiting and reading the daily sports section where he played the odds on college basketball. Trevor and Link stepped into the room together, and very quickly Trevor removed two twenty-dollar bills and handed them to Link. The closed-circuit cameras couldn't see them if they did this just inside the door. As part of the routine, Spicer pretended not to see the transaction.

Then the briefcase was opened and Link made a pretense of looking through it. He did this without touching a thing. Trevor removed a large manila envelope which was sealed and marked in bold

56

'Legal Papers.' Link took it and squeezed it to make sure it held only papers and not a gun or a bottle of pills, then he gave it back. They'd done this dozens of times.

Trumble regulations required a guard to be present in the room when all papers were removed and all envelopes were opened. But the two twenties got Link outside where he posted himself at the door because there was simply nothing else to guard at the moment. He knew letters were being passed back and forth, and he didn't care. As long as Trevor didn't traffic in weapons or drugs, Link wouldn't get involved. The place had so many silly regulations anyway. He leaned on the door, with his back to it, and before long was drifting into one of his many horse naps, one leg stiff, the other bent at the knee.

In the lawyers' room, little legal work was being done. Spicer was still absorbed in point spreads. Most inmates welcomed their guests. Spicer only tolerated his.

'Got a call last night from the brother of Jeff Daggett,' Trevor said. 'The kid from Coral Gables.'

'I know him,' Spicer said, finally lowering his newspaper because money was on the horizon. 'He got twelve years in a drug conspiracy.'

'Yep. His brother says that there's this ex-federal judge inside Trumble who's looked over his papers and thinks he might be able to knock off a few years. This judge wants a fee, so Daggett calls his brother, who calls me.' Trevor removed his rumpled blue seersucker jacket and flung it on a chair. Spicer hated his bow tie.

57

'How much can they pay?'

'Have you guys quoted a fee?' Trevor asked.

'Beech may have, I don't know. We try to get five thousand for a two-two-five-five reduction.' Spicer said this as if he had practiced criminal law in the federal courts for years. Truth was, the only time he'd actually seen a federal courtroom was the day he was sentenced.

'I know,' Trevor said. 'I'm not sure they can pay five thousand. The kid had a public defender for a lawyer.'

'Then squeeze whatever you can, but get at least a thousand up front. He's not a bad kid.'

'You're getting soft, Joe Roy.'

'No. I'm getting meaner.'

And in fact he was. Joe Roy was the managing partner of the Brethren. Yarber and Beech had the talent and the training, but they'd been too humiliated by their fall to have any ambition. Spicer, with no training and little talent, possessed enough manipulative skills to keep his colleagues on track. While they brooded, he dreamed of his comeback.

Joe Roy opened a file and withdrew a check. 'Here's a thousand bucks to deposit. Came from a pen pal in Texas named Curtis.'

'What's his potential?'

'Very good, I think. We're ready to bust Quince in Iowa.' Joe Roy withdrew a pretty lavender envelope, tightly sealed and addressed to Quince Garbe in Bakers, Iowa.

'How much?' Trevor asked, taking the envelope.

'A hundred thousand.'

'Wow.'

'He's got it, and he'll pay it. I've given him the wiring instructions. Alert the bank.'

In twenty-three years of practicing law, Trevor had never earned a fee anywhere close to $33,000. Suddenly, he could see it, touch it, and, though he tried not to, he began spending it – $33,000 for doing nothing but shuttling mail.

'You really think this will work?' he asked, mentally paying off the tab at Pete's Bar and telling MasterCard to take this check and shove it. He'd keep the same car, his beloved Beetle, but he might spring for an air conditioner.

'Of course it will,' Spicer said, without a trace of doubt.

He had two more letters, both written by Justice Yarber posing as young Percy in rehab. Trevor took them with anticipation.

'Arkansas is at Kentucky tonight,' Spicer said, returning to his newspaper. 'The line is fourteen. Whatta you think?'

'Much closer than that. Kentucky is very tough at home.'

'Are you in?'

'Are you?'

Trevor had a bookie at Pete's Bar, and though he gambled little he had learned to follow the lead of Justice Spicer.

'I'll put a hundred on Arkansas,' Spicer said.

'I think I will too.'

They played blackjack for half an hour, with Link occasionally glancing in and frowning his disapproval. Cards were prohibited during visitation, but who cared? Joe Roy played the game hard because he was training for his next career. Poker and gin rummy were the favorites in the rec room, and Spicer often had trouble finding a blackjack opponent.

Trevor wasn't particularly good, but he was always willing to play. It was, in Spicer's opinion, his only redeeming quality.

FIVE

The announcement had the festive air of a victory party, with red, white, and blue banners and bunting draped from the ceiling and parade music blasting through the hangar. Every D-L Trilling employee was required to be present, all four thousand of them, and to heighten their spirits they had been promised a full day of extra vacation. Eight hours paid, at an average wage of $22.40, but management didn't care because they had found their man. The hastily built stage was also covered in banners and packed with every suit in the company, all smiling broadly and clapping wildly as the music whipped the crowd into a frenzy. Three days earlier no one had heard of Aaron Lake. Now he was their savior.

He certainly looked like a candidate, with a new slightly trimmer haircut suggested by one consultant and a dark brown suit suggested by another. Only Reagan had been able to wear brown suits, and he'd won two landslides.

When Lake finally appeared, and strode purposefully across the stage, shaking vigorously the hands of corporate honchos he'd never see again, the laborers went wild. The music was carefully ratcheted up a couple of notches by a sound consultant who was a member of a sound team Lake's people had hired for $24,000 for the event. Money was of little concern.

Balloons fell like manna. Some were popped by workers who'd been asked to pop them, so for a few seconds the hangar sounded like the first wave of a ground attack. Get ready for it. Get ready for war. Lake Before It's Too Late.

The Trilling CEO clutched him as if they were fraternity brothers, when in fact they'd met two hours earlier. The CEO then took the podium and waited for the noise to subside. Working with notes he'd been faxed the day before, he began a long-winded and quite generous introduction of Aaron Lake, future President. On cue, the applause interrupted him five times before he finished.

Lake waved like a conquering hero and waited behind the microphone, then with perfect timing stepped forward and said, 'My name is Aaron Lake, and I am now running for President.' More roaring applause. More piped-in parade music. More balloons drifting downward.

When he'd had enough, he launched into his speech. The theme, the platform, the only reason for running was national security, and Lake hammered out the appalling statistics proving just how thoroughly the current Administration had depleted our military. No other issues were really that important, he said bluntly. Lure us into a war we can't win, and we'll forget about the tired old quarrels over abortion, race, guns, affirmative action, taxes. Concerned about family values? Start losing our sons and daughters in combat and you'd see some families with real problems.

Lake was very good. The speech had been written by him, edited by consultants, polished by other professionals, and the night before he'd delivered it to Teddy Maynard, alone, deep inside Langley. Teddy had approved, with minor changes.

Teddy was tucked under his quilts and watching the show with great pride. York was with him, silent as usual. The two often sat alone, staring at screens, watching the world grow more dangerous.

'He's good,' York said quietly at one point.

Teddy nodded, even managing a slight smile.

Halfway through his speech, Lake became wonderfully angry at the Chinese. 'Over a twenty-year period, we allowed them to steal forty percent of our nuclear secrets!' he said, and the laborers hissed.

'Forty percent!' he shouted.

It was closer to fifty, but Teddy chose to downplay it just a little. The CIA had received its share of blame for the Chinese thievery.

For five minutes Aaron Lake blistered the Chinese, and their looting and their unprecedented military buildup. The strategy was Teddy's. Use the Chinese to scare the American voters, not the Russians. Don't tip them. Protect the real threat until later in the campaign.

Lake's timing was near-perfect. His punch line brought down the house. When he promised to double the defense budget in the first four years of his Administration, the four thousand D-L Trilling employees who built military helicopters exploded in a frenzy.

Teddy watched it quietly, very proud of his creation. They had managed to upstage the spectacle in New Hampshire by simply snubbing it. Lake's name had not been on the ballot, and he was the first candidate in decades to be proud of that fact. 'Who needs New Hampshire?' he'd been quoted as saying. 'I'll take the rest of the country.'

Lake signed off amid thunderous applause, and reshook all the hands on the stage. CNN returned to its studio where the talking heads would spend fifteen minutes telling the viewers what they had just witnessed.

On his table, Teddy pushed buttons and the screen changed. 'Here's the finished product,' he said. 'The first installment.'

It was a television ad for candidate Lake, and it began with a brief glimpse of a row of grim Chinese generals standing rigidly at a military parade, watching massive hardware roll by. 'You think the world's a safer place?' a deep, rich ominous voice asked off-camera. Then, glimpses of the world's current madmen, all watching their armies parade by – Hussein, Qaddafi, Milosevic, Kim in North Korea. Even poor Castro, with the last of his ragtag army lumbering through Havana, got a split second of airtime. 'Our military could not now do what it did in 1991 during the Gulf War,' the voice said as gravely as if another war had already been declared. Then a blast, an atomic mushroom, followed by thousands of Indians

64

dancing in the streets. Another blast, and the Pakistanis were dancing next door.

'China wants to invade Taiwan,' the voice continued as a million Chinese soldiers marched in perfect step.'North Korea wants South Korea,' the voice said, as tanks rolled through the DMZ. 'And the United States is always an easy target.'

The voice changed quickly into one with a high pitch, and the ad shifted to a congressional hearing of some sort, with a heavily bemedaled general lecturing some subcommittee. 'You, the Congress,' he was saying, 'spend less on the military each year. This defense budget is smaller than it was fifteen years ago. You expect us to be ready for war in Korea, the Middle East, and now Eastern Europe, yet our budget keeps shrinking. The situation is critical.' The ad went blank, nothing but a dark screen, then the first voice said, 'Twelve years ago there were two superpowers. Now there are none.' The handsome face of Aaron Lake appeared, and the ad finished with the voice saying, 'Lake, Before It's Too Late.'

'I'm not sure I like it,' York said after a pause.

'Why not?'

'It's so negative.'

'Good. Makes you feel uncomfortable, doesn't it?'

'Very much so.'

'Good. We're going to flood television for a week, and I suspect Lake's soft numbers will get even softer. The ads will make people squirm, and they won't like them.'

York knew what was coming. The people would indeed squirm and dislike the ads, then get the hell scared out of them, and Lake would suddenly become a visionary. Teddy was working on the terror.

There were two TV rooms on each wing at Trumble; two small bare rooms where you could smoke and watch whatever the guards wanted you to watch. No remote – they'd tried that at first but it had caused too much trouble. By far the nastiest disagreements occurred when the boys couldn't agree on what to watch. So the guards made the selections.

Rules prohibited inmates from having their own TVs.

The guard on duty happened to like basketball. There was a college game on ESPN, and the room was packed with inmates. Hatlee Beech hated sports, and he sat alone in the other TV room and watched one banal sitcom after another. When he was on the bench and working twelve hours a day, he had never watched television. Who had the time? He'd had an office in his home where he dictated opinions until late while everyone else was glued to prime time. Now, watching the mindless crap, he realized how lucky he'd been. In so many ways.

He lit a cigarette. He hadn't smoked since college, and for the first two months at Trumble he'd resisted the temptation. Now it helped with the boredom, but only a pack a day. His blood pressure was up and down. Heart disease ran in the family. At fifty-six with nine years to go, he would leave in a box, he was certain.

Three years, one month, one week, and Beech

was still counting the days in as opposed to the days to go. Just four years ago he'd been building his reputation as a tough young federal judge who was going places. Four rotten years. When he traveled from one courthouse to the next in East Texas, he did so with a driver, a secretary, a clerk, and a U.S. Marshal. When he walked into a courtroom people stood out of respect. Lawyers gave him high marks for his fairness and hard work. His wife had been an unpleasant woman, but with her family's oil trust he'd managed to live peacefully with her. The marriage was stable, not exactly warm, but with three fine kids in college they had reason to be proud. They had weathered some rough times and were determined to grow old together. She had the money. He had the status. Together they'd raised a family. Where was there to go?

Certainly not to prison.

Four miserable years.

The drinking came from nowhere. Maybe it was pressure from work, maybe it was to escape his wife's bickering. For years, after law school, he'd been a light social drinker, nothing serious. Certainly not a habit. Once when the kids were small, his wife took them to Italy for two weeks. Beech was left alone, which suited him fine. For some reason he could never determine, or remember, he turned to bourbon. Lots of it, and he never stopped. The bourbon became important. He kept it in his study and sneaked it late at night. They had separate beds so he seldom got caught.

The trip to Yellowstone had been a three-day judicial conference. He'd met the young lady in a

67

bar in Jackson Hole. After hours of drinking they made the sad decision to take a ride. While Hatlee drove she took off her clothes, but for no other reason than to just do it. Sex had not been discussed, and at that point he was completely harmless.

The two hikers were from D.C., just college kids returning from the trails. Both died at the scene, slaughtered on the shoulder of a narrow road by a drunken driver who never saw them. The young lady's car was found in a ditch with Beech hugging the steering wheel, unable to remove himself. She was naked and knocked out.

He remembered nothing. When he awoke hours later he saw for the first time the inside of a cell. 'Better get used to it,' the sheriff had said with a sneer.

Beech called in every favor and pulled every string imaginable, all to no avail. Two young people were dead. He'd been caught with a naked woman. His wife had the oil money so his friends ran like scared dogs. In the end, no one stood up for the Honorable Hatlee Beech.

He was lucky to get twelve years. MADD mothers and SADD students protested outside the courthouse when he made his first official appearance. They wanted a life sentence. Life!

He himself, the Honorable Hatlee Beech, was charged with two counts of manslaughter, and there was no defense. There was enough alcohol in his blood to kill the next guy. A witness said he'd been speeding on the wrong side of the road.

Looking back, he'd been lucky his crime was on federal lands. Otherwise he would have been shipped away to some state pen where things were much tougher. Say what you want, but the feds knew how to run a prison.

He smoked alone in the semidarkness, watching prime-time comedy written by twelve-year-olds, and there was a political ad, one of many those days. It was one Beech had never seen, a menacing little segment with a somber voice predicting doom if we didn't hurry and build more bombs. It was very well done, ran for a minute and a half, cost a bundle, and delivered a message no one wanted to hear. Lake Before It's Too Late.

Who the hell's Aaron Lake?

Beech knew his politics. It had been his passion in another life, and at Trumble he was known as a fellow who watched Washington. He was one of the few who cared what happened there.

Aaron Lake? Beech had missed the guy. What an odd strategy, to enter the race as an unknown after New Hampshire. Never a shortage of clowns who want to be President.

Beech's wife kicked him out before he pled guilty to two counts of manslaughter. Quite naturally, she was angrier over the naked woman than the dead hikers. The kids sided with her because she had the money and because he'd screwed up so badly. It was an easy decision on their part. The divorce was final a week after he arrived at Trumble.

His youngest had been to see him twice in three years, one month, and one week. Both visits were on the sly, lest the mother find out about them. She had prohibited the kids from going to Trumble.

69

Then he got sued, two wrongful death cases brought by the families. With no friends willing to step forward, he'd tried to defend himself from prison. But there wasn't much to defend. A judgment of $5 million had been entered against him by the trial court. He appealed from Trumble, lost from Trumble, and appealed again.

In the chair beside him, next to his cigarettes, was an envelope brought earlier by Trevor, the lawyer. The court had rejected his final appeal. The judgment was now written in stone.

Didn't really matter, because he'd also filed for bankruptcy. He'd typed the papers himself in the law library and filed them with a pauper's oath, sent them to the same courthouse in Texas where he was once a god.

Convicted, divorced, disbarred, imprisoned, sued, bankrupt.

Most of the losers at Trumble handled their time because their falls had been so short. Most were repeat offenders who'd blown third and fourth chances. Most liked the damned place because it was better than any other prison they'd visited.

But Beech had lost so much, had fallen so far. Just four years ago he'd had a wife with millions and three kids who loved him and a big home in a small town. He was a federal judge, appointed by the President for life, making $140,000 a year, which was a lot less than her oil royalties but still not a bad salary. He got himself called to Washington twice a year for meetings at Justice. Beech had been important.

An old lawyer friend had been to see him twice,

70

on his way to Miami where he had kids, and he stayed long enough to deliver the gossip. Most of it was worthless, but there was a strong rumor that the ex-Mrs. Beech was now seeing someone else. With a few million bucks and slender hips it was only a matter of time.

Another ad. Lake Before It's Too Late again. This one began with a grainy video of men with guns slithering through the desert, dodging and shooting and undergoing some type of training. Then the sinister face of a terrorist – dark eyes and hair and features, obviously some manner of Islamic radical – and he said in Arabic with English subtitles, 'We will kill Americans wherever we find them. We will die in our holy war against the great Satan.' After that, quick videos of burning buildings. Embassy bombings. A busload of tourists. The remains of a jetliner scattered through a pasture.

A handsome face appeared, Mr. Aaron Lake himself. He looked directly at Hatlee Beech and said, 'I'm Aaron Lake, and you probably don't know me. I'm running for President because I'm scared. Scared of China and Eastern Europe and the Middle East. Scared of a dangerous world. Scared of what's happened to our military. Last year the federal government had a huge surplus, yet spent less on defense than we did fifteen years ago. We're complacent because our economy is strong, but the world today is far more dangerous than we realize. Our enemies are legion, and we cannot protect ourselves. If elected, I will double defense spending during my term of office.'

No smiles, no warmth. Just plain talk from a

71

man who meant what he said. A voice over said, 'Lake, Before It's Too Late.'

Not bad, thought Beech.

He lit another cigarette, his last of the night, and stared at the envelope on the empty chair – $5 million lodged against him by the two families. He'd pay the money if he could. Never saw the kids, not before he killed them. The paper the next day had their happy photos, a boy and a girl. Just college kids, enjoying the summer.

He missed the bourbon.

He could bankrupt half the judgment. The other half was for punitive damages, nonbankruptable. So it would follow wherever he went, which he assumed was nowhere. He'd be sixty-five when his sentence was over, but he'd be dead before then. They'd carry him out of Trumble in a box, send him home to Texas, where they'd bury him behind the little country church where he'd been baptized. Maybe one of the kids would spring for a head-stone.

Beech left the room without turning off the TV. It was almost ten, time for lights-out. He bunked with Robbie, a kid from Kentucky who'd broken into 240 houses before they caught him. He sold the guns and microwaves and stereos for cocaine. Robbie was a four-year veteran of Trumble, and because of his seniority he had chosen the bottom bunk. Beech crawled into the top one, said, 'Good night, Robbie,' and turned off the light.

'Night, Hatlee,' came the soft response.

Sometimes they chatted in the dark. The walls were cinderblock, the door was metal, their words were confined to their little room. Robbie was

72

twenty-five and would be forty-five before he left Trumble. Twenty-four years – one for every ten houses.

The time between bed and sleep was the worst of the day. The past came back with a vengeance – the mistakes, the misery, the could-haves and should-haves. Try as he might, Hatlee could not simply close his eyes and go to sleep. He had to punish himself first. There was a grandchild he'd never seen, and he always started with her. Then his three kids. Forget the wife. But he always thought about her money. And the friends. Ah, the friends. Where were they now?

Three years in, and with no future there was only the past. Even poor Robbie below dreamed of a new beginning at the age of forty-five. Not Beech. At times he almost longed for the warm Texas soil, layered upon his body, behind the little church.

Surely someone would buy him a headstone.

SIX

For Quince Garbe, February 3 would be the worst day of his life. It was almost the last, and it would've been had his doctor been in town. He couldn't get a prescription for sleeping pills, and he didn't have the courage to use a gun on himself.

It began pleasantly enough with a late breakfast, a bowl of oatmeal by the fire in the den, alone. His wife of twenty-six years had already left for town, for another day of charity teas and fund-raising and frantic small-town volunteerism that kept her busy and away from him.

It was snowing when he left their large and pretentious banker's home on the edge of Bakers, Iowa, and drove ten minutes to work in his long black Mercedes, eleven years old. He was an important man about town, a Garbe, a member of a family that had owned the bank for generations. He parked in his reserved spot behind the bank, which faced Main Street, and made a quick detour to the post office, something he did twice a week. For years he'd had a private box there, away from his wife and especially away from his secretary.

Because he was rich and few others were in

Bakers, Iowa, he seldom spoke to people on the street. He didn't care what they thought. They worshiped his father and that was enough to keep their business.

But when the old man died, would he have to change his personality? Would he be forced to smile on the sidewalks of Bakers and join the Rotary Club, the one founded by his grandfather?

Quince was tired of being dependent on the whims of the public for his security. He was tired of relying on his father to keep their customers happy. He was tired of banking and tired of Iowa and tired of snow and tired of his wife, and what Quince wanted more than anything that morning in February was a letter from his beloved Ricky. A nice, brief little note confirming their rendezvous.

What Quince really wanted was three warm days on a love boat with Ricky. He might never come back.

Bakers had eighteen thousand people, so the central post office on Main was usually busy. And there was always a different clerk behind the counter. That's how he'd rented the box – he'd waited until a new postal worker was on duty. CMT Investments was the official lessee. He went straight to the box, around a corner to a wall with a hundred others.

There were three letters, and as he snatched them and stuffed them in his coat pocket his heart froze as he saw that one was from Ricky. He hurried onto Main, and minutes later entered his bank, at exactly 10 A.M. His father had been there for four hours, but they had long since stopped bickering over Quince's work schedule. As always, he stopped at his secretary's desk to hurriedly remove his gloves as if important matters were waiting. She handed him his mail, his two phone messages, and reminded him that he had lunch in two hours with a local real estate agent.

He locked his door behind him, flung his gloves one way and his coat the other, and ripped open the letter from Ricky. He sat on his sofa and put on his reading glasses, breathing heavily not from the walk but from anticipation. He was on the verge of arousal when he started reading.

The words hit like bullets. After the second paragraph, he emitted a strange, painful 'Awwww.' Then a couple of 'Oh my gods.' Then a low, hissing 'Sonofabitch.'

Quiet, he told himself, the secretary is always listening. The first reading brought shock, the second disbelief. Reality began settling in with the third reading, and Quince's lip started to quiver. Don't cry, dammit, he told himself.

He threw the letter on the floor and paced around his desk, ignoring as best he could the cheerful faces of his wife and children. Twenty years' worth of class photos and family portraits were lined along his credenza, just under the window. He looked out and watched the snow, now heavier and accumulating on the sidewalks. God how he hated Bakers, Iowa. He'd thought he might leave and escape to the beach, where he could frolic with a handsome young pal and maybe never come home.

Now he would leave under different circumstances.

It was a joke, a hoax, he told himself, but he

76

instantly knew better. The scam was too tight. The punch line was too perfect. He'd been set up by a professional.

All his life he'd fought his desires. Somehow he'd finally found the nerve to crack the closet door, and now he got shot between the eyes by a con man. Stupid, stupid, stupid. How could this be so difficult?

Random thoughts hit from every direction as he watched the snow. Suicide was the easy answer, but his doctor was gone and he really didn't want to die. At least not at the moment. He wasn't sure where he'd find a hundred thousand bucks he could send off without raising suspicions. The old bastard next door paid him a pittance and kept his thumb on every dime. His wife insisted on balancing their checkbook. There was some money in mutuals, but he couldn't move it without her knowing. The life of a rich banker in Bakers, Iowa, meant a title and a Mercedes and a large mortgaged house and a wife with social activities. Oh how he wanted to escape!

He'd go to Florida anyway, and track the letter somehow, and confront this con man, expose his extortion attempt, find some justice. He, Quince Garbe, had done nothing wrong. Surely a crime was being perpetrated here. Perhaps he could hire an investigator, and maybe a lawyer, and they'd protect him. They'd get to the bottom of this scam.

Even if he found the money, and wired it as instructed, the gate would be opened and Ricky, whoever in hell Ricky was, might want more. What would stop Ricky from extorting again, and again?

If he had guts he'd run off anyway, run to Key

West or some hot spot where it never snowed and live any damn way he wanted to live, and let the pitiful little people of Bakers, Iowa, gossip about him for the next half-century. But he didn't have the guts, and that's what made Quince so sad.

His children were staring at him, freckled smiles with teeth wrapped in silver braces. His heart sank, and he knew he'd find the money and wire it precisely as directed. He had to protect them. They had done nothing wrong.

The bank's stock was worth about $10 million, all of it still tightly controlled by the old man, who at the moment was barking in the hallway. The old man was eighty-one, very much alive but still eighty-one. When he was gone, Quince would have to contend with a sister in Chicago, but the bank would be his. He'd sell the damned thing as fast as he could and leave Bakers with a few million in his pocket. Until then, though, he'd be forced to do what he'd always done, keep the old man content.

Quince's getting yanked out of the closet by some con man would devastate his father, and pretty much take care of the stock. Sister in Chicago would get all of it.

When the barking stopped outside, he eased through the door and passed his secretary for a cup of coffee. He ignored her as he returned to his room, locked his door, read the letter for the fourth time, and collected his thoughts. He'd find the money, and he'd wire it just as instructed, and he'd hope and pray with a fury that Ricky would go away. If not, if he came back for more, Quince would call his doctor and get some pills.

The real estate agent he was meeting for lunch was a high-roller who took chances and cut corners, probably a crook. Quince began to make plans. The two of them would arrange a few shady loans; overappraise some land, lend the money, sell to a strawman, etc. He would know how to do it.

Quince would find the money.

The Lake campaign's doomsday ads landed with a thud, at least in public opinion. Massive polling through the first week showed a dramatic increase in name recognition, from 2 to 20 percent, but the ads were universally disliked. They were frightening and people just didn't want to think about wars and terrorism and old nukes getting hauled across mountains in the dark. People saw the ads (they were impossible to miss), and they heard the message, but most voters simply didn't want to be bothered. They were too busy making money and spending it. When issues were confronted in the midst of a roaring economy, they were limited to the old standbys of family values and tax cuts.

Candidate Lake's early interviewers treated him as just another flake until he announced, live on the air, that his campaign had received in excess of $11 million in less than a week.

'We expect to have twenty million in two weeks,' he said without boasting, and real news started to happen. Teddy Maynard had assured him the money would be there.

Twenty million in two weeks had never been done before, and by the end of that day Washington was consumed with the story. The frenzy reached its peak when Lake was interviewed, live yet again, by two of the three networks on the evening news. He looked great; big smile, smooth words, nice suit and hair. The man was electable.

Final confirmation that Aaron Lake was a serious candidate came late in the day, when one of his opponents took a shot at him. Senator Britt of Maryland had been running for a year and had finished a strong second in New Hampshire. He'd raised $9 million, spent a lot more than that, and was forced to waste half of his time soliciting money rather than campaigning. He was tired of begging, tired of cutting staff, tired of worrying about TV ads, and when a reporter asked him about Lake and his $20 million Britt shot back, 'It's dirty money. No honest candidate can raise that much that fast.' Britt was shaking hands in the rain at the entrance to a chemical plant in Michigan.

The dirty money comment was seized with great gusto by the press and soon splattered all over the place.

Aaron Lake had arrived.

Senator Britt of Maryland had other problems, though he'd tried to forget them.

Nine years earlier he'd toured Southeast Asia to find some facts. As always, he and his colleagues from the Congress flew first class, stayed in nice hotels, and ate lobster, all in an effort to study poverty in the region and to get to the bottom of the raging controversy brought about by Nike and its use of cheap foreign labor. Early in the journey, Britt met a girl in Bangkok, and, feigning illness, decided to stay behind while his buddies continued their fact-finding into Laos and Vietnam.

Her name was Payka, and she was not a prostitute. She was a twenty-year-old secretary in the U.S. embassy in Bangkok, and because she was on his country's payroll Britt felt a slight proprietary interest. He was far away from Maryland, from his wife and five kids and his constituents. Payka was stunning and shapely, and anxious to study in the United States.

What began as a fling quickly turned into a romance, and Senator Britt had to force himself to return to Washington. Two months later he was back in Bangkok on, as he told his wife, pressing but secret business.

In nine months he made four trips to Thailand, all first class, all at taxpayer expense, and even the globe-trotters in the Senate were beginning to whisper. Britt pulled strings with the State Department and Payka appeared to be headed for the United States.

She never made it. During the fourth and final rendezvous, Payka confessed that she was pregnant. She was Catholic and abortion was not an option. Britt stiff-armed her, said he needed time to think, then fled Bangkok in the middle of the night. The fact-finding was over.

Early in his Senate career, Britt, a fiscal hardliner, had grabbed a headline or two by criticizing CIA wastefulness. Teddy Maynard said not a word, but certainly didn't appreciate the grandstanding. The rather thin file on Senator Britt was dusted off and given priority, and when he went to Bangkok for the second time the CIA went with him. Of course he didn't know it, but they sat near him on the flight, first class also, and they had people on the ground in Bangkok. They watched the hotel where the two lovebirds spent three days. They took pictures of them eating in fine restaurants. They saw everything. Britt was oblivious and stupid.

Later, when the child was born, the CIA obtained the hospital records, then the medical records to link the blood and DNA. Payka kept her job at the embassy, so she was easy to find.

When the child was a year old, he was photographed sitting on Payka's knee in a downtown park. More photos followed, and by the time he was four he was beginning to remotely favor Senator Dan Britt of Maryland.

His daddy was long gone. Britt's zeal for finding facts in Southeast Asia had faded dramatically, and he'd turned his attention to other critical areas of the world. In due course he was seized with presidential ambitions, the old senatorial affliction that sooner or later gets them all. He'd never heard from Payka, and that nightmare had been easy to forget.

Britt had five legitimate children, and a wife with a big mouth. They were a team, Senator and Mrs. Britt, both leading the juggernaut of family values and 'We've Got to Save Our Kids!' Together they wrote a book on how to raise children in a sick American culture, though their oldest was only thirteen. When the President was embarrassed by sexual misadventures, Senator Britt became the biggest virgin in Washington.

He and his wife struck a nerve, and the money

rolled in from conservatives. He did well in the Iowa caucuses, ran a close second in New Hampshire, but was running out of money and sinking in the polls.

He would sink even more. After a brutal day of campaigning, his entourage settled into a motel in Dearborn, Michigan, for a short night. It was there that the senator finally came face to face with child number six, though not in person.

The agent's name was McCord, and he'd been following Britt with phony press credentials for a week. He said he worked for a newspaper in Tallahassee, but in fact he'd been a CIA agent for eleven years. There were so many reporters swarming around Britt that no one thought to check.

McCord befriended a senior aide, and over a late drink in the Holiday Inn bar he confessed that he had something in his possession that would destroy candidate Britt. He said it was given to him by a rival camp, Governor Tarry's. It was a notebook, with a bomb on every page: an affidavit from Payka setting forth the broad details of their affair; two photos of the child, the last of which had been taken a month earlier and the child, now seven, looking more and more like his dad; blood and DNA summaries indelibly linking father and son; and travel records which showed in black and white that Senator Britt had burned $38,600 in taxpayers' money to carry on his affair on the other side of the world.

The deal was simple and straightforward: Withdraw from the race immediately, and the story would never be told. McCord, the journalist, was ethical and didn't have the stomach for such trash. Governor Tarry would keep it quiet if Britt disappeared. Quit, and not even Mrs. Britt would know.

Shortly after 1 A.M., in Washington, Teddy Maynard took the call from McCord. The package had been delivered. Britt was planning a press conference for noon the next day.

Teddy had dirt files on hundreds of politicians, past and present. As a group they were an easy bunch to trap. Place a beautiful young woman in their path, and you generally gathered something for the file. If women didn't work, money always did. Watch them travel, watch them crawl in bed with the lobbyists, watch them pander to any foreign government smart enough to send lots of cash to Washington, watch them set up their campaigns and committees to raise funds. Just watch them, and the files always grew thicker. He wished the Russians were so easy.

Though he despised politicians as a group, he did respect a handful of them. Aaron Lake was one. He'd never chased women, never drank much or picked up habits, never seemed preoccupied with cash, never had been inclined to grandstand. The more he watched Lake, the more he liked him.

He took his last pill of the night and rolled himself to bed. So Britt was gone. Good riddance. Too bad he couldn't leak the story anyway. The pious hypocrite deserved a good thrashing. Save it, he told himself. And use it again. President Lake might need Britt one day, and that little boy over in Thailand might come in handy.

SEVEN

Picasso was suing Sherlock and other unnamed defendants for injunctive relief in an effort to stop them from urinating on his roses. A little misdirected urine was not going to upset the balance of life at Trumble, but Picasso also wanted damages in the amount of five hundred dollars. Five hundred dollars was a serious matter.

The dispute had been festering since the past summer, when Picasso caught Sherlock in the act, and the assistant warden had finally intervened. He asked the Brethren to settle the matter. Suit was filed, then Sherlock hired an ex-lawyer named Ratliff, yet another tax evader, to stall, delay, postpone, and file frivolous pleadings, the usual routine for those practicing the art of law on the outside. But Ratliff's tactics didn't sit well with the Brethren, and neither Sherlock nor his lawyer was held in high esteem by the panel.

Picasso's rose garden was a carefully tended patch of dirt next to the gym. It had taken him three years of bureaucratic wars to convince some mid-level paper-pusher in Washington that such a hobby was and always had been therapeutic, since

85

Picasso suffered from several disorders. Once the garden was approved, the warden quickly signed off, and Picasso dug in with both hands. He got his roses from a supplier in Jacksonville, which in itself took another box of paperwork.

His real job was that of a dishwasher in the cafeteria, for which he earned thirty cents an hour. The warden refused his request to be classified as a gardener, so the roses were deemed a hobby. During the season, Picasso could be seen early and late in his little patch, on all fours, tilling and digging and watering. He even talked to his flowers.

The roses in question were Belinda's Dream, a pale pink rose, not particularly beautiful, but loved by Picasso nonetheless. When they arrived from the supplier everybody at Trumble knew that the Belindas were there. He lovingly planted them in the front and center of his garden.

Sherlock began urinating on them just for the sheer hell of it. He wasn't fond of Picasso anyway because he was a notorious liar, and peeing on the man's roses just seemed appropriate for some reason. Others caught on. Sherlock encouraged them by assuring that they were in fact helping the roses by adding fertilizer.

The Belindas lost their pinkness and began to fade, and Picasso was horrified. An informant left a note under his door, and the secret was out. His beloved garden had become a favorite watering hole. Two days later, he ambushed Sherlock, caught him in the act, and the two chubby middle-aged white men had an ugly wrestling match on the sidewalk.

The plants turned a dull yellow, and Picasso filed suit.

When it finally reached trial, after months of delays by Ratliff, the Brethren were already tired of it. They had quietly preassigned the case to Justice Finn Yarber, whose mother had once raised roses, and after a few hours of research he had informed the other two that urine would, in fact, not change the color of the plants. So two days before the hearing they reached their decision: They would grant the injunction to keep Sherlock and the other pigs from spraying Picasso's roses, but they would not award damages.

For three hours they listened to grown men bicker about who peed where and when, and how often. At times, Picasso, acting as his own attorney, was near tears as he begged his witnesses to squeal on their friends. Ratliff, counsel for the defense, was cruel and abrasive and redundant, and after an hour it was obvious he deserved his disbarment, whatever his crimes may have been.

Justice Spicer passed the time by studying the point spreads on college basketball games. When he couldn't contact Trevor he placed make-believe bets, every game. He was up $3,600 in two months, on paper. He was on a roll, winning at cards, winning at sports, and he had trouble sleeping at night dreaming about his next life, in Vegas or in the Bahamas, doing it as a pro. With or without his wife.

Justice Beech frowned with deep judicial deliberation and appeared to be taking exhaustive notes, when in fact he was drafting another letter to Curtis in Dallas. The Brethren had decided to

87

bait him again. Writing as Ricky, Beech explained that a cruel guard at the rehab unit was threatening all sorts of vile physical attacks unless Ricky could produce some 'protection money.' Ricky needed $5,000 to secure his safety from the beast, and could Curtis lend it to him?

'Could we move this along?' Beech said loudly, interrupting ex-lawyer Ratliff once again. When he was a real judge, Beech had mastered the practice of reading magazines while half-listening to lawyers drone on before juries. A blaring and well-timed admonition from the bench kept everyone sharp.

He wrote: 'It is such a vicious game they play here. We arrive broken into tiny pieces. Slowly, they clean us up, dry us out, put us back together, piece by piece. They clear our heads, teach us discipline and confidence, and prepare us for our return to society. They do a good job of this, yet they allow these ignorant thugs who guard the grounds to threaten us, fragile as we still are, and in doing so break down what we've worked so hard to produce. I am so scared of this man. I hide in my room when I'm supposed to be tanning and lifting weights. I cannot sleep. I long for booze and drugs as a means of escape. Please, Curtis, loan me the $5,000 so I can buy this guy off, so I can complete my rehab and leave here in one piece. When we meet, I want to be healthy and in great shape.'

What would his friends think? The Honorable Hatlee Beech, federal judge, writing prose like a faggot, extorting money out of innocent people.

He had no friends. He had no rules. The law he

once worshiped had placed him where he was, which, at the moment, was in a prison cafeteria wearing a faded green choir robe from a black church, listening to a bunch of angry convicts argue over urine.

'You've already asked that question eight times,' he barked at Ratliff, who'd obviously been watching too many bad lawyer shows on television.

Since the case was Justice Yarber's, he was expected to at least appear as if he were paying attention. He was not, nor was he concerned about appearances. As usual, he was naked under his robe, and he sat with his legs crossed wide, cleaning his long toenails with a plastic fork.

'You think they'd turn brown if I crapped on them?' Sherlock yelled at Picasso, and the cafeteria erupted with laughter.

'Language, please,' Justice Beech admonished.

'Order in the court,' said T. Karl, the court jester, under his bright gray wig. It was not his role in the courtroom to demand order, but it was something he did well and the Brethren let it slide. He rapped his gavel, said, 'Order, gentlemen.'

Beech wrote: 'Please help me, Curtis. I have no one else to turn to. I'm breaking again. I fear another collapse. I fear I will never leave this place. Hurry.'

Spicer put a hundred dollars on Indiana over Purdue, Duke over Clemson, Alabama over Vandy, Wisconsin over Illinois. What did he know about Wisconsin basketball? he asked himself. Didn't matter. He was a professional gambler, and a damned good one. If the $90,000 was still buried

89

behind the toolshed he'd parlay it into a million within a year.

'That's enough,' Beech said, holding up his hands.

'I've heard enough too,' Yarber said, forgetting his toenails and leaning on the table.

The Brethren huddled and deliberated as if the outcome might set a serious precedent, or at least have some profound impact on the future of American jurisprudence. They frowned and scratched their heads and appeared to even argue over the merits of the case. Meanwhile, poor Picasso sat by himself, ready to cry, thoroughly exhausted by Ratliff's tactics.

Justice Yarber cleared his throat and said, 'By a vote of two to one, we have reached a decision. We are issuing an injunction against all inmates urinating on the damned roses. Anyone caught doing so will be fined fifty dollars. No damages will be assessed at this time.'

With perfect timing T. Karl slammed his gavel and yelled, 'Court's adjourned until further notice. All rise.'

Of course, no one moved.

'I want to appeal,' Picasso yelled.

'So do I,' said Sherlock.

'Must be a good decision,' Yarber said, collecting his robe and standing. 'Both sides are unhappy.'

Beech and Spicer stood too, and the Brethren paraded out of the cafeteria. A guard walked into the middle of the litigants and witnesses and said, 'Court's over, boys. Get back to work.'

★

The CEO of Hummand, a company in Seattle which made missiles and radar-jamming machinery, had once been a congressman who'd been quite close to the CIA. Teddy Maynard knew him well. When the CEO announced at a press conference that his company had raised $5 million for the Lake campaign, CNN interrupted a liposuction segment to carry the story Live! Five thousand Hummand workers had written checks for $1,000 each, the maximum allowed under federal law. The CEO had the checks in a box that he showed to the cameras, then he flew with them on a Hummand jet to Washington, where he took them to the Lake headquarters.

Follow the money, and you'll find your winner. Since Lake's announcement, over eleven thousand defense and aerospace workers from thirty states had contributed just over $8 million. The Postal Service was delivering their checks in boxes. Their unions had sent almost that much, with another $2 million promised. Lake's people hired a D.C. accounting firm just to process and count the money.

The Hummand CEO arrived in Washington amid as much fanfare as could be generated. Candidate Lake was on another private jet, a Challenger freshly leased at $400,000 a month. When he landed in Detroit he was met by two black Suburbans, both brand new, both just leased at $1,000 a month each. Lake now had an escort, a group of people moving in sync with him wherever he went, and though he was certain he'd soon get used to it, it was unnerving at first. Strangers around him all the time. Grave young men in dark

91

suits with little microphones in their ears, guns strapped to their bodies. Two Secret Service agents were on the flight with him, and three more waited with the Suburbans.

And he had Floyd from his congressional office. Floyd was a dull-witted young man from a prominent family back in Arizona who was good for nothing but running errands. Now Floyd was a driver. Floyd took the wheel of one Suburban, Lake in the front seat, two agents and a secretary sitting behind. Two aides and three agents piled into the other, and away they went, headed for downtown Detroit where serious local TV journalists were waiting.

Lake had no time for stumping or walking neighborhoods or eating catfish or standing in the rain outside busy factories. He couldn't hike for the cameras or stage town meetings or stand amid rubble in ghettos and decry failed policies. There wasn't enough time to do all the things candidates were expected to do. He was entering late, with no groundwork in place, no grass roots, no local support of any kind. Lake had a handsome face, a pleasant voice, nice suits, an urgent message, and lots of cash.

If buying TV could buy an election, Aaron Lake was about to get himself a new job.

He called Washington, talked to his moneyman, and was given the news about the $5 million announcement. He'd never heard of Hummand. 'Is it a public company?' he asked. No, came the answer. Very private. Just under a billion in annual sales. An innovator in radar jamming. Could make billions if the right man took charge of the military and started spending again.

Nineteen million dollars was now in hand, a record, of course. And they were revising their projections. The Lake campaign would collect thirty million in its first two weeks.

There was no way to spend money that fast.

He folded the cell phone, handed it back to Floyd, who appeared to be lost in traffic. 'From now on we use helicopters,' Lake announced over his shoulder to the secretary, who actually wrote down the directive: Find helicopters.

Lake hid behind his sunglasses and tried to analyze thirty million bucks. The transition from a fiscal conservative to a freewheeling candidate was awkward, but the money had to be spent. It wasn't squeezed from the taxpayers; rather, it was freely given. He could rationalize. Once elected, he'd continue his fight for the workingman.

He thought again about Teddy Maynard, sitting in some dark room deep inside Langley, legs wrapped in a quilt, face squinting from pain, pulling strings only he could pull, making money fall from trees. Lake would never know the things Teddy was doing on his behalf, nor did he want to.

The Director of Middle East Operations was named Lufkin, a twenty-year man Teddy trusted implicitly. Fourteen hours earlier he'd been in Tel Aviv. Now he was in Teddy's war room, somehow looking fresh and alert. His message had to be delivered in person, mouth to mouth, no wires or signals or satellites. And what was said between

93

them would never be repeated. It had been that way for many years.

'An attack on our embassy in Cairo is now imminent,' Lufkin said. No reaction from Teddy; no frown, no surprise, no cutting of the eyes, nothing. He'd gotten such news many times before.

'Yidal?'

'Yes. His top lieutenant was seen in Cairo last week.'

'Seen by whom?'

'The Israelis. They've also followed two truck-loads of explosives from Tripoli. Everything seems to be in place.'

'When?'

'Imminent.'

'How imminent?'

'Within a week, I'd guess.'

Teddy pulled an earlobe and closed his eyes. Lufkin tried not to stare, and he knew better than to ask questions. He would leave soon, and return to the Middle East. And he would wait. The attack on the embassy might proceed with no warning. Dozens would be killed and maimed. A crater in the city would smolder for days, and in Washington fingers would point and accusations would fly. The CIA would be blamed again.

None of it would faze Teddy Maynard. As Lufkin had learned, sometimes Teddy needed the terror to accomplish what he wanted.

Or maybe the embassy would be spared, the attack thwarted by Egyptian commandos working with the United States. The CIA would be praised for its excellent intelligence. That wouldn't faze Teddy either.

'And you're certain?' he asked.

'Yes, as certain as one can be in these situations.'

Lufkin, of course, had no clue that the Director was now plotting to elect a President. Lufkin had barely heard of Aaron Lake. Frankly, he didn't care who won the election. He'd been in the Middle East long enough to know it didn't really matter who set American policy there.

He'd leave in three hours, on the Concorde to Paris, where he'd spend a day before going to Jerusalem.

'Go to Cairo,' Teddy said without opening his eyes.

'Sure. And do what?'

'Wait.'

'Wait for what?'

'Wait for the ground to shake. Stay away from the embassy.'

York's initial reaction was one of horror. 'You can't run this damned ad, Teddy,' he said. 'It's R-rated. I've never seen so much blood.'

'I like that,' Teddy said, pushing a button on the remote. 'An R-rated campaign ad. It's never been done before.'

They watched it again. It began with the sound of a bomb, then footage of the Marine barracks in Beirut; smoke, rubble, chaos, Marines being pulled from debris, mangled bodies, Marines lying dead in a neat row. President Reagan addressing the press and vowing revenge. But the threat

95

sounded hollow. Then the photo of an American soldier standing between two masked gunmen. A heavy, ominous voiceover said, 'Since 1980, hundreds of Americans have been murdered by terrorists around the world.' Another bomb scene, more bloody and dazed survivors, more smoke and chaos. 'We always vow revenge. We always threaten to find and punish those responsible.' Quick clips of President Bush on two separate occasions angrily promising retaliation – another attack, more bodies. Then footage of a terrorist standing in the door of a jetliner, dragging off the body of an American soldier. President Clinton, near tears, his voice ready to crack, saying, 'We will not rest until we find those responsible.' Next the handsome but serious face of Aaron Lake, looking sincerely at the camera, coming into our homes, saying, 'The fact is, we don't retaliate. We react with words, we swagger and threaten, but in reality we bury our dead, then forget about them. The terrorists are winning the war because we have lacked the guts to fight back. When I'm your President, we will use our new military to fight terrorism wherever we find it. No American death will go unanswered. I promise. We will not be humiliated by ragtag little armies hiding in mountains. We will destroy them.'

The ad ran for exactly sixty seconds, cost very little to make because Teddy already had the footage, and would start running during prime time in forty-eight hours.

'I don't know, Teddy,' York said. 'It's gruesome.'

'It's a gruesome world.'

Teddy liked the ad and that's all that mattered. Lake had objected to the blood, but came around quickly. His name recognition was up to 30 percent, but his ads were still disliked.

Just wait, Teddy kept telling himself. Wait until there are more bodies.

EIGHT

Trevor was sipping a carry-out double latte from Beach Java and debating whether to add a generous shot or two of Amaretto to help soothe away the morning's cobwebs when the call came. His cramped suite had no intercom system; one was not needed. Jan could simply yell any message down the hall, and he could yell back if he wanted. For eight years he and this particular secretary had been barking at each other.

'It's some bank in the Bahamas!' she announced. He almost spilled the coffee as he lunged for the phone.

It was a Brit whose accent had been softened by the islands. A substantial wire had been received, from a bank in Iowa.

How substantial, he wanted to know, covering his mouth so Jan couldn't hear.

A hundred thousand dollars.

Trevor hung up and added the Amaretto, three shots of it, and sipped the delightful brew while smiling goofily at the wall. In his career he'd never come close to a fee of $33,000. He'd settled a car wreck once for $25,000, taken a fee of $7,500, and within two months had spent all of it.

Jan knew nothing about the offshore account and the scam that diverted money to it, so he was forced to wait an hour, make a bunch of useless phone calls, and try to look busy before announcing he had to take care of some crucial business in downtown Jacksonville, then he was needed at Trumble. She didn't care. He disappeared all the time and she had some reading to keep her occupied.

He raced to the airport, almost missed his shuttle, and drank two beers during the thirty-minute flight to Fort Lauderdale, then two more on the way to Nassau. On the ground, he fell into the back of a cab, a 1974 Cadillac painted gold, without air-conditioning and with a driver who'd also been drinking. The air was hot and wet, the traffic slow, and Trevor's shirt was sticking to his back by the time they stopped downtown near the Geneva Trust Bank Building.

Inside, Mr. Brayshears came forward eventually and led Trevor to his small office. He presented a sheet of paper which gave the bare details: a $100,000 wire originating from the First Iowa Bank in Des Moines, remitter being a faceless entity named CMT Investments. The payee was another generic entity named Boomer Realty, Ltd. Boomer was the name of Joe Roy Spicer's favorite bird dog.

Trevor signed the forms to transfer $25,000 to his own, separate account with Geneva Trust, money he kept hidden from his secretary and from the IRS. The remaining $8,000 was handed to him

99

in a thick envelope, cash. He stuffed it deep into his khaki pants pocket, shook Brayshears' soft little hand, and raced out of the building. He was tempted to stay a couple of days, find a room on the beach, get a chair by the pool, and drink rum until they stopped bringing it to him. The temptation grew to the point that he almost bolted from the gate at the airport and raced to get another cab. But he reached deep, determined not to squander his money this time.

Two hours later he was in the Jacksonville airport, drinking strong coffee, without liquor, and making his plans. He drove to Trumble, arriving at four-thirty, and he waited for Spicer for almost half an hour.

'A pleasant surprise,' Spicer said dryly as he stepped into the attorney-conference room. Trevor had no briefcase to inspect, so the guard patted his pockets and stepped outside. His cash was hidden under the floor mat of his Beetle.

'We received a hundred thousand dollars from Iowa,' Trevor said, glancing at the door.

Spicer was suddenly happy to see his lawyer. He resented the 'we' in Trevor's announcement, and he resented the healthy cut he raked off the top. But the scam wouldn't work without help from the outside, and, as usual, the lawyer was a necessary evil. So far, Trevor could be trusted.

'It's in the Bahamas?'

'Yes. I just left there. The money's tucked away, all sixty-seven thousand of it.'

Spicer breathed deeply and savored the victory. A third of the loot gave him $22,000 and change. It was time to write some more letters!

100

He reached into the pocket of his olive prison shirt and removed a folded newspaper clipping. He stretched his arms, studied it for a second, then said, 'Duke's at Tech tonight. The line is eleven. Put five thousand bucks on Tech.'

'Five thousand?'

'Yep.'

'I've never put five thousand on a game before.'

'What kinda bookie you got?'

'Small time.'

'Look, if he's a bookie, he can handle the numbers. Call him as soon as you can. He may have to make a few calls, but he can do it.'

'All right, all right.'

'Can you come back tomorrow?'

'Probably.'

'How many other clients have ever paid you thirty-three thousand bucks?'

'None.'

'Right, so be here at four tomorrow. I'll have some mail for you.'

Spicer left him and walked quickly from the administration building with only a nod at a guard in a window. He walked with a purpose across the finely manicured lawn, the Florida sun heating the sidewalk even in February. His colleagues were deep in their unhurried labors in their little library, alone as always, so Spicer did not hesitate to announce: 'We got the hundred thousand from ole Quince in Iowa!'

Beech's hands froze on his keyboard. He peered over his reading glasses, his jaw dropping, and managed to say, 'You're kidding.'

'Nope. Just talked to Trevor. The money was

101

wired in exactly as instructed, arrived in the Bahamas this morning. Quincy baby came through.'

'Let's hit him again,' Yarber said, before the others could think of it.

'Quince?'

'Sure. The first hundred was easy, let's squeeze him one more time. What could we lose?'

'Not a damned thing,' Spicer said with a smile. He wished he'd said it first.

'How much?' asked Beech.

'Let's try fifty,' Yarber said, pulling numbers from the air as if anything was possible.

The other two nodded and pondered the next fifty thousand, then Spicer took charge and said, 'Look, let's evaluate where we are now. I think Curtis in Dallas is ripe. We'll hit Quince again. This thing is working, and I think we should shift gears, get more aggressive, know what I mean? Let's take each pen pal, analyze them one by one, and step up the pressure.'

Beech turned off his computer and reached for a file. Yarber cleared his small desk. Their little Angola scam had just received a fresh infusion of capital, and the smell of ill-gotten cash was intoxicating.

They began reading all the old letters, and drafting new ones. More victims were needed, they quickly decided. More ads would be placed in the back pages of those magazines.

Trevor made it as far as Pete's Bar and Grill, arriving there just in time for happy hour, which at Pete's began at 5 P.M. and ran until the first fistfight. He found Prep, a thirty-two-year-old sophomore at North Florida, shooting nine-ball for twenty bucks a game. Prep's dwindling trust fund required the family lawyer to pay him $2,000 a month as long as he was enrolled as a full-time student. He'd been a sophomore for eleven years.

Prep was also the busiest bookie at Pete's, and when Trevor whispered that he had serious money to place on the Duke-Tech game, Prep asked, 'How much?'

'Fifteen thousand,' Trevor said, then gulped his longneck beer.

'You serious?' Prep asked, chalking his cue stick and glancing around the smoky table. Trevor had never bet more than a hundred bucks on any game.

'Yep.' Another long pull on the bottle. He was feeling lucky. If Spicer had the guts to lay $5,000 on the game, Trevor would double it. He'd just earned 33,000 tax-free dollars. So what if he lost ten? That much belonged to the IRS anyway.

'I'll have to make a call,' Prep said, pulling out a cell phone.

'Hurry. The game starts in thirty minutes.'

The bartender was a local who'd never left the state of Florida but had somehow developed an intense passion for Australian Rules Football. A game was on from Down Under, and it took a $20 bribe from Trevor to get the channel changed to ACC basketball.

With $15,000 riding on Georgia Tech, there was no way Duke could miss a shot, at least not in the first half. Trevor ate french fries, drank one bottle after another, and tried to ignore Prep, who was

103

standing near a pool table in a dark corner, watching.

In the second half, Trevor almost bribed the bartender to switch back to the Aussie game. He was getting drunker, and with ten minutes to go was openly cursing Joe Roy Spicer to anyone who would listen. What did that redneck know about ACC basketball? Duke led by twenty with nine minutes to go, when Tech's point guard got hot and nailed four straight threes. Trevor had Tech and eleven.

The game was tied with a minute to go. Trevor didn't care who won. He'd beat the spread. He paid his tab, tipped the bartender another $100, then flashed a smart-ass salute to Prep as he walked out the door. Prep flipped him the bird.

In the cool darkness, Trevor skipped along Atlantic Boulevard, away from the lights, past the cheap summer rentals packed tightly together, past the neat little retirement homes with their fresh paint and perfect lawns, down the old wooden steps to the sand, where he took off his shoes and strolled along the edge of the water. The temperature was in the forties, not unusual for Jacksonville in February, and before long his feet were cold and wet.

Not that he felt much – $43,000 in one day, tax-free, all hidden from the government. Last year after expenses he'd cleared $28,000, and that was working practically full time – haggling with clients too poor or too cheap to pay, avoiding courtrooms, dealing with penny-ante real estate agents and bankers, bickering with his secretary, cutting corners on taxes.

Ah, the joy of quick cash. He'd been suspicious of the Brethren's little scam, but now it seemed so brilliant. Extort from those who can't complain. How thoroughly clever.

And since it was working so well, he knew Spicer would turn up the heat. The mail would get heavier, the visits to Trumble more frequent. Hell, he'd be there every day if necessary, hauling letters in and out, bribing guards.

He splashed his feet in the water as the wind picked up and the waves roared in.

Even more clever would be to steal from the extortionists, court-certified crooks who certainly couldn't complain. It was a nasty thought, one he was almost ashamed of, but a valid one nonetheless. All options would be kept open. Since when were thieves known for their loyalty?

He needed a million dollars, nothing more or less. He'd done the math many times, driving to Trumble, drinking at Pete's, sitting at his desk with the door locked. A lousy million bucks, and he could close his sad little office, surrender his law license, buy a sailboat, and spend eternity drifting with the winds around the Caribbean.

He was closer than he would ever be.

Justice Spicer rolled over again on the bottom bunk. Sleep was a rare gift in his tiny room, on his tiny bed with a small, smelly roommate named Alvin snoring above him. Alvin had roamed North America as a hobo for decades, but late in life had grown weary and hungry. His crime had been the robbery of a rural mail carrier in Oklahoma. His apprehension had been aided mightily when Alvin walked into the FBI office in Tulsa and declared, 'I did it.' The FBI scrambled for six hours to find the crime. Even the judge knew Alvin planned it all. He wanted a federal bed, certainly not one provided by the state.

Sleep was even more difficult than usual because Spicer was worried about the lawyer. Now that the scam had hit its stride, there was serious cash lying around. And more on the way. The more Boomer Realty collected in the Bahamas, the more tempting it would become for Trevor. He and he alone could steal their ill-gotten loot and get away with it.

But the scam worked only with an outside conspirator. Someone had to sneak the mail back and forth. Someone had to collect the money.

There had to be a way to bypass the lawyer, and Joe Roy was determined to find it. If he didn't sleep for a month, he didn't care. No slimy lawyer would take a third of his money, then steal the rest.

NINE

Defensepac, or D-PAC as it would quickly and widely become known, made a roaring entry onto the loose and murky field of political finance. No political-action committee in recent history had appeared with as much muscle behind it.

Its seed money came from a Chicago financier named Mitzger, an American with dual Israeli citizenship. He put up the first $1 million, which lasted about a week. Other Jewish high-rollers were quickly brought into the fold, though their identities were shielded by corporations and offshore accounts. Teddy Maynard knew the dangers of having a bunch of rich Jews contribute openly and in an organized fashion to Lake's campaign. He relied on old friends in Tel Aviv to organize the money in New York.

Mitzger was a liberal when it came to politics, but no issue was as dear as the security of Israel. Aaron Lake was much too moderate on social matters, but he was also dead serious about a new military. Middle East stability depended on a strong America, at least in Mitzger's opinion.

He rented a suite at the Willard in D.C. one day,

and by noon the next he had leased an entire floor of an office building near Dulles. His staff from Chicago worked around the clock plowing through the myriad details required to instantly outfit forty thousand square feet with the latest technology. He had a 6 A.M. breakfast with Elaine Tyner, a lawyer/lobbyist from a gigantic Washington firm, one she'd built with her own iron will and lots of oil clients. Tyner was sixty years old and currently regarded as the most powerful lobbyist in town. Over bagels and juice she agreed to represent D-PAC for an initial retainer of $500,000. Her firm would immediately dispatch twenty associates and that many clerks to the new D-PAC offices where one of her partners would take charge. One section would do nothing but raise money. One would analyze congressional support for Lake and begin, gently at first, the delicate process of lining up endorsements from senators and representatives and even governors. It would not be easy; most were already committed to other candidates. Yet another section would do nothing but research – military hardware, its costs, new gadgets, futuristic weapons, Russian and Chinese innovations – anything that candidate Lake might need to know.

Tyner herself would work on raising money from foreign governments, one of her specialties. She was very close to the South Koreans, having been their presence in Washington for the past decade. She knew the diplomats, the businessmen, the big shots. Few countries would sleep easier with a beefed-up United States military than South Korea.

'I feel sure they'll be good for at least five million,' she said confidently. 'Initially, anyway.'

From memory, she made a list of twenty French and British companies that derived at least a fourth of their annual sales from the Pentagon. She'd start working on them immediately.

Tyner was very much the Washington lawyer these days. She hadn't seen a courtroom in fifteen years, and every meaningful world event originated within the Beltway and somehow affected her.

The challenge at hand was unprecedented – electing an unknown, last-minute candidate who, at the moment, enjoyed 30 percent name recognition and 12 percent positives. What their candidate had, though, unlike the other flakes who dropped in and out of the presidential derby, was seemingly unlimited cash. Tyner had been well paid to elect and defeat scores of politicians, and she held the unwavering belief that money would always win. Give her the money, and she could elect or beat anybody.

During the first week of its existence, D-PAC buzzed with unbridled energy. The offices were open twenty-four hours a day as Tyner's people set up shop and charged forward. Those raising money produced an exhaustive computerized list of 310,000 hourly workers in defense and related industries, then hit them hard with a slick mail-out pleading for money. Another list had the names of twenty-eight thousand white-collar defense workers who earned in excess of $50,000 a year. They were mailed a different type of solicitation.

The D-PAC consultants looking for endorsements found the fifty members of Congress with the most defense jobs in their districts. Thirty-seven were up for reelection, which would make the arm-twisting that much easier. D-PAC would go to the grassroots, to the defense workers and their bosses, and orchestrate a massive phone campaign in support of Aaron Lake and more military spending. Six senators from defense-heavy states had tough opponents in November, and Elaine Tyner planned a lunch with each of them.

Unlimited cash cannot go unnoticed for long in Washington. A rookie congressman from Kentucky, one of the lowest of the 435, desperately needed money to fight what appeared to be a losing campaign back home. No one had heard of the poor boy. He hadn't said a word during his first two years, and now his rivals back home had found an attractive opponent. No one would give him money. He heard rumors, tracked down Elaine Tyner, and their conversation went something like this:

'How much money do you need?' she asked.

'A hundred thousand dollars.' He flinched, she did not.

'Can you endorse Aaron Lake for President?'

'I'll endorse anybody if the price is right.'

'Good. We'll give you two hundred thousand and run your campaign.'

'It's all yours.'

Most were not that easy, but D-PAC managed to buy eight endorsements in the first ten days of its existence. All were insignificant congressmen who'd served with Lake and liked him well

110

enough. The strategy was to line them up before the cameras a week or two before big Super Tuesday, March 7. The more the merrier.

Most, however, had already committed to other candidates.

Tyner hurriedly made the rounds, sometimes eating three power meals a day, all happily covered by D-PAC. Her goal was to let the town know that her brand-new client had arrived, had plenty of money, and was backing a dark horse soon to break from the pack. In a city where talk was an industry in itself, she had no trouble spreading her message.

Finn Yarber's wife arrived unannounced at Trumble, her first visit in ten months. She wore fraying leather sandals, a soiled denim skirt, a baggy blouse adorned with beads and feathers, and all sorts of old hippie crap around her neck and wrists and head. She had a gray butch cut and hair under her arms, and looked very much like the tired, worn-out refugee from the sixties that she really was. Finn was less than thrilled when word got to him that his wife was waiting up front.

Her name was Carmen Topolski-Yocoby, a mouthful that she had used as a weapon all of her adult life. She was a radical feminist lawyer in Oakland whose speciality was representing lesbians suing for sexual harassment at work. So every single client was an angry woman battling an angry employer. Work was a bitch.

She had been married to Finn for thirty years – married, but not always living together. He'd lived with other women; she'd lived with other men.

111

Once when they were newlyweds, they lived with an entire houseful of others, different combinations each week. Both came and went. For one six-year stretch they lived together in chaotic monogamy, and produced two children, neither of whom had amounted to much.

They'd met on the battlefields of Berkeley in 1965, both protesting the war and all other evils, both law students, both committed to the high moral ground of social change. They worked diligently to register voters. They fought for the dignity of migrant workers. They got arrested during the Tet Offensive. They chained themselves to redwoods. They fought the Christians in the schools. They sued on behalf of the whales. They marched the streets of San Francisco in every parade, for any and every cause.

And they drank heavily, partied with great enthusiasm, and relished the drug culture; they moved in and out and slept around, and this was okay because they defined their own morality. They were fighting for the Mexicans and the redwoods, dammit! They had to be good people!

Now they were just tired.

She was embarrassed that her husband, a brilliant man who'd somehow stumbled his way onto the California Supreme Court, was now locked away in a federal prison. He was quite relieved that the prison was in Florida and not California; otherwise she might visit more often. His first digs had been near Bakersfield, but he managed to get himself transferred away.

They never wrote each other, never called. She

112

was passing through because she had a sister in Miami.

'Nice tan,' she said. 'You're looking good.'

And you're shriveling like an old prune, he thought. Damn, she looked ancient and tired.

'How's life?' he asked, not really caring.

'Busy. I'm working too hard.'

'That's good.' Good that she was working and making a living, something she'd done off and on for many years. Finn had five years to go before he could shake Trumble's dust from his gnarled and bare feet. He had no intention of returning to her, or to California. If he survived, something he doubted every day, he'd leave at the age of sixty-five, and his dream was to find a land where the IRS and the FBI and all the rest of those alphabetized government thugs had no jurisdiction. Finn hated his own government so much he planned to renounce his citizenship and find another nationality.

'Are you still drinking?' he asked. He, of course, was not, though he did manage a little pot occasionally from one of the guards.

'I'm still sober, thanks for asking.'

Every question was a barb, every reply a retort. He honestly wondered why she had stopped by. Then he found out.

'I've decided to get a divorce,' she said.

He shrugged as if to say, 'Why bother?' Instead he said, 'Probably not a bad idea.'

'I've found someone else,' she said.

'Male or female?' he asked, more curious than anything else. Nothing would surprise him.

'A younger man.'

113

He shrugged again and almost said, 'Go for it, old girl.'

'He's not the first,' Finn said.

'Let's not go there,' she said.

Fine with Finn. He had always admired her exuberant sexuality, her stamina, but it was difficult to imagine this old woman doing it with any regularity. 'Show me the papers,' he said. 'I'll sign them.'

'They'll be here in a week. It's a clean break, since we own so little these days.'

At the height of his rise to power, Justice Yarber and Ms. Topolski-Yocoby had jointly applied for a mortgage on a home in the marina district of San Francisco. The application, properly sanitized to remove any hint of chauvinism or sexism or racism or ageism, blandly worded by spooked California lawyers terrified of being sued by some offended soul, showed a gap between assets and liabilities of almost a million dollars.

Not that a million dollars had mattered to either one of them. They were too busy fighting timber interests and ruthless farmers, etc. In fact, they'd taken pride in the scantness of their assets.

California was a community property state, which roughly meant an equal split. The divorce papers would be easy to sign, for many reasons.

And there was one reason Finn would never mention. The Angola scam was producing money, hidden and dirty, and off-limits to any and every greedy agency. Ms. Carmen would damned sure never know about it.

Finn wasn't certain how the tentacles of community property might reach a secret bank account

114

in the Bahamas, but he had no plans to find out. Show him the papers, he'd be happy to sign.

They managed to chat a few minutes about old friends, a brief conversation indeed because most friends were gone. When they said good-bye, there was no sadness, no remorse. The marriage had been dead for a long time. They were relieved at its passing.

He wished her well, without so much as a hug, then went to the track, where he stripped to his boxers and walked an hour in the sun.

TEN

Lufkin was finishing his second day in Cairo with dinner at a sidewalk café on Shari' el-Corniche, in the Garden City section of the city. He sipped strong black coffee and watched the merchants close their shops – sellers of rugs and brass pots and leather bags and linens from Pakistan, all for the tourists. Less than twenty feet away, an ancient vendor meticulously folded his tent, then left his spot without a trace.

Lufkin looked very much the part of a modern Arab – white slacks, light khaki jacket, a white vented fedora with the bill down close to his eyes. He watched the world from behind a hat and a pair of sunshades. He kept his face and arms tanned and his dark hair cut very short. He spoke perfect Arabic and moved with ease from Beirut to Damascus to Cairo.

His room was at the Hotel El-Nil on the edge of the Nile River, six crowded blocks away, and as he drifted through the city he was suddenly joined by a tall thin foreigner of some breed with only passable English. They knew each other well

116

enough to trust each other, and continued their walk.

'We think tonight is the night,' the contact said, his eyes also hidden.

'Go on.'

'There's a party at the embassy.'

'I know.'

'Yes, a nice setting. Lots of traffic. The bomb will be in a van.'

'What kind of van?'

'We don't know.'

'Anything else?'

'No,' he said, then vanished in a swarming crowd.

Lufkin drank a Pepsi in a hotel bar, alone, and thought about calling Teddy. But it had been four days since he'd seen him at Langley, and Teddy had made no contact. They'd been through this before. Teddy was not going to intervene. Cairo was a dangerous place for Westerners these days, and no one could effectively blame the CIA for not stopping an attack. There would be the usual grandstanding and finger pointing, but the terror would quickly be shoved into the recesses of the national memory, then forgotten. There was a campaign at hand, and the world moved fast anyway. With so many attacks, and assaults, and mindless violence both at home and abroad, the American people had become hardened. Twenty-four-hour news, nonstop flash points, the world always with a crisis somewhere. Late-breaking stories, a shock here and a shock there, and before long you couldn't keep up with events.

Lufkin left the bar and went to his room. From

his window on the fourth floor the city rambled forever, built helter-skelter over the centuries. The roof of the American embassy was directly in front of him, a mile away.

He opened a paperback Louis L'Amour, and waited for the fireworks.

The truck was a two-ton Volvo panel van, loaded from floor to ceiling with three thousand pounds of plastic explosives made in Romania. Its door happily advertised the services of a well-known caterer in the city, a company which made frequent visits to most of the Western embassies. It was parked near the service entrance, in the basement.

The driver of the truck had been a large, friendly Egyptian called Shake by the Marines who guarded the embassy. Shake passed through often, hauling food and supplies to and from social events. Shake was now dead on the floor of his truck, a bullet in his brain.

At twenty minutes after ten, the bomb was detonated by a remote device, operated by a terrorist hiding across the street. As soon as he pushed the right buttons, he ducked behind a car, afraid to look.

The explosion ripped out supporting columns deep in the basement, so the embassy fell to one side. Debris rained for blocks. Most of the nearby buildings suffered structural damage. Windows within a quarter of a mile were cracked.

Lufkin was napping in his chair when the quake came. He jumped to his feet, walked onto his narrow balcony, and watched the cloud of dust.

The roof of the embassy was no longer visible. Within minutes flames were seen and the interminable sirens began. He propped his chair against the railing of the balcony, and settled in for the duration. There would be no sleep. Six minutes after the explosion, the electricity in Garden City went out, and Cairo was dark except for the orange glow of the American embassy.

He called Teddy.

When the technician, Teddy's sanitizer, assured Lufkin the line was secure, the old man's voice came through as clearly as if they were chatting from New York to Boston. 'Yes, Maynard here.'

'I'm in Cairo, Teddy. Watching our embassy go up in smoke.'

'When did it happen?'

'Less than ten minutes ago.'

'How big –'

'Hard to tell. I'm in a hotel a mile away. Massive, I'd say.'

'Call me in an hour. I'll stay here at the office tonight.'

'Done.'

Teddy rolled himself to a computer, punched a few buttons, and within seconds found Aaron Lake. The candidate was en route from Philadelphia to Atlanta, aboard his shiny new airplane. There was a phone in Lake's pocket, a secure digital unit as slim as a cigarette lighter.

Teddy punched more numbers, the phone was summoned, and Teddy spoke to his monitor. 'Mr. Lake, it's Teddy Maynard.'

Who else could it be? Lake thought. No one else could use the phone.

'Are you alone?' Teddy asked.

'Just a minute.'

Teddy waited, then the voice returned. 'I'm in the kitchen now,' Lake said.

'Your plane has a kitchen?'

'A small one, yes. It's a very nice plane, Mr. Maynard.'

'Good. Listen, sorry to bother you, but I have some news. They bombed the American embassy in Cairo fifteen minutes ago.'

'Who?'

'Don't ask that.'

'Sorry.'

'The press will be all over you. Take a moment, prepare some remarks. It will be a good time to express concern for the victims and their families. Keep the politics to a minimum, but also keep the hard line. Your ads are prophetic now, so your words will be repeated many times.'

'I'll do it right now.'

'Call me when you get to Atlanta.'

'Yes, I will.'

Forty minutes later, Lake and his group landed in Atlanta. The press had been duly notified of his arrival, and with the dust just settling in Cairo, there was a crowd waiting. No live pictures had yet emerged of the embassy, yet several agencies were already reporting that 'hundreds' had been killed.

In the small terminal for private aircraft, Lake stood before an eager group of reporters, some

120

with cameras and mikes, others with slim recorders, others still with just plain old notepads. He spoke solemnly, without notes: 'At this moment, we should be in prayer for those who've been injured and killed by this act of war. Our thoughts and prayers are with them and their families, and also with the rescue people. I am not going to politicize this event, but I will say that it is absurd for this country to once again suffer at the hands of terrorists. When I am President, no American life will go unaccounted for. I will use our new military to track down and annihilate any terrorist group that preys upon innocent Americans. That's all I have to say.'

He walked off, ignoring the shouts and questions from the pack of shaggy dogs.

Brilliant, thought Teddy, watching live from his bunker. Quick, compassionate, yet tough as hell. Superb! He once again patted himself on the back for choosing such a wonderful candidate.

When Lufkin called again it was past midnight in Cairo. The fires had been extinguished and they were hauling out bodies as fast as they could. Many were buried in the rubble. He was a block away, behind an army barricade, watching with thousands of others. The scene was chaos, smoke and dust thick in the air. Lufkin had been to several bomb sites in his career, and this was a bad one, he reported.

Teddy rolled around his room and poured another decaf coffee. The Lake terror ads would begin at prime time. On this very night the campaign would spend $3 million in a coast-to-coast deluge of fear and doom. They'd pull the ads

121

tomorrow, and announce it beforehand. Out of respect for the dead and their families, the Lake campaign would temporarily suspend its little prophecies. And they'd start polling at noon tomorrow, massive polling.

High time candidate Lake's positives shot upward. The Arizona and Michigan primaries were less than a week away.

The first pictures from Cairo were of a harried reporter with his back to an army barricade, soldiers watching him fiercely, as he might get shot if he tried once more to charge forward. Sirens wailed all around; lights flashed. But the reporter knew little. A massive bomb had exploded deep in the embassy at ten-twenty when a party was breaking up; no idea of the casualties, but there'd be plenty, he promised. The area was cordoned off by the army, and for good measure they'd sealed the airspace so, dammit, there'd be no helicopter shots. As of yet, no one had claimed responsibility, but for good measure he gave the names of three radical groups as the usual suspects.

'Could be one of these, could be someone else,' he said helpfully. With no carnage to film, the camera was forced to stay with the reporter, and since he had nothing to say he prattled on about how dangerous the Middle East had become, as if this were breaking news and he was there to report it!

Lufkin called around 8 P.M. D.C. time to tell Teddy that the American ambassador to Egypt could not be located, and they were beginning to fear he might be in the rubble. At least that was the word on the street. While talking to Lufkin on the

122

phone, Teddy watched the muted reporter; a Lake terror ad appeared on another screen. It showed the rubble, the carnage, the bodies, the radicals from some other attack, then the smooth but earnest voice of Aaron Lake promising revenge.

How perfect the timing, Teddy thought.

An aide woke Teddy at midnight with lemon tea and a vegetable sandwich. As he so often did, he'd napped in his wheelchair, the wall of TV screens alive with images but no sound. When the aide left, he pushed a button and listened.

The sun was well up in Cairo. The ambassador had not been found, and it was now being assumed he was somewhere in the rubble.

Teddy had never met the ambassador to Egypt, an absolute unknown anyway, who was now being idolized by the chattering reporters as a great American. His death didn't particularly bother Teddy, though it would increase the criticism of the CIA. It would also add gravity to the attack, which, in the scheme of things, would benefit Aaron Lake.

Sixty-one bodies had been recovered so far. The Egyptian authorities were blaming Yidal, the likeliest of suspects because his little army had bombed three Western embassies in the past sixteen months, and because he was openly calling for war against the United States. The current CIA dossier on Yidal gave him thirty soldiers and an annual budget of around $5 million, almost all originating from Libya and Saudi Arabia. But to the press, the leaks suggested an army of a thousand with unlimited funds with which to terrorize innocent Americans.

The Israelis knew what Yidal had for breakfast and where he ate it. They could've taken him out a dozen times, but so far he'd kept his little war away from them. As long as he killed Americans and Westerners, the Israelis really didn't care. It was to their benefit for the West to loathe the Islamic radicals.

Teddy ate slowly, then napped some more. Lufkin called before noon Cairo time with the news that the bodies of the ambassador and his wife had been found. The count was now at eighty-four; all but eleven were Americans.

The cameras caught up with Aaron Lake outside a plant in Marietta, Georgia, shaking hands in the dark as the shift changed, and when asked about events in Cairo, he said: 'Sixteen months ago these same criminals bombed two of our embassies, killing thirty Americans, and we've done nothing to stop them. They're operating with impunity because we lack the commitment to fight. When I'm President, we'll declare war on these terrorists and stop the killing.'

The tough talk was contagious, and as America woke up to the terrible news in Cairo, the country was also treated to a brash chorus of threats and ultimatums from the other seven candidates. Even the more passive among them now sounded like gunslingers.

ELEVEN

It was snowing again in Iowa, a steady swirl of snow and wind that turned to slush on the streets and sidewalks and made Quince Garbe once again long for a beach. He covered his face on Main Street as if to protect himself, but the truth was he didn't want to speak to anyone. Didn't want anyone to see him darting yet again into the post office.

There was a letter in the box. One of those letters. His jaw fell and his hands froze when he saw it, just lying there with some junk mail, innocent, like a note from an old friend. He glanced over both shoulders – a thief racked with guilt – then yanked it out and thrust it into his coat.

His wife was at the hospital planning a ball for crippled children, so the house was empty except for a maid who spent her day napping down in the laundry room. He hadn't given her a raise in eight years. He took his time driving there, fighting the snow and the drifts, cursing the con man who'd entered his life under the ruse of love, anticipating

125

the letter, which grew heavier near his heart with each passing minute.

No sign of the maid as he entered the front door, making as much noise as possible. He went upstairs to his bedroom, where he locked the door. There was a pistol under the mattress. He flung his overcoat and his gloves onto an armchair, then his jacket, and he sat on the edge of his bed and examined the envelope. Same lavender paper, same handwriting, same everything with a Jacksonville postmark, two days old. He ripped it open and removed a single page.

Dear Quince:
Thanks so much for the money. So that you won't think I'm a total thug, I think you should know the money went to my wife and children. They are suffering so. My incarceration has left them destitute. My wife is clinically depressed and cannot work. My four children are fed by welfare and food stamps.
(A hundred thousand bucks should certainly fatten them up, Quince thought.)
They live in government housing and have no dependable transportation. So, thanks again for your help. Another $50,000 should get them out of debt and start a nice college fund.
Same rules as before; same wiring instructions; same promises to expose your secret life if the money is not received quickly. Do it now, Quince, and I swear this is my last letter.

Thanks again, Quince.

Love, Ricky

He went to the bathroom, to the medicine cabinet, where he found his wife's Valium. He took two, but thought about eating all of them. He needed to lie down but he couldn't use the bed because it would be wrinkled and someone would ask questions. So he stretched himself out on the floor, on the worn but clean carpet, and waited for the pills to work.

He'd begged and scraped and even lied a little to borrow the first installment for Ricky. There was no way he could squeeze another $50,000 from a personal balance sheet already heavily padded and still teetering on the edge of insolvency. His nice large house was choked with a fat mortgage held by his father. His father signed his paychecks. His cars were large and imported, but they had a million miles on them and little value. Who in Bakers, Iowa, would want to buy an eleven-year-old Mercedes?

And what if he managed to somehow steal the money? The criminal otherwise known as Ricky would simply thank him again, then demand more.

It was over.

Time for the pills. Time for the gun.

The phone startled him. Without thinking, he scrambled to his feet and grabbed the receiver. 'Hello,' he grunted.

'Where the hell are you?' It was his father, with a tone he knew so well.

'I'm, uh, not feeling well,' he managed to say,

127

staring at his watch and now remembering the ten-thirty meeting with a very important inspector from the FDIC.

'I don't give a damn how you feel. Mr. Colthurst from the FDIC has been waiting in my office for fifteen minutes.'

'I'm vomiting, Dad,' he said, and cringed again with the word Dad. Fifty-one years old, still using the word Dad.

'You're lying. Why didn't you call if you're sick? Gladys told me she saw you just before ten walking toward the post office. What the hell's going on here?'

'Excuse me. I gotta go to the toilet. I'll call you later.' He hung up.

The Valium rolled in like a pleasant fog, and he sat on the edge of his bed staring at the lavender squares scattered on the floor. Ideas were slow in coming, hampered by the pills.

He could hide the letters, then kill himself. His suicide note would place the bulk of the blame on his father. Death was not an altogether unpleasant prospect; no more marriage, no more bank, no more Dad, no more Bakers, Iowa, no more hiding in the closet.

But he would miss his children and grandchildren.

And what if this Ricky monster didn't learn of the suicide, and sent another letter, and they found it, and somehow Quince got himself outed anyway, long after his funeral?

The next lousy idea involved a conspiracy with his secretary, a woman he trusted marginally to begin with. He would tell her the truth, then ask

128

her to write a letter to Ricky and break the news of Quince Garbe's suicide. Together, Quince and his secretary could scheme and fake their way through a suicide, and in the process take some measure of revenge against Ricky.

But he'd rather be dead than tell his secretary.

The third idea occurred after the Valium had settled in at full throttle, and it made him smile. Why not try a little honesty? Write a letter to Ricky and plead poverty. Offer another $10,000 and tell him that's all. If Ricky was determined to destroy him, then he, Quince, would have no choice but to come after Ricky. He'd inform the FBI, let them track the letters and the wire transfers, and both men would go down in flames.

He slept on the floor for thirty minutes, then gathered his jacket, gloves, and overcoat. He left the house without seeing the maid. As he drove to town, flush with the desire to confront the truth, he admitted aloud that only the money mattered. His father was eighty-one. The bank's stock was worth about $10 million. Someday it would be his. Stay in the closet until the cash was in hand, then live any way he damned well pleased.

Don't screw up the money.

Coleman Lee owned a taco hut in a strip mall on the outskirts of Gary, Indiana, in a section of town now ruled by the Mexicans. Coleman was forty-eight, with two bad divorces decades earlier, no children, thank God. Because of all the tacos, he was thick and slow, with a drooping stomach and large fleshy cheeks. Coleman was not pretty, but he was certainly lonely.

His employees were mainly young Mexican boys, illegal immigrants, all of whom he, sooner or later, tried to molest, or seduce, or whatever you'd call his clumsy efforts. Rarely was he successful, and his turnover was high. Business was slow too because people talked and Coleman was not well regarded. Who wanted to buy tacos from a pervert?

He rented two small boxes at the post office at the other end of the strip mall – one for his business, the other for his pleasure. He collected porno and gathered it almost daily from the post office. The mail carrier at his apartment was a curious type, and it was best to keep some things as quiet as possible.

He strolled along the dirty sidewalk at the edge of the parking lot, past the discount stores for shoes and cosmetics, past a XXX video dive he'd been banned from, past a welfare office, one brought to the suburbs by a desperate politician looking for votes. The post office was crowded with Mexicans taking their time because it was cold out.

His daily haul was two hard-core magazines sent to him in plain brown wrappers, and a letter which looked vaguely familiar. It was a square yellow envelope, no return address, postmarked in Atlantic Beach, Florida. Ah, yes, he remembered as he held it. Young Percy in rehab.

Back in his cramped little office between the kitchen and the utility room, he quickly flipped through the magazines, saw nothing new, then stacked them in a pile with a hundred others. He opened the letter from Percy. Like the two before,

it was handprinted, and addressed to Walt, a name
he used to collect all his porn. Walt Lee.

Dear Walt:

I really enjoyed your last letter. I've read it
many times. You have a nice way with words.
As I told you, I've been here for almost
eighteen months, and it gets very lonely. I
keep your letters under my mattress, and
when I feel really isolated I read them over
and over. Where did you learn to write like
that? Please send another one as soon as
possible.

With a little luck, I'll be released in April.
I'm not sure where I'll go or what I'll do. It's
frightening, really, to think that I'll just walk
out of here after almost two years, and have
no one to be with. I hope we're still pen pals
by then.

I was wondering, and I really hate to ask
this, but since I have no one else I'll do it
anyway, and please feel free to say no, it
won't hurt our friendship, but could you loan
me a thousand bucks? They have this little
book and music shop here at the clinic, and
they let us buy paperbacks and CDs on
credit, and, well, I've been here so long that
I've run up quite a tab.

If you can make the loan, I'd really
appreciate it. If not, I completely understand.

Thanks for being there, Walt. Please write
me soon. I treasure your letters.

Love, Percy

131

A thousand bucks? What kinda little creep was this? Coleman smelled a con. He ripped the letter into pieces and threw them in the trash.

'A thousand bucks,' he mumbled to himself, reaching for the magazines again.

Curtis was not the real name of the jeweler in Dallas. Curtis worked fine when corresponding with Ricky in rehab, but the real name was Vann Gates.

Mr. Gates was fifty-eight years old, on the surface happily married, the father of three and the grandfather of two, and he and his wife owned six jewelry stores in the Dallas area, all located in malls. On paper they had $2 million, and they'd made it themselves. They had a very nice new home in Highland Park, with separate bedrooms at opposite ends. They met in the kitchen for coffee and in the den for TV and grandkids.

Mr. Gates ventured from the closet now and then, always with excruciating caution. No one had a clue. His correspondence with Ricky was his first attempt at finding love through the want ads, and so far he'd been thrilled with the results. He rented a small box in a post office near one of the malls, and used the name Curtis V. Cates.

The lavender envelope was addressed to Curtis Cates, and as he sat in his car and carefully opened it, he at first had no clue anything was wrong. Just another sweet letter from his beloved Ricky. Lightning hit, though, with the first words:

Dear Vann Gates:
The party's over, pal. My name ain't Ricky,

132

and you're not Curtis. I'm not a gay boy looking for love. You, however, have an awful secret, which I'm sure you want to keep. I want to help.

Here's the deal: Wire $100,000 to Geneva Trust Bank, Nassau, Bahamas, account number 144-DXN-9593, for Boomer Realty, Ltd., routing number 392844–22.

Do so immediately! This is not a joke. It's a scam, and you've been hooked. If the money is not received within ten days, I will send to your wife, Ms. Glenda Gates, a little packet filled with copies of all letters, photos, etc.

Wire the money, and I'll simply go away.

Love, Ricky

With time, Vann found the Dallas I-635 loop, and before long he was on the I-820 loop around Fort Worth, then back to Dallas, driving at exactly fifty-five, in the right-hand lane, oblivious to the traffic stacked up behind him. If crying would help, then he would've certainly had a good one. He had no qualms about weeping, especially in the privacy of his Jaguar.

But he was too angry to cry, too bitter to be wounded. And he was too frightened to waste time yearning for someone who did not exist. Action was needed – quick, decisive, secretive.

Heartache, though, overcame him, and he finally pulled onto the shoulder and parked with the engine running. All those wonderful dreams of Ricky, those countless hours staring at his handsome face with his crooked little smile, and reading

133

his letters – sad, funny, desperate, hopeful – how could so many emotions be conveyed with the written word? He'd practically memorized the letters.

And he was just a boy, so young and virile, yet lonely and in need of mature companionship. The Ricky he'd come to love needed the loving embrace of an older man, and Curtis/Vann had been making plans for months. The ploy of a diamond show in Orlando while his wife was in El Paso at her sister's. He'd sweated the details and left no tracks.

He did, finally, cry. Poor Vann shed tears without shame or embarrassment. No one could see him; the other cars were flying past at eighty miles per hour.

He vowed revenge, like any jilted lover. He'd track down this beast, this monster who'd posed as Ricky and broken his heart.

When the sobbing began to subside, he thought of his wife and family and that helped greatly in drying up the tears. She'd get all six stores and the $2 million and the new house with separate bedrooms, and he would get nothing but ridicule and scorn and gossip in a town that loved it so. His children would follow the money, and for the rest of their lives his grandchildren would hear the whispers about their grandfather.

Back in the right lane at fifty-five, back through Mesquite for the second time, reading the letter again as eighteen-wheelers roared past.

There was no one to call, no banker he could trust to check out the account in the Bahamas, no

lawyer to run to for advice, no friend to hear his
sorry tale.

For a man who'd carefully lived a double life,
the money would not be insurmountable. His wife
watched every dime, both at home and at the
stores, and for that reason Vann had long since
mastered the scheme of hiding money. He did it
with gems, rubies and pearls and sometimes small
diamonds he placed aside and later sold to other
dealers for cash. It was common in the business.
He had boxes of cash – shoe boxes neatly stacked
in a fireproof safe in a mini-storage out in Plano.
Post-divorce cash. Cash for the afterlife when he
and Ricky would sail the world and spend it all in
one endless voyage.

'Sonofabitch!' he said through gritted teeth. And
again and again.

Why not write this con man and plead poverty?
Or threaten to expose his little extortion scheme?
Why not fight back?

Because the sonofabitch knew exactly what he
was doing. He'd tracked Vann well enough to
learn his real name, and the name of his wife. He
knew Vann had the money.

He pulled into his driveway and there was
Glenda sweeping the sidewalk. 'Where have you
been, honey?' she asked pleasantly.

'Running errands,' he said with a smile.

'Took a long time,' she said, still sweeping.

He was so sick of it. She timed his movements!
For thirty years he'd been under her thumb, with a
stopwatch clicking in the palm of her hand.

He pecked her on the cheek out of habit, then
went to the basement where he locked a door and

135

began to cry again. The house was his prison (with a mortgage of $7,800 a month, it certainly felt like it). She was the guard, the keeper of the keys. His sole means of escape had just collapsed, replaced by a cold-blooded extortionist.

TWELVE

Eighty coffins required a lot of space. They were laid in perfect rows, all neatly wrapped in red, white, and blue, all the same length and width. They'd arrived thirty minutes earlier aboard an Air Force cargo plane, and were removed with great pomp and ceremony. Almost a thousand friends and relatives sat on folding chairs, on the concrete floor of the hangar, and stared in shock at the sea of flags arranged before them. They were outnumbered only by the shaggy dogs, all quarantined behind barricades and military police.

Even for a country well accustomed to foreign policy boondoggles, it was an impressive body count. Eighty Americans, eight Brits, eight Germans – no French because they'd been boycotting Western diplomatic functions in Cairo. Why were eighty Americans still in the embassy after 10 P.M.? That was the question of the hour, and so far no good answer had surfaced. So many of those who made such decisions were now lying in their coffins. The best theory buzzing around D.C. was that the caterer had been late, and the band even later.

But the terrorists had proved all too well that they would strike at any hour, so what difference did it make how late the ambassador and his wife and their staff and colleagues and guests wanted to party?

The second great question of the hour was just exactly why did we have eighty people in our embassy in Cairo to begin with? The State Department had yet to acknowledge the question.

After some mournful music from an Air Force band, the President spoke. His voice broke and he managed to summon a tear or two, but after eight years of such theatrics the act had worn thin. He'd already promised revenge many times, so he dwelt on comfort and sacrifice and the promise of a better life in the hereafter.

The Secretary of State called the names of the dead, a morbid recitation designed to capture the gravity of the moment. The sobbing increased. Then some more music. The longest speech was delivered by the Vice President, fresh from the campaign trail and filled with a newly discovered commitment to eradicate terrorism from the face of the earth. Though he'd never worn a military uniform, he seemed eager to start tossing grenades.

Lake had them all on the run.

Lake watched the grim ceremony while flying from Tucson to Detroit, late for another round of interviews. On board was his pollster, a newly acquired magician who now traveled with him. While Lake and his staff watched the news, the pollster worked feverishly at the small conference

138

table upon which he had two laptops, three phones, and more printouts than any ten people could digest.

The Arizona and Michigan primaries were three days away, and Lake's numbers were climbing, especially in his home state, where he was in a dead heat with the long-established front-runner, Governor Tarry of Indiana. In Michigan, Lake was ten points down, but people were listening. The fiasco in Cairo was working beautifully in his favor.

Governor Tarry was suddenly scrambling for money. Aaron Lake was not. It was coming in faster than he could spend it.

When the Vice President finally finished, Lake left the screen and returned to his leather swivel recliner and picked up a newspaper. A staff member brought him coffee, which he sipped while watching the flatlands of Kansas eight miles below him. Another staff member handed him a message – one that was supposed to require an urgent call from the candidate. Lake glanced around the plane, and counted thirteen people, pilots not included.

For a private man who still missed his wife, Lake was not adjusting well to the complete lack of privacy. He moved with a group, every half hour slotted by someone, every action coordinated by a committee, every interview preceded by written guesses about the questions and suggested responses. He got six hours each night alone, in his hotel room, and damned if the Secret Service wouldn't sleep on the floor if he'd allow it. Because of the fatigue, he slept like an infant. His only true moments of quiet reflection occurred in the bath-room, either in the shower or on the toilet.

But he wasn't kidding himself. He, Aaron Lake, quiet congressman from Arizona, had become an overnight sensation. He was charging while the rest were faltering. Big money was aimed at him. The press followed like bloodhounds. His words got repeated. He had very powerful friends, and as the pieces were falling in place the nomination looked realistic. He hadn't dreamed of such things a month earlier.

Lake was savoring the moment. The campaign was madness, but he could control the tempo of the job itself. Reagan was a nine-to-five President, and he'd been far more effective than Carter, an avid workaholic. Just get to the White House, he told himself over and over, suffer these fools, gut it through the primaries, endure with a smile and a quick wit, and one day very soon he'd sit in the Oval Office, alone, with the world at his feet.

And he would have his privacy.

Teddy sat with York in his bunker, watching the live scene from Andrews Air Force Base. He preferred York's company when things were rough. The accusations had been brutal. Scape-goats were in demand, and many of the idiots chasing the cameras blamed the CIA because that's who they always blamed.

If they only knew.

He'd finally told York of Lufkin's warnings, and York understood completely. Unfortunately, they'd been through this before. When you police the world you lose a lot of cops, and Teddy and

140

York had shared many sad moments watching the flag-covered coffins roll off the C-130s, evidence of another debacle abroad. The Lake campaign would be Teddy's final effort at saving American lives.

Failure seemed unlikely. D-PAC had collected more than $20 million in two weeks, and was in the process of hauling the money around Washington. Twenty-one congressmen had been recruited for Lake endorsements, at a total cost of $6 million. But the biggest prize so far was Senator Britt, the ex-candidate, the father of a little Thai boy. When he abandoned his quest for the White House he owed close to $4 million, with no viable plan to cover his deficit. Money tends not to follow those who pack up and go home. Elaine Tyner, the lawyer running D-PAC, met with Senator Britt. It took her less than an hour to cut the deal. D-PAC would pay off all his campaign debts, over a three-year period, and he would make a noisy endorsement of Aaron Lake.

'Did we have a projection of casualties?' York asked.

After a while Teddy said, 'No.'

Their conversations were never hurried.

'Why so many?'

'Lots of booze. Happens all the time in the Arab countries. Different culture, life is dull, so when our diplomats throw a party, they throw a good one. Many of the dead were quite drunk.'

Minutes passed. 'Where's Yidal?' asked York.

'Right now he's in Iraq. Yesterday, Tunisia.'

'We really should stop him.'

141

'We will, next year. It'll be a great moment for President Lake.'

Twelve of the sixteen congressmen endorsing Lake wore blue shirts, a fact that was not lost on Elaine Tyner. She counted such things. When a D.C. politician got near a camera, odds were he'd put on his best blue cotton shirt. The other four wore white.

She arranged them before the reporters in a ballroom of the Willard Hotel. The senior member, Representative Thurman of Florida, opened things up by welcoming the press to this very important occasion. Working from prepared notes, he offered his opinions on the current state of world events, commented on things in Cairo and China and Russia, and said that the world was a lot more dangerous than it looked. He rattled off the usual statistics about our reduced military. Then he launched into a long soliloquy about his close friend Aaron Lake, a man he'd served with for ten years and whom he knew better than most. Lake was a man with a message, one we didn't particularly want to hear, but a very important one nonetheless.

Thurman was breaking ranks with Governor Tarry, and though he did so with great reluctance and no small feeling of betrayal, he had become convinced through painful soul-searching that Aaron Lake was needed for the safety of our nation. What Thurman didn't say was that a recent poll showed Lake becoming very popular back in Tampa-St. Pete.

The mike was then passed to a congressman

from California. He covered no new territory, but rambled for ten minutes anyway. In his district north of San Diego were forty-five thousand defense and aerospace workers, and all of them, it seemed, had written or called. He'd been an easy convert; the pressure from home plus $250,000 from Ms. Tyner and D-PAC, and he had his marching orders.

When the questions started, the sixteen bunched together in a tight little pack, all anxious to answer and say something, all afraid their faces might not get wedged into the picture.

Though there were no committee chairmen, the group was not unimpressive. They managed to convey the image that Aaron Lake was a legitimate candidate, a man they knew and trusted. A man the nation needed. A man who could be elected.

The event was well staged and well covered, and instantly made news. Elaine Tyner would trot out five more the following day, then save Senator Britt for the day before big Super Tuesday.

The letter in Ned's glove box was from Percy, young Percy in rehab who got his mail through Laurel Ridge, Post Office Box 4585, Atlantic Beach, FL 32233.

Ned was in Atlantic Beach, had been for two days, with the letter and with the determination to track down young Percy because he smelled a hoax. He had nothing better to do. He was retired with plenty of money, no family to speak of, and besides, it was snowing in Cincinnati. He had a room at the Sea Turtle Inn, on the beach, and at night he hit the bars along Atlantic Boulevard.

143

He'd found two excellent restaurants, crowded little places with lots of young pretty girls and boys. He'd discovered Pete's Bar and Grill a block away, and for the last two nights he'd staggered from the place, drunk on cold drafts. The Sea Turtle was just around the corner.

During the day Ned watched the post office, a modern brick and glass government job on First Street, parallel to the beach. A small, windowless box midway from the floor, 4585 was on a wall with eighty others, in an area of medium traffic. Ned had inspected the box, tried to open it with keys and wire, and had even asked questions at the front desk. The postal workers had been most unhelpful. Before leaving the first day, he had stuck a two-inch strand of thin black thread to the bottom of the box's door. It was imperceptible to anyone else, but Ned would know if the mail was checked.

He had a letter in there, in a bright red envelope, one he'd mailed three days earlier from Cincinnati, then raced south. In it he'd sent Percy a check for $1,000, money the boy needed for a set of artist's supplies. In an earlier letter, Ned had revealed that he had once owned a modern art gallery in Greenwich Village. It was a lie, he had not, but he doubted everything Percy said too.

Ned had been suspicious from the beginning. Before he answered the solicitation, he had tried to verify Laurel Ridge, the fancy detox unit supposedly holding Percy. There was a telephone, a private number he'd been unable to pry out of directory assistance. There was no street address. Percy had explained in his first letter that the place

144

was top-secret because many of its patients were high-powered corporate executives and top-level government officials, all of whom had, in one way or another, succumbed to chemicals. It sounded good. The boy had a way with words.

And a very pretty face. That's why Ned kept writing. The photo was something he admired every day.

The request for money had caught him by surprise, and since he was bored he decided to make the drive to Jacksonville.

From his spot in the parking lot, low behind the steering wheel of his car, with his back to First Street, he could watch the wall of boxes and the postal customers as they came and went. It was a long shot, but what the hell. He used a small pair of foldable binoculars, and on occasion caught a stare from someone walking by. The task grew monotonous after two days, but as the time passed he became more and more convinced that his letter would be retrieved. Surely someone checked the box at least once every three days. A rehab clinic with patients would get plenty of mail, wouldn't it? Or was it simply a front for a con man who dropped by once a week to check his traps?

The con man showed up late in the afternoon of the third day. He parked a Beetle next to Ned, then ambled into the post office. He wore wrinkled khakis, white shirt, straw hat, bow tie, and had the disheveled air of a would-be beach Bohemian.

Trevor had enjoyed a long midday break at Pete's, then slept off his liquid lunch with an hour nap at his desk, and was just stirring about, making his rounds. He put the key in Box 4585 and

145

removed a handful of correspondence, most of it junk mail, which he threw away as he flipped through the letters on his way out of the building.

Ned watched every move. After three days of tedium, he was thrilled that his surveillance had paid off. He followed the Beetle, and when it parked and the driver walked into a small, run-down law office, Ned drove away, scratching his temple, repeating out loud, 'A lawyer?'

He kept driving, down Highway A1A, along the shore, away from the sprawl of Jacksonville, south through Vilano Beach and Crescent Beach and Beverly Beach and Flagler Beach and finally to a Holiday Inn outside Port Orange. He went to the bar before he went to his room.

It wasn't the first scam he'd flirted with. In fact, it was the second. He'd sniffed the other one out too before any damage was done. Over his third martini he swore it would be his last.

146

THIRTEEN

The day before the Arizona and Michigan primaries, the Lake campaign unleashed a media blitz, the likes of which had never been seen before in presidential politics. For eighteen hours, the two states were bombarded with one ad after another. Some were fifteen seconds, little softies with not much more than his handsome face and the promises of decisive leadership and a safer world. Others were one-minute documentaries on the dangers of the post-cold war. Still others were macho, in-your-face promises to the terrorists of the world – kill people simply because they are Americans, and you will pay a very dear price. Cairo was still very fresh, and the assurances hit their mark.

The ads were bold, put together by high-powered consultants, and the only downside was oversaturation. But Lake was too new to the scene to bore anyone, not now anyway. His campaign spent $10 million on television in the two states, a staggering amount.

They ran at a slower clip during voting hours on Tuesday, February 22, and when the polls closed the exit analysts predicted Lake would win his home state and run a close second in Michigan. Governor Tarry, after all, was from Indiana, another midwestern state, and he'd spent weeks in Michigan during the previous three months.

Evidently, he hadn't spent enough time there. The voters in Arizona opted for their native son, and those in Michigan liked the new fellow too. Lake got 60 percent at home, and 55 percent in Michigan where Governor Tarry got a paltry 31 percent. The balance was divided among the noncontenders.

It was a devastating loss for Governor Tarry, just two weeks before big Super Tuesday and three weeks before the little one.

Lake watched the vote counting from on board his airplane, en route from Phoenix, where'd he'd voted for himself. An hour from Washington, CNN declared him the surprise winner in Michigan, and his staff opened the champagne. He savored the moment, even allowed himself two glasses.

History was not lost on Lake. No one had ever started so late, and come so far so fast. In the darkened cabin, they watched the analysts on four screens, the experts all marveling at this man Lake and what he'd done. Governor Tarry was gracious, but also worried about the enormous sums of money being spent by his heretofore unknown opponent.

Lake chatted politely with the small group of reporters waiting for him at Reagan National Airport, then rode in yet another black Suburban

148

to his national campaign headquarters where he thanked his highly paid staff and told them to go home and get some sleep.

It was almost midnight when he got to Georgetown, to his quaint little rowhouse on Thirty-fourth, near Wisconsin. Two Secret Service agents got out of the car behind Lake, and two more were waiting on the front steps. He had adamantly refused an official request to put guards inside his home.

'I do not want to see you people lurking around here,' he said harshly at his front door. He resented their presence, didn't know their names, and didn't care if they disliked him. They had no names, as far as he was concerned. They were simply 'You people,' said with as much contempt as possible.

Once he was locked inside, he went upstairs to his bedroom and changed clothes. He turned out the lights as if he were asleep, waited fifteen minutes, then eased downstairs to the den to see if anyone was looking in, then down another flight to the small basement. He climbed through a window, and stepped into the cold night near his tiny patio. He paused, listened, heard nothing, then quietly opened a wooden gate and darted between the two buildings behind his. He surfaced on Thirty-fifth Street, alone, in the dark, dressed like a jogger with a running cap pulled low to his brow. Three minutes later he was on M Street, in the crowds. He found a taxi and disappeared into the night.

Teddy Maynard had gone to sleep reasonably

149

content with his candidate's first two victories, but he was awakened by the news that something had gone wrong. When he rolled himself into the bunker at ten minutes after 6 A.M., he was more frightened than angry, though his emotions had run the gamut in the past hour. York was waiting, along with a supervisor named Deville, a tiny nervous man who'd obviously been wired for many hours.

'Let's hear it,' Teddy growled, still rolling and looking for coffee.

Deville did the talking. 'At twelve-o-two this morning he said good-bye to the Secret Service and entered his house. At twelve-seventeen he exited through a small window in the basement. We, of course, have wires and timers on every door and window. We've leased a rowhouse across the street, and we were on alert anyway. He hasn't been home in six days.' Deville waved a small pill, the size of an aspirin. 'This is a little device known as a T-Dec. They're in the soles of all of his shoes, including his jogging shoes. So if he's not barefoot we know where he is. Once pressure is applied from the foot, the bug emits a signal that is broadcast for two hundred yards without a trans-mitter. When pressure is relaxed, it will continue to provide a signal for fifteen minutes. We scrambled and picked him up on M Street. He was dressed in sweats with a cap over his eyes. We had two cars in place when he jumped in a cab. We followed him to Chevy Chase, to a suburban shopping center. While the cab waited, he darted into a place called Mailbox America, one of these new places where you can send and receive mail

150

outside the Postal Service. Some, including this one, are open twenty-four hours for mail pickup. He was inside for less than a minute, just long enough to open his box with a key, remove several pieces of mail, throw it all away, then return to the cab. One of our cars followed him back to M Street, where he got out and sneaked back home. The other car stayed at the mailbox place. We went through the waste can just inside the door, and found six pieces of junk mail, evidently his. The address is A1 Konyers, Box 455, Mailbox America, 39380 Western Avenue, Chevy Chase.'

'So he didn't find what he was looking for?' Teddy asked.

'It looks as though he tossed everything he took from his box. Here's the video.'

A screen dropped from the ceiling as the lights faded. Footage from a video camera zoomed across a parking lot, past the cab, and onto the figure of Aaron Lake in his baggy sweats as he disappeared around a corner inside Mailbox America. Seconds later he reappeared, flipping through letters and papers in his right hand. He stopped briefly at the door and then dumped everything in a tall wastebasket.

'What the hell's he looking for?' Teddy mumbled to himself.

Lake left the building and quickly ducked inside the cab. The video stopped; the lights became brighter.

Deville resumed his narrative. 'We're confident we found the right papers in the trash can. We were there within seconds, and no one else entered the premises while we waited. The time was twelve fifty-eight. An hour later, we entered again and keyed the lock to Box 455, so we'll have access anytime we need it.'

'Check it every day,' Teddy said. 'Inventory every piece of mail. Leave the junk, but when something arrives I want to know it.'

'You got it. Mr. Lake reentered the basement window at one twenty-two and stayed at home for the rest of the night. He's there now.'

'That's all,' Teddy said, and Deville left the room.

A minute passed as Teddy stirred his coffee. 'How many addresses does he have?'

York knew the question was coming. He glanced at some notes. 'He gets most of his personal mail at his home in Georgetown. He has at least two addresses on Capitol Hill, one at his office, the other at the Armed Services Committee. He has three offices back home in Arizona. That's six that we know about.'

'Why would he need a seventh?'

'I don't know the reason, but it can't be good. A man who has nothing to hide does not use an alias or a secret address.'

'When did he rent the box?'

'We're still working on that.'

'Maybe he rented the box after he decided to enter the race. He's got the CIA doing his thinking for him, so maybe he figures we're watching everything too. And he figures he might need a little privacy, thus the box. Maybe it's a girlfriend we missed somehow. Maybe he likes dirty magazines or videos, something that is shipped through the mail.'

After a long pause, York said, 'Could be. What

152

if the box was rented months ago, long before he entered the race?'

'Then he's not hiding from us. He's hiding from the world, and his secret is truly dreadful.'

They silently contemplated the dreadfulness of Lake's secret, neither wanting to venture a guess. They decided to step up surveillance even more, and to check the mailbox twice a day. Lake would be leaving town in a matter of hours, off to do battle in other primaries, and they would have the box to themselves.

Unless someone else was also checking it for him.

Aaron Lake was the man of the hour in Washington. From his office on Capitol Hill he graciously granted live interviews to the early morning news programs. He received senators and other members of Congress, friends and former enemies alike, all bearing tidings of great joy and congratulations. He had lunch with his campaign staff, and followed it with long meetings on strategy. After a quick dinner with Elaine Tyner, who brought wonderful news of tons of new cash over at D-PAC, he left the city and flew to Syracuse to make plans for the New York primary.

A large crowd welcomed him. He was, after all, now the front-runner.

FOURTEEN

The hangovers were becoming more frequent, and as Trevor opened his eyes for another day he told himself that he simply had to get a grip. You can't lay out at Pete's every night, drinking cheap longnecks with coeds, watching meaningless basketball games just because you've got a thousand bucks on them. Last night it had been Logan State and somebody, some team with green uniforms. Who the hell cared about Logan State?

Joe Roy Spicer, that's who. Spicer put $500 on them, Trevor backed it up with a thousand of his own, and Logan won it for them. In the past week, Spicer had picked ten out of twelve winners. He was up $3,000 in real cash, and Trevor, happily following along, was up $5,500 for himself. His gambling was proving to be much more profitable than his lawyering. And someone else was picking the winners!

He went to the bathroom and splashed water on his face without looking at the mirror. The toilet was still clogged from the day before, and as he stomped around his dirty little house looking for a plunger the phone rang. It was a wife from a

154

previous life, a woman he loathed and one who loathed him, and when he heard her voice he knew she needed money. He said no angrily and got in the shower.

Things were worse at the office. A divorcing couple had arrived in separate cars to finish the negotiations for their property settlement. The assets they were fighting over were of no consequence to anyone else – pots, pans, a toaster – but since they had nothing, they had to fight over something. The fights are nastiest when the stakes are smallest.

Their lawyer was an hour late, and they had used the time to simmer and boil until finally Jan had separated them. The wife was parked in Trevor's office when he stumbled in from the back door.

'Where the hell you been?' she demanded loud enough for husband to hear up front. Husband charged down the hall, past Jan, who did not give chase, and burst into Trevor's small office.

'We've been waiting for an hour!' he announced.

'Shut up, both of you!' Trevor screamed, and Jan left the building. His clients were stunned at the volume.

'Sit down!' he screamed again, and they fell into the only empty chairs. 'You people pay five hundred bucks for a lousy divorce and you think you own the place!'

They looked at his red eyes and red face and decided this was not a man to mess with. The phone started ringing and no one answered it. Nausea hit again, and Trevor bolted out of his office and across the hall to the bathroom, where he puked, as quietly as possible. The toilet failed to flush, the little metal chain clinking harmlessly inside the tank.

The phone was still ringing. He staggered down the hall to fire Jan, and when he couldn't find her he left the building too. He walked to the beach, took off his shoes and socks, and splashed his feet in the cool salt water.

Two hours later, Trevor sat motionless at his desk, door locked to keep out clients, bare feet on the desk, with sand still wedged between the toes. He needed a nap and he needed a drink, and he stared at the ceiling trying to organize his priorities. The phone rang, this time duly answered by Jan, who was still employed but secretly checking want ads.

It was Brayshears, in the Bahamas. 'We have a wire, sir,' he said.

Trevor was instantly on his feet. 'How much?'

'A hundred thousand, sir.'

Trevor glanced at his watch. He had about an hour to catch a flight. 'Can you see me at three-thirty?' he asked.

'Certainly, sir.'

He hung up and yelled toward the front, 'Cancel my appointments for today and tomorrow. I'm leaving.'

'You don't have any appointments,' Jan yelled back. 'You're losing money faster than ever.'

He wouldn't bicker. He slammed the back door and drove away.

The flight to Nassau stopped first in Fort Lauderdale, though Trevor hardly knew it. After two quick beers he was sound asleep. Two more over the Atlantic, and a flight attendant had to wake him when the plane was empty.

The wire was from Curtis in Dallas, as expected. It was remitted by a Texas bank, payable to Boomer Realty, care of Geneva Trust Bank, Nassau. Trevor raked his one third off the top, again hiding $25,000 in his own secret account, and taking $8,000 in cash. He thanked Mr. Brayshears, said he hoped to see him soon, and staggered out of the building.

The thought of going home had not crossed his mind. He headed for the shopping district, where packs of heavy American tourists choked the sidewalks. He needed shorts and a straw hat and a bottle of sunscreen.

Trevor eventually made it to the beach, where he found a room in a nice hotel, $200 a night but what did he care? He lathered himself in oil and stretched out by the pool, close enough to the bar. A waitress in a thong fetched him drinks.

He woke up after dark, sufficiently cooked but not burned. A security guard escorted him to his room, where he fell on the bed and returned to his coma. The sun was up again before he moved.

After such a long period of rest, he awoke surprisingly clear-headed, and very hungry. He ate some fruit and went looking for sailboats, not exactly shopping for one, but paying close attention to the details. A thirty-footer would be sufficient, just large enough to live on yet manageable by a crew of one. There would be no passengers; just the lonely skipper hopping from

157

island to island. The cheapest one he found was $90,000 and it needed some work.

Noon found him back at the pool with a cell phone trying to placate a client or two, but his heart wasn't in it. The same waitress brought another drink. Off the phone, he hid behind dark sunshades and tried to crunch the numbers. But things were wonderfully dull between his ears.

In the past month he'd earned about $80,000 in tax-free graft. Could the pace continue? If so, he'd have his million bucks in a year, and he could abandon his office and what was left of his career, and he could buy his little boat and hit the sea.

For the first time ever, the dream almost seemed real. He could see himself at the wheel, shirtless, shoeless, cold beer at the ready, gliding across the water from St. Barts to St. Kitts, from Nevis to St. Lucia, from one island to a thousand others, wind popping his mainsail, not a damned thing in the world to worry about. He closed his eyes and longed even harder for an escape.

His snoring woke him. The thong was nearby. He ordered some rum and checked his watch.

Two days later Trevor finally made it back to Trumble. He arrived with mixed feelings. First, he was quite anxious to pick up the mail and facilitate the scam, anxious to keep the extortion going and the money rolling in. On the other hand, he was tardy and Judge Spicer would not be happy.

'Where the hell you been?' Spicer growled at him as soon as the guard left the attorney-conference room. It seemed to be the standard question these days. 'I've missed three games because of you, and I picked nothing but winners.'

'The Bahamas. We got a hundred thousand from Curtis in Dallas.'

Spicer's mood changed dramatically. 'It took three days to check on a wire in the Bahamas?' he asked.

'I needed a little rest. Didn't know I was supposed to visit this place every day.'

Spicer was mellowing by the second. He'd just picked up another $22,000. It was safely tucked away with his other loot, in a place no one could find, and as he handed the lawyer yet another stack of pretty envelopes he was thinking of ways to spend the money.

'Aren't we busy,' Trevor said, taking the letters.

'Any complaints? You're making more than we are.'

'I have more to lose than you do.'

Spicer handed over a sheet of paper. 'I've picked ten games here. Five hundred bucks on each.'

Great, thought Trevor. Another long weekend at Pete's, watching one game after another. Oh well, there could be worse things. They played blackjack at a dollar a hand until the guard broke up the meeting.

Trevor's increased visits had been discussed by the warden and the higher-ups at the Bureau of Prisons in Washington. Paperwork had been created on the subject. Restrictions had been contemplated, but then abandoned. The visits were useless, and besides, the warden didn't want to alienate the Brethren. Why pick a fight?

The lawyer was harmless. After a few phone

calls around Jacksonville they decided that Trevor was basically unknown and probably had nothing better to do than hang out in the attorney-conference room of a prison.

The money gave new life to Beech and Yarber. Spending it would necessarily entail getting to it, and that would require they one day walk away as free men, free to do whatever they wanted with their growing fortunes.

With $50,000 or so now in the bank, Yarber was busy plotting an investment portfolio. No sense letting it sit there at 5 percent per annum, even if it was tax-free. One day very soon he'd roll it over into aggressive growth funds, with emphasis on the Far East. Asia would boom again, and his little pile of dirty money would be there to share in the wealth. He had five years to go, and if he earned between 12 and 15 percent on his money until then the $50,000 would grow to roughly $100,000 by the time he left Trumble. Not a bad start for a man who would be sixty-five, and hopefully still in good health.

But if he (and Percy and Ricky) could keep adding to the principal, he might indeed be rich when they turned him loose. Five lousy years – months and weeks he'd been dreading. Now he was suddenly wondering if he had enough time to extort all he needed. As Percy, he was writing letters to over twenty pen pals across North America. No two were in the same town. It was Spicer's job to keep the victims separated. Maps were being used in the law library to make certain neither Percy nor Ricky was corresponding with men who appeared to live near one another.

When he wasn't writing letters, Yarber caught himself thinking about the money. Thankfully, the divorce papers from his wife had come and gone. He'd be officially single in a few months, and by the time he was paroled she'd have long since forgotten about him. Nothing would be shared. He'd be free to walk away without a single string attached.

Five years, and he had so much work to do. He'd cut out the sugar and walk an extra mile each day.

In the darkness of his top bunk, during sleepless nights, Hatlee Beech had done the same math as his colleagues. Fifty thousand dollars in hand, a healthy rate of return somewhere, add to the principal by squeezing from as many victims as they could catch, and one day there'd be a fortune. Beech had nine years, a marathon that once seemed endless. Now there was a flicker of hope. The death sentence they'd handed him was slowly becoming a time of harvest. Conservatively, if the scam netted him only $100,000 a year for the next nine years, plus a healthy rate of return, then he'd be a multimillionaire when he danced through the gates, also at the age of sixty-five.

Two, three, four million was not out of the question.

He knew exactly what he'd do. Since he loved Texas, he'd go to Galveston and buy one of those ancient Victorians near the sea, and he'd invite old friends to stop by and see how rich he was. Forget the law, he'd put in twelve-hour days working the money, nothing but work, nothing but money, so that by the time he was seventy he'd have more than his ex-wife.

For the first time in years, Hatlee Beech thought he might live to see sixty-five, maybe seventy.

He, too, gave up sugar, and butter, and he cut his cigarettes in half with the goal of going cold turkey real soon. He vowed to stay away from the infirmary and stop taking pills. He began walking a mile every day, in the sun, like his colleague from California. And he wrote his letters, he and Ricky.

And Justice Spicer, already equipped with sufficient motivation, was finding it difficult to sleep. He wasn't plagued by guilt or loneliness or humiliation, nor was he depressed by the indignity of prison. He was simply counting money, and juggling rates of return, and analyzing point spreads. With twenty-one months to go, he could see the end.

His lovely wife Rita had passed through the week before, and they'd spent four hours together over two days. She'd cut her hair, stopped drinking, and lost eighteen pounds, and she promised to be even skinnier when she picked him up at the front gate in less than two years. After four hours with her, Joe Roy was convinced the $90,000 was still buried behind the toolshed.

They'd move to Vegas, buy a new condo, and say to hell with the rest of the world.

With the Percy-and-Ricky scam working so well, Spicer had found a new worry. He'd leave Trumble first, happily, gladly, without looking back. But what about the money to be made after he was gone? If the scam was still printing money, what would happen to his share of the future earnings, money he was clearly entitled to? It had been, after all, his idea, one he'd borrowed from the prison in Louisiana. Beech and Yarber had been reluctant conspirators at first.

He had time to devise an exit strategy, just as he had time to contrive a way to get rid of the lawyer. But it would cost him some sleep.

The letter from Quince Garbe in Iowa was read by Beech: "'Dear Ricky (or whoever the hell you are): I don't have any more money. The first $100,000 was borrowed from a bank using a bogus financial statement. I'm not sure how I'll pay it back. My father owns our bank and all its money. Why don't you write him some letters, you thug! I can possibly scrape together $10,000 if we can agree that the extortion will stop there. I'm on the verge of suicide, so don't push. You're scum, you know that. I hope you get caught. Sincerely, Quince Garbe.'"

'Sounds pretty desperate,' Yarber said, looking up from his own pile of mail.

Spicer said, toothpick hanging from his bottom lip, 'Tell him we'll take twenty-five thousand.'

'I'll write him and tell him to wire it,' Beech said, opening another envelope addressed to Ricky.

163

FIFTEEN

During lunch, when experience had shown that traffic picked up somewhat at Mailbox America, an agent nonchalantly entered the place behind two other customers, and for the second time that day placed a key in Box 455. Lying on top of three pieces of junk mail – one from a pizza carryout, one from a car wash, one from the U.S. Postal Service – he noticed something new. It was an envelope, light orange in color, five by eight. With a pair of tweezers he kept on his key ring, he clamped the end of the envelope, slid it quickly from the box, and dropped it in a small leather briefcase. The junk mail was left undisturbed.

At Langley, it was carefully opened by experts. Two handwritten pages were removed, and copied.

An hour later, Deville entered Teddy's bunker, holding a file. Deville was in charge of what was commonly referred to, deep inside Langley, as the 'Lake mess.' He gave copies of the letter to Teddy and York, then scanned it to a large screen, where Teddy and York at first just stared at it. The printing was bold, in block form, easily readable,

164

as if the author had labored over each word. It read:

Dear Al:

Where you been? Did you get my last letter? I wrote three weeks ago and I haven't heard a word. I guess you're busy, but please don't forget about me. I get very lonely here, and your letters have always inspired me to keep going. They give me strength and hope because I know somebody out there cares. Please don't give up on me, Al.

My counselor says that I might be released in two months. There's a halfway house in Baltimore, actually a few miles from where I grew up, and the people here are trying to get me a spot there. It would be for ninety days, enough time for me to find a job, some friends, etc., you know, get used to society again. It's a lockdown place at night, but I'd be free during the day.

There aren't many good memories, Al. Every person who ever loved me is now dead, and my uncle, the guy who's paying for this rehab, is very rich but very cruel.

I need friends so desperately, Al.

By the way, I've lost another five pounds, and my waist is now a thirty-two. The photo I sent you is getting outdated. I've never liked the way my face looks in it – too much flesh on the cheeks.

I'm much leaner now, and tanned. They let us tan for up to two hours a day here, weather permitting. It's Florida, but some

165

days are too cool. I'll send you another
photo, maybe one from the chest up. I'm
lifting weights like crazy. I think you'll like
the next photo.

You said you would send me one of you.
I'm still waiting. Please don't forget me, Al. I
need one of your letters.

Love, Ricky

Since York had had the responsibility of investigating every aspect of Lake's life, he felt compelled
to try and speak first. But he could think of
nothing to say. They read the letter in silence
again, and again.

Finally, Deville broke the ice by saying, 'Here's
the envelope.' He flashed it on the wall. It was
addressed to Mr. Al Konyers, at Mailbox America.
The return address was: Ricky, Aladdin North,
P.O. Box 44683, Neptune Beach, FL 32233.

'It's a front,' Deville said. 'There's no such place
as Aladdin North. There's a telephone number,
and you get an answering service. We've called ten
times with questions, but the operators know
nothing. We've called every rehab and treatment
clinic in North Florida, and no one's heard of this
place.'

Teddy was silent, still staring at the wall.

'Where's Neptune Beach?' York grunted.

'Jacksonville.'

Deville was excused, but told to stand by. Teddy
began making notes on a green legal pad. 'There
are other letters, and at least one photo,' he said, as
if the problem were just part of the routine. Panic
was a state unknown to Teddy Maynard.

'We have to find them,' he said.

'We've done two thorough searches of his home,' York said.

'Then do a third. I doubt if he would keep such stuff at his office.'

'How soon – '

'Do it now. Lake is in California looking for votes. We have no time on this, York. There may be other secret boxes, other men writing letters and bragging about their tans and waistlines.'

'Do you confront him?'

'Not yet.'

Since they had no sample of Mr. Konyers' handwriting, Deville made a suggestion that Teddy eventually liked. They would use the ruse of a new laptop, one with a built-in printer. The first draft was composed by Deville and York, and after an hour or so the fourth draft read as follows:

Dear Ricky:

I got your letter of the twenty-second; forgive me for not writing sooner. I've been on the road a lot lately, and I'm behind on everything. In fact, I'm writing this letter at thirty-five thousand feet, somewhere over the Gulf, en route to Tampa. And I'm using a new laptop, one so small it almost fits in my pocket. Amazing technology. The printer leaves something to be desired. I hope you can read it okay.

Wonderful news about your release, and the halfway house in Baltimore. I have some business interests there, and I'm sure I can help you find a job.

Keep your head up, only two months to go. You're a much stronger person now, and you're ready to live life to its fullest. Don't be discouraged.

I'll help in any way possible. When you get to Baltimore, I'll be happy to spend some time with you, show you around, you know.

I promise I'll write sooner. I can't wait to hear from you.

Love, Al

They decided Al was in a hurry and forgot to sign his name. The letter was marked up, revised, redrafted, pored over with more care than a treaty. The final version was printed on a piece of stationery from the Royal Sonesta Hotel in New Orleans, and placed in a thick, plain brown envelope with optic wiring hidden along the bottom edge. In the lower right-hand corner, in a spot that looked as if it had been slightly damaged and knotted in transit, a tiny transmitter the size of a pinhead was installed. When activated, it would send a signal a hundred yards for up to three days.

Since Al was traveling to Tampa, the envelope was stamped with a Tampa postmark, dated that day. This was done in less than half an hour by a team of very strange people down in Documents on the second floor.

At 4 P.M., a green van with many miles on it stopped at the curb in front of Aaron Lake's townhouse, near one of the many shade trees on Thirty-fourth, in a lovely section of Georgetown.

Its door advertised a plumbing company in the District. Four plumbers got out and began removing tools and equipment.

After a few minutes, the only neighbor who'd noticed grew bored and returned to her television. With Lake in California, the Secret Service was with him, and his home had yet to qualify for round-the-clock surveillance, at least by the Secret Service. That scrutiny would come quickly, though.

The ploy was a clogged sewer line in the small front lawn, something that could be done without entering the home. An outside job, one that would pacify the Secret Service in case they happened to drop by.

But two of the plumbers did indeed enter the home, with their own keys. Another van stopped by to check on progress, and to drop off a tool. Two plumbers from the second van mixed with those already there, and a regular unit began to form.

Inside the house, four of the agents began their tedious search for hidden files. They moved from room to room, inspecting the obvious, prying for the secrets.

The second van left, and a third one came from the other direction and parked with its tires on the sidewalk, as service vans often do. Four more plumbers joined the sewer cleaning, and two eventually drifted inside. After dark, a spotlight was rigged in the front yard, over the sewer cover, and directed into the home so the lights inside would not be noticed. The four men left outside

169

sipped coffee and told jokes and tried to stay warm. Neighbors hurried by on foot.

After six hours the sewer was clean, as was the home. Nothing unusual was found, certainly no hidden file with correspondence from one Ricky in rehab. No sign of a photo. The plumbers turned off their lights, packed their tools, and disappeared without a trace.

At eight-thirty the next morning, when the doors opened at the Neptune Beach post office, an agent named Barr walked hurriedly in as if he were late for something. Barr was an expert on locks and keys, and he'd spent five hours the previous afternoon at Langley studying various boxes used by the Postal Service. He had four master keys, one of which he was certain would open number 44683. If not, he'd be forced to key it, which might take sixty seconds or so and could possibly draw attention. The third key worked, and Barr placed the brown envelope, postmarked the day before from Tampa, addressed to Ricky with no last name, care of Aladdin North, inside the box. There were two other letters already there. For good measure, he removed a piece of junk mail, then closed the door to the box, wadded up the mail, and threw it in the wastebasket.

Barr and two others waited patiently in a van in the parking lot, sipping coffee and videoing every postal customer. They were seventy yards away from the box. Their handheld receiver beeped with the faint signal from the envelope. A diverse group came and went with the flow – a black female in a short brown dress, a white male with a beard and

170

leather jacket, a white female in a jogging suit, a black male in jeans – all agents of the CIA, all watching the box without a clue about who wrote the letter or where it was going. Their job was simply to find the person who'd rented the box.

They found him after lunch.

Trevor drank his lunch at Pete's, but only two beers. Cold drafts with salty peanuts from the community bowl, consumed while losing fifty bucks on a dogsled race in Calgary. Back at the office, he napped for an hour, snoring so loudly his long-suffering secretary finally had to close his door. She slammed it actually, but not loud enough to wake him.

Dreaming of sailboats, he made his trek to the post office, this time choosing to walk because the day was beautiful, he had nothing better to do, and his head needed clearing. He was delighted to find four of the little treasures angled neatly in Aladdin North's box. He placed them carefully in the pocket of his well-worn seersucker jacket, straightened his bow tie, and ambled forth, certain that another payday was fast approaching.

He'd never been tempted to read the letters. Let the Brethren do the dirty work. He could keep his hands clean, shuttle the mail, rake his third off the top. And besides, Spicer would kill him if he delivered mail that had been tampered with.

Seven agents watched him stroll back to his office.

Teddy was napping in his wheelchair when Deville

entered. York had gone home; it was after 10 P.M. York had a wife, Teddy did not.

Deville delivered his narrative while referring to pages of scribbled notes: 'The letter was removed from the box at one-fifty P.M. by a local lawyer named Trevor Carson. We followed him to his office in Neptune Beach, where he stayed for eighty minutes. It's a small one-man office, one secretary, not a lot of clients. Carson is a small-timer along the beaches, does divorces, real estate, two-bit stuff. He's forty-eight, divorced at least twice, native of Pennsylvania, college at Furman, law school at Florida State, got his license suspended eleven years ago for commingling client funds, then got it back.'

'All right, all right,' Teddy said.

'At three-thirty, he left his office, drove an hour to the federal prison at Trumble, Florida. Took the letters with him. We followed but lost the signal when he entered the prison. Since then, we've gathered some information about Trumble. It's a minimum-security prison, commonly referred to as a camp. No walls or fences, very low risk inmates. A thousand of them at Trumble. According to a source within the Bureau of Prisons here in Washington, Carson visits all the time. No other lawyer, no other person visits as much as Carson. Up until a month ago he went once a week, now it's at least three times a week. Sometimes four. All visits are official attorney-client conferences.'

'Who is his client?'

'It's not Ricky. He is the attorney of record for three judges.'

'Three judges?'

'Yes.'

'Three judges in prison?'

'That's right. They call themselves the Brethren.'

Teddy closed his eyes and rubbed his temples. Deville let things sink in for a moment, then continued: 'Carson was in the prison for fifty-four minutes, and when he exited we could not pick up the signal from the envelope. By this time, we were parked next to his car. He walked within five feet of our receiver, and we're certain he did not have the letter. We followed him back to Jacksonville, back to the beaches. He parked near a place called Pete's Bar and Grill, where he stayed for three hours. We searched his car, found his briefcase, and inside there were eight letters addressed to various men all over the country. All letters were outbound from the prison, none were inbound. Evidently, Carson shuttles mail back and forth to his clients. As of thirty minutes ago, he was still in the bar, quite drunk, betting on college basketball games.'

'A loser.'

'Very much so.'

The loser staggered out of Pete's after the second overtime of a game on the West Coast. Spicer had picked three out of four winners. Trevor had dutifully followed suit, and was up a thousand bucks for the night.

Drunk as he was, he was smart enough not to drive. His DUI three years earlier was still a painful memory, and besides the damned cops were all over the place. The restaurants and bars around

173

the Sea Turtle Inn attracted the young and restless, thus the cops.

Walking was a challenge, though. He made it well enough to his office, a straight shot south, past the quiet little summer rentals and retirement cottages, all dark and tucked in for the night. He carried his briefcase with the letters from Trumble.

He pressed onward, searching for his house. He crossed the street for no reason, and half a block later recrossed it. There was no traffic. When he began to circle back, he came within twenty yards of an agent who'd ducked behind a parked car. The silent army watched him, suddenly fearful that the drunken fool might stumble into one of them.

At some point he gave up, and managed to find his office again. He rattled keys on the front steps, dropped his briefcase and forgot about it, and less than a minute after opening the door he was at his desk, sprawled in his swivel rocker, fast asleep, the front door half open.

The back door had been unlocked throughout the night. Following orders from Langley, Barr and company had entered the office and wired everything. There was no alarm system, no locks on the windows, nothing of value to attract thievery in the first place. Tapping the phones and bugging the walls had been an easy task, made so by the obvious fact that no one on the outside observed anything inside the offices of L. Trevor Carson, Attorney and Counselor-at-Law.

The briefcase was emptied, its contents cataloged at Langley's instructions. Langley wanted a precise record of the letters the lawyer had taken

174

from Trumble. When everything had been inspected and photographed, the briefcase was placed in the hallway near his office. The snoring was impressive, and uninterrupted.

Shortly before 2, Barr managed to start the Beetle parked near Pete's. He drove it down the empty street and left it innocently on the curb in front of the law office, so that the drunk would rub his eyes in a few hours and pat himself on the back for such a nice job of driving. Or maybe he would shrink in horror at the thought of having driven while intoxicated once again. Either way, they'd be listening.

SIXTEEN

Thirty-seven hours before the polls opened in Virginia and Washington, the President appeared live on national television to announce that he had ordered an air attack in and around the Tunisian city of Talah. The Yidal terrorist unit was believed to train there, in a well-stocked compound on the edge of town.

And so the country became glued to yet another mini-war, one of pushbuttons and smart bombs and retired generals on CNN prattling on about this strategy or that. It was dark in Tunisia, thus no footage. The retired generals and their clueless interviewers did a lot of guessing. And waiting. Waiting for sunlight so the smoke and rubble could be broadcast to a jaded nation.

But Yidal had its sources, most likely the Israelis. The compound was empty when the smart bombs dropped in from nowhere. They hit their targets, shook the desert, destroyed the compound, but killed not a single terrorist. A couple strayed, however, one venturing into the center of Talah, where it hit a hospital. Another hit a small

176

house where a family of seven was fast asleep. Fortunately, they never knew what happened.

Tunisian television was quick to cover the burning hospital, and at daybreak on the East Coast the country learned that the smart bombs weren't so smart after all. At least fifty bodies had been recovered, all very innocent civilians.

At some point during the early morning, the President developed a sudden uncharacteristic aversion to reporters, and could not be reached for comment. The Vice President, a man who'd said plenty when the attack started, was in seclusion with his staff somewhere in Washington.

The bodies piled up, the cameras kept rolling, and by midmorning world reaction was swift, brutal, and unanimous. The Chinese were threatening war. The French seemed inclined to join them. Even the Brits said the United States was trigger-happy.

Since the dead were nothing more than Tunisian peasants, certainly not Americans, the politicians were quick to politicize the debacle. The usual finger-pointing and grandstanding and calls for investigations happened before noon in Washington. And on the campaign circuit, those still in the race took a few moments to reflect on just how ill-fated the mission had been. None of them would have engaged in such desperate retaliation without better intelligence. None but the Vice President, who was still in seclusion. As the bodies were being counted, not a single candidate thought the raid was worthy of the risks. All condemned the President.

But it was Aaron Lake who attracted the most

177

attention. He found it difficult to move without tripping over cameramen. In a carefully worded statement, he said, without notes, 'We are inept. We are helpless. We are feeble. We should be ashamed of our inability to wipe out a ragtag little army of less than fifty cowards. You cannot simply push buttons and run for cover. It takes guts to fight wars on the ground. I have the guts. When I am President, no terrorist with American blood on his hands will be safe. That is my solemn promise.'

In the fury and chaos of the morning, Lake's words found their mark. Here was a man who meant what he said, who knew precisely what he would do. We wouldn't slaughter innocent peasants if a man with guts were making the decisions. Lake was the man.

In the bunker, Teddy weathered another storm. Bad intelligence was blamed for every disaster. When the raids were successful, the pilots and the brave boys on the ground and their commanders and the politicians who sent them into battle got the credit. But when the raids went wrong, as they usually did, the CIA got the blame.

He had advised against the attack. The Israelis had a tenuous and very secret agreement with Yidal – don't kill us, and we won't kill you. As long as the targets were Americans and an occasional European, then the Israelis would not get involved. Teddy knew this, but it was information he had not shared. Twenty-four hours before the attack, he had advised the President, in writing, that he doubted the terrorists would be in the compound when the bombs arrived. And, because of the

178

target's proximity to Talah, there was an excellent chance of collateral damage.

Hatlee Beech opened the brown envelope without noticing that the right lower corner was somewhat wadded and slightly damaged. He was opening so many personal envelopes these days, he looked only at the return address to see who and where they came from. Nor did he notice the Tampa postmark.

He hadn't heard from Al Konyers in several weeks. He read the letter through without stopping, and found little if no interest in the fact that Al was using a new laptop. It was perfectly believable that Ricky's pen pal had taken a sheet of stationery from the Royal Sonesta in New Orleans, and was pecking out the letter at thirty-five thousand feet.

Wonder if he was flying first class? he asked himself. Probably so. They wouldn't have computer hookups back in coach, would they? Al had been in New Orleans on business, stayed at a very nice hotel, then flew first class to his next destination. The Brethren were interested in the financial conditions of all their pen pals. Nothing else mattered.

After he read the letter, he handed it to Finn Yarber, who was in the process of writing another one as poor Percy. They were working in the small conference room in the corner of the law library, their table littered with files and mail and a pretty assortment of soft pastel correspondence cards. Spicer was outside, at his table, guarding the door and studying point spreads.

179

'Who's Konyers?' Finn asked.

Beech was flipping through some files. They kept a neat folder on every pen pal, complete with the letters they received and copies of all letters they'd sent.

'Don't know much,' Beech said. 'Lives in the D.C. area, fake name, I'm sure. Uses one of those mailbox services. That's his third letter, I think.'

From the Konyers file Beech pulled out the first two letters. The one from December 11 read:

Dear Ricky:

Hello. My name is Al Konyers. I'm in my fifties. I like jazz, old movies, Humphrey Bogart, and I like to read biographies. I don't smoke and don't like people who do. Fun is Chinese take-out, a little wine, a black-and-white western with a good friend. Drop me a line.

Al Konyers

It was typewritten on plain white paper, the way most of them were at first. Fear was stamped between every line – fear of getting caught, fear of starting a long-distance relationship with a complete stranger. Every letter of every word was typewritten. He didn't even sign his name.

Ricky's first response was the standard letter Beech had written a hundred times now: Ricky's twenty-eight, in rehab, bad family, rich uncle, etc. And dozens of the same enthusiastic questions: What kind of work do you do? How about your family? Do you like to travel? If Ricky could bare his soul, then he needed something in return. Two

180

pages of the same crap Beech had been writing for five months. He wanted so desperately to simply Xerox the damned thing. But he couldn't. He was forced to personalize each one, on nice pretty paper. And he sent Al the same handsome photo he'd sent to the others. The picture was the bait that hooked almost all of them.

Three weeks passed. On January 9, Trevor had delivered a second letter from Al Konyers. It was as clean and sterile as the first, probably typed with rubber gloves.

Dear Ricky:

I enjoyed your letter. I have to admit I felt sorry for you at first, but you seem to have adjusted well to rehab and know where you're going. I've never had problems with drugs and alcohol, so it's difficult for me to understand. It sounds as though you're getting the best treatment money can buy. You shouldn't be so harsh on your uncle. Think of where you might be if not for him.

You ask many questions about me. I'm not ready to discuss a lot of personal matters, but I understand your curiosity. I was married for thirty years, but not anymore. I live in D.C., and work for the government. My job is challenging and fulfilling.

I live alone. I have few close friends and prefer it that way. When I travel, it's usually to Asia. I adore Tokyo.

I'll keep you in my thoughts in the days to come.

Al Konyers

Just above the typewritten name, he'd scribbled the name 'Al,' with a black-felt pen, fine point.

The letter was most unimpressive for three reasons. First, Konyers did not have a wife, or at least he said he didn't. A wife was crucial for extortion. Threaten to tell the wife, to send her copies of all the letters from the gay pen pal, and the money rolled in.

Second, Al worked for the government, so he probably didn't have a lot of money.

Third, Al was much too scared to waste time with. Getting information was like pulling teeth. The Quince Garbes and Curtis Cateses were much more fun because they'd spent their lives in the closet and were now anxious to escape. Their letters were long and windy and filled with all the damning little facts an extortionist might need. Not Al. Al was boring. Al wasn't sure what he wanted.

So Ricky raised the stakes with his second letter, another piece of boilerplate Beech had perfected with practice. Ricky had just learned that he would be released in a few months! And he was from Baltimore. What a coincidence! And he might need some help getting a job. His rich uncle was refusing to help anymore, he was afraid of life on the outside without the help of friends, and he really couldn't trust his old friends because they were still on drugs, etc., etc.

The letter went unanswered, and Beech assumed that Al Konyers was frightened by it. Ricky was on his way to Baltimore, just an hour from Washington, and that was too close for Al.

While waiting for an answer from Al, the Quince

Garbe money landed, followed by the wire from Curtis in Dallas, and the Brethren found renewed energy in their scam. Ricky wrote Al the letter that was intercepted and analyzed at Langley.

Now, suddenly, Al's third letter had a very different tone. Finn Yarber read it twice, then reread the second letter from Al. 'Sounds like a different person, doesn't it?' he said.

'Yes, it does,' Beech said, looking at both letters. 'I think the old boy is finally excited about meeting Ricky.'

'I thought he worked for the government.'

'Says he does.'

'Then what's this about having business interests in Baltimore?'

'We worked for the government, didn't we?'

'Sure.'

'What was your highest salary on the bench?'

'When I was chief justice I made a hundred and fifty thousand.'

'I made a hundred and forty. Some of those professional bureaucrats make more than that. Plus, he's not married.'

'That's a problem.'

'Yeah, but let's keep pushing. He's got a big job, which means he's got a big boss, lots of colleagues, typical Washington hotshot. We'll find a pressure point somewhere.'

'What the hell,' Finn said.

What the hell, indeed. What was there to lose? So what if they pushed a little too hard, and Mr. Al got scared or got mad and decided to throw the letters away? You can't lose what you don't have.

Serious money was being made here. It was not

a time to be timid. Their aggressive tactics were producing spectacular results. The mail was growing each week, as was their offshore account. Their scam was foolproof because their pen pals lived double lives. Their victims had no one to complain to.

Negotiations were quick because the market was ripe. It was still winter in Jacksonville, and because the nights were chilly and the ocean was too cool to swim in, the busy season was a month away. There were hundreds of small rentals available along Neptune Beach and Atlantic Beach, including one almost directly across the street from Trevor. A man from Boston offered $600 cash for two months, and the real estate agent snatched it. The place was furnished with odds and ends no flea market would handle. The old shag carpet was well worn and emitted a permanent musty smell. It was perfect.

The renter's first chore was to cover the windows. Three of them faced the street and looked across to Trevor's, and during the first few hours of surveillance it became obvious how few clients came and went. There was so little business over there! When work surfaced it was usually done by the secretary, Jan, who also read a lot of magazines.

Others quietly moved into the rental, men and women with old suitcases and large duffel bags filled with electronic wizardry. The fragile furnishings were shoved to the rear of the cottage, and the front rooms were quickly filled with screens and monitors and listening devices of a dozen varieties.

Trevor himself would make an interesting case study for third-year law students. He arrived around 9 A.M., and spent the first hour reading newspapers. His morning client seemed to always arrive at ten-thirty, and after an exhaustive half-hour conference he was ready for lunch, always at Pete's Bar and Grill. He carried a phone with him, to prove his importance to the bartenders there, and he usually made two or three unnecessary calls to other lawyers. He called his bookie a lot.

Then he walked back to his office, past the rental where the CIA monitored every step, back to his desk where it was time for a nap. He came to life around three, and hit it hard for two hours. By then he needed another longneck from Pete's.

The second time they followed him to Trumble, he left the prison after an hour and returned to his office about 6 P.M. While he was having dinner in an oyster bar on Atlantic Boulevard, alone, an agent entered his office and found his old brief-case. In it were five letters from Percy and Ricky.

The commander of the silent army in and around Neptune Beach was a man named Klock-ner, the best Teddy had in the field of domestic street spying. Klockner had been instructed to intercept all mail flowing through the law office.

When Trevor went straight home after leaving the oyster bar, the five letters were taken across the street to the rental, where they were opened, copied, then resealed and replaced in Trevor's briefcase. None of the five was for Al Konyers.

At Langley, Deville read the five letters as they came off the fax. They were examined by two handwriting experts who agreed that Percy and

185

Ricky were not the same people. Using samples taken from their court files, it was determined, without much effort, that Percy was really former Justice Finn Yarber, and that Ricky was former U.S. District Judge Hatlee Beech.

Ricky's address was the Aladdin North box at the Neptune Beach post office. Percy, to their surprise, used a postal box in Atlantic Beach, one rented to an outfit called Laurel Ridge.

SEVENTEEN

For his next visit to Langley, the first in three weeks, the candidate arrived in a caravan of shiny black vans, all going too fast but who would complain. They were cleared and waved onward, deeper into the complex, until they roared to a collective stop near a very convenient door where all sorts of grim-faced, thick-necked young men were waiting. Lake rode the wave into the building, losing escorts as he went until finally he arrived not at the usual bunker but in Mr. Maynard's formal office, with a view of a small forest. Everyone else was left at the door. Alone, the two great men shook hands warmly and actually appeared happy to see one another.

Important things first. 'Congratulations on Virginia,' Teddy said.

Lake shrugged as if he wasn't sure. 'Thank you, in more ways than one.'

'It's a very impressive win, Mr. Lake,' Teddy said. 'Governor Tarry worked hard there for a year. Two months ago he had commitments from every precinct captain in the state. He looked unbeatable. Now, I think he's fading fast. It's often

187

a disadvantage to be the front-runner early in the race.'

'Momentum is a strange animal in politics,' Lake observed wisely.

'Cash is even stranger. Right now, Governor Tarry can't find a dime because you've got it all. Money follows momentum.'

'I'm sure I'll say this many times, Mr. Maynard, but, well, thanks. You've given me an opportunity I'd hardly dreamed of.'

'Are you having any fun?'

'Not yet. If we win, the fun will come later.'

'The fun starts next Tuesday, Mr. Lake, with big Super Tuesday. New York, California, Massachusetts, Ohio, Georgia, Missouri, Maryland, Maine, Connecticut, all in one day. Almost six hundred delegates!' Teddy's eyes were dancing as if he could almost count the votes. 'And you're ahead in every state, Mr. Lake. Can you believe it?'

'No, I cannot.'

'It's true. You're neck and neck in Maine, for some damned reason, and it's close in California, but you're going to win big next Tuesday.'

'If you believe the polls,' Lake said, as if he didn't trust them himself. Fact was, like every candidate, Lake was addicted to the polls. He was actually gaining in California, a state with 140,000 defense workers.

'Oh, I believe them. And I believe that a landslide is coming on little Super Tuesday. They love you down South, Mr. Lake. They love guns and tough talk and such, and right now they're falling in love with Aaron Lake. Next Tuesday will be fun, but the following Tuesday will be a romp.'

188

Teddy Maynard was predicting a romp, and Lake couldn't help but smile. His polls showed the same trends, but it just sounded better coming from Teddy. He lifted a sheet of paper and read the latest polling data from around the country. Lake was ahead by at least five points in every state.

They reveled in their momentum for a few minutes, then Teddy turned serious. 'There's something you should know,' he said, and the smile was gone. He flipped a page and glanced at some notes. 'Two nights ago, in the Khyber Pass in the mountains of Afghanistan, a Russian long-range missile with nuclear warheads was moved by truck into Pakistan. It is now en route to Iran, where it will be used for God knows what. The missile has a range of three thousand miles, and the capability of delivering four nuclear bombs. The price was about thirty million dollars U.S., cash up front paid by the Iranians through a bank in Luxembourg. It's still there, in an account believed to be controlled by Natty Chenkov's people.'

'I thought he was stockpiling, not selling.'

'He needs cash, and he's getting it. In fact, he's probably the only man we know who's collecting it faster than you.'

Teddy didn't do humor well, but Lake laughed out of politeness anyway.

'Is the missile operational?' Lake asked.

'We think so. It originated from a collection of silos near Kiev, and we believe it's of a recent make and model. With so many lying around, why would the Iranians buy an old one? Yes, it's safe to assume it's fully operational.'

'Is it the first?'

'There've been some spare parts and plutonium, to Iran and Iraq and India and others, but I think this is the first fully assembled, ready-to-shoot missile.'

'Are they anxious to use it?'

'We don't think so. It appears as if the transaction was instigated by Chenkov. He needs the money to buy other kinds of weapons. He's shopping his wares, things he doesn't need.'

'Do the Israelis know it?'

'No. Not yet. You have to be careful with them. Everything is give and take. Someday, if we need something from them, then we might tell them about this transaction.'

For a moment, Lake longed to be President, and immediately. He wanted to know everything Teddy knew, then he realized he probably never would. There was, after all, a sitting President right then, at that moment, albeit a lame duck, and Teddy wasn't chatting with him about Chenkov and his missiles.

'What do the Russians think about my campaign?' he asked.

'At first, they weren't concerned. Now they're watching closely. But you have to remember, there is no such thing as a Russian voice anymore. The free marketers speak favorably of you because they fear the Communists. The hard-liners are scared of you. It's very complex.'

'And Chenkov?'

'I'm ashamed to say we're not that close to him,

yet. But we're working on it. We should have some ears in the vicinity soon.'

Teddy tossed his papers onto his desk, and rolled himself closer to Lake. The many wrinkles in his forehead pinched closer together, downward. His bushy eyebrows fell hard on his sad eyes. 'Listen to me, Mr. Lake,' he said, his voice much more somber. 'You have this thing won. There will be a bump or two in the road, things we cannot foresee, and even if we could we'd be powerless to prevent them. We'll ride them out together. The damage will be slight. You're something brand new and the people like you. You're doing a marvelous job and communicating. Keep the message simple – our security is at risk, the world is not as safe as it looks. I'll take care of the money, and I'll certainly keep the country frightened. That missile in the Khyber Pass, we could've detonated it. Five thousand people would've been killed, five thousand Pakistanis. Nuclear bombs exploding in the mountains. You think we'd wake up and worry about the stock market? Not a chance. I'll take care of the fear, Mr. Lake. You keep your nose clean and run hard.'

'I'm running as hard as I can.'

'Run harder, and no surprises, okay?'

'Certainly not.'

Lake wasn't sure what he meant by surprises, but he let it pass. Just a bit of grandfatherly wisdom, perhaps.

Teddy rolled away again. He found his buttons and a screen dropped from the ceiling. They spent twenty minutes viewing rough cuts of the next series of Lake ads, then said their goodbyes.

191

Lake sped away from Langley, two vans in front and one behind, all racing to Reagan National Airport, where the jet was waiting. He wanted a quiet night in Georgetown, at home where the world was held at bay, where he could read a book in solitude, with no one watching or listening. He longed for the anonymity of the streets, the nameless faces, the Arab baker on M Street who made a perfect bagel, the used-book dealer on Wisconsin, the coffeehouse where they roasted beans from Africa. Would he ever be able to walk the streets again, like a normal person, doing whatever he pleased? Something told him no, that those days were gone, probably forever.

When Lake was airborne, Deville entered the bunker and announced to Teddy that Lake had come and gone without trying to check the mailbox. It was time for the daily briefing on the Lake mess. Teddy was spending more time than he'd planned worrying about what his candidate might do next.

The five letters Klockner and his group intercepted from Trevor had been thoroughly researched. Two had been written by Yarber as Percy; the other three by Beech as Ricky. The five pen pals were in different states. Four were using fictitious names; one was bold enough not to hide behind an alias. The letters were basically the same: Percy and Ricky were troubled young men in rehab, trying desperately to pull their lives together, both talented and still able to dream big dreams, but in need of moral and physical support from new friends because the old ones were dangerous. They

192

freely divulged their sins and foibles, their weaknesses and heartaches. They rambled about their lives after rehab, their hopes and dreams of all the things they wanted to do. They were proud of their tans and their muscles, and seemed anxious to show their new hardened bodies to their pen pals.

Only one letter asked for money. Ricky wanted a loan of $1,000 from a correspondent named Peter in Spokane, Washington. He said the money was needed to cover some expenses his uncle was refusing to pay.

Teddy had read the letters more than once. The request for money was important because it began to shed light on the Brethren's little game. Perhaps it was just a two-bit enterprise someone taught them, some other con who'd finished his time at Trumble and was now roaming at large stealing anew.

But the size of the stakes was not the issue. It was a flesh game – thinner waists and bronze skin and firm biceps – and their candidate was in the middle of it.

There were still questions, but Teddy was patient. They would watch the mail. The pieces would fall into place.

With Spicer guarding the door to the conference room, and daring anyone to use the law library, Beech and Yarber labored away with their mail. To Al Konyers, Beech wrote:

Dear Al:
 Thanks for your last letter. It means so much to me to hear from you. I feel like I've

been living in a cage for months, and I'm slowly seeing daylight. Your letters help to open the door. Please don't stop writing.

I'm sorry if I've bored you with too much personal stuff. I respect your privacy and hope I haven't asked too many questions. You seem like a very sensitive man who enjoys solitude and the finer things of life. I thought about you last night when I watched *Key Largo,* the old Bogart and Bacall film. I could almost taste the Chinese carry-out. The food here is pretty good, I guess, but they simply can't do Chinese.

I have a great idea. In two months when I get out of here, let's rent *Casablanca and African Queen,* get the carry-out, get a bottle of nonalcoholic wine, and spend a quiet evening on the sofa. God, I get excited just thinking about life on the outside and doing real things again.

Forgive me if I'm going too fast, Al. It's just that I've done without a lot of things here, and not just booze and good food. Know what I mean?

The halfway house in Baltimore is willing to take me if I can find a part-time job of some type. You said you had some interests there. I know I'm asking a lot because you don't know me, but can you arrange this? I will be forever grateful.

Please write me soon, Al. Your letters, and the hopes and dreams of leaving here in two months with a job on the outside, sustain me in my darkest hours.

194

Thanks, friend.

Love, Ricky

The one to Quince Garbe had a very different tone. Beech and Yarber had kicked it around for several days. The final draft read:

Dear Quince:
Your father owns a bank, yet you say you can only raise another $10,000. I think you're lying, Quince, and it really ticks me off. I'm tempted to send the file to your father and wife anyway.
I'll settle for $25,000, immediately, same wiring instructions.
And don't threaten suicide. I really don't care what you do. We'll never meet, and I think you're a sicko anyway.
Wire the damned money, Quince, and now!

Love, Ricky

Klockner worried that Trevor might visit Trumble one day before noon, then drop off the mail at some point along the way before returning to his office or his home. There was no way to intercept it while en route. It was imperative that he haul it back, and leave it overnight so they could get their hands on it.

He worried, but at the same time Trevor was proving to be a late starter. He showed few signs of life until after his two o'clock nap.

So when he informed his secretary that he was about to leave for Trumble at 11 A.M., the rental across the street sprang into action. A call was

195

immediately placed to Trevor's office by a middle-aged woman claiming to be a Mrs. Beltrone, who explained to Jan that she and her rich husband were in dire need of a quick divorce. The secretary put her on hold, and yelled down the hallway for Trevor to wait a second. Trevor was gathering papers from his desk and placing them in his briefcase. The camera in the ceiling above him caught his look of displeasure at having been interrupted by a new client.

'She says she's rich!' Jan yelled, and Trevor's frown disappeared. He sat down and waited.

Mrs. Beltrone unloaded on the secretary. She was wife number three, the husband was much older, they had a home in Jacksonville but spent most of their time at their home in Bermuda. Also had a home in Vail. They'd been planning the divorce for some time, everything had been agreed upon, no fighting at all, very amicable, just needed a good lawyer to handle the paperwork. Mr. Carson had come highly recommended, but they had to act fast for some undisclosed reason.

Trevor took over and listened to the same story. Mrs. Beltrone was sitting across the street in the rental, working from a script the team had put together just for this occasion.

'I really need to see you,' she said after fifteen minutes of baring her soul.

'Well, I'm awfully busy,' Trevor said, as if he were flipping pages in half a dozen daily appointment books. Mrs. Beltrone was watching him on the monitor. His feet were on the desk, his eyes closed, his bow tie crooked. The life of an awfully busy lawyer.

'Please,' she begged. 'We need to get this over with. I must see you today.'

'Where's your husband?'

'He's in France, but he'll be here tomorrow.'

'Well, uh, let's see,' Trevor mumbled, playing with his bow tie.

'What's your fee?' she asked, and his eyes flew open.

'Well, this is obviously more complicated than your simple no-fault. I'd have to charge a fee of ten thousand dollars.' He grimaced when he said it, holding his breath for the response.

'I'll bring it today,' she said. 'Can I see you at one?'

He was on his feet, hovering over the phone. 'How about one-thirty?' he managed to say.

'I'll be there.'

'Do you know where my office is?'

'My driver can find it. Thanks, Mr. Carson.'

Just call me Trevor, he almost said. But she was gone.

They watched as he wrung his hands together, then pumped his fists, gritted his teeth, said, 'Yes!' He'd hooked a big one.

Jan appeared from the hall and said, 'Well?'

'She'll be here at one-thirty. Get this place cleaned up a little.'

'I'm not a maid. Can you get some money up front? I need to pay bills.'

'I'll get the damned money.'

Trevor attacked his bookshelves, straightening volumes he hadn't touched in years, dusting the planks with a paper towel, stuffing files in drawers.

When he charged his desk, Jan finally felt a twinge of guilt and began vacuuming the reception area.

They labored through lunch, their bitching and straining making for great amusement across the street.

No sign of Mrs. Beltrone at one-thirty.

'Where the hell is she?' Trevor barked down the hall just after two.

'Maybe she checked around, got some more references,' Jan said.

'What did you say?' he yelled.

'Nothing, boss.'

'Call her,' he demanded at two-thirty.

'She didn't leave a number.'

'You didn't get a number?'

'That's not what I said. I said she didn't leave a number.'

At three-thirty, Trevor stormed out of his office, still trying desperately to uphold his end of a raging argument with a woman he'd fired at least ten times in the past eight years.

They followed him straight to Trumble. He was in the prison for fifty-three minutes, and when he left it was after five, too late to drop off mail in either Neptune Beach or Atlantic Beach. He returned to his office and left his briefcase on his desk. Then, predictably, he went to Pete's for drinks and dinner.

EIGHTEEN

The unit from Langley flew to Des Moines, where the agents rented two cars and a van, then drove forty minutes to Bakers, Iowa. They arrived in the quiet, snowbound little town two days before the letter. By the time Quince picked it up at the post office, they knew the names of the postmaster, the mayor, the chief of police, and the short-order cook at the pancake house next to the hardware store. But no one in Bakers knew them.

They watched Quince hurry to the bank after leaving the post office. Thirty minutes later, two agents known only as Chap and Wes found the corner of the bank where Mr. Garbe, Jr., did business, and they presented themselves to his secretary as inspectors from the Federal Reserve. They certainly looked official – dark suits, black shoes, short hair, long overcoats, clipped speech, efficient manners.

Quince was locked inside, and at first seemed unwilling to come out. They impressed upon his secretary the urgency of their visit, and after almost forty minutes the door opened slightly. Mr. Garbe looked as though he'd been crying. He was pale, shaken, unhappy with the prospect of entertaining anyone. But he showed them in anyway, too unnerved to ask for identification. He didn't even catch their names.

He sat across the massive desk, and looked at the twins facing him. 'What can we do for you?' he asked, with a very faint smile.

'Is the door locked?' Chap asked.

'Why yes, it is.' The twins got the impression that most of Mr. Garbe's day was spent behind locked doors.

'Can anyone hear us?' Wes asked.

'No.' Quince was even more rattled now.

'We're not reserve officials,' Chap said. 'We lied.'

Quince wasn't sure if he should be angry or relieved or even more frightened, so he just sat there for a second, mouth open, frozen, waiting to be shot.

'It's a long story,' Wes said.

'You've got five minutes.'

'Actually, we have as long as we want.'

'This is my office. Get out.'

'Not so fast. We know some things.'

'I'll call security.'

'No you won't.'

'We've seen the letter,' Chap said. 'The one you just got from the post office.'

'I picked up several.'

'But only one from Ricky.'

Quince's shoulders sagged, his eyes closed slowly. Then they opened again and looked at the tormentors in total, absolute defeat. 'Who are you?' he mumbled.

'We're not enemies.'

'You're working for him, aren't you?'

'Him?'

'Ricky, or whoever the hell he is.'

'No,' Wes said. 'He's our enemy too. Let's just say that we have a client who's in the same boat you're in, more or less. We've been hired to protect him.'

Chap pulled a thick envelope from his coat pocket and tossed it on the desk. 'There's twenty-five thousand cash. Send it to Ricky.'

Quince stared at the envelope, his mouth open wide. His poor brain was choked with so many thoughts he was dizzy. So he closed his eyes again, and squinted fiercely in a vain effort to organize things. Forget the question of who they were. How did they read the letter? Why were they offering him money? How much did they know?

He sure as hell couldn't trust them.

'The money's yours,' Wes said. 'In return, we need some information.'

'Who is Ricky?' Quince asked, his eyes barely open.

'What do you know about him?' Chap asked.

'His name's not Ricky.'

'True.'

'He's in prison.'

'True,' Chap said again.

'Says he has a wife and children.'

'Partially true. The wife is now an ex-wife. The children are still his.'

'Says they're destitute, and that's why he's scamming people.'

'Not exactly. His wife is quite wealthy, and his

201

children have followed the money. We're not sure why he's scamming people.'

'But we'd like to stop him,' Chap added. 'We need your help.'

Quince suddenly realized that for the first time in his life, in all of his fifty-one years, he was sitting in the presence of two living, breathing people who knew he was a homosexual. The knowledge terrified him. For a second he wanted to deny it, to concoct some story of how he came to know Ricky, but invention failed him. He was too scared to be inspired.

Then he realized that these two, whoever they were, could ruin him. They knew his little secret, and they had the power to wreck his life.

And they were offering $25,000 cash?

Poor Quince covered his eyes with his knuckles and said, 'What do you want?'

Chap and Wes thought he was about to cry. They didn't particularly care, but there was no need for it. 'Here's the deal, Mr. Garbe,' said Chap. 'You take the money lying there on your desk, and you tell us everything about Ricky. Show us your letters. Show us everything. If you have a file or a box or some secret place where you've hidden everything, we'd like to see it. Once we've gathered all we need, then we'll leave. We'll disappear as quickly as we've come, and you'll never know who we are or who we're protecting.'

'And you'll keep the secrets?'

'Absolutely.'

'There's no reason for us to tell anyone about you,' Wes added.

'Can you make him stop?' Quince asked, staring at them.

Chap and Wes paused and glanced at each other. Their responses had been perfect so far, but this question had no clear answer. 'We can't promise, Mr. Garbe,' Wes said. 'But we'll try our best to put this Ricky character out of business. As we said, he's upsetting our client too.'

'You've got to protect me on this.'

'We'll do all we can.'

Suddenly Quince stood and leaned forward with his palms flat on the desk. 'Then I have no choice,' he announced. He didn't touch the money, but walked a few steps to an ancient glass bookcase filled with weathered and peeling volumes. With one key he unlocked the case, and with another he opened a small, hidden safe on the second shelf from the floor. Carefully, he withdrew a thin, letter-sized folder, which he delicately placed next to the envelope filled with cash.

Just as he opened the file, an offensive, high-pitched voice squawked through the intercom, 'Mr. Garbe, your father would like to see you immediately.'

Quince bolted upright in horror, his cheeks instantly pale, his face contorted in panic. 'Uh, tell him I'm in a meeting,' he said, trying to sound reassuring but coming off as a hopeless liar.

'You tell him,' she said, and the intercom clicked.

'Excuse me,' he said, actually trying to smile. He picked up the receiver, punched three numbers, and turned his back on Wes and Chap so that maybe they wouldn't hear.

'Dad, it's me. What's up?' he said, head low.

A long pause as the old man filled his ear.

Then, 'No, no, they're not from the Federal Reserve. They're, uh, they're lawyers from Des Moines. They represent the family of an old college buddy of mine. That's all.'

A shorter pause.

'Uh, Franklin Delaney, you wouldn't remember him. He died four months ago, without a will, a big mess. No, Dad, uh, it has nothing to do with the bank.'

He hung up. Not a bad piece of lying. The door was locked. That's all that mattered.

Wes and Chap stood and moved in tandem to the edge of the desk, where they leaned forward together as Quince opened the file. The first thing they noticed was the photo, paper-clipped to the inside flap. Wes gently removed it, and said, 'Is this supposed to be Ricky?'

'That's him,' Quince said, ashamed but determined to get through it.

'A nice-looking young man,' Chap said, as if they were staring at a *Playboy* centerfold. All three were immediately uncomfortable.

'You know who Ricky is, don't you?' Quince asked.

'Yes.'

'Then tell me.'

'No, it's not part of the deal.'

'Why can't you tell me? I'm giving you everything you want.'

'That's not what we agreed on.'

'I want to kill the bastard.'

204

'Relax, Mr. Garbe. We have a deal. You get the money, we get the file, nobody gets hurt.'

'Let's go back to the beginning,' Chap said, looking down at the fragile and suffering little man in the oversized chair. 'How did it all start?'

Quince moved some papers around in the file and produced a thin magazine. 'I bought this at a bookstore in Chicago,' he said, sliding it around so they could read it. The title was *Out and About*, and it described itself as a publication for mature men with alternative lifestyles. He let them take in the cover, then flipped to the back pages. Wes and Chap didn't try to touch it, but their eyes took in as much as possible. Very few pictures, lots of small print. It wasn't pornography by any means.

On page forty-six was a small section of personals. One was circled with a red pen. It read:

> SWM in 20s looking for kind and
> discreet gentleman in 40s or 50s
> to pen pal with.

Wes and Chap leaned lower to read it, then came back up together. 'So you answered this ad?' Chap said.

'I did. I sent a little note, and about two weeks later I heard from Ricky.'

'Do you have a copy of your note?'

'No. I didn't copy my letters. Nothing left this office. I was afraid to make copies around here.'

Wes and Chap frowned in disbelief, then great disappointment. What kind of dumb ass were they dealing with here?

'Sorry,' Quince said, tempted to grab the cash before they changed their minds.

Moving things along, he removed the first letter from Ricky and thrust it at them. 'Just lay it down,' Wes said, and they leaned in again, inspecting without touching. They were very slow readers, Quince noticed, and they read with incredible concentration. His mind was beginning to clear, and a glimmer of hope emerged. How sweet it was to have the money and not have to worry about another crooked loan, another pack of lies to cover his trail. And now he had allies, Wes and Chap here, and God knows who else working against Ricky. His heart slowed a little and his breathing was not as labored.

'The next letter please,' Chap said.

Quince laid them out in sequence, one beside the other, three lavender in color, one a soft blue, one yellow, all written in the tedious block handwriting of a person with plenty of time. When they finished one page, Chap would carefully arrange the next one with a pair of tweezers. Their fingers touched nothing.

The odd thing about the letters, as Chap and Wes would whisper to each other much later, was that they were so thoroughly believable. Ricky was wounded and tortured and in dire need of someone to talk to. He was pitiful and sympathetic. And there was hope because the worst was over for him and he would soon be free to pursue new friendships. The writing was superb!

After a deafening silence, Quince said, 'I need to make a phone call.'

'To whom?'

'It's business.'

Wes and Chap looked at each other with uncertainty, then nodded. Quince walked with the phone to his credenza and watched Main Street below while talking to another banker.

At some point, Wes began making notes, no doubt in preparation for the cross-examination to come. Quince loitered by the bookcase, trying to read a newspaper, trying to ignore the note-taking. He was calm now, thinking as clearly as possible, plotting his next move, the one after these goons left him.

'Did you send a check for a hundred thousand dollars?' Chap asked.

'I did.'

Wes, the grimmer-faced of the two, glared at him with contempt, as if to say, 'What a fool.'

They read some more, took a few notes, whispered and mumbled between themselves.

'How much money has your client sent?' Quince asked, just for the hell of it.

Wes got even grimmer and said, 'We can't say.'

No surprise to Quince. The boys had no sense of humor.

They sat down after an hour, and Quince took his seat in his banker's chair.

'Just a couple of questions,' Chap said, and Quince knew they'd be talking for another hour.

'How'd you book the gay cruise?'

'It's in the letter there. This thug gave me the name and number of a travel agency in New York. I called, then sent a money order. It was easy.'

'Easy? Have you done it before?'

'Are we here to talk about my sex life?'

207

'No.'

'So let's stick to the issues,' Quince said like a real ass, and he felt good again. The banker in him boiled for a moment. Then he thought of something he simply couldn't resist. With a straight face, he said, 'The cruise is still paid for. You guys wanna go?'

Fortunately, they laughed. It was a quick flash of humor, then back to business. Chap said, 'Did you consider using a pseudonym?'

'Yes, of course. It was stupid not to. But I'd never done this before. I thought the guy was legitimate. He's in Florida, I'm in Podunk, Iowa. It never crossed my mind the guy was a fraud.'

'We'll need copies of all this,' Wes said.

'That could be a problem.'

'Why?'

'Where would you copy it?'

'The bank doesn't have a copier?'

'It does, but you're not copying that file in this bank.'

'Then we'll take it to a quick print somewhere.'

'This is Bakers. We don't have a quick print.'

'Do you have an office supply store?'

'Yes, and the owner owes my bank eighty thousand dollars. He sits next to me at the Rotary Club. You're not copying it there. I'm not going to be seen with that file.'

Chap and Wes looked at each other, then at Quince. Wes said, 'Okay, look. I'll stay here with you. Chap will take the file and find a copier.'

'Where?'

'The drugstore,' Wes said.

'You've found the drugstore?'

'Sure, we needed some tweezers.'

'That copier's twenty years old.'

'No, they have a new one.'

'You must be careful, okay? The pharmacist is my secretary's second cousin. This is a very small town.'

Chap took the file and walked to the door. It clicked loudly when he unlocked it, and when he stepped through he was immediately under scrutiny. The secretary's desk was crowded with older women, all busy doing nothing until Chap emerged and they froze and gawked. Old Mr. Garbe was not far away, holding a ledger, pretending to be busy but himself consumed with curiosity. Chap nodded to them all and eased away, passing as he went virtually every employee of the bank.

The door clicked loudly again as Quince locked the damned thing before anyone could barge in. He and Wes chatted awkwardly about this and that for a few minutes, the conversation almost dying at times for lack of common ground. Forbidden sex had brought them together, and they certainly had to avoid that subject. Life in Bakers was of little interest. Quince could ask nothing about Wes' background.

Finally, he said, 'What should I say in my letter to Ricky?'

Wes warmed to the idea immediately. 'Well, I would wait, first of all. Wait a month. Let him sweat. If you hurry back with a response, and with the money, he might think it's too easy.'

'What if he gets mad?'

'He won't. He has plenty of time, and he wants the money.'

'Do you see all his mail?'

'We think we have access to most of it.'

Quince was overcome with curiosity. Sitting with a man who now knew his deepest secret, he felt as though he could prod. 'How will you stop him?'

And Wes, for no reason he would ever understand, said simply, 'We'll probably just kill him.'

A radiant peace broke out around the eyes of Quince Garbe, a warm calming glow that spread through his tortured countenance. His wrinkles softened. His lips spread into a tiny smile. His inheritance would be safe after all, and when the old man was gone and the money was his he'd flee this life and live as he pleased.

'How nice,' he said softly. 'How very nice.'

Chap took the file to a motel room where a leased color copier was waiting with other members of the unit. Three sets were made, and thirty minutes later he was back at the bank. Quince inspected his originals; everything was in order. He carefully relocked the file, then said to his guests, 'I think it's time for you to go.'

They left without shaking hands or the usual good-byes. What was there to say?

A private jet was waiting at the local airport, whose runway was barely long enough. Three hours after leaving Quince, Chap and Wes reported to Langley. Their mission was a resounding success.

★

210

A summary of the account in the Geneva Trust Bank was procured with a bribe of $40,000 to a Bahamian banking official, a man they'd used before. Boomer Realty had a balance of $189,000. Its lawyer had about $68,000 in his account. The summary listed all the transactions – money wired in, money taken out. Deville's people were trying desperately to track down the originators of the wires. They knew about Mr. Garbe's remitting bank in Des Moines, and they knew that another wire of $100,000 had been sent from a bank in Dallas. They could not, however, find out who'd originated that wire.

They were scrambling on many fronts when Teddy summoned Deville to the bunker. York was with him. The table was covered with copies of Garbe's file and copies of the bank summaries.

Deville had never seen his boss so dejected. York too had little to say. York was bearing the brunt of the Lake screwup, though Teddy was blaming himself.

'The latest,' Teddy said softly.

Deville never sat while in the bunker. 'We're still tracking the money. We've made contact with the magazine *Out and About*. It's published in New Haven, a very small outfit, and I'm not sure if we'll be able to penetrate. Our contact in the Bahamas is on retainer and we'll know if and when any wires are received. We have a unit ready to search Lake's offices on Capitol Hill, but that's a long shot. I'm not optimistic. We have twenty people on the ground in Jacksonville.'

'How many of our people are shadowing Lake?'

'We've just gone from thirty to fifty.'

211

'He must be watched. We cannot turn our backs. He is not the person we thought he was, and if we lose sight of him for one hour he might mail a letter, or buy another magazine.'

'We know. We're doing the best we can.'

'This is our highest domestic priority.'

'I know.'

'What about planting someone inside the prison?' Teddy asked. It was a new idea, one hatched by York within the past hour.

Deville rubbed his eyes and chewed his nails for a moment, then said, 'I'll go to work on it. We'll have to pull strings we've never pulled before.'

'How many prisoners are in the federal system?' York asked.

'One hundred thirty-five thousand, give or take,' Deville said.

'Surely we could slip in another, couldn't we?'

'I'll give it a look.'

'Do we have contacts at the Bureau of Prisons?'

'It's new territory, but we're working on it. We're using an old friend at Justice. I'm optimistic.'

Deville left them for a while. He'd get called back in an hour or so. York and Teddy would have another checklist of questions and thoughts and errands for him to tend to.

'I don't like the idea of searching his office on Capitol Hill,' York said. 'It's too risky. And besides, it would take a week. Those guys have a million files.'

'I don't like it either,' Teddy said softly.

'Let's get our guys in Documents to write a

212

letter from Ricky to Lake. We'll wire the envelope, track it, maybe it will lead us to his file.'

'That's an excellent idea. Tell Deville.'

York made a note on a pad filled with many other notes, most of which had been scratched through. He scribbled to pass the time, then asked the question he'd been saving. 'Will you confront him?'

'Not yet.'

'When?'

'Maybe never. Let's gather the intelligence, learn all we can. He seems to be very quiet about his other life, perhaps it came about after his wife died. Who knows? Maybe he can keep it quiet.'

'But he has to know that you know. Otherwise, he might take another chance. If he knows we're always watching, he'll behave himself. Maybe.'

'Meanwhile the world's going to hell. Nuclear arms are bought and sold and sneaked across borders. We're tracking seven small wars with three more on the brink. A dozen new terrorist groups last month alone. Maniacs in the Middle East building armies and hoarding oil. And we sit here hour after hour plotting against three felonious judges who are at this very moment probably playing gin rummy.'

'They're not stupid,' York said.

'No, but they're clumsy. Their nets have snared the wrong person.'

'I guess we picked the wrong person.'

'No, they did.'

213

NINETEEN

The memo arrived by fax from the Regional Supervisor, Bureau of Prisons, Washington. It was directed to M. Emmitt Broon, the warden of Trumble. In terse but standard language the supervisor said he'd reviewed the logs from Trumble and was bothered by the number of visits by one Trevor Carson, attorney for three of the inmates. Lawyer Carson had reached the point of logging in almost every day.

While every inmate certainly had a constitutional right to meet with his attorney, the prison likewise had the power to regulate the traffic. Beginning immediately, attorney-client visits would be restricted to Tuesdays, Thursdays, and Saturdays, between the hours of 3 and 6 P.M. Exceptions would be granted liberally for good cause shown.

The new policy would be utilized for a period of ninety days, after which time it would be reviewed.

Fine with the warden. He too had grown suspicious of Trevor's almost daily appearances. He'd questioned the front desk and the guards in a vain effort to determine what, exactly, was the

214

nature of all this legal work. Link, the guard who usually escorted Trevor to the conference room, and who usually pocketed a couple of twenties on each visit, told the warden that the lawyer and Mr. Spicer talked about cases and appeals and such. 'Just a bunch of law crap,' Link said.

'And you always search his briefcase?' the warden had asked.

'Always,' Link had replied.

Out of courtesy, the warden dialed the number of Mr. Trevor Carson in Neptune Beach. The phone was answered by a woman who said rudely, 'Law office.'

'Mr. Trevor Carson, please.'

'Who's calling?'

'This is Emmitt Broon.'

'Well, Mr. Broon, he's taking a nap right now.'

'I see. Could you possibly wake him? I'm the warden at the federal prison at Trumble, and I need to speak with him.'

'Just a minute.'

He waited for a long time, and when she returned she said, 'I'm sorry. I couldn't wake him up. Could I have him return your call?'

'No, thank you. I'll just fax him a note.'

The idea of a reverse scam was hatched by York, while playing golf on a Sunday, and as his game progressed, occasionally on the fairways but more often in the sand and trees, the scheme grew and grew and became brilliant. He abandoned his pals after fourteen holes and called Teddy.

They would learn the tactics of their adversaries.

And they could divert attention away from Al Konyers. There was nothing to lose.

The letter was created by York, and assigned to one of the top forgers in Documents. The pen pal was christened Brant White, and the first note was handwritten on a plain, white, but expensive correspondence card.

Dear Ricky:

Saw your ad, liked it. I'm fifty-five, in great shape, and looking for more than a pen pal. My wife and I just bought a home in Palm Valley, not far from Neptune Beach. We'll be down in three weeks, with plans to stay for two months.

If interested, send photo. If I like what I see, then I'll give more details.

Brant

The return address was from Brant, P.O. Box 88645, Upper Darby, PA 19082.

To save two or three days, a Philadelphia postmark was applied in Documents, and the letter was flown to Jacksonville where agent Klockner himself delivered it to Aladdin North's little box in the Neptune Beach post office. It was a Monday.

After his nap the following day, Trevor picked up the mail and headed west, out of Jacksonville, along the familiar route to Trumble. He was greeted by the same guards, Mackey and Vince, at the front door, and he signed the same logbook Rufus shoved in front of him. He followed Link into the visitors' area and to a corner where Spicer

216

was waiting in one of the small attorney-conference rooms.

'I'm catchin some heat,' Link said as they stepped into the room. Spicer did not look up. Trevor handed two twenties to Link, who took them in a flash.

'From who?' Trevor asked, opening his brief-case. Spicer was reading a newspaper.

'The warden.'

'Hell, he's cut back on my visits. What else does he want?'

'Don't you understand?' Spicer said, without lowering the newspaper. 'Link here is upset because he's not collecting as much. Right, Link?'

'You got that right. I don't know what kinda funny business you boys are runnin here, but if I tightened up on my inspections you'd be in trouble, wouldn't you?'

'You're being paid well,' Trevor said.

'That's what you think.'

'How much do you want?' Spicer said, staring at him now.

'A thousand a month, cash,' he said, looking at Trevor. 'I'll pick it up at your office.'

'A thousand bucks and the mail doesn't get checked,' Spicer said.

'Yep.'

'And not a word to anybody.'

'Yep.'

'It's a deal. Now get outta here.'

Link smiled at both of them and left the room. He positioned himself outside the door, and for the benefit of the closed-circuit cameras looked through the window occasionally.

217

Inside, the routine varied little. The exchange of mail happened first and took only a second. From a worn manila folder, the same one every time, Joe Roy Spicer removed the outgoing letters and handed them to Trevor, who took the incoming mail from his briefcase and gave it to his client.

There were six letters to be mailed. Some days there were as many as ten, seldom less than five. Though Trevor didn't keep records, or copies, or documents in a file that would serve as proof that he had anything whatsoever to do with the Brethren's little scam, he knew there had to be twenty or thirty potential victims currently being set up. He recognized some of the names and addresses.

Twenty-one to be exact, according to Spicer's precise records. Twenty-one serious prospects, with another eighteen who were marginal. Almost forty pen pals currently hiding in their various closets, some terrified of their shadows, others getting bolder by the week, still others on the verge of kicking down the door and dashing off to meet Ricky or Percy.

The difficult part was being patient. The scam was working, money was changing hands, the temptation was to squeeze them too quickly. Beech and Yarber were proving to be workhorses, laboring over their letters for hours at a time while Spicer directed operations. It took discipline to hook a new pen pal, one with money, then ply him with enough pretty words to earn his trust.

'Aren't we due for a bust?' Trevor said.

Spicer was flipping through the new letters. 'Don't tell me you're broke,' he said. 'You're making more than we are.'

218

'My money's tucked away just like yours. I'd just like to have some more of it.'

'So would I.' Spicer looked at the envelope from Brant in Upper Darby, Pa. 'Ah, a new one,' he mumbled to himself, then opened it. He read it quickly, and was surprised by its tone. No fear, no wasted words, no peeking around corners. This man was ready for action.

'Where's Palm Valley?' he asked.

'Ten miles south of the beaches. Why?'

'What kinda place is it?'

'It's one of the gated golf communities for rich retirees, almost all from up North.'

'How much are the houses?'

'Well, I've never been there, okay. They keep the damned gate locked, guards everywhere like somebody might break in and steal their golf carts, but –'

'How much are the houses?'

'Nothing less than a million. I've seen a couple advertised for three million.'

'Wait here,' Spicer said, gathering his file and walking to the door.

'Where you going?' Trevor asked.

'To the library. I'll be back in half an hour.'

'I got things to do.'

'No you don't. Read the newspaper.'

Spicer said something to Link, who escorted him through the visitors' area and out of the administration building. He walked quickly along the manicured grounds. The sun was warm, and the gardeners were earning their fifty cents an hour.

So were the keepers of the law library. Beech

219

and Yarber were hiding in their little conference room, taking a break from their writings with a game of chess, when Spicer entered in a rush, with an uncharacteristic smile. 'Boys, we've finally hooked the big one,' he said, and tossed Brant's letter on the table. Beech read it aloud.

'Palm Valley is one of the golf communities for rich folks,' Spicer explained proudly. 'Houses go for about three million. The boy's got plenty of dough and he ain't much for letters.'

'He does seem anxious,' Yarber observed.

'We need to move fast,' Spicer said. 'He wants to come down in three weeks.'

'What's the upside potential?' Beech asked. He loved the jargon of those who invested millions.

'At least a half a million,' Spicer said. 'Let's do the letter now. Trevor is waiting.'

Beech opened one of his many files and displayed his wares; sheets of paper in soft pastels. 'I think I'll try the peach,' he said.

'Oh definitely,' Spicer said. 'Gotta do peach.'

Ricky wrote a scaled-down version of the initial contact letter. Twenty-eight years old, college graduate, locked down in rehab but on the verge of release, probably in ten days, very lonely, looking for a mature man to start a relationship. How convenient that Brant would be living nearby, because Ricky had a sister in Jacksonville and he'd be staying with her. There were no obstacles, no hurdles to cross. He'd be ready for Brant when he came South. But he'd like a photo first. Was Brant really married? Would his wife be living at Palm Valley too? Or would she stay up there in Pennsylvania? Wouldn't it be great if she did?

220

They enclosed the same color photo they'd used a hundred times. It had proved to be irresistible.

The peach envelope was taken by Spicer back to the attorney-conference room where Trevor was napping. 'Mail this immediately,' Spicer barked at him.

They spent ten minutes on their basketball bets, then said goodbye without a handshake.

Driving back to Jacksonville, Trevor called his bookie, a new one, a bigger bookie, now that he was a player. The digital line was indeed more secure, but the phone wasn't. Agent Klockner and his band of operatives were listening as usual, and tracking Trevor's bets. He wasn't doing badly, up $4,500 in the past two weeks. By contrast, his law firm had put $800 on the books during the same period.

In addition to the phone, there were four mikes in the Beetle, most of them of little value but operational nonetheless. And under each bumper was a transmitter, both wired to the car's electrical system and checked every other night when Trevor was either drinking or sleeping. A powerful receiver in the rental across the street tracked the Beetle wherever it went. As Trevor puttered down the highway, talking on his phone like a big shot, tossing money around like a Vegas high roller, sipping scalded coffee from a quick-stop grocery, he was emitting more signals than most private jets.

March 7. Big Super Tuesday. Aaron Lake bounced triumphantly across the stage in a large

221

banquet room of a Manhattan hotel, while thousands cheered and music roared and balloons fell from above. He'd taken New York with 43 percent of the vote. Governor Tarry had a rather weak 29 percent, and the other also-rans got the rest. Lake hugged people he'd never seen before and waved to people he'd never see again, and he delivered without notes a stirring victory speech.

Then he was off, on his way to L.A. for another victory celebration. For four hours, in his new Boeing jet that would hold a hundred and leased for $1 million a month and flew at a speed of five hundred miles per hour, thirty-eight thousand feet above the country, he and his staff monitored the returns from the twelve states participating in big Super Tuesday. Along the East Coast, where the polls had already closed, Lake barely won in Maine and Connecticut, but put up big margins in New York, Massachusetts, Maryland, and Georgia. He lost Rhode Island by eight hundred votes, and won Vermont by a thousand. As he was flying over Missouri, CNN declared him the winner of that state by four percentage points over Governor Tarry. Ohio was just as close.

By the time Lake reached California, the rout was over. Of the 591 delegates at stake, he'd captured 390. He'd also solidified the momentum. And most important, Aaron Lake now had the money. Governor Tarry was falling hard and fast, and all bets were on Lake.

TWENTY

Six hours after claiming victory in California, Lake awoke to a frenzied morning of live interviews. He suffered through eighteen in two hours, then flew to Washington.

He went straight to his new campaign headquarters, on the ground floor of a large office building on H Street, a stone's throw from the White House. He thanked his workers, almost none of whom were volunteers. He worked his crowd, shook their hands, all the while asking himself, 'Where did these people come from?'

We're gonna win, he said over and over, and everybody believed it. Why not?

He met for an hour with his top people. He had $65 million, no debt. Tarry had less than $1 million on hand and he was still trying to count the money he owed. In fact, the Tarry campaign had missed a federal filing deadline because its books were in such a mess. All cash had vanished. Contributions had stopped. Lake was getting all the money.

The names of three potential Vice Presidents were debated with great enthusiasm. It was an exhilarating exercise because it meant the nomination was in the bag. Lake's first choice, Senator Nance from Michigan, was drawing fire because he'd had some shady business deals in another life. His partners had been of Italian extraction, from Detroit, and Lake could close his eyes and see the press peeling skin off Nance. A committee was appointed to explore the issue further.

And a committee was appointed to begin planning Lake's presence at the convention in Denver. Lake wanted a new speech-writer, now, and he wanted him working on the acceptance speech.

Lake secretly marveled at his own overhead. His campaign chairman was getting $150,000 for the year, not for twelve months, but until Christmas. There was a chairman of finance, of policy, of media relations, of operations, and of strategic planning, and all had contracts for $120,000 for about ten months of work. Each chairman had two or three immediate underlings, people Lake hardly knew, and they earned $90,000 apiece. Then there were the campaign assistants, or CAs, not the volunteers that most candidates attracted, but real employees who earned $50,000 each and kept the offices in a frenzy. There were dozens of them. And dozens of clerks and secretaries and, hell, nobody made less than $40,000.

And on top of all this waste, Lake kept telling himself, if I make it to the White House then I'll have to find jobs for them there. Every damned one of them. Kids now running around with Lake buttons on every lapel will expect to have West Wing clearances and jobs paying $80,000 a year.

It's a drop in the bucket, he kept reminding

224

himself. Don't get hung up on the small stuff when so much more is at stake.

Negatives were pushed to the end of the meeting and given short shrift. A reporter for the *Post* had been digging into Lake's early business career. Without too much effort he'd stumbled upon the GreenTree mess, a failed land development, twenty-two years in the past. Lake and a partner had bankrupted GreenTree, legally shafting creditors out of $800,000. The partner had been indicted for bankruptcy fraud, but a jury let him walk. No one laid a glove on Lake, and seven times after that the people of Arizona elected him to Congress.

'I'll answer any question about GreenTree,' Lake said. 'It was just a bad business deal.'

'The press is about to shift gears,' said the chairman of media relations. 'You're new and you haven't been subjected to enough scrutiny. It's time for them to get nasty.'

'It's already started,' Lake said. 'I have no skeletons.'

For an early dinner he was whisked away to Mortimer's, the current power place to be seen, just down Pennsylvania, where he met Elaine Tyner, the lawyer running D-PAC. Over fruit and cottage cheese she laid out the current financials of the newest PAC on the block. Cash in hand of $29 million, no significant debt, money being churned around the clock, coming in from all directions, from everywhere in the world.

Spending it was the challenge. Since it was considered 'soft money,' or money that couldn't go directly to the Lake campaign, it had to be used elsewhere. Tyner had several targets. The first was a series of generic ads similar to the doomsday ads Teddy had put together. D-PAC was already buying prime-time spots for the fall. The second, and by far the most enjoyable, were the Senate and congressional races. 'They're lining up like ants,' she said with great amusement. 'It's amazing what a few million bucks can do.'

She told the story of a House race in a district in Northern California where the incumbent, a twenty-year veteran Lake knew and despised, started the year with a forty-point lead against an unknown challenger. The unknown found his way to D-PAC and surrendered his soul to Aaron Lake. 'We've basically taken over his campaign,' she said. 'We're writing speeches, polling, doing all his print and TV ads, we even hired a new staff for him. So far we've spent one-point-five million, and our boy has cut the lead to ten points. And we have seven months to go.'

In all, Tyner and D-PAC were meddling in thirty House races and ten in the Senate. She expected to raise a total of $60 million, and spend every dime of it by November.

Her third area of 'focus' was taking the pulse of the country. D-PAC was polling nonstop, every day, fifteen hours a day. If labor in western Pennsylvania was bothered by an issue, D-PAC would know it. If the Hispanics in Houston were pleased with a new welfare policy, D-PAC would know it. If the women in greater Chicago liked or disliked a Lake ad, D-PAC knew yes or no and by what percentage. 'We know everything,' she boasted. 'We're like Big Brother, always watching.'

226

The polling cost $60,000 a day, a bargain. No one could touch it. For the important matters, Lake was nine points ahead of Tarry in Texas, even in Florida, a state Lake had yet to visit, and very close in Indiana, Tarry's home state.

'Tarry's tired,' she said. 'Morale is low because he won in New Hampshire and the money was rolling in. Then you came from nowhere, a fresh face, no baggage, new message, you start winning, and suddenly the money finds you. Tarry can't raise fifty bucks at a church bake sale. He's losing key people because he can't pay them, and because they smell another winner.'

Lake chewed a piece of pineapple and savored the words. They weren't new; he'd heard them from his own people. But coming from a seasoned insider like Tyner, they were even more reassuring.

'What are the Vice President's numbers?' Lake asked. He had his own set, but for some reason trusted her more.

'He'll squeak out the nomination,' she said, offering nothing new. 'But the convention will be bloody. Right now, you're only a few points behind him on the big question: Who will you vote for in November?'

'November is far away.'

'It is and it isn't.'

'A lot can change,' Lake said, thinking of Teddy, and wondering what sort of crisis he'd create to terrify the American people.

The dinner was more of a snack, and from Mortimer's Lake he was driven to a small dining room at the Hay-Adams Hotel. It was a long, late dinner with friends, two dozen of his colleagues

227

from the House. Few of them had rushed to endorse him when he'd entered the race, but now they were all wildly enthusiastic about their man. Most had their own pollsters. The bandwagon was rolling down the mountain.

Lake had never seen his old pals so happy to be around him.

The letter was prepared in Documents by a woman named Bruce, one of the agency's three best counterfeiters. Tacked to the corkboard just above the worktable in her small lab were letters written by Ricky. Excellent samples, much more than she needed. She had no idea who Ricky was, but there was no doubt his handwriting was contrived. It was fairly consistent, with the more recent samples clearly showing an ease that came only with practice. His vocabulary was not remarkable, but then she suspected he was trying to downplay it. His sentence structure showed few mistakes. Bruce guessed him to be between the ages of forty and sixty, with at least a college education.

But it wasn't her job to make such inferences, at least not in this case. With the same pen and paper as Ricky, she wrote a nice little note to Al. The text had been prepared by someone else, she did not know who. Nor did she care.

It was, 'Hey, Al, where have you been? Why haven't you written? Don't forget about me.' That kind of letter, but with a nice little surprise. Since Ricky couldn't use the phone, he was sending Al a cassette tape with a brief message from deep inside rehab.

Bruce fit the letter onto one page, then worked

228

for an hour on the envelope. The postmark she applied was from Neptune Beach, Florida.

She didn't seal the envelope. Her little project was inspected, then taken to another lab. The tape was recorded by a young agent who'd studied drama at Northwestern. In a soft, accentless voice he said, 'Hey, Al, this is Ricky. Hope you're surprised to hear my voice. They won't let us use the phones around here, I don't know why, but for some reason we can send tapes back and forth. I can't wait to get out of this place.' Then he rambled for five minutes about his rehab and how much he hated his uncle and the people who ran Aladdin North. But he did concede that they had rid him of his addictions. He was certain he would look back and not judge the place too harshly.

His entire narrative was nothing but babble. No plans were discussed for his release, no hint of where he might go or what he might do, only a vague reference about seeing Al one day.

They were not yet ready to bait Al Konyers. The sole purpose of the tape was to hide within its casing a transmitter strong enough to lead them to Lake's hidden file. A tiny bug in the envelope was too risky. Al might be smart enough to find it.

At Mailbox America in Chevy Chase, the CIA now controlled eight boxes, duly rented for one year by eight different people, each of whom had the same twenty-four-hour access that Mr. Konyers had. They came and went at all hours, checking their little boxes, picking up mail they'd sent themselves, occasionally taking a peek at Al's box if no one was looking.

Since they knew his schedule better than he

229

knew it himself, they waited patiently until he'd made his rounds. They felt certain he'd sneak out as before, dressed like a jogger, so they held the envelope with the tape until almost ten one night. Then they placed it in his box.

Four hours later, with a dozen agents watching every move, Lake the jogger jumped from a cab in front of Mailbox America, darted inside, his face hidden by the long bill of a running cap, went to his box, pulled out the mail, and hurried back into the cab.

Six hours later he left Georgetown for a prayer breakfast at the Hilton, and they waited. He addressed an association of police chiefs at nine, and a thousand high school principals at eleven. He lunched with the Speaker of the House. He taped a stressful Q&A session with some talking heads at three, then returned home to pack. His itinerary called for him to depart Reagan National at eight and fly to Dallas.

They followed him to the airport, watched the Boeing 707 take off, then called Langley. When the two Secret Service agents arrived to check the perimeter of Lake's townhouse, the CIA was already inside.

The search ended in the kitchen ten minutes after it began. A handheld receptor caught the signal from the cassette tape. They found it in the wastebasket, along with an empty half-gallon milk jug, two torn packages of oatmeal, some soiled paper towels, and that morning's edition of the *Washington Post*. A maid came twice a week. Lake had simply left the garbage for her to take care of.

They couldn't find Lake's file because he didn't have one. Smart man, he tossed away the evidence.

Teddy was almost relieved when he got word. The team was still in the townhouse, hiding and waiting for the Secret Service to leave. Whatever Lake did in his secret life, he worked hard not to leave a trail.

The tape unnerved Aaron Lake. Reading Ricky's letters and looking at his handsome face had given him a nervous thrill. The young man was far away and odds were they'd never meet. They could be pen pals and play tag at a distance and move slowly, at least that's what Lake had contemplated initially.

But hearing Ricky's voice had brought him much closer, and Lake was rattled. What had begun a few months earlier as a curious little game now held horrible possibilities. It was much too risky. Lake trembled at the thought of getting caught.

It still seemed impossible, though. He was well hidden behind the mask of Al Konyers. Ricky had not a clue. It was 'Al this' and 'Al that' on the tape. The post office box was his shield.

But he had to end it. At least for now.

The Boeing was packed with Lake's well-paid people. They didn't make an airplane big enough to haul his entire entourage. If he leased a 747, within two days it would be filled with CAs and advisers and consultants and pollsters, not to mention his own growing army of bodyguards from the Secret Service.

The more primaries he won, the heavier his

plane became. It might be wise to lose a couple of states so he could jettison some of the baggage.

In the darkness of the plane, Lake sipped tomato juice and decided to write a final letter to Ricky. Al would wish him the best, and simply terminate the correspondence. What could the boy do?

He was tempted to write the note right then, sitting in his deep recliner, his feet in the air. But at any moment an assistant of some variety would emerge with another breathless report that the candidate had to hear immediately. He had no privacy. He had no time to think or loaf or daydream. Every pleasant thought was interrupted by a new poll or a late-breaking story or an urgent need to make a decision.

Surely he'd be able to hide in the White House. Loners had lived there before.

TWENTY-ONE

The case of the stolen cell phone had fascinated the inmates at Trumble for the past month. Mr. T-Bone, a wiry street kid from Miami serving twenty for drugs, had taken original possession of the phone by means that were still unclear. Cell phones were strictly prohibited at Trumble, and the method by which he got one had created more rumors than T. Karl's sex life. The few who'd actually seen it had described it, not in court, but around the camp, as being no larger than a stopwatch. Mr. T-Bone had been seen lurking in the shadows, hunched at the waist, chin to his chest, back to the world, mumbling into the phone. No doubt he was still directing street operations in Miami.

Then it disappeared. Mr. T-Bone let it be known that he might kill whoever took it, and when the threats of violence didn't work he offered a reward of $1,000 cash. Suspicion soon fell upon another young drug dealer, Zorro, from a section of Atlanta just as rough as Mr. T-Bone's. A killing seemed likely, so the guards and the suits up front intervened and convinced the two that they'd be shipped away if things got out of hand. Violence was not tolerated at Trumble. The punishment was a trip to a medium-security pen with inmates who understood violence.

Someone told Mr. T-Bone about the weekly dockets the Brethren held, and in due course he found T. Karl and filed suit. He wanted his phone back, plus a million bucks in punitive damages.

When it was first set for trial, an assistant warden appeared in the cafeteria to observe the proceedings, and the matter was quickly postponed by the Brethren. The same thing happened just before the second trial. Allegations of who did or did not have possession of an outlawed cell phone could not be heard by anyone in administration. The guards who watched the weekly shows wouldn't repeat a word.

Justice Spicer finally convinced a prison counselor that the boys had a private matter to reconcile, without interference from the front. 'We're trying to settle a little matter,' he whispered. 'And we need to do it in private.'

The request worked its way upward, and at the third trial date the cafeteria was packed with spectators, most of whom were hoping to see bloodshed. The only prison official in the room was a solitary guard, sitting in the back, half asleep.

Neither of the litigants was a stranger to courtrooms, so it was no surprise that Mr. T-Bone and Zorro acted as their own attorneys. Justice Beech spent most of the first hour trying to keep the language out of the gutter. He finally gave up. Wild accusations spewed forth from the plaintiff, charges that couldn't have been proved with the aid of a thousand FBI agents. The denials were just as loud and preposterous from the defense. Mr. T-Bone scored heavy blows with two affidavits, signed by inmates whose names were revealed only to the Brethren, which contained eyewitness accounts of seeing Zorro trying to hide while talking on a tiny phone.

Zorro's angry response described the affidavits in language the Brethren had never before encountered.

The knockout punch came from nowhere. Mr. T-Bone, in a move that even the slickest lawyer would admire, produced documentation. His phone records had been smuggled in, and he showed the court in black and white that exactly fifty-four calls had been made to numbers in southeast Atlanta. His supporters, by far the majority but whose loyalty could vanish in an instant, whooped and hollered until T. Karl slammed his plastic gavel and got them quiet.

Zorro had trouble regrouping, and his hesitation killed him. He was ordered to immediately turn over the phone to the Brethren within twenty-four hours, and to reimburse Mr. T-Bone $450 for long-distance charges. If twenty-four hours passed with no phone, the matter would be referred to the warden, along with a finding of fact from the Brethren that Zorro did indeed possess an illegal cell phone.

The Brethren further ordered the two to maintain a distance of at least fifty feet from one another at all times, even when eating.

T. Karl rapped a gavel and the crowd began a

235

noisy exit. He called the next case, another petty gambling dispute, and waited for the spectators to leave. 'Quiet!' he shouted, and the racket only grew louder. The Brethren went back to their newspapers and magazines.

'Quiet!' he barked again, slamming his gavel.

'Shut up,' Spicer yelled at T. Karl. 'You're making more noise than they are.'

'It's my job,' T. Karl snapped back, the curls of his wig bouncing in all directions.

When the cafeteria was empty, only one inmate remained. T. Karl looked around and finally asked him, 'Are you Mr. Hooten?'

'No sir,' the young man said.

'Are you Mr.Jenkins?'

'No sir.'

'I didn't think so. The case of Hooten versus Jenkins is hereby dismissed for failure to show,' T. Karl said, and made a dramatic entry into his docket book.

'Who are you?' Spicer asked the young man, who was sitting alone and glancing around as if he wasn't sure he was welcome. The three men in the pale green robes were now looking at him, as was the clown with the gray wig and the old maroon pajamas and the lavender shower shoes, no socks. Who were these people!

He slowly got to his feet and moved forward with great apprehension until he stood before the three. 'I'm looking for some help,' he said, almost afraid to speak.

'Do you have business before the court?' T.Karl growled from the side.

'No sir.'

'Then you'll have to –'

'Shut up!' Spicer said. 'Court's adjourned. Leave.'

T.Karl slammed his docket book, kicked back his folding chair, and stormed out of the room, his shower shoes sliding on the tile, his wig bouncing behind him.

The young man appeared ready to cry. 'What can we do for you?' Yarber asked.

He was holding a small cardboard box, and the Brethren knew from experience that it was filled with the papers that had brought him to Trumble. 'I need some help,' he said again. 'I got here last week, and my roommate said you guys could help with my appeals.'

'Don't you have a lawyer?' Beech asked.

'I did. He wasn't very good. He's one reason I'm here.'

'Why are you here?' asked Spicer.

'I don't know. I really don't know.'

'Did you have a trial?'

'Yes. A long one.'

'And you were found guilty by a jury?'

'Yes. Me and a bunch of others. They said we were part of a conspiracy.'

'A conspiracy to do what?'

'Import cocaine.'

Another druggie. They were suddenly anxious to get back to their letter writing. 'How long is your sentence?' asked Yarber.

'Forty-eight years.'

'Forty-eight years! How old are you?'

'Twenty-three.'

The letter writing was momentarily forgotten.

237

They looked at his sad young face and tried to picture it fifty years later. Released at the age of seventy-one; it was impossible to imagine. Each of the Brethren would leave Trumble a younger man than this kid.

'Pull up a chair,' Yarber said, and the kid grabbed the nearest one and placed it in front of their table. Even Spicer felt a little sympathy for him.

'What's your name?' Yarber asked.

'I go by Buster.'

'Okay, Buster, what'd you do to get yourself forty-eight years?'

The story came in torrents. Balancing his box on his knees, and staring at the floor, he began by saying he'd never been in trouble with the law, nor had his father. They owned a small boat dock together in Pensacola. They fished and sailed and loved the sea, and running the dock was the perfect life for them. They sold a used fishing boat, a fifty-footer, to a man from Fort Lauderdale, an American who paid them in cash – $95,000. The money went in the bank, or at least Buster thought it did. A few months later the man was back for another boat, a thirty-eight-footer for which he paid $80,000. Cash for boats was not unusual in Florida. A third and fourth boat followed. Buster and his dad knew where to find good used fishing boats, which they overhauled and renovated. They enjoyed doing the work themselves. After the fifth boat, the narcs came calling. They asked questions, made vague threats, wanted to see the books and records. Buster's dad refused initially, then

238

they hired a lawyer who advised them not to cooperate. Nothing happened for months.

Buster and his father were arrested at 3 A.M. on a Sunday morning by a pack of goons wearing vests and enough guns to hold Pensacola hostage. They were dragged half-dressed from their small home near the bay, lights flashing all over the place. The indictment was an inch thick, 160 pages, eighty-one counts of conspiracy to smuggle cocaine. He had a copy of it in his box. Buster and his dad were barely mentioned in the 160 pages, but they were nonetheless named as defendants and lumped together with the man they'd sold the boats to, along with twenty-five other people they'd never heard of. Eleven were Colombians. Three were lawyers. Everybody else was from South Florida.

The U.S. Attorney offered them a deal – two years each in return for guilty pleas and cooperation against the other codefendants. Pleading guilty to what? They'd done nothing wrong. They knew exactly one of their twenty-six coconspirators. They'd never seen cocaine.

Buster's father remortgaged their home to raise $20,000 for a lawyer, and they made a bad selection. At trial, they were alarmed to find themselves sitting at the same table with the Colombians and the real drug traffickers. They were on one side of the courtroom, all the coconspirators, sitting together as if they'd once been a well-oiled drug machine. On the other side, near the jury, were the government lawyers, groups of pompous little bastards in dark suits, taking notes, glaring at them as if they were child molesters. The jury glared at them too.

During seven weeks of trial, Buster and his father were practically ignored. Three times their names were mentioned. The government's principal charge against them was that they had conspired to procure and rebuild fishing boats with souped-up engines to transport drugs from Mexico to various drop-offs along the Florida panhandle. Their lawyer, who complained that he wasn't getting paid enough to handle a seven-week trial, proved ineffective at rebutting these loose charges. Still, the government lawyers did little damage and were much more concerned with nailing the Colombians.

But they didn't have to prove much. They had done a superior job of picking the jury. After eight days of deliberation, the jurors, obviously tired and frustrated, found every conspirator guilty of all charges. A month after they were sentenced, Buster's father killed himself.

As the narrative wound down, the kid looked as if he might cry. But he stuck out his jaw, gritted his teeth, and said, 'I did nothing wrong.'

He certainly wasn't the first inmate at Trumble to declare his innocence. Beech watched and listened and remembered a young man he'd sentenced once to forty years for drug trafficking back in Texas. The defendant had a rotten childhood, no education, a long record as a juvenile offender, not much of a chance in life. Beech had lectured him from the bench, high and lordly from above, and had felt good about himself for handing down such a brutal sentence. Gotta get these damned drug dealers off the streets!

A liberal is a conservative who's been arrested.

After three years on the inside of a prison Hatlee Beech agonized over many of the people he'd thrown the book at. People far guiltier than Buster here. Kids who just needed a break.

Finn Yarber watched and listened and felt immense pity for the young man. Everybody at Trumble had a sad story, and after a month or so of hearing them he'd learned to believe almost nothing. But Buster was believable. For the next forty-eight years he would wither and decline, all at taxpayer expense. Three meals a day. A warm bed at night – $31,000 a year was the latest guess of what a federal inmate cost the government. Such a waste. Half the inmates at Trumble had no business being there. They were non-violent men who should've been punished with stiff fines and community service.

Joe Roy Spicer listened to Buster's compelling story, and he sized the boy up for future use. There were two possibilities. First, in Spicer's opinion, the telephones were not being properly utilized in the Angola scam. The Brethren were old men writing letters as if they were young. It would be too risky to call Quince Garbe in Iowa, for example, and pretend to be Ricky, a robust twenty-eight-year-old. But with a kid like Buster working for them, they could convince any potential victim. There were plenty of young guys at Trumble, and Spicer had considered several of them. But they were criminals, and he didn't trust them. Buster was fresh off the streets, seemingly innocent, and he was coming to them for help. The boy could be manipulated.

The second possibility was an offshoot of the

241

first. If Buster joined their conspiracy, he would be in place when Joe Roy was released. The scam was proving too profitable to simply walk away from. Beech and Yarber were splendid at writing the letters, but they had no business sense. Perhaps Spicer could train young Buster here to fill his shoes, and to divert his share to the outside.

Just a thought.

'Do you have any money?' Spicer asked.

'No sir. We lost everything.'

'No family, no uncles, aunts, cousins, friends who could help you with your legal fees?'

'No sir. What kinda legal fees?'

'We usually charge for reviewing cases and helping with the appeals.'

'I'm dead broke, sir.'

'I think we can help,' Beech said. Spicer didn't work on the appeals anyway. The man never finished high school.

'Sort of a pro bono case, wouldn't you say?' Yarber said to Beech.

'A pro what?' Spicer asked.

'Pro bono.'

'What's that?'

'Free legal work,' Beech said.

'Free legal work. Done by whom?'

'By lawyers,' Yarber explained. 'Every lawyer is expected to donate a few hours of his time to help people who can't afford to hire him.'

'It's part of the Old English common law,' Beech added, further clouding the issue.

'It never caught on over here, did it?' Spicer said.

'We'll review your case,' Yarber said to Buster. 'But please do not be optimistic.'

'Thank you.'

They left the cafeteria in a group, three ex-judges in green choir robes followed by a scared young inmate. Frightened, but also quite curious.

TWENTY-TWO

Brant's reply from Upper Darby, Pa., had an urgent tone to it:

Dear Ricky:
    Wow! What a photo! I'm coming down even sooner. I'll be there on April 20. Are you available? If so, we'll have the house to ourselves because my wife will stay here for another two weeks. Poor woman. We've been married for twenty-two years and she doesn't have a clue.
    Here's a picture of me. That's my Learjet in the background, one of my favorite toys. We'll buzz around in it if you want.
    Write me immediately, please.
                                    Sincerely, Brant

There was still no last name, not that that was a problem. They would dig for it soon enough.
    Spicer inspected the postmark, and for a passing moment thought about how quickly the mail was running between Jacksonville and Philadelphia. But the photo kept his attention. It was a four-by-

six candid shot, very similar to an ad for a get-rich-quick scheme where the huckster is pictured with a proud smile, flanked by his jet, his Rolls, and possibly his latest wife. Brant was standing beside a plane, smiling, dressed neatly in tennis shorts and a sweater, with no Rolls in sight but with an attractive middle-aged woman next to him.

It was the first photo, in their growing collection, in which one of their pen pals had included his wife. Odd, thought Spicer, but then Brant had mentioned her in both letters. Nothing surprised him anymore. The scam would work forever because there was an endless supply of potential victims willing to ignore the risks.

Brant himself was fit and tanned, short dark hair with shades of gray, and a mustache. He was not particularly handsome, but what did Spicer care?

Why would a man with so much be so careless? Because he'd always taken chances and never been caught. Because it was a way of life. And after they squeezed him and took his money, Brant would slow down for a while. He'd avoid the personal ads, and the anonymous lovers. But an aggressive type like Brant would soon return to his old ways.

Spicer figured the thrill of finding random partners overshadowed the risks. He was still bothered by the fact that he, of all people, spent time each day trying to think like a homosexual.

Beech and Yarber read the letter and studied the photo. The small cramped room was completely silent. Could this be the big one?

'Reckon how much that jet cost,' Spicer said, and all three laughed. It was nervous laughter, as if they weren't sure they could believe it.

245

'A couple of million,' Beech said. Since he was from Texas, and had been married to a rich woman, the other two assumed he knew more about jets than they. 'It's a small Lear.'

Spicer would settle for a small Cessna, anything that would lift him off the ground and take him away. Yarber didn't want a plane. He wanted tickets, in first class where they brought you champagne and two menus and you had your choice of movies. First class over the ocean, far away from this country.

'Let's bust him,' Yarber said.

'How much?' asked Beech, still staring at the photo.

'At least a half a million,' Spicer said. 'And if we get that, we'll go back for more.'

They sat in silence, each playing with his portion of half a million dollars. Trevor's third was suddenly getting in the way. He'd take $167,000 off the top, leaving each of them $111,000. Not bad for prisoners, but it should be a helluva lot more. Why was the lawyer making so much?

'We're going to cut Trevor's fee,' Spicer announced. 'I've been thinking about this for some time. Beginning now, the money will be split four ways. He takes an equal share.'

'He won't do it,' Yarber said.

'He has no choice.'

'It's only fair,' Beech said. 'We're doing the work, and he's getting more than each of us. I say we cut it.'

'I'll do it Thursday.'

Two days later, Trevor arrived at Trumble just

246

after four with a particularly bad hangover, one deadened by neither the two-hour lunch nor the one-hour nap.

Joe Roy seemed particularly edgy. He passed across the outgoing mail, but held a large, red, oversized envelope. 'We're getting ready to bust this guy,' he said, tapping it on the table.

'Who is he?'

'Brant somebody, near Philadelphia. He's hiding behind the post office, so you need to flush him out.'

'How much?'

'A half a million bucks.'

Trevor's red eyes narrowed and his dry lips fell open. He did the math – $167,000 in his pocket. His sailing career was suddenly drawing closer. Perhaps he didn't need a full million bucks before he slammed his office door and left for the Caribbean. Maybe half that would do it. And he was getting so close.

'You're kidding,' he said, knowing that Spicer was not. Spicer had no sense of humor, and he certainly took his money seriously.

'No. And we're changing your percentage.'

'I'll be damned if we are. A deal's a deal.'

'Deals can always be changed. From now on you get the same piece we do. One fourth.'

'No way.'

'Then you're fired.'

'You can't fire me.'

'I just did. What, you think we can't find another crooked lawyer to run mail for us?'

'I know too much,' Trevor said, his cheeks flashing pink and his tongue suddenly parched.

247

'Don't overestimate yourself. You're not that valuable.'

'Yes I am. I know everything that's going on here.'

'And so do we, hotshot. Difference is, we're already in jail. You're the one with the most to lose. You play hardball with me and you'll be sittin on this side of the table.'

Bolts of pain shot through Trevor's forehead and he closed his eyes. He was in no condition to argue. Why had he stayed at Pete's so late last night? He had to be sharp when he met with Spicer. Instead, he was tired and half-drunk.

His head spun and he thought he might be sick again. He did the math. They were arguing over the difference between $167,000 and $125,000. Frankly, both sounded good to Trevor. He couldn't run the risk of being fired because he'd managed to alienate what few clients he had. He spent less time in the office; he wouldn't return their calls. He'd found a far richer source of income, so to hell with the small-time foot traffic along the beaches.

And he was no match for Spicer. The man had no conscience. He was mean and conniving and desperate to stash away as much money as possible.

'Are Beech and Yarber in favor of this?' he asked, knowing damned well they were, and knowing that even if they weren't he'd never know the difference.

'Sure. They're doing all the work. Why should you make more than them?'

It did seem a little unfair. 'Okay, okay,' Trevor said, still in pain. 'There's a good reason you're in prison.'

'Are you drinking too much?'

'No! Why do you ask?'

'I've known drunks. Lots of them. You look like hell.'

'Thanks. You take care of your business, I'll take care of mine.'

'It's a deal. But nobody wants a drunk for a lawyer. You're handling all our money, in an enterprise that's very illegal. A little loose talk in a bar and somebody starts asking questions.'

'I can handle myself.'

'Good. Watch your back too. We're squeezing people, making them hurt. If I were on the other end of our little sting, I'd be tempted to come down and try to get some answers before I coughed up the money.'

'They're too scared.'

'Keep your eyes open anyway. It's important for you to stay sober and alert.'

'Thank you very much. Anything else?'

'Yeah, I got some games for you.' On to the important stuff. Spicer opened a newspaper and they began making their bets.

Trevor bought a quart of beer at a country store on the edge of Trumble, and sipped it slowly as he puttered back to Jacksonville. He tried his best not to think of their money, but his thoughts were out of control. Between his account and their account, there was just over $250,000 sitting offshore, money he could take anytime he wanted. Add a

249

half a million bucks to it, and, well, he just couldn't stop adding – $750,000!

He'd never get caught stealing dirty money; that was the beauty of it. The victims of the Brethren weren't complaining now because they were too ashamed. They weren't breaking any laws. They were just scared. The Brethren, on the other hand, were committing crimes. So who would they run to if their money disappeared?

He had to stop thinking such thoughts.

But how could they, the Brethren, catch him? He'd be on a sailboat drifting between islands they'd never heard of. And when they were finally released, would they have the energy and money and willpower to track him down? Of course not. They were old men. Beech would probably die at Trumble.

'Stop it,' he yelled at himself.

He walked to Beach Java for a triple-shot latte, and returned to his office determined to do something productive. He went online and found the names of several private investigators in Phila-delphia. It was almost six when he began calling. The first two went to answering machines.

The third, to the offices of Ed Pagnozzi, was answered by the investigator himself. Trevor explained that he was a lawyer in Florida and needed a quick job in Upper Darby.

'Okay. What kinda job?'

'I'm trying to track some mail here,' Trevor said glibly. He'd done this enough to have it well rehearsed. 'Pretty big divorce case. I got the wife, and I think the husband's hiding money. Anyway,

I need somebody up there to find out who's renting a certain post office box.'

'You gotta be kiddin.'

'Well, no, I'm pretty serious about this.'

'You want me to go snoopin around a post office?'

'It's just basic detective work.'

'Look, pal, I'm very busy. Call somebody else.' Pagnozzi was gone, off to more important matters. Trevor cursed him under his breath and punched the next number. He tried two more, and hung up on both when the machines answered. He'd try again tomorrow.

Across the street, Klockner listened to the brief chat with Pagnozzi one more time, then called Langley. The final piece of the puzzle had just fallen into place, and Mr. Deville would want to know it immediately.

While dependent on fancy words and smooth talk and compelling photos, the scam was basic in its operation. It preyed on human desire and it paid off by sheer terror. Its mechanics had been solved by Mr. Garbe's file, and by the Brant White reverse scam, and by the other letters they'd intercepted.

Only one question had gone unanswered: When aliases were used to rent post office boxes, how did the Brethren find the real names of their victims? The phone calls to Philadelphia had just given them their answer. Trevor simply hired a local private detective, evidently one with less business than Mr. Pagnozzi.

It was almost ten when Deville was finally

cleared to see Teddy. The North Koreans had shot another American soldier in the DMZ, and Teddy had been dealing with the fallout since noon. He was eating cheese and crackers and sipping a Diet Coke when Deville entered the bunker.

After a quick briefing, Teddy said, 'That's what I thought.'

His instincts were uncanny, especially with hindsight.

'This means, of course, that the lawyer could hire a local here to somehow uncover the real identity of Al Konyers,' Deville said.

'But how?'

'We can think of several ways. First is surveillance, the same way we caught Lake sneaking to his box. Watch the post office. That's somewhat risky because there's a good chance you'll get noticed. Second is bribery. Five hundred bucks cash to a postal clerk will work in a lot of places. Third is computer records. This is not highly classified material. One of our guys just hacked his way into the central post office in Evansville, Indiana, and got the list of all box leases. It was a random test, took him about an hour. That's high tech. Low tech is to simply break into the post office at night and have a look around.'

'How much does he pay for this?'

'Don't know, but we'll find out soon when he hires an investigator.'

'He has to be neutralized.'

'Eliminated?'

'Not yet. I'd rather buy him first. He is our window. If he's working for us, then we know

everything and we keep him away from Konyers.
Put together a plan.'

'And for his removal?'

'Go ahead and plan it, but we're in no hurry.
Not yet anyway.'

TWENTY-THREE

The South did indeed like Aaron Lake, with his love of guns and bombs and tough talk and military readiness. He flooded Florida, Mississippi, Tennessee, Oklahoma, and Texas with ads that were even bolder than his first ones. And Teddy's people flooded the same states with more cash than had ever changed hands the night before an election.

The result was another rout, with Lake getting 260 of the 312 delegates at stake on little Super Tuesday. After the votes were counted on March 14, 1,301 of the 2,066 total delegates had been decided. Lake held a commanding lead over Governor Tarry – 801 to 390.

The race was over, barring an unforeseen catastrophe.

Buster's first job at Trumble was running a Weed Eater, for which he earned a starting wage of twenty cents an hour. It was either that or mopping floors in the cafeteria. He chose the weed eating because he liked the sun and vowed that his skin would not turn as pale as some of the

254

bleached-out inmates he'd seen. Nor would he get fat like some of them. This is prison, he kept telling himself, how can they be so fat?

He worked hard in the bright sun, kept his tan, vowed to keep his flat stomach, and tried gamely to go through the motions. But after ten days Buster knew he would not last for forty-eight years.

Forty-eight years! He couldn't begin to comprehend such time. Who could?

He'd cried for the first forty-eight hours.

Thirteen months earlier he and his father were running their dock, working on boats, fishing twice a week in the Gulf.

He worked slowly around the concrete edge of the basketball court where a rowdy game was in progress. Then to the big sandbox where they sometimes played volleyball. In the distance, a solitary figure was walking around the track, an old-looking man with his long gray hair in a ponytail and with no shirt. He looked vaguely familiar. Buster worked both edges of a sidewalk, making his way to the track.

The lone walker was Finn Yarber, one of the judges who was trying to help him. He moved around the oval at a steady pace, head level, back and shoulders stiff and erect, not a picture of athleticism but not bad for a sixty-year-old man. He was barefoot and barebacked, sweat rolling off his leathery skin.

Buster turned off the Weed Eater and placed it on the ground. When Yarber drew near, he saw the kid and said, 'Hello, Buster. How's it goin?'

'I'm still here,' the kid said. 'Mind if I walk with you?'

'Not at all,' Finn said without breaking stride.

They did an eighth of a mile before Buster could find the courage to say, 'So how about my appeals?'

'Judge Beech is lookin at it. The sentencing appears to be in order, which is not good news. A lot of guys get here with flaws in their sentencing, and we can usually file a couple of motions and knock off a few years. Not so with you. I'm sorry.'

'That's okay. What's a few when you have forty-eight? Twenty-eight, thirty-eight, forty-eight, what does it matter?'

'You still have your appeals. There's a chance the decision can be overturned.'

'A slim chance.'

'You can't give up hope, Buster,' Yarber said, without the slightest trace of conviction. Keeping some measure of hope meant keeping some faith in the system. Yarber certainly had none. He'd been framed and railroaded by the same law he'd once defended.

But at least Yarber had enemies, and he could almost understand why they came after him.

This poor boy had done nothing wrong. Yarber had read enough of his file to believe Buster was completely innocent, another victim of an over-zealous prosecutor.

It appeared, at least from the record, that the kid's father may have been hiding some cash, but nothing serious. Nothing to warrant a 160-page conspiracy indictment.

Hope. He felt like a hypocrite for even thinking the word. The appeals courts were now packed with right-wing law and order types, and it was a rare drug case that got reversed. They'd slamdunk the kid's appeal with a rubber stamp, and tell themselves they were making the streets safer.

The biggest coward had been the trial judge. Prosecutors are expected to indict the world, but the judges are supposed to weed out the fringe defendants. Buster and his father should've been separated from the Colombians and their cohorts, and sent home before the trial began.

Now one was dead. The other was ruined. And nobody in the federal criminal system gave a damn. It was just another drug conspiracy.

At the first curve of the oval, Yarber slowed, then stopped. He looked off in the distance, beyond a grassy field to the edge of a treeline. Buster looked too. For ten days he'd been looking at the perimeter of Trumble, and seeing what wasn't there – fences, razor wire, guard towers.

'Last guy who left here,' Yarber said, gazing at nothing, 'left through those trees. They're thick for a few miles, then you come to a country road.'

'Who was he?'

'A guy named Tommy Adkins. He was a banker in North Carolina, got caught with his hand in the cookie jar.'

'What happened to him?'

'He went crazy and walked away one day. He was gone six hours before anybody knew it. A month later they found him in a motel room in Cocoa Beach, not the cops but the maids. He was curled in the fetal position on the floor, naked, suckin his thumb, his mind completely gone. They put him in some mental joint.'

'Six hours, huh?'

'Yeah, it happens about once a year. Somebody just walks away. They notify the cops in your hometown, put your name in the national computers, the usual drill.'

'How many get caught?'

'Almost all.'

'Almost.'

'Yeah, but they get caught because they do dumb things. Get drunk in bars. Drive cars with no taillights. Go see their girlfriends.'

'So if you had a brain you could pull it off?'

'Sure. Careful planning, a little cash, it would be easy.'

They began walking again, a bit slower. 'Tell me something, Mr. Yarber,' Buster said. 'If you were facing forty-eight years, would you take a walk?'

'Yes.'

'But I don't have a dime.'

'I do.'

'Then you'll help me.'

'We'll see. Give it some time. Settle in here. They're watchin you a bit closer because you're new, but with time they'll forget about you.'

Buster actually smiled. His sentence had just been reduced dramatically.

'You know what happens if you get caught?' Yarber said.

'Yeah, they add some more years. Big deal. Maybe I'll get fifty-eight. No sir, if I get caught, I blow my brains out.'

'That's what I'd do. You have to be prepared to leave the country.'

'And go where?'

'Go someplace where you look like the locals, and where they don't extradite to the U.S.'

'Anyplace in particular?'

'Argentina or Chile. You speak any Spanish?'

'No.'

'Start learnin. We have Spanish lessons here, you know. Some of the Miami boys teach them.'

They walked a lap in silence as Buster reconsidered his future. His feet were lighter, his shoulders straighter, and he couldn't keep a grin off his face.

'Why are you helping me?' he asked.

'Because you're twenty-three years old. Too young and too innocent. You've been screwed by the system, Buster. You have the right to fight back any way you can. Do you have a girlfriend?'

'Sort of.'

'Forget about her. She'll only get you in trouble. Besides, you think she'll wait forty-eight years?'

'She said she would.'

'She's lyin. She's already playin the field. Forget about her, unless you want to get caught.'

Yeah, he's probably right, thought Buster. He'd yet to get a letter from her, and though she lived only four hours away she hadn't made it to Trumble. They'd talked twice on the phone, and all she seemed to care about was whether he'd been attacked.

'Any kids?' asked Yarber.

'No. Not that I know of.'

'What about your mother?'

'She died when I was very young. My dad raised me. It was just the two of us.'

'Then you're the perfect guy to walk away.'

'I'd like to leave now.'

259

'Be patient. Let's plan it carefully.'

Another lap, and Buster wanted to sprint. He couldn't think of a damned thing he'd miss in Pensacola. He'd made As and Bs in Spanish in high school, and while he couldn't remember any of it, he hadn't struggled with the material. He'd pick it up fast. He'd take the courses and hang out with the Latins.

The more he walked the more he wanted his conviction to be affirmed. And the quicker the better. If it got reversed, he'd be forced to have another trial, and he had no confidence in the next jury.

Buster wanted to run, starting over there in the grassy field, to the treeline, through the woods to the country road where he wasn't sure what to do next. But if an insane banker could walk away and make it to Cocoa Beach, so could he.

'Why haven't you walked away?' he asked Yarber.

'I've thought about it. But in five years they'll let me go. I can last that long. I'll be sixty-five, in good health, with a life expectancy of sixteen years. That's what I'm livin for, Buster, the last sixteen years. I don't wanna be lookin over my shoulder.'

'Where will you go?'

'Don't know yet. Maybe a little village in the Italian countryside. Maybe the mountains of Peru. I've got the whole world to choose from, and I spend hours every day just dreamin about it.'

'So you have plenty of money?'

'No, but I'm gettin there.'

That raised a number of questions, but Buster

let them pass. He was learning that in prison you kept most of your questions to yourself.

When Buster was tired of walking, he stopped near his Weed Eater. 'Thanks, Mr. Yarber,' he said.

'No problem. Just keep it between the two of us.'

'Sure. I'm ready whenever you are.'

Finn was off, pacing another lap, his shorts now soaked with sweat, his gray ponytail dripping with moisture. Buster watched him go, then for a second looked across the grassy field, into the trees.

At that moment, he could see all the way to South America.

TWENTY-FOUR

For two long, hard months Aaron Lake and Governor Tarry had gone head to head, toe to toe, coast to coast, in twenty-six states with almost 25 million votes cast. They'd pushed themselves with eighteen-hour days, brutal schedules, relentless travel, the typical madness of a presidential race.

Yet they'd worked just as hard to avoid a face-to-face debate. Tarry didn't want one in the early primaries because he was the front-runner. He had the organization, the cash, the favorable polls. Why legitimize the opposition? Lake didn't want one because he was a newcomer to the national scene, a novice at highstakes campaigning, and besides it was much easier to hide behind a script and a friendly camera and make ads whenever needed. The risks of a live debate were simply too high.

Teddy didn't like the thought of one either.

But campaigns change. Front-runners fade, small issues become big ones, the press can create a crisis simply out of boredom.

Tarry decided he needed a debate because he was broke, and losing one primary after another. 'Aaron Lake is trying to buy this election,' he said

262

over and over. 'And I want to confront him, man to man.' It sounded good, and the press had beaten it to death.

'He's running from a debate,' Tarry declared, and the pack liked that too.

'The governor's been dodging a debate since Michigan' was Lake's standard response.

And so for three weeks they played the he's-running-from-me game until their people quietly worked out the details.

Lake was reluctant, but he also needed a forum. Though he was winning week after week, he was rolling over an opponent who'd been fading for a long time. His polls and D-PAC's polls showed a great deal of voter interest in him, but mainly because he was new and handsome and seemingly electable.

Unknown to outsiders, the polls also showed some very soft areas. The first was on the question of Lake's single-issue campaign. Defense spending can excite the voters for only so long, and there was great concern, in the polls, about where Lake stood on other issues.

Second, Lake was still five points behind the Vice President in their hypothetical November matchup. The voters were tired of the Vice President, but at least they knew who he was. Lake remained a mystery to many. Also, the two would debate several times prior to November. Lake, who had the nomination in hand, needed the experience.

Tarry didn't help matters with his constant query, 'Who is Aaron Lake?' With some of his few remaining funds, he authorized the printing of

263

bumper stickers with the now famous question –
Who is Aaron Lake?

(It was a question Teddy asked himself almost
every hour, but for a different reason.)

The setting of the debate was in Pennsylvania at
a small Lutheran college with a cozy auditorium,
good acoustics and light, a controllable crowd.
Even the smallest of details were haggled over by
the two camps, but because both sides now needed
a debate agreements were eventually reached. The
precise format had nearly caused fistfights, but
once ironed out it gave everybody something. The
media got three reporters on the stage to ask direct
questions during one segment. The spectators got
twenty minutes to ask about anything, with nothing screened. Tarry, a lawyer, wanted five minutes
for opening remarks and a ten-minute closing
statement. Lake wanted thirty minutes of one-on-
one debate with Tarry, no holds barred, no one to
referee, just the two of them slugging it out
without rules. This had terrified the Tarry camp,
and had almost broken the deal.

The moderator was a local public radio figure,
and when he said, 'Good evening, and welcome to
the first and only debate between Governor Wen-
dell Tarry and Congressman Aaron Lake,' an
estimated 18 million people were watching.

Tarry wore a navy suit his wife had selected,
with the standard blue shirt and the standard red
and blue tie. Lake wore a dashing light brown suit,
a white shirt with a spread collar, and a tie of red
and maroon and a half-dozen other colors. The
entire ensemble had been put together by a fashion
consultant, and was designed to complement the

colors of the set. Lake's hair had received a tinting. His teeth had been bleached. He'd spent four hours in a tanning bed. He looked thin and fresh, and anxious to be onstage.

Governor Tarry was himself a handsome man. Though he was only four years older than Lake, the campaign was taking a heavy toll. His eyes were tired and red. He'd gained a few pounds, especially in his face. When he began his opening remarks, beads of sweat popped up along his forehead and glistened in the lights.

Conventional wisdom held that Tarry had more to lose because he'd already lost so much. Early in January, he'd been declared, by prophets as prescient as *Time* magazine, to have the nomination within his grasp. He'd been running for three years. His campaign was built on grassroots support and shoe leather. Every precinct captain and poll worker in Iowa and New Hampshire had drunk coffee with him. His organization was impeccable.

Then came Lake with his slick ads and single-issue magic.

Tarry badly needed either a stunning performance by himself, or a major gaffe by Lake.

He got neither. By a flip of the coin, he was chosen to go first. He stumbled badly in his opening remarks as he moved stiffly around the stage, trying desperately to look at ease but forgetting what his notes said. Sure he'd once been a lawyer, but his specialty had been securities. As he forgot one point after another, he returned to his common theme – Mr. Lake here is trying to buy this election because he has nothing to say. A

265

nasty tone developed quickly. Lake smiled handsomely; water off a duck's back.

Tarry's weak beginning emboldened Lake, gave
him a shot of confidence, and convinced him to
stay behind the podium where it was safe and
where his notes were. He began by saying that he
wasn't there to throw mud, that he had respect for
Governor Tarry, but they had just listened to him
speak for five minutes and eleven seconds and he'd
said nothing positive.

He then ignored his opponent, and briefly
covered three issues that needed to be discussed.
Tax relief, welfare reform, and the trade deficit.
Not a word about defense.

The first question from the panel of reporters
was directed at Lake, and it dealt with the budget
surplus. What should be done with the money? It
was a soft pitch, lobbed by a friendly reporter, and
Lake was all over it. Save Social Security, he
answered, then in an impressive display of financial straight talk he outlined precisely how the
money should be used. He gave figures and
percentages and projections, all from memory.

Governor Tarry's response was simply to cut
taxes. Give the money back to the people who'd
earned it.

Few points were scored during the questioning.
Both candidates were well prepared. The surprise
was that Lake, the man who wanted to own the
Pentagon, was so well versed in all other issues.

The debate settled into the usual give and take.
The questions from the spectators were thoroughly
predictable. The fireworks began when the candidates were allowed to quiz one another. Tarry

went first, and, as expected, asked Lake if he was trying to buy the election.

'You weren't concerned about money when you had more than everybody else,' Lake shot back, and the audience came to life.

'I didn't have fifty million dollars,' Tarry said.

'Neither do I,' Lake said. 'It's more like sixty million, and it's coming in faster than we can count it. It's coming from working people and middle-income folks. Eighty-one percent of our contributors are people earning less than forty thousand dollars a year. Something wrong with those people, Governor Tarry?'

'There should be a limit on how much a candidate should spend.'

'I agree. And I've voted for limits eight different times in Congress. You, on the other hand, never mentioned limits until you ran out of money.'

Governor Tarry looked Quayle-like at the camera, the frozen stare of a deer in headlights. A few of Lake's people in the audience laughed just loud enough to be heard.

The beads of sweat returned to the governor's forehead as he shuffled his oversized notecards. He wasn't actually a sitting governor, but he still preferred the title. In fact, it had been nine years since the voters of Indiana sent him packing, after only one term. Lake saved this ammo for a few minutes.

Tarry then asked why Lake had voted for fifty-four new taxes during his fourteen years in Congress.

'I don't recall fifty-four taxes,' Lake said. 'But a lot of them were on tobacco and alcohol and

267

gambling. I also voted against increases in personal income taxes, corporate income taxes, federal withholding taxes, and Social Security taxes. I'm not ashamed of that record. And speaking of taxes, Governor, during your four years in Indiana, how do you explain the fact that individual tax rates increased by an average of six percent?'

No quick response was forthcoming, so Lake plowed ahead. 'You want to cut federal spending, yet in your four years in Indiana state spending increased eighteen percent. You want to cut corporate income taxes, yet during your four years in Indiana, corporate income taxes went up three percent. You want to end welfare, yet when you were governor forty thousand people were added to the welfare rolls in Indiana. How do you explain this?'

Each blow from Indiana drew blood, and Tarry was on the ropes. 'I disagree with your figures, sir,' he managed to say. 'We created jobs in Indiana.'

'Is that so?' Lake said sardonically. He pulled up a sheet of paper from his podium as if it were a federal indictment against Governor Tarry. 'Maybe you did, but during your four years almost sixty thousand ex-workers signed up for unemployment,' he announced without looking at the paper.

Sure Tarry had had a bad four years as governor, but the economy had gone south on him. He had explained all this before and he'd love to do it again, but, gosh, he had only a few short minutes on national television. Surely he shouldn't waste it splitting hairs about the past. 'This race is not about Indiana,' he said, managing a smile. 'It's about all fifty states. It's about working people everywhere who'll be expected to pay more taxes to finance your gold-plated defense projects, Mr. Lake. You can't be serious about doubling the Pentagon's budget.'

Lake looked hard at his opponent. 'I'm very serious about it. And if you wanted a strong military, you'd be serious too.' He then rattled off a string of statistics that went on and on, each building on the other. It was conclusive proof of our military unreadiness, and when he finally finished our armed forces would've been hard-pressed to invade Bermuda.

But Tarry had a study to the contrary, a thick glossy manuscript produced by a think tank run by ex-admirals. He waved it for the cameras and argued such a buildup was unnecessary. The world was at peace, with the exception of a few civil and regional wars, disputes in which we had no national interest, and the United States was by far the only superpower left standing. The cold war was history. The Chinese were decades away from achieving anything remotely resembling parity. Why burden the taxpayers with tens of billions in new hardware?

They argued for a while about how to pay for it, and Tarry scored minor points. But they were on Lake's turf, and as the issue dragged on it became evident that Lake knew far more than the governor.

Lake saved his best for last. During his ten-minute recap, he returned to Indiana and continued the miserable list of Tarry's failures there during his sole term. The theme was simple, and

269

very effective: If he can't run Indiana, how can he run the entire nation?

'I'm not knocking the people of Indiana,' Lake said at one point. 'In fact, they had the wisdom to return Mr. Tarry to private life after only one term. They knew he was doing a terrible job. That's why only thirty-eight percent of them voted for him when he asked for four more years. Thirty-eight percent! We should trust the people of Indiana. They know this man. They've seen him govern. They made a mistake, and they got rid of him. It would be sad if the rest of the country now made the same mistake.'

The instant polls gave a solid win to Lake. D-PAC called a thousand voters immediately after the debate. Almost 70 percent thought Lake was the better of the two.

On a late flight from Pittsburgh to Wichita, several bottles of champagne were opened on Air Lake and a small party began. The debate poll results were flowing in, each better than the last, and the mood was victorious.

Lake hadn't banned alcohol on his Boeing, but he had discouraged it. If and when a member of his staff took a drink, it was always a quick one, and always on the sly. But some moments called for a little celebration. He enjoyed two glasses of champagne himself. Only his closest people were present. He thanked them and congratulated them, and just for fun they watched the highlights of the debate while another bottle was opened. They paused the video each time Governor Tarry looked particularly puzzled, and the laughs grew louder.

But the party was brief; fatigue hit hard. These were people who'd been sleeping five hours a night for weeks. Most had slept even less the night before the debate. Lake himself was exhausted. He finished a third glass, the first time in many years he'd drunk that much, and settled into his massive leather recliner with a heavy quilt. Bodies sprawled everywhere in the darkness of the cabin.

He couldn't sleep; he seldom did on airplanes. There were too many things to think and worry about. It was impossible not to savor the victory in the debate, and as he kicked around under the quilt Lake repeated his best lines of the night. He had been brilliant, something he'd never admit to anyone else.

The nomination was his. He would be showcased at the convention, then for four months he and the Vice President would slug it out in the grandest of American traditions.

He turned on the small overhead reading light. Someone else was reading down the aisle, near the flight deck. Another insomniac, with the only other light on in the cabin. People were actually snoring under their blankets, the sleep of hurried young people running on fumes.

Lake opened his briefcase and pulled out a small leather folder filled with his personal correspondence cards. They were four by six, heavy stock, off-white in color, and in light black Old English print had the name of 'Aaron Lake' printed at the top. With a thick, antique Mont Blanc pen, Lake scribbled a brief word to his college roommate, now a professor of Latin at a small college in Texas. He wrote a thank-you to the moderator of the debate, and one to his Oregon coordinator. Lake loved Clancy novels. He'd just finished the latest one, the thickest yet, and he wrote the author a complimentary note.

Sometimes his notes ran long, and for this reason he had plain cards, same size and color but without his name. He looked around to make sure everyone was sound asleep, and he quickly wrote:

Dear Ricky:
   I think it's best if we end our correspondence. I wish you well with your rehab.
                              Sincerely, Al

He addressed an unmarked envelope. The address of Aladdin North came from memory. Then he returned to his personalized cards and wrote a series of thank-you notes to serious contributors. He wrote twenty of them before fatigue finally settled in. With the cards still in front of him, and his reading light still on, he yielded to exhaustion and within minutes was napping.

He'd slept less than an hour when panicked voices awakened him. Lights were on, people were moving, and there was smoke in the cabin. A buzzer of some sort was ringing loudly from the cockpit, and once he got his bearings Lake realized the nose of the Boeing was pointed downward. Total panic set in quickly as the air masks dropped from above. After years of half-watching flight attendants give their routine demonstrations before takeoff, the damned masks were actually going to be used. Lake snapped his into place and inhaled mightily.

The pilot announced they were making an emergency landing in St. Louis. The lights flickered, and someone actually screamed. Lake wanted to move about the cabin and reassure everyone, but the mask wouldn't move with him. In the section behind him were two dozen reporters and about that many Secret Service people.

Maybe the air masks didn't drop back there, he thought, then felt guilty.

The smoke got thicker, and the lights faded. After the onset of panic, Lake managed a rational thought or two, if only for a brief second. He quickly gathered the correspondence cards and envelopes. The one to Ricky got his attention just long enough to place it in the envelope to Aladdin North. He sealed it, and stuffed the folder back into his briefcase. The lights flickered again, then went out for good.

The smoke burned their eyes and warmed their faces. The plane was descending at a rapid pace. Warning bells and sirens shrieked from the flight deck.

This can't be happening, Lake told himself as he gripped his armrests. I'm about to be elected President of the United States. He thought of Rocky Marciano, Buddy Holly, Otis Redding, Thurman Munson, Senator Tower of Texas, Mickey Leland from Houston, a friend of his. And JFK, Jr., and Ron Brown.

The air suddenly turned cold and the smoke

273

dissipated rapidly. They were below ten thousand feet, and the pilot had somehow managed to vent the cabin. The plane leveled and from the windows they could see lights on the ground.

'Please continue to use the oxygen masks,' the pilot said in the darkness. 'We'll be on the ground in a few minutes. The landing should be uneventful.'

Uneventful? He must be kidding, thought Lake. He needed to find the nearest toilet.

Relief settled uneasily through the plane. Just before it touched down, Lake saw the flashing lights of a hundred emergency vehicles. They bounced a little, a typical landing, and when they stopped at the end of the runway the emergency doors flew open.

A controlled stampede occurred, and within minutes they were grabbed by rescue personnel and rushed to ambulances. The fire, in the luggage area of the Boeing, was still spreading when they landed. As Lake jogged away from the plane, firemen rushed toward it. Smoke boiled from under the wings.

Just a few more minutes, Lake said to himself, and we would be dead.

'That was a close one, sir,' a paramedic said as they raced away. Lake clutched his briefcase, with his little letters inside, and for the first time went rigid with horror.

The near miss, and the obligatory nonstop media barrage after it, probably did little to boost Lake's popularity. But the publicity certainly didn't hurt. He was everywhere on the morning news, one

274

moment talking about his decisive victory over Governor Tarry in the debate, and the next giving details of what could've been his last flight.

'I think I'll take the bus for a while,' he said with a laugh. He used as much humor as he could muster, and took the high road of aw-shucks-it-was-nothing. His staff members had different stories, of breathing oxygen in the dark while the smoke grew thicker and hotter. And the reporters on board were eager sources of information, providing detailed narratives of the terror.

Teddy Maynard watched it all from his bunker. Three of his men were on the plane, and one had called him from the hospital in St. Louis.

It was a perplexing event. On the one hand, he still believed in the importance of a Lake presidency. The security of the nation depended on it.

On the other hand, a crash wouldn't have been a catastrophe. Lake and his double life would be gone. A huge headache wiped out. Governor Tarry had learned firsthand the power of unlimited cash. Teddy could cut a deal with him in time to win in November.

But Lake was still standing, taller than ever now. His tanned face was on the front of every newspaper and close to every camera. His campaign had progressed far faster than Teddy had dreamed.

So why was there so much angst in the bunker? Why was Teddy not celebrating?

Because he had yet to solve the puzzle of the Brethren. And he couldn't simply start killing people.

TWENTY-FIVE

The team in Documents used the same laptop
they'd used to write the last letter to Ricky. This
letter was composed by Deville himself, and
approved by Mr. Maynard. It read:

Dear Ricky:
  Good news about your release to the
halfway house in Baltimore. Give me a few
days and I think I'll have a full-time job lined
up for you there. It's a clerical position, not a
lot of money, but a pretty good place to start.
  I suggest we go a bit slower than you want.
Maybe a nice lunch at first, then we'll see
where things go. I'm not the type to rush in.
  Hope you're doing well. I'll write you next
week with the details of the job. Hang in
there.

Best Wishes, Al

Only the 'Al' was handwritten. A D.C. postmark
was applied, and the letter was flown and hand-
delivered to Klockner in Neptune Beach.
  Trevor happened to be in Fort Lauderdale,

oddly enough tending to legitimate legal business, and so the letter sat in the Aladdin North box for two days. When he returned, exhausted, he stopped by his office just long enough to commence a nasty argument with Jan, then stormed out, got back in his car, and went straight to the post office. To his delight, the box was full. He sorted out the junk mail, then drove a half mile to the Atlantic Beach post office and checked the box for Laurel Ridge, Percy's fancy rehab spa.

Once all the mail was collected, and much to the dismay of Klockner, Trevor left for Trumble. He made one call en route, to his bookie. He'd lost $2,500 in three days on hockey, a sport Spicer knew nothing about and refused to bet on. Trevor was picking his own favorites, with predictable results.

Spicer didn't answer the page at the courtyard at Trumble, so Beech met with Trevor in the attorney-conference room. They did their mail swap – eight letters going out, fourteen coming in.

'What about Brant in Upper Darby?' Beech asked, flipping through the envelopes.

'What about him?'

'Who is he? We're ready to bust him.'

'I'm still searching. I've been out of town for a few days.'

'Get it done, okay. This guy could be the biggest fish yet.'

'I'll do it tomorrow.'

Beech had no Vegas lines to ponder and he didn't want to play cards. Trevor left after twenty minutes.

★

Long after they should've eaten dinner, and long after the library should've been closed, the Brethren remained locked in their little room, saying little, avoiding eye contact with one another, each staring at the walls, deep in thought.

On the table were three letters. One was from Al's laptop, postmarked two days earlier in D.C. One was Al's handwritten note ending his correspondence with Ricky, postmarked from St. Louis, three days earlier. These two conflicted sharply, and were obviously written by different people. Someone was tampering with their mail.

The third letter had stopped them cold. They'd read it over and over, one by one, collectively, in silence, in unison. They'd picked at its corners, held it up to the light, even smelled it. There was a very faint smoky odor, same as the envelope and the note from Al to Ricky.

Handwritten in ink, it was dated April 18, at 1:20 A.M., and addressed to a woman named Carol.

Dear Carol:
   What a great night! The debate couldn't have gone better, thanks in part to you and the Pennsylvania volunteers. Many thanks! Let's push harder and win this thing. We're ahead in Pennsylvania, let's stay there. See you next week.

It was signed by Aaron Lake. The card had his name personalized across the top. The handwriting was identical to that on the terse note Al had sent Ricky.

The envelope was addressed to Ricky at Aladdin North, and when Beech opened it he did not notice the second card stuck behind the first. Then it fell on the table, and when he picked it up he saw the name 'Aaron' Lake engraved in black.

That had happened sometime around 4 P.M., not long after Trevor had left. For almost five hours they'd studied the mail, and they were now almost certain that (a) the laptop letter was a fake, with the name 'Al' signed by someone who was quite good at forging; (b) the forged 'Al' signature was virtually identical to the original 'Al,' so the forger at some point had gained access to Ricky's correspondence with Al; (c) the notes to Ricky and Carol were handwritten by Aaron Lake; and (d) the one to Carol had obviously been sent to them by mistake.

Above all, Al Konyers was really Aaron Lake.

Their little scam had snared the most famous politician in the country.

Other, less important pieces of evidence also pointed toward Lake. His front was a mailbox service in the D.C. area, a place where Congressman Lake spent almost all of his time. Being a high-profile elected official, subject to the whims of voters every so often, he would certainly hide behind an alias. And he'd use a machine with a printer to hide his handwriting. Al had not sent a photograph, another sign that he had a lot to conceal.

They'd checked recent newspapers in the library to get the dates straight. The handwritten notes had been mailed from St. Louis the day after the

279

debate, when Lake was there because his airplane had caught fire.

The timing seemed perfect for Lake to call off the letters. He'd started the correspondence before he entered the race. In three months he'd taken the country by storm and become very famous. Now, he had so much to lose.

Slowly, with no concern for time, they built their case against Aaron Lake. And when it looked airtight, they tried to break it down. The most compelling counterpoint came from Finn Yarber.

Suppose, he said, someone on Lake's staff had access to his stationery? Not a bad question, and one they'd kicked around for an hour. Wouldn't Al Konyers do such a thing in order to hide himself? What if he lived in the D.C. area and worked for Lake? Suppose Lake, a very busy man, trusted this assistant to write personal notes for him. Yarber couldn't remember allowing an assistant such authority back when he was Chief Justice. Beech had never let anyone write his personal notes. Spicer had never fooled with such nonsense. That's what phones were for.

But Yarber and Beech had never known the stress and fury of anything remotely similar to a presidential campaign. They'd been busy men in their times, they reflected with sadness, but nothing like Lake.

Say it was an assistant to Lake. So far he had a perfect cover because he'd told them almost nothing. No photo. Only the vaguest details about career and family. He liked old movies and Chinese food, and that was about all they'd extracted. Konyers was on their list of pen pals to

280

soon dispose of because he was too timid. Why, then, would he call off the relationship at this moment?

There was no ready answer.

And the argument was a long shot anyway. Beech and Yarber concluded that no man in Lake's position, someone with a good chance of becoming President of the United States, would allow anyone else to write and sign personal notes. Lake had a hundred staff members to type letters and memos, all of which could be signed by him at a rapid clip.

Spicer had posed a more serious question. Why would Lake run the risk of a handwritten note? His prior letters had been typed on plain white paper, and mailed in a plain white envelope. They could spot a coward by his choice of stationery, and Lake was as fainthearted as anyone who'd answered their ad. The campaign, rich as it was, had plenty of word processors and typewriters and laptops, no doubt the latest in technology.

To find the answer, they went back to the little evidence they had. The letter to Carol had been written at 1:20 A.M. According to a newspaper, the emergency landing happened around 2:15, less than an hour later.

'He wrote it on the plane,' Yarber said. 'It was late, the plane was filled with people, almost sixty according to the paper, these people were exhausted, and maybe he couldn't get his hands on a computer.'

'Then why not wait?' asked Spicer. He'd proved to be excellent at asking questions no one, especially him, could answer.

'He made a mistake. He thought he was being smart, and he probably was. Somehow the mail got mixed.'

'Look at the big picture,' Beech said. 'The nomination is in the bag. He's just wiped out his only opponent, before a national audience, and he's finally convinced that his name will be on the ballot in November. But he's got this secret. He's got Ricky, and he's been thinking for weeks about what to do with Ricky. The boy's going to be released, he wants to have a rendezvous, etc. Lake feels the pressure on both fronts – from Ricky, and from the realization that he might just be elected President. So he decides to stiff Ricky. He writes a note that has one chance in a billion of getting screwed up, then the plane catches on fire. He makes a small mistake, but it turns into a monster.'

'And he doesn't know it,' Yarber added. 'Yet.'

Beech's theory settled in. They absorbed it in the heavy stillness of their little room. The gravity of their discovery weighed down their words and thoughts. The hours passed, and it slowly sank in.

For the next great question they grappled with the baffling reality that someone was meddling with their mail. Who? And why would anyone want to? How had they intercepted the letters? The puzzle seemed hopeless.

Again, they argued the scenario that the culprit was someone very close to Lake, perhaps an assistant with access who'd stumbled across the letters. And maybe he was trying to protect Lake from Ricky by commandeering the correspondence, with the goal of somehow, someday ending the relationship.

But there were too many unknowns to build any evidence. They scratched their heads and bit their nails, and finally admitted they would have to sleep on it. They couldn't plot the next move because the situation before them had more riddles than answers.

They slept little, and they were red-eyed and unshaved when they reconvened just after 6 A.M. with black coffee steaming from Styrofoam cups. They locked the door, pulled out the letters, placed them exactly where they'd been the night before, and began thinking.

'I think we should scope out the box in Chevy Chase,' said Spicer. 'It's easy, safe, usually quick. Trevor's been able to do it almost everywhere. If we know who's renting it, then a lot of questions will be answered.'

'It's hard to believe a man like Aaron Lake would be renting a box so he could hide letters like these,' Beech said.

'It's not the same Aaron Lake,' Yarber said. 'When he rented the box and began writing to Ricky, he was just a simple congressman, one of four hundred and thirty-five. You'd never heard of him. Now, things have changed dramatically.'

'And that's exactly why he's trying to end the relationship,' Spicer said. 'Things are very different now. He has much more to lose.'

The first step would be to get Trevor to investigate the post office box in Chevy Chase.

The second step was not as clear. They were concerned that Lake, and they assumed that Lake was Al and Al was Lake, might realize his screwup

283

with the letters. He had tens of millions of dollars (a fact they had certainly not overlooked), and he could easily use some of it to track down Ricky. Given the enormity of the stakes, Lake, if he did realize his mistake, would do almost anything to neutralize Ricky.

So they debated whether to write him a note, in which Ricky would beg Al not to slam the door like this. Ricky needed his friendship, nothing more, etc. The purpose would be to give the impression that everything was fine, nothing out of the ordinary. They hoped Lake would read it and scratch his head and wonder to himself just where, exactly, did that damned card to Carol get off to.

Such a note was unwise, they decided, because someone else was also reading the letters. Until they knew who, they couldn't risk any more contact with Al.

They finished their coffee and walked to the cafeteria. They ate alone, cereal and fruit and yogurt, healthy stuff because they would now live again on the outside. They walked four smoke-free laps together, at a leisurely pace, then returned to their chamber to finish the morning deep in thought.

Poor Lake. He was scrambling from one state to the next with fifty people in tow, late for three engagements at once, a dozen aides whispering in both ears. He had no time to think for himself.

And the Brethren had all day, hours upon hours to sit with their thoughts and their schemes. It was not an equal match.

TWENTY-SIX

There were two types of phones at Trumble; secured and unsecured. In theory, all calls made on unsecured lines were taped and subject to review by little elves in a booth somewhere who did nothing but listen to a million hours of useless chatter. In reality, about half the calls were actually taped, at random, and only about 5 percent were ever heard by anybody working for the prison. Not even the federal government could hire enough elves to handle all the listening.

Drug dealers had been known to direct their gangs from unsecured lines. Mafia bosses had been known to order hits on their rivals. The odds were very high against getting caught.

The secured lines were fewer in number, and by law could not be wired for surveillance. The secured calls went only to lawyers, and always with a guard posted nearby.

When Spicer's turn finally came to make a secured call, the guard had drifted away.

'Law office,' came the rude hello from the free world.

'Yes, this is Joe Roy Spicer, calling from the Trumble prison, and I need to speak with Trevor.'

'He's asleep.'

It was 1:30 P.M. 'Then wake the sonofabitch up,' Spicer growled.

'Hang on.'

'Would you please hurry? I'm on a prison phone.'

Joe Roy glanced around and wondered, not for the first time, what kind of lawyer they'd crawled in bed with.

'Why are you calling?' were Trevor's first words.

'Never mind. Wake your ass up and get to work. We need something done quickly.'

By now, the rental across from Trevor's office was buzzing. This was the first call from Trumble.

'What is it?'

'We need a box checked out. Quickly. And we want you to go supervise it. Don't leave until it's finished.'

'Why me?'

'Just do it, dammit, okay? This could be the biggest one yet.'

'Where is it?'

'Chevy Chase, Maryland. Write this down. Al Konyers, Box 455, Mailbox America, 39380 Western Avenue, Chevy Chase. Be very careful because this guy could have some friends, and there's a good chance someone else is already watching the box. Take some cash and hire a couple of good investigators.'

'I'm pretty busy around here.'

'Yeah, sorry I woke you up. Do it now, Trevor.

286

Leave today. And don't come back until you know who rented the box.'

'All right, all right.'

Spicer hung up, and Trevor put his feet back on his desk and appeared to return to his nap. But he was just contemplating matters. A moment later he yelled for Jan to check the flights to Washington.

In fourteen years as a field supervisor, Klockner had never seen so many people watch one person do so little. He made a quick call to Deville at Langley, and the rental sprang into action. It was time for the Wes and Chap show.

Wes walked across the street and entered the creaking and peeling door of Mr. L. Trevor Carson, Attorney and Counselor-at-Law. Wes was dressed in khakis and a pullover knit, loafers, no socks, and when Jan offered him her customary sneer she couldn't tell if he was a native or a tourist. 'What can I do for you?' she asked.

'I really need to see Mr. Carson,' Wes said with an air of desperation.

'Do you have an appointment?' she asked, as if her boss was so busy she couldn't keep track of his meetings.

'Well, no, it's sort of an emergency.'

'He's very busy,' she said, and Wes could almost hear the laughter from the rental.

'Please, I've got to talk to him.'

She rolled her eyes and didn't budge. 'What kind of matter is it?'

'I've just buried my wife,' he said, on the verge of tears, and Jan finally cracked a bit. 'I'm very sorry,' she said. Poor guy.

'She was killed in a car wreck on I–95, just north of Jacksonville.'

Jan was standing now and wishing she'd made fresh coffee. 'I'm so sorry,' she said. 'When did this happen?'

'Twelve days ago. A friend recommended Mr. Carson.'

Not much of a friend, she wanted to say. 'Would you like some coffee?' she asked, putting the top on her nail polish. Twelve days ago, she thought. Like all good legal secretaries, she read the newspapers with a keen eye on the accidents. Who knows, one might walk in the door.

Never Trevor's door. Until now.

'No, thanks,' Wes said. 'She was hit by a Texaco truck. The driver was drunk.'

'Oh my god!' she exclaimed, hand over her mouth. Even Trevor could handle this one.

Serious money, big fees, right here in the reception area, and that fool back there snoring off his lunch.

'He's in a deposition,' she said. 'Let me see if I can disturb him. Please have a seat.' She wanted to lock the front door so he couldn't escape.

'The name's Yates. Yates Newman,' he said, trying to help her.

'Oh yes,' she said, racing down the hall. She knocked politely on Trevor's door, then stepped inside. 'Wake up, asshole!' she hissed through clenched teeth, loud enough for Wes to hear up front.

'What is it?' Trevor said, standing, ready for a fistfight. He wasn't sleeping after all. He'd been reading an old *People*.

288

'Surprise! You have a client.'

'Who is it?'

'A man whose wife got run over by a Texaco truck twelve days ago. He wants to see you right now.'

'He's here?'

'Yep. Hard to believe, isn't it? Three thousand lawyers in Jacksonville and this poor guy falls through the cracks. Said a friend recommended you.'

'What'd you tell him?'

'I told him he needed to find new friends.'

'No, really, what did you tell him?'

'That you're in a deposition.'

'I haven't had a deposition in eight years. Send him back.'

'Be cool. I'll make him some coffee. Act like you're finishing some important stuff back here. Why don't you straighten this place up?'

'You just make sure he can't get out.'

'The Texaco driver was drunk,' she said, opening the door. 'Don't screw this up.'

Trevor froze, slack-jawed, glassy-eyed, his deadened mind suddenly springing to life. One third of $2 million, $4 million, hell, $10 million if he was really drunk and punitive damages kicked in. He wanted to at least straighten his desk, but he couldn't move.

Wes stared out the front window, stared at the rental, where his buddies were staring at him. He kept his back to the ruckus down the hall because he was struggling to keep a straight face. Footsteps, then Jan said, 'Mr. Carson will see you in just a moment.'

289

'Thanks,' he said softly, without turning around.

Poor guy's still grieving, she thought, then walked to the dirty kitchen to make coffee.

The deposition was over in a flash, and the other participants miraculously vanished without a trace. Wes followed her down the hall to Mr. Carson's cluttered office. Introductions were made. She brought them fresh coffee, and when she was finally gone, Wes made an unusual request.

'Is there any place to get a strong latte around here?'

'Why, certainly, yes, of course,' Trevor said, the words jumping across the desk. 'There's a place called Beach Java just a few blocks away.'

'Could you send her to get me one?'

Absolutely. Anything!

'Yes, of course. Tall or grande?'

'Tall's fine.'

Trevor bounced out of his office, and a few seconds later Jan hit the front door and practically ran down the street. When she was out of sight, Chap left the rental and walked to Trevor's. The front door was locked, so he opened it with a key of his own. Inside, he latched the chain, so poor Jan would be stuck on the porch with a cup of scalding latte.

Chap eased down the hall and made a sudden entrance into the lawyer's office.

'Excuse me,' Trevor said.

'It's okay,' Wes said. 'He's with me.'

Chap closed and locked the door, then he yanked a 9-millimeter pistol from his jacket and almost pointed it at poor Trevor, whose eyes bulged and heart froze.

'What –' he managed to emit in a high-pitched painful voice.

'Just shut up, okay,' said Chap, handing the pistol to Wes, who was sitting. Trevor's wild eyes followed it from one to the other, then it disappeared. What have I done? Who are these thugs? All my gambling debts are paid.

He was very happy to shut up. Whatever they wanted.

Chap leaned on the wall, pretty damned close to Trevor, as if he might lunge at any moment. 'We have a client,' he began. 'A wealthy man, who has been snagged in the little scam run by you and Ricky.'

'Oh my god,' Trevor mumbled. His worst nightmare.

'It's a wonderful idea,' Wes said. 'Extorting from rich gay men who are still hiding in the closet. They can't complain. Ricky's already in prison, so what does he have to lose?'

'Almost perfect,' Chap said. 'Until you hook the wrong fish, which is exactly what you've done.'

'It's not my scam,' Trevor said, his voice still two octaves above normal, his eyes still searching for the pistol.

'Yes, but it wouldn't work without you, would it?' Wes asked. 'There has to be a crooked lawyer on the outside to shuttle mail. And Ricky needs someone to direct the money and do a little investigative work.'

'You're not cops, are you?' Trevor asked.

'No. We're private thugs,' Chap said.

'Because if you're cops then I'm not sure I wanna talk anymore.'

291

'We're not cops, okay.'

Trevor was breathing and thinking again, the breathing going much faster than the thinking, but his training kicked in. 'I think I'll record this,' he said. 'Just in case you're cops.'

'I said we're not cops.'

'I don't trust cops, especially the FBI. The fibbies would walk in here just like the two of you, wave a gun around, and swear that they weren't fibbies. I just don't like cops. I think I'll get this on tape.'

Don't worry, pal, they wanted to say. It was all being recorded, live and in high-density digital color from a tiny camera in the ceiling a few feet behind where they were sitting. And there were mikes planted all around Trevor's littered desk so that when he snored or burped or even cracked his knuckles somebody across the street heard it.

The pistol was back. Wes held it with both hands and examined it carefully.

'You're not recording anything,' Chap said. 'As I told you, we're private boys. And we're calling the shots right now.' He took a step closer along the wall. Trevor watched him with one eye, and with the other helped Wes examine the pistol.

'In fact, we come in peace,' Chap said.

'We have some money for you,' Wes said, and put the damned thing away again.

'Money for what?'Trevor asked.

'We want you on our side. We want to retain your services.'

'To do what?'

'To help us protect our client,' Chap said. 'Here's the way we see it. You're a conspirator in

292

an extortion scheme operating from inside a federal prison, and you've been discovered by us. We could go to the feds, get you and your client busted, you'd be sent away for thirty months, probably to Trumble, where you'd fit right in. You'd be automatically disbarred, which means you'd lose all this.' Chap casually waved his right hand, dismissing the clutter and dust and heaps of old files untouched in years.

Wes jumped right in. 'We're prepared to go to the feds right now, and we could probably stop the mail out of Trumble. Our client would probably be spared any embarrassment. But there's an element of risk our client is not willing to take. What if Ricky has another cohort, either inside or out of Trumble, somebody we haven't found yet, and he somehow manages to expose our client in retaliation?'

Chap was already shaking his head. 'It's too risky. We'd rather work with you, Trevor. We'd rather buy you off, and kill the scam from this office.'

'I cannot be bought,' Trevor said with only a trace of conviction.

'Then we'll lease you for a while, how about that?' Wes said. 'Aren't all lawyers leased by the hour anyway?'

'I suppose, but you're asking me to sell out a client.'

'Your client is a felon who's committing crimes every day from inside a federal prison. And you're just as guilty as he is. Let's not get too sanctimonious here.'

'When you become a criminal, Trevor,' Chap

said gravely, 'you lose the privilege of being self-righteous. Don't preach to us. We know it's just a question of how much money.'

Trevor forgot about the gun for a moment, and he forgot about his law license hanging on the wall behind him, slightly crooked. As he so often did these days when faced with yet another unpleasantry from the practice of law, he closed his eyes and dreamed of his forty-foot schooner, anchored in the warm, still waters of a secluded bay, topless girls on the beach a hundred yards away, and himself barely clad, sipping a beverage on the deck. He could smell the salt water, feel the gentle breeze, taste the rum, hear the girls.

He opened his eyes and tried to focus on Wes across the desk. 'Who is your client?' he asked.

'Not so fast,' Chap said. 'Let's cut the deal first.'

'What deal?'

'We give you some money, and you work as a double agent. We get access to everything. We wire you when you talk to Ricky. We see all the mail. You don't make a move until we discuss it.'

'Why don't you just pay the extortion money?' Trevor asked. 'It'd be a whole lot easier.'

'We've thought of that,' Wes said. 'But Ricky doesn't play fair. If we paid him, then he'd come back for more. And more.'

'No, he wouldn't.'

'Really? What about Quince Garbe in Bakers, Iowa?'

Oh my god, thought Trevor, and he almost said it aloud. How much do they know? All he could manage was a very weak 'Who's he?'

'Come on, Trevor,' Chap said. 'We know where

the money is hidden in the Bahamas. We know about Boomer Realty, and about your little account, currently with a balance of almost seventy thousand bucks.'

'We've dug as far as we can dig, Trevor,' Wes said, jumping in with perfect timing. Trevor was watching tennis, back and forth, back and forth. 'But we've finally hit a rock. That's why we need you.'

Truthfully, Trevor had never liked Spicer. He was a cold, ruthless, nasty little man who'd had the gall to cut Trevor's percentage. Beech and Yarber were okay, but what the hell. It wasn't as if Trevor had a lot of choices here. 'How much?' he asked.

'Our client is prepared to pay a hundred thousand dollars, cash,' Chap said.

'Of course it's cash,' Trevor replied. 'A hundred thousand is a joke. That would be Ricky's first installment. My self-respect is worth a helluva lot more than a hundred thousand.'

'Two hundred thousand,' Wes said.

'Let's do it this way,' Trevor said, trying to willfully suppress his racing heart. 'How much is it worth to your client to have his little secret buried?'

'And you're willing to bury it?' Wes asked.

'Yep.'

'Give me a second,' Chap said, yanking a tiny phone from his pocket. He punched numbers as he opened the door and stepped into the hallway, then mumbled several sentences Trevor could barely hear. Wes stared at a wall, the gun lying peacefully beside his chair. Trevor couldn't see it, though he tried.

Chap returned and stared hard at Wes, as if his

eyebrows and wrinkles could somehow deliver a crucial message. In the brief hesitation, Trevor rushed in. 'I think it's worth a million bucks,' he said. 'It could be my last case. You're asking me to divulge confidential client information, a rather egregious act for a lawyer. It would get me disbarred in an instant.'

Disbarment would be a step up for old Trevor, but Wes and Chap let it pass. Nothing good could come from an argument about how valuable his law license might be.

'Our client will pay a million dollars,' Chap said.

And Trevor laughed. He couldn't help it. He cackled as if he'd just heard the perfect punch line, and across the street in the rental they laughed because Trevor was laughing.

Trevor managed to control himself. He stopped chuckling but couldn't wipe off the smile. A million bucks. Cash. Tax-free. Hidden offshore, in another bank, of course, away from the clutches of the IRS and every other branch of the government.

Then he managed to arrange a lawyerly frown, a little embarrassed that he'd reacted so unprofessionally. He was about to say something important when three sharp raps on glass came from the front. 'Oh yes,' he said. 'That would be the coffee.'

'She's gotta go,' Chap said.

'I'll send her home,' Trevor said, standing for the first time, a little light-headed.

'No. Permanently. Get her out of the office.'

'How much does she know?' Wes asked.

'She's dumb as a rock,' Trevor said happily.

'It's part of the deal,' Chap said. 'She goes, and

296

now. We have a lot to discuss, and we don't want her around.'

The knocking grew louder. Jan had unlocked the door but was caught by the security chain. 'Trevor! It's me!' she shouted through the two-inch crack.

Trevor walked slowly down the hall, scratching his head, searching for words. He came face to face with her through the window of the front door, and he looked very confused.

'Open up,' she growled. 'This coffee is hot.'

'I want you to go home,' he said.

'Why?'

'Why?'

'Yes, why?'

'Because, well, uh –' Words failed him for a second, then he thought of the money. Her exit was part of the deal. 'Because you're fired,' he said.

'What?'

'I said you're fired!' he yelled, loud enough for his new pals in the back to hear.

'You can't fire me! You owe me too much money.'

'I don't owe you a damned thing!'

'How about a thousand bucks in back salary!'

The windows of the rental were crowded with faces hidden by one-way shading. The voices echoed down the quiet street.

'You're crazy!' Trevor screamed. 'I don't owe you a dime!'

'One thousand forty bucks, to be exact!'

'You're nuts.'

'You sonofabitch! I stick with you for eight years, making minimum wage, then you finally get

297

the big case, and you fire me. Is that what you're doing, Trevor!?'

'Something like that! Now leave!'

'Open the door, you little coward!'

'Leave, Jan!'

'Not until I get my things!'

'Come back tomorrow. I'm meeting with Mr. Newman.' With that, Trevor took a step back. When she saw he wasn't opening the door, she lost it. 'You sonofabitch!' she screamed even louder, then hurled the tall latte at the door. The thin, rickety window shook but didn't break, and was instantly covered with creamy brown liquid.

Trevor, safe on the inside, flinched anyway and watched in horror as this woman he knew so well lost her mind. She stormed away, red-faced and cursing, and took a few steps until a rock caught her attention. It was a remnant of a long-forgotten, low-budget landscaping project he'd once okayed at her insistence. She grabbed it, gritted her teeth, cursed some more, then launched it toward the door.

Wes and Chap had done a masterful job of playing it straight, but when the rock crashed through the door window, they couldn't help but laugh. Trevor yelled, 'You crazy bitch!' They laughed again and looked away from each other, trying gamely to tighten up.

Silence followed. Peace had broken out in and around the reception area.

Trevor appeared in the doorway of his office, unscathed, no visible injuries. 'Sorry about that,' he said softly, and went to his chair.

'You okay?' Chap asked.

298

'Sure. No problem. How about plain coffee?' he asked Wes.

'Forget about it.'

The details were hammered out during lunch, which Trevor insisted they enjoy at Pete's. They found a table in the back, near the pinball machines. Wes and Chap were concerned with privacy, but they soon realized that nobody listened because nobody conducted business at Pete's.

Trevor knocked down three longnecks with his french fries. They had soft drinks and burgers.

Trevor wanted all the money in hand before he betrayed his client. They agreed to deliver a hundred thousand cash that afternoon, and immediately start a wire transfer for the balance. Trevor demanded a different bank, but they insisted on keeping Geneva Trust in Nassau. They assured him their access was limited only to observing the account; they could not tamper with the funds. Besides, the money would arrive there by late afternoon. If they changed banks, then it might take a day or two. Both sides were anxious to complete the deal. Wes and Chap wanted full, immediate protection for their client. Trevor wanted his fortune. After three beers he was already spending it.

Chap left early to fetch the money. Trevor ordered a longneck to go, and they got into Wes' car for a ride around town. The plan was to meet Chap at some spot and take possession of the cash. As they rode south on Highway A1A, along the beach, Trevor began talking.

'Isn't it amazing,' he said, his eyes hidden behind cheap sunglasses, his head back on the headrest.

'What's amazing?'

'The risks people are willing to take. Your client, for example. A rich man. He could hire all the young boys he wanted, yet he answers an ad in a gay magazine and starts writing letters to a complete stranger.'

'I don't understand it,' Wes said, and the two straight boys bonded for a second. 'It's not my job to ask questions.'

'I suppose the thrill is in the unknown,' Trevor said and took a small sip.

'Yeah, probably so. Who's Ricky?'

'I'll tell you when I get the money. Which one's your client?'

'Which one? How many victims are you working on right now?'

'Ricky's been busy lately. Probably twenty or so in the works.'

'How many have you extorted?'

'Two or three. It's a nasty business.'

'How'd you get involved?'

'I'm Ricky's lawyer. He's very bright, very bored, somehow he cooked up this scheme to put the squeeze on gays still in the closet. Against my better judgment, I signed on.'

'Is he gay?' Wes asked. Wes knew the names of Beech's grandchildren. He knew Yarber's blood type. He knew who Spicer's wife was dating back in Mississippi.

'No,' said Trevor.

'He's a sicko then.'

'No, he's a nice guy. So who's your client?'

'Al Konyers.'

Trevor nodded and tried to remember how many letters he'd handled between Ricky and Al. 'What a coincidence. I was making plans to go to Washington to do some background work on Mr. Konyers. Not his real name, of course.'

'Of course not.'

'Do you know his real name?'

'No. We were hired by some of his people.'

'How interesting. So none of us knows the real Al Konyers?'

'That's correct. And I'm sure it'll stay that way.'

Trevor pointed to a convenience store and said, 'Pull in there. I need a beer.'

Wes waited near the gas pumps. It had been determined that they would not say anything about his drinking until the money changed hands and he'd told them everything. They would build some trust, then gently try to nudge him closer to sobriety. The last thing they needed was Trevor at Pete's every night, drinking and talking too much.

Chap was waiting in a matching rental car, in front of a Laundromat five miles south of Ponte Vedra Beach. He handed Trevor a thin, cheap briefcase and said, 'It's all there. A hundred thousand. I'll meet you guys back at the office.'

Trevor didn't hear him. He opened the briefcase and began counting the money. Wes turned around and headed north. Ten stacks of $10,000, all in $100 bills.

Trevor closed it, and crossed over to the other side.

TWENTY-SEVEN

Chap's first task as Trevor's new paralegal was to organize the front desk and rid it of anything remotely female. He put Jan's things in a cardboard box, everything from lipstick tubes and nail files to peanut candy and several X-rated romance novels. There was an envelope with eighty dollars and change. The boss claimed it for himself, said it was petty cash.

Chap wrapped her photos in old newspapers and placed them carefully in another box, along with the breakable knickknacks you find on most front desks. He copied her appointment books so they would know who was scheduled to appear in the future. The traffic would be light, he saw with little surprise. Not a single court date anywhere on the horizon. Two office appointments this week, two the next, then nothing. As Chap studied the calendars, it was obvious that Trevor had shifted to a slower gear at about the time the money arrived from Quince Garbe.

They knew Trevor's gambling had picked up in recent weeks, and probably his drinking. Several times Jan had told friends on the phone that

302

Trevor was spending more time at Pete's than at the office.

As Chap busied himself in the front room, packing her junk, rearranging her desk, dusting and vacuuming and throwing away old magazines, the phone rang occasionally. His job description covered the phone, and he stayed close to it. Most of the calls were for Jan, and he politely explained that she no longer worked there. 'Good for her' seemed to be the general feeling.

An agent dressed as a carpenter arrived early to replace the front door. Trevor marveled at Chap's efficiency. 'How'd you find one so quick?' he asked.

'You just have to work the yellow pages,' Chap said.

Another agent posing as a locksmith followed the carpenter and changed every lock in the building.

Their agreement included the provision that Trevor would see no new clients for at least the next thirty days. He'd argued long and hard against this, as if he had a stellar reputation to protect. Think of all the people who might need him, he'd complained. But they knew how slow the last thirty days had been, and they pressed him until he conceded. They wanted the place to themselves. Chap called those clients with scheduled appointments and told them that Mr. Carson would be tied up in court on the day they were supposed to stop by. Rescheduling would be difficult, Chap explained, but he'd give them a call when there was a break in the action.

303

'I didn't think he went to court,' one of them said.

'Oh yes,' Chap said. 'It's a really big case.'

When the client list was pared to the core, only one case required an office visit. It was an ongoing child support matter, and Trevor had represented the woman for three years. He couldn't simply give her the boot.

Jan stopped by to cause trouble, and brought with her a boyfriend of sorts. He was a wiry young man with a goatee, polyester pants, white shirt, and tie, and Chap figured he probably sold used cars. No doubt he could have easily thrashed Trevor, but he wanted no part of Chap.

'I'd like to speak to Trevor,' Jan said, her eyes darting around her newly organized desk.

'Sorry. He's in a meeting.'

'And who the hell are you?'

'I'm a paralegal.'

'Yeah, well get your money up front.'

'Thank you. Your things are in those two boxes over there,' Chap said, pointing.

She noticed the magazine racks were purged and neat, the wastebasket was empty, the furniture had been polished. There was a smell of antiseptic, as if they'd fumigated the place where she'd once sat. She was no longer needed.

'Tell Trevor he owes me a thousand dollars in unpaid salary,' she said.

'I will,' Chap replied. 'Anything else?'

'Yeah, that new client yesterday, Yates Newman. Tell Trevor I checked the newspapers. In the past two weeks there's been no accident deaths on

I-95. No record of a female named Newman getting killed either. Something's up.'

'Thank you. I'll tell him.'

She looked around for the last time, and smirked again when she saw the new door. Her boyfriend glared at Chap as if he might just step over and break his neck anyway, but the glaring was done as he headed for the door. They left without breaking anything, both of them carrying a box as they lumbered down the sidewalk.

Chap watched them leave, then began preparing for the challenge of lunch.

Dinner the night before had been nearby, at a crowded new seafood place two blocks from the Sea Turtle Inn. Given the size of the portions, the prices were outrageous, and that was exactly why Trevor, the newest millionaire in Jacksonville, had insisted they eat there. Of course the evening was on him and he spared no expense. He was drunk after the first martini, and didn't remember what he ate. Wes and Chap had explained that their client did not allow them to drink. They sipped designer water and kept his wineglass full.

'I'd find me another client,' Trevor said, laughing at his own humor.

'Guess I'll have to drink for all three of us,' he said halfway through dinner, then proceeded to do just that.

Much to their relief, they learned that he was a docile drunk. They kept pouring, in an effort to see how far he would go. He got quieter and lower in his seat, and long after dessert he tipped the waiter

$300 in cash. They helped him to their car and drove him home.

He slept with the new briefcase across his chest. When Wes turned off his light, Trevor was lying on his bed in his rumpled pants and white cotton shirt, bow tie undone, shoes still on, snoring, and clutching the briefcase tightly with both arms.

The wire had arrived just before five. The money was in place. Klockner had told them to get him drunk, see how he behaved in that condition, then start working in the morning.

At 7:30 A.M. they returned to his house, unlocked the door with their key, and found him pretty much as they'd left him. One shoe was off, and he was curled on his side with the briefcase tucked away like a football.

'Let's go! Let's go!' Chap had yelled while Wes turned on lights and raised shades and made as much noise as possible. Trevor, to his credit, scrambled from bed, raced to the bathroom, took a quick shower, and twenty minutes later walked into his den with a fresh bow tie and not a wrinkle anywhere. His eyes were slightly swollen, but he was smiling and determined to tackle the day.

The million dollars helped. In fact, he'd never conquered a hangover as quickly.

They had a quick muffin and strong coffee at Beach Java, then attacked his little office with vigor. While Chap took care of the front, Wes kept Trevor in his office.

Some of the pieces had fallen into place over dinner. The names of the Brethren had finally been extracted from Trevor, and Wes and Chap had done a splendid job of being surprised.

306

'Three judges?' they'd both repeated, in apparent disbelief.

Trevor had smiled and nodded with great pride, as if he and he alone had been the architect of this masterful scheme. He wanted them to believe that he'd had the brains and skill to convince three former judges that they should spend their time writing letters to lonely gay men so he, Trevor, could rake off a third of their extortion. Hell, he was practically a genius.

Other pieces of the puzzle remained unclear, and Wes was determined to keep Trevor locked away until he had answers.

'Let's talk about Quince Garbe,' he said. 'His post office box was rented to a fake corporation. How'd you learn his true identity?'

'It was easy,' Trevor said, very proud of himself. Not only was he a genius now, but he was a very rich one. He had awakened yesterday morning with a headache, and had spent the first half hour in bed, worrying about his gambling losses, worrying about his dwindling law practice, worrying about his increasing reliance on the Brethren and their scam. Twenty-four hours later, he'd awakened with a worse headache, but one soothed with the balm of a million bucks.

He was euphoric, giddy, and anxious to finish the task at hand so he could get on with life.

'I found a private investigator in Des Moines,' he said, sipping coffee, his feet on his desk, where they belonged. 'Sent him a check for a thousand bucks. He spent two days in Bakers – you been to Bakers?'

'Yep.'

'I was afraid I'd have to go. The scam works best if you can snare some prominent guy with money. He'll pay anything to keep you quiet. Anyway, this investigator found a postal clerk who needed some money. She was a single mother, houseful of kids, old car, small apartment, you get the picture. He called her at night and said he'd give her five hundred dollars cash if she could tell him who was renting Box 788 in the name of CMT Investments. Next morning he called her at the post office. They met in a parking lot during her lunch break. She gave him a piece of paper with the name of Quince Garbe, and he gave her an envelope with five one-hundred-dollar bills. She never asked who he was.'

'Is that a typical method?'

'It worked with Garbe. Curtis Cates, the guy in Dallas, the second one we scammed, was a little more complicated. The investigator we hired there couldn't find anyone on the inside, so he had to watch the post office for three days. Cost eighteen hundred dollars, but he finally saw him and got his license number.'

'Who's next?'

'Probably this guy in Upper Darby, Pennsylvania. His alias is Brant White, and he appears to be a hot prospect.'

'Do you ever read the letters?'

'Never. I don't know what's being said back and forth; don't wanna know. When they're ready to bust somebody, they'll tell me to scope out the box and get a real name. That's if their pen pal is using a front, like your client Mr. Konyers. You'd be

308

amazed how many men use their real names. Unbelievable.'

'Do you know when they send the extortion letters?'

'Oh yeah. They tell me so I can alert the bank in the Bahamas that a wire might be on the way. The bank calls me as soon as the money hits.'

'Tell me about this Brant White in Upper Darby,' Wes said. He was taking pages of notes, as if something might be missed. Every word was being recorded on four different machines across the street.

'They're ready to bust him, that's all I know. He seems hot to trot because they've just swapped a couple of letters. Some of these guys, it's like pulling teeth, judging by the number of letters.'

'But you don't keep track of the letters?'

'There are no records here. I was afraid the feds would show up one day with a search warrant, and I wanted no evidence of my involvement.'

'Smart, very smart.'

Trevor smiled and savored his shrewdness. 'Yeah, well, I've done a lot of criminal law. After a while, you start thinking like a criminal. Anyway, I've been unable to find the right investigator in the Philadelphia area. Still working on it though.'

Brant White was a Langley creation. Trevor could hire every investigator in the Northeast and they'd never find a real person behind the post office box.

'In fact,' he continued, 'I was preparing to go up there myself when I got the call from Spicer telling me to go to Washington and track down Al Konyers. Then you guys showed up, and, well, the

309

rest is history.' His words trailed away as he once again thought of the money. Sure it was a coincidence that Wes and Chap entered his life just hours after he was supposed to go searching for their client. But he didn't care. He could hear the seagulls and feel the hot sand. He could hear the reggae from the island bands, and feel the wind pushing his little boat.

'Is there another contact on the outside?' Wes asked.

'Oh no,' he said vainly. 'I don't need any help. The fewer people involved, the easier the operation works.'

'Very smart,' Wes said.

Trevor leaned back even deeper in his chair. The ceiling above him was cracked and peeling and in need of a fresh coat of enamel. A couple of days ago that might have worried him. Now he knew it would never get painted, not if they expected him to foot the bill. He'd walk out of the place one day very soon, once Wes and Chap here had finished with the Brethren. He'd spend a day or two boxing up his files to store for what reason he was not certain, and he'd give away his outdated and unused law books. He'd find some broke rookie fresh out of law school and looking for a few crumbs around city court, and he'd sell him the furniture and computer for a very reasonable price. And when all the loose ends were covered, he, L. Trevor Carson, Attorney and Counselor-at-Law, would walk out of the office and never look back.

What a glorious day that would be.

Chap interrupted the brief daydream with a sack

of tacos and soft drinks. Lunch had not been discussed among the three, but Trevor had already been checking his watch in anticipation of another long meal at Pete's. He grudgingly took a taco and seethed for a moment. He needed a drink.

'I think it's a good idea to lay off the booze during lunch,' Chap said as they huddled around Trevor's desk and tried not to spill black beans and ground beef.

'Do as you please,' Trevor said.

'I was talking to you,' Chap said. 'At least for the next thirty days.'

'That wasn't part of our deal.'

'It is now. You need to be sober and alert.'

'Why, exactly?'

'Because our client wants you that way. And he's paying you a million dollars.'

'Does he want me to floss twice a day and eat my spinach?'

'I'll ask him.'

'Tell him to kiss my ass while you're at it.'

'Don't overreact, Trevor,' Wes said. 'Just cut back on the drinking for a few days. It'll be good for you.'

If the money had set him free, these two were beginning to choke him. They'd now spent twenty-four hours together, and they showed no signs of leaving. In fact, the opposite was happening. They were moving in.

Chap left early to collect the mail. They'd convinced Trevor that he'd been very sloppy in his habits, and that's how they'd tracked him so easily. Suppose other victims were lurking out there? Trevor'd had little trouble in finding the real names of their victims. Why couldn't the victims do the same to the person behind Aladdin North and Laurel Ridge? From now on, Wes and Chap would take turns collecting the mail. They'd mix things up, visit the post offices at different times, use disguises, real cloak-and-dagger stuff.

Trevor eventually agreed. They seemed to know what they were doing.

There were four letters for Ricky waiting in the Neptune Beach post office, and two for Percy in Atlantic Beach. Chap quickly made the rounds, with a team behind him, watching anyone who might be watching him. The letters were taken to the rental, where they were quickly opened, and copied, then put back together.

The copies were read and analyzed by agents anxious to have something to do. Klockner read them too. Of the six, they'd seen five of the names before. All were lonely middle-aged men trying to muster the nerve to take the next step with Ricky or Percy. None seemed particularly aggressive.

One wall in a converted bedroom of the rental had been painted white and a large map of the fifty states had been stenciled on it. Red pushpins were used to mark Ricky's pen pals. Green for Percy. The names and hometowns of the correspondents were printed in black under the pins.

The nets were getting wider. Ricky had twenty-three men actively writing him; Percy, eighteen. Thirty states were represented. The Brethren were fine-tuning their venture with each passing week. They were now running ads in three magazines, as far as Klockner could tell. They held firm to their profile, and by the third letter they usually knew if a new guy had any money. Or a wife.

It was a fascinating game to watch, and now that they had complete access to Trevor they wouldn't miss a letter.

The day's mail was summarized in two pages, then given to an agent who took off to Langley. Deville had it in hand by 7 P.M.

The first call of the afternoon, at three-ten, came when Chap was washing windows. Wes was still in Trevor's office, grilling him with one question after another. Trevor was weary. He'd missed his nap and he desperately needed a drink.

'Law office,' Chap answered.

'Is this Trevor's office?' the caller asked.

'It is. Who's calling?'

'Who are you?'

'I'm Chap, the new paralegal.'

'What happened to the girl?'

'She no longer works here. What can I do for you?'

'This is Joe Roy Spicer. I'm a client of Trevor's, and I'm calling from Trumble.'

'Calling from where?'

'Trumble. It's a federal prison. Is Trevor there?'

'No sir. He's in Washington, and he should be back here in a couple of hours.'

'Okay. Tell him I'll call back at five.'

'Yes sir.'

Chap hung up and took a deep breath, as did Klockner across the street. The CIA had just had its first live contact with one of the Brethren.

★

313

The second call came at exactly five. Chap answered the phone and recognized the voice. Trevor was waiting in his office. 'Hello.'

'Trevor, this is Joe Roy Spicer.'

'Hello, Judge.'

'What'd you find in Washington?'

'We're still working on it. It's gonna be a tough one, but we'll find him.'

There was a long pause, as if Spicer didn't like this news and was uncertain about how much to say. 'Are you comin tomorrow?'

'I'll be there at three.'

'Bring five thousand dollars cash.'

'Five thousand dollars?'

'That's what I said. Get the money and bring it here. All in twenties and fifties.'

'What are you gonna do –'

'Don't ask stupid questions, Trevor. Bring the damned money. Put it in an envelope with the other mail. You've done it before.'

'All right.'

Spicer hung up without another word. Then Trevor spent an hour discussing the economics of Trumble. Cash was prohibited. Every inmate had a job and his wages were credited to his account. Expenditures, such as long-distance calls, commissary charges, copying expenses, stamps, were all debited against his account.

But cash was present, though seldom seen. It was smuggled in and hidden, and it was used to pay gambling debts and bribe guards for small favors. Trevor was afraid of it. If he, as the attorney, got caught sneaking it in, his visiting privileges would be permanently eliminated. He'd smuggled on two previous occasions, both times $500, in tens and twenties.

He couldn't imagine what they wanted with $5,000.

TWENTY-EIGHT

After three days of stepping over and around Wes and Chap, Trevor needed a break. They wanted breakfast, lunch, and dinner together. They wanted to drive him home and pick him up for work, very early in the morning. They were running what was left of his practice – Chap the paralegal, Wes the office manager, both of them drilling him with endless questions because there was precious little lawyering to be done.

So it was no surprise when they announced they would drive him to Trumble. He didn't need a driver, he explained. He'd made the trip many times, in his trusty little Beetle, and he'd go it alone. This upset them, and they threatened to call their client for guidance.

'Call the damned client, for all I care,' Trevor yelled at them, and they backed down. 'Your client is not running my life.'

But the client was, and they all knew it. Only the money mattered now. Trevor had already performed his Judas act.

He left Neptune Beach in his Beetle, alone, followed by Wes and Chap in their rental car, and

316

behind them was a white van occupied by people Trevor would never see. Nor did he want to see them. Just for the hell of it, he made a sudden turn into a convenience store for a six-pack, and laughed when the rest of the caravan slammed on brakes and barely avoided a wreck. Once out of town, he drove painfully slow, sipping his beer, savoring his privacy, telling himself he could suffer through the next thirty days. He could suffer through anything for a million bucks.

As he neared the village of Trumble, he had the first pangs of guilt. Could he pull this off? He was about to face Spicer, a client who trusted him, a prisoner who needed him, a partner in crime. Could he keep a straight face and act as if things were fine, while every word was being captured by a high-frequency mike in his briefcase? Could he swap letters with Spicer as if nothing had changed, knowing that the mail was being monitored? Plus, he was throwing away his law career, something he'd worked hard to attain and had once been proud of.

He was selling his ethics, his standards, even his morals for money. Was his soul worth a million bucks? Too late now. The money was in the bank. He took a sip of beer and washed away the fading twinges of guilt.

Spicer was a crook, and so were Beech and Yarber, and he, Trevor Carson, was just as culpable. There's no honor among thieves, he kept repeating silently.

Link got a whiff of the beer wafting off Trevor as they walked down the hall and into the visitors' area. At the lawyers' room Trevor looked inside.

He saw Spicer, partially hidden by a newspaper, and was suddenly nervous. What kind of low-life lawyer carries an electronic listening device into a confidential meeting with a client? The guilt hit Trevor like a brick, but there was no turning back.

The mike was almost as big as a golf ball, and had been meticulously installed by Wes in the bottom of Trevor's beaten-up and scruffy black leather briefcase. It was extremely powerful, and would easily transmit everything to the faceless boys in the white van. Wes and Chap were there too, ready with their earphones, anxious to hear it all.

'Afternoon, Joe Roy,' Trevor said.

'Same to you,' Spicer said.

'Lemme see the briefcase,' Link said. He gave a cursory look, then said, 'It looks fine.' Trevor had warned Wes and Chap that Link sometimes took a peek into the briefcase. The mike was covered by a pile of papers.

'Here's the mail,' Trevor said.

'How many?' Link asked.

'Eight.'

'You got any?' Link asked Spicer.

'No. None today,' Spicer replied.

'I'll be outside,' Link said.

The door closed; feet shuffled, and suddenly there was silence. A very long silence. Nothing. Not a word between lawyer and client. They waited in the white van for an eternity, until it was obvious something had gone wrong.

As Link stepped from the small room, Trevor quickly and deftly set the briefcase outside the door, on the floor, where it rested benignly during the remainder of the attorney-client conference. Link noticed it, and thought nothing about it.

'What'd you do that for?' Spicer asked.

'It's empty,' Trevor said, shrugging. 'Let the closed-circuit see it. We have nothing to hide.' Trevor had had one final, brief attack of ethics. Maybe he'd bug the next chat with his client, but not this one. He'd simply tell Wes and Chap that the guard took his briefcase, something that happened occasionally.

'Whatever,' Spicer said, riffling through the mail until he came to two envelopes that were slightly thicker. 'Is this the money?'

'It is. I had to use some hundreds.'

'Why? I plainly said twenties and fifties.'

'That's all I could find, okay. I didn't anticipate needing that much cash.'

Joe Roy studied the addresses on the other letters. Then he asked, rather caustically, 'So what happened in Washington?'

'It's a tough one. One of those rent-a-box outfits in the suburbs, open twenty-four hours, seven days a week, always somebody on duty, lots of traffic. Security is tight. We'll figure it out.'

'Who are you using?'

'Some outfit in Chevy Chase.'

'Gimme a name.'

'Whatta you mean, gimme a name?'

'Give me the name of the investigator in Chevy Chase.'

Trevor drew a blank; invention failed him. Spicer was on to something, his dark liquid eyes

319

glowing with intensity. 'I can't remember,' Trevor said.

'Where'd you stay?'

'What is this, Joe Roy?'

'Give me the name of your hotel.'

'Why?'

'I have the right to know. I'm the client. I'm paying for your expenses. Where did you stay?'

'Ritz-Carlton.'

'Which one?'

'I don't know. The Ritz-Carlton.'

'There are two. Which one was it?'

'I don't know. Not downtown.'

'What flight did you take?'

'Come on, Joe Roy. What is this?'

'What airline?'

'Delta.'

'The flight number?'

'I don't remember.'

'You got back yesterday. Less than twenty-four hours ago. What was your flight number?'

'I don't recall.'

'Are you sure you went to Washington?'

'Of course I went,' Trevor said, but his voice broke a little from a lack of sincerity. He had not planned his lies, and they were breaking down as fast as he put them up.

'You don't know your flight number, which hotel you stayed in, or the name of the investigator you spent the last two days with. You must think I'm stupid.'

Trevor didn't answer. He could only think of the mike in the briefcase and how lucky he was to have it outside. Getting flogged like this was something he'd rather Wes and Chap not hear.

'You've been drinking, haven't you?' Spicer asked, on the attack.

'Yes,' Trevor said, a temporary pause in the lying. 'I stopped and bought a beer.'

'Or two.'

'Yes, two.'

Spicer leaned on his elbows, his face halfway across the table. 'I got some bad news for you, Trevor. You're fired.'

'What?'

'Terminated. Sacked. Gone for good.'

'You can't fire me.'

'I just did. Effective immediately. By unanimous vote of the Brethren. We're notifying the warden so your name will be removed from the list of attorneys. When you leave today, Trevor, don't come back.'

'Why?'

'Lying, drinking too much, sloppy habits, a general lack of trust on behalf of your clients.'

It sounded true enough, but Trevor nevertheless took it hard. It had never crossed his mind that they'd have the guts to fire him. He clenched his teeth and asked, 'What about our little enterprise?'

'It's a clean break. You keep your money, we'll keep ours.'

'Who'll run it on the outside?'

'We'll worry about that. You can pursue an honest living, if you're able.'

'What would you know about an honest living?'

'Why don't you just leave, Trevor? Get up, walk out, it's been lovely.'

'Sure,' he mumbled, his thoughts a blur but two coming to the forefront. First, Spicer had brought no letters, the first time that had happened in many weeks. Second, the cash. What did they need the five grand for? Probably to bribe their new lawyer. They'd planned their ambush well, which was always an advantage they held because they had so much time on their hands. Three very bright men, with lots of idle time. It wasn't fair.

Pride made him stand. He extended a hand and said, 'Sorry it had to happen.'

Spicer shook it reluctantly. Just get out of here, he wanted to say.

When they made eye contact for the last time, Trevor said, almost in a whisper, 'Konyers is the man. Very rich. Very powerful. He knows about you.'

Spicer leapt up like a cat. With their faces just inches apart, he said, also in a whisper, 'Is he watching you?'

Trevor nodded and winked. Then he grabbed the door. He picked up his briefcase without a word to Link. What was he supposed to say to the guard? Sorry, old boy, but the thousand bucks a month in cash you were getting under the table just got cut off. Sad about it? Then ask Judge Spicer here why it happened.

But he let it pass. He was reeling and almost dizzy, and the alcohol didn't help. What would he tell Wes and Chap? That was the question of the moment. They would hammer him as soon as they could catch him.

He said good-bye to Link, and Vince, Mackey,

and Rufus up front, same as always but now for the last time, and walked into the hot sun.

Wes and Chap were parked three cars down. They wanted to talk but played it safe. Trevor ignored them as he tossed his briefcase into the passenger's seat and got in the Beetle. The caravan followed him away from the prison, and slowly down the highway toward Jacksonville.

Their decision to dispose of Trevor had been reached with a maximum of judicial deliberation. They'd spent hours hiding in their little room, studying the Konyers file until every word of every letter was memorized. They'd walked miles around the track, just the three of them, playing one scenario against another. They ate together, played cards together, all the while whispering new theories of who might be watching their mail.

Trevor was the nearest culprit, and the only one they could control. If their victims got sloppy, they could do nothing about it. But if their lawyer had failed to watch his trail, then he had to be fired. He was not the type to evoke a lot of trust in the first place. How many good, busy lawyers would be willing to risk their careers in a gay extortion scheme?

The only hesitation in ridding themselves of Trevor was the fear of what he might do with their money. They expected him to steal it, frankly, and they couldn't stop him. But they were willing to run that risk in return for a bigger score with Mr. Aaron Lake. To get to Lake, they felt they had to eliminate Trevor.

Spicer gave them the details of their meeting,

word for word. Trevor's muted message at the end stunned them. Konyers was watching Trevor. Konyers knew about the Brethren. Did that mean Lake knew about the Brethren? Who was really Konyers now? Why did Trevor whisper this and why did he leave his briefcase outside the door?

With the scrutiny that only a team of bored judges could generate, the questions poured forth. And then the strategies.

Trevor was making coffee in his newly cleaned and shined kitchen when Wes and Chap made their quiet entry and came straight at him.

'What happened?' Wes asked. They were frowning and gave the impression they'd been fretting for some time.

'What do you mean?' Trevor asked, as if things were splendid.

'What happened to the mike?'

'Oh that. The guard took the briefcase and kept it outside.'

They frowned at each other some more. Trevor poured the water into his coffee machine. The fact that it was almost five and he was making coffee was duly noted by the agents.

'Why did he do that?'

'It's routine. About once a month the guard will keep the briefcase during the visit.'

'Did he search it?'

Trevor busied himself by watching the coffee drip. Absolutely nothing was wrong. 'He made his usual quick exam, which I think he does with his eyes closed. He removed the ingoing letters, then took it. The mike was safe.'

'Did he notice the thick envelopes?'

'Of course not. Relax.'

'And the meeting went well?'

'It was routine, except that Spicer had no outgoing mail, which is a bit unusual these days, but it happens. I'll go back in two days and he'll have a stack of letters, and the guard will not even touch the briefcase. You'll get to hear every word. Want some coffee?'

They relaxed in unison. 'Thanks, but we'd better go,' Chap said. There were reports to make, questions to answer. They started for the door, but Trevor stopped them.

'Look, fellas,' he said very politely. 'I'm perfectly capable of getting dressed by myself, and of having a quick bowl of cereal, alone, the way I've done it for many years. And I like to open my office here no earlier than nine. Since it's my office, we'll open at nine, and not a minute sooner. You're welcome to be here at that unholy hour, but not at eight fifty-nine. Stay away from my house, and stay away from this office until nine. Understood?'

'Sure,' one of them said, and they were gone. It didn't really matter to them. They had bugs crawling all over the office, the house, the car, even the briefcase now. They knew where he bought his toothpaste.

Trevor drank the entire pot of coffee and sobered up. Then he began his movements, all carefully planned. He'd started preparing the moment he left Trumble. He assumed they were watching, back there with the boys from the white van. They had the gadgets and the toys, the mikes and the bugs, and Wes and Chap certainly knew

325

how to use them. Money was no object. He told himself to believe they knew everything, just let his imagination run wild and assume they heard every word, followed every turn, and knew exactly where he was at all times.

The more paranoid he was, the better his chances of escape.

He drove to a mall sixteen miles away near Orange Park, in the sprawl south of Jacksonville. He roamed and window-shopped and ate pizza in a near-empty food court. It was difficult not to dart behind a rack of clothes in a store and wait for the shadows to walk by. But he resisted. In a Radio Shack, he bought a small cell phone. One month of long distance with a local service came with the package, and Trevor had what he needed.

He returned home after nine, certain that they were watching. He turned the television on full volume, and made more coffee. In the bathroom he stuffed his cash into pockets.

At midnight, with the house dark and quiet and Trevor evidently asleep, he slipped out the back door and into the night. The air was brisk, the moon full, and he tried his best to look as though he was simply going for a walk on the beach. He wore baggy cargo pants with pockets from the waist down, two denim shirts, and an oversized windbreaker with money stuffed inside the liner. In all, Trevor had $80,000 hidden on himself as he wandered aimlessly south, along the edge of the water, just another beachcomber out for a midnight stroll.

After a mile his pace quickened. When he'd

gone three miles he was exhausted, but he was in a desperate hurry. Sleep and rest would have to wait.

He left the beach and walked into the grungy lobby of a rundown motel. There was no traffic along Highway A1A; nothing was open except for the motel and a convenience store in the distance.

The door rattled enough for the clerk to come to life. A television was on somewhere in the back. A chubby young man of no more than twenty emerged and said, 'Good evening. Need a room?'

'No sir,' Trevor said, as he slowly drew a hand from a pocket and produced a thick roll of bills. He began peeling them off and placing them in a neat row on the counter. 'I need a favor.'

The clerk stared at the money, then rolled his eyes. The beach attracted all kinds. 'These rooms ain't that expensive,' he said.

'What's your name?' Trevor asked.

'Oh, I don't know. Let's say it's Sammy Sosa.'

'All right, Sammy. There's a thousand bucks. It's yours if you'll drive me to Daytona Beach. Take you ninety minutes.'

'It'll take me three hours because I have to drive back.'

'Whatever. That's more than three hundred bucks an hour. When's the last time you made three hundred bucks an hour?'

'It's been a while. I can't do it. I run the night shift, you see. My job is to be on duty from ten until eight.'

'Who's the boss?'

'He's in Atlanta.'

'When's the last time he stopped by?'

'I've never met him.'

'Of course you haven't. If you owned a dump like this, would you stop by?'

'It's not that bad. We have free color TVs and most of the air-conditioning works.'

'It's a dump, Sammy. You can lock that door, drive away, and come back three hours later, and no one will ever know it.'

Sammy looked at the money again. 'You runnin from the law or something?'

'No. And I'm not armed. I'm just in a hurry.'

'So what's up?'

'A bad divorce, Sammy. I have a little money. My wife wants it all and she has some pretty nasty lawyers. I gotta get out of town.'

'You got money, but no car?'

'Look, Sammy. You want the deal or not? If you say no, then I'll walk down the street to the convenience store and find somebody smart enough to take my cash.'

'Two thousand.'

'You'll do it for two thousand?'

'Yep.'

The car was worse than Trevor had expected. It was an old Honda, uncleaned by Sammy or any of the previous five owners. But A1A was deserted, and the trip to Daytona Beach took exactly ninety-eight minutes.

At 3:20 A.M., the Honda stopped in front of an all-night waffle grill, and Trevor got out. He thanked Sammy, said good-bye, and watched him drive away. Inside, he drank coffee and chatted with the waitress long enough to persuade her to go fetch a local phone directory. He ordered

328

pancakes and used his new Radio Shack cell phone to find his way around town.

The nearest airport was Daytona Beach International. A few minutes after four, his cab stopped at the general aviation terminal. Dozens of small planes sat in neat rows on the tarmac. He stared at them as the cab drove away. Surely, he told himself, one of them was available for a quick charter. He just needed one, preferably a twin-engine.

TWENTY-NINE

The back bedroom of the rental had been converted into the meeting room, with four folding tables pushed together to make one large one. It was covered with newspapers, magazines, and doughnut boxes. Every morning at seven-thirty Klockner and his team met over coffee and pastries to review the night and plan the day. Wes and Chap were always there, and six or seven others joined them, depending on who was in town from Langley. The technicians from the front room sometimes sat in, though Klockner did not require their attendance. Now that Trevor was on their side, they needed fewer people to track him.

Or so they thought. Surveillance detected no movement inside his home before seven-thirty, which was not altogether unusual for a man who often went to bed drunk and woke up late. At eight, while Klockner was still meeting in the back, a technician called the house under the ruse of a wrong number. After three rings, the recorder came on and Trevor announced he was not in, please leave a message. This happened occasionally when he was trying to sleep late, but it usually worked well enough to roust him from bed.

Klockner was notified at eight-thirty that the house was completely still; no shower, no radio, no television, no stereo, not a sound from the normal routine.

It was entirely possible he'd gotten drunk at home, by himself, but they knew he had not spent last night at Pete's. He'd gone to a mall and arrived home apparently sober.

'He could be sleeping,' Klockner said, unconcerned. 'Where's his car?'

'In his driveway.'

At nine, Wes and Chap knocked on Trevor's door, then opened it when there was no answer. The rental sprang to life when they reported there was no sign of him, and that his car was still there. Without panic, Klockner sent people to the beach, to the coffee shops near the Sea Turtle, even to Pete's, which was not yet open. They canvassed the area around his house and office, by foot and by car, and saw nothing.

At ten, Klockner called Deville at Langley. The lawyer's missing, was the message.

Every flight to Nassau was checked; nothing turned up, no sign of a Trevor Carson. Deville's contact in Bahamian customs could not be located, nor could he find the banking supervisor they'd been bribing.

Teddy Maynard was in the middle of a briefing on North Korean troop movements when he was interrupted by an urgent message that Trevor Carson, their drunken lawyer in Neptune Beach, Florida, was missing.

'How can you lose a fool like him?' Teddy growled at Deville, in a rare display of anger.

'I don't know.'

'I don't believe this!'

'Sorry, Teddy.'

Teddy shifted his weight and grimaced from the pain. 'Find him, dammit!' he hissed.

The plane was a Beech Baron, a twin-engine owned by some doctors and chartered by Eddie, the pilot Trevor had coaxed out of bed at six in the morning with the promise of cash on the spot and more under the table. The official quote was $2,200 for a round-trip between Daytona Beach and Nassau – two hours each way, total of four at $400 an hour, plus some fees for landing and immigration and pilot downtime. Trevor kicked in another $2,000 for Eddie's pocket if the trip took place immediately.

The Geneva Trust Bank in downtown Nassau opened at 9 EST, and Trevor was waiting when the doors were unlocked. He barged into the office of Mr. Brayshears and demanded immediate assistance. He had almost a million dollars in his account – $900,000 from Mr. Al Konyers, through Wes and Chap; about $68,000 from his dealings with the Brethren.

With one eye on the door, he pressed Brayshears to help him move the money, and quickly. The money was owned by Trevor Carson, and no one else. Brayshears had no choice. There was a bank in Bermuda managed by a friend of his, which suited Trevor just fine. He didn't trust Brayshears,

332

and he planned to keep moving the money until he felt safe.

For a moment, Trevor cast a lustful eye at the account of Boomer Realty, currently with a balance of $189,000 and change. It was within his power, during that fleeting moment, to snatch their money too. They were nothing but felons – Beech, Yarber, the odious Spicer, all crooks. And they'd had the arrogance to fire him. They had forced him to run. He tried to hate them enough to take their money, but as he wavered back and forth he felt a soft spot for them. Three old men wasting away in prison.

A million was enough. Besides, he was in a hurry. If Wes and Chap suddenly charged in with guns, it wouldn't have surprised him. He thanked Brayshears and ran from the building.

When the Beech Baron lifted off the runway at Nassau International, Trevor couldn't help but laugh. He laughed at the heist, at the getaway, at his luck, at Wes and Chap and their rich client now minus a million, at his shabby little law office now mercifully idle. He laughed at his past and at his glorious future.

At three thousand feet he gazed downward at the still blue waters of the Caribbean. A lonely sailboat rocked along, its captain at the wheel, a scantily clad lady nearby. That would be him down there in just a few short days.

He found a beer in a carry-on cooler. He drank it and fell sound asleep. They landed on the island of Eleuthera, a place Trevor had seen in a travel magazine he'd bought the night before. There were beaches and hotels and all the water sports.

He paid Eddie in cash, then waited an hour at the small airport for a taxi to happen by.

He bought clothes at a tourist shop in Governor's Harbour, then walked to a hotel on the beach. He was amused at how quickly he stopped watching the shadows. Sure Mr. Konyers had plenty of money, but no one could afford a secret army big enough to track someone through the Bahamas. His future would be one of sheer delight. He would not ruin it by looking over his shoulder.

He drank rum by the pool as fast as the bar maid could bring it. At the age of forty-eight, Trevor Carson welcomed his new life in pretty much the same condition he'd left his old one.

The law office of Trevor Carson opened on time and things proceeded as if nothing was amiss. Its owner had fled, but its paralegal and office manager were on duty to take care of any business that might unexpectedly develop. They listened in all the right places, and heard nothing. The phone rang twice before noon, two misguided inquiries from souls lost in the yellow pages. Not a single client needed Trevor. Not a single friend called to say hello. Wes and Chap busied themselves by going through the few drawers and files they had not yet inspected. Nothing of consequence was found.

Another crew combed every inch of Trevor's house, primarily looking for the cash he'd been paid. Not surprisingly, they didn't find it. The cheap briefcase was in a closet, empty. There was

334

no trail. Trevor had just walked away, with his cash.

The Bahamian banking official was tracked to New York, where he was visiting on government business. He was reluctant to get involved from such a long distance, but he eventually made his calls. Around 1 P.M. it was confirmed that the money had been moved. Its owner had done so in person, and the official would divulge nothing else.

Where did the money go? It was moved by wire, and that's all he would tell Deville. His country's banking reputation depended upon secrecy, and he could reveal only so much. He was corrupt, but he did have his limits.

U.S. Customs cooperated after some initial reluctance. Trevor's passport had been scanned at Nassau International early that morning, and so far he had not left the Bahamas, at least not officially. His passport was red-listed. If he used it to enter another country, U.S. Customs would know it within two hours.

Deville delivered a quick update to Teddy and York, his fourth of the day, then hung around for further instructions.

'He'll make a mistake,' York said. 'He'll use his passport somewhere, and we'll catch him. He doesn't know who's chasing him.'

Teddy seethed but said nothing. His agency had toppled governments and killed kings, yet he was constantly amazed at how the little things often got botched. One bumbling and witless lawyer from Neptune Beach slipped through their net while a dozen people were supposed to be watching. He thought he was beyond surprises.

335

The lawyer was to be their link, their bridge to the inside of Trumble. For a million dollars they thought they could trust him. There'd been no contingency plan for his sudden flight. Now they were scrambling to develop one.

'We need someone inside the prison,' Teddy said.

'We're close,' Deville answered. 'We're working with Justice and the Bureau of Prisons.'

'How close?'

'Well, in light of what's happened today, I think we can have a man there, inside Trumble, within forty-eight hours.'

'Who is he?'

'His name is Argrow, eleven years with the agency, age thirty-nine, solid credentials.'

'His story?'

'He'll transfer into Trumble from a federal prison in the Virgin Islands. His paperwork will be cleared by the Bureau here in Washington so the warden down there won't ask any questions. He's just another federal prisoner who requested a transfer.'

'And he's ready to go?'

'Almost. Forty-eight hours.'

'Do it now.'

Deville left, again with the burden of a difficult task that suddenly had to be done overnight.

'We have to find out how much they know,' Teddy said, almost in a mumble.

'Yes, but we have no reason to believe they suspect anything,' York said. 'I've read all their mail. There's nothing to indicate they are particularly excited about Konyers. He's just one of their

336

potential victims. We bought the lawyer to stop him from snooping around behind Konyers' post office box. He's off in the Bahamas now, drunk with his money, so he's not a threat.'

'But we still dispose of him,' Teddy said. It was not a question.

'Of course.'

'I'll feel better when he's gone,' Teddy said.

A guard with a uniform but no gun entered the law library in mid-afternoon. He first encountered Joe Roy Spicer, who was by the door to the chamber.

'The warden would like to see you,' the guard said. 'You and Yarber and Beech.'

'What's this about?' Spicer asked. He was reading an old copy of *Field & Stream*.

'None of my business. He wants you now. Up front.'

'Tell him we're busy.'

'I ain't tellin him nothin. Let's go.'

They followed him to the administration building, picking up other guards along the way until a regular entourage emerged from the elevator and stood before the warden's secretary. She and she alone somehow managed to escort the Brethren into the big office where Emmitt Broon was waiting. When she was gone, he said abruptly, 'I have been notified by the FBI that your lawyer is missing.'

No visible response from the three, but each instantly thought about the money hidden offshore.

He continued, 'He disappeared this morning,

337

and there's some money missing. I don't have the details.'

Whose money? they wanted to ask. No one knew about their hidden funds. Had Trevor stolen from someone else?

'Why are you telling us?' Beech asked.

The real reason was that the Justice Department in Washington had asked Broon to inform the three of the latest news. But the reason he gave was 'Just thought you'd want to know in case you needed to call him.'

They'd fired Trevor the day before, and had not yet informed the administration that he was no longer their attorney of record.

'What're we gonna do for a lawyer?' Spicer asked, as if life couldn't go on.

'That's your problem. Frankly, I'd say you gentlemen have had enough legal counsel to last you many years.'

'What if he contacts us?' Yarber asked, knowing full well they'd never hear from Trevor again.

'You are to notify me immediately.'

They agreed to do so. Whatever the warden wanted. He excused them.

Buster's escape was less complicated than a trip to the grocery. They waited until the next morning, until breakfast was over and most of the inmates were busy with their menial jobs. Yarber and Beech were on the track, walking an eighth of a mile apart so that one was always watching the prison while the other watched the woods in the distance. Spicer loitered near the basketball court, on the lookout for guards.

With no fences or towers or pressing security concerns, guards were not that critical at Trumble. Spicer saw none.

Buster was lost in the whining noise of his Weed Eater, which he slowly worked toward the track. He took a break to wipe his face and look around. Spicer, from fifty yards away, heard the engine die. He turned and quickly gave a thumbs-up, the sign to do it quickly. Buster stepped onto the track, caught up with Yarber, and for a few steps they walked together.

'Are you sure you want to do this?' Yarber asked.

'Yes. I'm positive.' The kid appeared calm and ready.

'Then do it now. Pace yourself. Be cool.'

'Thanks, Finn.'

'Don't get caught, son.'

'No way.'

At the turn, Buster kept walking, off the track, across the freshly cut grass, a hundred yards to some brush, then he was gone. Beech and Yarber saw him go, then turned to watch the prison. Spicer was calmly walking toward them. There was no sign of alarm around the courtyards or dorms or any of the other buildings on the prison grounds. Not a guard in sight.

They walked three miles, twelve laps, at the leisurely pace of fifteen minutes per mile, and when they'd had enough they retired to the coolness of the chamber to relax and listen for news of the escape. It would be hours before they heard a word.

Buster's pace was much faster. Once into the

339

woods, he began to jog without looking back. Watching the sun, he moved due south for half an hour. The woods were not thick; the undergrowth was thin and did not slow him. He passed a deer stand twenty feet up in an oak tree, and soon found a trail that ran to the southwest.

In his left front pants pocket he had $2,000 cash, given to him by Finn Yarber. In his other front pocket he had a map Beech had drawn by hand. And in his rear pocket he had a yellow envelope addressed to a man named Al Konyers in Chevy Chase, Maryland. All three were important, but the envelope had received the most attention from the Brethren.

After an hour, he stopped to rest, and to listen. Highway 30 was his first landmark. It ran east and west and Beech figured he would find it within two hours. He heard nothing, and started running again.

He had to pace himself. There was a chance his absence would be noticed just after lunch, when the guards sometimes walked the grounds in a very casual inspection. If one of them thought to look for Buster, then other questions might follow. But after two weeks of watching the guards, neither Buster nor any of the Brethren thought this was a possibility.

So he had at least four hours. And probably a lot more because his workday ended at five when he turned in his Weed Eater. When he didn't show, they'd start looking around the prison. After two hours of that, they'd notify the surrounding police agencies that another one had walked away from Trumble. They were never armed and dangerous,

340

and no one got too excited. No search parties. No bloodhounds. No helicopters hovering over the woods. The county sheriff and his deputies would patrol the main roads and warn the citizens to lock their doors.

The escapee's name went into a national computer. They watched his home and watched his girlfriend, and they waited for him to do something stupid.

After ninety minutes of freedom, Buster stopped for a moment and heard the whine of an eighteen-wheeler not far away. The woods stopped abruptly at a right-of-way ditch, and there was the highway. According to Beech's map, the nearest town was several miles to the west. The plan was to hike along the highway, dodging traffic by using ditches and bridges, until civilization in some form was found.

Buster wore the standard prison issue of khaki pants and an olive-colored short-sleeve shirt, both darkened with sweat. The locals knew what the prisoners wore, and if he were spotted walking down Highway 30 someone would call the sheriff. Get to town, Beech and Spicer had told him, and find different clothes. Then pay cash for a bus ticket, and never stop running.

It took him three hours of ducking behind trees and jumping over roadside ditches before he saw the first buildings. He moved away from the highway, and cut through a hay field. A dog growled at him as he stepped onto a street lined with house trailers. Behind one of them he noticed a clothesline with someone's laundry hanging in

341

the windless air. He took a red and white pullover and threw away his olive shirt.

Downtown was nothing more than two blocks of stores, a couple of gas stations, a bank, some sort of town hall, and a post office. He bought denim shorts, a tee shirt, and a pair of boots at a discount store, and changed in the employee restroom. He found the post office inside the town hall. He smiled and thanked his friends at Trumble as he dropped their precious envelope into the Out-of-Town slot.

Buster caught a bus to Gainesville, where he purchased, for $480, the right to ride a bus anywhere in the United States for sixty days. He headed west. He wanted to get lost in Mexico.

THIRTY

The Pennsylvania primary on April 25 was to be Governor Tarry's last mighty effort. Undaunted by his dismal showing in the debate there two weeks earlier, he campaigned with great enthusiasm, but with very little money. 'Lake has it all,' he proclaimed at every stop, feigning pride at being the pauper. He did not leave the state for eleven straight days. Reduced to traveling in a large Winnebago camper, he ate his meals in the homes of supporters, stayed in cheap motels, and worked himself ragged shaking hands and walking neighborhoods.

'Let's talk about the issues,' he pleaded. 'Not about money.'

Lake, too, worked very hard in Pennsylvania. His jet traveled ten times faster than Tarry's RV. Lake shook more hands, made more speeches, and he certainly spent more money.

The result was predictable. Lake received 71 percent of the vote, a landslide so embarrassing to Tarry that he openly talked about quitting. But he vowed to hang on for at least another week, until the Indiana primary. His staff had left him. He was

343

$11 million in debt. He'd been evicted from his campaign headquarters in Arlington.

Yet, he wanted the good people of Indiana to have the opportunity to see his name on the ballot.

And who knew, Lake's shiny new jet might catch on fire, just like the previous one.

Tarry licked his rather deep wounds, and the day after the primary he promised to fight on.

Lake almost felt sorry for him, and he sort of admired his determination to endure until the convention. But Lake, along with everybody else, could do the math. Lake needed just forty more delegates to lock up the nomination, and there were almost five hundred still out there. The race was over.

After Pennsylvania, newspapers across the country confirmed his nomination. His happy handsome face was everywhere, a political miracle. He was praised by many as a symbol of why the system works – an unknown with a message who came from nowhere and captured the attention of the people. Lake's campaign gave hope to every person who dreamed of running for President. It didn't take months of pounding the back roads of Iowa. Skip New Hampshire, it was such a small state anyway.

And he was condemned for buying his nomination. Before Pennsylvania, it was estimated he'd spent $40 million. A more precise number was difficult because the money was being burned on so many fronts. Another $20 million had been spent by D-PAC and half a dozen other high-powered lobbying groups, all working on Lake's behalf.

No other candidate in history had spent anything close.

The criticism stung Lake, and it dogged him day and night. But he'd rather have the money and the nomination than suffer the alternative.

Big money was hardly taboo. Online entrepreneurs were making billions. The federal government, of all bumbling entities, was showing a surplus! Nearly everybody had a job, and an affordable mortgage, and a couple of cars. Lake's nonstop polling led him to believe that the big money was not yet an issue with the voters. In a November matchup against the Vice President, Lake was now practically even.

He once again returned to Washington, from the wars of the West, as a triumphant hero. Aaron Lake, lowly congressman from Arizona, was now the man of the hour.

Over a quiet and very long breakfast, the Brethren read the Jacksonville morning paper, the only one allowed inside Trumble. They were very happy for Aaron Lake. In fact, they were thrilled with his nomination. They were now among his most ardent supporters. Run, Aaron, run.

The news of Buster's walk to freedom had created hardly a stir. Good for him, the inmates were saying. He was just a kid with a long sentence. Run, Buster, run.

The escape wasn't mentioned in the morning paper. They passed it around, reading every word but the want ads and the obituaries. They were waiting now. No more letters would be written; none would be brought in because they'd lost their courier. Their little scam was on hold until they heard from Mr. Lake.

Wilson Argrow arrived at Trumble in an unmarked green van, handcuffed, with two marshals pulling at his elbows. He'd flown with his escorts from Miami to Jacksonville, of course at the expense of the taxpayers.

According to his paperwork, he had served four months of a sixty-month sentence for bank fraud. He had requested a transfer for reasons that were not clear, but his reasons were of no concern to anyone at Trumble. He was just another low-security prisoner in the federal system. They moved around all the time.

He was thirty-nine years old, divorced, college-educated, and his home address, for prison records, was in Coral Gables, Florida. His real name was Kenny Sands, an eleven-year veteran of the CIA, and though he'd never seen the inside of a prison, he'd had much tougher assignments than Trumble. He'd be there a month or two, then request another transfer.

Argrow maintained the cool facade of an old prison hand as he was processed, but his stomach churned. He'd been assured that violence was not tolerated at Trumble, and he could certainly take care of himself. But prison was prison. He suffered through a one-hour orientation by an assistant warden, then was given a quick tour of the grounds. He began to relax when he saw Trumble for himself. The guards had no guns, and most of the inmates looked rather harmless.

His cell mate was an old man with a spotty white

346

beard, a career criminal who'd seen many prisons and loved Trumble. He told Argrow he planned to die there. The man took Argrow to lunch and explained the vagaries of the menu. He showed him the game room, where groups of thick men bunched around folding tables studying their cards, every one with a cigarette stuck to the lips. 'Gambling's illegal,' his cell mate said with a wink.

They walked to the lifting area outdoors where the younger men sweated in the sun, polishing their tans while their muscles expanded. He pointed to the track in the distance and said, 'You gotta love the federal government.'

He showed Argrow the library, a place he never visited, and he pointed to a corner and said, 'That's the law library.'

'Who uses it?' Argrow asked.

'We usually have some lawyers here. Right now we have some judges too.'

'Judges?'

'Three of 'em.'

The old man had no interest in the library. Argrow followed him to the chapel, then around the grounds again.

Argrow thanked him for the tour, then excused himself and returned to the library, which was empty except for an inmate mopping a floor. Argrow went to the corner, and opened a door to the law library.

Joe Roy Spicer glanced up from his magazine and saw a man he'd never seen before. 'Lookin for something?' he asked, with no effort at being helpful.

Argrow recognized the face from the file. An ex-

Justice of the Peace caught stealing bingo profits. What a low-life.

'I'm new,' he said, forcing a smile. 'Just got here. This is the law library?'

'It is.'

'I guess anybody can use it, huh?'

'I guess,' Spicer said. 'You a lawyer?'

'Nope, a banker.'

A few months earlier, Spicer would've hustled him for some legal work, under the table, of course. But not now. They no longer needed the nickel-and-dime stuff. Argrow looked around and did not see Beech and Yarber. He excused himself and returned to his room.

Contact was made.

Lake's plan to rid himself of any memories of Ricky and their ill-fated correspondence depended upon someone else. He, Lake, was simply too scared and too famous to sneak away again in the middle of the night, in a disguise, in the back of a taxi, dashing through the suburbs to an all-night mailbox. The risks were too great; plus he seriously doubted if he could shake the Secret Service anymore. He couldn't count the number of agents now assigned to protect him. Count, hell, he couldn't see them all.

The young lady's name was Jayne. She'd joined the campaign in Wisconsin and had quickly worked her way into the inner circle. A volunteer at first, she now earned $55,000 a year as a personal aide to Mr. Lake, who trusted her completely. She seldom left his side, and they'd

348

already had two little chats about Jayne's future job in the White House.

At the right moment, Lake would give Jayne the key to the box rented by Mr. Al Konyers, and instruct her to get the mail, close out the rental, and leave no forwarding address. He would tell her it was a box he'd rented in an effort to monitor the sale of classified defense contracts, back when he was convinced the Iranians were buying data they should never see. Or some such tale. She would believe him because she wanted to believe him.

If he were incredibly lucky, there would be no letter from Ricky. The box would be forever closed. And if a letter was waiting for Jayne, and if she was the least bit curious, Lake would simply tell her he had no idea who the person was. She would ask nothing further. Blind allegiance was her strong suit.

He waited for the right moment. He waited too long.

THIRTY-ONE

It arrived safely with a million other letters, tons of paperwork shipped into the capital to sustain the government for one more day. It was sorted by zip code, then by street. Three days after Buster dropped it off, Ricky's last letter to Al Konyers made it to Chevy Chase. A routine check of Mailbox America by a surveillance team found it. The envelope was examined, then quickly taken to Langley.

Teddy was between briefings, alone for a moment in his office, when Deville rushed in, holding a thin file. 'We got this thirty minutes ago,' he said as he handed over three sheets of paper. 'It's a copy. The original is in the file.'

The Director adjusted his bifocals and looked at the copies before he began reading. There was the Florida postmark, same as always. The handwriting was too familiar. He knew it was serious trouble before he began reading.

Dear Al:
   In your last letter you tried to end our correspondence. Sorry, it won't be that easy.

350

I'll get right to the point. I'm not Ricky, and you're not Al. I'm in a prison, not some fancy drug rehab clinic.

I know who you are, Mr. Lake. I know you're having a great year, just wrapped up the nomination and all, and you have all that money pouring in. They give us newspapers here at Trumble, and we've been following your success with great pride.

Now that I know who Al Konyers really is, I'm sure you'd like for me to keep quiet about our little secret. I'll be happy to remain silent, but it will cost you dearly.

I need money, and I want out of prison. I can keep secrets and I know how to negotiate.

The money is the easy part, because you have so much of it. My release will be more complicated, but you're collecting all sorts of very powerful friends. I'm sure you'll think of something.

I have nothing to lose, and I'm willing to ruin you if you don't negotiate with me.

My name is Joe Roy Spicer. I'm an inmate at Trumble Federal Prison. You figure out a way to contact me, and do it quickly.

I will not go away.

Sincerely,

Joe Roy Spicer

The next briefing was canceled. Deville found York, and ten minutes later they were locked away in the bunker.

Killing them was the first option discussed.

Argrow could do it with the right tools; pills and poisons and such. Yarber could die in his sleep. Spicer could drop dead on the track. Beech the hypochondriac could get a bad prescription from the prison pharmacy. They were not particularly fit or healthy, and certainly no match for Argrow. A nasty fall, a broken neck. There were many ways to make it look natural or accidental.

It would have to be done quickly, while they were still waiting for a reply from Lake.

But it would be messy, and unduly complicated. Three dead bodies all at once, in a harmless little prison like Trumble. And the three were close friends who spent most of their time together, and they would each die in different ways within a very short period of time. It would create an avalanche of suspicion. What if Argrow became a suspect? His background was hidden to begin with.

And the Trevor factor frightened them. Wherever he was, there was the chance he would hear of their deaths. The news would scare him even more, but it might also make him unpredictable. There was a chance he knew more than they thought.

Deville would work on plans to take them out, but Teddy was very reluctant. He had no qualms about killing the three, but he was not convinced it would protect Lake.

What if the Brethren had told someone else?

There were too many unknowns. Make the plans, Deville was told, but they would be used only when every other option was gone.

All scenarios were on the table. York suggested, for the sake of argument, that the letter be

352

returned to the box so Lake could find it. It was his screwup to begin with.

'He wouldn't know what to do,' Teddy said.

'Do we?'

'Not yet.'

The thought of Aaron Lake reacting to this ambush and somehow trying to silence the Brethren was almost amusing, but there was a strong element of justice to it. Lake had created this mess; let him handle it.

'Actually, we created this mess,' Teddy said, 'and we'll deal with it.'

They couldn't predict, and thus they couldn't control, what Lake would do. Somehow the fool had avoided their net long enough to drop something in the mail to Ricky. And he'd been so stupid that the Brethren now knew who he was.

Not to mention the obvious: Lake was the type of person who secretly swapped letters with a gay pen pal. He was living a double life, and didn't deserve a lot of confidence.

Confronting Lake was discussed for a moment. York had been advocating a showdown since the first letter from Trumble, but Teddy wasn't convinced. The sleep he'd lost fretting over Lake was always filled with thoughts and hopes of stopping the mail long before now. Quietly take care of the problem, then have a chat with the candidate.

Oh, how he'd love to confront Lake. He'd love to sit him in a chair over there and start flashing copies of all those damned letters up on a screen. And a copy of the ad from *Out and About*. He'd tell him about Mr. Quince Garbe in Bakers, Iowa, another idiot who fell for the scam, and Curtis

Vann Gates in Dallas. 'How could you be so stupid!?' he wanted to scream at Aaron Lake.

But Teddy kept his eye on the bigger picture. The problems with Lake were small when compared to the urgency of national defense. The Russians were coming, and when Natty Chenkov and the new regime seized power the world would change forever.

Teddy had neutralized men far more powerful than three felonious judges rotting away in a federal prison. Meticulous planning was his strong suit. Patient, tedious planning.

The meeting was interrupted by a message from Deville's office. Trevor Carson's passport had been scanned at a departure checkpoint at the airport in Hamilton, Bermuda. He left on a flight to San Juan, Puerto Rico, that was scheduled to land in about fifty minutes.

'Did we know he was in Bermuda?' York asked.

'No, we did not,' Deville answered. 'Evidently he entered without using his passport.'

'Maybe he's not as drunk as we thought.'

'Do we have someone in Puerto Rico?' Teddy asked, his voice only a shade more excited.

'Of course,' said York.

'Let's pick up the scent.'

'Have the plans changed for ole Trevor?' Deville asked.

'No, not at all,' Teddy said. 'Not at all.'

Deville left to deal with the latest Trevor crisis. Teddy called an assistant and ordered mint tea. York was reading the letter again. When they were alone, he asked, 'What if we separate them?'

'Yes, I was thinking of that. Do it quickly, before

354

they have time to confer. Send them to three prisons far apart, put them in isolation for a period of time, make sure they have no phone privileges, no mail. Then what? They still have their secret. Any one of them could conceivably ruin Lake.'

'I'm not sure we have the contacts within the Bureau of Prisons.'

'It can be done. If necessary, I'll have a chat with the Attorney General.'

'Since when did you become friends with the Attorney General?'

'It's a matter of national security.'

'Three crooked judges sitting in a federal prison in Florida can somehow affect national security? I'd like to hear that conversation.'

Teddy sipped his tea with his eyes closed, all ten fingers on the cup. 'It's too risky,' he whispered. 'We make them mad, they become even more erratic. We can't take chances here.'

'Suppose Argrow can find their records,' York said. 'Think about it – these are con men, convicted criminals. No one will believe their story about Lake unless they have proof. The proof is documentation, pieces of paper, originals and copies of the correspondence. The proof exists somewhere. We find it, take it from them, then who will listen?'

Another small sip with his eyes closed, another long pause. Teddy shifted slightly in his chair and grimaced from the pain. 'True,' he said softly. 'But I'm worried about somebody on the outside, somebody we know nothing about. These guys are a step ahead of us, and they always will be. We're trying to figure out what they've known for some time. I'm not sure we'll ever catch up. Maybe they've thought about losing their little files. I'm sure the prison has rules against maintaining such paperwork, so they're already hiding things. The Lake letters are much too valuable not to copy again and stash on the outside.'

'Trevor was their mailman. We've seen every letter he's carried out of Trumble for the past month.'

'We think we have. But we don't know for certain.'

'But who?'

'Spicer has a wife. She's been to see him. Yarber's getting a divorce, but who knows what they're doing. She's visited in the past three months. Or maybe they're bribing guards to run mail for them. These people are bored and they're smart and they're very creative. We can't just assume we know everything they're up to. And if we make a mistake here, if we assume too much, then Mr. Aaron Lake gets himself shoved out of the closet.'

'How? How would they do it?'

'Probably contact a reporter, feed him one letter at a time until he was convinced. It would work.'

'The press would go insane.'

'It can't happen, York. We simply cannot allow it to happen.'

Deville returned in a rush. U.S. Customs had been notified by the authorities in Bermuda ten minutes after the flight departed for San Juan. Trevor would be landing in eighteen minutes.

Trevor was just following his money. He had

quickly grasped the fundamentals of wire transfers, and was now perfecting the art. In Bermuda, he had sent half of it to a bank in Switzerland, and the other half to a bank in Grand Cayman. East or west? That had been the great question. The quickest flight out of Bermuda went to London, but the idea of sneaking through Heathrow scared him. He was not a wanted man, at least not by the government. No charges were filed or pending. But the Brits were so efficient at customs. He'd go west and take his chances in the Caribbean.

He landed in San Juan and went straight to a bar where he ordered a tall draft and studied the flights. No hurry, no pressure, a pocket full of cash. He could go anywhere, do anything, and take as long as he wanted. He had another draft and decided to spend a few days in Grand Cayman, with his money. He went to the Air Jamaica counter and bought a ticket, then back to the bar because it was almost five and he had thirty minutes before boarding.

Of course he flew first class. He boarded early so he could get another drink, and as he watched the other passengers file by he saw a face he'd seen before.

Where was it now? Just moments ago, some-where in the airport. A long thin face, with a salt-and-pepper goatee, and little narrow slits for eyes behind square glasses. The eyes glanced at him just long enough to meet Trevor's, then looked away, down the aisle, as if nothing had been seen.

It had been near the airline counter, as Trevor was turning to leave after buying his ticket. The face was watching him. The man was standing nearby, studying the departure notices.

When you're on the run, the stray glances and second looks and drifting eyes all seem more suspicious. See a face once, and you don't even know it. See it again a half hour later, and somebody is watching every move you make.

Stop drinking, Trevor ordered himself. He asked for coffee after takeoff, and drank it quickly. He was the first passenger off the plane in Kingston, and he walked quickly through the terminal, through immigration. No sign of the man behind him.

He grabbed his two small bags and raced for the taxi stand.

THIRTY-TWO

The Jacksonville paper arrived at Trumble each morning around seven. Four copies were taken to the game room where they were to be read and left behind for any of the inmates who cared about life on the outside. Most of the time Joe Roy Spicer was the only one waiting at seven, and he usually took one paper for himself because he needed to study the Vegas lines throughout the day. The scene rarely changed: Spicer with a tall Styrofoam cup of coffee, feet on a card table, waiting for Roderick the guard to bring the papers.

So Spicer saw the story first, at the bottom of the front page. Trevor Carson, a local lawyer who'd been missing for some vague reason, found dead outside a hotel in Kingston, Jamaica, shot twice in the head last night, just after dark. The story had no picture of Trevor, Spicer noticed. Why would the paper have one on file? Why would anyone care if Trevor died?

According to Jamaican officials, Carson was a tourist who'd apparently been robbed. An unidentified source close to the scene had tipped the police as to the identity of Mr. Carson, since his wallet was missing. The source seemed to know a lot.

The paragraph recapping Trevor's legal career was quite brief. A former secretary, Jan something or other, had no comment. The story had been thrown together, and placed on the front page only because the victim was a murdered lawyer.

Finn was at the far end of the track, rounding the turn, walking at a rapid clip in the damp early morning air, his shirt already off. Spicer waited at the homestretch, and handed him the paper without a word.

They found Beech waiting in line in the cafeteria, holding his plastic tray and staring forlornly at the crude piles of freshly scrambled eggs. They sat together in a corner, away from everyone else, picking at their food, talking in muted voices.

'If he was running, who the hell was he running from?'

'Maybe Lake was after him.'

'He didn't know it was Lake. He didn't have a clue, did he?'

'Okay, then he was running from Konyers. The last time he was here he said Konyers was the big one. He said Konyers knew about us, then he disappeared the next day.'

'Maybe he was just scared. Konyers confronted him, threatened to expose his role in our scam, and so Trevor, who wasn't the most stable guy to begin with, decided to steal all he could and disappear.'

'Whose money was missing, that's what I want to know.'

'Nobody knows about our money. How could it be missing?'

360

'Trevor probably stole from everybody he could, then vanished. Happens all the time. Lawyers get in trouble, crack up. They raid their clients' trust funds and bolt.'

'Really?' asked Spicer.

Beech could think of three examples, and Yarber added a couple more for good measure.

'So who killed him?'

'There's a good chance he was just in the wrong part of town.'

'Outside the Sheraton Hotel? I don't think so.'

'Okay, what if Konyers iced him?'

'That's possible. Konyers somehow smoked out Trevor, learned he was the outside contact for Ricky. He put pressure on Trevor, threatened to nail him or whatever, and Trevor ran off to the Caribbean. Trevor didn't know Konyers was Aaron Lake.'

'And Lake certainly has the money and power to track down a drunken lawyer.'

'What about us? By now, Lake knows Ricky ain't Ricky, that Joe Roy here is the man, and that he has friends with him in prison.'

'Question is, can he get to us?'

'I guess I'll find out first,' Spicer said with a nervous laugh.

'And there's always the chance that Trevor was down there in Jamaica hanging around in the wrong part of town, probably drunk and trying to pick up a woman, and he got himself shot.'

They all agreed on this, that Trevor was perfectly capable of getting himself killed.

May he rest in peace. But only if he didn't steal their money.

361

They scattered for an hour or so. Beech went to the track, to walk and think. Yarber was on the clock, twenty cents an hour trying to fix a computer in the chaplain's office. Spicer went to the library, where he found Mr. Argrow reading law books.

The law library was open, no appointments were necessary, but the unwritten rule was that you should at least ask one of the Brethren before using their books. Argrow was new, and obviously had not yet learned the rules. Spicer decided to give him a break.

They acknowledged each other with a nod, then Spicer got busy clearing tables and straightening books.

'Rumor has it you guys do legal work,' Argrow said from across the room. No one else was present.

'You hear a lot of rumors around here.'

'My case is on appeal.'

'What happened at trial?'

'Jury nailed me on three counts of bank fraud, hiding money offshore, in the Bahamas. The judge gave me sixty months. I've served four. I'm not sure I'm gonna last for fifty-six more. I need some help with my appeals.'

'What court?'

'Virgin Islands. I worked for a big bank in Miami. Lots of drug money.'

Argrow was glib and fast and very anxious to talk, and this irritated Spicer, but only slightly. The reference to the Bahamas had his attention.

'For some reason, I developed a fascination for money laundering. I dealt with tens of millions every day, and it was intoxicating. I could move dirty money quicker than any banker in South Florida. Still can. But I made some bad friends, and bad choices.'

'You admit you're guilty?'

'Sure.'

'That puts you in the distinct minority around here.'

'No, I was wrong, but I think the sentence was too harsh. Somebody said you guys can get some time knocked off.'

Spicer was no longer concerned with the untidy tables and disorganized books. He took a chair nearby and had time to talk. 'We can take a look at your papers,' he said, as if he'd handled a thousand appeals.

You idiot, Argrow wanted to say. You dropped out of high school in the tenth grade, and stole a car when you were nineteen. Your father pulled some strings and got the charges dropped. You got yourself elected Justice of the Peace by voting dead people and stuffing absentee ballots, and now you're stuck in a federal pen and trying to play the big shot.

And, Argrow conceded, you, Mr. Spicer, now have the power to bring down the next President of the United States.

'What will it cost?' Argrow asked.

'How much do you have?' Spicer asked, just like a real lawyer.

'Not much.'

'I thought you knew how to hide money off-shore.'

'Oh, I do, believe me. And at one point I had a nice bundle, but I let it get away.'

'So you can't pay anything?'

'Not much. Maybe a couple of thousand or so.'

'What about your lawyer?'

'He got me convicted. I don't have enough to hire a new one.'

Spicer pondered the situation for a moment. He realized he did indeed miss Trevor. Things had been much simpler when they had him on the outside collecting money. 'You still got contacts in the Bahamas?'

'I have contacts all over the Caribbean. Why?'

'Because you'll have to wire the money. Cash is forbidden around here.'

'You want me to wire two thousand dollars?'

'No. I want you to wire five thousand dollars. That's our minimum fee.'

'Where's your bank?'

'In the Bahamas.'

Argrow's eyes narrowed. His eyebrows pushed together, and while he was deep in thought so was Spicer. The minds were in the process of meeting.

'Why the Bahamas?' Argrow asked.

'Same reason you used the Bahamas.'

Thoughts rattled around in both heads. 'Lemme ask you something,' Spicer said. 'You said you could move dirty money quicker than anybody else.'

Argrow nodded and said, 'No problem.'

'Can you still do it?'

'You mean, from in here?'

'Yes. From here.'

Argrow laughed and shrugged as if nothing could be easier. 'Sure. I still have some friends.'

'Meet me here in an hour. I might have a deal for you.'

An hour later, Argrow returned to the law library and found the three judges already in position, behind a table with papers and law books scattered about as if the Supreme Court of Florida were in session. Spicer introduced him to Beech and Yarber, and he took a seat across the table. No one else was present.

They talked for a moment about his appeal, and he was sufficiently vague on the details. His file was en route from the other prison, and they couldn't do much without it.

The appeal was a preliminary topic of conversation, and both sides of the table knew it.

'Mr. Spicer tells us you're an expert on moving dirty money,' Beech said.

'I was until I got caught,' Argrow said modestly. 'I take it you have some.'

'We have a little account offshore, money we've earned doing legal work and a few other things we can't be too open about. As you know, we can't charge for legal work.'

'But we do anyway,' added Yarber. 'And we get paid for it.'

'How much is in the account?' Argrow asked, knowing yesterday's closing balance to the exact penny.

'Let's wait on that,' Spicer said. 'There's a good chance the money may have disappeared.'

Argrow let the words hang for a second, and managed to appear confused. 'I'm sorry?' he said.

'We had a lawyer,' Beech said slowly, each word measured. 'He disappeared and he may have taken the money.'

'I see. And this account is in a bank in the Bahamas?'

'It was. We're not sure if it still is.'

'We doubt the money is still there,' Yarber added.

'But we'd like to know for sure,' Beech added.

'Which bank?' Argrow asked.

'Geneva Trust, in Nassau,' Spicer answered, glancing at his colleagues.

Argrow nodded smugly, as if he knew dark little dirty secrets about the bank.

'You know the bank?' Beech asked.

'Sure,' he said, and let them hang for a long second.

'And?' Spicer said.

Argrow was overcome with smugness and insider knowledge, so he stood rather dramatically and walked around the small library for a moment, deep in thought, then moved closer to the table again. 'Look, what do you guys want me to do? Let's cut to the chase.'

The three looked at him, then at each other, and it was obvious they weren't sure of two things: (a) how much they trusted this man they'd just met, and (b) what they really wanted from him.

But they figured the money was gone anyway, so what was there to lose. Yarber said, 'We're not too sophisticated when it comes to moving dirty money. That was not our original calling, you understand. Forgive our lack of knowledge, but is there any way to verify if the money is still where it once was?'

'We're just not sure if the lawyer stole it,' Beech added.

'You want me to verify the balance of a secret account?' Argrow asked.

'Yes, that's it,' said Yarber.

'We figure that maybe you still have some friends in the business,' Spicer said, treading water. 'And we're just curious as to whether there's any way to do this.'

'You're lucky,' Argrow said, and allowed the words to settle.

'How's that?' Beech asked.

'You picked the Bahamas.'

'Actually, the lawyer picked the Bahamas,' Spicer said.

'Anyway, the banks are pretty loose there. Lots of secrets get told. Lots of officials get bribed. Most of the serious money launderers stay away from the Bahamas. Panama is the current hot spot, and, of course, Grand Cayman is still rock solid.'

Of course, of course, they all three nodded. Offshore was offshore, wasn't it? Just another example of trusting an idiot like Trevor.

Argrow watched them with their puzzled faces and thought how truly clueless they were. For three men with the ability to totally wreck the American electoral process, they seemed awfully naive.

'You haven't answered our question,' Spicer said.

'Anything's possible in the Bahamas.'

'So you can do it?'

'I can try. No guarantees.'

'Here's the deal,' Spicer said. 'You verify the account, and we'll do your appeals for free.'

'That's not a bad deal,' Argrow said.

'We didn't think so. Agreed?'

'Agreed.'

For an awkward second they just looked at one another, proud of their mutual agreement but not sure who moved next. Finally, Argrow said, 'I'll need to know something about the account.'

'Such as?' Beech asked.

'Such as a name or a number.'

'The account name is Boomer Realty, Ltd. The account number is 144-DXN-9593.'

Argrow scribbled some notes on a sheet of scrap paper.

'Just curious,' Spicer said as they watched him closely. 'How do you plan to communicate with your contacts outside?'

'Phone,' Argrow said without looking up.

'Not these phones,' Beech said.

'These phones are not secure,' Yarber said.

'You can't use these phones,' Spicer said with an edge.

Argrow smiled and acknowledged their concerns, then he glanced over his shoulder and removed from his pants pocket an instrument of some sort, not much larger than a pocketknife. He held it between his thumb and index finger, and said, 'This is a phone, gentlemen.'

They stared in disbelief, then watched as he quickly unfolded it from the top and the bottom and from one side so that when properly opened it still looked much too small for any meaningful conversation. 'It's digital,' he said. 'Very secure.'

'Who gets the monthly bill?' asked Beech.

'I have a brother in Boca Raton. The phone and the service were gifts from him.' He snapped it back smartly, and it vanished before their eyes. Then he pointed to the small conference room behind them, to their chamber. 'What's in there?' he asked.

'Just a conference room,' Spicer said.

'It has no windows, right?'

'None, except for that small one in the door.'

'All right. What if I go in there, get on the phone, and go to work. You three stay here and watch out for me. If anyone enters the library, come knock on the door.'

The Brethren readily agreed, though they did not believe Argrow could pull it off.

The call went to the white van, parked a mile and a half from Trumble, on a gravel road sometimes maintained by the county. The road was next to a hay field, farmed by a man they'd yet to meet. The property line for the acreage owned by the federal government was a quarter of a mile away, but from where the van was sitting there was no sign of a prison.

Only two technicians were in the van, one fully asleep in the front seat, the other half asleep in the back with a headset on. When Argrow pressed the Send button on his fancy little gadget, a receiver in the van was activated, and both men came to life.

'Hello,' he said. 'This is Argrow.'

369

'Yes, Argrow, Chevy One here, go ahead,' said the technician in the back.

'I'm near the three stooges, going through the motions, supposedly making calls to friends on the outside to verify the existence of their account offshore. So far things are progressing even faster than I'd hoped.'

'Sounds like it.'

'Roger. I'll check in later.' He pushed the End button, but kept the phone at his head and appeared to be deep in conversation. He sat on the edge of the table, then he walked around some, glancing occasionally at the Brethren and beyond.

Spicer couldn't help but sneak a look through the window of the door. 'He's making calls,' he said excitedly.

'What do you expect him to be doing?' asked Yarber, who was actually reading recent court decisions.

'Relax, Joe Roy,' Beech said. 'The money disappeared with Trevor.'

Twenty minutes passed, and things became dull as usual. While Argrow worked the phones, the judges killed time, waiting at first, then returning to more pressing business. It had been six days since Buster had left with their letter. No word from Buster meant he'd walked away clean, dropped off the note to Mr. Konyers, and was now somewhere far away. Give it three days to travel to Chevy Chase, and the way they had it figured Mr. Aaron Lake should now be scrambling with a plan to deal with them.

Prison had taught them patience. Only one deadline worried them. Lake had the nomination, which meant he would be vulnerable to their blackmail until November. If he won, they would have four years in which to torment him. But if he lost he would fade quickly away, like all the losers. 'Where's Dukakis now?' Beech had asked.

They had no plans to wait until November. Patience was one thing, release was another. Lake was their one fleeting opportunity to walk away with enough money to coast forever.

They intended to give it a week, then write another letter to Mr. Al Konyers in Chevy Chase. They weren't sure how to smuggle it out, but they would think of something. Link, the guard up front whom Trevor had been bribing for months, was their first prospect.

Argrow's phone presented an option. 'If he'll let us use it,' Spicer said, 'then we can call Lake, call his campaign office, his congressional office, call every damned number we can get from directory assistance. Leave the message that Ricky in rehab really needs to see Mr. Lake. That'll scare the hell out of him.'

'But Argrow will have a record of our calls, or at least his brother will,' Yarber said.

'So? We'll pay him for the calls, and so what if they know we're trying to call Aaron Lake. Right now, half the country is trying to call him. Argrow won't have a clue why we're doing it.'

A brilliant idea, one they pondered for a long time. Ricky in rehab could make the calls and leave the messages. Spicer in Trumble could do the same. Poor Lake would get hounded.

Poor Lake. The man had money pouring in so fast he couldn't count it.

371

After an hour, Argrow emerged from the chamber and announced he was making progress. 'I need to wait an hour, then make a few more calls,' he said. 'What about lunch?'

They were anxious to continue their discussion, and they did so over sloppy joes and coleslaw.

THIRTY-THREE

Pursuant to Mr. Lake's precise instructions, Jayne drove alone to Chevy Chase. She found the shopping center on Western Avenue, and parked in front of Mailbox America. With Mr. Lake's key, she opened the box, removed eight pieces of junk mail, and placed them in a folder. There were no personal letters. She walked to the counter and informed the clerk that she wished to close the box on behalf of her employer, Mr. Al Konyers.

The clerk pecked a few times on a keyboard. The records indicated that a man named Aaron L. Lake had rented the box in the name of Al Konyers about seven months earlier. The rental had been paid for twelve months, so nothing was owed.

'That guy running for President?' the clerk asked as she slid a form across the counter.

'Yes,' Jayne said, signing where indicated.

'No forwarding address?'

'No.'

She left with the folder and headed south, back into the city. She had not stopped to question Lake's story about renting the box in a clandestine

373

effort to expose fraud at the Pentagon. It didn't matter to her, nor did she have time to ask a lot of questions. Lake had them sprinting eighteen hours a day, and she had far more important things to worry about.

He was waiting in his campaign office, alone for the moment. The offices and hallways around him were choked with assistants of a dozen varieties, all running back and forth as if war were imminent. But Lake was enjoying a lull in the action. She gave him the folder and left.

Lake counted eight pieces of junk mail – taco delivery, long-distance service, a car wash, coupons for this and for that. And nothing from Ricky. The box was closed, there was no forwarding address. The poor boy would have to find someone else to help him through his new life. Lake fed the junk mail and the cancellation agreement through a small shredder under his desk, then paused a moment to count his blessings. He carried little baggage in life, and he'd made few mistakes. Writing to Ricky had been a stupid thing to do, yet he was walking away unscathed. What a lucky man!

He smiled and almost giggled to himself, then he bounced from his chair, grabbed his jacket, and rounded up his entourage. The candidate had meetings to attend, then a lunch with defense contractors.

Oh what a lucky man!

Back in the corner of the law library, with his three new friends guarding the perimeter like sleepy sentries, Argrow fiddled with the phone long

374

enough to convince them he'd pulled strings all through the dark and murky world of offshore banking. Two hours of pacing and mumbling and holding the phone to his head like a frantic stockbroker, and he finally came out of the room.

'Good news, gentlemen,' he said with a tired smile.

They huddled around, eager for the results.

'It's still there,' he said.

Then the great question, the one they'd been planning, the one that would verify whether Argrow was a fraud or a player.

'How much?' asked Spicer.

'A hundred and ninety thousand, and small change,' he said, and they exhaled in unison. Spicer smiled. Beech looked away. Yarber looked at Argrow with a quizzical frown, but a rather pleasant one.

According to their figures, the balance was $189,000, plus whatever paltry rate of interest the bank was paying.

'He didn't steal it,' Beech mumbled, and they shared a pleasant memory of their dead lawyer, who suddenly was not the devil they'd made him out to be.

'I wonder why not,' Spicer mused, almost to himself.

'Well, it's still there,' Argrow said. 'That's a lot of legal work.'

It certainly appeared to be, and since neither of the three could think of a quick fib, they just let it pass.

'I suggest you move it, if you don't mind my

saying so,' Argrow said. 'This bank is known for its leaks.'

'Move it where?' Beech asked.

'If the money were mine, I'd move it to Panama immediately.'

This was a new issue, a train of thought they had not pursued because they had been obsessed with Trevor and his certain theft. But they weighed it carefully anyway, as if the matter had been discussed many times.

'Why would you move it?' Beech asked. 'It's safe, isn't it?'

'I guess,' Argrow answered, quick with a response. He knew where he was going, they did not. 'But you see how loose the confidentiality can be. I wouldn't use banks in the Bahamas these days, especially this one.'

'And we don't know if Trevor told anyone about it,' Spicer said, always anxious to nail the lawyer.

'If you want the money protected, move it,' Argrow said. 'It takes less than a day and you won't have to worry about it. And put the money to work. This account is just sitting there, drawing a few pennies in interest. Put it with a fund manager and let it earn fifteen or twenty percent. You're not gonna be using it any time soon.'

That's what you think, pal, they thought. But he made perfect sense.

'And I assume you can move it?' Yarber said.

'Of course I can. Do you doubt me now?'

All three shook their heads. No sir, they did not doubt him.

'I have some nice contacts in Panama. Think about it.' Argrow glanced at his watch as if he had

376

lost interest in their account and had a hundred pressing matters elsewhere. A punch line was coming, and he didn't want to push.

'We've thought about it,' Spicer said. 'Let's move it now.'

He looked at three sets of eyes, all looking back at him. 'There's a fee involved,' he said, like a seasoned money launderer.

'What kinda fee?' Spicer asked.

'Ten percent, for the transfer.'

'Who gets ten percent?'

'I do.'

'That's rather steep,' said Beech.

'It's a sliding scale. Anything under a million pays ten percent. Anything over a hundred million pays one percent. It's pretty common in the business, and it's exactly the reason I'm wearing an olive prison shirt and not a thousand-dollar suit.'

'That's pretty sleazy,' said Spicer, the man who'd skimmed bingo profits from a charity.

'Let's not preach, okay. We're talking about a small cut from money that's already tainted, both here and there. Take it or leave it.' His tone was aloof, an icy veteran who'd cut much larger deals.

It was only $19,000, and this from a stash they'd been certain was gone. After his 10 percent, they still had $170,000, roughly $60,000 each, and it would've been more if treacherous Trevor hadn't raked so much off the top. And, besides, they were confident of greener pastures just around the corner. The loot in the Bahamas was pocket change.

'It's a deal,' Spicer said as he looked at the other two for approval. They both nodded slowly. All three were thinking the same thing now. If the shakedown of Aaron Lake proceeded as they dreamed it would, then serious money was coming their way. They would need a place to hide it, and maybe someone to help them. They wanted to trust this new guy Argrow. Let's give him the chance.

'Plus, you do my appeals,' Argrow said.

'Yes, we'll do the appeals.'

Argrow smiled and said, 'Not a bad deal. Lemme make some more calls.'

'There's one thing you should know,' Beech said.

'Okay.'

'The lawyer's name was Trevor Carson. He set up the account, directed the deposits, did everything really. And he was murdered night before last in Kingston, Jamaica.'

Argrow searched their faces for more. Yarber handed him a copy of the newspaper, which he read very deliberately. 'Why was he missing?' he asked after a long silence.

'We don't know,' Beech said. 'He left town, and we got word through the FBI that he was missing. We just assumed that he'd stolen our money.'

Argrow handed the paper back to Yarber, and crossed his arms over his chest. He cocked his head, narrowed his eyes, and managed to look suspicious. Let them sweat.

'How dirty is this money?' he asked, as if he might not want to get involved with it after all.

'It's not drug money,' Spicer said quickly, on the defensive, as if all other money was clean.

'We really can't say,' Beech replied.

'You've got a deal,' Yarber said. 'Take it or leave it.'

Good move, old boy, Argrow said to himself. 'The FBI is involved?' he asked.

'Only with the lawyer's disappearance,' Beech said. 'The feds know nothing about the offshore account.'

'Let me get this straight. You got a dead lawyer, the FBI, an offshore account hiding dirty money, right? What've you boys been up to?'

'You don't wanna know,' Beech said.

'I think you're right.'

'No one's forcing you to get involved,' Yarber said.

So a decision had to be made. For Argrow, the red flags were up, the minefield was marked. If he went forward, then he did so armed with sufficient warnings that his three new friends could be dangerous. This, of course, meant nothing to Argrow. But to Beech, Spicer, and Yarber, the opening in their tight little partnership, however slight it might be, meant they were admitting another conspirator. They would never tell him about their scam, and certainly not about Aaron Lake, nor would he share in any more of their loot, unless he earned it with his wiring prowess. But he already knew more than he should. They had no choice.

Desperation played no small role in their decision. With Trevor, they'd had access to the outside, something they'd taken for granted. Now that he was gone, their world had shrunk considerably.

Though they had yet to admit it, firing him had

been a mistake. With perfect hindsight, they should've warned him, and told him everything about Lake and the tampered mail. He'd been far from perfect, but they needed all the help they could get.

Perhaps they would've hired him back a day or two later, but they never had the chance. Trevor bolted, and now he was gone forever.

Argrow had access. He had a phone and friends; he had guts and he knew how to get things done. Perhaps they might need him, but they would take it slowly.

He scratched his head and frowned as if a headache was coming. 'Don't tell me anything else,' he said. 'I don't wanna know.'

He returned to the conference room and closed the door behind him, then perched on the edge of the table and once again seemed to be firing calls all over the Caribbean.

They heard him laugh twice, probably a joke with an old friend surprised to hear his voice. They heard him swear once, but had no idea at whom or for what reason. His voice rose and fell, and try as they might to read court decisions and dust off old books and study Vegas odds, they couldn't ignore the noise from the room.

Argrow put on quite a show, and after an hour of useless chatter he came out and said, 'I think I can finish it tomorrow, but we need an affidavit signed by one of you stating that you are the sole owners of Boomer Realty.'

'Who sees the affidavit?' Beech asked.

'Only the bank in the Bahamas. They're getting a copy of the story about Mr. Carson, and they want verification about the ownership of the account.'

The idea of actually signing any type of document in which they admitted they had anything to do with the dirty money terrified them. But the request made sense.

'Is there a fax machine around here?' Argrow asked.

'No, not for us,' Beech replied.

'I'm sure the warden has one,' Spicer said. 'Just trot up there and tell him you need to send a document to your offshore bank.'

It was unnecessarily sarcastic. Argrow glared at him, then let it pass. 'Okay, tell me how to get the affidavit from here to the Bahamas. How does the mail run?'

'The lawyer was our mail runner,' Yarber said. 'Everything else is subject to inspection.'

'How close do they inspect the legal mail?'

'They glance at it,' Spicer said. 'But they can't open it.'

Argrow paced around a bit, deep in thought. Then, for the benefit of his audience he stepped between two racks of books, so that he could not be seen from outside the law library. He deftly unfolded his gadget, punched numbers, and stuck it to his ear. He said, 'Yes, Wilson Argrow here. Is Jack in? Yes, tell him it's important.' He waited.

'Who the hell's Jack?' Spicer asked from across the room. Beech and Yarber listened but watched for passersby.

'My brother in Boca,' Argrow said. 'He's a real estate lawyer. He's visiting me tomorrow.' Then, into the phone, he said, 'Hey, Jack, it's me. You

381

comin tomorrow? Good, can you come in the morning? Good. Around ten. I'll have some mail going out. Good. How's Mom? Good. I'll see you in the morning.'

The prospect of the resumption of mail intrigued the Brethren. Argrow had a brother who was a lawyer. And he had a phone, and brains, and guts.

He slid the gadget back into his pocket and walked from the racks. 'I'll give the affidavit to my brother in the morning. He'll fax it to the bank. By noon the next day the money will be in Panama, safe and sound and earning fifteen percent. Piece of cake.'

'We're assuming we can trust your brother?' Yarber said.

'With your life,' Argrow said, almost offended by the question. He was walking to the door. 'I'll see you guys later. I need some fresh air.'

THIRTY-FOUR

Trevor's mother arrived from Scranton. She was with her sister, Trevor's aunt Helen. They were both in their seventies and in reasonably good health. They got lost four times between the airport and Neptune Beach, then meandered through the streets for an hour before stumbling on Trevor's house, a place his mother hadn't seen in six years. She hadn't seen Trevor in two years. Aunt Helen hadn't seen him in at least ten, not that she particularly missed him.

His mother parked the rental car behind his little Beetle, and had a good cry before getting out.

What a dump, Aunt Helen said to herself.

The front door was unlocked. The place had been abandoned, but long before its owner fled the dishes had collected in the sink, the garbage had gone unattended, the vacuum hadn't left the closet.

The odor drove Aunt Helen out first, and Trevor's mother soon followed. They had no clue what to do. His body was still in Jamaica, in a crowded morgue, and according to the unfriendly

383

young man she'd talked to at the State Department it would cost $600 to ship him home. The airlines would cooperate, but the paperwork was tied up in Kingston.

It took a half hour of bad driving to find his office. By then, word was out. Chap the paralegal was waiting at the reception desk, trying to look sad and busy at the same time. Wes the office manager was in a back room, just to listen and observe. The phone had rung constantly the day the news broke, but after a round of condolences from fellow lawyers and a client or two it went silent again.

On the front door was a cheap wreath, paid for by the CIA. 'Ain't that nice,' his mother said as they waddled up the sidewalk.

Another dump, thought Aunt Helen.

Chap greeted them and introduced himself as Trevor's paralegal. He was in the process of trying to close the office, a most difficult task.

'Where's the girl?' his mother asked, her eyes red from grieving.

'She left some time back. Trevor caught her stealing.'

'Oh dear.'

'Would you like some coffee?' he asked.

'That would be nice, yes.' They sat on the dusty and uneven sofa, while Chap fetched three coffees from a pot that just happened to be fresh. He sat across from them in an unstable wicker chair. The mother was bewildered. The aunt was curious, her eyes darting around the office, looking for any sign of prosperity. They were not poor, but at their ages affluence would never be attained.

'I'm very sorry about Trevor,' Chap said.

'It's just awful,' Mrs. Carson said, her lip quivering. Her cup shook and coffee splashed onto her dress. She didn't notice it.

'Did he have a lot of clients?' Aunt Helen asked.

'Yes, he was very busy. A good lawyer. One of the best I've ever worked with.'

'And you're a secretary?' Mrs. Carson asked.

'No, I'm a paralegal. I go to law school at night.'

'Are you handling his affairs?' Aunt Helen asked.

'Well, not really,' Chap said. 'I was hoping that's why the two of you were here.'

'Oh, we're too old,' his mother said.

'How much money did he leave?' asked the aunt.

Chap stepped it up a notch. This old bitch was a bloodhound. 'I have no idea. I didn't handle his money.'

'Who did?'

'I guess his accountant.'

'Who's his accountant?'

'I don't know. Trevor was very private about most things.'

'He certainly was,' his mother said sadly. 'Even as a boy.' She splashed her coffee again, this time on the sofa.

'You pay the bills around here, don't you?' asked the aunt.

'No. Trevor took care of his money.'

'Well, listen, young man, they want six hundred dollars to fly him home from down in Jamaica.'

'Why was he down there?' his mother interrupted.

385

'It was a short vacation,' Chap said.

'And she doesn't have six hundred dollars,' Helen finished.

'Yes I do.'

'Oh, there's some cash here,' Chap said, and Aunt Helen looked satisfied.

'How much?' she asked.

'A little over nine hundred dollars. Trevor liked to keep plenty of petty cash.'

'Give it to me,' Aunt Helen demanded.

'Do you think we should?' asked his mother.

'You'd better take it,' Chap said gravely. 'If not, it will just go into his estate and the IRS will get it all.'

'What else will go into his estate?' asked the aunt.

'All this,' Chap said, waving his arms at the office while he walked to the desk. He removed a wrinkled envelope stuffed with bills of all denominations, money they'd just transferred from the rental across the street. He gave it to Helen, who snatched it and counted the money.

'Nine twenty, and some change,' Chap said.

'Which bank did he use?' Helen asked.

'I have no idea. Like I said, he was very private about his money.' And in one respect, Chap was telling the truth. Trevor had wired the $900,000 from the Bahamas to Bermuda, and from there the trail had disappeared. The money was now hidden in a bank somewhere, in a numbered account accessible only by Trevor Carson. They knew he was headed for Grand Cayman, but the bankers there were famous for their secrecy. Two days of intense digging had revealed nothing. The man

386

who shot him took his wallet and room key, and while the police were inspecting the crime scene the gunman searched the hotel room. There was about $8,000 in cash hidden in a drawer, and nothing else of any significance. Not a clue as to where Trevor had parked his money.

It was the collected wisdom at Langley that Trevor, for some reason, suspected he was being followed closely. The bulk of the cash was missing, though he could have deposited it in a bank in Bermuda. His hotel room had been secured without a reservation – he simply walked in from the street and paid cash for one night.

A person on the run, chasing $900,000 from one island to the next, would have, somewhere on his body or in his effects, evidence of banking activities. Trevor had none.

While Aunt Helen riffled through what would surely be the only cash they'd net from the estate, Wes thought about the fortune lost somewhere in the Caribbean.

'What do we do now?' Trevor's mother asked.

Chap shrugged and said, 'I guess you need to bury him.'

'Can you help us?'

'That's not really something I do. I –'

'Should we take him back to Scranton?' Helen asked.

'That's up to you.'

'How much would that cost?' Helen asked.

'I have no idea. I've never had to do anything like this.'

'But all his friends are here,' his mother said, touching her eyes with a tissue.

'He left Scranton a long time ago,' Helen said, her eyes cutting in all directions, as if there was a long story behind Trevor's leaving Scranton. No doubt, thought Chap.

'I'm sure his friends here will want a memorial service,' Mrs. Carson said.

'Actually, one is already planned,' Chap said.

'It is!' she said, thrilled.

'Yes, it's tomorrow at four o'clock.'

'Where?'

'A place called Pete's, just down the street a few blocks.'

'Pete's?' Helen said.

'It's, well, it's sort of a restaurant.'

'A restaurant. What about a church?'

'I don't think he went.'

'He did when he was a boy,' his mother said in defense.

In memory of Trevor, the five o'clock happy hour would begin at four, and run until midnight. Fifty-cent longnecks, Trevor's favorite.

'Should we go?' asked Helen, sensing trouble.

'I wouldn't think so.'

'Why not?' asked Mrs. Carson.

'It could be a rough crowd. A bunch of lawyers and judges, you know the scene.' He frowned at Helen, and she got the message.

They asked about funeral parlors and cemetery lots, and Chap felt himself getting dragged deeper and deeper into their problems. The CIA killed Trevor. Was it expected to send him off with a proper burial?

Klockner thought not.

After the ladies left, Wes and Chap finished the

removal of the cameras, wires, mikes, and phone taps. They tidied up the place, and when they locked the doors for the last time Trevor's office had never been so orderly.

Half of Klockner's team had already left town. The other half monitored Wilson Argrow inside Trumble. And they waited.

When the forgers at Langley finished with Argrow's court file it fit in a cardboard box, and was flown to Jacksonville on a small jet along with three agents. It contained, among many other things, a fifty-one-page indictment handed down by a grand jury in Dade County, a correspondence file filled with letters from Argrow's defense lawyer and the U.S. Attorney's office, a thick file of motions and other pretrial maneuverings, research memos, a list of witnesses and summaries of their testimonies, a trial brief, jury analysis, an abstract of the trial, presentencing reports, and the final sentence itself. It was reasonably well organized, though not too neat to arouse suspicion. Copies were smudged, and pages were missing, and staples were hanging off, little touches of reality carefully added by the good folks in Documents to create authenticity. Ninety percent of it would not be needed by Beech and Yarber, but its sheer heft made it impressive. Even the cardboard box had some age on it.

The box was delivered to Trumble by Jack Argrow, a semiretired real estate lawyer in Boca Raton, Florida, and brother of the inmate. Lawyer Argrow's state bar certification had been faxed to the proper bureaucrat at Trumble, and his name was on the approved list of attorneys.

Jack Argrow was Roger Lyter, a thirteen-year man with a law degree from Texas. He'd never met Kenny Sands, who was Wilson Argrow. The two shook hands and said hello while Link looked suspiciously at the cardboard box sitting on the table.

'What's in there?' he asked.

'It's my court records,' Wilson said.

'Just paperwork,' Jack said.

Link stuck a hand in the box and moved some files around, and in a few seconds the search was over and he stepped out of the room.

Wilson slid a paper across the desk, and said, 'This is the affidavit. Wire the money to the bank in Panama, then get me written verification so I'll have something to show them.'

'Less ten percent.'

'Yes, that's what they think.'

The Geneva Trust Bank in Nassau had not been contacted. To do so would've been futile and risky. No bank would release funds under the circumstances Argrow was creating. And questions would be raised if he tried.

The wire transfer going to Panama was new money.

'Langley is quite anxious,' the lawyer said.

'I'm ahead of schedule,' the banker replied.

The box was emptied on a table in the law library. Beech and Yarber began sifting through its contents while Argrow, their new client, watched with feigned interest. Spicer had better things to do. He was in the middle of his weekly poker game.

'Where's the sentencing report?' Beech asked, scratching through the pile.

'I want to see the indictment,' Yarber mumbled to himself.

They found what they wanted, and both settled into their chairs for a long afternoon of reading. Beech's choice was quite dull. Yarber's, however, was not.

The indictment read like a crime narrative. Argrow, along with seven other bankers, five accountants, five securities brokers, two lawyers, eleven men identified only as drug traffickers, and six gentlemen from Colombia, had organized and run an elaborate enterprise designed to take drug proceeds in the form of cash and turn them into respectable deposits. At least $400 million had been laundered before the ring was infiltrated, and it appeared as though their man Argrow was right in the thick of things. Yarber admired him. If half the allegations were true, then Argrow was a very smart and talented financier.

Argrow became bored with the silence, and left to stroll around the prison. When Yarber finished reading the indictment, he interrupted Beech and made him read it. Beech enjoyed it too. 'Surely,' he said, 'he's got some of the loot buried some-where.'

'You know he does,' Yarber agreed. 'Four hundred million bucks, and that's just what they could find. What about his appeal?'

'Doesn't look good. The judge followed the guidelines. I see no error.'

'Poor guy.'

'Poor guy, my ass. He'll be out four years before me.'

'I don't think so, Mr. Beech. We've spent our last Christmas in prison.'

'Do you really believe that?' Hatlee asked.

'Indeed I do.'

Beech placed the indictment back on the table, then stood and stretched and paced around the room 'We should've heard something by now,' he said, very softly though no one else was there.

'Patience.'

'But the primaries are almost over. He's back in Washington most of the time. He's had the letter for a week.'

'He can't ignore it, Hatlee. He's trying to figure out what to do. That's all.'

The latest memo from the Bureau of Prisons in Washington baffled the warden. Who in hell's name up there had nothing better to do than to stare at a map of the federal prisons and decide which one to meddle with that day? He had a brother making $150,000 selling used cars, and there he was making half that much running a prison and reading idiotic memos from pencil-pushers making $100,000 and not doing a productive damned thing. He was so sick of it!

RE: Attorney Visitation, Trumble Federal Prison

Disregard prior order, said order restricting attorney visitation to Tuesdays, Thursdays, and Saturdays, from 3 to 6 P.M.

Attorneys are now permitted to visit seven days a week, from 9 to 7 P.M.

'It takes a dead lawyer to get the rules changed,' he mumbled to himself.

THIRTY-FIVE

Deep in a basement garage, they rolled Teddy Maynard into his van and locked the doors. York and Deville sat with him. A driver and a bodyguard handled the van, which had a television, a stereo, and a small bar with bottled water and sodas, all of which were ignored by Teddy. He was subdued, and dreading the next hour. He was tired – tired of his work, tired of the fight, tired of forcing himself through another day, then another. Fight it six more months, he kept telling himself, then give it up and let someone else worry about saving the world. He'd go quietly to his small farm in West Virginia where he'd sit by the pond, watch the leaves fall into the water, and wait for the end. He was so tired of the pain.

There was a black car in front of them and a gray one behind, and the little convoy made its way around the Beltway, then east across the Roosevelt Bridge and onto Constitution Avenue.

Teddy was silent, so therefore York and Deville were too. They knew how much he loathed what he was about to do.

He talked to the President once a week, usually

on Wednesday morning, always by phone if Teddy had his way. They last saw each other nine months earlier when Teddy was in the hospital and the President needed to be briefed.

The favors usually fell to an equal level, but Teddy hated to be on the same footing with any President. He'd get the favor he wanted, but it was the asking that humiliated him.

In thirty years he'd survived six Presidents, and his secret weapon had been the favors. Gather the intelligence, hoard it, rarely tell the President everything, and occasionally gift-wrap a small miracle and deliver it to the White House.

This President was still pouting over the humiliating defeat of a nuclear test ban treaty Teddy had helped sabotage. The day before the Senate killed it, the CIA leaked a classified report raising legitimate concerns about the treaty, and the President got flattened in the stampede. He was leaving office, a lame duck more concerned with his legacy than with the pressing matters of the country.

Teddy had dealt with lame ducks before, and they were impossible. Since they wouldn't face the voters again, they dwelt on the big picture. In their waning days, they liked to travel, with lots of their friends, to foreign lands where they held summits with other lame ducks. They worried about their presidential libraries. And their portraits. And their biographies, so they spent time with historians. As the clock ticked they became wiser and more philosophical, and their speeches became grander. They talked of the future, of the challenges and the way things ought to be, conveniently ignoring the fact that they'd had eight years to do all the things that needed to be done.

There was nothing worse than a lame duck. And Lake would be just as bad if and when he had the chance.

Lake. The very reason Teddy was trekking to the White House, hat in hand, to grovel for a while.

They were cleared through the West Wing, where Teddy suffered the indignity of having his wheelchair examined by a Secret Service agent. Then they rolled him to a small office next to the cabinet room. A busy appointment secretary explained with no apology that the President was running late. Teddy smiled and waved her off and mumbled something to the effect that this President had never been on time for anything. He'd suffered a dozen fussy secretaries just like her, in the same position she was now in, and the others were long gone. She led York and Deville and the others away, down to the dining room where they would eat by themselves.

Teddy waited, as he knew he would. He read a thick report as if time meant nothing. Ten minutes passed. They brought him coffee. Two years ago the President had visited Langley, and Teddy had made him wait for twenty-one minutes. He needed a favor then, the President did, needed a little matter kept quiet.

The only advantage to being crippled was that he didn't have to jump to his feet when the President entered the room. He finally arrived in a rush, with aides scrambling behind him, as if this would impress Teddy Maynard. They shook hands and made the required greetings as the aides got rid of themselves. A waiter appeared and placed small green salads before them.

'It's good to see you,' the President said with a soft voice and drippy smile. Save it for television, Teddy thought, and he couldn't bring himself to return the lie. 'You're looking well,' he said, only because it was partially true. The President had a new tint to his hair, and he looked younger. They ate their salads, and a quietness settled around them.

Neither wanted a long lunch. 'The French are selling toys to the North Koreans again,' Teddy said, offering a crumb.

'What kinds of toys?' the President asked, though he knew precisely about the trafficking. And Teddy knew he knew.

'It's their version of stealth radar, which is quite stupid because they haven't perfected it yet. But the North Koreans are even dumber because they're paying for it. They'll buy anything from France, especially if the French try to hide it. The French, of course, know this, so it's all cloak and dagger and the North Koreans pay top dollar.'

The President pushed a button and the waiter appeared to remove their plates. Another brought chicken and pasta.

'How's your health?' the President asked.

'About the same. I'll probably leave when you do.'

This pleased them both, the prospect of the other leaving. For no apparent reason, the President then launched into a windy narrative about his Vice President, and what a wonderful job he would do in the Oval Office. He ignored his lunch and became very earnest in his opinions of what a fine human being and brilliant thinker and capable leader the man was. Teddy played with his chicken.

'How do you see the race?' the President asked.

'I honestly don't care,' Teddy said, lying again. 'As I told you, I'm leaving Washington when you do, Mr. President. I'm retiring to my little farm where there's no television, no newspapers, nothing but a little fishing and a lot of rest. I'm tired, sir.'

'Aaron Lake scares me,' the President said.

You don't know the half of it, Teddy thought. 'Why?' he asked, taking a bite. Eat, and let him talk.

'A single issue. Nothing but defense. You give the Pentagon unlimited resources and they'll waste enough to feed the third world. And all this money worries me.'

It never worried you before. The last thing Teddy wanted was a long, useless conversation about politics. They were wasting time. The sooner he finished his business, the sooner he could return to the safety of Langley. 'I'm here to ask a favor,' he said slowly.

'Yes, I know. What can I do for you?' The President was smiling and chewing, enjoying both the chicken and the rare moment of having the upper hand.

'It's a little out of the ordinary. I'd like clemency for three federal prisoners.'

The chewing and smiling stopped, not out of shock but out of confusion. Clemency was usually a simple matter, unless it involved spies or terrorists or infamous politicians. 'Spies?' the President asked.

'No. Judges. One from California, one from Texas, one from Mississippi. They're serving their time together in a federal prison in Florida.'

'Judges?'

'Yes, Mr. President.'

'Do I know these people?'

'I doubt it. The one from California was once the Chief Justice of the Supreme Court out there. He got himself recalled, then had a little trouble with the IRS.'

'I think I remember that.'

'He was convicted of tax evasion and sentenced to seven years. He's served two. The one from Texas was a trial judge, a Reagan appointee. He got drunk and killed a couple of hikers in Yellowstone.'

'I do remember that, but vaguely.'

'It was several years ago. The one from Mississippi was a Justice of the Peace who got caught embezzling bingo profits.'

'I must've missed that one.'

There was a long pause as they considered the questions. The President was bewildered and not certain where to start. Teddy wasn't sure what was coming, so they finished eating in silence. Neither wanted dessert.

The request was an easy one, at least for the President. The felons were virtually unknown, as were their victims. Any fallout would be quick and painless, especially for a politician whose career was less than seven months from being over. He'd

399

been pressured to grant far more difficult pardons. The Russians always had a few spies they lobbied to get back. There were two Mexican businessmen locked away in Idaho for drug trafficking, and every time a treaty of some sort was on the table their clemency became an issue. There was a Canadian Jew serving a life sentence for spying, and the Israelis were determined to get him out.

Three unknown judges? The President could sign his name three times and the matter would be over. Teddy would owe him.

It would be a simple matter, but that was no reason to make things easy for Teddy.

'I'm sure there's a good reason for this request,' he said.

'Of course.'

'A matter of grave national security?'

'Not really. Just a few favors for old friends.'

'Old friends? Do you know these men?'

'No. But I know their friends.'

The lie was so obvious the President almost jumped at it. How could Teddy know the friends of three judges who just happened to be serving time together?

Nothing would come from grilling Teddy Maynard, nothing but frustration. And the President would not stoop that low. He would not beg for information he'd never get. Whatever Teddy's motives were, he would take them to his grave.

'This is a bit confusing,' the President said with a shrug.

'I know. Let's leave it at that.'

'What's the fallout?'

'Not much. The families of the two kids who

400

were killed in Yellowstone might squawk, and I wouldn't blame them.'

'How long ago was it?'

'Three and a half years.'

'You want me to pardon a Republican federal judge?'

'He's not a Republican now, Mr. President. They have to swear off politics once they take the bench. Now that he's been convicted, he can't even vote. I'm sure if you granted clemency he'd become a big fan of yours.'

'I'm sure he would.'

'If it'll make matters easier, these gentlemen will agree to leave the country for at least two years.'

'Why?'

'It might look bad if they return home. Folks will know that they somehow got out early. This can be kept very quiet.'

'Did the judge from California pay the taxes he tried to evade?'

'He did.'

'And did the guy from Mississippi repay the money he stole?'

'Yes sir.'

All the questions were superficial. He had to ask something.

The last favor had dealt with nuclear spying. The CIA had a report documenting widespread infiltration of Chinese spies in and through virtually all levels of the U.S. nuclear arms program. The President learned of the report just days before he was scheduled to visit China for a highly touted summit. He asked Teddy to come have lunch, and over the same chicken and pasta he

401

asked that the report be held for a few weeks. Teddy agreed. Later, he wanted the report modified to place more blame on prior administrations. Teddy rewrote it himself. When it was finally released, the President deflected most of the blame.

Chinese spying and national security, versus three obscure ex-judges. Teddy knew he would get the pardons.

'If they leave the country, where will they go?' the President asked.

'We're not sure yet.'

The waiter brought coffee. When he was gone, the President asked, 'Will this in any way hurt the Vice President?'

And with the same expressionless face, Teddy said, 'No. How could it?'

'You tell me. I have no clue what you're doing.'

'There's nothing to worry about, Mr. President. I'm asking for a small favor. With a little luck, this will not be reported anywhere.'

They sipped their coffee and both wanted to leave. The President had a full afternoon with more pleasant matters. Teddy needed a nap. The President was relieved it was such a benign request. Teddy was thinking, If you only knew.

'Give me a few days to do the background,' the President said. 'These requests are pouring in, as you might guess. Seems everybody wants something now that my days are numbered.'

'Your last month here will be your happiest,' Teddy said with a rare grin. 'I've seen enough Presidents to know.'

After forty minutes together, they shook hands and promised to talk in a few days.

There were five ex-lawyers at Trumble, and the newest one was using the library when Argrow entered. Poor guy was up to his elbows in briefs and legal pads, working feverishly, no doubt pursuing his last feeble appeal.

Spicer was rearranging law books and managing to look sufficiently busy. Beech was in the chamber, writing something. Yarber was absent.

Argrow removed a folded sheet of white paper from his pocket, and gave it to Spicer. 'I just saw my lawyer,' he whispered.

'What is it?' Spicer asked, holding the paper.

'It's a wire confirmation. Your money is now in Panama.'

Spicer looked at the lawyer across the room, but he was oblivious to everything except his legal pad. 'Thanks,' he whispered. Argrow left the room, and Spicer took the paper to Beech, who examined it carefully.

Their loot was now safely guarded by the First Coast Bank of Panama.

THIRTY-SIX

Joe Roy had dropped eight more pounds, was down to ten cigarettes a day and averaging twenty-five miles a week around the track. Argrow found him there, walking and pacing in the late afternoon heat.

'Mr. Spicer, we need to talk,' Argrow said.

'Two more laps,' Joe Roy said without breaking stride.

Argrow watched him for a few seconds, then jogged fifty yards until he caught up. 'Mind if I join?' he asked.

'Not at all.'

They went into the first turn, stride for stride. 'I just met with my lawyer again,' Argrow said.

'Your brother?' Spicer asked, breathing heavily. His paces were not nearly as graceful as Argrow's, a man twenty years younger.

'Yes. He's talked to Aaron Lake.'

Spicer stopped as if he'd hit a wall. He glared at Argrow, then looked at something in the distance.

'Like I said, we need to talk.'

'I suppose we do,' Spicer said.

'I'll meet you in the law library in half an hour,'

404

Argrow said, and walked away. Spicer watched him until he disappeared.

There was no Jack Argrow, Attorney-at-Law, in the Boca Raton yellow pages, and this initially caused concern. Finn Yarber frantically worked the unsecured phone, seeking directory assistance all over South Florida. When he asked for Pompano Beach, the operator said, 'One moment, please,' and Finn actually smiled. He scribbled down the number, then dialed it. A recorded voice said, 'You've reached the law offices of Jack Argrow. Mr. Argrow keeps hours by appointment only, so please leave your name and number and a brief description of the real estate you're interested in, and we'll get in touch with you.' Finn hung up and walked quickly across the lawn to the law library, where his colleagues were waiting. Argrow was already ten minutes late.

A moment before he arrived, the same ex-lawyer entered the room carrying a bulky file, evidently ready to spend hours trying to save himself. To ask him to leave would cause a fight and create suspicion, and besides he wasn't the type who respected judges anyway. One by one they retired to the small conference room, where Argrow joined them. The room was cramped when Beech and Yarber worked there, writing their letters. With Argrow as the fourth man in, and bringing no small amount of pressure, the room had never felt so crowded. They sat around the small table, each able to reach and touch the other three.

'I know only what I've been told,' Argrow began. 'My brother is a semiretired lawyer in Boca

Raton. He has some money, and for years he's been active in Republican politics in South Florida. Yesterday he was approached by some people who work for Aaron Lake. They had investigated matters and knew that I was his brother, and that I was here in Trumble along with Mr. Spicer. They made promises, swore him to secrecy, and now he's sworn me to secrecy. Now that everything is nice and confidential, I think you can connect the dots.'

Spicer had not showered. His shirt and face were still wet, but his breathing had slowed. Not the slightest sound from either Beech or Yarber. The Brethren were in a collective trance. Keep going, they said with their eyes.

Argrow looked at the three faces, and pushed onward. He reached into his pocket and removed a sheet of paper, which he unfolded and laid before them. It was a copy of their last letter to Al Konyers, the outing letter, the extortion demand, signed by Joe Roy Spicer, current address of Trumble Federal Prison. They had the words memorized, so there was no need to read it again. They recognized the handwriting, that of poor little Ricky, and they realized that it had now come full circle. From the Brethren to Mr. Lake, from Mr. Lake to Argrow's brother, from Argrow's brother back to Trumble, all in thirteen days.

Spicer finally picked it up, and glanced at the words. 'I guess you know everything, don't you?' he asked.

'I don't know how much I know.'

'Tell us what they've told you.'

'You're running a scam, the three of you. You

406

advertise in gay magazines, you develop relation-
ships with older men, by mail, you somehow learn
their true identities, then you extort money from
them.'

'That's a pretty fair summary of the game,'
Beech said.

'And Mr. Lake made the mistake of answering
one of your ads. I don't know when he did this,
and I don't know how you found out who he was.
There are some gaps in the plot, as far as I'm
concerned.'

'It's best to keep it that way,' Yarber said.

'Fair enough. I didn't volunteer for this job.'

'What will you get out of it?' Spicer asked.

'Early release. I'll spend a few more weeks
around here, then they'll move me again. I'll walk
by the end of the year, and if Mr. Lake gets elected
then I'll get a full pardon. Not a bad deal. My
brother gets a huge favor from the next President.'

'So you're the negotiator?' Beech said.

'No, I'm the messenger.'

'Then shall we begin?'

'The first move belongs to you.'

'You've got the letter. We want some money
and we want out of this place.'

'How much money?'

'Two million each,' Spicer said, and it was
obvious this had been discussed many times
already. All six eyes watched Argrow, waiting for
the twitch, the frown, the shock. But there was no
reaction, just a pause as he returned their stares. 'I
have no authority here, okay? I can't say yes or no
to your demands. All I do is relay the details to my
brother.'

'We read the newspaper every day,' Beech said. 'Mr. Lake has more money than he can spend right now. Six million is a drop in the bucket.'

'He has seventy-eight million on hand, with no debt,' Yarber added.

'Whatever,' Argrow said. 'I'm just the courier, the mail runner, sort of like Trevor.'

They froze again, with the mention of their dead lawyer. They glared at Argrow, whose fingernails had caught his attention, and they wondered if the Trevor comment had been laid across the table as some sort of warning. How deadly had their game become? They were giddy with thoughts of money and freedom, but how safe were they now? How safe would they be in the future?

They would always know Lake's secret.

'And the terms of the money?' Argrow asked.

'Very simple,' Spicer said. 'All of it up front, all of it wired to some delightful little place, probably Panama.'

'Okay. Now what about your release?' Argrow asked.

'What about it?' asked Beech.

'Any suggestions?'

'Not really. We thought Mr. Lake could take care of that. He has lots of friends these days.'

'Yes, but he's not the President yet. He can't lean on the right people yet.'

'We're not waiting until January when he's inaugurated,' Yarber said. 'In fact, we're not waiting until November to see if he wins.'

'So you want to be released now?'

'Pretty damned quick,' Spicer said.

'Does it matter how you're released?'

408

They thought for a moment, then Beech said, 'It has to be clean. We're not running for the rest of our lives. We're not looking over our shoulders.'

'Do you leave together?'

'Yes,' Yarber said. 'And we have some definite plans on how we want to do it. First, though, we need to agree on the important things – money, and exactly when we walk out of here.'

'Fair enough. From this side of the table, they'll want your files, all of the letters and notes and records from your scam. Obviously, Mr. Lake has to receive assurances that the secrets will be buried.'

'If we get what we want,' Beech said, 'he has nothing to worry about. We'll gladly forget we ever heard of Aaron Lake. But we must warn you, so you can warn Mr. Lake, that if anything happens to us, his story will be told anyway.'

'We have an outside contact,' Yarber said.

'It's a delayed reaction,' Spicer added, as if he were helping explain the unexplainable. 'Something happens to us, like, for instance, the same thing that happened to Trevor, and a few days later a little delay bomb goes off. Mr. Lake gets himself outed anyway.'

'That won't happen,' Argrow said.

'You're the messenger. You don't know what will or will not happen,' Beech said, lecturing. 'These are the same people who killed Trevor.'

'You're not sure of that.'

'No, but we have our opinions.'

'Let's not argue something we can't prove, gentlemen,' Argrow said, ending the session. 'I'll see my brother at nine in the morning. Let's meet here at ten.'

Argrow left the room, left them sitting trance-like, deep in thought, counting their money but afraid to start spending it. He headed for the track, but turned away when he saw a group of inmates jogging. He roamed the grounds until he found a secluded spot behind the cafeteria, then he called Klockner.

Within an hour, Teddy was briefed.

THIRTY-SEVEN

The 6 A.M. bell shrieked through Trumble, through the corridors of the dorms, across the lawns, around the buildings, into the surrounding woods. It lasted for exactly thirty-five seconds, most inmates could tell you, and by the time it quit no one was left asleep. It jolted them to life, as if important events were planned that day, and they had to hurry and get ready. But the only pressing matter was breakfast.

The bell startled Beech, Spicer, and Yarber, but it didn't wake them. Sleep had been elusive, the reasons obvious. They lived in different dorms, but not surprisingly they met in line for coffee, at ten minutes after six. With their tall cups, and without a word, they walked to the basketball court where they sat on a bench and sipped in the early dawn. They watched the prison grounds; the track was behind them.

How many more days would they wear their olive shirts and sit in the Florida heat, getting paid pennies by the hour for doing nothing, just waiting, dreaming, drinking endless cups of coffee? Would it be a month, or two? Were they talking

411

days now? The possibilities had robbed them of sleep.

'There are only two possible ways,' Beech was saying. He was the federal judge, and they listened carefully, though it was familiar ground. 'The first is to go back to the sentencing jurisdiction and file a motion for reduced time. Under very narrow circumstances, the trial judge has the authority to release an inmate. It's rarely done, though.'

'Did you ever do it?' Spicer asked.

'No.'

'Asshole.'

'For what reasons?' Yarber asked.

'Only when the prisoner has provided new information about old crimes. If the prisoner provides substantial assistance to the authorities, then he might get a few years off.'

'That's not encouraging,' Yarber said.

'What's number two?' Spicer asked.

'We're shipped out to a halfway house, a really nice one where they don't expect us to live by the rules. The Bureau of Prisons has sole authority in placing inmates. If the right pressure is applied by our new friends in Washington, then the Bureau could move us out and basically forget about us.'

'Don't you have to live in a halfway house?' Spicer asked.

'Yes, in most of them. But they're all different. Some are locked down at night, with strict rules. Others are very laid back. You can phone in once a day, or once a week. It's all up to the Bureau.'

'But we'll still be convicted felons,' Spicer said.

'Doesn't bother me,' Yarber said. 'I'll never vote again.'

412

'I have an idea,' Beech said. 'It came to me last night. As part of our negotiations, we make Lake agree to pardon us if he's elected.'

'I thought of that too,' Spicer said.

'So did I,' said Yarber. 'But who cares if we have a record? The only thing that matters is that we get out.'

'It won't hurt to ask,' Beech replied. They concentrated on their coffee for a few minutes.

'Argrow's making me nervous,' Finn finally said.

'How's that?'

'Well, he drops in here from nowhere, and suddenly becomes our best friend. He does a magic trick with our money, gets it wired to a safer bank. Now he's the point man for Aaron Lake. Keep in mind, somebody out there was reading our mail. And it wasn't Lake.'

'He doesn't bother me,' Spicer said. 'Lake had to find somebody to talk to us. He pulled some strings, did some research, found out that Argrow was here and that he had a brother they could talk to.'

'That's awfully convenient, don't you think?' Beech asked.

'You too, huh?'

'Maybe. Finn's got a point. We know for a fact that somebody else got involved.'

'Who?'

'That's the big question,' Finn said. 'That's why I haven't slept in a week. There's somebody else out there.'

'Do we really care?' Spicer asked. 'If Lake can get us outta here, fine. If somebody else can get us outta here, what's wrong with that?'

413

'Don't forget Trevor,' Beech said. 'Two bullets in the back of the head.'

'This place might be safer than we think.'

Spicer was not convinced. He finished a drink and said, 'Do you really think that Aaron Lake, a man about to be elected President of the United States, would order a hit on a worthless lawyer like Trevor?'

'No,' replied Yarber. 'He would not. It's much too risky. And he wouldn't kill us. But the mystery man would. The guy who killed Trevor is the same guy who read our mail.'

'I'm not convinced.'

They were together where Argrow expected to find them, in the law library, and they seemed to be waiting. He entered in a rush, and when he was sure they were alone, he said, 'I just met with my brother again. Let's talk.'

They scurried into their little conference room, closed the door, and crowded around the table.

'Things are about to happen very fast,' Argrow said nervously. 'Lake will pay the money. It'll be wired anywhere you want it. I can help if you want; otherwise you can handle it any way you wish.'

Spicer cleared his throat. 'That's two million each?'

'That's what you asked for. I don't know Mr. Lake, but evidently he moves fast.' Argrow glanced at his watch, then looked over his shoulder at the door. 'There are some people from Washington here to meet with you. Big shots.' He yanked some papers from his pocket, unfolded them, and laid a single sheet before each of the three. 'These are presidential pardons, signed yesterday.'

With great reserve, they reached forward, took the papers, and tried to read them. The copies certainly looked official. They gawked at the bold letters across the top, the paragraphs of fussy prose, the compact signature of the President of the United States, and not a single word could be summoned. They were just stunned.

'We've been pardoned?' Yarber finally managed to ask, his voice dry.

'Yes. By the President of the United States.'

They kept reading. They fidgeted and chewed their lips and clenched their jaws, and tried to quietly hide their shock.

'They're gonna come get you, take you to the warden's office where the big shots from Washington will deliver the good news. Act surprised, okay?'

'No problem.'

'That should be easy.'

'How did you get these copies?' Yarber asked.

'They were given to my brother. I have no idea how. Lake has powerful friends. Anyway, here's the deal. You'll be released within the hour. A van will take you to Jacksonville, to a hotel where my brother will meet you. You will wait there until the wire transfers are confirmed, then you will hand over all of your dirty little files. Everything. Understood?'

They nodded in unison. For two million bucks, they could have it all.

'You will agree to leave the country immediately, and not to return for at least two years.'

'How can we leave the country?' Beech asked. 'We have no passports, no papers.'

'My brother will have all of that. You will be given new identities, with a complete set of papers, including credit cards. It's all waiting for you.'

'Two years?' Spicer asked, and Yarber looked at him as if he'd lost his mind.

'That's right. Two years. It's part of the deal. Agreed?'

'I don't know,' Spicer said, his voice shaking. Spicer had never left the United States.

'Don't be foolish,' Yarber snapped at him. 'A complete pardon, a million bucks a year for two years to live abroad. Hell, yes, we'll take the deal.'

A sudden knock on the door terrified them. Two guards were looking in. Argrow grabbed the copies of the pardons and stuffed them in his pocket. 'Do we have a deal, gentlemen?'

They nodded yes, and all three shook hands with him.

'Good,' he said. 'Remember, act surprised.'

They followed the guards to the warden's office where they were introduced to two very stern-faced men from Washington, one from Justice, one from the Bureau of Prisons. The warden completed the stiff introductions without getting any of the names confused, then he handed each of the three a legal-sized document. They were the originals of what Argrow had just shown them.

'Gentlemen,' the warden announced with as much drama as he could muster, 'you've just been pardoned by the President of the United States.' He smiled warmly as if he were responsible for this good news.

416

They stared at their pardons, still in shock, still dizzy with a thousand questions, the biggest of which was, How in the world did Argrow scoop the warden and show them the documents first?

'I don't know what to say,' Spicer managed to mumble, then the other two mumbled something else.

The man from Justice said, 'The President reviewed your cases, and he felt that you have served enough time. He feels very strongly that you have more to offer your country and your communities by once again becoming productive citizens.'

They stared blankly at him. This fool didn't know they were about to assume new names and flee their country and their communities for at least two years? Who was on which side here?

And why was the President granting them clemency when they had enough dirt to destroy Aaron Lake, the man who was primed to defeat the Vice President? It was Lake who wanted them silenced, not the President? Right?

How could Lake convince the President to pardon them?

How could Lake convince the President to do anything, at this stage of the campaign?

They clutched their pardons and sat speechless, their faces drawn tight as the questions hammered away inside.

The man from the Bureau said, 'You should feel honored. Clemency is very rare.'

Yarber managed to acknowledge him with a quick nod, but even then he was thinking, Who's waiting for us on the outside?

417

'I think we're in shock,' Beech said.

It was a first for Trumble, inmates so important that the President decided to pardon them. The warden was quite proud of the three, but uncertain as to how the moment should be commemorated. 'When would you like to leave?' he asked, as if they might want to stick around for a party.

'Immediately,' Spicer said.

'Very well. We'll drive you to Jacksonville.'

'No thanks. We'll have someone pick us up.'

'Okay, then, well, there's some paperwork.'

'Make it quick,' Spicer said.

They were each given a duffel bag to collect their things in. As they walked rather briskly across the grounds, all still very close together and in perfect step, with a guard trailing behind, Beech said, under his breath, 'So who got us the damned pardons?'

'It wasn't Lake,' Yarber said, just barely loud enough to be heard.

'Of course it wasn't Lake,' Beech said. 'The President wouldn't do a damned thing Aaron Lake asked him to.'

They walked faster.

'What difference does it make?' Spicer asked.

'It doesn't make any sense,' Yarber said.

'So what're you gonna do, Finn?' Spicer asked without looking. 'Stay here for a few days and ponder the situation? And then if you figure out who's responsible for the pardon, then maybe you won't accept it? Gimme a break.'

'Somebody else is behind this,' Beech said.

'Then I love this somebody else, okay?' Spicer said. 'I'm not sticking around to ask questions.'

418

They ransacked their rooms in a mad rush, never slowing to say good-bye to anyone. Most of their friends were scattered around the camp anyway.

They had to hurry before the dream was over, or before the President changed his mind.

At eleven-fifteen, they walked through the front door of the administration building, the same door they'd each entered years ago, and waited on the hot sidewalk for their ride. None of the three looked back.

The van was driven by Wes and Chap, though they gave other names. They used so many.

Joe Roy Spicer lay down on the backseat, and covered his eyes with a forearm, determined not to see anything until he was far away. He wanted to cry and he wanted to scream, but he was numb with euphoria – sheer, uncut, unabashed euphoria. He hid his eyes and smiled a goofy smile. He wanted a beer and he wanted a woman, preferably his wife. He'd call her soon. The van was rolling now.

The suddenness of the release had them rattled. Most inmates count the days, and in doing so know with some measure of accuracy when the moment will come. And they know where they're going, and who's waiting for them there.

But the Brethren knew so little. And the few things they knew, they didn't really believe. The pardons were a hoax. The money was nothing but bait. They were being taken away to be slaughtered, same as poor Trevor. The van would stop any minute, and the two goons up front would search their bags, find their dirty files, then murder them in a roadside ditch.

Maybe. But, at the moment, they did not miss the safety of Trumble.

Finn Yarber sat behind the driver and watched the road ahead. He held his pardon, ready to present it to anyone who might stop them and tell them the dream was over. Next to him was Hatlee Beech, who after a few minutes on the road began to cry, not loud, but with his eyes tightly closed and his lips quivering.

Beech had reason to cry. With almost eight and a half years to go, clemency meant more to him than to his two colleagues combined.

Not a word was uttered between Trumble and Jacksonville. As they approached the city, and the roads became wider and the traffic heavier, the three watched the scenery with great curiosity. People were driving, moving about. Planes overhead. Boats on the rivers. Things were normal again.

They inched through the traffic on Atlantic Boulevard, thoroughly enjoying every moment of the congestion. The weather was hot, the tourists were out, ladies with long bronze legs. They saw the seafood restaurants and bars with signs advertising cold beer and cheap oysters. When the street ended, the beach began, and they pulled under the veranda of the Sea Turtle. They followed one of their escorts through the lobby, where they caught a look or two because they were still dressed alike. Up to the fifth floor, and off the elevator before Chap said, 'Your rooms are right here, these

420

three.' He was pointing down the hall. 'Mr. Argrow would like to see you as soon as possible.'

'Where is he?' Spicer asked.

Chap pointed again. 'Over there, in the corner suite. He's waiting.'

'Let's go,' Spicer said, and they followed Chap into the corner, their duffel bags bouncing against one another.

Jack Argrow looked nothing like his brother. He was much shorter, and his hair was blond and wavy where his brother's was dark and thinning. It was just a casual observation, but the three noticed it and mentioned it later. He shook their hands quickly, but only to be polite. He was edgy and talked very fast. 'How's my brother?' he asked.

'He's doing well,' Beech said.

'We saw him this morning,' Yarber added.

'I want him out of prison,' Jack snapped, as if they'd put him there in the first place. 'That's what I'll get outta this deal, you know. I'll get my brother out of prison.'

They glanced at each other; nothing could be said.

'Have a seat,' Argrow said. 'Look, I don't know how or why I'm in the middle of this, you understand. It makes me very nervous. I'm here on behalf of Mr. Aaron Lake, a man I believe will be elected, and make a great President. I suppose I can then get my brother outta prison. But anyway, I've never met Mr. Lake. Some of his people approached me about a week ago, and asked me to get involved in a very secret and delicate matter. That's why I'm here. It's a favor, okay? I don't know everything, you understand?' The sentences

421

were clipped and rapid. He talked with his hands and his mouth, and he couldn't be still.

The Brethren offered no response, none was really expected.

Two hidden cameras captured the scene and sent it immediately to Langley, where Teddy, York, and Deville watched it on a wide screen in the bunker. The ex-judges, now ex-inmates, looked like freshly released POWs, dazed and subdued, still in uniform, still in disbelief. They sat close together, watching Agent Lyter give a splendid performance.

After trying to outthink and outmaneuver them for three months, it was fascinating to finally see them. Teddy studied their faces, and grudgingly admitted a little admiration. They'd been shrewd and lucky enough to hook the right victim; now they were free and about to be well compensated for their ingenuity.

'Okay, look, the first thing is the money,' Argrow barked. 'Two million each. Where do you want it?'

It was not the sort of question they'd had much experience with. 'What are the options?' asked Spicer.

'You have to wire it somewhere,' Argrow snapped back.

'How about London?' Yarber asked.

'London?'

'We'd like the money, all of it, all six million, to be wired at one time, to one account, to a bank in London,' Yarber said.

'We can wire it anywhere. Which bank?'

'Can you help us with the details?' Yarber asked.

422

'I'm told we can do anything you want. I'll have to make a few calls. Why don't you go to your rooms, take a shower, change clothes. Give me fifteen minutes.'

'We don't have any clothes,' Beech said.

'There are some things in your rooms.'

Chap led them down the hall and gave them their keys.

Spicer stretched out on his king-sized bed and stared at the ceiling. Beech stood in the window of his room and looked north, for miles along the beach, the blue water gently rolling onto the white sand. Children played near their mothers. Couples strolled hand in hand. A fishing boat inched along on the horizon. Free at last, he said to himself. Free at last.

Yarber took a long hot shower – complete privacy, no time limit, plenty of soap, thick towels. Someone had placed a selection of toiletries on the vanity – deodorant, shaving cream, razors, toothpaste, toothbrush, floss. He took his time, then changed into a pair of Bermuda shorts, sandals, and a white tee shirt. He'd be the first to leave, and he needed to find a clothing store.

Twenty minutes later they reconvened in Argrow's suite, and they brought with them their collection of files wrapped neatly in a pillowcase. Argrow was just as anxious as before. 'There's a large bank in London called Metropolitan Trust. We can send the money there, then you can do with it whatever you want.'

'That's fine,' Yarber said. 'The account will be in my name only.'

Argrow looked at Beech and Spicer, and they

423

nodded their approval. 'Very well. I assume you have a plan of some sort.'

'We do,' Spicer said. 'Mr. Yarber here will leave for London this afternoon, and when he gets there he'll go to the bank and take care of the money. If all goes well, then we'll leave soon afterward.'

'I assure you things will go well.'

'And we believe you. We're just being careful.'

Argrow handed two sheets of paper to Finn. 'I need your signature to start the wire and open the account.' Yarber scribbled his name.

'Have you had lunch?' he asked.

They shook their heads. Lunch was certainly on their minds, but they weren't sure how to proceed.

'You're free men now. There are some nice restaurants just a few blocks from here. Go enjoy yourselves. Give me an hour to start the wire. Let's meet here at two-thirty.'

Spicer was holding the pillowcase. He sort of waved it at Argrow and said, 'Here are the files.'

'Right. Just throw them on the sofa there.'

THIRTY-EIGHT

They left the hotel on foot, without escorts, without restrictions, but with their pardons in their pockets, just in case. And though the sun was warmer near the beach, the air was certainly lighter. The sky was clearer. The world was pretty again. Hope filled the air. They smiled and laughed at almost anything. They strolled along Atlantic Boulevard, and mixed easily with the tourists.

Lunch was steak and beer at a sidewalk café, under an umbrella, so they could watch the foot traffic. Little was said as they ate and drank. Everything was seen, though, especially the younger ladies in shorts and skimpy tops. Prison had turned them into old men. Now they felt the urge to party.

Especially Hatlee Beech. He'd had wealth and status and ambition, and as a federal judge he'd had what was all but impossible to lose – a lifetime appointment. He'd fallen hard, lost everything, and during his first two years at Trumble he'd existed in a state of depression. He had accepted the fact that he would die there, and he'd seriously considered suicide. Now, at the age of fifty-six, he was emerging from the darkness in a rather splendid fashion. He was fifteen pounds lighter, nicely tanned, in good health, divorced from a woman who had money but not much else to offer, and about to collect a fortune. Not a bad middle-aged rally, he told himself. He missed his children, but they'd followed the money and forgotten about him.

Hatlee Beech was ready for some fun.

Spicer was also looking for a party, preferably one at a casino. His wife had no passport, so it would be a few weeks before she could join him in London, or wherever he might land. Did they have casinos in Europe? Beech thought so. Yarber had no idea, and didn't care.

Finn was the most reserved of the three. He drank a soda instead of beer, and he wasn't as interested in the flesh passing by. Finn was already in Europe. He'd never leave, never return to his native land. He was sixty, very fit, now with lots of money, and was about to bum around Italy and Greece for the next ten years.

Across the street, they found a small bookstore and bought several travel books. In a shop specializing in beachwear, they found just the right sunglasses. Then it was time to see Jack Argrow again, and finish the deal.

Klockner and company watched them stroll back to the Sea Turtle. Klockner and company were weary of Neptune Beach and Pete's and the Sea Turtle and the crowded rental. Six agents, including Chap and Wes, were still there, all very anxious

426

for another assignment. The unit had discovered the Brethren, plucked them from inside Trumble, brought them to the beach, and now they just wanted them to leave the country.

Jack Argrow had not touched the files, or at least they appeared untouched. They were still wrapped in the pillowcase, on the sofa, in the exact spot Spicer had left them.

'The wire is under way,' Argrow said as they settled into his suite.

Teddy was still watching from Langley. The three were now wearing all manner of beach garb. Yarber had a fishing cap with a six-inch bill. Spicer had a straw hat and a yellow tee shirt of some variety. Beech, the Republican, wore khaki shorts, a knit pullover, and a golf cap.

There were three large envelopes on the dining table. Argrow handed one to each of the Brethren. 'Inside, you'll find your new identities. Birth certificates, credit cards, Social Security cards.'

'What about passports?' asked Yarber.

'We have a camera set up in the next room. The passports and driver's licenses will need photos. It'll take thirty minutes. There's also five thousand dollars cash in those small envelopes there.'

'I'm Harvey Moss?' Spicer asked, looking at his birth certificate.

'Yes. You don't like Harvey?'

'I guess I do now.'

'You look like a Harvey,' Beech said.

'And who are you?'

'Well, I'm James Nunley.'

'Nice to meet you, James.'

Argrow never cracked a smile, never relaxed for

a second. 'I need to know your travel plans. The people in Washington really want you out of the country.'

'I need to check flights to London,' Yarber said.

'We've already done that. A flight to Atlanta leaves Jacksonville in two hours. At seven-ten tonight, there's a flight leaving Atlanta for London Heathrow that arrives early tomorrow morning.'

'Can you get me a seat?'

'It's already done. First class.'

Finn closed his eyes and smiled.

'And what about you?' Argrow asked, looking at the other two.'

'I kinda like it here,' Spicer said.

'Sorry. We have a deal.'

'We'll take the same flights tomorrow afternoon,' Beech said. 'Assuming all goes well with Mr. Yarber.'

'Do you want us to handle the reservations?'

'Yes, please.'

Chap eased into the room without making a sound, and took the pillowcase from the sofa. He left with the files.

'Let's do the photos,' Argrow said.

Finn Yarber, now traveling as a Mr. William McCoy of San Jose, California, flew to Atlanta without incident. For an hour he walked the concourses of the airport, rode the underground shuttles, and thoroughly enjoyed the frenzy and chaos of being in the midst of a million people in a hurry.

His first-class seat was a massive leather recliner. After two glasses of champagne, he began to drift, and to dream. He was afraid to sleep because he was afraid to wake up. He was certain he would be back on his top bunk, staring at the ceiling, counting off another day at Trumble.

From a pay phone next to Beach Java, Joe Roy finally caught his wife. At first, she thought the call was a hoax and refused to accept the collect charges. 'Who is this?' she asked.

'It's me, dear. I'm no longer in prison.'

'Joe Roy?'

'Yes, now listen. I'm out of prison, okay. Are you there?'

'I think so. Where are you?'

'I'm staying at a hotel near Jacksonville, Florida. I was released from prison this morning.'

'Released? But how –'

'Don't ask, okay. I'll explain everything later. I'm leaving tomorrow for London. I want you to go to the post office first thing in the morning, and get an application for a passport.'

'London? Did you say London?'

'Yes.'

'England?'

'That's it, yes. I have to go there for a while. It's part of the deal.'

'For how long?'

'A couple of years. Listen, I know it's hard to believe, but I'm free and we're gonna live abroad for a couple of years.'

'What kinda deal? Have you escaped, Joe Roy? You said it'd be easy to do.'

'No. I have been released.'

'But you got more than twenty months to go.'

'Not anymore. Listen, get the application for a passport and follow the instructions.'

'Why do I need a passport?'

'So we can meet in Europe.'

'For two years?'

'Yes, that's it.'

'But Mother's sick. I can't just run off and leave Mother.'

He thought of all the things he'd like to say about her mother, then let it pass. A deep breath, a glance down the street. 'I'm going away,' he said. 'I have no choice.'

'Just come home,' she said.

'I can't. I'll explain it later.'

'An explanation would be nice.'

'I'll call you tomorrow.'

Beech and Spicer ate seafood in a restaurant crowded with people much younger. They roamed the sidewalks and eventually found their way to Pete's Bar and Grill, where they watched the Braves and enjoyed the noise.

Finn was somewhere over the Atlantic, following their money.

The customs agent at Heathrow barely glanced at Finn's passport, which was a marvel of forgery. It was well used and had accompanied Mr. William McCoy around the world. Aaron Lake did indeed have powerful friends.

Finn took a taxi to the Basil Street Hotel in Knightsbridge, and paid cash for the smallest room available. He and Beech had selected the hotel at random from a travel guide. It was an old-fashioned place, filled with antiques, and it rambled

430

from floor to floor. At the small restaurant upstairs, he had breakfast of coffee, eggs, and black sausage, then went for a walk. At ten, his taxi stopped in front of the Metropolitan Trust in the City. The receptionist didn't care for his attire – jeans and a pullover – but when she realized he was an American she shrugged and seemed to tolerate it.

They made him wait for an hour, but he didn't mind it at all. Finn was nervous, but didn't show it. He'd wait for days, weeks, months to get the money. He'd learned how to be patient. The Mr. MacGregor who was in charge of the wire finally came for him. The money had just arrived, sorry for the delay. All six million bucks had crossed the Atlantic safely, and was now on British soil.

But not for long. 'I'd like to wire it to Switzerland,' Finn said, with the proper dose of confidence and experience.

That afternoon, Beech and Spicer flew to Atlanta. Like Yarber, they roamed the airport with unrestrained freedom while waiting for their London flight. They sat together in first class, ate and drank for hours, watched movies, tried to sleep as they crossed the ocean.

Much to their surprise, Yarber was waiting when they cleared customs at Heathrow. He delivered the wonderful news that the money had come and gone. It was hidden in Switzerland. He surprised them again with the idea of leaving immediately.

'They know we're here,' he said over coffee in an airport bar. 'Let's shake them.'

'You think they're following us?' Beech asked.

431

'Let's assume they are.'

'But why?' Spicer asked.

They discussed it for half an hour, then began looking for flights. Alitalia to Rome caught their attention. First class, of course.

'Do they speak English in Rome?' Spicer asked as they were boarding.

'Actually, they speak Italian,' Yarber said.

'You think the Pope will see us?'

'He's probably busy.'

THIRTY-NINE

Buster zigzagged westward for days until he made his final bus stop in San Diego. The ocean attracted him, the first water he'd seen in months. He hung around the docks looking for odd jobs and chatting with the regulars. A charter boat captain hired him as a gopher, and he jumped ship in Los Cabos, Mexico, at the southern tip of the Baja. The harbor there was filled with expensive fishing boats, much nicer than the ones he and his father once traded. He met a few of the captains, and within two days had a job as a deckhand. The customers were wealthy Americans from Texas and California, and they spent more time drinking than fishing. He earned no wages or salary, but worked for tips, which invariably got larger the more the clients drank. A slow day would net him $200; a good day, $500, all cash. He lived in an inexpensive motel, and after a few days stopped looking over his shoulder. Los Cabos quickly became his home.

Wilson Argrow was suddenly transferred out of

Trumble and sent to a halfway house in Milwaukee, where he stayed exactly one night before walking away. Since he didn't exist he couldn't be found. Jack Argrow met him at the airport with tickets, and they flew together to D.C. Two days after leaving Florida, the Argrow brothers, Kenny Sands and Roger Lyter, reported to Langley for their next assignment.

Three days before he was scheduled to depart D.C. for the convention in Denver, Aaron Lake arrived at Langley for lunch with the Director. It was to be a joyful occasion, the conquering candidate once again thanking the genius who'd asked him to run. His acceptance speech had been written for a month, but Teddy had a few suggestions he wanted to discuss.

He was escorted to Teddy's office, where the old man was waiting under his quilt, as always. He looked so pale and tired, Lake thought. The aides vanished, the door was closed, and Lake noticed that no table had been prepared. They sat away from the desk, face to face, very close together.

Teddy liked the speech and made just a few comments. 'Your speeches are getting too long,' he said quietly. But Lake had so much to say these days.

'We're still editing,' he said.

'This election belongs to you, Mr. Lake,' Teddy said, quite feebly.

'I feel good, but it will be a brawl.'

'You'll win by fifteen points.'

Lake stopped smiling and listened hard. 'That's, uh, quite a margin.'

434

'You're up slightly in the polls. Next month the Vice President will be up. It will go back and forth until the middle of October. Then, there will be a nuclear situation that will terrify the world. And you, Mr. Lake, will become the messiah.'

The prospect frightened even the messiah. 'A war?' Lake asked quietly.

'No. There will be casualties, but they won't be Americans. Natty Chenkov will get the blame, and the good voters of this republic will flock to the polls. You could win by as much as twenty points.'

Lake breathed deeply. He wanted to ask more questions, even perhaps object to the bloodshed. But it would be futile. Whatever terror Teddy had planned for October was already in the works. There was nothing Lake could say or do to stop it.

'Keep beating the same drum, Mr. Lake. The same message. The world is about to become a lot crazier, and we have to be strong to protect our way of life.'

'The message has worked so far.'

'Your opponent will become desperate. He'll attack you for the single issue, and he'll whine about the money. He'll beat you up and score some points. Don't panic. The world will be turned upside down in October, trust me.'

'I do.'

'You've got this thing won, Mr. Lake. Keep preaching the same message.'

'Oh, I will.'

'Good,' Teddy said, and closed his eyes for a moment as if he needed a quick nap. Then he opened them and said, 'Now, on an entirely

435

different topic, I'm a little curious about your plans once you get to the White House.'

Lake was puzzled, and his face showed it.

Teddy continued the ambush: 'You need a partner, Mr. Lake, a First Lady, someone to grace the White House with her presence. Someone to entertain and decorate, a pretty woman, one young enough to have children. It's been a long time since we had children in the White House, Mr. Lake.'

'You must be kidding.' Lake was flabbergasted.

'I like this Jayne Cordell on your staff. She's thirty-eight, smart, articulate, quite pretty though she needs to drop fifteen pounds. Her divorce was twelve years ago, and it's forgotten. I think she'd make a fine First Lady.'

Lake cocked his head to one side, and was suddenly angry. He wanted to lash out at Teddy, but for the moment words failed him. He managed to mumble, 'Have you lost your mind?'

'We know about Ricky,' Teddy said, very coolly, with his eyes penetrating Lake's.

The wind was sucked out of Lake's lungs, and as he exhaled he said, 'Oh my god.' He studied his feet for a moment, his entire body frozen in shock.

To make matters worse, Teddy handed over a sheet of paper. Lake took it, and instantly recognized it as a copy of his last note to Ricky.

Dear Ricky:
   I think it's best if we end our correspondence. I wish you well with your rehab.
Sincerely, Al

Lake almost said that he could explain things; they were not as they seemed. But he decided to say nothing, at least not for a while. The questions flooded his thoughts – How much do they know? How in hell did they intercept the mail? Who else knows?

Teddy let him suffer in silence. There was no hurry.

When his thoughts cleared somewhat, the politician in Lake came to the surface. Teddy was offering a way out. Teddy was saying, 'Just play ball with me, son, and things will be fine. Do it my way.'

And so Lake swallowed hard and said, 'I actually like her.'

'Of course you do. She's perfect for the job.'

'Yes. She's very loyal.'

'Are you sleeping with her?'

'No. Not yet.'

'Start soon. Hold hands with her during the convention. Let the gossip start, let nature take its course. A week before the election, announce a Christmas wedding.'

'Big or small?'

'Huge. The social event of the year in Washington.'

'I like that.'

'Get her pregnant quickly. Just before your inauguration, announce that the First Lady is expecting. It'll make a marvelous story. And it will be so nice to see young children in the White House again.'

Lake smiled and nodded and appeared to like

the thought, then he suddenly frowned. 'Will anyone ever know about Ricky?' he asked.

'No. He's been neutralized.'

'Neutralized?'

'He'll never write another letter, Mr. Lake. And you'll be so busy playing with all your little children that you won't have time to think about people like Ricky.'

'Ricky who?'

'Atta boy, Lake. Atta boy.'

'I'm very sorry, Mr. Maynard. Very sorry. It won't happen again.'

'Of course it won't. I've got the file, Mr. Lake. Always remember that.' Teddy began rolling himself backward, as if the meeting was over.

'It was an isolated moment of weakness,' Lake said.

'Never mind, Lake. Take care of Jayne. Get her a new wardrobe. She works too hard and she looks tired. Ease up on her. She's going to make a wonderful First Lady.'

'Yes sir.'

Teddy was at the door. 'No more surprises, Lake.'

'No sir.'

Teddy opened the door and rolled himself away.

By late November, they had settled in Monte Carlo, primarily because of its beauty and warm weather, but also because so much English was spoken there. And there were casinos, a must for Spicer. Neither Beech nor Yarber could tell if he was winning or losing, but he was certainly enjoying himself. His wife was still tending to her mother, who'd yet to die. Things were tense because Joe Roy wouldn't go home, and she wouldn't leave Mississippi.

They lived in the same small but handsome hotel on the edge of town, and they usually had breakfast together twice a week before scattering. As the months passed and they settled into their new lives, they saw less and less of each other. They had differing interests. Spicer wanted to gamble and drink and spend time with the ladies. Beech preferred the sea and enjoyed fishing. Yarber traveled and studied the history of southern France and northern Italy.

But each always knew where the others were. If one disappeared, the other two wanted to know it.

They'd read nothing about their pardons. Beech and Yarber had spent hours in a library in Rome, reading American newspapers just after they fled. Not a word about them. They'd had no contact with anyone from home. Spicer's wife claimed to have told no one that he was out of prison. She still thought he'd escaped.

On Thanksgiving Day, Finn Yarber was enjoying an espresso at a sidewalk café in downtown Monte Carlo. It was warm and sunny, and he was only vaguely aware that it was an important holiday back home. He didn't care because he would never go back. Beech was asleep in his hotel room. Spicer was in a casino three blocks away.

A vaguely familiar face appeared from nowhere. In a flash, the man sat across from Yarber and said, 'Hello, Finn. Remember me?'

Yarber calmly took a sip of coffee and studied the face. He'd last seen it at Trumble.

439

'Wilson Argrow, from prison,' the man said, and Yarber put down his cup before he dropped it.

'Good morning, Mr. Argrow,' Finn said slowly, calmly, though there were many other things he wanted to say.

'I guess you're surprised to see me.'

'Yes, as a matter of fact.'

'Wasn't that exciting news about Aaron Lake's landslide?'

'I suppose. What can I do for you?'

'I just want you to know that we're always close by, just in case you need us.'

Finn actually chuckled, then said, 'That doesn't seem likely.' It had been five months since their release. They had moved from country to country, from Greece to Sweden, from Poland to Portugal, slowly heading south as the weather changed. How on earth could Argrow track them down?

It was impossible.

Argrow pulled a magazine from inside his jacket. 'I ran across this last week,' he said, handing it over. The magazine was turned to a page in the back where a personal ad was circled with a red marker:

> SWM in 20s looking for kind and discreet American gentleman in 40s or 50s to pen pal with.

Yarber had certainly seen it before, but he shrugged as if he hadn't a clue.

'Looks familiar, doesn't it?' Argrow asked.

'They all look the same to me,' Finn said. He

440

tossed the magazine on the table. It was the European edition of *Out and About*.

'We traced the address to the post office here in Monte Carlo,' Argrow said. 'A brand-new box rental, with a fake name and everything. What a coincidence.'

'Look, I don't know who you work for, but I have a very strong hunch that we're not in your jurisdiction. We haven't broken a single law. Why don't you bug off?'

'Sure, Finn, but two million bucks isn't enough?'

Finn smiled and looked around the lovely café. He took a sip of coffee and said, 'You gotta keep busy.'

'I'll see you around,' Argrow said, then jumped to his feet and vanished.

Yarber finished his coffee as if nothing had happened. He watched the street and the traffic for a while, then left to gather his colleagues.

The Summons

THE SUMMONS

THE SUMMONS

Chapter 1

It came by mail, regular postage, the old-fashioned way since the Judge was almost eighty and distrusted modern devices. Forget e-mail and even faxes. He didn't use an answering machine and had never been fond of the telephone. He pecked out his letters with both index fingers, one feeble key at a time, hunched over his old Underwood manual on a rolltop desk under the portrait of Nathan Bedford Forrest. The Judge's grandfather had fought with Forrest at Shiloh and throughout the Deep South, and to him no figure in history was more revered. For thirty-two years, the Judge had quietly refused to hold court on July 13, Forrest's birthday.

It came with another letter, a magazine, and two invoices, and was routinely placed in the law school mailbox of Professor Ray Atlee. He recognized it immediately since such envelopes had been a part of his life for as long as he could remember. It was from his father, a man he too called the Judge.

Professor Atlee studied the envelope, uncertain whether he should open it right there or wait a moment. Good news or bad, he never knew with the Judge, though the old man was dying and good news had been rare. It was thin and appeared to contain only one sheet of paper; nothing unusual about that. The Judge was frugal with the written word, though he'd once been known for his windy lectures from the bench.

It was a business letter, that much was certain. The Judge was not one for small talk, hated gossip and idle chitchat, whether written or spoken. Ice tea with him on the porch would be a refighting of the Civil War, probably at Shiloh, where he would once again lay all blame for the Confederate defeat at the shiny, untouched boots of General Pierre G. T. Beauregard, a man he would hate even in heaven, if by chance they met there.

He'd be dead soon. Seventy-nine years old with cancer in his stomach. He was overweight, a diabetic, a heavy pipe smoker, had a bad heart that had survived three attacks, and a host of lesser ailments that had tormented him for twenty years and were now finally closing in for the kill. The pain was constant. During their last phone call three weeks earlier, a call initiated by Ray because the Judge thought long distance was a rip-off, the old man sounded weak and strained. They had talked for less than two minutes.

2

The return address was gold-embossed: Chancellor Reuben V. Atlee, 25th Chancery District, Ford County Courthouse, Clanton, Mississippi. Ray slid the envelope into the magazine and began walking. Judge Atlee no longer held the office of chancellor. The voters had retired him nine years earlier, a bitter defeat from which he would never recover. Thirty-two years of diligent service to his people, and they tossed him out in favor of a younger man with radio and television ads. The Judge had refused to campaign. He claimed he had too much work to do, and, more important, the people knew him well and if they wanted to reelect him then they would do so. His strategy had seemed arrogant to many. He carried Ford County but got shellacked in the other five.

It took three years to get him out of the courthouse. His office on the second floor had survived a fire and had missed two renovations. The Judge had not allowed them to touch it with paint or hammers. When the county supervisors finally convinced him that he had to leave or be evicted, he boxed up three decades' worth of useless files and notes and dusty old books and took them home and stacked them in his study. When the study was full, he lined them down the hallways into the dining room and even the foyer.

Ray nodded to a student who was seated in the hall. Outside his office, he spoke to a colleague. Inside, he locked the door behind him and placed the mail in the center of his desk. He took off his jacket, hung it on the back of the door, stepped over a stack of thick law books he'd been stepping over for half a year, and then to himself uttered his daily vow to organize the place.

The room was twelve by fifteen, with a small desk and a small sofa, both covered with enough work to make Ray seem like a very busy man. He was not. For the spring semester he was teaching one section of antitrust. And he was supposed to be writing a book, another drab, tedious volume on monopolies that would be read by no one but would add handsomely to his pedigree. He had tenure, but like all serious professors he was ruled by the 'publish or perish' dictum of academic life.

He sat at his desk and shoved papers out of the way.

The envelope was addressed to Professor N. Ray Atlee, University of Virginia School of Law, Charlottesville, Virginia. The *e*'s and *o*'s were smudged together. A new ribbon had been needed for a decade. The Judge didn't believe in zip codes either.

The N was for Nathan, after the general, but few people knew it. One of their uglier fights had been over the son's decision to drop Nathan altogether and plow through life simply as Ray.

The Judge's letters were always sent to the law school, never to his son's apartment in downtown Charlottesville. The Judge liked titles and

4

important addresses, and he wanted folks in Clanton, even the postal workers, to know that his son was a professor of law. It was unnecessary. Ray had been teaching (and writing) for thirteen years, and those who mattered in Ford County knew it.

He opened the envelope and unfolded a single sheet of paper. It too was grandly embossed with the Judge's name and former title and address, again minus the zip code. The old man probably had an unlimited supply of the stationery.

It was addressed to both Ray and his younger brother, Forrest, the only two offspring of a bad marriage that had ended in 1969 with the death of their mother. As always, the message was brief:

> Please make arrangements to appear in my study on Sunday, May 7, at 5 P.M., to discuss the administration of my estate.
> Sincerely, Reuben V. Atlee.

The distinctive signature had shrunk and looked unsteady. For years it had been emblazoned across orders and decrees that had changed countless lives. Decrees of divorce, child custody, termination of parental rights, adoptions. Orders settling will contests, election contests, land disputes, annexation fights. The Judge's autograph had been authoritative and well known; now it was the vaguely familiar scrawl of a very sick old man.

5

Sick or not, though, Ray knew that he would be present in his father's study at the appointed time. He had just been summoned, and as irritating as it was, he had no doubt that he and his brother would drag themselves before His Honor for one more lecture. It was typical of the Judge to pick a day that was convenient for him without consulting anybody else.

It was the nature of the Judge, and perhaps most judges for that matter, to set dates for hearings and deadlines with little regard for the convenience of others. Such heavy-handedness was learned and even required when dealing with crowded dockets, reluctant litigants, busy lawyers, lazy lawyers. But the Judge had run his family in pretty much the same manner as he'd run his courtroom, and that was the principal reason Ray Atlee was teaching law in Virginia and not practicing it in Mississippi.

He read the summons again, then put it away, on top of the pile of current matters to deal with. He walked to the window and looked out at the courtyard where everything was in bloom. He wasn't angry or bitter, just frustrated that his father could once again dictate so much. But the old man was dying, he told himself. Give him a break. There wouldn't be many more trips home.

The Judge's estate was cloaked with mystery. The principal asset was the house – an antebellum hand-me-down from the same Atlee who'd fought with General Forrest. On a shady street

6

in old Atlanta it would be worth over a million dollars, but not in Clanton. It sat in the middle of five neglected acres three blocks off the town square. The floors sagged, the roof leaked, paint had not touched the walls in Ray's lifetime. He and his brother could sell it for perhaps a hundred thousand dollars, but the buyer would need twice that to make it livable. Neither would ever live there; in fact, Forrest had not set foot in the house in many years.

The house was called Maple Run, as if it were some grand estate with a staff and a social calendar. The last worker had been Irene the maid. She'd died four years earlier and since then no one had vacuumed the floors or touched the furniture with polish. The Judge paid a local felon twenty dollars a week to cut the grass, and he did so with great reluctance. Eighty dollars a month was robbery, in his learned opinion.

When Ray was a child, his mother referred to their home as Maple Run. They never had dinners at their home, but rather at Maple Run. Their address was not the Atlees on Fourth Street, but instead it was Maple Run on Fourth Street. Few other folks in Clanton had names for their homes.

She died from an aneurysm and they laid her on a table in the front parlor. For two days the town stopped by and paraded across the front porch, through the foyer, through the parlor for last respects, then to the dining room for punch and cookies. Ray and Forrest hid in the attic and

7

cursed their father for tolerating such a spectacle. That was their mother lying down there, a
pretty young woman now pale and stiff in an
open coffin.

Forrest had always called it Maple Ruin. The
red and yellow maples that once lined the street
had died of some unknown disease. Their rotted
stumps had never been cleared. Four huge oaks
shaded the front lawn. They shed leaves by the
ton, far too many for anyone to rake and gather.
And at least twice a year the oaks would lose a
branch that would fall and crash somewhere
onto the house, where it might or might not get
removed. The house stood there year after year,
decade after decade, taking punches but never
falling.

It was still a handsome house, a Georgian
with columns, once a monument to those who'd
built it, and now a sad reminder of a declining
family. Ray wanted nothing to do with it. For
him the house was filled with unpleasant memories and each trip back depressed him. He
certainly couldn't afford the financial black hole
of maintaining an estate that ought to be
bulldozed. Forrest would burn it before he
owned it.

The Judge, however, wanted Ray to take the
house and keep it in the family. This had been
discussed in vague terms over the past few years.
Ray had never mustered the courage to ask,
'What family?' He had no children. There was
an ex-wife but no prospect of a current one.

8

Same for Forrest, except he had a dizzying collection of ex-girlfriends and a current housing arrangement with Ellie, a three-hundred-pound painter and potter twelve years his senior.

It was a biological miracle that Forrest had produced no children, but so far none had been discovered.

The Atlee bloodline was thinning to a sad and inevitable halt, which didn't bother Ray at all. He was living life for himself, not for the benefit of his father or the family's glorious past. He returned to Clanton only for funerals.

The Judge's other assets had never been discussed. The Atlee family had once been wealthy, but long before Ray. There had been land and cotton and slaves and railroads and banks and politics, the usual Confederate portfolio of holdings that, in terms of cash, meant nothing in the late twentieth century. It did, however, bestow upon the Atlees the status of 'family money.'

By the time Ray was ten he knew his family had money. His father was a judge and his home had a name, and in rural Mississippi this meant he was indeed a rich kid. Before she died his mother did her best to convince Ray and Forrest that they were better than most folks. They lived in a mansion. They were Presbyterians. They vacationed in Florida, every third year. They occasionally went to the Peabody Hotel in Memphis for dinner. Their clothes were nicer.

Then Ray was accepted at Stanford. His

bubble burst when the Judge said bluntly, 'I can't afford it.'

'What do you mean?' Ray had asked.

'I mean what I said. I can't afford Stanford.'

'But I don't understand.'

'Then I'll make it plain. Go to any college you want. But if you go to Sewanee, then I'll pay for it.'

Ray went to Sewanee, without the baggage of family money, and was supported by his father, who provided an allowance that barely covered tuition, books, board, and fraternity dues. Law school was at Tulane, where Ray survived by waiting tables at an oyster bar in the French Quarter.

For thirty-two years, the Judge had earned a chancellor's salary, which was among the lowest in the country. While at Tulane Ray read a report on judicial compensation, and he was saddened to learn that Mississippi judges were earning fifty-two thousand dollars a year when the national average was ninety-five thousand.

The Judge lived alone, spent little on the house, had no bad habits except for his pipe, and he preferred cheap tobacco. He drove an old Lincoln, ate bad food but lots of it, and wore the same black suits he'd been wearing since the fifties. His vice was charity. He saved his money, then he gave it away.

No one knew how much money the Judge donated annually. An automatic ten percent went to the Presbyterian Church. Sewanee got two thousand dollars a year, same for the Sons of Confederate Veterans. Those three gifts were carved in granite. The rest were not.

Judge Atlee gave to anyone who would ask. A crippled child in need of crutches. An all-star team traveling to a state tournament. A drive by the Rotary Club to vaccinate babies in the Congo. A shelter for stray dogs and cats in Ford County. A new roof for Clanton's only museum.

The list was endless, and all that was necessary to receive a check was to write a short letter and ask for it. Judge Atlee always sent money and had been doing so ever since Ray and Forrest left home.

Ray could see him now, lost in the clutter and dust of his rolltop, pecking out short notes on his Underwood and sticking them in his chancellor's envelopes with scarcely readable checks drawn on the First National Bank of Clanton – fifty dollars here, a hundred dollars there, a little for everyone until it was all gone.

The estate would not be complicated because there would be so little to inventory. The ancient law books, threadbare furniture, painful family photos and mementos, long forgotten files and papers – all a bunch of rubbish that would make an impressive bonfire. He and Forrest would sell the house for whatever it might bring and be quite happy to salvage anything from the last of the Atlee family money.

He should call Forrest, but those calls were

always easy to put off. Forrest was a different set of issues and problems, much more complicated than a dying, reclusive old father hell-bent on giving away his money. Forrest was a living, walking disaster, a boy of thirty-six whose mind had been deadened by every legal and illegal substance known to American culture.

What a family, Ray mumbled to himself.

He posted a cancellation for his eleven o'clock class, and went for therapy.

Chapter 2

Spring in the Piedmont, calm clear skies, the foothills growing greener by the day, the Shenandoah Valley changing as the farmers crossed and recrossed their perfect rows. Rain was forecast for tomorrow, though no forecast could be trusted in central Virginia.

With almost three hundred hours under his belt, Ray began each day with an eye on the sky as he jogged five miles. The running he could do come rain or shine, the flying he could not. He had promised himself (and his insurance company) that he would not fly at night and would not venture into clouds. Ninety-five percent of all small plane crashes happened either in weather or in darkness, and after nearly three years of flying Ray was still determined to be a coward. 'There are old pilots and bold pilots,' the adage went, 'but no old bold pilots.' He believed it, and with conviction.

Besides, central Virginia was too beautiful to buzz over in clouds. He waited for perfect weather – no wind to push him around and make landings complicated, no haze to dim the horizon and get him lost, no threat of storms or moisture. Clear skies during his jog usually determined the rest of his day. He could move lunch up or back, cancel a class, postpone his research to a rainy day, or a rainy week for that matter. The right forecast, and Ray was off to the airport.

It was north of town, a fifteen-minute drive from the law school. At Docker's Flight School he was given the normal rude welcome by Dick Docker, Charlie Yates, and Fog Newton, the three retired Marine pilots who owned the place and had trained most of the private aviators in the area. They held court each day in the Cockpit, a row of old theater chairs in the front office of the flight school, and from there they drank coffee by the gallon and told flying tales and lies that grew by the hour. Each customer and student got the same load of verbal abuse, like it or not, take it or leave it, they didn't care. They were drawing nice pensions.

The sight of Ray prompted the latest round of lawyer jokes, none of which were particularly funny, all of which drew howls at the punch lines.

'No wonder you don't have any students,' Ray said as he did the paperwork.

'Where you going?' demanded Docker.

'Just punching a few holes in the sky.'

'We'll alert air traffic control.'

14

'You're much too busy for that.'

Ten minutes of insults and rental forms, and Ray was free to go. For eighty bucks an hour he could rent a Cessna that would take him a mile above the earth, away from people, phones, traffic, students, research, and, on this day, even farther from his dying father, his crazy brother, and the inevitable mess facing him back home.

There were tie-downs for thirty light aircraft at the general aviation ramp. Most were small Cessnas with high wings and fixed landing gears, still the safest airplanes ever built. But there were some fancier rigs. Next to his rented Cessna was a Beech Bonanza, a single-engine, two-hundred-horsepower beauty that Ray could handle in a month with a little training. It flew almost seventy knots faster than the Cessna, with enough gadgets and avionics to make any pilot drool. Even worse, the Bonanza was for sale – $450,000 – off the charts, of course, but not that far off. The owner built shopping centers and wanted a King Air, according to the latest analysis from the Cockpit.

Ray stepped away from the Bonanza and concentrated on the little Cessna sitting next to it. Like all new pilots, he carefully inspected his plane with a checklist. Fog Newton, his instructor, had begun each lesson with a gruesome tale of fire and death caused by pilots too hurried or lazy to use checklists.

When he was certain all outside parts and

surfaces were perfect, he opened the door and strapped himself inside. The engine started smoothly, the radios sparked to life. He finished a pre-takeoff list and called the tower. A commuter flight was ahead of him, and ten minutes after he locked his doors he was cleared for takeoff. He lifted off smoothly and turned west, toward the Shenandoah Valley.

At four thousand feet, he crossed Afton Mountain, not far below him. A few seconds of mountain turbulence bounced the Cessna, but it was nothing out of the ordinary. When he was past the foothills and over the farmlands, the air became still and quiet. Visibility was officially twenty miles, though at this altitude he could see much farther. No ceiling, not a cloud anywhere. At five thousand feet, the peaks of West Virginia rose slowly on the horizon. Ray completed an in-flight checklist, leaned his fuel mixture for normal cruise, and relaxed for the first time since taxiing into position for takeoff.

Radio chatter disappeared, and it wouldn't pick up again until he switched to the Roanoke tower, forty miles to the south. He decided to avoid Roanoke and stay in uncontrolled airspace.

Ray knew from personal experience that psychiatrists worked for two hundred dollars an hour in the Charlottesville area. Flying was a bargain, and much more effective, though it was a very fine shrink who'd suggested he pick up a new hobby, and quickly. He was seeing the fellow because he had to see someone. Exactly a month after the former Mrs. Atlee filed for divorce, quit her job, and walked out of their townhouse with only her clothes and jewelry, all done with ruthless efficiency in less than six hours, Ray left the psychiatrist for the last time, drove to the airport, stumbled into the Cockpit, and took his first insult from either Dick Docker or Fog Newton, he couldn't remember which.

The insult felt good, someone cared. More followed, and Ray, wounded and confused as he was, had found a home. For three years now he had crossed the clear, solitary skies of the Blue Ridge Mountains and the Shenandoah Valley, soothing his anger, shedding a few tears, hashing out his troubled life to an empty seat beside him. She's gone, the empty seat kept saying.

Some women leave and come back eventually. Others leave and endure a painful reconsideration. Still others leave with such boldness they never look back. Vicki's departure from his life was so well planned and her execution of it was so cold-blooded that Ray's lawyer's first comment was, 'Give it up, pal.'

She'd found a better deal, like an athlete swapping teams at the trading deadline. Here's the new uniform, smile for the cameras, forget the old arena. While Ray was at work one fine morning, she left in a limousine. Behind it was a van with her things. Twenty minutes later, she walked into her new place, a mansion on a horse farm east of town where Lew the Liquidator was waiting with open arms and a prenuptial agreement. Lew was a corporate vulture whose raids had netted him a half a billion or so, according to Ray's research, and at the age of sixty-four he'd cashed in his chips, left Wall Street, and for some reason picked Charlottesville as his new nest.

Somewhere along the way he'd bumped into Vicki, offered her a deal, gotten her pregnant with the children Ray was supposed to father, and now with a trophy wife and another family he wanted to be taken seriously as the new Big Fish.

Enough of this, Ray said aloud. He talked loudly at five thousand feet, and no one talked back.

He was assuming, and hoping, that Forrest was clean and sober, though such assumptions were usually wrong and such hopes were often misguided. After twenty years of rehab and relapse, it was doubtful if his brother would ever overcome his addictions. And Ray was certain that Forrest would be broke, a condition that went hand in hand with his habits. And being broke, he'd be looking for money, as in his father's estate.

What money the Judge had not given away to charities and sick children, he had poured down the black hole of Forrest's detoxification. So much money had been wasted there, along with so many years, that the Judge, as only he could do, had basically excommunicated Forrest from

18

their father-son relationship. For thirty-two years he had terminated marriages, taken children away from parents, given children to foster homes, sent mentally ill people away forever, ordered delinquent fathers to jail – all manner of drastic and far-reaching decrees that were accomplished merely by signing his name. When he first went on the bench, his authority had been granted by the State of Mississippi, but late in his career he took his orders only from God.

If anyone could expel a son, it was Chancellor Reuben V. Atlee.

Forrest pretended to be unbothered by his banishment. He fancied himself as a free spirit and claimed he had not set foot inside the house at Maple Run in nine years. He had visited the Judge once in the hospital, after a heart attack when the doctors rounded up the family. Surprisingly, he'd been sober then. 'Fifty-two days, Bro,' he'd whispered proudly to Ray as they huddled in the ICU corridor. He was a walking scoreboard when rehab was working.

If the Judge had plans to include Forrest in his estate, no one would have been more surprised than Forrest. But with the chance that money or assets were about to change hands, Forrest would be there looking for crumbs and leftovers.

Over the New River Gorge near Beckley, West Virginia, Ray turned around and headed back. Though flying cost less than professional therapy, it wasn't cheap. The meter was ticking.

If he won the lottery, he would buy the Bonanza and fly everywhere. He was due a sabbatical in a couple of years, a respite from the rigors of academic life. He'd be expected to finish his eight-hundred-page brick on monopolies, and there was an even chance that that might happen. His dream, though, was to lease a Bonanza and disappear into the skies.

Twelve miles west of the airport, he called the tower and was directed to enter the traffic pattern. The wind was light and variable, the landing would be a cinch. On final approach, with the runway a mile away and fifteen hundred feet down, and Ray and his little Cessna gliding at a perfect descent, another pilot came on the radio. He checked in with the controller as 'Challenger-two-four-four-delta-mike,' and he was fifteen miles to the north. The tower cleared him to land, number two behind Cessna traffic.

Ray pushed aside thoughts of the other aircraft long enough to make a textbook landing, then turned off the runway and began taxiing to the ramp.

A Challenger is a Canadian-built private jet that seats eight to fifteen, depending on the configuration. It will fly from New York to Paris, nonstop, in splendid style, with its own flight attendant serving drinks and meals. A new one sells for somewhere around twenty-five million dollars, depending on the endless list of options.

20

The 244DM was owned by Lew the Liquidator, who'd pinched it out of one of the many hapless companies he'd raided and fleeced. Ray watched it land behind him, and for a second he hoped it would crash and burn right there on the runway, so he could enjoy the show. It did not, and as it sped along the taxiway toward the private terminal, Ray was suddenly in a tight spot.

He'd seen Vicki twice in the years since their divorce, and he certainly didn't want to see her now, not with him in a twenty-year-old Cessna while she bounded down the stairway of her gold-plated jet. Maybe she wasn't on board. Maybe it was just Lew Rodowski returning from yet another raid.

Ray cut the fuel mixture, the engine died, and as the Challenger moved closer to him he began to sink as low as possible in his captain's seat.

By the time it rolled to a stop, less than a hundred feet from where Ray was hiding, a shiny black Suburban had wheeled out onto the ramp, a little too fast, lights on, as if royalty had arrived in Charlottesville. Two young men in matching green shirts and khaki shorts jumped out, ready to receive the Liquidator and whoever else might be on board. The Challenger's door opened, the steps came down, and Ray, peeking above his instrument deck with a complete view, watched with fascination as one of the pilots came down first, carrying two large shopping bags.

21

Then Vicki, with the twins. They were two years old now, Simmons and Ripley, poor children given genderless last names as first names because their mother was an idiot and their father had already sired nine others before them and probably didn't care what they were called. They were boys, Ray knew that much for sure because he'd watched the vitals in the local paper – births, deaths, burglaries, etc. They were born at Martha Jefferson Hospital seven weeks and three days after the Atlees' no-fault divorce became final, and seven weeks and two days after a very pregnant Vicki married Lew Rodowski, his fourth trip down the aisle, or whatever they used that day at the horse farm.

Clutching the boys' hands, Vicki carefully descended the steps. A half a billion dollars was looking good on her – tight designer jeans on her long legs, legs that had become noticeably thinner since she had joined the jet set. In fact, Vicki appeared to be superbly starved – bone-thin arms, small flat ass, gaunt cheeks. He couldn't see her eyes because they were well hidden behind black wrap-arounds, the latest style from either Hollywood or Paris, take your pick.

The Liquidator had not been starving. He waited impatiently behind his current wife and current litter. He claimed he ran marathons, but then so little of what he said in print turned out to be true. He was stocky, with a thick belly. Half his hair was gone and the other half was gray with age. She was forty-one and could pass for thirty. He was sixty-four and looked seventy, or at least Ray thought so, with great satisfaction.

They finally made it into the Suburban while the two pilots and two drivers loaded and reloaded luggage and large bags from Saks and Bergdorf. Just a quick shopping jaunt up to Manhattan, forty-five minutes away on your Challenger.

The Suburban sped off, the show was over, and Ray sat up in the Cessna.

If he hadn't hated her so much, he would have sat there a long time reliving their marriage.

There had been no warnings, no fights, no change in temperature. She'd simply stumbled upon a better deal.

He opened the door so he could breathe and realized his collar was wet with sweat. He wiped his eyebrows and got out of the plane.

For the first time in memory, he wished he'd stayed away from the airport.

Chapter 3

The law school was next to the business school, and both were at the northern edge of a campus that had expanded greatly from the quaint academic village Thomas Jefferson designed and built.

To a university that so revered the architecture of its founder, the law school was just another modern campus building, square and flat, brick and glass, as bland and unimaginative as many others built in the seventies. But recent money had renovated and landscaped things nicely. It was ranked in the Top Ten, as everybody who worked and studied there knew so well. A few of the Ivys were ranked above it, but no other public school. It attracted a thousand top students and a very bright faculty.

Ray had been content teaching securities law at Northeastern in Boston. Some of his writings caught the attention of a search committee, one thing led to another, and the chance to move South to a better school became attractive. Vicki was from Florida, and though she thrived in the city life of Boston, she could never adjust to the winters. They quickly adapted to the slower pace of Charlottesville. He was awarded tenure, she earned a doctorate in romance languages. They were discussing children when the Liquidator wormed his way into the picture.

Another man gets your wife pregnant, then takes her, and you'd like to ask him some questions. And perhaps have a few for her. In the days right after her exit he couldn't sleep for all the questions, but as time passed he realized he would never confront her. The questions faded, but seeing her at the airport brought them back. Ray was cross-examining her again as he parked in the law school lot and returned to his office.

He kept office hours late in the afternoon, no appointment was necessary. His door was open and any student was welcome. It was early May, though, and the days were warm. Student visits had become rare. He reread the directive from his father, and again became irked at the usual heavy-handedness.

At five o'clock he locked his office, left the law school, and walked down the street to an intramural sports complex where the third-year students were playing the faculty in the second of a three-game softball series. The professors had lost the first game in a slaughter. Games two and three were not really necessary to determine the better team.

Smelling blood, first- and second-year students filled the small bleachers and hung on the fence along the first-base line, where the faculty team was huddled for a useless pregame pep talk. Out in left field some first-years of dubious reputation were bunched around two large coolers, the beer already flowing.

There's no better place to be in the springtime than on a college campus, Ray thought to himself as he approached the field and looked for a pleasant spot to watch the game. Girls in shorts, a cooler always close by, festive moods, impromptu parties, summer approaching. He was forty-three years old, single, and he wanted to be a student again. Teaching keeps you young, they all said, perhaps energetic and mentally sharp, but what Ray wanted was to sit on a cooler out there with the hell-raisers and hit on the girls.

A small group of his colleagues loitered behind the backstop, smiling gamely as the faculty took the field with a most unimpressive lineup. Several were limping. Half wore some manner of knee brace. He spotted Carl Mirk, an associate dean and his closest friend, leaning on a fence, tie undone, jacket slung over his shoulder.

'Sad-looking crew out there,' Ray said.

'Wait till you see them play,' Mirk said. Carl was from a small town in Ohio where his father was a local judge, a local saint, everybody's

26

grandfather. Carl, too, had fled and vowed never to return.

'I missed the first game,' Ray said.

'It was a hoot. Seventeen to nothing after two innings.'

The leadoff hitter for the students ripped the first pitch into the left-field gap, a routine double, but by the time the left fielder and center fielder hobbled over, corralled the ball, kicked it a couple of times, fought over it, then flung it toward the infield, the runner walked home and the shutout was blown. The rowdies in left field were hysterical. The students in the bleachers yelled for more errors.

'It'll get worse,' Mirk said.

Indeed it did. After a few more fielding disasters, Ray had seen enough. 'I'll be out of town early next week,' he said between batters. 'I've been called home.'

'I can tell you're excited,' Mirk said. 'Another funeral?'

'Not yet. My father is convening a family summit to discuss his estate.'

'I'm sorry.'

'Don't be. There's not much to discuss, nothing to fight over, so it'll probably be ugly.'

'Your brother?'

'I don't know who'll cause more trouble, brother or father.'

'I'll be thinking of you.'

'Thanks. I'll notify my students and give them assignments. Everything should be covered.'

'Leaving when?'

'Saturday, should be back Tuesday or Wednesday, but who knows.'

'We'll be here,' Mirk said. 'And hopefully this series will be over.'

A soft ground ball rolled untouched between the legs of the pitcher.

'I think it's over now,' Ray said.

Nothing soured Ray's mood like thoughts of going home. He hadn't been there in over a year, and if he never went back it would still be too soon.

He bought a burrito from a Mexican takeout and ate at a sidewalk café near the ice rink where the usual gang of black-haired Goths gathered and spooked the normal folks. The old Main Street was a pedestrian mall – a very nice one with cafés and antique stores and book dealers – and if the weather was pleasant, as it usually was, the restaurants spread outdoors for long evening meals.

When he'd suddenly become single again, Ray unloaded the quaint townhouse and moved downtown, where most of the old buildings had been renovated for more urban-style housing. His six-room apartment was above a Persian rug dealer. It had a small balcony over the mall, and at least once a month Ray had his students over for wine and lasagne.

It was almost dark when he unlocked the door on the sidewalk and trudged up the noisy steps to his place. He was very much alone – no mate, no dog, no cat, no goldfish. In the past few years he'd met two women he'd found attractive and had dated neither. He was much too frightened for romance. A saucy third-year student named Kaley was making advances, but his defences were in place. His sex drive was so dormant he had considered counseling, or perhaps wonder drugs. He flipped on lights and checked the phone.

Forrest had called, a rare event indeed, but not completely unexpected. Typical of Forrest, he had simply checked in, without leaving a number. Ray fixed tea with no caffeine and put on some jazz, trying to stall as he prepped himself for the call. Odd that a phone chat with his only sibling should take so much effort, but chatting with Forrest was always depressing. They had no wives, no children, nothing in common but a name and a father.

Ray punched in the number to Ellie's house in Memphis. It rang for a long time before she answered. 'Hello, Ellie, this is Ray Atlee,' he said pleasantly.

'Oh,' she grunted, as if he'd called eight times already. 'He's not here.'

Doing swell, Ellie, and you? Fine, thanks for asking. Great to hear your voice. How's the weather down there?

'I'm returning his call,' Ray said.

'Like I said, he's not here.'

'I heard you. Is there a different number?'

'For what?'

'For Forrest. Is this still the best number to reach him?'

'I guess. He stays here most of the time.'

'Please tell him I called.'

They met in detox, she for booze, Forrest for an entire menu of banned substances. At the time she weighed ninety-eight pounds and claimed she'd lived on nothing but vodka for most of her adult life. She kicked it, walked away clean, tripled her body weight, and somehow got Forrest in the deal too. More mother than girlfriend, she now had him a room in the basement of her ancestral home, an eerie old Victorian in midtown Memphis.

Ray was still holding the phone when it rang. 'Hey, Bro,' Forrest called out. 'You rang?'

'Returning yours. How's it going?'

'Well, I was doing fairly well until I got a letter from the old man. You get one too?'

'It arrived today.'

'He thinks he's still a judge and we're a couple of delinquent fathers, don't you think?'

'He'll always be the Judge, Forrest. Have you talked to him?'

A snort, then a pause. 'I haven't talked to him on the phone in two years, and I haven't set foot in the house in more years than I can remember. And I'm not sure I'll be there Sunday.'

'You'll be there.'

'Have you talked to him?'

'Three weeks ago. I called, he didn't. He

30

sounded very sick, Forrest, I don't think he'll be around much longer. I think you should seriously consider –'

'Don't start, Ray. I'm not listening to a lecture.'

There was a gap, a heavy stillness in which both of them took a breath. Being an addict from a prominent family, Forrest had been lectured to and preached at and burdened with unsolicited advice for as long as he could remember.

'Sorry,' Ray said. 'I'll be there. What about you?'

'I suppose so.'

'Are you clean?' It was such a personal question, but one that was as routine as How's the weather? With Forrest the answer was always straight and true.

'A hundred and thirty-nine days, Bro.'

'That's great.'

It was, and it wasn't. Every sober day was a relief, but to still be counting after twenty years was disheartening.

'And I'm working too,' he said proudly.

'Wonderful. What kind of work?'

'I'm running cases for some local ambulance chasers, a bunch of sleazy bastards who advertise on cable and hang around hospitals. I sign 'em up and get a cut.'

It was difficult to appreciate such a seedy job, but with Forrest any employment was good news. He'd been a bail bondsman, process

31

server, collection agent, security guard, investigator, and at one time or another had tried virtually every job at the lesser levels of the legal profession.

'Not bad,' Ray said.

Forrest started a tale, this one involving a shoving match in a hospital emergency room, and Ray began to drift. His brother had also worked as a bouncer in a strip bar, a calling that was short-lived when he was beaten up twice in one night. He'd spent one full year touring Mexico on a new Harley-Davidson; the trip's funding had never been clear. He had tried leg-breaking for a Memphis loan shark, but again proved deficient when it came to violence.

Honest employment had never appealed to Forrest, though, in all fairness, interviewers were generally turned off by his criminal record. Two felonies, drug-related, both before he turned twenty but permanent blotches nonetheless.

'Are you gonna talk to the old man?' he was asking.

'No, I'll see him Sunday,' Ray answered.

'What time will you get to Clanton?'

'I don't know. Sometime around five, I guess. You?'

'God said five o'clock, didn't he?'

'Yes, he did.'

'Then I'll be there sometime after five. See you, Bro.'

Ray circled the phone for the next hour, deciding yes, he would call his father and just

32

say hello, then deciding no, that anything to be said now could be said later, and in person. The Judge detested phones, especially those that rang at night and disrupted his solitude. More often than not he would simply refuse to answer. And if he picked up he was usually so rude and gruff that the caller was sorry for the effort.

He would be wearing black trousers and a white shirt, one with tiny cinder holes from the pipe ashes, and the shirt would be heavily starched because the Judge had always worn them that way. For him a white cotton dress shirt lasted a decade, regardless of the number of stains and cinder holes, and it got laundered and starched every week at Mabe's Cleaners on the square. His tie would be as old as his shirt and the design would be some drab print with little color. Navy blue suspenders, always.

And he would be busy at his desk in his study, under the portrait of General Forrest, not sitting on the porch waiting for his sons to come home. He would want them to think he had work to do, even on a Sunday afternoon, and that their arrivals were not that important.

Chapter 4

The drive to Clanton took fifteen hours, more or less, if you went with the truckers on the busy four-lanes and fought the bottlenecks around the cities, and it could be done in one day if you were in a hurry. Ray was not.

He packed a few things in the trunk of his Audi TT roadster, a two-seat convertible he'd owned for less than a week, and said farewell to no one because no one really cared when he came or went, and left Charlottesville. He would not exceed the speed limits and he would not drive on a four-lane, if he could possibly avoid it. That was his challenge – a trip without sprawl. On the leather seat next to him he had maps, a thermos of strong coffee, three Cuban cigars, and a bottle of water.

A few minutes west of town he turned left on the Blue Ridge Parkway and began snaking his way south on the tops of the foothills. The TT was a 2000 model, just a year or two off the drawing board. Ray had read Audi's announcement of a brand-new sports car about eighteen months earlier, and he'd rushed to order the first one in town. He had yet to see another one, though the dealer assured him they would become popular.

At an overlook, he put the top down, lit a Cuban, and sipped coffee, then took off again at the maximum speed of forty-five. Even at that pace Clanton was looming

Four hours later, in search of gas, Ray found himself sitting at a stoplight on Main Street in a small town in North Carolina. Three lawyers walked in front of him, all talking at once, all carrying old briefcases that were scuffed and worn almost as badly as their shoes. He looked to his left and noticed a courthouse. He looked to his right and watched as they disappeared into a diner. He was suddenly hungry, both for food and for sounds of people.

They were in a booth near the front window, still talking as they stirred their coffee. Ray sat at a table not too far away and ordered a club sandwich from an elderly waitress who'd been serving them for decades. One glass of ice tea, one sandwich, and she wrote it all down in great detail. Chef's probably older, he thought.

The lawyers had been in court all morning haggling over a piece of land up in the mountains. The land was sold, a lawsuit followed, etc., etc., and now they were having the trial. They had called witnesses, quoted precedents to the judge, disputed everything the others had said, and in general had gotten themselves heated up to the point of needing a break.

And this is what my father wanted me to do, Ray almost said aloud. He was hiding behind the local paper, pretending to read but listening to the lawyers.

Judge Reuben Atlee's dream had been for his sons to finish law school and return to Clanton. He would retire from the bench, and together they would open an office on the square. There, they would follow an honorable calling and he would teach them how to be lawyers – gentleman lawyers, country lawyers.

Broke lawyers was the way Ray had figured things. Like all small towns in the South, Clanton was brimming with lawyers. They were packed in the office buildings opposite the courthouse square. They ran the politics and banks and civic clubs and school boards, even the churches and Little Leagues. Where, exactly, around the square was he supposed to fit in?

During summer breaks from college and law school, Ray had clerked for his father. For no salary, of course. He knew all the lawyers in Clanton. As a whole, they were not bad people. There were just too many of them.

Forrest's turn for the worse came early in life and put even more pressure on Ray to follow the old man into a life of genteel poverty. The pressure was resisted, though, and by the time

Ray had finished one year of law school he had promised himself he would not remain in Clanton. It took another year to find the courage to tell his father, who went eight months without speaking to him. When Ray graduated from law school, Forrest was in prison. Judge Atlee arrived late for the commencement, sat in the back row, left early, and said nothing to Ray. It took the first heart attack to reunite them.

But money wasn't the primary reason Ray fled Clanton. Atlee & Atlee never got off the ground because the junior partner wanted to escape the shadow of the senior.

Judge Atlee was a huge man in a small town.

Ray found gas at the edge of town, and was soon back in the hills, on the parkway, driving forty-five miles an hour. Sometimes forty. He stopped at the overlooks and admired the scenery. He avoided the cities and studied his maps. All roads led, sooner or later, to Mississippi.

Near the North Carolina state line, he found an old motel that advertised air conditioning, cable TV, and clean rooms for $29.99, though the sign was crooked and rusted around the edges. Inflation had arrived with the cable because the room was now $40. Next door was an all-night café where Ray choked down dumplings, the nightly special. After dinner he sat on a bench in front of the motel, smoked another cigar, and watched the occasional car go by.

Across the road and down a hundred yards

was an abandoned drive-in movie theater. The marquee had fallen and was covered with vines and weeds. The big screen and the fences around the perimeter had been crumbling for many years.

Clanton had once had such a drive-in, just off the main highway entering town. It was owned by a chain from up North and provided the locals with the typical lineup of beach romps, horror flicks, kung-fu action, movies that attracted the younger set and gave the preachers something to whine about. In 1970, the powers up North decided to pollute the South once again by sending down dirty movies.

Like most things good and bad, pornography arrived late in Mississippi. When the marquee listed *The Cheerleaders* it went unnoticed by the passing traffic. When *XXX* was added the next day, traffic stopped and tempers rose in the coffee shops around the square. It opened on a Monday night to a small, curious, and somewhat enthusiastic crowd. The reviews at school were favorable, and by Tuesday packs of young teenagers were hiding in the woods, many with binoculars, watching in disbelief. After Wednesday night prayer meeting, the preachers got things organized and launched a counterattack, one that relied more on bullying than on shrewd tactics.

Taking a lesson from the civil rights protectors, a group they had had absolutely no sympathy for, they led their flocks to the highway in front of the drive-in, where they carried posters and prayed and sang hymns and hurriedly scribbled down the license plate numbers of those cars trying to enter.

Business was cut off like a faucet. The corporate guys up North filed a quick lawsuit, seeking injunctive relief. The preachers put together one of their own, and it was no surprise that all of this landed in the courtroom of the Honorable Reuben V. Atlee, a lifelong member of the First Presbyterian Church, a descendant of the Atlees who'd built the original sanctuary, and for the past thirty years the teacher of a Sunday School class of old goats who met in the church's basement kitchen.

The hearings lasted for three days. Since no Clanton lawyer would defend *The Cheerleaders*, the owners were represented by a big firm from Jackson. A dozen locals argued against the movie and on behalf of the preachers.

Ten years later, when he was in law school at Tulane, Ray studied his father's opinion in the case. Following the most current federal cases, Judge Atlee's ruling protected the rights of the protestors, with certain restrictions. And, citing a recent obscenity case ruling by the U.S. Supreme Court, he allowed the show to go on.

Judicially, the opinion could not have been more perfect. Politically, it could not have been uglier. No one was pleased. The phone rang at night with anonymous threats. The preachers denounced Reuben Atlee as a traitor. Wait till the next election, they promised from their pulpits.

Letters flooded the *Clanton Chronicle* and *The Ford County Times,* all castigating Judge Atlee for allowing such filth in their unblemished community. When the Judge was finally fed up with the criticism, he decided to speak. He chose a Sunday at the First Presbyterian Church as his time and place, and word spread quickly, as it always did in Clanton. Before a packed house, Judge Atlee strode confidently down the aisle, up the carpeted steps and to the pulpit. He was over six feet tall and thick, and his black suit gave him an aura of dominance. 'A Judge who counts votes before the trial should burn his robe and run for the county line,' he began sternly.

Ray and Forrest were sitting as far away as possible, in a corner of the balcony, both near tears. They had begged their father to allow them to skip the service, but missing church was not permissible under any circumstances.

He explained to the less informed that legal precedents have to be followed, regardless of personal views or opinions, and that good judges follow the law. Weak judges follow the crowd. Weak judges play for the votes and then cry foul when their cowardly rulings are appealed to higher courts.

'Call me what you want,' he said to a silent crowd, 'but I am no coward.'

Ray could still hear the words, still see his

40

father down there in the distance, standing alone like a giant.

After a week or so the protestors grew weary, and the porno ran its course. Kung-fu returned with a vengeance and everybody was happy. Two years later, Judge Atlee received his usual eighty percent of the vote in Ford County.

Ray flipped the cigar into a shrub and walked to his room. The night was cool so he opened a window and listened to the cars as they left town and faded over the hills.

Chapter 5

Every street had a story, every building a memory. Those blessed with wonderful child- hoods can drive the streets of their hometowns and happily roll back the years. The rest are pulled home by duty and leave as soon as possible. After Ray had been in Clanton for fifteen minutes he was anxious to get out.

The town had changed, but then it hadn't. On the highways leading in, the cheap metal build- ings and mobile homes were gathering as tightly as possible next to the roads for maximum visibility. Ford County had no zoning whatso- ever. A landowner could build anything with no permit, no inspection, no code, no notice to adjoining landowners, nothing. Only hog farms and nuclear reactors required approvals and paperwork. The result was a slash-and-build clutter that got uglier by the year.

But in the older sections, nearer the square, the town had not changed at all. The long shaded streets were as clean and neat as when

Ray had roamed them on his bike. Most of the houses were still owned by people he knew, or if those folks had passed on the new owners kept the lawns clipped and the shutters painted. Only a few were being neglected. A handful had been abandoned.

This deep in Bible country, it was still an unwritten rule that little was done on Sundays except go to church, sit on porches, visit neighbors, rest and relax the way God intended.

It was cloudy, quite cool for May, and as he toured his old turf, killing time until the appointed hour, he tried to dwell on the good memories from Clanton. There was Dizzy Dean Park where he had played Little League for the Pirates, and there was the public pool he'd swum in every summer except 1969 when the city closed it rather than admit black children. There were the churches – Baptist, Methodist, and Presbyterian – facing each other at the intersection of Second and Elm like wary sentries, their steeples competing for height. They were empty now, but in an hour or so the more faithful would gather for evening services.

The square was as lifeless as the streets leading to it. With eight thousand people, Clanton was just large enough to have attracted the discount stores that had wiped out so many small towns. But here the people had been faithful to their downtown merchants, and there wasn't a single empty or boarded-up building around the square – no small miracle. The retail

43

shops were mixed in with the banks and law offices and cafés, all closed for the Sabbath.

He inched through the cemetery and surveyed the Atlee section in the old part, where the tombstones were grander. Some of his ancestors had built monuments for their dead. Ray had always assumed that the family money he'd never seen must have been buried in those graves. He parked and walked to his mother's grave, something he hadn't done in years. She was buried among the Atlees, at the far edge of the family plot because she had barely belonged.

Soon, in less than an hour, he would be sitting in the Judge's study, sipping bad instant tea and receiving instructions on exactly how his father would be laid to rest. Many orders were about to be given, many decrees and directions, because the Judge was a great man and cared deeply about how he was to be remembered.

Moving again, Ray passed the water tower he'd climbed twice, the second time with the police waiting below. He grimaced at his old high school, a place he'd never visited since he'd left it. Behind it was the football field where Forrest Atlee had romped over opponents and almost became famous before getting bounced off the team.

It was twenty minutes before five, Sunday, May 7. Time for the family meeting.

There was no sign of life at Maple Run. The front lawn had been cut within the past few days, and the Judge's old black Lincoln was parked in the rear, but other than those two pieces of evidence there was no sign that anyone had lived there for many years.

The front of the house was dominated by four large round columns under a portico, and when Ray had lived there these columns were painted white. Now they were green with vines and ivy. The wisteria was running wildly along the tops of the columns and onto the roof. Weeds choked everything – flower beds, shrubs, walkways.

Memories hit hard, as they always did when he pulled slowly into the drive and shook his head at the condition of a once fine home. And there was always the same wave of guilt. He should've stayed, should've gone in with the old man and founded the house of Atlee & Atlee, should've married a local girl and sired a half-dozen descendants who would live at Maple Run, where they would adore the Judge and make him happy in his old age.

He slammed his door as loudly as possible, hoping to alert anyone who might need to be alerted, but the noise fell softly on Maple Run. The house next door to the east was another relic occupied by a family of spinsters who'd been dying off for decades. It was also an antebellum but without the vines and weeds, and it was completely shadowed by five of the largest oak trees in Clanton.

The front steps and the front porch had been swept recently. A broom was leaning near the door, which was open slightly. The Judge refused to lock the house, and since he also refused to use air conditioning he left windows and doors open around the clock.

Ray took a deep breath and pushed the door open until it hit the doorstop and made noise. He stepped inside and waited for the odor to hit, whatever it might be this time. For years the Judge kept an old cat, one with bad habits, and the house bore the results. But the cat was gone now, and the smell was not unpleasant at all. The air was warm and dusty and filled with the heavy scent of pipe tobacco.

'Anybody home?' he said, but not too loudly. No answer.

The foyer, like the rest of the house, was being used to store the boxes of ancient files and papers the Judge clung to as if they were important. They had been there since the county evicted him from the courthouse. Ray glanced to his right, to the dining room where nothing had changed in forty years, and he stepped around the corner to the hallway that was also cluttered with boxes. A few soft steps and he peeked into his father's study.

The Judge was napping on the sofa.

Ray backed away quickly and walked to the kitchen, where, surprisingly, there were no dirty dishes in the sink and the counters were clean. The kitchen was usually a mess, but not today. He found a diet soda in the refrigerator and sat at the table trying to decide whether to wake his

46

father or to postpone the inevitable. The old man was ill and needed his rest, so Ray sipped his drink and watched the clock above the stove move slowly toward 5 P.M.

Forrest would show up, he was certain. The meeting was too important to blow off. He'd never been on time in his life. He refused to wear a watch and claimed he never knew what day it was, and most folks believed him.

At exactly five, Ray decided he was tired of waiting. He had traveled a long way for this moment, and he wanted to take care of business. He walked into the study, noticed his father hadn't moved, and for a long minute or two was frozen there, not wanting to wake him, but at the same time feeling like a trespasser.

The Judge wore the same black pants and the same white starched shirt he'd worn as long as Ray could remember. Navy suspenders, no tie, black socks, and black wing tips. He'd lost weight and his clothes swallowed him. His face was gaunt and pale, his hair thin and slicked back. His hands were crossed at his waist and were almost as white as the shirt.

Next to his hands, attached to his belt on the right side, was a small white plastic container. Ray took a step closer, a silent step, for a better look. It was a morphine pack.

Ray closed his eyes, then opened them and glanced around the room. The rolltop desk under General Forrest had not changed in his lifetime. The ancient Underwood typewriter still

47

sat there, a pile of papers beside it. A few feet away was the large mahogany desk left behind by the Atlee who'd fought with Forrest.

Under the stern gaze of General Nathan Bedford Forrest, and standing there in the center of a room that was timeless, Ray began to realize that his father was not breathing. He comprehended this slowly. He coughed, and there was not the slightest response. Then he leaned down and touched the Judge's left wrist. There was no pulse.

Judge Reuben V. Atlee was dead.

Chapter 6

There was an antique wicker chair with a torn cushion and a frayed quilt over the back. No one had ever used it but the cat. Ray backed into it because it was the nearest place to sit, and for a long time he sat there across from the sofa, waiting for his father to start breathing, to wake up, sit up, take charge of matters, and say, 'Where is Forrest?'

But the Judge was motionless. The only breathing at Maple Run was Ray's rather labored efforts to get control of himself. The house was silent, the still air even heavier. He stared at the pallid hands resting peacefully, and waited for them to rise just slightly. Up and down, very slowly as the blood began pumping again and the lungs filled and emptied. But nothing happened. His father was straight as a board, with hands and feet together, chin on chest, as if he knew when he lay down that this last nap would be eternal. His lips were together with a hint of a smile. The powerful drug had stopped the pain.

As the shock began to fade, the questions took over. How long had he been dead? Did the cancer get him or did the old man just crank up the morphine? What was the difference? Was this staged for his sons? Where the hell was Forrest? Not that he would be of any help.

Alone with his father for the last time, Ray fought back tears and fought back all the usual tormenting questions of why didn't I come earlier, and more often, and why didn't I write and call and the list could go on if he allowed it.

Instead, he finally moved. He knelt quietly beside the sofa, put his head on the Judge's chest, whispered, 'I love you, Dad,' then said a short prayer. When he stood he had tears in his eyes, and that was not what he wanted. Younger brother would arrive in a moment, and Ray was determined to handle the situation with no emotion.

On the mahogany desk he found the ashtray with two pipes. One was empty. The bowl of the other was full of tobacco that had recently been smoked. It was slightly warm, at least Ray thought so, though he was not certain. He could see the Judge having a smoke while he tidied up the papers on his desk, didn't want the boys to see too much of a mess, then when the pain hit he stretched out on the sofa, a touch of morphine for a little relief, then he drifted away.

Next to the Underwood was one of the

Judge's official envelopes, and across the front he had typed, 'Last Will and Testament of Reuben V. Atlee.' Under it was yesterday's date, May 6, 2000. Ray took it and left the room. He found another diet soda in the refrigerator and walked to the front porch, where he sat on the swing and waited for Forrest.

Should he call the funeral home and have his father moved before Forrest arrived? He debated this with a fury for a while, then he read the will. It was a simple, one-page document with no surprises.

He decided he would wait until precisely 6 P.M., and if Forrest hadn't arrived he would call the funeral home.

The Judge was still dead when Ray returned to his study, and that was not a complete surprise. He replaced the envelope next to the typewriter, shuffled through some more papers, and at first felt odd doing so. But he would be executor of his father's estate, and would soon be in charge of all the paperwork. He would inventory the assets, pay the bills, help lead the last remnants of the Atlee family money through probate, and finally put it to rest. The will split everything between the two sons, so the estate would be clean and relatively simple.

As he watched the time and waited for his brother, Ray poked around the study, each step watched carefully by General Forrest. Ray was quiet, still not wanting to disturb his father. The drawers to the rolltop were filled with stationery.

51

There was a pile of current mail on the mahogany desk.

Behind the sofa was a wall of bookshelves crammed with law treatises that appeared to have been neglected for decades. The shelves were made of walnut and had been built as a gift by a murderer freed from prison by the Judge's grandfather late in the last century, according to family lore, which as a rule went unquestioned, until Forrest came along. The shelves rested on a long walnut cabinet that was no more than three feet high. The cabinet had six small doors and was used for storage. Ray had never looked inside. The sofa was in front of the cabinet, almost entirely blocking it from view.

One of the cabinet doors was open. Inside, Ray could see an orderly stack of dark green Blake & Son stationer's boxes, the same ones he'd seen as long as he could remember. Blake & Son was an ancient printing company in Memphis. Virtually every lawyer and judge in the state bought letterheads and envelopes from Blake & Son, and had been doing so forever. He crouched low and moved behind the sofa for a better look. The storage spaces were tight and dark.

A box of envelopes without a top had been left sitting in the open door, just a few inches above the floor. There were no envelopes, however. The box was filled with cash – one-hundred-dollar bills. Hundreds of them packed neatly in a box that was twelve inches across, eighteen inches long, and maybe five inches deep. He lifted the box, and it was heavy. There were dozens more tucked away in the depths of the cabinet.

Ray pulled another one from the collection. It too was filled with one-hundred-dollar bills. Same for the third. In the fourth box, the bills were wrapped with yellow paper bands with '$2,000' printed on them. He quickly counted fifty-three bands.

One hundred and six thousand dollars.

Crawling on all fours along the back of the sofa, and careful not to touch it and disturb anybody, Ray opened the other five doors of the cabinet. There were at least twenty dark green Blake & Son boxes.

He stood and walked to the door of the study, then through the foyer onto the front porch for fresh air. He was dizzy, and when he sat on the top step a large drop of sweat rolled down the bridge of his nose and fell onto his pants.

Though clear thinking was not entirely possible, Ray was able to do some quick math. Assuming there were twenty boxes and that each held at least a hundred thousand dollars, then the stash greatly exceeded whatever the Judge had grossed in thirty-two years on the bench. His office of chancellor had been full time, nothing on the side, and not much since his defeat nine years earlier.

53

He didn't gamble, and to Ray's knowledge, had never bought a single share of stock.

A car approached from down the street. Ray froze, instantly fearful that it was Forrest. The car passed, and Ray jumped to his feet and ran to the study. He lifted one end of the sofa and moved it six inches away from the bookshelves, then the same for the other end. He dropped to his knees and began withdrawing the Blake & Son boxes. When he had a stack of five, he carried them through the kitchen to a small room behind the pantry where Irene the maid had always kept her brooms and mops. The same brooms and mops were still there, evidently untouched since Irene's death. Ray swatted away spiderwebs, then set the boxes on the floor.

The broom closet had no window and could not be seen from the kitchen.

From the dining room, he surveyed the front driveway, saw nothing, then raced back to the study where he balanced seven Blake & Son boxes in one stack and took them to the broom closet. Back to the dining room window, nobody out there, back to the study where the Judge was growing colder by the moment. Two more trips to the broom closet and the job was finished. Twenty-seven boxes in total, all safely stored where no one would find them.

It was almost 6 P.M. when Ray went to his car and removed his overnight bag. He needed a dry shirt and clean pants. The house was filled with

54

dust and dirt and everything he touched left a smudge. He washed and dried himself with a towel in the only downstairs bathroom. Then he tidied up the study, moved the sofa back in place, and went from room to room looking for more cabinets.

He was on the second floor, in the Judge's bedroom with the windows up, going through his closets, when he heard a car in the street. He ran downstairs and managed to slip into the swing on the porch just as Forrest parked behind his Audi. Ray took deep breaths and tried to calm himself.

The shock of a dead father was enough for one day. The shock of the money had left him shaking.

Forrest crept up the steps, as slowly as possible, hands stuck deep in his white painter's pants. Shiny black combat boots with bright green laces. Always different.

'Forrest,' Ray said softly, and his brother turned to see him.

'Hey, Bro.'

'He's dead.'

Forrest stopped and for a moment studied him, then he gazed at the street. He was wearing an old brown blazer over a red tee shirt, an ensemble no one but Forrest would attempt to pull off. And no one but Forrest could get by with it. As Clanton's first self-proclaimed free spirit, he had always worked to be cool, offbeat, avant-garde, hip.

55

He was a little heavier and was carrying the weight well. His long sandy hair was turning gray much quicker than Ray's. He wore a battered Cubs baseball cap.

'Where is he?' Forrest asked.

'In there.'

Forrest pulled open the screen and Ray followed him inside. He stopped in the door of the study and seemed uncertain as to what to do next. As Forrest stared at his father his head fell slightly to one side, and Ray thought for a second he might collapse. As tough as he tried to act, Forrest's emotions were always just under the surface. He mumbled, 'Oh my God,' then moved awkwardly to the wicker chair where he sat and looked in disbelief at the Judge.

'Is he really dead?' he managed to say with his jaws clenched.

'Yes, Forrest.'

He swallowed hard and fought back tears and finally said, 'When did you get here?'

Ray sat on a stool and turned it to face his brother. 'About five, I guess. I walked in, thought he was napping, then realized he was dead.'

'I'm sorry you had to find him,' Forrest said, wiping the corners of his eyes.

'Somebody had to.'

'What do we do now?'

'Call the funeral home.'

Forrest nodded as if he knew that was exactly what you're supposed to do. He stood slowly and unsteadily and walked to the sofa. He touched his father's hands. 'How long has he been dead?' he mumbled. His voice was hoarse and strained.

'I don't know. Couple of hours.'

'What's that?'

'A morphine pack.'

'You think he cranked it up a little too much?'

'I hope so,' Ray said.

'I guess we should've been here.'

'Let's not start that.'

Forrest looked around the room as if he'd never been there before. He walked to the rolltop and looked at the typewriter. 'I guess he won't need a new ribbon after all,' he said.

'I guess not,' Ray said, glancing at the cabinet behind the sofa. 'There's a will there if you want to read it. Signed yesterday.'

'What does it say?'

'We split everything. I'm the executor.'

'Of course you're the executor.' He walked behind the mahogany desk and gave a quick look at the piles of papers covering it. 'Nine years since I set foot in this house. Hard to believe, isn't it?'

'It is.'

'I stopped by a few days after the election, told him how sorry I was that the voters had turned him out, then I asked him for money. We had words.'

'Come on, Forrest, not now.'

Stories of the war between Forrest and the Judge could be told forever.

'Never did get that money,' he mumbled as he opened a desk drawer. 'I guess we'll need to go through everything, won't we?'

'Yes, but not now.'

'You do it, Ray. You're the executor. You handle the dirty work.'

'We need to call the funeral home.'

'I need a drink.'

'No, Forrest, please.'

'Lay off, Ray. I'll have a drink anytime I want a drink.'

'That's been proven a thousand times. Come on, I'll call the funeral home and we'll wait on the porch.'

A policeman arrived first, a young man with a shaved head who looked as though someone had interrupted his Sunday nap and called him into action. He asked questions on the front porch, then viewed the body. Paperwork had to be done, and as they went through it Ray fixed a pitcher of instant tea with heavy sugar.

'Cause of death?' the policeman asked.

'Cancer, heart disease, diabetes, old age,' Ray said. He and Forrest were rocking gently in the swing.

'Is that enough?' Forrest asked, like a true smart-ass. Any respect he might've once had for cops had long since been abandoned.

'Will you request an autopsy?'

58

'No,' they said in unison.

He finished the forms and took signatures from both Ray and Forrest. As he drove away, Ray said, 'Word will spread like wildfire now.'

'Not in our lovely little town.'

'Hard to believe, isn't it? Folks actually gossip around here.'

'I've kept them busy for twenty years.'

'Indeed you have.'

They were shoulder to shoulder, both holding empty glasses. 'So what's in the estate?' Forrest finally asked.

'You want to see the will?'

'No, just tell me.'

'He listed his assets – the house, furniture, car, books, six thousand dollars in the bank.'

'Is that all?'

'That's all he mentioned,' Ray said, avoiding the lie.

'Surely, there's more money than that around here,' Forrest said, ready to start looking.

'I guess he gave it all away,' Ray said calmly.

'What about his state retirement?'

'He cashed out when he lost the election, a huge blunder. Cost him tens of thousands of dollars. I'm assuming he gave everything else away.'

'You're not going to screw me, are you, Ray?'

'Come on, Forrest, there's nothing to fight over.'

'Any debts?'

'He said he had none.'

'Nothing else?'

'You can read the will if you want.'

'Not now.'

'He signed it yesterday.'

'You think he planned everything?'

'Sure looks like it.'

A black hearse from Magargel's Funeral Home rolled to a stop in front of Maple Run, then turned slowly into the drive.

Forrest leaned forward, elbows on knees, face in hand, and began crying.

Chapter 7

Behind the hearse was the county coroner,
Thurber Foreman, in the same red Dodge
pickup he'd been driving since Ray was in
college, and behind Thurber was Reverend Silas
Palmer of the First Presbyterian Church, an
ageless little Scot who'd baptized both Atlee
sons. Forrest slipped away and hid in the
backyard while Ray met the party on the front
porch. Sympathies were exchanged. Mr. B. J.
Magargel from the funeral home and Reverend
Palmer appeared to be near tears. Thurber had
seen countless dead bodies. He had no financial
interest in this one, however, and appeared to be
indifferent, at least for the moment.

Ray led them to the study where they respect-
fully viewed Judge Atlee long enough for
Thurber to officially decide he was dead. He did
this without words, but simply nodded at Mr.
Magargel with a somber, bureaucratic dip of the
chin that said, 'He's dead. You can take him

61

now.' Mr. Magargel nodded, too, thus completing a silent ritual they'd gone through many times together.

Thurber produced a single sheet of paper and asked the basics. The Judge's full name, date of birth, place of birth, next of kin. For the second time, Ray said no to an autopsy.

Ray and Reverend Palmer stepped away and took a seat at the dining room table. The minister was much more emotional than the son. He adored the Judge and claimed him as a close friend.

A service befitting a man of Reuben Atlee's stature would draw many friends and admirers and should be well planned. 'Reuben and I talked about it not long ago,' Palmer said, his voice low and raspy, ready to choke up at any moment.

'That's good,' Ray said.

'He picked out the hymns and scriptures, and he made a list of the pallbearers.'

Ray hadn't yet thought of such details. Perhaps they would've come to mind had he not stumbled upon a couple of million in cash. His overworked brain listened to Palmer and caught most of his words, then it would switch to the broom closet and start swirling again. He was suddenly nervous that Thurber and Magargel were alone with the Judge in the study. Relax, he kept telling himself.

'Thank you,' he said, genuinely relieved that

the details had been taken care of. Mr. Magargel's assistant rolled a gurney through the front door, through the foyer, and struggled to get it turned into the Judge's study.

'And he wanted a wake,' the reverend said. Wakes were traditional, a necessary prelude to a proper burial, especially among the older folks.

Ray nodded.

'Here in the house.'

'No,' Ray said instantly. 'Not here.'

As soon as he was alone, he wanted to inspect every inch of the house in search of more loot. And he was very concerned with the stash already in the broom closet. How much was there? How long would it take to count it? Was it real or counterfeit? Where did it come from? What to do with it? Where to take it? Who to tell? He needed time alone to think, to sort things out and develop a plan.

'Your father was very plain about this,' Palmer said.

'I'm sorry, Reverend. We will have a wake, but not here.'

'May I ask why not?'

'My mother.'

He smiled and nodded and said, 'I remember your mother.'

'They laid her on the table over there in the front parlor, and for two days the entire town paraded by. My brother and I hid upstairs and cursed my father for such a spectacle.' Ray's voice was firm, his eyes hot. 'We will not have a wake in this house, Reverend.'

Ray was utterly sincere. He was also concerned about securing the premises. A wake would require a thorough scouring of the house by a cleaning service, and the preparation of food by a caterer, and flowers hauled in by a florist. And all of this activity would begin in the morning.

'I understand,' the reverend said.

The assistant backed out first, pulling the gurney, which was being pushed gently by Mr. Magargel. The Judge was covered from head to foot by a starched white sheet that was tucked neatly under him. With Thurber following behind, they rolled him out, across the front porch and down the steps, the last Atlee to live at Maple Run.

Half an hour later, Forrest materialized from somewhere in the back of the house. He was holding a tall clear glass that was filled with a suspicious-looking brown liquid, and it wasn't ice tea. 'They gone?' he asked, looking at the driveway.

'Yes,' Ray said. He was sitting on the front steps, smoking a cigar. When Forrest sat down next to him, the aroma of sour mash followed quickly.

'Where'd you find that?' Ray asked.

'He had a hiding place in his bathroom. Want some?'

'No. How long have you known that?'

'Thirty years.'

A dozen lectures leapt forward, but Ray fought them off. They'd been delivered many times before, and evidently they had failed because here was Forrest sipping bourbon after 141 days of sobriety.

'How's Ellie?' Ray asked after a long puff.

'Crazy as hell, the same.'

'Will I see her at the funeral?'

'No, she's up to three hundred pounds. One-fifty is her limit. Under one-fifty and she'll leave the house. Over one-fifty, and she locks herself up.'

'When was she under one-fifty?'

'Three or four years ago. She found some wacko doctor who gave her pills. Got all the way down to a hundred pounds. Doctor went to jail and she gained another two hundred. Three hundred is her max, though. She weighs every day and freaks out if the big needle goes beyond three.'

'I told Reverend Palmer that we would have a wake, but not here, not in the house.'

'You're the executor.'

'You agree?'

'Sure.'

A long pull on the bourbon, another long puff on the cigar.

'What about that hosebag who ditched you? What's her name?'

'Vicki.'

65

'Yeah, Vicki, I hated that bitch even at your wedding.'

'I wish I had.'

'She still around?'

'Yep, saw her last week, at the airport, getting off her private jet.'

'She married that old fart, right, some crook from Wall Street?'

'That's him. Let's talk about something else.'

'You brought up women.'

'Always a big mistake.'

Forrest slugged another drink, then said, 'Let's talk about money. Where is it?'

Ray flinched slightly and his heart stopped, but Forrest was gazing at the front lawn and didn't notice. What money are you talking about, dear brother? 'He gave it away.'

'But why?'

'It was his money, not ours.'

'Why not leave some for us?'

Not too many years earlier, the Judge had confided to Ray that over a fifteen-year period he had spent more than ninety thousand dollars on legal fees, court fines, and rehab for Forrest. He could leave the money for Forrest to drink and snort, or he could give it away to charities and needy families during his lifetime. Ray had a profession and could take care of himself.

'He left us the house,' Ray said.

'What happens to it?'

'We'll sell it if you want. The money goes in a

pot with everything else. Fifty percent will go for estate taxes. Probate will take a year.'

'Gimme the bottom line.'

'We'll be lucky to split fifty thousand a year from now.'

Of course there were other assets. The loot was sitting innocently in the broom closet, but Ray needed time to evaluate it. Was it dirty money? Should it be included in the estate? If so, it would cause terrible problems. First, it would have to be explained. Second, at least half would get burned in taxes. Third, Forrest would have his pockets filled with cash and would probably kill himself with it.

'So I'll get twenty-five thousand bucks in a year?' Forrest said.

Ray couldn't tell if he was anxious or disgusted. 'Something like that.'

'Do you want the house?'

'No, do you?'

'Hell no. I'll never go back in there.'

'Come on, Forrest.'

'He kicked me out, you know, told me I'd disgraced this family long enough. Told me to never set foot on this soil again.'

'And he apologized.'

A quick sip. 'Yes, he did. But this place depresses me. You're the executor, you deal with it. Just mail me a check when probate is over.'

'We should at least go through his things together.'

'I'm not touching them,' he said and got to his

feet. 'I want a beer. It's been five months, and I want a beer.' He was walking toward his car as he talked. 'You want one?'

'No.'

'You wanna ride with me?'

Ray wanted to go so he could protect his brother, but he felt a stronger urge to sit tight and protect the Atlee family assets. The Judge never locked the house. Where were the keys? 'I'll wait here,' he said.

'Whatever.'

The next visitor was no surprise. Ray was in the kitchen digging through drawers, looking for keys, when he heard a loud voice bellowing at the front door. Though he hadn't heard it in years, there was no doubt it belonged to Harry Rex Vonner.

They embraced, a bear hug from Harry Rex, a retreating squeeze from Ray. 'I'm so sorry,' Harry Rex said several times. He was tall with a large chest and stomach, a big messy bear of a man who worshiped Judge Atlee and would do anything for his boys. He was a brilliant lawyer trapped in a small town, and it was to Harry Rex that Judge Atlee had always turned during Forrest's legal problems.

'When did you get here?' he asked.

'Around five. I found him in his study.'

'I've been in trial for two weeks, hadn't talked to him. Where's Forrest?'

'Gone to buy beer.'

They both digested the gravity of this. They sat in the rocking chairs near the swing. 'It's good to see you, Ray.'

'And you too, Harry Rex.'

'I can't believe he's dead.'

'Nor can I. I thought he'd always be here.'

Harry Rex wiped his eyes with the back of a sleeve. 'I'm so sorry,' he mumbled. 'I just can't believe it. I saw him two weeks ago, I guess it was. He was movin' around, sharp as a tack, in pain but not complainin'.'

'They gave him a year, and that was about twelve months ago. I thought he'd hang on, though.'

'Me too. Such a tough old fart.'

'You want some tea?'

'That'd be nice.'

Ray went to the kitchen and poured two glasses of instant ice tea. He took them back to the porch and said, 'This stuff isn't very good.'

Harry Rex took a drink and concurred. 'At least it's cold.'

'We need to have a wake, Harry Rex, and we're not doing it here. Any ideas?'

He pondered this only for a second, then leaned in with a big smile. 'Let's put him in the courthouse, first floor in the rotunda, lay him in state like a king or somethin'.'

'You're serious?'

'Why not. He'd love it. The whole town could parade by and pay their respects.'

'I like it.'

'It's brilliant, trust me. I'll talk to the sheriff and get it approved. Ever'body'll love it. When's the funeral?'

'Tuesday.'

'Then we'll have us a wake tomorrow afternoon. You want me to say a few words?'

'Of course. Why don't you just organize the whole thing?'

'Done. Y'all picked out a casket?'

'We were going in the morning'

'Do oak, forget that bronze and copper crap. We buried Momma last year in oak and it was the prettiest damned thang I'd ever seen. Magargel can get one out of Tupelo in two hours. And forget the vault, too. They're just rip-offs. Ashes to ashes, dust to dust, bury 'em and let 'em rot is the only way to go. The Episcopalians do it right.'

Ray was a little dazed by the torrent of advice, but was thankful nonetheless. The Judge's will had not mentioned the casket but had specifically requested a vault. And he wanted a nice headstone. He was, after all, an Atlee, and he was to be buried among the other great ones.

If anyone knew anything about the Judge's business, it was Harry Rex. As they watched the shadows fall across the long front lawn of Maple Run, Ray said, as nonchalantly as possible, 'Looks like he gave all his money away.'

'I'm not surprised. Are you?'

'No.'

'There'll be a thousand folks at his funeral

70

who were touched by his generosity. Crippled children, sick folks with no insurance, black kids he sent to college, every volunteer fire department, civic club, all-star team, school group headed for Europe. Our church sent some doctors to Haiti and the Judge gave us a thousand bucks.'

'When did you start going to church?'

'Two years ago.'

'Why?'

'Got a new wife.'

'How many is that?'

'Four. I really like this one, though.'

'Lucky for her.'

'She's very lucky.'

'I like this courthouse wake, Harry Rex. All those folks you just mentioned can pay their respects in public. Plenty of parking, don't have to worry about seating.'

'It's brilliant.'

Forrest wheeled into the drive and slammed on his brakes, stopping inches behind Harry Rex's Cadillac. He crawled out and lumbered toward them in the semidarkness, carrying what appeared to be a whole case of beer.

Chapter 8

When he was alone, Ray sat in the wicker chair across from the empty sofa, and tried to convince himself that life without his father would not be greatly different than life apart from him. This day was long in coming, and he would simply take it in stride and go on with a small measure of mourning. Just go through the motions, he told himself, wrap things up in Mississippi and race back to Virginia.

The study was lit by one weak bulb under the shade of a dust-covered lamp on the rolltop, and the shadows were long and dark. Tomorrow he would sit at the desk and plunge into the paperwork, but not tonight.

Tonight he needed to think.

Forrest was gone, hauled away by Harry Rex, both of them drunk. Forrest, typically, became sullen and wanted to drive to Memphis. Ray suggested he simply stay there. 'Sleep on the porch if you don't want to sleep in the house,' he said, without pushing. Pushing would only cause a fight. Harry Rex said he would, under normal circumstances, invite Forrest to stay with him, but the new wife was a hard-ass and two drunks were probably too much.

'Just stay here,' Harry Rex said, but Forrest wouldn't budge. Bullheaded enough when he was cold sober, he was intractable after a few drinks. Ray had seen it more times than he cared to remember and sat quietly as Harry Rex argued with his brother.

The issue was settled when Forrest decided he would rent a room at the Deep Rock Motel north of town. 'I used to go there when I was seeing the mayor's wife, fifteen years ago,' he said.

'It's full of fleas,' Harry Rex said.

'I miss it already.'

'The mayor's wife?' Ray asked.

'You don't want to know,' Harry Rex said.

They left a few minutes after eleven, and the house had been growing quieter by the minute.

The front door had a latch and the patio door had a deadbolt. The kitchen door, the only one at the rear of the house, had a flimsy knob with a lock that was not working. The Judge could not operate a screwdriver and Ray had inherited this lack of mechanical skill. Every window had been closed and latched, and he was certain that the Atlee mansion had not been this secure in decades. If necessary, he would sleep in the kitchen where he could guard the broom closet.

He tried not to think about the money. Sitting

in his father's sanctuary, he mentally worked on an unofficial obituary.

Judge Atlee was elected to the bench of the 25th Chancery District in 1959 and was reelected by a landslide every four years until 1991. Thirty-two years of diligent service. As a jurist, his record was impeccable. Rarely did the Appellate Court reverse one of his decisions. Often he was asked by his colleagues to hear untouchable cases in their districts. He was a guest lecturer at the Ole Miss Law School. He wrote hundreds of articles on practice, procedure, and trends. Twice he turned down appointments to the Mississippi Supreme Court; he simply didn't want to leave the trial bench.

When he wasn't wearing a robe, Judge Atlee kept his finger in all local matters – politics, civic work, schools, and churches. Few things in Ford County were approved without his endorsement, and few things he opposed were ever attempted. At various times he served on every local board, council, conference, and ad hoc committee. He quietly selected candidates for local offices and he quietly helped defeat the ones who didn't get his blessing.

In his spare time, what little of it there had been, he studied history and the Bible and wrote articles on the law. Never once had he thrown a baseball with his sons, never once had he taken them fishing.

He was preceded in death by his wife, Margaret, who died suddenly of an aneurysm in 1969. He was survived by two sons.

And somewhere along the way he managed to siphon off a fortune in cash.

Maybe the mystery of the money would be solved over there on the desk, somewhere in the stacks of papers or perhaps hidden in the drawers. Surely his father had left a clue, if not an outright explanation. There had to be a trail. Ray couldn't think of a single person in Ford County with a net worth of two million dollars, and to hold that much in cash was unthinkable.

He needed to count it. He'd checked on it twice during the evening. Just counting the twenty-seven Blake & Son's boxes had made him anxious. He would wait until early morning, when there was plenty of light and before the town began moving. He'd cover the kitchen windows and take one box at a time.

Just before midnight, Ray found a small mattress in a downstairs bedroom and dragged it into the dining room, to a spot twenty feet from the broom closet, where he could see the front drive and the house next door. Upstairs he found the Judge's .38-caliber Smith & Wesson in the drawer of his night table. With a pillow that smelled of mildew and a wool blanket that smelled of mold, he tried in vain to sleep.

The rattling noise came from the other side of the house. It was a window, though it took Ray minutes to wake up, clear his head, realize where he was and what he was hearing. A pecking sound, then a more violent shaking, then silence. A long pause as he poised himself on the mattress and gripped the .38. The house was much darker than he wanted because almost all the lightbulbs had burned out and the Judge had been too cheap to replace them.

Too cheap. Twenty-seven boxes of cash.

Put lightbulbs on the list, first thing in the morning.

There was the noise again, too firm and too rapid to be leaves or limbs brushing in the wind. Tap, tap, tap, then a hard push or shove as someone tried again to pry it open.

There were two cars in the drive – Ray's and Forrest's. Any fool could see the house had people in it, so whoever this fool was he didn't care. He probably had a gun, too, and he certainly knew how to handle it better than Ray.

Ray slid across the foyer on his stomach, wiggling like a crab and breathing like a sprinter. He stopped in the dark hallway and listened to the silence. Lovely silence. Just go away, he kept saying to himself. Please go away.

Tap, tap, tap, and he was sliding again toward the rear bedroom with the pistol aimed in front of him. Was it loaded? he asked himself, much too late. Surely the Judge kept his bedside gun loaded. The noise was louder and coming from a small bedroom they had once used for guests, but for decades now it had been collecting boxes

76

of junk. He slowly nudged the door open with his head and saw nothing but cardboard boxes. The door swung wider and hit a floor lamp, which pitched forward and crashed near the first of three dark windows.

Ray almost began firing, but he held his ammo, and his breath. He lay still on the sagging wooden floor for what seemed like an hour, sweating, listening, swatting spiders, hearing nothing. The shadows rose and fell. A light wind was hitting every branch out there, and somewhere up near the roof a limb was gently rubbing the house.

It was the wind after all. The wind and the old ghosts of Maple Run, a place of many spirits, according to his mother, because it was an old house where dozens had died. They had buried slaves in the basement, she said, and their ghosts grew restless and roamed about.

The Judge hated ghost stories and refuted them all.

When Ray finally sat up, his elbows and knees were numb. With time he stood and leaned on the door frame, watching the three windows with his gun ready. If there had actually been an intruder, the noise evidently spooked him. But the longer Ray stood there the more he convinced himself that the racket had been nothing but the wind.

Forrest had the better idea. As grungy as the Deep Rock was, it had to be more restful than this place.

77

Tap, tap, tap, and he hit the floor again, stricken with fear once more, except this was worse because the noise came from the kitchen. He made the tactical decision to crawl instead of slide, and by the time he got back to the foyer his knees were screaming. He stopped at the French doors that led to the dining room and waited. The floor was dark but a faint porch light slanted feebly through the blinds and shone along the upper walls and ceiling.

Not for the first time, he asked himself what, exactly, was he, a professor of law at a prestigious university, doing hiding in the darkness of his childhood home, armed, frightened out of his mind, ready to jump out of his skin, and all because he wanted desperately to protect a mysterious hoard of cash he had stumbled upon. 'Answer that one,' he mumbled to himself.

The kitchen door opened onto a small wooden deck. Someone was shuffling around out there, just beyond the door, footsteps on boards. Then the doorknob rattled, the flimsy one with the malfunctioning lock. Whoever he was, he had made the bold decision to walk straight through the door instead of sneaking through a window.

Ray was an Atlee, and this was his soil. This was also Mississippi, where guns were expected to be used for protection. No court in the state would frown on drastic action in this situation. He crouched beside the kitchen table, took aim at a spot high in the window above the sink, and began squeezing the trigger. One loud gunshot, cracking through the darkness, coming from inside and shattering a window, would no doubt terrify any burglar.

Just as the door rattled again, he squeezed harder, the hammer clicked, and nothing happened. The gun had no bullets. The chamber spun, he squeezed again, and there was no discharge. In a panic, Ray grabbed the empty pitcher of tea on the counter and hurled it at the door. To his great relief, it made more noise than any bullet could possibly have done. Scared out of his wits, he hit a light switch and went charging to the door, brandishing the gun and yelling, 'Get the hell outta here!' When he yanked it open and saw no one, he exhaled mightily and began breathing again.

For half an hour he swept glass, making as much noise as possible.

The cop's name was Andy, nephew of a guy Ray finished high school with. That relationship was established within the first thirty seconds of his arrival, and once they were linked they talked about football while the exterior of Maple Run was inspected. No sign of entry at any of the downstairs windows. Nothing at the kitchen door but broken glass. Upstairs, Ray looked for bullets while Andy went from room to room. Both searches produced nothing. Ray brewed coffee and they drank it on the porch, chatting quietly in the early morning hours. Andy was the only cop protecting Clanton at that time, and he confessed he wasn't really needed. 'Nothin' ever happens this early Monday morning,' he said. 'Folks are asleep, gettin' ready for work.' With a little prodding, he reviewed the crime scene in Ford County – stolen pickups, fights at the honky-tonks, drug activity in Lowtown, the colored section. Hadn't had a murder in four years, he said proudly. A branch bank got robbed two years ago. He prattled on and took a second cup. Ray would keep pouring it, and brewing it if necessary, until sunrise. He was comforted by the presence of a well-marked patrol car sitting out front.

Andy left at three-thirty. For an hour Ray lay on the mattress, staring holes in the ceiling, holding a gun that was useless. He fought sleep by plotting strategies to protect the money. Not investment schemes, those could wait. More pressing was a plan to get the money out of the broom closet, out of the house, and into a safe place somewhere. Would he be forced to haul it to Virginia? He certainly couldn't leave it in Clanton, could he? And when could he count it?

At some point, fatigue and the emotional drain of the day overcame him, and he drifted away. The tapping came back, but he did not hear it. The kitchen door, now secured by a jammed chair and a piece of rope, was rattled and pushed, but Ray slept through it all.

Chapter 9

At seven-thirty, sunlight woke him. The money was still there, untouched. The doors and windows had not been opened, as far as he could tell. He fixed a pot of coffee, and as he drank the first cup at the kitchen table he made an important decision. If someone was after the money, then he could not leave it, not for a moment.

But the twenty-seven Blake & Son boxes would not fit in the small trunk of his little Audi roadster.

The phone rang at eight. It was Harry Rex, reporting that Forrest had been delivered to the Deep Rock Motel, that the county would allow a ceremony in the rotunda of the courthouse that afternoon at four-thirty, that he had already lined up a soprano and a color guard. And he was working on a eulogy for his beloved friend.

'What about the casket?' he asked.

'We're meeting with Magargel at ten,' Ray answered.

'Good. Remember, go with the oak. The Judge would like that.'

They talked about Forrest for a few minutes, the same conversation they'd had many times. When he hung up, Ray began moving quickly. He opened windows and blinds so he could see and hear any visitors. Word was spreading through the coffee shops around the square that Judge Atlee had died, and visitors were certainly possible.

The house had too many doors and windows, and he couldn't stand guard around the clock. If someone was after the money, then that someone could get it. For a few million bucks, a bullet to Ray's head would be a solid investment.

The money had to be moved.

Working in front of the broom closet, he took the first box and dumped the cash into a black plastic garbage bag. Eight more boxes followed, and when he had about a million bucks in bag number one he carried it to the kitchen door and peeked outside. The empty boxes were returned to the cabinet under the bookshelves. Two more garbage bags were filled. He backed his car close to the deck, as close to the kitchen as possible, then surveyed the landscape in search of human eyes. There were none. The only neighbors were the spinsters next door, and they couldn't see the television in their own den. Darting from the door to the car, he loaded the fortune into the trunk, shoved the bags this way and that, and when it looked as though the lid might not close he slammed it down anyway. It clicked and locked and Ray Atlee was quite relieved.

He wasn't sure how he would unload the loot in Virginia and carry it from a parking lot down the busy pedestrian mall to his apartment. He would worry about that later.

The Deep Rock had a diner, a hot cramped greasy place Ray had never visited, but it was the perfect spot to eat on the morning after Judge Atlee's death. The three coffee shops around the square would be busy with gossip and stories about the great man, and Ray preferred to stay away.

Forrest looked decent. Ray had certainly seen much him worse. He wore the same clothes and he hadn't showered, but with Forrest that was not unusual. His eyes were red but not swollen. He said he'd slept well, but needed grease. Both ordered bacon and eggs.

'You look tired,' Forrest said, gulping black coffee.

Ray indeed felt tired. 'I'm fine, couple of hours of rest and I'm ready to roll.' He glanced through the window at his Audi, which was parked as close to the diner as possible. He would sleep in the damned thing if necessary.

'It's weird,' Forrest said. 'When I'm clean, I sleep like a baby. Eight, nine hours a night, a

83

hard sleep. But when I'm not clean, I'm lucky to get five hours. And it's not a deep sleep either.'

'Just curious – when you're clean, do you think about the next round of drinking?'

'Always. It builds up, like sex. You can do without it for a while, but the pressure's building and sooner or later you gotta have some relief. Booze, sex, drugs, they all get me eventually.'

'You were clean for a hundred and forty days.'

'A hundred and forty-one.'

'What's the record?'

'Fourteen months. I came out of rehab a few years back, this great detox center that the old man paid for, and I kicked ass for a long time. Then I crashed.'

'Why? What made you crash?'

'It's always the same. When you're an addict you can lose it any time, any place, for any reason. They haven't designed a wagon that can hold me. I'm an addict, Bro, plain and simple.'

'Still drugs?'

'Sure. Last night it was booze and beer, same tonight, same tomorrow. By the end of the week I'll be doing nastier stuff.'

'Do you want to?'

'No, but I know what happens.'

The waitress brought their food. Forrest quickly buttered a biscuit and took a large bite. When he could speak he said, 'The old man's dead, Ray, can you believe it?'

84

Ray was anxious to change the subject too. If they dwelt on Forrest's shortcomings they would be fighting soon enough. 'No, I thought I was ready for it, but I wasn't.'

'When was the last time you saw him?'

'November, when he had prostate surgery. You?'

Forrest sprinkled Tabasco sauce on his scrambled eggs and pondered the question. 'When was his heart attack?'

There had been so many ailments and surgeries that they were difficult to remember. 'He had three.'

'The one in Memphis.'

'That was the second one,' Ray said. 'Four years ago.'

'That's about right. I spent some time with him at the hospital. Hell, it wasn't six blocks away. I figured it was the least I could do.'

'What did you talk about?'

'Civil War. He still thought we'd won.'

They smiled at this and ate in silence for a few moments. The silence ended when Harry Rex found them. He helped himself to a biscuit while offering the latest details of the splendid ceremony he was planning for Judge Atlee.

'Everybody wants to come out to the house,' he said with a mouthful.

'It's off limits,' Ray said.

'That's what I'm tellin' them. Y'all want to receive guests tonight?'

'No,' said Forrest.

85

'Should we?' asked Ray.

'It's the proper thing to do, either at the house or at the funeral home. But if you don't, it's no big deal. Ain't like folks'll get pissed and refuse to speak to you.'

'We're doing the courthouse wake and a funeral, isn't that enough?' Ray asked.

'I think so.'

'I'm not sittin' around a funeral home all night huggin' old ladies who've been talkin' about me for twenty years,' Forrest said. 'You can if you want, but I will not be there.'

'Let's pass on it,' Ray said.

'Spoken like a true executor,' Forrest said with a sneer.

'Executor?' said Harry Rex.

'Yes, there was a will on his desk, dated Saturday. A simple, one-page, holographic will, leaving everything to the two of us, listing his assets, naming me as the executor. And he wants you to do the probate, Harry Rex.'

Harry Rex had stopped chewing. He rubbed the bridge of his nose with a chubby finger and gazed across the diner. 'That's odd,' he said, obviously puzzled by something.

'What?'

'I did a long will for him a month ago.'

All had stopped eating. Ray and Forrest exchanged looks that conveyed nothing because neither had a clue what the other was thinking.

'I guess he changed his mind,' Harry Rex said.

'What was in the other will?' Ray asked.

'I can't tell you. He was my client, so it's confidential.'

'I'm lost here, fellas,' Forrest said. 'Forgive me for not being a lawyer.'

'The only will that matters is the last one,' said Harry Rex. 'It revokes all prior wills, so whatever the Judge put in the will I prepared is irrelevant.'

'Why can't you tell us what's in the old will?' Forrest asked.

'Because I, as a lawyer, cannot discuss a client's will.'

'But the will you prepared is no good, right?'

'Right, but I still can't talk about it.'

'That sucks,' Forrest said, and glared at Harry Rex. All three took a deep breath, then a large bite.

Ray knew in an instant that he would have to see the other will and see it soon. If it mentioned the loot hidden in the cabinet, then Harry Rex knew about it. And if he knew, then the money would quickly be removed from the trunk of the little TT convertible and repackaged in Blake & Son boxes and put back where it came from. It would then be included in the estate, which was a public record.

'Won't there be a copy of your will in his office?' Forrest asked, in the general direction of Harry Rex.

'No.'

'Are you sure?'

'I'm reasonably sure,' Harry Rex said. 'When you make a new will you physically destroy the old one. You don't want someone finding the old one and probating it. Some folks change their wills every year, and as lawyers we know to burn the old ones. The Judge was a firm believer in destroying revoked wills because he spent thirty years refereeing will contests.'

The fact that their close friend knew something about their dead father, and that he was unwilling to share it, chilled the conversation. Ray decided to wait until he was alone with Harry Rex to grill him.

'Magargel's waiting,' he said to Forrest.

'Sounds like fun.'

They rolled the handsome oak casket down the east wing of the courthouse on a funeral gurney draped with purple velvet. Mr. Magargel led while an assistant pushed. Behind the casket were Ray and Forrest, and behind them was a Boy Scout color guard with flags and pressed khaki uniforms.

Because Reuben V. Atlee had fought for his country, his casket was covered with the Stars and Stripes. And because of this a contingent of Reservists from the local armory snapped to attention when Retired Captain Atlee was stopped in the center of the courthouse rotunda. Harry Rex was waiting there, dressed in a fine black suit, standing in front of a long row of floral arrangements.

Every other lawyer in the county was present, too, and, at Harry Rex's suggestion, they were cordoned off in a special section close to the casket. All city and county officials, courthouse clerks, cops, and deputies were present, and as Harry Rex stepped forward to begin the crowd pressed closer. Above, on the second and third levels of the courthouse, another crowd leaned on the iron railings and gawked downward.

Ray wore a brand-new navy suit he'd purchased just hours earlier at Pope's, the only men's clothier in town. At $310 it was the most expensive in the store, and slashed from that hefty price was a ten percent discount that Mr. Pope insisted on giving. Forrest's new suit was dark gray. It cost $280 before the discount, and it had also been paid for by Ray. Forrest had not worn a suit in twenty years and swore he would not wear one for the funeral. Only a tongue lashing by Harry Rex got him to Pope's.

The sons stood at one end of the casket, Harry Rex at the other, and near the center of it Billy Boone, the ageless courthouse janitor, had carefully placed a portrait of Judge Atlee. It had been painted ten years earlier by a local artist, for free, and everyone knew the Judge had not been particularly fond of it. He hung it in his chambers behind his courtroom, behind a door so no one could see it. After his defeat, the county fathers placed it in the main courtroom, high above the bench.

Programs had been printed for the 'Farewell

to Judge Reuben Atlee.' Ray studied his intently because he didn't wish to look around the gathering. All eyes were on him, and Forrest. Reverend Palmer delivered a windy prayer. Ray had insisted that the ceremony be brief. There was a funeral tomorrow.

The Boy Scouts stepped forward with the flag and led the congregation in the Pledge of Allegiance, then Sister Oleda Shumpert from the Holy Ghost Church of God in Christ stepped forward and sang a mournful rendition of 'Shall We Gather at the River,' a cappella because she certainly didn't need any support. The words and melody brought tears to the eyes of many, including Forrest, who stayed close to his brother's shoulder with his chin low.

Standing next to the casket, listening to her rich voice echo upward through the rotunda, Ray for the first time felt the burden of his father's death. He thought of all the things they could have done together, now that they were men, all the things they had not done when he and Forrest were just boys. But he had lived his life and the Judge had lived his, and this had suited them both.

It wasn't fair now to relive the past just because the old man was dead. He kept telling himself this. It was only natural at death to wish he'd done more, but the truth was that the Judge had carried a grudge for years after Ray left Clanton. And, sadly, he had become a recluse since leaving the bench.

90

A moment of weakness, and Ray stiffened his back. He would not beat himself up because he had chosen a path that was not the one his father wanted.

Harry Rex began what he promised would be a brief eulogy. 'Today we gather here to say good-bye to an old friend,' he began. 'We all knew this day was coming, and we all prayed it would never get here.' He hit the highlights of the Judge's career, then told of his first appearance in front of the great man, thirty years ago, when Harry Rex was fresh out of law school. He was handling an uncontested divorce, which he somehow managed to lose.

Every lawyer had heard the story a hundred times, but they still managed a good laugh at the appropriate time. Ray glanced at them, then began studying them as a group. How could one small town have so many lawyers? He knew about half of them. Many of the old ones he'd known as a child and as a student were either dead or retired. Many of the younger ones he'd never seen before.

Of course they all knew him. He was Judge Atlee's boy.

Ray was slowly realizing that his speedy exit from Clanton after the funeral would only be temporary. He would be forced to return very soon, to make a brief court appearance with Harry Rex and begin probate, to prepare an inventory and do a half-dozen other duties as executor of his father's estate. That would be easy and routine and take just a few days. But weeks and perhaps months were looming out there as he tried to solve the mystery of the money.

Did one of those lawyers over there know something? The money had to originate from a judicial setting, didn't it? The Judge had no life outside of the law. Looking at them, though, Ray could not imagine a source rich enough to generate the kind of money now hidden in the trunk of his little car. They were small-town ham-and-egg lawyers, all scrambling to pay their bills and outhustle the guy next door. There was no real money over there. The Sullivan firm had eight or nine lawyers who represented the banks and insurance companies, and they earned just enough to hang out with the doctors at the country club.

There wasn't a lawyer in the county with serious cash. Irv Chamberlain over there with the thick eyeglasses and bad hairpiece owned thousands of acres handed down through generations, but he couldn't sell it because there were no buyers. Plus, it was rumored he was spending time at the new casinos in Tunica.

As Harry Rex droned on, Ray dwelt on the lawyers. Someone shared the secret. Someone knew about the money. Could it be a distinguished member of the Ford County bar?

Harry Rex's voice began to break, and it was time to quit. He thanked them all for coming and announced that the Judge would lie in state in the courthouse until 10 P.M. He directed the procession to begin where Ray and Forrest were standing. The crowd moved obediently to the east wing and formed a line that snaked its way outside.

For an hour, Ray was forced to smile and shake hands and graciously thank everyone for coming. He listened to dozens of brief stories about his father and the lives the great man had touched. He pretended to remember the names of all those who knew him. He hugged old ladies he'd never met before. The procession moved slowly by Ray and Forrest, then to the casket, where each person would stop and gaze forlornly at the Judge's bad portrait, then to the west wing where registers were waiting. Harry Rex moved about, working the crowd like a politician.

At some point during the ordeal, Forrest disappeared. He mumbled something to Harry Rex about going home, to Memphis, and something about being tired of death.

Finally, Harry Rex whispered to Ray, 'There's a line around the courthouse. You could be here all night.'

'Get me out of here,' Ray whispered back.

'You need to go to the rest room?' Harry Rex asked, just loud enough for those next in line to hear.

'Yes,' Ray said, already stepping away. They eased back, whispering importantly, and ducked into a narrow hallway. Seconds later they emerged behind the courthouse.

They drove away, in Ray's car of course, first circling the square and taking in the scene. The flag in front of the courthouse was at half-mast. A large crowd waited patiently to pay their respects to the Judge.

Chapter 10

Twenty-four hours in Clanton, and Ray was desperate to leave. After the wake, he ate dinner with Harry Rex at Claude's, the black diner on the south side of the square where the Monday special was barbecued chicken and baked beans so spicy they served ice tea by the half-gallon. Harry Rex was reveling in the success of his grand send-off for the Judge and after dinner was anxious to return to the courthouse and monitor the rest of the wake.

Forrest had evidently left town for the evening Ray hoped he was in Memphis, at home with Ellie, behaving himself, but he knew better. How many times could he crash before he died? Harry Rex said there was a fifty-fifty chance Forrest would make it to the funeral tomorrow.

When Ray was alone he drove away, out of Clanton, headed west to no place in particular. There were new casinos along the river, seventy miles away, and with each trip back to Missis-sippi he heard more talk and gossip about the state's newest industry. Legalized gambling had arrived in the state with the lowest per capita income in the country.

An hour and a half from Clanton, he stopped for gas and as he pumped it he noticed a new motel across the highway. Everything was new in what had recently been cotton fields. New roads, new motels, fast-food restaurants, gas stations, billboards, all spillover from the casinos a mile away.

The motel had rooms on two levels, with doors that opened to face the parking lot. It appeared to be a slow night. He paid $39.99 for a double on the ground level, around back where there were no other cars or trucks. He parked the Audi as close as possible to his room, and within seconds had the three garbage bags inside.

The money covered one bed. He did not stop to admire it because he was convinced it was dirty. And it was probably marked in some way. Maybe it was counterfeit. Whatever it was, it was not his to keep.

All the bills were one-hundred-dollar notes, some brand new and never used, others passed around a little. None were worn badly, and none were dated before 1986 or after 1994. About half were banded together in two-thousand-dollar stacks, and Ray counted those first – one hundred thousand dollars in one-hundred-dollar bills was about fifteen inches high. He counted the money from one bed, then arranged

96

it on the other in neat rows and sections. He was very deliberate, time was of no concern. As he touched the money, he rubbed it between his forefingers and thumbs and even smelled it to see if it was counterfeit. It certainly appeared to be real.

Thirty-one sections, plus a few leftovers – $3,118,000 to be exact. Retrieved like buried treasure from the crumbling home of a man who had earned less than half that during his lifetime.

It was impossible not to admire the fortune spread before him. How many times in his life would he gaze upon three million bucks? How many others ever got the chance? Ray sat in a chair with his face in his hands, staring at the tidy rows of cash, dizzy with thoughts of where it came from and where it was headed.

A slamming car door somewhere outside jolted him back. This would be an excellent place to get robbed. When you travel around with millions in cash everybody becomes a potential thief.

He rebagged it, stuffed it back into the trunk of his car, and drove to the nearest casino.

His involvement with gambling was limited to a weekend junket to Atlantic City with two other law professors, both of whom had read a book on successful crap shooting and were convinced they could beat the house. They did not. Ray had rarely played cards. He found a home at the five-dollar blackjack table, and after two miserable days in a noisy dungeon he cleared sixty dollars and vowed not to return. His colleagues' losses were never nailed down, but he learned that those who gamble quite often lie about their success.

For a Monday night, there was a respectable crowd at the Santa Fe Club, a hastily built box the size of a football field. A ten-floor tower attached to it housed the guests, mostly retirees from up North who had never dreamed of setting foot in Mississippi but were now lured by unlimited slots and free gin while they gambled.

In his pocket he had five bills taken from five different sections of the loot he'd counted in the motel room. He walked to an empty blackjack table where the dealer was half-asleep and placed the first bill on the table. 'Play it,' he said.

'Playing a hundred,' the dealer said over her shoulder, where no one was there to hear it. She picked up the bill, rubbed it with little interest, then put it in play.

It must be real, he thought, and relaxed a little. She sees them all day long. She shuffled one deck, dealt the cards, promptly hit twenty-four, then took the bill from Judge Atlee's buried treasure and put down two black chips. Ray played them both, two hundred dollars a bet, nerves of steel. She dealt the cards quickly, and with fifteen showing she hit a nine. Ray now had four black chips. In less than a minute he'd won three hundred dollars.

Rattling the four black chips in his pocket, he strolled through the casino, first through the slots where the crowd was older and subdued, almost brain-dead as they sat on their stools, pulling the arm down again and again, staring sadly at the screens. At the craps table, the dice were hot and a rowdy bunch of rednecks were hollering instructions that made no sense to him. He watched for a moment, completely bewildered by the dice and the bets and the chips changing hands.

At another empty blackjack table, he tossed down the second hundred-dollar bill, more like a seasoned gambler now. The dealer pulled it close to his face, held it up to the lights, rubbed it, and took it a few steps over to the pit boss, who was immediately distrustful of it. The pit boss produced a magnifying device that he stuck in his left eye and examined the bill like a surgeon. Just as Ray was about to break and bolt through the crowd, he heard one of them say, 'It's good.' He wasn't sure which one said it because he was looking wildly around the casino for armed guards. The dealer returned to the table and placed the suspicious money in front of Ray, who said, 'Play it.' Seconds later, the queen of hearts and the king of spades were staring at Ray, and he'd won his third hand in a row.

Since the dealer was wide awake and his supervisor had done a close inspection, Ray decided to settle the matter once and for all. He pulled the other three hundred-dollar bills from his pocket and laid them on the table. The dealer inspected each carefully, then shrugged and said, 'You want change?'

'No, play them.'

'Playing three hundred cash,' the dealer said loudly, and the pit boss loomed over his shoulder.

Ray stood on a ten and a six. The dealer hit on a ten and a four, and when he turned over the jack of diamonds, Ray won his fourth straight hand. The cash disappeared and was replaced with six black chips. Ray now had ten, a thousand dollars, and he also had the knowledge that the other thirty thousand bills stuffed into the back of his car were not counterfeit. He left one chip for the dealer and went to find a beer.

The sports bar was elevated a few feet, so that if you wanted you could have a drink and take in all the action on the floor. Or you could watch pro baseball or NASCAR reruns or bowling on any of the dozen screens. But you couldn't gamble on the games; it wasn't allowed yet.

He was aware of the risks the casino posed. Now that the money was real, the next question was whether it was marked in some way. The suspicions of the second dealer and his supervisor would probably be enough to get the bills examined by the boys upstairs. They had Ray on video, he was certain, same as everybody else. Casino surveillance was extensive; he knew that

from his two bright pals who'd planneu
the bank at the craps table.

If the money set off alarms, they could easily
find him. Couldn't they?

But where else could he get the money
examined? Walk in the First National in Clanton and hand the teller a few of the bills? 'Mind
taking a look at these, Mrs. Dempsey, see if
they're real or not?' No teller in Clanton had
ever seen counterfeit money, and by lunch the
entire town would know Judge Atlee's boy was
sneaking around with a pocketful of suspicious
money.

He'd thought of waiting until he was back in
Virginia. He would go to his lawyer who could
find an expert to examine a sample of the
money, all nice and confidential. But he
couldn't wait that long. If the money was fake,
he'd burn it. Otherwise, he wasn't sure what to
do with it.

He drank his beer slowly, giving them time to
send down a couple of goons in dark suits who
would walk up and say, 'Gotta minute?' They
couldn't work that fast, and Ray knew it. If the
money was marked, it would take days to link it
to wherever it came from.

Suppose he got caught with marked money.
What was his crime? He had taken it from his
deceased father's house, a place that had been
willed to him and his brother. He was the
executor of the estate, soon to be charged with
the responsibility of protecting its assets. He had

months to report it to both the probate court and the tax authorities. If the Judge had somehow accumulated the money by illegal means, then sorry, he's dead now. Ray had done nothing wrong, at least for the moment.

He took his winnings back to the first blackjack table and placed a five-hundred-dollar bet. The dealer got the attention of her supervisor, who ambled over with his knuckles to his mouth and one finger tapping an ear, smugly, as if five hundred dollars on one hand of blackjack happened all the time at the Santa Fe Club. He was dealt an ace and a king, and the dealer slid over seven hundred fifty dollars.

'Would you like something to drink?' asked the pit boss, all smiles and bad teeth.

'Beck's beer,' Ray said, and a cocktail waitress appeared from nowhere.

He bet a hundred dollars on the next hand and lost. Then quickly he slid three chips out for the next hand, which he won. He won eight of the next ten hands, alternating his bets from a hundred to five hundred dollars as if he knew precisely what he was doing. The pit boss lingered behind the dealer. They had a potential card counter on their hands, a professional blackjack player, one to be watched and filmed. The other casinos would be notified.

If they only knew.

He lost consecutive bets of two hundred dollars, then just for the hell of it pushed ten chips out for a bold and reckless wager of a thousand dollars. He had another three million in the trunk. This was chicken feed. When two queens landed next to his chips, he kept a perfect poker face as if he'd been winning like this for years.

'Would you like dinner, sir?' the pit boss asked.

'No,' Ray said.

'Can we get anything for you?'

'A room would be nice.'

'King or a suite?'

A jerk would've said, 'A suite, of course,' but Ray caught himself. 'Any room will be fine,' he said. He'd had no plans to stay there, but after two beers he thought it best not to drive. What if he got stopped by a rural deputy? And what would the deputy do if he searched the trunk?

'No problem, sir,' said the pit boss. 'I'll get you checked in.'

For the next hour he broke even. The cocktail waitress stopped by every five minutes, pushing beverages, trying to loosen him up, but Ray nursed the first beer. During a shuffle, he counted thirty-nine black chips.

At midnight he began yawning, and he remembered how little he'd slept the night before. The room key was in his pocket. The table had a thousand-dollar limit per hand; otherwise he would've played it all at one time and gone down in a blaze of glory. He placed ten black chips in the circle and with an audience hit blackjack. Another ten chips, and the dealer blew it with twenty-two. He gathered his chips, left four for the dealer, and went to the cashier. He'd been in the casino for three hours.

From his fifth-floor room he could see the parking lot, and because his sports car was within view he felt compelled to watch it. As tired as he was, he could not fall asleep. He pulled a chair to the window and tried to doze, but couldn't stop thinking.

Had the Judge discovered the casinos? Could gambling be the source of his fortune, a lucrative little vice that he'd kept to himself?

The more Ray told himself that the idea was too far-fetched, the more convinced he became that he'd found the source of the money. To his knowledge, the Judge had never played the stock market, and if he had, if he'd been another Warren Buffett, why would he take his profits in cash and hide it under the bookshelves? Plus, the paperwork would be thick.

If he'd lived the double life of a judge on the take, there wasn't three million dollars to steal on the court dockets in rural Mississippi. And taking bribes would involve too many other people.

It had to be gambling. It was a cash business. Ray had just won six thousand dollars in one night. Sure it was blind luck, but wasn't all gaming? Perhaps the old man had a knack for cards or dice. Maybe he hit one of the big jackpots in the slot machines. He lived alone and answered to no one.

He could've pulled it off.

But three million dollars over seven years?

Didn't the casinos require paperwork for substantial winnings? Tax forms and such?

And why hide it? Why not give it away like the rest of his money?

Shortly after three, Ray gave it up and left his complimentary room. He slept in his car until sunrise.

Chapter 11

The front door was slightly cracked, and at eight o'clock in the morning with no one living there it was indeed an ominous sign. Ray stared at it for a long minute, not certain if he wanted to step inside but knowing he had no choice. He shoved it wider, clenched his fists as if the thief just might still be in there, and took a very deep breath. It swung open, creaking every inch of the way, and when the light fell upon the stacks of boxes in the foyer Ray saw muddy footprints on the floor. The assailant had entered from the rear lawn where there was mud and for some reason had chosen to leave through the front door.

Ray slowly removed the pistol from his pocket.

The twenty-seven green Blake & Son boxes were scattered around the Judge's study. The sofa was overturned. The doors to the cabinet below the bookshelves were open. The rolltop appeared to be unmolested but the papers from the desk were scattered on the floor.

The intruder had removed the boxes, opened them, and finding them empty, had evidently stomped them and thrown them in a fit of rage. As still as things were, Ray felt the violence and it made him weak.

The money could get him killed.

When he was able to move he fixed the sofa and picked up the papers. He was gathering boxes when he heard something on the front porch. He peeked through the window and saw an old woman tapping on the front door.

Claudia Gates had known the Judge like no one else. She had been his court reporter, secretary, driver, and many other things, according to gossip that had been around since Ray was a small boy. For almost thirty years, she and the Judge had traveled the six counties of the 25th District together, often leaving Clanton at seven in the morning and returning long after dark. When they were not in court, they shared the Judge's office in the courthouse, where she typed the transcripts while he did his paperwork.

A lawyer named Turley had once caught them in a compromising position during lunch at the office, and he made the awful mistake of telling others about it. He lost every case in Chancery Court for a year and couldn't buy a client. It took four years for Judge Atlee to get him disbarred.

'Hello, Ray,' she said through the screen. 'May I come in?'

'Sure,' he said, and opened the door wider.

Ray and Claudia had never liked each other. He had always felt that she was getting the attention and affection that he and Forrest were not, and she viewed him as a threat as well. When it came to Judge Atlee, she viewed everyone as a threat.

She had few friends and even fewer admirers. She was rude and callous because she spent her life listening to trials. And she was arrogant because she whispered to the great man.

'I'm very sorry,' she said.

'So am I.'

As they walked by the study, Ray pulled the door closed and said, 'Don't go in there.' Claudia did not notice the intruder's footprints.

'Be nice to me, Ray,' she said.

'Why?'

They went to the kitchen, where he put up some coffee and they sat across from each other. 'Can I smoke?' she asked.

'I don't care,' he said. Smoke till you choke, old gal. His father's black suits had always carried the acrid smell of her cigarettes. He'd allowed her to smoke in the car, in chambers, in his office, probably in bed. Everywhere but the courtroom.

The raspy breath, the gravelly voice, the countless wrinkles clustered around the eyes, ah, the joys of tobacco.

She'd been crying, which was not an insignificant event in her life. When he was clerking for his father one summer, Ray had had the misfortune of sitting through a gut-wrenching child abuse case. The testimony had been so sad and pitiful that everyone, including the Judge and all the lawyers, were moved to tears. The only dry eyes in the courtroom belonged to old stone-faced Claudia.

'I can't believe he's dead,' she said, then blew a puff of smoke toward the ceiling.

'He's been dying for five years, Claudia. This is no surprise.'

'It's still sad.'

'It's very sad, but he was suffering at the end. Death was a blessing.'

'He wouldn't let me come see him.'

'We're not rehashing history, okay?'

The history, depending on which version you believed, had kept Clanton buzzing for almost two decades. A few years after Ray's mother died, Claudia divorced her husband for reasons that were never clear. One side of town believed the Judge had promised to marry her after her divorce. The other side of town believed the Judge, forever an Atlee, never intended to marry such a commoner as Claudia, and that she got a divorce because her husband caught her fooling around with yet another man. Years passed with the two enjoying the benefits of married life, except for the paperwork and actual cohabitation. She continued to press the Judge to get married, he continued to postpone things. Evidently, he was getting what he wanted.

Finally she put forth an ultimatum, which proved to be a bad strategy. Ultimatums did not impress Reuben Atlee. The year before he got booted from office, Claudia married a man nine years younger. The Judge promptly fired her, and the coffee shops and knitting clubs talked of nothing else. After a few rocky years, her younger man died. She was lonely, so was the Judge. But she had betrayed him by remarrying, and he never forgave her.

'Where's Forrest?' she asked.

'He should be here soon.'

'How is he?'

'He's Forrest.'

'Do you want me to leave?'

'It's up to you.'

'I'd rather talk to you, Ray. I need to talk to someone.'

'Don't you have friends?'

'No. Reuben was my only friend.'

He cringed when she called him Reuben. She stuck the cigarette between her gluey red lips, a pale red for mourning, not the bright red she was once known for. She was at least seventy, but wearing it well. Still straight and slim, and wearing a tight dress that no other seventy-year-old woman in Ford County would attempt. She had diamonds in her ears and one on her finger, though he couldn't tell if they were real. She was also wearing a pretty gold pendant and two gold bracelets.

She was an aging tart, but still an active volcano. He would ask Harry Rex whom she was seeing these days.

He poured more coffee and said, 'What would you like to talk about?'

'Reuben.'

'My father is dead. I don't like history.'

'Can't we be friends?'

'No. We've always despised each other. We're not going to kiss and hug now, over the casket. Why would we do that?'

'I'm an old woman, Ray.'

'And I live in Virginia. We'll get through the funeral today, then we'll never see each other again. How's that?'

She lit another one and cried some more. Ray was thinking about the mess in the study, and what he would say to Forrest if he barged in now and saw the footprints and scattered boxes. And if Forrest saw Claudia sitting at the table, he might go for her neck.

Though they had no proof, Ray and Forrest had long suspected that the Judge had paid her more than the going rate for court reporters. Something extra, in exchange for the extras she was providing. It was not difficult holding a grudge.

'I want something to remember, that's all,' she said.

'You want to remember me?'

'You are your father, Ray. I'm clinging here.'

'Are you looking for money?'

'No.'

'Are you broke?'

'I'm not set for life, no.'

'There's nothing here for you.'

'Do you have his will?'

'Yes, and your name is not mentioned.'

She cried again, and Ray began a slow burn. She got the money twenty years ago when he was waiting tables and living on peanut butter and trying to survive another month of law school without getting evicted from his cheap apartment. She always had a new Cadillac when he and Forrest were driving wrecks. They were expected to live like impoverished gentry while she had the wardrobe and the jewelry.

'He always promised to take care of me,' she said.

'He broke it off years ago, Claudia. Give it up.'

'I can't. I loved him too much.'

'It was sex and money, not love. I'd rather not talk about it.'

'What's in the estate?'

'Nothing. He gave it all away.'

'He what?'

'You heard me. You know how he loved to write checks. It got worse after you left the picture.'

112

'What about his retirement?' She wasn't crying now, this was business. Her green eyes were dry and glowing.

'He cashed in the year after he left office. It was a terrible financial blunder, but he did it without my knowledge. He was mad and half-crazy. He took the money, lived on some of it, and gave the rest to the Boy Scouts, Girl Scouts, Lions Club, Sons of the Confederacy, Committee to Preserve Historic Battlefields, you name it.'

If his father had been a crooked judge, something Ray was not willing to believe, then Claudia would know about the money. It was obvious she did not. Ray never suspected she knew, because if she had then the money would not have remained hidden in the study. Let her have a rip at three million bucks and everybody in the county would know about it. If she had a dollar, you were going to see it. As pitiful as she looked across the table, Ray suspected she had very few dollars.

'I thought your second husband had some money,' he said, with a little too much cruelty.

'So did I,' she said and managed a smile. Ray chuckled a bit. Then they both laughed, and the ice thawed dramatically. She had always been known for her bluntness.

'Never found it, huh?'

'Not a dime. He was this nice-looking guy, nine years younger, you know –'

'I remember it well. A regular scandal.'

'He was fifty-one years old, a smooth talker, had a line about making money in oil. We drilled like crazy for four years and I came up with nothing.'

Ray laughed louder. He could not, at that moment, ever remember having a talk about sex and money with a seventy-year-old woman. He got the impression she had plenty of stories. Claudia's greatest hits.

'You're looking good, Claudia, you have time for another one.'

'I'm tired, Ray. Old and tired. I'd have to train him and all. It's not worth it.'

'What happened to number two?'

'He croaked with a heart attack and I didn't even find a thousand dollars,' she said.

'The Judge left six.'

'Is that all?' she asked in disbelief.

'No stocks, no bonds, nothing but an old house and six thousand dollars in the bank.'

She lowered her eyes, shook her head, and believed everything Ray was saying. She had no clue about the cash.

'What will you do with the house?'

'Forrest wants to burn it and collect the insurance.'

'Not a bad idea.'

'We'll sell it.'

There was noise on the porch, then a knock. Reverend Palmer was there to discuss the funeral service, which would begin in two hours. Claudia hugged Ray as they walked to her car.

She hugged him again and said good-bye. 'I'm sorry I wasn't nicer to you,' she whispered as he opened her car door.

'Good-bye, Claudia. I'll see you at the church.'

'He never forgave me, Ray.'

'I forgive you.'

'Do you really?'

'Yes. You're forgiven. We're friends now.'

'Thank you so much.' She hugged him a third time and started crying. He helped her into the car, always a Cadillac. Just before she turned the ignition, she said, 'Did he ever forgive you, Ray?'

'I don't think so.'

'I don't think so either.'

'But it's not important now. Let's get him buried.'

'He could be a mean old sumbitch, couldn't he?' she said, smiling through the tears.

Ray had to laugh. His dead father's seventy-year-old former lover had just called the great man a son of a bitch.

'Yes,' he agreed. 'He certainly could be.'

Chapter 12

They rolled Judge Atlee down the center aisle in his fine oak casket and parked him at the altar in front of the pulpit where Reverend Palmer was waiting in a black robe. The casket was left unopened, much to the disappointment of the mourners, most of whom still clung to the ancient Southern ritual of viewing the deceased one last time in a strange effort to maximize the grief. 'Hell no,' Ray had said politely to Mr. Magargel when asked about opening things up. When the pieces were in place, Palmer slowly stretched out his arms, then lowered them, and the crowd sat.

In the front pew to his right was the family, the two sons. Ray wore his new suit and looked tired. Forrest wore jeans and a black suede jacket and looked remarkably sober. Behind them were Harry Rex and the other pallbearers, and behind them was a sad collection of ancient judges, not far from the casket themselves. In the front pew to his left were all sorts of dignitaries – politicians, an ex-governor, a couple of Mississippi Supreme Court justices. Clanton had never seen such power assembled at one time.

The sanctuary was packed, with folks standing along the walls under the stained-glass windows. The balcony above was full. One floor below, the auditorium had been wired for audio and more friends and admirers were down there.

Ray was impressed by the crowd. Forrest was already looking at his watch. He had arrived fifteen minutes earlier and got cursed by Harry Rex, not Ray. His new suit was dirty, he'd said, and besides Ellie had bought him the black suede jacket years ago and she thought it would do just fine for the occasion.

She, at three hundred pounds, would not leave the house, and for that Ray and Harry Rex were grateful. Somehow she'd kept him sober, but a crash was in the air. For a thousand reasons, Ray just wanted to get back to Virginia.

The reverend prayed, a short, eloquent message of thanks for the life of a great man. Then he introduced a youth choir that had won national honors at a music competition in New York. Judge Atlee had given them three thousand dollars for the trip, according to Palmer. They sang two songs Ray had never heard before, but they sang them beautifully.

The first eulogy – and there would be only two short ones per Ray's instructions – was

117

delivered by an old man who barely made it to the pulpit, but once there startled the crowd with a rich and powerful voice. He'd been in law school with the Judge a hundred years ago. He told two humorless stories and the potent voice began to fade.

The reverend read some scripture and delivered words of comfort for the loss of a loved one, even an old one who had lived a full life.

The second eulogy was given by a young black man named Nakita Poole, something of a legend in Clanton. Poole came from a rough family south of town, and had it not been for a chemistry teacher at the high school he would have dropped out in the ninth grade and become another statistic. The Judge met him during an ugly family matter in court, and he took an interest in the kid. Poole had an amazing capacity for science and math. He finished first in his class, applied to the best colleges, and was accepted everywhere. The Judge wrote powerful letters of recommendation and pulled every string he could grab. Nakita picked Yale, and its financial package covered everything but spending money. For four years Judge Atlee wrote him every week, and in each letter there was a check for twenty-five dollars.

'I wasn't the only one getting the letters or the checks,' he said to a silent crowd. 'There were many of us.'

Nakita was now a doctor and headed for Africa for two years of volunteer work. 'I'm gonna miss those letters,' he said, and every lady in the church was in tears.

The coroner, Thurber Foreman, was next. He'd been a fixture at funerals in Ford County for many years, and the Judge specifically wanted him to play his mandolin and sing 'Just a Closer Walk with Thee.' He sang it beautifully, and somehow managed to do so while weeping.

Forrest finally began wiping his eyes. Ray just stared at the casket, wondering where the cash came from. What had the old man done? What, exactly, did he think would happen to the money after he died?

When the reverend finished a very brief message, the pallbearers rolled Judge Atlee out of the sanctuary. Mr. Magargel escorted Ray and Forrest down the aisle and down the front steps to a limo waiting behind the hearse. The crowd spilled out and went to their cars for the ride to the cemetery.

Like most small towns, Clanton loved a funeral procession. All traffic stopped. Those not driving in the procession were on the sidewalks, standing sadly and gazing at the hearse and the endless parade of cars behind it. Every part-time deputy was in uniform and blocking something, a street, an alley, parking spaces.

The hearse led them around the courthouse, where the flag was at half-mast and the county employees lined the front sidewalk and lowered

119

their heads. The merchants around the square came out to bid farewell to Judge Atlee.

He was laid to rest in the Atlee plot, next to his long-forgotten wife and among the ancestors he so revered. He would be the last Atlee returned to the dust of Ford County, though no one knew it. And certainly no one cared. Ray would be cremated and his ashes scattered over the Blue Ridge Mountains. Forrest admitted he was closer to death than his older brother, but he had not nailed down his final details. The only thing for certain was that he would not be buried in Clanton. Ray was lobbying for crema-tion. Ellie liked the idea of a mausoleum. Forrest preferred not to dwell on the subject.

The mourners crowded under and around a crimson Magargel Funeral Home tent, which was much too small. It covered the grave and four rows of folding chairs. A thousand were needed.

Ray and Forrest sat with their knees almost touching the casket and listened as Reverend Palmer wrapped it all up. Sitting in a folding chair at the edge of his father's open grave, Ray found it odd the things he thought about. He wanted to go home. He missed his classroom and his students. He missed flying and the views of the Shenandoah Valley from five thousand feet. He was tired and irritable and did not want to spend the next two hours lingering in the cemetery making small talk with people who remembered when he was born.

The wife of a Pentecostal preacher had the final words. She sang 'Amazing Grace,' and for five minutes time stood still. In a beautiful soprano, her voice echoed through the gentle hills of the cemetery, comforting the dead, giving hope to the living. Even the birds stopped flying.

An Army boy with a trumpet played 'Taps,' and everybody had a good cry. They folded the flag and handed it to Forrest, who was sobbing and sweating under the damned suede jacket. As the final notes faded into the woods, Harry Rex started bawling behind them. Ray leaned forward and touched the casket. He said a silent farewell, then rested with his elbows on his knees, his face in his hands.

The burial broke up quickly. It was time for lunch. Ray figured that if he just sat there and stared at the casket, then folks would leave him alone. Forrest flung a heavy arm across his shoulders, and together they looked as though they might stay until dark. Harry Rex regained his composure and assumed the role of family spokesman. Standing outside the tent, he thanked the dignitaries for coming, complimented Palmer on a fine service, praised the preacher's wife for such a beautiful rendition, told Claudia that she could not sit with the boys, that she needed to move along, and on and on. The gravediggers waited under a nearby tree, shovels in hand.

When everybody was gone, including Mr.

Magargel and his crew, Harry Rex fell into the chair on the other side of Forrest and for a long time the three of them sat there, staring, not wanting to leave. The only sound was that of a backhoe somewhere in the distance, waiting. But Forrest and Ray didn't care. How often do you bury your father?

And how important is time to a gravedigger?

'What a great funeral,' Harry Rex finally said. He was an expert on such matters.

'He would've been proud,' said Forrest.

'He loved a good funeral,' Ray added. 'Hated weddings though.'

'I love weddings,' said Harry Rex.

'Four or five?' asked Forrest.

'Four, and counting.

A man in a city work uniform approached and quietly asked, 'Would you like for us to lower it now?'

Neither Ray nor Forrest knew how to respond. Harry Rex had no doubt. 'Yes, please,' he said. The man turned a crank under the grave apron. Very slowly, the casket began sinking. They watched it until it came to rest deep in the red soil.

The man removed the belts, the apron, and the crank, and disappeared.

'I guess it's over,' Forrest said.

Lunch was tamales and sodas at a drive-in on the edge of town, away from the crowded places where someone would undoubtedly interrupt them with a few kind words about the Judge. They sat at a wooden picnic table under a large umbrella and watched the cars go by.

'When are you heading back?' Harry Rex asked.

'First thing in the morning,' Ray answered.

'We have some work to do.'

'I know. Let's do it this afternoon.'

'What kinda work?' Forrest asked.

'Probate stuff,' Harry Rex said. 'We'll open the estate in a couple of weeks, whenever Ray can get back. We need to go through the Judge's papers now and see how much work there is.'

'Sounds like a job for the executor.'

'You can help.'

Ray was eating and thinking about his car, which was parked on a busy street near the Presbyterian church. Surely it was safe there. 'I went to a casino last night,' he announced with his mouth full.

'Which one?' asked Harry Rex.

'Santa Fe something or other, the first one I came to. You been there?'

'I've been to all of them,' he said, as if he'd never go back. With the exception of illegal narcotics, Harry Rex had explored every vice.

'Me too,' said Forrest, a man with no exceptions.

'How'd you do?' Forrest asked.

'I won a couple of thousand at blackjack. They comped me a room.'

'I paid for that damned room,' Harry Rex said. 'Probably the whole floor.'

'I love their free drinks,' said Forrest. 'Twenty bucks a pop.'

Ray swallowed hard and decided to set the bait. 'I found some matches from the Santa Fe on the old man's desk. Was he sneaking over there?'

'Sure,' said Harry Rex. 'He and I used to go once a month. He loved the dice.'

'The old man?' Forrest asked. 'Gambling?'

'Yep.'

'So there's the rest of my inheritance. What he didn't give away, he gambled away.'

'No, he was actually a pretty good player.'

Ray pretended to be as shocked as Forrest, but he was relieved to pick up his first clue, slight as it was. It seemed almost impossible that the Judge could've amassed such a fortune shooting craps once a week.

He and Harry Rex would pursue it later.

Chapter 13

As he approached the end, the Judge had been diligent in organizing his affairs. The important records were in his study and easily found.

They went through his mahogany desk first. One drawer had ten years' worth of bank statements, all arranged nearly in chronological order. His tax returns were in another. There were thick ledger books filled with entries of the donations he'd made to everybody who'd asked. The largest drawer was filled with letter-size manila files, dozens of them. Files on property taxes, medical records, old deeds and titles, bills to pay, judicial conferences, letters from his doctors, his retirement fund. Ray flipped through the row of files without opening them, except for the bills to pay. There was one – $13.80 to Wayne's Lawnmower Repair – dated a week earlier.

'It's always weird going through the papers of someone who just died,' Harry Rex said. 'I feel dirty, like a peeping Tom.'

'More like a detective looking for clues,' Ray said. He was on one side of the desk, Harry Rex the other, their ties off and sleeves rolled up, with piles of evidence between them. Forrest was his usual helpful self. He'd drained half a six-pack for dessert after lunch, and was now snoring it off in the swing on the front porch.

But he was there, instead of lost in one of his patented binges. He had disappeared so many times over the years. If he'd blown off his father's funeral, no one in Clanton would've been surprised. Just another black mark against that crazy Atlee boy, another story to tell.

In the last drawer they found personal odds and ends – pens, pipes, pictures of the Judge with his cronies at bar conventions, a few photos of Ray and Forrest from years ago, his marriage license, and their mother's death certificate. In an old, unopened envelope there was her obituary clipped from the *Clanton Chronicle*, dated October 12, 1969, complete with a photograph. Ray read it and handed it to Harry Rex.

'Do you remember her?' Ray asked.

'Yes, I went to her funeral,' he said, looking at it. 'She was a pretty lady who didn't have many friends.'

'Why not?'

'She was from the Delta, and most of those folks have a good dose of blue blood. That's what the Judge wanted in a wife, but it didn't work too well around here. She thought she was marrying money. Judges didn't make squat back

126

then, so she had to work hard at being better than everybody else.'

'You didn't like her.'

'Not particularly. She thought I was unpolished.'

'Imagine that.'

'I loved your father, Ray, but there weren't too many tears at her funeral.'

'Let's get through one funeral at a time.'

'Sorry.'

'What was in the will you prepared for him? The last one.'

Harry Rex laid the obituary on the desk and sat back in his chair. He glanced at the window behind Ray, then spoke softly. 'The Judge wanted to set up a trust so that when this place was sold the money would go there. I'd be the trustee and as such I'd have the pleasure of doling out the money to you and him.' He nodded toward the porch. 'But his first hundred thousand would be paid back to the estate. That's how much the Judge figured Forrest owed him.'

'What a disaster.'

'I tried to talk him out of it.'

'Thank God he burned it.'

'Yes indeed. He knew it was a bad idea, but he was trying to protect Forrest from himself.'

'We've been trying for twenty years.'

'He thought of everything. He was going to leave it all to you, cut him out completely, but he knew that would only cause friction. Then he got mad because neither of you would ever live here, so he asked me to do a will that gave the house to the church. He never signed it, then Palmer pissed him off over the death penalty and he ditched that idea, said he would have it sold after his death and give the money to charity.' He stretched his arms upward until his spine popped. Harry Rex had had two back surgeries and was seldom comfortable. He continued. 'I'm guessing the reason he called you and Forrest home was so the three of you could decide what to do with the estate.'

'Then why did he do a last-minute will?'

'We'll never know, will we? Maybe he got tired of the pain. I suspect he'd grown fond of the morphine, like most folks at the end. Maybe he knew he was about to die.'

Ray looked into the eyes of General Nathan Bedford Forrest, who'd been gazing sternly on the Judge's study from the same perch for almost a century. Ray had no doubt that his father had chosen to die on the sofa so that the general could help him through it. The general knew. He knew how and when the Judge died. He knew where the cash came from. He knew who had broken in last night and trashed the office.

'Did he ever include Claudia in anything?' Ray asked.

'Never. He could hold a grudge, you know that.'

'She stopped by this morning.'

'What'd she want?'

'I think she was looking for money. She said the Judge had always promised to take care of her, and she wanted to know what was in the will.'

'Did you tell her?'

'With pleasure.'

'She'll be all right, never worry about that woman. You remember old Walter Sturgis, out from Karraway, a dirt contractor for years, tight as a tick?' Harry Rex knew everybody in the county, all thirty thousand souls – blacks, whites, and now the Mexicans.

'I don't think so.'

'He's rumored to have a half a million bucks in cash, and she's after it. Got the ole boy wearing golf shirts and eating at the country club. He told his buddies he takes Viagra every day.'

'Atta boy.'

'She'll break him.'

Forrest shifted somehow in the porch swing and the chains creaked. They waited a moment, until all was quiet out there. Harry Rex opened a file and said, 'Here's the appraisal. We had it done late last year by a guy from Tupelo, probably the best appraiser in north Mississippi.'

'How much?'

'Four hundred thousand.'

'Sold.'

'I thought he was high. Of course, the Judge thought the place was worth a million.'

'Of course.'

'I figure three hundred is more likely.'

'We won't get half that much. What's the appraisal based on?'

'It's right here. Square footage, acreage, charm, comps, the usual.'

'Give me a comp.'

Harry Rex flipped through the appraisal. 'Here's one. A house about the same age, same size, thirty acres, on the edge of Holly Springs, sold two years ago for eight hundred grand.'

'This is not Holly Springs.'

'No, it's not.'

'That's an antebellum town, with lots of old houses.'

'You want me to sue the appraiser?'

'Yeah, let's go after him. What would you give for this place?'

'Nothing. You want a beer?'

'No.'

Harry Rex lumbered into the kitchen, and returned with a tall can of Pabst Blue Ribbon. 'I don't know why he buys this stuff,' he mumbled, then gulped a fourth of it.

'Always been his brand.'

Harry Rex peeked through the blinds and saw nothing but Forrest's feet hanging off the swing. 'I don't think he's too worried about his father's estate.'

'He's like Claudia, just wants a check.'

'Money would kill him.'

It was reassuring to hear Harry Rex share this belief. Ray waited until he returned to the desk because he wanted to watch his eyes carefully. 'The Judge earned less than nine thousand dollars last year,' Ray said, looking at a tax return.

'He was sick,' Harry Rex said, stretching and twisting his substantial back, then sitting down. 'But he was hearing cases until this year.'

'What kind of cases?'

'All sorts of stuff. We had this Nazi right-wing governor a few years back –'

'I remember him.'

'Liked to pray all the time when he campaigned, family values, anti-everything but guns. Turned out he liked the ladies, his wife caught him, big stink, really juicy stuff. The local judges down in Jackson wanted no part of the case for obvious reasons, so they asked the Judge to ride in and referee things.'

'Did it go to trial?'

'Oh hell yeah, big ugly trial. The wife had the goods on the governor, who thought he could intimidate the Judge. She got the governor's house and most of the money. Last I heard he was living above his brother's garage, with bodyguards, of course.'

'Did you ever see the old man intimidated?'

'Never. Not once in thirty years.'

Harry Rex worked on his beer and Ray looked at another tax return. Things were quiet, and when he heard Forrest snore again, Ray said, 'I found some money, Harry Rex.'

His eyes conveyed nothing. No conspiracy, no surprise, no relief. They didn't blink and they didn't stare. He waited, then finally shrugged and said, 'How much?'

'A boxful.' The questions would follow, and Ray had tried to predict them.

Again Harry Rex waited, then another innocent shrug. 'Where?'

'Over there, in that cabinet behind the sofa. It was cash in a box, over ninety thousand bucks.'

So far he had not told a lie. He certainly hadn't given the entire truth, but he wasn't lying. Not yet.

'Ninety thousand bucks?' Harry Rex said, a little too loudly and Ray nodded toward the porch.

'Yes, in one-hundred-dollar bills,' he said in a lower voice. 'Any idea where it came from?'

Harry Rex gulped from the can, then squinted his eyes at the wall and finally said, 'Not really.'

'Gambling? You said he could throw the dice.'

Another sip. 'Yeah, maybe. The casinos opened six or seven years ago, and he and I would go once a week, at least in the beginning.'

'You stopped?'

'I wish. Between me and you, I was going all the time. I was gambling so much I didn't want the Judge to know it, so whenever he and I went

132

I always played it light. Next night, I'd sneak over and lose my ass again.'

'How much did you lose?'

'Let's talk about the Judge.'

'Okay, did he win?'

'Usually. On a good night he'd win a coupla thousand.'

'On a bad night?'

'Five hundred, that was his limit. If he was losin', he knew when to quit. That's the secret to gamblin', you gotta know when to quit, and you gotta have the guts to walk away. He did. I did not.'

'Did he go without you?'

'Yeah, I saw him once. I sneaked over one night and picked a new casino, hell they got fifteen now, and while I was playin' blackjack things got hot at a craps table not too far away. In the thick of things, I saw Judge Atlee. Had on a baseball cap so folks wouldn't recognize him. His disguises didn't always work because I'd hear things around town. A lot of folks go to the casinos and there were sightings.'

'How often did he go?'

'Who knows? He answered to no one. I had a client, one of those Higginbotham boys who sell used cars, and he told me he saw old Judge Atlee at the craps table at three o'clock one mornin' at Treasure Island. So I figured the Judge sneaked over at odd hours so folks wouldn't see him.'

Ray did some quick math. If the Judge gambled three times a week for five years and won two thousand dollars every time, his winnings would have been somewhere around one and a half million.

'Could he have rat-holed ninety thousand?' Ray asked. It sounded like such a small amount.

'Anything's possible, but why hide it?'

'You tell me.'

They pondered this for a while. Harry Rex finished the beer and lit a cigar. A sluggish ceiling fan above the desk pushed the smoke around. He shot a cloud of exhaust toward the fan and said, 'You gotta pay taxes on your winnings, and since he didn't want anybody to know about his gambling, maybe he just kept it all quiet.'

'But don't the casinos require paperwork if you win a certain amount?'

'I never saw any damned paperwork.'

'But if you'd won?'

'Yeah, they do. I had a client who won eleven thousand at the five-dollar slots. They gave him a form ten-ninety-nine, a notice to the IRS.'

'What about shooting craps?'

'If you cash in more than ten thousand in chips at one time, then there's paperwork. Keep it under ten, and there's nothin'. Same as cash transactions at a bank.'

'I doubt if the Judge wanted records.'

'I'm sure he did not.'

'He never mentioned any cash when y'all were doing his wills?'

'Never. The money is a secret, Ray. I can't

134

explain it. I have no idea what he was thinkin'. Surely he knew it would be found.'

'Right. The question now is what do we do with it.'

Harry Rex nodded and stuck the cigar in his mouth. Ray leaned back and watched the fan. For a long time they contemplated what to do with the money. Neither wanted to suggest that they simply continue to hide it. Harry Rex decided to fetch another beer. Ray said he'd take one too. As the minutes passed it became obvious that the money would not be discussed again, not that day. In a few weeks, when the estate was opened and an inventory of assets was filled, they could visit the issue again. Or perhaps they would not.

For two days, Ray had debated whether or not to tell Harry Rex about the cash, not the entire fortune, but just a sample of it. After doing so, there were more questions than answers.

Little light had been shed on the money. The Judge enjoyed the dice and was good at gambling, but it seemed unlikely he could have cleared $3.1 million in seven years. And to do so without creating paperwork and leaving a trail seemed impossible.

Ray returned to the tax records while Harry Rex plowed through the ledgers of donations. 'Which CPA are you gonna use?' Ray asked after a long period of silence.

'There are several.'

'Not local.'

'No, I stay away from the guys around here. It's a small town.'

'Looks to me like the records are in good shape,' Ray said, closing a drawer.

'It'll be easy, except for the house.'

'Let's put it on the market, the sooner the better. It won't be a quick sell.'

'What's the asking price?'

'Let's start at three hundred.'

'Are we spending money to fix it up?'

'There is no money, Harry Rex.'

Just before dark, Forrest announced he was tired of Clanton, tired of death, tired of hanging around a depressing old house he had never particularly cared for, tired of Harry Rex and Ray, and that he was going home to Memphis where wild women and parties were waiting.

'When are you coming back?' he asked Ray.

'Two or three weeks.'

'For probate?'

'Yes,' Harry Rex answered. 'We'll make a brief appearance before the judge. You're welcome to be there, but it's not required.'

'I don't do court. Been there enough.'

The brothers walked down the drive to Forrest's car. 'You okay?' Ray asked, but only because he felt compelled to show concern.

'I'm fine. See you, Bro,' Forrest said, in a hurry to leave before his brother blurted something stupid. 'Call me when you come back,' he

136

said. He started the car and drove away. Ray knew he would pull over somewhere between Clanton and Memphis, either at a joint with a bar and a pool table, or maybe just a beer store where he would buy a case and slug it as he drove. Forrest had survived his father's funeral in an impressive way, but the pressure had been building. The meltdown would not be pretty.

Harry Rex was hungry, as usual, and asked if Ray wanted fried catfish. 'Not really,' he answered.

'Good, there's a new place on the lake.'

'What's it called?'

'Jeter's Catfish Shack.'

'You're kidding.'

'No, it's delicious.'

They dined on an empty deck jutting over a swamp, on the backwaters of the lake. Harry Rex ate catfish twice a week; Ray, once every five years. The cook was heavy on the batter and peanut oil, and Ray knew it would be a long night, for several reasons.

He slept with a loaded gun in the bed of his old room, upstairs, with the windows and doors locked, and the three garbage bags packed with money at his feet. With such an arrangement, it was difficult to look around in the dark and conjure up any pleasant childhood memories that would normally be just under the surface. The house had been dark and cold back then, especially after his mother died.

Instead of reminiscing, he tried to sleep by

137

counting little round black chips, a hundred bucks each, hauled by the Judge from the tables to the cashiers. He counted with imagination and ambition, and he got nowhere near the fortune he was in bed with.

Chapter 14

The Clanton square had three cafés, two for the whites and one for the blacks. The Tea Shoppe crowd leaned toward banking and law and retail, more of a white-collar bunch, where the chatter was a bit heavier – the stock market, politics, golf. Claude's, the black diner, had been around for forty years and had the best food.

The Coffee Shop was favored by the farmers, cops, and factory workers who talked football and bird hunting. Harry Rex preferred it, as did a few other lawyers who liked to eat with the people they represented. It opened at five every morning but Sunday, and was usually crowded by six. Ray parked near it on the square and locked his car. The sun was inching above the hills to the east. He would drive fifteen hours or so and hopefully be home by midnight.

Harry Rex had a table in the window and a Jackson newspaper that had already been rearranged and folded to the point of being useless to anyone else. 'Anything in the news?' Ray asked. There was no television at Maple Run.

'Not a damned thang,' Harry Rex grumbled with his eyes glued to the editorials. 'I'll send you all the obituaries.' He slid across a crumpled section the size of a paperback. 'You wanna read this?'

'No, I need to go.'

'You're eating first?'

'Yes.'

'Hey, Dell!' Harry Rex yelled across the café. The counter and booths and other tables were crowded with men, only men, all eating and talking.

'Dell is still here?' Ray asked.

'She doesn't age,' Harry Rex said, waving. 'Her mother is eighty and her grandmother is a hundred. She'll be here long after we're buried.'

Dell did not appreciate being yelled at. She arrived with a coffeepot and an attitude, which vanished when she realized who Ray was. She hugged him and said, 'I haven't seen you in twenty years.' Then she sat down, clutched his arm, and began saying how sorry she was about the Judge.

'Wasn't it a great funeral?' Harry Rex said.

'I can't remember a finer one,' she said, as if Ray was supposed to be both comforted and impressed.

'Thank you,' he said, his eyes watering not from sadness but from the medley of cheap perfumes swirling about her.

Then she jumped up and said, 'What're y'all eatin'? It's on the house.'

Harry Rex decided on pancakes and sausage, for both of them, a tall stack for him, short for Ray. Dell disappeared, a thick cloud of fragrances lingering behind.

'You got a long drive. Pancakes'll stick to your ribs.'

After three days in Clanton, everything was sticking to his ribs. Ray looked forward to some long runs in the countryside around Charlottesville, and to much lighter cuisine.

To his great relief, nobody else recognized him. There were no other lawyers in the Coffee Shop at that hour, and no one else who'd known the Judge well enough to attend his funeral. The cops and mechanics were too busy with their jokes and gossip to look around. Remarkably, Dell kept her mouth shut. After the first cup of coffee, Ray relaxed and began to enjoy the waves of conversation and laughter around him.

Dell was back with enough food for eight; pancakes, a whole hog's worth of sausage, a tray of hefty biscuits with a bowl of butter, and a bowl of somebody's homemade jam. Why would anyone need biscuits to eat with pancakes? She patted his shoulder again and said, 'And he was such a sweet man.' Then she was gone.

'Your father was a lot of things,' Harry Rex said, drowning his hotcakes with at least a quart of somebody's homemade molasses. 'But he wasn't sweet.'

'No he was not,' Ray agreed. 'Did he ever come in here?'

'Not that I recall. He didn't eat breakfast, didn't like crowds, hated small talk, preferred to sleep as late as possible. I don't think this was his kind of place. For the past nine years, he hasn't been seen much around the square.'

'Where'd Dell meet him?'

'In court. One of her daughters had a baby. The daddy already had a family. A real mess.' He somehow managed to shovel into his mouth a serving of pancakes that would choke a horse. Then a bite of sausage.

'And of course you were in the middle of it.'

'Of course. Judge treated her right.' Chomp, chomp.

Ray felt compelled to take a large bite of his food. With molasses dripping everywhere, he leaned forward and lifted a heavy fork to his mouth.

'The Judge was a legend, Ray, you know that. Folks around here loved him. He never got less than eighty percent of the vote in Ford County.'

Ray nodded as he worked on the pancakes. They were hot and buttery, but not particularly tasty.

'If we spend five thousand bucks on the house,' Harry Rex said without showing food, 'then we'll get it back several times over. It's a good investment.'

142

'Five thousand for what?'

He wiped his mouth with one long swipe. 'Clean the damned thing first. Spray it, wash it, fumigate it, clean the floors and walls and furniture, make it smell better. Then paint the outside and the downstairs. Fix the roof so the ceilings won't spot. Cut the grass, pull the weeds, just spruce it up. I can find folks around here to do it.' He thrust another serving into his jaws and waited for Ray to respond.

'There's only six thousand in the bank,' Ray said.

Dell dashed by and somehow managed to refill both coffee cups and pat Ray on the shoulder without missing a stride.

'You got more in that box you found,' Harry Rex said, carving another wedge of pancakes.

'So we spend it?'

'I been thinking about it,' he said, gulping coffee. 'Fact, I's up all night thinking about it.'

'And?'

'Got two issues, one's important, the other's not.' A quick bite of modest proportions, then using the knife and fork to help him talk, he continued: 'First, where'd it come from? That's what we want to know, but it ain't really that important. If he robbed a bank, he's dead. If he hit the casinos and didn't pay taxes, he's dead. If he simply liked the smell of cash and saved it over the years, he's still dead. You follow?'

Ray shrugged as if he was waiting for something complicated. Harry Rex used the break in

143

his monologue to eat sausage, then began stabbing the air again: 'Second, what are you going to do with it? That's what's important. We're assuming nobody knows about the money, right?'

Ray nodded and said, 'Right. It was hidden.' Ray could hear the windows being rattled. He could see the Blake & Son boxes scattered and crushed.

He couldn't help but glance through the window and look at his TT roadster, packed and ready to flee.

'If you include the money in the estate, half will go to the IRS.'

'I know that, Harry Rex. What would you do?'

'I'm not the right person to ask. I've been at war with the IRS for eighteen years, and guess who's winnin'? Not me. Screw 'em.'

'That's your advice as an attorney?'

'No, as a friend. If you want legal advice, then I will tell you that all assets must be collected and properly inventoried pursuant to the Mississippi Code, as annotated and amended.'

'Thank you.'

'I'd take twenty thousand or so, put it in the estate to pay the up-front bills, then wait a long time and give Forrest his half of the rest.'

'Now, that's what I call legal advice.'

'Nope, it's just common sense.'

The mystery of the biscuits was solved when Harry Rex attacked them. 'How 'bout a biscuit?' he said, though they were closer to Ray.

144

'No thanks.'

Harry Rex sliced two in half, buttered them, added a thick layer of jam, then, at the last moment, inserted a patty of sausage. 'You sure?'

'Yes, I'm sure. Could the money be marked in any way?'

'Only if it's ransom or drug money. Don't reckon Reuben Atlee was into those sorts of things, you?'

'Okay, spend five thousand.'

'You'll be pleased.'

A small man with matching khaki pants and shirt stopped at the table, and with a warm smile said, 'Excuse me, Ray, but I'm Loyd Darling.' He stuck out a hand as he spoke. 'I have a farm just east of town.'

Ray shook his hand and half-stood. Mr. Loyd Darling owned more land than anybody in Ford County. He had once taught Ray in Sunday School. 'So good to see you,' Ray said.

'Keep your seat,' he said, gently shoving Ray down by the shoulder. 'Just wanted to say how sorry I am about the Judge.'

'Thank you, Mr. Darling.'

'There was no finer man than Reuben Atlee. You have my sympathies.'

Ray just nodded. Harry Rex had stopped eating and appeared to be ready to cry. Then Loyd was gone and breakfast resumed. Harry Rex launched into a war story about IRS abuse. After another bite or two Ray was stuffed, and as he pretended to listen he thought of all the fine folks who so greatly admired his father, all the Loyd Darlings out there who revered the old man.

What if the cash didn't come from the casinos? What if a crime had been committed, some secret horrible sting perpetrated by the Judge? Sitting there among the crowd in the Coffee Shop, watching Harry Rex but not listening to him, Ray Atlee made a decision. He vowed to himself that if he ever discovered that the cash now crammed into the trunk of his car had been collected by his father in some manner that was less than ethical, then no one would ever know it. He would not desecrate the stellar reputation of Judge Reuben Atlee.

He signed a contract with himself, shook hands, made a blood oath, swore to God. Never would anyone know.

They said good-bye on the sidewalk in front of yet another law office. Harry Rex bear-hugged him, and Ray tried to return the embrace but his arms were pinned to his sides.

'I can't believe he's gone,' Harry Rex said, his eyes moist again.

'I know, I know.'

He walked away, shaking his head and fighting back tears. Ray jumped in his Audi and left the square without looking back. Minutes later he was on the edge of town, past the old drive-in where porno had been introduced, past the shoe factory where a strike had been mediated by the Judge. Past everything until he was in the

146

country, away from the traffic, away from the legend. He glanced at his speedometer and realized he was driving almost ninety miles an hour.

Cops should be avoided, as well as rear-end collisions. The drive was long, but the timing of the arrival in Charlottesville was crucial. Too early and there would be foot traffic on the downtown mall. Too late and the night patrol might see him and ask questions.

Across the Tennessee line, he stopped for gas and a rest room break. He'd had too much coffee. And too much food. He tried to call Forrest on his cell phone, but there was no answer. He took it as neither good news or bad – with Forrest nothing was predictable.

Moving again, he kept his speed at fifty-five and the hours began to pass. Ford County faded into another lifetime. Everyone has to be from somewhere, and Clanton was not a bad place to call home. But if he never saw it again, he would not be unhappy.

Exams were over in a week, graduation the week after, then the summer break. Because he was supposed to be researching and writing, he'd have no classes to teach for the next three months. Which meant he had very little to do at all.

He would return to Clanton and take the oath as executor of his father's estate. He would make all the decisions that Harry Rex asked him to

make. And he would try to solve the mystery of
the money.

Chapter 15

With ample time to plan his movements, he was not surprised when nothing went right. His arrival time was suitable, 11:20 P.M., Wednesday, May 10. He had hoped to park illegally at the curb, just a few feet from the ground-level door to his apartment, but other drivers had the same idea. The curb had never been so completely blocked with a line of cars, and, to his anxious satisfaction, every one of them had a citation under a windshield wiper.

He could park in the street while he dashed back and forth, but that would invite trouble. The small lot behind his building had four spaces, one reserved for him, but they locked the gate at eleven.

So he was forced to use a dark and almost completely abandoned parking garage three blocks away, a large cavernous multilevel that was sold out during the day and eerily empty at night. He'd thought about this alternative off and on for many hours, as he drove north and east and plotted the offensive, and it was the least attractive of all options. It was plan D or E, somewhere way down the list of ways he wanted to transfer the money. He parked on level one, got out with his overnight bag, locked the car, and with great anxiety left it there. He hurried away, eyes darting around as if armed gangs were watching and waiting. His legs and back were stiff from the drive, but he had work to do.

The apartment looked precisely the same as when he'd left it, which was an odd relief. Thirty-four messages awaited him, no doubt colleagues and friends calling with their sympathies. He would listen later.

At the bottom of a tiny closet in the hall, under a blanket and a poncho and other things that had been tossed in, as opposed to being placed or stored, he found a red Wimbledon tennis bag that he hadn't touched in at least two years. Aside from luggage, which he thought would appear too suspicious, it was the largest bag he could think of.

If he'd had a gun he would've stuck it in his pocket. But crime was rare in Charlottesville, and he preferred to live without weapons. After the episode Sunday in Clanton, he was even more terrified of pistols and such. He'd left the Judge's guns hidden in a closet at Maple Run.

With the bag slung over a shoulder, he locked his door on the street and tried his best to walk casually along the downtown mall. It was well lit, there was a cop or two always watching, and

150

the pedestrians at this hour were the wayward kids with green hair, an occasional wino, and a few stragglers working their way home. Charlottesville was a quiet town after midnight.

A thundershower had passed through not long before his arrival. The streets were wet and the wind was blowing. He passed a young couple walking hand in hand but saw no one else on the way to the garage.

He'd given some thought to simply hauling the garbage bags themselves, just throwing them over a shoulder like Santa, one at a time, and walking hurriedly from wherever he was parked to his apartment. He could move the money in three trips and cut his exposure on the street. Two things stopped him. First, what if one ripped, and a million bucks hit the pavement? Every thug and wino in town would come out of the alleys, drawn like sharks to blood. Second, the sight of anyone hauling bags of what appeared to be trash into an apartment, as opposed to away from it, might be suspicious enough to attract the attention of the police.

'What's in the bag, sir?' a cop might ask.

'Nothing. Garbage. A million dollars.' No answer seemed correct.

So the plan was to be patient, take all the time that was necessary, move the loot in small loads, and not worry about how many trips might be required because the least important factor was Ray's fatigue. He could rest later.

The terrifying part was the transferring of the

151

money from one bag to another while crouching over his trunk and trying not to look guilty. Fortunately, the garage was deserted. He crammed money into the tennis bag until it would barely zip, then slammed the trunk down, looked around as if he'd just smothered someone, and left.

Perhaps a third of a garbage bag – three hundred thousand dollars. Much more than enough to get him arrested or knifed. Nonchalance was what he desperately wanted, but there was nothing fluid about his steps and movements. Eyes straight ahead, though the eyes wanted to dart up and down, right and left, nothing could be missed. A frightening teenager with studs in his nose stumbled by, stoned out of his wasted mind. Ray walked even faster, not sure if he had the nerves for eight or nine more trips to the parking garage.

A drunk on a dark bench yelled something unintelligible at him. He lurched forward, then caught himself, and was thankful he had no gun. At that moment, he might've shot anything that moved. The cash got heavier with each block, but he made it without incident. He spilled the money onto his bed, locked every door possible, and took another route back to his car.

During the fifth trip, he was confronted by a deranged old man who jumped from the shadows and demanded, 'What the hell are you doing?' He was holding something dark in his hand. Ray assumed it was a weapon with which to slaughter him.

'Get out of the way,' he said as rudely as possible, but his mouth was dry.

'You keep going back and forth,' the old man yelled. He stank and his eyes were glowing like a demon's.

'Mind your own business.' Ray had never stopped walking, and the old man was in front of him, bouncing along. The village idiot.

'What's the problem?' came a clear crisp voice from behind them. Ray stopped and a policeman ambled over, nightstick in hand.

Ray was all smiles. 'Evening, Officer.' He was breathing hard and his face was sweaty.

'He's up to something!' the old man yelled. 'Keeps going back and forth, back and forth. Goes that way, the bag is empty. Goes that way, the bag is full.'

'Relax, Gilly,' the cop said, and Ray took a deeper breath. He was horrified that someone had been watching, but relieved because that someone was of Gilly's ilk. Of all the characters on the mall, Ray had never seen this one.

'What's in the bag?' the cop asked.

It was a dumb question, far into foul territory, and for a split second Ray, the law professor, considered a lecture on stops, searches, seizures, and permissible police questioning. He let it pass, though, and smoothly delivered the prepared line. 'I played tennis tonight at Boar's Head. Got a bad hamstring, so I'm just walking

153

it off. I live over there.' He pointed to his apartment two blocks down.

The cop turned to Gilly and said, 'You can't be yelling at people, Gilly, I've told you that. Does Ted know you're out?'

'He's got something in that bag,' Gilly said, much softer. The cop was leading him away.

'Yes, it's cash,' said the cop. 'I'm sure the guy's a bank robber, and you caught him. Good work.'

'But it's empty, then it's full.'

'Good night, sir,' the officer said over his shoulder.

'Good night.' And Ray, the wounded tennis player, actually limped for half a block for the benefit of other characters lurking in the darkness. When he dumped the fifth load on his bed, he found a bottle of scotch in his small liquor cabinet and poured a stiff one.

He waited for two hours, ample time for Gilly to return to Ted, who hopefully could keep him medicated and confined for the rest of the night, and time perhaps for a shift change so a different cop would be walking the beat. Two very long hours, in which he imagined every possible scenario involving his car in the parking garage. Theft, vandalism, fire, towed away by some misguided wrecker, everything imaginable.

At 3 A.M., he emerged from his apartment wearing jeans, hiking boots, and a navy sweatshirt with VIRGINIA across the chest. He'd ditched the red tennis bag in favor of a battered

154

leather briefcase, one that would not hold as much money but wouldn't catch the attention of the cop either. He was armed with a steak knife stuck in his belt, under the sweatshirt, ready to be withdrawn in a flash and used on the likes of Gilly or any other assailant. It was foolish and he knew it, but he wasn't himself either and he was quite aware of that. He was dead-tired, sleep-deprived for the third night in a row, just a little tipsy from three scotches, determined to get the money safely hidden, and scared of getting stopped again.

Even the winos had given up at three in the morning. The downtown streets were deserted. But as he entered the parking garage, he saw something that terrified him. At the far end of the mall, passing under a street lamp, was a group of five or six black teenagers. They were moving slowly in his general direction, yelling, talking loudly, looking for trouble.

It would be impossible to make a half-dozen more deliveries without running into them. The final plan was created on the spot.

Ray cranked the Audi and left the garage. He circled around and stopped in the street next to the cars parked illegally on the curb, close to the door to his apartment. He killed the engine and the lights, opened the trunk, and grabbed the money. Five minutes later, the entire fortune was upstairs, where it belonged.

★

155

At 9 A.M. the phone woke him. It was Harry Rex. 'Wake your ass up, boy,' he growled. 'How was the trip?'

Ray swung to the edge of his bed and tried to open his eyes. 'Wonderful,' he grunted.

'I talked to a Realtor yesterday, Baxter Redd, one of the better ones in town. We walked around the place, kicked the tires, you know, whatta mess. Anyway, he wants to stick to the appraised value, four hundred grand, and he thinks we can get at least two-fifty. He gets the usual six percent. You there?'

'Yeah.'

'Then say something, okay?'

'Keep going.'

'He agrees we need to spend some dough to fix it up, a little paint, a little floor wax, a good bonfire would help. He recommended a cleaning service. You there?'

'Yes.' Harry Rex had been up for hours, no doubt refueled with another feast of pancakes, biscuits, and sausage.

'Anyway, I've already hired a painter and a roofer. We'll need an infusion of capital pretty soon.'

'I'll be back in two weeks, Harry Rex, can't it wait?'

'Sure. You hungover?'

'No, just tired.'

'Well, get your ass in gear, it's after nine there.'

'Thanks.'

156

'Speaking of hangovers,' he said, his voice suddenly lower, his words softer, 'Forrest called me last night.'

Ray stood and arched his back. 'This can't be good,' he said.

'No, it's not. He's tanked, couldn't tell if it was booze or drugs, probably both. Whatever he's on, there's plenty of it. He was so mellow I thought he was falling asleep, then he'd fire up and cuss me.'

'What did he want?'

'Money. Not now, he says, claims he's not broke, but he's concerned about the house and the estate and wants to make sure you don't screw him.'

'Screw him?'

'He was bombed, Ray, so you can't hold it against him. But he said some pretty bad things.'

'I'm listening.'

'I'm tellin' you so you'll know, but please don't get upset. I doubt he'll remember it this mornin'.'

'Go ahead, Harry Rex.'

'He said the Judge always favored you and that's why he made you the executor of his estate, that you've always gotten more out of the old man, that it's my job to watch you and protect his interests in the estate because you'll try to screw him out of the money, and so on.'

'That didn't take long, did it? We've hardly got him in the ground.'

'No.'

'I'm not surprised.'

'Keep your guard up. He's on a binge and he might call you with the same crap.'

'I've heard it before, Harry Rex. His problems are not his fault. Somebody's always out to get him. Typical addict.'

'He thinks the house is worth a million bucks, and said it's my job to get that much for it. Otherwise, he might have to hire his own lawyer, blah, blah, blah. It didn't bother me. Again, he was blitzed.'

'He's pitiful.'

'He is indeed, but he'll bottom out and sober up in a week or so. Then I'll cuss him. We'll be fine.'

'Sorry, Harry Rex.'

'It's part of my job. Just one of the joys of practicin' law.'

Ray fixed a pot of coffee, a strong Italian blend he was quite attached to and had missed sorely in Clanton. The first cup was almost gone before his brain woke up.

Any trouble with Forrest would run its course. In spite of his many problems, he was basically harmless. Harry Rex would handle the estate and there would be an equal division of everything left over. In a year or so, Forrest would get a check for more money than he had ever seen.

The image of a cleaning service turned loose at Maple Run bothered him for a while. He could see a dozen women buzzing around like

158

ants, happy with so much to clean. What if they stumbled upon another treasure trove fiendishly left behind by the Judge? Mattresses stuffed with cash? Closets filled with loot? But it wasn't possible. Ray had pored over every inch of the house. You find three million bucks tucked away and you get motivated to pry under every board. He'd even clawed his way through spiderwebs in the basement, a dungeon no cleaning lady would enter.

He poured another cup of strong coffee and walked to his bedroom, where he sat in a chair and stared at the piles of cash. Now what?

Through the blur of the last four days, he had concentrated only on getting the money to the spot where it was now located. Now he had to plan the next step, and he had very few ideas. It had to be hidden and protected, he knew that much for sure.

Chapter 16

There was a large floral arrangement in the center of his desk, with a sympathy card signed by all fourteen students in his antitrust class. Each had written a small paragraph of condolences, and he read them all. Beside the flowers was a stack of cards from his colleagues on the faculty.

Word spread fast that he was back, and throughout the morning the same colleagues dropped by with a quick hello, welcome back, sorry about your loss. For the most part the faculty was a close group. They could bicker with the best of them on the trivial issues of campus politics, but they were quick to circle the wagons in times of need. Ray was very happy to see them. Alex Duffman's wife sent a platter of her infamous chocolate brownies, each weighing a pound and proven to add three more to your waist. Naomi Kraig brought a small collection of roses she'd picked from her garden.

Late in the morning Carl Mirk stopped by

and closed the door. Ray's closest friend on the faculty, his journey to the law school had been remarkably similar. They were the same age, and both had fathers who were small-town judges who'd ruled their little counties for decades. Carl's father was still on the bench, and still holding a grudge because his son did not return to practice law in the family firm. It appeared, though, that the grudge was fading with the years, whereas Judge Atlee apparently carried his to his death.

'Tell me about it,' Carl said. Before long he would make the same trip back to his hometown in northern Ohio.

Ray began with the peaceful house, too peaceful, he recalled now. He described the scene when he found the Judge.

'You found him dead?' Carl asked. The narrative continued, then, 'You think he speeded things up a bit?'

'I hope so. He was in a lot of pain.'

'Wow.'

The story unfolded in great detail, as Ray remembered things he had not thought about since last Sunday. The words poured forth, the telling became therapeutic. Carl was an excellent listener.

Forrest and Harry Rex were colorfully described. 'We don't have characters like that in Ohio,' Carl said. When they told their small-town stories, usually to colleagues from the cities, they stretched the facts and the characters

161

became larger. Not so with Forrest and Harry Rex. The truth was sufficiently colorful.

The wake, the funeral, the burial. When Ray closed with 'Taps' and the lowering of the casket, both had moist eyes. Carl bounced to his feet and said, 'What a great way to go. I'm sorry.'

'Just glad it's over.'

'Welcome back. Let's do lunch tomorrow.'

'What's tomorrow?'

'Friday.'

'Lunch it is.'

For his noon antitrust class, Ray ordered pizzas from a carryout and ate them outside in the courtyard with his students. Thirteen of the fourteen were there. Eight would be graduating in two weeks. The students were more concerned about Ray and the death of his father than about their final exams. He knew that would change quickly.

When the pizza was gone, he dismissed them and they scattered. Kaley lingered behind, as she had been doing in the past months. There was a rigid no-fly zone between faculty and students, and Ray Atlee was not about to venture into it. He was much too content with his job to risk it fooling around with a student. In two weeks, though, Kaley would no longer be a student, but a graduate, and thus not covered by the rules. The flirting had picked up a bit – a serious question after class, a drop-in at his office to get a missed assignment, and always

162

that smile with the eyes that lingered for just a second too long.

She was an average student with a lovely face and a rear-end that stopped traffic. She had played field hockey and lacrosse at Brown and kept a lean athletic figure. She was twenty-eight, a widow with no kids and loads of money she'd received from the company that made the glider her deceased husband had been flying when it cracked up a few miles off the coast at Cape Cod. They found him in sixty feet of water, still strapped in, both wings snapped in two. Ray had researched the accident report online. He'd also found the court file in Rhode Island where she had sued. The settlement gave her four million up front and five hundred thousand a year for the next twenty years. He had kept this information to himself.

After chasing the boys for the first two years of law school, she was now chasing the men. Ray knew of at least two other law professors who were getting the same lingering routine as he. One just happened to be married. Evidently, all were as wary as Ray.

They strolled into the front entrance of the law school, chatting aimlessly about the final exam. She was easing closer with each flirtation, warming up to the zone, the only one who knew where she might be headed with this.

'I'd like to go flying sometime,' she announced.

Anything but flying. Ray thought of her young

163

husband and his horrible death, and for a second could think of nothing to say. Finally, with a smile he said, 'Buy a ticket.'

'No, no, with you, in a small plane. Let's fly somewhere.'

'Anyplace in particular?'

'Just buzz around for a while. I'm thinking of taking lessons.'

'I was thinking of something more traditional, maybe lunch or dinner, after you graduate.' She had stepped closer, so that anyone who walked by at that moment would have no doubt that they, student and professor, were discussing illicit activity.

'I graduate in fourteen days,' she said, as if she might not be able to wait that long before they hopped in the sack.

'Then I'll ask you to dinner in fifteen days.'

'No, let's break the rule now, while I'm still a student. Let's have dinner before I graduate.'

He almost said yes. 'Afraid not. The law is the law. We're here because we respect it.'

'Oh yes. It's so easy to forget. But we have a date?'

'No, we will have a date.'

She flashed another smile and walked away. He tried mightily not to admire her exit, but it was impossible.

The rented van came from a moving company north of town, sixty dollars a day. He tried for a half-day rate because he would need it only for

164

a few hours, but sixty it was. He drove it exactly four tenths of a mile and stopped at Chaney's Self-Storage, a sprawling arrangement of new cinder-block rectangles surrounded by chain link and shiny new razor wire. Video cameras on light poles watched his every move as he parked and walked into the office.

Plenty of space was available. A ten-by-ten bay was forty-eight dollars a month, no heating, no air, a roll-down door, and plenty of lighting.

'Is it fireproof?' Ray asked.

'Absolutely,' said Mrs. Chaney herself, fighting off the smoke from the cigarette stuck between her lips as she filled in forms. 'Nothing but concrete block.' Everything was safe at Chaney's. They featured electronic surveillance, she explained, as she waved at four monitors on a shelf to her left. On a shelf to her right was a small television wherein folks were yelling and fighting, a Springer-style gabfest that was now a brawl. Ray knew which shelf received the most attention.

'Twenty-four-hour guards,' she said, still doing the paperwork. 'Gate's locked at all times. Never had a break-in, and if one happens then we got all kinds of insurance. Sign right here. Fourteen B.'

Insurance on three million bucks, Ray said to himself as he scribbled his name. He paid cash for six months and took the keys to 14B.

He was back two hours later with six new storage boxes, a pile of old clothes, and a stick or

165

two of worthless furniture he'd picked up at a flea market downtown for authenticity. He parked in the alley in front of 14B and worked quickly to unload and store his junk.

The cash was stuffed into forty-two-ounce freezer bags, zipped tight to keep air and water out, fifty-three in all. The freezer bags were arranged in the bottoms of the six storage boxes, then carefully covered with papers and files and research notes that Ray had until very recently deemed useful. Now his meticulous files served a much higher calling. A few old paperbacks were thrown in for good measure.

If, by chance, a thief penetrated 14B, he would probably abandon it after a cursory look into the boxes. The money was well hidden and as well protected as possible. Short of a safety deposit box in a bank, Ray could think of no better place to secure the money.

What would ultimately become of the money was a mystery that grew by the day. The fact that it was now safely tucked away in Virginia provided little comfort, contrary to what he had hoped.

He watched the boxes and the other junk for a while, not really anxious to leave. He vowed to himself that he would not stop by every day to check on things, but as soon as the vow was made he began to doubt it.

He secured the roll-down door with a new padlock. As he drove away, the guard was awake, the video cameras scanning, the gate locked.

Fog Newton was worrying about the weather. He had a student-pilot on a cross-country to Lynchburg and back, and thunderstorms were moving in quickly, according to radar. The clouds had not been expected, and no weather had been forecast during the student's preflight briefing.

'How many hours does he have?' Ray asked.

'Thirty-one,' Fog said gravely. Certainly not enough experience to handle thunderstorms. There were no airports between Charlottesville and Lynchburg, only mountains.

'You're not flying, are you?' Fog asked.

'I want to.'

'Forget it. This storm is coming together quickly. Let's go watch it.'

Nothing frightened an instructor more than a student up in heavy weather. Each cross-country training flight had to be carefully planned – route, time, fuel, weather, secondary airports, and emergency procedures. And each flight had to be approved in writing by the instructor. Fog had once grounded Ray because there was a slight chance of icing at five thousand feet, on a perfectly clear day.

They walked through the hangar to the ramp where a Lear was parking and shutting down its engines. To the west beyond the foothills was the first hint of clouds. The wind had picked up

167

noticeably. 'Ten to fifteen knots, gusting,' Fog said. 'A direct crosswind.' Ray would not want to attempt a landing in such conditions.

Behind the Lear was a Bonanza taxiing to the ramp, and as it got closer Ray noticed that it was the one he'd been coveting for the past two months. 'There's your plane,' Fog said.

'I wish,' Ray said.

The Bonanza parked and shut down near them, and when the ramp was quiet again Fog said, 'I hear he's cut the price.'

'How much?'

'Somewhere around four twenty-five. Four-fifty was a little steep.'

The owner, traveling alone, crawled out and pulled his bags from the rear. Fog was gazing at the sky and glancing at his watch. Ray kept his eyes on the Bonanza, where the owner was locking the door and putting it to rest.

'Let's take it for a spin,' Ray said.

'The Bonanza?'

'Sure. What's the rent?'

'It's negotiable. I know the guy pretty well.'

'Let's get it for a day, fly up to Atlantic City, then back.'

Fog forgot about the approaching clouds and the rookie student. He turned and looked at Ray. 'You're serious?'

'Why not? Sounds like fun.'

Aside from flying and poker, Fog had few other interests. 'When?'

'Saturday. Day after tomorrow. Leave early, come back late.'

Fog was suddenly deep in thought. He glanced at his watch, looked once more to the west, then to the south. Dick Docker yelled from a window, 'Yankee Tango is ten miles out.'

'Thank God,' Fog mumbled to himself and visibly relaxed. He and Ray walked to the Bonanza for a closer look. 'Saturday, huh?' Fog said.

'Yep, all day.'

'I'll catch the owner. I'm sure we can work a deal.'

The winds relented for a moment and Yankee Tango landed with little effort. Fog relaxed even more and managed a smile. 'Didn't know you liked the action,' he said as they walked across the ramp.

'Just a little blackjack, nothing serious,' Ray said.

Chapter 17

The solitude of a late Friday morning was broken by the doorbell. Ray had slept late, still trying to shake off the fatigue from the trip home. Three newspapers and four coffees later he was almost fully awake.

It was a FedEx box from Harry Rex, and it was filled with letters from admirers and newspaper clippings. Ray spread them on the dining table and began with the articles. The *Clanton Chronicle* ran a front-page piece on Wednesday that featured a dignified photo of Reuben Atlee, complete with black robe and gavel. The picture was at least twenty years old. The Judge's hair was thicker and darker, and he filled out the robe. The headline read JUDGE REUBEN ATLEE DEAD AT 79. There were three stories on the front page. One was a flowery obituary. One was a collection of comments from his friends. The third was a tribute to the Judge and his amazing gift of charity.

The *Ford County Times* likewise had a picture,

one taken just a few years earlier. In it Judge Atlee was sitting on his front porch holding his pipe, looking much older but offering a rare smile. He wore a cardigan and looked like a grandfather. The reporter had cajoled him into a feature with the ruse of chatting about the Civil War and Nathan Bedford Forrest. There was the hint of a book in the works, one about the general and the men from Ford County who'd fought with him.

The Atlee sons were barely mentioned in the stories about their father. Referring to one would require referring to the other, and most folks in Clanton wanted to avoid the subject of Forrest. It was painfully obvious that the sons were not a part of their father's life.

But we could've been, Ray said to himself. It was the father who'd chosen early on to have limited involvement with the sons, not the other way around. This wonderful old man who'd given so much to so many had had so little time for his own family.

The stories and photos made him sad, which was frustrating because he had not planned to be sad this Friday. He had held up quite well since discovering his father's body five days earlier. In moments of grief and sorrow, he had dug deep and found the strength to bite his lip and push forward without breaking down. The passage of time and the distance to Clanton had helped immensely, and now from nowhere had come the saddest reminders yet.

The letters had been collected by Harry Rex from the Judge's post office box in Clanton, from the courthouse, and from the mailbox at Maple Run. Some were addressed to Ray and Forrest and some to the family of Judge Atlee. There were lengthy letters from lawyers who'd practiced before the great man and had been inspired by his passion for the law. There were cards of sympathy from people who, for one reason or another, had appeared before Judge Atlee in a divorce, or adoption, or juvenile matter, and his fairness had changed their lives. There were notes from people all over the state – sitting judges, old law school pals, politicians Judge Atlee had helped over the years, and friends who wanted to pass along their sympathies and fond memories.

The largest batch came from those who had received the Judge's charity. The letters were long and heartfelt, and all the same. Judge Atlee had quietly sent money that was desperately needed, and in many cases it had made a dramatic change in the life of someone.

How could a man so generous die with more than three million dollars hidden below his bookshelves? He certainly buried more than he gave away. Perhaps Alzheimer's had crept into his life, or some other affliction that had gone undetected. Had he slipped toward insanity? The easy answer was that the old man had simply gone nuts, but how many crazy people could put together that kind of money?

After reading twenty or so letters and cards, Ray took a break. He walked to the small balcony overlooking the downtown mall and watched the pedestrians below. His father had never seen Charlottesville, and though Ray was certain he had asked him to visit, he could not remember a specific invitation. They had never traveled anywhere together. There were so many things they could have done.

The Judge had always talked of seeing Gettysburg, Antietam, Bull Run, Chancellorsville, and Appomatox, and he would have done so had Ray shown an interest. But Ray cared nothing for the refighting of an old war, and he had always changed the subject.

The guilt hit hard, and he couldn't shake it. What a selfish ass he'd been.

There was a lovely card from Claudia. She thanked Ray for talking to her and expressing his forgiveness. She had loved his father for years and would carry her grief to her grave. Please call me, she begged, then signed off with hugs and kisses. And she's got her current boyfriend on Viagra, according to Harry Rex.

The nostalgic journey home came to an abrupt halt with a simple anonymous card that froze his pulse and sent goose bumps down the backs of both legs.

The only pink envelope in the pile contained a card with the words 'With Sympathy' on the outside. Taped to the inside was a small square piece of paper with a typed message that read:

'It would be a mistake to spend the money. The IRS is a phone call away.' The envelope had been postmarked in Clanton on Wednesday, the day after the funeral, and was addressed to the family of Judge Atlee at Maple Run.

Ray placed it aside while he scanned the other cards and letters. They were all the same at this point, and he'd read enough. The pink one sat there like a loaded gun, waiting for him to return to it.

He repeated the threat on the balcony as he grasped the railing and tried to analyze things. He mumbled the words in the kitchen as he fixed more coffee. He'd left the note on the table so he could see it from any part of his rambling den.

Back on the balcony he watched the foot traffic pick up as noon approached, and anyone who glanced up was a person who might know about the money. Bury a fortune, then realize you're hiding it from someone, and your imagination can get crazy.

The money didn't belong to him, and it was certainly enough to get him stalked, followed, watched, reported, even hurt.

Then he laughed at his own paranoia. I will not live like this, he said, and went to take a shower.

Whoever it was knew exactly where the Judge had hidden the money. Make a list, Ray told himself as he sat on the edge of his bed, naked, with water dripping onto the floor. The felon who cut the lawn once a week. Perhaps he was a smooth talker who'd befriended the Judge and spent time in the house. Entry was easy. When the Judge sneaked off to the casinos, maybe the grasscutter slinked through the house, pilfering.

Claudia would be at the top of the list. Ray could easily see her easing over to Maple Run whenever the Judge beckoned. You don't sleep with a woman for years then cut her off without a replacement. Their lives had been so connected it was easy to imagine their romance continuing. No one had been closer to Reuben Atlee than Claudia. If anyone knew where the money came from, it was her.

If she wanted a key to the house, she could've had one, though a key was not necessary. Her visit on the morning of the funeral could've been for surveillance and not sympathy, though she'd played it well. Tough, smart, savvy, calloused, and old but not too old. For fifteen minutes he dwelt on Claudia and convinced himself that she was the one tracking the money.

Two other names came to mind, but Ray could not add them to the list. The first was Harry Rex, and as soon as he mumbled the name he felt ashamed. The other was Forrest, and it too was a ridiculous idea. Forrest had not been inside the house for nine years. Assuming, just for the sake of argument, that he somehow had known about the money, he would never have left it. Give Forrest three million in cash and he would've done serious damage to himself and those around him.

The list took great effort but there was little to show for it. He wanted to go for a quick run, but instead stuffed some old clothes into two pillowcases, then drove to Chaney's, where he unloaded them into 14B. Nothing had been touched, the boxes were just as he'd left them the day before. The money was still well hidden. As he loitered there, not wanting to leave until the last second, he was hit with the thought that perhaps he was creating a trail. Obviously, someone knew he had taken it from the Judge's study. For that kind of money, private investigators could be hired to follow Ray.

They could follow him from Clanton to Charlottesville, from his apartment to Chaney's Self-Storage.

He cursed himself for being so negligent. Think, man! The money doesn't belong to you!

He locked up 14B as tightly as possible. Driving across town to meet Carl for lunch, he glanced at his mirrors and watched other drivers, and after five minutes of this he laughed at himself and vowed that he would not live like wounded prey.

Let them have the damned money! One less thing to worry about. Break into 14B and haul it away. Wouldn't affect his life in the least. No sir.

Chapter 18

The estimated flying time to Atlantic City was eighty-five minutes in the Bonanza, which was exactly thirty-five minutes faster than the Cessna Ray had been renting. Early Saturday morning he and Fog did a thorough preflight under the intrusive and often obnoxious supervision of Dick Docker and Charlie Yates, who walked around the Bonanza with their tall Styrofoam cups of bad coffee as if they were flying instead of just watching. They had no students that morning, but the gossip around the airport was that Ray was buying the Bonanza and they had to see things for themselves. Hangar gossip was as reliable as coffee shop rumors.

'How much does he want now?' Docker asked in the general direction of Fog Newton, who was crouched under a wing draining a fuel sump, checking for water and dirt in the tanks.

'He's down to four-ten,' Fog said, with an air of importance because he was in charge of this flight, not them.

'Still too high,' Yates said.

'You gonna make an offer?' Docker said to Ray.

'Mind your own business,' Ray shot back without looking. He was checking the engine oil.

'This is our business,' Yates said, and they all laughed.

In spite of the unsolicited help, the preflight was completed without a problem. Fog climbed in first and buckled himself into the left seat. Ray followed in the right, and when he pulled the door hard and latched it and put on the headset he knew he had found the perfect flying machine. The two-hundred-horsepower engine started smoothly. Fog slowly went through the gauges, instruments, and radios, and when they finished a pre-takeoff checklist he called the tower. He would get it airborne, then turn it over to Ray.

The wind was light and the clouds were high and scattered, almost a perfect day for flying. They lifted off the runway at seventy miles per hour, retracted the landing gear, and climbed eight hundred feet per minute until they reached their assigned cruising altitude of six thousand feet. By then, Ray had the controls and Fog was explaining the autopilot, the radar weather, the traffic collision avoidance system. 'She's loaded,' Fog said more than once.

Fog had flown Marine fighters for one career, but for the past ten years he'd been relegated to the little Cessnas in which he'd taught Ray and a thousand others to fly. A Bonanza was the Porsche of single engines, and Fog was delighted for the rare chance to fly one. The route assigned by air traffic control took them just south and east of Washington, away from the busy airspace around Dulles and Reagan National. Thirty miles away and more than a mile up, they could see the dome of the Capitol, then they were over the Chesapeake with the skyline of Baltimore in the distance. The bay was beautiful, but the inside of the airplane was far more interesting. Ray was flying it himself without the help of the autopilot. He maintained a course, kept the assigned altitude, talked to Washington control, and listened to Fog chat incessantly about the performance ratings and features of the Bonanza.

Both pilots wanted the flight to last for hours, but Atlantic City was soon ahead. Ray descended to four thousand feet, then to three thousand, and then switched to the approach frequency. With the runway in sight, Fog took the controls and they glided to a soft touchdown. Taxiing to the general aviation ramp, they passed two rows of small Cessnas and Ray couldn't help but think that those days were behind him. Pilots were always searching for the next plane, and Ray had found his.

Fog's favorite casino was the Rio, on the boardwalk with several others. They agreed to meet for lunch in a second-floor cafeteria, then quickly lost each other. Each wanted to keep his gambling private. Ray wandered among the slots and scoped out the tables. It was Saturday and the Rio was busy. He circled around and eased up on the poker tables. Fog was in a crowd around a table, lost in his cards with a stack of chips under his hands.

Ray had five thousand dollars in his pocket – fifty of the hundred-dollar bills picked at random from the stash he'd hauled back from Clanton. His only goal that day was to drop the money in the casinos along the boardwalk and make certain it was not counterfeit, not marked, not traceable in any way. After his visit to Tunica last Monday night, he was fairly certain the money was for real.

Now he almost hoped it was marked. If so, then maybe the FBI would track him down and tell him where the money came from. He'd done nothing wrong. The guilty party was dead. Bring on the feds.

He found an empty chair at a blackjack table and laid five bills down for chips. 'Greens,' he said like a veteran gambler.

'Changing five hundred,' the dealer said, barely looking up.

'Change it,' came the reply from a pit boss. The tables were busy. Slots were ringing in the background. A crap game was hot off in the distance, men were yelling at the dice.

The dealer picked up the bills as Ray froze for a second. The other players watched with

180

detached admiration. All were playing five- and ten-dollar chips. Amateurs.

The dealer stuffed the Judge's bills, all perfectly valid, into the money box and counted twenty twenty-five-dollar green chips for Ray, who lost half of them in the first fifteen minutes and left to find some ice cream. Down two hundred fifty and not the least bit worried about it.

He ventured near the crap tables and watched the confusion. He could not imagine his father mastering such a complicated game. Where did one learn to shoot dice in Ford County, Mississippi?

According to a thin little gambling guide he'd picked up in a bookstore, a basic wager is a come-bet, and when he mustered the courage he wedged his way between two other gamblers and placed the remaining ten chips on the pass line. The dice rolled twelve, the money was scraped away by the dealer, and Ray left the Rio to visit the Princess next door.

Inside, the casinos were all the same. Old folks staring hopelessly at the slots. Just enough coins rattling in the trays to keep them hooked. Blackjack tables crowded with subdued players slugging free beer and whiskey. Serious gamblers packed around the crap tables hollering at the dice. A few Asians playing roulette. Cocktail waitresses in silly costumes showing skin and hauling drinks.

He picked out a blackjack table and repeated

181

the procedure. His next five bills passed the dealer's inspection. Ray bet a hundred dollars on the first hand, but instead of quickly losing his money, he began winning.

He had too much untested cash in his pocket to waste time accumulating chips, so when he'd doubled his money, he pulled out ten more bills and asked for hundred-dollar chips. The dealer informed the pit boss, who offered a gapped smile, and said, 'Good luck.' An hour later, he left the table with twenty-two chips.

Next on his tour was the Forum, an older-looking establishment with an odor of stale cigarette smoke partially masked by cheap disinfectant. The crowd was older too because, as he soon realized, the Forum's specialty was quarter slots and those over sixty-five got a free breakfast, lunch, or dinner, take your pick. The cocktail waitresses were on the downhill side of forty and had given up the notion of showing flesh. They hustled about in what appeared to be track suits with matching sneakers.

The limit at blackjack was ten dollars a hand. The dealer hesitated when he saw Ray's cash hit the table, and he held the first bill up to the light as if he'd finally caught a counterfeiter. The pit boss inspected it too, and Ray was rehearsing his lines about procuring that particular bill down the street at the Rio. 'Cash it,' said the pit boss, and the moment passed. He lost three hundred dollars in an hour.

Fog claimed to be breaking the casino when they met for a quick sandwich. Ray was down a hundred dollars, but like all gamblers lied and said he was up slightly. They agreed to leave at 5 P.M. and fly back to Charlottesville.

The last of Ray's cash was converted to chips at a fifty-dollar table in Canyon Casino, the newest of those on the boardwalk. He played for a while but soon grew tired of cards and went to the sports bar, where he sipped a soda and watched boxing from Vegas. The five thousand he brought to Atlantic City had been thoroughly flushed through the system. He would leave with forty-seven hundred, and a wide trail. He had been filmed and photographed in seven casinos. At two of them he had filled in paperwork when cashing in chips at the cashiers' windows. At two others he had used his credit cards to make small withdrawals, just to leave more evidence behind.

If the Judge's cash was traceable, then they would know who he was and where to find him.

Fog was quiet as they rode back to the airport. His luck had turned south during the afternoon. 'Lost a couple hundred,' he finally admitted, but his demeanor suggested he'd lost much more.

'You?' he asked.

'I had a good afternoon,' Ray said. 'Won enough to pay for the charter.'

'That's not bad.'

'Don't suppose I could pay for it in cash, could I?'

'Cash is still legal,' Fog said, perking up a bit. 'Then cash it is.'

During the preflight, Fog asked if Ray wanted to fly in the left seat. 'We'll call it a lesson,' he said. The prospect of a cash transaction had raised his spirits.

Behind two commuter flights, Ray taxied the Bonanza into position and waited for traffic to clear. Under the close eye of Fog, he began the takeoff roll, accelerated to seventy miles per hour, then lifted smoothly into the air. The turbocharged engine seemed twice as powerful as the Cessna's. They climbed with little effort to seventy-five hundred feet and were soon on top of the world.

Dick Docker was napping in the Cockpit when Ray and Fog walked in to log the trip and turn in headsets. He jumped to attention and made his way to the counter. 'Didn't expect you back so soon,' he mumbled, half-asleep, as he pulled paperwork from a drawer.

'We broke the casino,' Ray said.

Fog had disappeared down into the study room of the flight school.

'Gee, I never heard that before.'

Ray was flipping through the logbook.

'You paying now?' Dick asked, scribbling numbers.

'Yes, and I want the cash discount.'

'Didn't know we had one.'

'You do now. It's ten percent.'

184

'We can do that. Yep, it's the old cash discount.' He figured again, then said, 'Total's thirteen hundred and twenty bucks.'

Ray was counting money from his wad of bills. 'I don't carry twenties. Here's thirteen.' As Dick was recounting the money, he said, 'Some guy came poking around today, said he wanted to take lessons and somehow your name came up.'

'Who was he?'

'Never saw him before.'

'Why was my name used?'

'It was kinda weird. I was giving him the spiel about costs and such, and out of the blue he asked if you owned an airplane. Said he knew you from someplace.'

Ray had both hands on the counter. 'Did you get his name?'

'I asked. Dolph something or other, wasn't real clear. Started acting suspicious and finally left. I watched him. He stopped by your car in the parking lot, walked around it like he might break in or something, then left. You know a Dolph?'

'I've never known a Dolph.'

'Me neither. I've never heard of a Dolph. Like I said, it was weird.'

'What'd he look like?'

'Fiftyish, small, thin, head full of grey hair slicked back, dark eyes like a Greek or something, used-car-salesman type, pointed-toe boots.'

185

Ray was shaking his head. Not a clue.

'Why didn't you just shoot him?' Ray asked.

'Thought he was a customer.'

'Since when are you nice to your customers?'

'You buying the Bonanza?'

'Nope. Just dreaming.'

Fog was back and they congratulated each other on a wonderful trip, promised to do it again, the usual. Driving away, Ray watched every car and every turn.

They were following him.

Chapter 19

A week passed, a week without FBI or Treasury agents knocking on his door with badges and questions about bad money tracked down in Atlantic City, a week with no sign of Dolph or anyone else following him, a week of the normal routine of running five miles in the morning and being a law professor after that.

He flew the Bonanza three times, each a lesson with Fog at his right elbow, and each lesson paid for on the spot with cash. 'Casino money,' he said with a grin, and it wasn't a lie. Fog was anxious to return to Atlantic City to reclaim his lost assets. Ray had no interest, but it wasn't a bad idea. He could boast of another good day at the tables and keep paying cash for his flying lessons.

The money was now in 37F – 14B was still rented to Ray Atlee, and it still held the old clothes and the cheap furniture; 37F was rented to NDY Ventures, named in honor of the three flight instructors at Docker's. Ray's name was nowhere on the paperwork for 37F. He leased it for three months, in cash.

'I want this confidential,' he'd said to Mrs. Chaney.

'Everything's confidential around here. We get all types.' She gave him a conspiratorial look as if to say, 'I don't care what you're hiding. Just pay me.'

He'd moved it one box at a time, hauling it at night, under the cover of darkness, with a security guard watching from a distance. Storage space 37F was identical to 14B, and when the six boxes were safely tucked away he had vowed once again to leave it alone and not stop by every day. It had never occurred to him that hauling around three million bucks could be such a chore.

Harry Rex had not called. He'd sent another overnight package with more of the same letters of sympathy and such. Ray was compelled to read them all, or least scan them just in case there was a second cryptic note. There was not.

Exams came and went and after graduation the law school would be quiet for the summer. Ray said good-bye to his students, all but Kaley, who, after her last exam, informed Ray she had decided to stay in Charlottesville through the summer. She pressed him again for a pregraduation rendezvous of some sort. Just for the hell of it.

'We are waiting until you are no longer a student,' Ray said, holding his ground but wanting to yield. They were in his office with the door open.

'That's a few days away,' she said.

'Yes it is.'

'Then let's pick a date.'

'No, let's graduate first, then we'll pick a date.'

She left him with the same lingering smile and look, and Ray knew that she was trouble. Carl Mirk caught him gazing down the hall as she walked away in very tight jeans. 'Not bad,' Carl said.

Ray was slightly embarrassed, but kept watching anyway. 'She's after me,' he said.

'You're not alone. Be careful.'

They were standing in the hallway next to the door to Ray's office. Carl handed him an odd-looking envelope and said, 'Thought you'd get a kick out of this.'

'What is it?'

'It's an invitation to the Buzzard Ball.'

'The what?' Ray was pulling out the invitation.

'The first ever Buzzard Ball, probably the last too. It's a black-tie gala to benefit the preservation of bird life in the Piedmont. Look at the hosts.'

Ray read it slowly. 'Vicki and Lew Rodowski cordially invite you to . . . '

'The Liquidator is now saving our birds. Touching, huh?'

'Five thousand bucks a couple!'

189

'I think that's a record for Charlottesville. It was sent to the Dean. He's on the A list, we are not. Even his wife was shocked at the price.'

'Suzie's shockproof, isn't she?'

'Or so we thought. They want two hundred couples. They'll raise a million or so and show everybody how it's done. That's the plan anyway. Suzie says they'll be lucky to get thirty couples.'

'She's not going?'

'No, and the Dean is very relieved. He thinks it's the first black-tie shindig they'll miss in the last ten years.'

'Music by the Drifters?' Ray said as he scanned the rest of the invitation.

'That'll cost him fifty grand.'

'What a fool.'

'That's Charlottesville. Some clown bails out from Wall Street, gets a new wife, buys a big horse farm, starts throwing money around, and wants to be the big man in a small town.'

'Well, I'm not going.'

'You're not invited. Keep it.'

Carl was off, and Ray returned to his desk, invitation in hand. He put his feet on his desk, closed his eyes, and began daydreaming. He could see Kaley in a slinky black dress with no back at all, slits up past her thighs, very low V-neck, drop-dead gorgeous, thirteen years younger than Vicki, a helluva lot fitter, out there on the dance floor with Ray, who was not a bad dancer himself, bobbing and jerking to the Motown rhythms of the Drifters, while everybody watched and whispered, 'Who's that?'

And in response Vicki would be forced to drag old Lew out onto the floor, Lew in his designer tux, which could not hide his dumpy little belly; Lew with shrubs of bright grey hair above his ears; Lew the old goat trying to buy respect by saving the birds; Lew with the arthritic back and slow feet who moves like a dump truck; Lew proud of his trophy wife in her million-dollar dress, which reveals too much of her magnificently starved bones.

Ray and Kaley would look much better, dance much better, and, well, what would all that prove?

A nice scene to visit, but give it up. Now that he had the money he wouldn't waste it on nonsense like that.

The drive to Washington was only two hours, and more than half of it was fairly scenic and enjoyable. But his preferred method of travel had changed. He and Fog flew the Bonanza for thirty-eight minutes to Reagan National, where they were reluctantly allowed to land, even with a preapproved slot. Ray jumped in a taxi and fifteen minutes later was at the Treasury Department on Pennsylvania Avenue.

A colleague at the law school had a brother-in-law with some clout in Treasury. Phone calls had been made, and Mr. Oliver Talbert welcomed Professor Atlee into his rather comfortable office in the BEP, Bureau of Engraving and Printing. The professor was doing research on a vaguely defined project and needed less than an hour of someone's time. Talbert was not the brother-in-law, but he was asked to fill in.

They began with the topic of counterfeiting, and in broad strokes Talbert laid out the current problems, almost all blamed on technology – primarily inkjet printers and computer-generated counterfeit currency. He had samples of some of the best imitations. With a magnifier, he pointed out the flaws – the lack of detail in Ben Franklin's forehead, the missing thin thread lines running through the design background, the bleeding ink in the serial numbers. 'This is very good stuff,' he said. 'And counterfeiters are getting better.'

'Where'd you find this?' Ray asked, though the question was completely irrelevant. Talbert looked at the tag on the back of the display board. 'Mexico,' he said, and that was all.

To outpace the counterfeiters, Treasury was investing heavily in its own technology. Printers that gave the bills an almost holographic effect, watermarks, color-shifting inks, fine line printing patterns, enlarged off-center portraits, and scanners that could spot a fake in less than a second. The most effective method so far was one that had not yet been used. Simply change the color of the money. Go from green to blue to

192

yellow then to pink. Gather up the old, flood the banks with the new, and the counterfeiters could not catch up, at least not in Talbert's opinion. 'But Congress won't allow it,' he said, shaking his head.

Tracing real money was Ray's primary concern, and they eventually got around to it. Money is not actually marked, Talbert explained, for obvious reasons. If the crook could look at the bills and see markings, then the sting would fall apart. Marking simply meant recording serial numbers, once a very tedious task because it was done manually. He told a kidnapping and ransom story. The cash arrived just minutes before the drop was planned. Two dozen FBI agents worked furiously to write down the serial numbers of the hundred-dollar bills. 'The ransom was a million bucks,' he was saying, 'and they simply ran out of time. Got about eighty thousand recorded, but it was enough. They caught the kidnappers a month later with some of the marked bills, and that broke the case.'

But a new scanner had made the job much easier. It photographs ten bills at a time, one hundred in forty seconds.

'Once the serial numbers are recorded, how do you find the money?' Ray asked, taking notes on a yellow legal pad. Would Talbert have expected anything else?

'Two ways. First, if you find the crook with the money, you simply put two and two together

193

and nail him. That's how the DEA and FBI catch drug dealers. Bust a street dealer, cut him a deal, give him twenty thousand in marked bills to buy coke from his supplier, then catch the bigger fish holding the government's money.'

'What if you don't catch the crook?' Ray asked, and in doing so could not help but think of his departed father.

'That's the second way, and it's much more diffficult. Once the money is lifted out of circulation by the Federal Reserve, a sample of it is routinely scanned. If a marked bill is found, it can be traced back to the bank that submitted it. By then it's too late. Occasionally, a person with marked money will use it in one general location over a period of time, and we've caught a few crooks that way.'

'Sounds like a long shot.'

'Very much so,' Talbert admitted.

'I read a story a few years ago about some duck hunters who stumbled across a wrecked airplane, a small one,' Ray said casually. The tale had been rehearsed. 'There was some cash on board, seems like it was almost a million bucks. They figured it was drug money, so they kept it. Turns out it they were right, the money was marked, and it soon surfaced in their small town.'

'I think I remember that,' Talbert said.

I must be good, thought Ray. 'My question is this: could they, or could anyone else who finds money, simply submit it to the FBI or DEA or

194

Treasury and have it scanned to see if it was marked, and if so, where it came from?'

Talbert scratched his cheek with a bony finger and contemplated the question, then shrugged and said, 'I don't see why they couldn't. The problem, though, is obvious. They would run the risk of losing the money.'

'I'm sure it's not a common occurrence,' Ray said, and they both laughed.

Talbert had a story about a judge in Chicago who was skimming from the lawyers, small sums, five hundred and a thousand bucks a pop, to get cases moved up the docket, and for friendly rulings. He'd done it for years before the FBI got a tip. They busted some of the lawyers and convinced them to play along. Serial numbers were taken from the bills, and during the two-year operation three hundred fifty thousand was sneaked across the bench into the judge's sticky fingers. When the raid happened, the money had vanished. Someone tipped the judge. The FBI eventually found the money in the judge's brother's garage in Arizona, and everybody went to jail.

Ray caught himself squirming. Was it a coincidence, or was Talbert trying to tell him something? But as the narrative unfolded he relaxed and tried to enjoy it, close as it was. Talbert knew nothing about Ray's father.

Riding in a cab back to the airport, Ray did the math on his legal pad. For a judge like the one in Chicago, it would take eighteen years,

195

stealing at the rate of a hundred seventy-five thousand a year, to accumulate three million. And that was Chicago, with a hundred courts and thousands of wealthy lawyers handling cases worth much more than the ones in north Mississippi. The judicial system there was an industry where things could slip through, heads could be turned, wheels greased. In Judge Atlee's world a handful of people did everything, and if money was offered or taken folks would know about it. Three million dollars could not be taken from the 25th Chancery District because there wasn't that much in the system to begin with.

He decided that one more trip to Atlantic City was necessary. He would take even more cash and flush it through the system. A final test. He had to be certain the Judge's money wasn't marked.

Fog would be thrilled.

Chapter 20

When Vicki fled and moved in with the Liquidator, a professor friend recommended Axel Sullivan as a divorce specialist. Axel proved to be a fine lawyer, but there wasn't much he could do on the legal front. Vicki was gone, she wasn't coming back, and she didn't want anything from Ray. Axel supervised the paperwork, recommended a good shrink, and did a commendable job of getting Ray through the ordeal. According to Axel, the best private investigator in town was Corey Crawford, a black ex-cop who'd pulled time for a beating.

Crawford's office was above a bar his brother owned near the campus. It was a nice bar, with a menu and unpainted windows, live music on the weekends, no unseemly traffic other than a bookie who worked the college crowd. But Ray parked three blocks away just the same. He did not want to be seen entering the premises. A sign that read CRAWFORD INVESTIGATIONS pointed to stairs on one side of the building.

There was no secretary, or at least none was present. He was ten minutes early but Crawford was waiting. He was in his late thirties with a shaved head and handsome face, no smile whatsoever. He was tall and lean and his expensive clothes were well fitted. A large pistol was strapped to his waist in a black leather holster.

'I think I'm being followed,' Ray began.

'This is not a divorce?' They were on opposite sides of a small table in a small office that overlooked the street.

'No.'

'Who would want to follow you?'

He had rehearsed a story about family trouble back in Mississippi, a dead father, some inheritances that may or may not happen, jealous siblings, a rather vague tale that Crawford seemed to buy none of. Before he could ask questions, Ray told him about Dolph at the airport and gave him his description.

'Sounds like Rusty Wattle,' Crawford said.

'And who's that?'

'Private eye from Richmond, not very good. Does some work around here. Based on what you've said, I don't think your family would hire someone from Charlottesville. It's a small town.'

The name of Rusty Wattle was duly recorded and locked away forever in Ray's memory.

'Is there a chance that these bad guys back in Mississippi would want you to know that you're being followed?' Crawford asked.

198

Ray looked completely baffled, so Crawford continued. 'Sometimes we get hired to intimidate, to frighten. Sounds like Wattle or whoever it was wanted your buddies at the airport to give you a good description. Maybe he left a trail.'

'I guess it's possible.'

'What do you want me to do?'

'Determine if someone is following me. If so, who is it, and who's paying for it.'

'The first two might be easy. The third might be impossible.'

'Let's give it a try.'

Crawford opened a thin file. 'I charge a hundred bucks an hour,' he said, his eyes staring right through Ray's, looking for indecision. 'Plus expenses. And a retainer of two thousand.'

'I prefer to deal in cash,' Ray said, staring right back. 'If that's acceptable.'

The first hint of a smile. 'In my business, cash is always preferred.'

Crawford filled in some blanks in a contract.

'Would they tap my phones, stuff like that?' Ray asked.

'We'll search everything. Get another cell phone, digital, and don't register it in your name. Most of our correspondence will be by cell phone.'

'What a surprise,' Ray mumbled, taking the contract, scanning it, then signing.

Crawford put it back in the file and returned to his notepad. 'For the first week, we'll coordinate your movements. Everything will be planned. Go about your normal routine, just give us notice so we can have people in place.'

I'll have a traffic jam behind me, Ray thought. 'It's a pretty dull life,' Ray said. 'I jog, I go to work, sometimes I go fly an airplane, I go home, alone, no family.'

'Other places?'

'Sometimes I do lunch, dinner, not a breakfast guy though.'

'You're putting me to sleep,' Crawford said and almost smiled. 'Women?'

'I wish. Maybe a prospect or two, nothing serious. If you find one, give her my name.'

'These bad guys in Mississippi, they're looking for something. What is it?'

'It's an old family with lots of stuff handed down. Jewelry, rare books, crystal, and silver.' It sounded natural and this time Crawford bought it.

'Now we're getting somewhere. And you have possession of the family heirloom?'

'That's right.'

'It's here?'

'Tucked away in Chaney's Self-Storage, on Berkshire Road.'

'What's it worth?'

'Not nearly as much as my relatives think.'

'Gimme a ballpark.'

'Half a million, on the high side.'

'And you have a legitimate claim to it?'

'Let's say the answer is yes. Otherwise, I'll be forced to give you the family history, which

200

could take the next eight hours and give us both a migraine.'

'Fair enough.'

Crawford finished a lengthy paragraph and was ready to wrap things up. 'When can you get a new cell phone?'

'I'll go now.'

'Great. And when can we check your apartment?'

'Anytime.'

Three hours later, Crawford and a sidekick he called Booty finished what was known as a sweep. Ray's phones were clear, no taps or bugs. The air vents hid no secret cameras. In the cramped attic they found no receivers or monitors hidden behind boxes.

'You're clean,' Crawford said as he left.

He didn't feel very clean as he sat on his balcony. You open up your life to complete strangers, albeit some selected and paid by you, and you feel compromised.

The phone was ringing.

Forrest sounded sober – strong voice, clear words. As soon as he said 'Hello, Bro,' Ray listened to see what kind of shape he was in. It was instinctive now, after years of phone calls at all hours, from all places, many of which he, Forrest, never remembered. He said he was fine, which meant he was sober and clean, no booze or drugs, but he did not say for how long. Ray was not about to ask.

Before either could mention the Judge or his estate or the house or Harry Rex, Forrest blurted out, 'I got a new racket.'

'Tell me about it,' Ray said, settling into his recliner. The voice on the other end was full of excitement. Ray had plenty of time to listen.

'Ever heard of Benalatofix?'

'No.'

'Me neither. The nickname is Skinny Ben. Ring a bell?'

'No, sorry.'

'It's a diet pill put out by a company called Luray Products, out of California, a big private outfit that no one's ever heard of. For the last five years doctors have been prescribing Skinny Bens like crazy because the drug works. It's not for the woman who needs to drop twenty pounds, but it does wonders for the really obese, talking linebackers, defensive ends. You there?'

'I'm listening.'

'Trouble is, after a year or two these poor women develop leaky heart valves. Tens of thousands of them have been treated, and Luray is getting sued like crazy in California and Florida. Food and Drug stepped in eight months ago, and last month Luray yanked Skinny Bens off the market.'

'Where, exactly, do you come in, Forrest?'

'I am now a medical screener.'

'And what does a medical screener do?'

'Thanks for asking. Today, for example, I was

202

in a hotel suite in Dyersburg, Tennessee, helping these hefty darlings on to a treadmill. The doctor, paid by the lawyers who pay me, checks their heart capacity, and if they're not up to snuff, guess what?'

'You have a new client.'

'Absolutely. Signed up forty today.'

'What's the average case worth?'

'About ten thousand bucks. The lawyers I'm now working with have eight hundred cases. That's eight million bucks, the lawyers get half, the women get screwed again. Welcome to the world of mass torts.'

'What's in it for you?'

'A base salary, a bonus for new clients, and a piece of the back end. There could be a half a million cases out there, so we're scrambling to round them up.'

'That's five billion dollars in claims.'

'Luray's got eight in cash. Every plaintiff's lawyer in the country is talking about Skinny Bens.'

'Aren't there some ethical problems?'

'There are no ethics anymore, Bro. You're in la-la land. Ethics are only for people like you to teach to students who'll never use them. I hate to be the one to break it to you.'

'I've heard it before.'

'Anyway, I'm mining for gold. Just thought you'd want to know.'

'That's good to hear.'

'Is anybody up there doing Skinny Bens?'

'Not to my knowledge.'

'Keep your eyes open. These lawyers are teaming up with other lawyers around the country. That's how mass tort stuff works, as I'm learning. The more cases you have in a class, the bigger the settlement.'

'I'll put out the word.'

'See you, Bro.'

'Be careful, Forrest.'

The next call came shortly after 2:30 A.M., and like every call at such an hour the phone seemed to ring forever, both during sleep and afterward. Ray finally managed to grab it and switch on a light.

'Ray, this is Harry Rex, sorry to call.'

'What is it?' he said, knowing too well that it was not good.

'Forrest. I've spent the last hour talking to him and some nurse at Baptist Hospital in Memphis. They've got him there, I think with a broken nose.'

'Back up, Harry Rex.'

'He went to a bar, got drunk, got in a fight, the usual. Looks like he picked on the wrong guy, now he's getting his face stitched up. They want to keep him overnight. I had to talk to the staff there and guarantee payment. I also asked them not to give him painkillers and drugs. They have no idea who they've got there.'

'I'm sorry you're in the middle of this, Harry Rex.'

'I've been here before, and I don't mind. But he's crazy, Ray. He started again about the estate and how he's getting screwed out of his rightful share, all that crap. I know he's drunk and all, but he just won't leave it alone.'

'I talked to him five hours ago. He was fine.'

'Well, he must've been headed for the bar. They finally had to sedate him to reset his nose, otherwise it would've been impossible. I'm just worried about all the drugs and stuff. What a mess.'

'I'm sorry, Harry Rex,' Ray said again because he could think of nothing else to say. There was a pause as Ray tried to collect his thoughts. 'He was fine, just a few hours ago, clean, sober, seemed so anyway.'

'Did he call you?' Harry Rex asked.

'Yeah, he was excited about a new job.'

'That Skinny Ben crap?'

'Yeah, is it a real job?'

'I think so. There are a bunch of lawyers down here chasing those cases. Quantity's crucial. They hire guys like Forrest to go out and round 'em up.'

'They ought to be disbarred.'

'Half of us should. I think you need to come home. The sooner we can open the estate the sooner we can get Forrest calmed down. I hate these accusations.'

'Do you have a court date?'

'We can do it Wednesday of next week. I think you ought to stay for a few days.'

'I was planning on it. Book it, I'll be there.'

'I'll notify Forrest in a day or so, try to catch him sober.'

'Sorry, Harry Rex.'

Not surprisingly, Ray couldn't sleep. He was reading a biography when his new cell phone rang. Had to be a wrong number. 'Hello,' he said suspiciously.

'Why are you awake?' asked the deep voice of Corey Crawford.

'Because my phone keeps ringing. Where are you?'

'We're watching. You okay?'

'I'm fine. It's almost four in the morning. You guys ever sleep?'

'We nap a lot. I'd keep the lights out if I were you.'

'Thank you. Anybody else watching my lights?'

'Not yet.'

'That's good.'

'Just checking in.'

Ray turned off the lights in the front of his apartment and retreated to his bedroom, where he read with aid of a small lamp. Sleep was made even more difficult with the knowledge that he was being billed a hundred dollars an hour through the night.

It's a wise investment, he kept telling himself.

At exactly 5 A.M. he sneaked down his hallway as if someone on the ground down there might see him, and he brewed coffee in the dark.

206

Waiting for the first cup, he called Crawford, who, not surprisingly, sounded groggy.

'I'm brewing coffee, you want some?' Ray asked.

'Not a good idea, but thanks.'

'Look, I'm flying to Atlantic City this afternoon. You got a pen?'

'Yeah, let's have it.'

'I'm leaving from general aviation in a white Beech Bonanza, tail number eight-one-five-romeo, at three P.M., with a flight instructor named Fog Newton. We'll stay tonight at the Canyon Casino, and return around noon tomorrow. I'll leave my car at the airport, locked as usual. Anything else?'

'You want us in Atlantic City?'

'No, that's not necessary. I'll move around a lot up there and try to watch my rear.'

Chapter 21

The consortium was put together by one of Dick Docker's flying buddies. It was built around two local ophthalmologists who had clinics in West Virginia. Both had just learned to fly and needed to shuttle back and forth at a faster pace. Docker's pal was a pension consultant who needed the Bonanza for about twelve hours a month. A fourth partner would get the deal off the ground. Each would put up $50,000 for a quarter interest, then sign a bank loan for the balance of the purchase price, which was currently at $390,000 and not likely to move lower. The note was spread over six years and would cost each partner $890 per month.

That was about eleven hours in a Cessna for Pilot Atlee.

On the plus side, there was depreciation and potential charter business when the partners were not using the plane. On the negative, there were hangar fees, fuel, maintenance, and a list that seemed to go on too long. Unsaid by the pal of Dick Docker, and also very much on the negative side, was the possibility of getting into business with three strangers, two of whom were doctors.

But Ray had $50,000, and he could swing $890 a month, and he wanted desperately to own the airplane that he secretly considered to be his.

Bonanzas held their value, according to a rather persuasive report that was attached to the proposal. Demand had remained high in the used-aircraft market. The Beech safety record was second only to Cessna and practically as strong. Ray carried the consortium deal around with him for two days, reading it at the office, in his apartment, at the lunch counter. The other three partners were in. Just sign his name in four places, and he would own the Bonanza.

The day before he left for Mississippi, he studied the deal for the last time, said to hell with everything else, and signed the papers.

If the bad guys were watching him, they were doing an excellent job of covering their tracks. After six days of trying to find the surveillance, Corey Crawford was of the opinion that there was nobody back there. Ray paid him thirty-eight hundred in cash and promised to call if he got suspicious again.

Under the guise of storing more junk, he went to Chaney's Self-Storage every day to check on the money. He hauled in boxes filled with anything he could find around his apartment. Both 14B and 37F were slowly taking on the appearance of an old attic.

The day before he left town, he went to the front office and asked Mrs. Chaney if someone had vacated 18R. Yes, two days ago.

'I'd like to rent it,' he said.

'That makes three,' she said.

'I'm going to need the space.'

'Why don't you just rent one of our larger units?'

'Maybe later. For now, I'll use the three small ones.'

It really didn't matter to her. He rented 18R in the name of Newton Aviation and paid cash for a six-month lease. When he was certain no one was watching, he moved the money out of 37F and into 18R, where new boxes were waiting. They were made of aluminum-coated vinyl and guaranteed to resist fire up to three hundred degrees Fahrenheit. They were also waterproof, and they locked. The money fit into five of them. For good measure, Ray threw some old quilts and blankets and clothes over the boxes so things would look a little more normal. He wasn't sure whom he was trying to impress with the randomness of his little room, but he felt better when it looked disheveled.

A lot of what he was doing these days was for the benefit of someone else. A different route from his apartment to the law school. A new jogging trail. A different coffee bar. A new

210

downtown bookstore to browse through. And always with an eye for the unusual, an eye in the rearview mirror, a quick turnaround when he walked or jogged, a peek through shelves after he entered a shop. Someone was back there, he could feel it.

He had decided to have dinner with Kaley before he went South for a while, and before she technically became a former student. Exams were over, what was the harm? She would be around for the summer and he was determined to pursue her, with great caution. Caution because that's what every female got from him. Caution because he thought he saw potential in this one.

But the first phone call to her number was a disaster. A male voice answered, a younger voice, Ray thought, and whoever he was, he wasn't too pleased that Ray had called. When Kaley got on the phone she was abrupt. Ray asked if he could call at a better time. She said no, she'd ring him back.

He waited three days then wrote her off, something he could do as easily as flipping the calendar to the next month.

So he departed Charlottesville with nothing left undone. With Fog in the Bonanza, he flew four hours to Memphis, where he rented a car and went to look for Forrest.

His first and only visit to the home of Ellie Crum had been for the same purpose as this one.

Forrest had cracked up, disappeared, and his family was curious as to whether he might be dead or thrown in jail somewhere. The Judge was still presiding back then, and life was normal, including the hunt for Forrest. Of course the Judge had been too busy to search for his youngest son, and why should he when Ray could do it?

The house was an old Victorian in midtown Memphis, a hand-me-down from Ellie's father, who'd once been prosperous. Not much else was inherited. Forrest had been attracted to the notion of trust funds and real family money, but after fifteen years he'd given up hope. In the early days of the arrangement he had lived in the main bedroom. Now his quarters were in the basement. Others lived in the house too, all rumored to be struggling artists in need of refuge.

Ray parked by the curb in the street. The shrubs needed trimming and the roof was old, but the house was aging nicely. Forrest painted it every October, always in a dazzling color scheme he and Ellie would argue over for a year. Now it was a pale blue trimmed with reds and oranges. Forrest said he'd painted it teal one year.

A young woman with snow-white skin and black hair greeted him at the door with a rude, 'Yes?'

Ray was looking at her through a screen.

Behind her the house was dark and eerie, same as last time. 'Is Ellie in?' Ray asked, as rudely as possible.

'She's busy. Who's calling?'

'I'm Ray Atlee, Forrest's brother.'

'Who?'

'Forrest, he lives in the basement.'

'Oh, that Forrest.' She disappeared and Ray heard voices somewhere in the back of the house.

Ellie was wearing a bedsheet, white with streaks and spots of clay and water and slits for her head and arms. She was drying her hands on a dirty dish towel and looked frustrated that her work had been interrupted. 'Hello, Ray,' she said like an old friend and opened the door.

'Hello, Ellie.' He followed her through the foyer and into the living room.

'Trudy, bring us some tea, will you?' she called out. Wherever Trudy was, she didn't answer. The walls of the room were covered with a collection of the wackiest pots and vases Ray had ever seen. Forrest said she sculpted ten hours a day and couldn't give the stuff away.

'I'm sorry about your father,' she said. They sat across a small glass table from each other. The table was unevenly mounted on three phallic cylinders, each a different shade of blue. Ray was afraid to touch it.

'Thank you,' he said stiffly. No calls, no cards, no letters, no flowers, not one word of

213

sympathy uttered until now, in this happen-stance meeting. An opera could barely be heard in the background.

'I guess you're looking for Forrest,' she said.
'Yes.'

'I haven't seen him lately. He lives in the basement, you know, comes and goes like an old tomcat. I sent a girl down this morning to have a look – she said she thinks he's been gone for a week or so. The bed hasn't been made in five years.'

'That's more than I wanted to know.'

'And he hasn't called.'

Trudy arrived with the tea tray, another of Ellie's hideous creations. And the cups were mismatched little pots with large handles. 'Cream and sugar?' she asked, pouring and stirring.

'Just sugar.'

She handed him his brew and he took it with both hands. Dropping it would've crushed a foot.

'How is he?' Ray asked when Trudy was gone.

'He's drunk, he's sober, he's Forrest.'

'Drugs?'

'Don't go there. You don't want to know.'

'You're right,' Ray said and tried to sip his tea. It was peach-flavored something and one drop was enough. 'He was in a fight the other night, did you know about it? I think he broke his nose.'

'It's been broken before. Why do men get

214

drunk and beat up each other?' It was an excellent question and Ray had no answer. She gulped her tea and closed her eyes to savor it. Many years ago, Ellie Crum had been a lovely woman. But now, in her late forties, she had stopped trying.

'You don't care for him, do you?' Ray asked.

'Of course I do.'

'No, really?'

'Is it important?'

'He's my brother. No one else cares about him.'

'We had great sex in the early years, then we just lost interest. I got fat, now I'm too involved with my work.'

Ray glanced around the room.

'And besides, there's always sex,' she said, nodding to the door from which Trudy had come and gone.

'Forrest is a friend, Ray. I suppose I love him, at some level. But he's also an addict who seems determined to always be an addict. After a point, you get frustrated.'

'I know. Believe me, I know.'

'And I think he's one of the rare ones. He's strong enough to pick himself up at the last possible moment.'

'But not strong enough to kick it.'

'Exactly. I kicked it, Ray, fifteen years ago. Addicts are tough on each other. That's why he's in the basement.'

He's probably happier down there, Ray

thought. He thanked her for the tea and the time, and she walked him to the door. She was still standing there, behind the screen, when he raced away.

Chapter 22

The estate of Reuben Vincent Atlee was opened for probate in the courtroom where he had presided for thirty-two years. High on the oak-paneled wall behind the bench, a grim-faced Judge Atlee looked down upon the proceedings from between the Stars and Stripes and the state flag of Mississippi. It was the same portrait they had placed near his coffin during the courthouse wake three weeks earlier. Now it was back where it belonged, in a place where it would undoubtedly hang forever.

The man who had ended his career, and sent him into exile and seclusion at Maple Run, was Mike Farr from Holly Springs. He'd been reelected once and according to Harry Rex was doing a credible job. Chancellor Farr reviewed the petition for letters of administration, and he studied the one-page will attached to the filings.

The courtroom was busy with lawyers and clerks milling about, filing papers and chatting with clients. It was a day set aside for uncontested matters and quick motions. Ray sat in the front row while Harry Rex was at the bench, whispering back and forth with Chancellor Farr. Next to Ray was Forrest, who, other than the faded bruises under his eyes, looked as normal as possible. He had insisted that he would not be present when probate was opened, but a tongue-lashing from Harry Rex had persuaded him otherwise.

He'd finally come home to Ellie's, the usual return from the streets without a word to anyone about where he'd been or what he'd been up to. No one wanted to know. There was no mention of a job, so Ray was assuming his brief career as a medical screener for the Skinny Ben lawyers was over.

Every five minutes, a lawyer would crouch in the aisle, stick out a hand, and tell Ray what a fine man his father had been. Of course Ray was supposed to know all of them because they knew him. No one spoke to Forrest.

Harry Rex motioned for Ray to join them at the bench. Chancellor Farr greeted him warmly. 'Your father was a fine man and a great judge,' he said, leaning down.

'Thank you,' Ray replied. Then why, during the campaign, did you say he was too old and out of touch? Ray wanted to ask. It had been nine years earlier and seemed like fifty. With the passing of his father, everything in Ford County was now decades older.

218

'You teach law?' Chancellor Farr asked.

'Yes, at the University of Virginia.'

He nodded his approval and asked, 'All the heirs are present?'

'Yes sir,' answered Ray. 'It's just my brother, Forrest, and myself.'

'And both of you have read this one-page document that purports to be the last will and testament of Reuben Atlee?'

'Yes sir.'

'And there is no objection to this will being probated?'

'No sir.'

'Very well. Pursuant to this will, I will appoint you as the executor of your late father's estate. Notice to creditors will be filed today and published in a local paper. I'll waive the bond. Inventory and accounting will be due pursuant to the statute.'

Ray had heard his father utter those same instructions a hundred times. He glanced up at Judge Farr.

'Anything further, Mr. Vonner?'

'No, Your Honor.'

'I'm very sorry, Mr. Atlee,' he said.

'Thank you, Your Honor.'

For lunch they went to Claude's and ordered fried catfish. Ray had been back for two days and he could already feel his arteries choking. Forrest had little to say. He was not clean and his system was polluted.

Ray's plans were vague. He wanted to visit

some friends around the state, he said. There was no hurry to return to Virginia. Forrest left them after lunch, said he was going back to Memphis.

'Will you be at Ellie's?' Ray asked.

'Maybe.' was his only reply.

Ray was sitting on the porch, waiting for Claudia when she arrived promptly at 5 P.M. He met her beside her car where she stopped and looked at the Realtor's For Sale sign in the front yard, near the street.

'Do you have to sell it?' she asked.

'Either that or give it away. How are you?'

'I'm fine, Ray.' They managed to hug with just the minimum of contact. She was dressed for the occasion in slacks, loafers, a checkered blouse, and a straw hat, as if she'd just stepped from the garden. The lips were red, the mascara perfect. Ray had never seen her when she wasn't properly turned out.

'I'm so glad you called,' she said as they slowly walked up the drive to the house.

'We went to court today, opened the estate.'

'I'm sorry, must've been tough on you.'

'It wasn't too bad. I met Judge Farr.'

'Did you like him?'

'Nice enough, I guess, in spite of the history.'

He took her arm and led her up the steps, though Claudia was fit and could climb hills, in spite of the two packs a day. 'I remember when he was fresh out of law school,' she said. 'Didn't

220

know a plaintiff from a defendant. Reuben could've won that race, you know, if I'd been around.'

'Let's sit here,' Ray said, pointing to two rockers.

'You've cleaned up the place,' she said, admiring the porch.

'It's all Harry Rex. He's hired painters, roofers, a cleaning service. They had to sandblast the dust off the furniture, but you can breathe now.'

'Mind if I smoke?' she said.

'No.' It didn't matter. She was smoking regardless.

'I'm so happy you called,' she said again, then lit a cigarette.

'I have tea and coffee,' Ray said.

'Ice tea, please, lemon and sugar,' she said, and crossed her legs. She was perched in the rocker like a queen, waiting for her tea. Ray recalled the tight dresses and long legs of many years ago as she sat just below the bench, scribbling elegantly away in her shorthand while every lawyer in the courtroom watched.

They talked about the weather, as folks do in the South when there's a gap in the conversation, or when there's nothing else to talk about. She smoked and smiled a lot, truly happy to be remembered by Ray. She was clinging. He was trying to solve a mystery.

They talked about Forrest and Harry Rex, two loaded topics, and when she'd been there for half an hour Ray finally got to the point.

221

'We've found some money, Claudia,' he said, and let the words hang in the air. She absorbed them, analyzed them, and proceeded cautiously. 'Where?'

It was an excellent question. Found where, as in the bank with records and such? Found where, as in stuffed in the mattress with no trail?

'In his study, cash. Left behind for some reason.'

'How much?' she asked, but not too quickly.

'A hundred thousand.' He watched her face and eyes closely. Surprise registered, but not shock. He had a script so he pressed on. 'His records are meticulous, checks written, deposits, ledgers with every expense, and this money seems to have no source.'

'He never kept a lot of cash,' she said slowly.

'That's what I remember too. I have no idea where it came from, do you?'

'None,' she said with no doubts whatsoever. 'The Judge didn't deal in cash. Period. Everything went through the First National Bank. He was on the board for a long time, remember?'

'Yes, very well. Did he have anything on the side?'

'Such as?'

'I'm asking you, Claudia, you knew him better than anyone. And you knew his business.'

'He was completely devoted to his work. To him, being a chancellor was a great calling, and he worked very hard at it. He had no time for anything else.'

222

'Including his family,' Ray said, then immediately wished he had not.

'He loved his boys, Ray, but he was from a different generation.'

'Let's stay away from that.'

'Let's.'

They took a break and each regrouped. Neither wanted to dwell on the family. The money had their attention. A car eased down the street and seemed to pause just long enough for the occupants to see the For Sale sign and take a long look at the house. One look was enough because it sped away.

'Did you know he was gambling?' Ray asked.

'The Judge? No.'

'Hard to believe, isn't it? Harry Rex took him to the casinos once a week for a while. Seems as if the Judge had a knack for it and Harry Rex did not.'

'You hear rumors, especially about the lawyers. Several of them have gotten into trouble over there.'

'But you've heard nothing about the Judge?'

'No. I still don't believe it.'

'The money came from somewhere, Claudia. And something tells me it was dirty, otherwise he would have included it with the rest of his assets.'

'And if he won at gambling he would have considered that dirty, don't you think?' Indeed, she knew the Judge better than anyone.

'Yes, and you?'

223

'Sounds like Reuben Atlee to me.'

They finished that round of conversation and took a break, both rocking gently in the cool shade of the front porch, as if time had stopped, neither bothered by the silence. Porch-sitting allowed great lapses while thoughts were gathered, or while there was no thinking at all.

Finally Ray, still plodding through an unwritten script, mustered the courage to ask the toughest question of the day. 'I need to know something, Claudia, and please be honest.'

'I'm always honest. It's one of my faults.'

'I have never questioned my father's integrity.'

'Nor should you now.'

'Help me out here, okay.'

'Go on.'

'Was there anything on the side – a little extra from a lawyer, a slice of the pie from a litigant, a nice backhander as the Brits like to say?'

'Absolutely not.'

'I'm throwing darts, Claudia, hoping to hit something. You don't just find a hundred thousand dollars in nice crisp bills tucked away on a shelf. When he died he had six thousand dollars in the bank. Why keep a hundred buried?'

'He was the most ethical man in the world.'

'I believe that.'

'Then stop talking about bribes and such.'

'Gladly.'

She lit another cigarette and he left to fill up the tea glasses. When he returned to the porch

Claudia was deep in thought, her gaze stretching far beyond the street. They rocked for a while.

Finally, he said, 'I think the Judge would want you to have some of it.'

'Oh you do?'

'Yes. We'll need some of it now to finish fixing up the place, probably twenty-five thousand or so. What if you, me, and Forrest split the remainder?'

'Twenty-five each?'

'Yep. What do you think?'

'You're not running it through the estate?' she asked. She knew the law better than Harry Rex.

'Why bother? It's cash, nobody knows about it, and if we report it then half will go for taxes.'

'And how would you explain it?' she asked, as always, one step ahead. They used to say that Claudia would have the case decided before the lawyers began their opening statements.

And the woman loved money. Clothes, perfume, always a late-model car, and all these things from a poorly paid court reporter. If she was drawing a state pension, it couldn't be much.

'It cannot be explained,' Ray said.

'If it's from gambling, then you'll have to go back and amend his tax returns for the past years,' she said, quickly on board. 'What a mess.'

'A real mess.'

The mess was quietly put to rest. No one would ever know about her share of the money.

'We had a case once,' she said, gazing across the front lawn. 'Over in Tippah County, thirty years ago. A man named Childers owned a scrap yard. He died with no will.' A pause, a long drag on the cigarette. 'Had a bunch of kids, and they found money hidden all over the place, in his office, in his attic, in a utility shed behind his house, in his fireplace. It was a regular Easter egg hunt. Once they'd scoured every inch of the place, they counted it up and it was about two hundred thousand dollars. This, from a man who wouldn't pay his phone bill and wore the same pair of overalls for ten years.' Another pause, another long puff. She could tell these stories forever. 'Half the kids wanted to split the money and run, the other half wanted to tell the lawyer and include the money in the probate. Word leaked out, the family got scared, and the money got added to the old man's estate. The kids fought bitterly. Five years later all the money was gone – half to the government, half to the lawyers.'

She stopped, and Ray waited for the resolution. 'What's the point?' he asked.

'The Judge said it was a shame, said the kids should've kept the money quiet and split it. After all, it was the property of their father.'

'Sounds fair to me.'

'He hated inheritance taxes. Why should the government get a large portion of your wealth just because you die? I heard him grumble about it for years.'

Ray took an envelope from behind his rocker and handed it to her. 'That's twenty-five thousand in cash.'

She stared at it, then looked at him in disbelief.

'Take it,' he said, inching it closer to her. 'No one will ever know.'

She took it and for a second was unable to speak. Her eyes watered, and for Claudia that meant serious emotions were at work. 'Thank you,' she whispered, and clutched the money even tighter.

Long after she left, Ray sat in the same chair, rocking in the darkness, quite pleased with himself for eliminating Claudia as a suspect. Her ready acceptance of twenty-five thousand dollars was convincing proof that she knew nothing of the much larger fortune.

But there was no suspect to take her place on the list.

Chapter 23

The meeting had been arranged through a Virginia law alumnus who was now a partner in a New York megafirm, which in turn was counsel to a gaming group that operated Canyon Casinos across the country. Contacts had been made, favors exchanged, arms twisted slightly and very diplomatically. It was in the delicate area of security, and no one wanted to step over the line. Professor Atlee needed just the basics.

Canyon had been on the Mississippi River, in Tunica County, since the mid-nineties, arriving in the second wave of construction and surviving the first shakeout. It had ten floors, four hundred rooms, eighty thousand square feet of gaming opportunities, and had been very successful with old Motown acts. Mr. Jason Piccolo, a vice president of some sort from the home office in Vegas, was on hand to greet Ray, and with him was Alvin Barker, head of security. Piccolo was in his early thirties and dressed like an Armani model. Barker was in his fifties and had the look of a weathered old cop in a bad suit.

They began by offering a quick tour, which Ray declined. He'd seen enough casino floors in the past month to last him forever. 'How much of the upstairs is off-limits?' he asked.

'Well, let's see,' Piccolo said politely, and they led him away from the slots and tables to a hallway behind the cashiers' booths. Up the stairs and down another hallway, and they stopped in a narrow room with a long wall of one-way mirrors. Through it, there was a large, low room filled with round tables covered with closed-circuit monitors. Dozens of men and women were glued to the screens, seemingly afraid to miss anything.

'This is the eye-in-the-sky,' Piccolo was saying. 'Those guys on the left are watching the blackjack tables. In the center, craps and roulette, to the right, slots and poker.'

'And what are they watching?'

'Everything. Absolutely everything.'

'Give me the list.'

'Every player. We watch the big hitters, the pros, the card counters, the crooks. Take blackjack. Those guys over there can watch ten hands and tell if a player is counting cards. That man in the gray jacket studies faces, looking for the serious players. They bounce around, here today, Vegas tomorrow, then they'll lay low for a week and surface in Atlantic City or the

229

Bahamas. If they cheat or count cards, he'll spot them when they sit down.' Piccolo was doing the talking. Barker was watching Ray as if he might be a potential cheater.

'How close is the camera view?' Ray asked.

'Close enough to read the serial number of any bill. We caught a cheater last month because we recognized a diamond ring he'd worn before.'

'Can I go in there?'

'Sorry.'

'What about the craps tables?'

'The same. It's a bigger problem because the game is faster and more complicated.'

'Are there professional cheaters at craps?'

'They're rare. Same with poker and roulette. Cheating is not a huge problem. We worry more about employee theft and mistakes at the table.'

'What kind of mistakes?'

'Last night a blackjack player won a forty-dollar hand, but our dealer made a mistake and pulled the chips. The player objected and called the pit boss over. Our guys up here saw it happen and we corrected the situation.'

'How?'

'We sent a security guy down with instructions to pay the customer his forty bucks, give him an apology, and comp a dinner.'

'What about the dealer?'

'He has a good record, but one more screwup and he's gone.'

'So everything's recorded?'

'Everything. Every hand, every throw of the dice, every slot. We have two hundred cameras rolling right now.'

Ray walked along the wall and tried to absorb the level of surveillance. There seemed to be more people watching above than gambling below.

'How can a dealer cheat with all this?' he asked, waving a hand.

Piccolo said, 'There are ways,' and gave Barker a knowing look. 'Many ways. We catch one a month.'

'Why do you watch the slots?' Ray asked, changing the subject. He would kill some time scatter-shooting since he'd been promised only one visit upstairs.

'Because we watch everything,' Piccolo said. 'And because there have been some instances where minors won jackpots. The casinos refused to pay, and they won the lawsuits because they had videos showing the minors ducking away while adults stepped in. Would you like something to drink?'

'Sure.'

'We have a secret little room with a better view.'

Ray followed them up another flight of stairs to a small enclosed balcony with views of the gaming floor and the surveillance room. A waitress materialized from thin air and took their drink orders. Ray asked for cappuccino. Waters for his hosts.

'What's your biggest security concern?' Ray asked. He was looking at a list of questions he'd pulled from his coat pocket.

'Card counters and sticky-fingered dealers,' Piccolo answered. 'Those little chips are very easy to drop into cuffs and pockets. Fifty bucks a day is a thousand dollars a month, tax free, of course.'

'How many card counters do you see in here?'

'More and more. There are casinos in forty states now, so more people are gambling. We keep extensive files on suspected counters, and when we think we have one here, then we simply ask them to leave. We have that right, you know.'

'What's your biggest one-day winner?' Ray asked.

Piccolo looked at Barker, who said, 'Excluding slots?'

'Yes.'

'We had a guy win a buck eighty in craps one night.'

'A hundred and eighty thousand?'

'Right.'

'And your biggest loser?'

Barker took his water from the waitress and scratched his face for a second. 'Same guy dropped two hundred grand three nights later.'

'Do you have consistent winners?' Ray asked, looking at his notes as if serious academic research was under way.

'I'm not sure what you mean,' Piccolo said.

232

'Let's say a guy comes in two or three times every week, plays cards or dice, wins more than he loses, and over time racks up some nice gains. How often do you see that?'

'It's very rare,' said Piccolo. 'Otherwise, we wouldn't be in business.'

'Extremely rare,' Barker said. 'A guy might get hot for a week or two. We'll zero in on him, watch him real close, nothing suspicious, but he is taking our money. Sooner or later he's gonna take one chance too many, do something stupid, and we'll get our money back.'

'Eighty percent lose over time,' Piccolo added.

Ray stirred his cappuccino and glanced at his notes. 'A guy walks in, complete stranger, lays down a thousand bucks on a blackjack table and wants hundred-dollar chips. What happens up here?'

Barker smiled and cracked his thick knuckles. 'We perk up. We'll watch him for a few minutes, see if he knows what he's doing. The pit boss'll ask him if he wants to be rated, or tracked, and if so then we'll get his name. If he says no, then we'll offer him a dinner. The cocktail waitress will keep the drinks coming, but if he doesn't drink then that's another sign that he might be serious.'

'The pros never drink when they gamble,' Piccolo added. 'They might order a drink for cover, but they'll just play with it.'

'What is rating?'

233

'Most gamblers want some extras,' explained Piccolo. 'Dinner, tickets to a show, room discounts, all kinds of goodies we can throw in. They have membership cards that we monitor to see how much they're gambling. The guy in your hypothetical has no card, so we'll ask him if he wants to be rated.'

'And he says no.'

'Then it's no big deal. Strangers come and go all the time.'

'But we sure try to keep up with them,' Barker admitted.

Ray scribbled something meaningless on his folded sheet of paper. 'Do the casinos pool their surveillance?' he asked, and for the first time Piccolo and Barker squirmed in unison.

'What do you mean by pool?' Piccolo asked with a smile, which Ray returned, Barker quickly joining in.

While all three were smiling, Ray said, 'Okay, another hypothetical about our consistent winner. Let's say the guy plays one night at the Monte Carlo, the next night at Treasure Cove, the next night at Aladdin, and so on down the strip here. He works all the casinos, and he wins a lot more than he loses. And this goes on for a year. How much will you know about this guy?'

Piccolo nodded at Barker, who was pinching his lips between a thumb and an index finger. 'We'll know a lot,' he admitted.

'How much?' Ray pressed.

'Go on,' Piccolo said to Barker, who reluctantly began talking.

'We'll know his name, his address, his occupation, phone number, automobile, bank. We'll know where he is each night, when he arrives, when he leaves, how much he wins or loses, how much he drinks, did he have dinner, did he tip the waitress, and if so then how much, how much did he tip the dealer.'

'And you keep records on these people?'

Barker looked at Piccolo, who nodded yes, very slowly, but said nothing. They were clamming up because he was getting too close. On second thought, a tour was just what he needed. They walked down to the floor where, instead of looking at the tables, Ray was looking up at the cameras. Piccolo pointed out the security people. They stood close to a blackjack table where a kid who seemed like a young teenager was playing with stacks of hundred-dollar chips.

'He's from Reno,' Piccolo whispered. 'Hit Tunica last week, took us for thirty grand. Very very good.'

'And he doesn't count cards,' Barker whispered, joining the conspiracy.

'Some people just have the talent for it, like golf or heart surgery,' Piccolo said.

'Is he working all the casinos?' Ray asked.

'Not yet, but they're all waiting for him.' The kid from Reno made both Barker and Piccolo very nervous.

The visit was finished in a lounge where they

235

drank sodas and wrapped things up. Ray had completed his list of questions, all of which had been leading up to the grand finale.

'I have a favor,' he asked the two of them. Sure, anything.

'My father died a few weeks ago, and we have reason to believe he was sneaking over here, shooting dice, perhaps winning a lot more than he was losing. Can this be confirmed?'

'What was his name?' asked Barker.

'Reuben Atlee, from Clanton.'

Barker shook his head no while pulling a phone from his pocket.

'How much?' asked Piccolo.

'Don't know, maybe a million over a period of years.'

Barker was still shaking his head. 'No way. Anybody who wins or loses that kinda money, we'll know him well.' And then, into the phone, Barker asked the person on the other end if he could check on a Reuben Atlee.

'You think he won a million dollars?' Piccolo asked.

'Won and lost,' Ray replied. 'Again, we're just guessing.'

Barker slammed his phone shut. 'No record of any Reuben Atlee anywhere. There's no way he gambled that much around here.'

'What if he never came to this casino?' Ray asked, certain of the answer.

'We would know,' they said together.

Chapter 24

He was the only morning jogger in Clanton, and for this he got curious stares from the ladies in their flower beds and the maids sweeping the porches and the summer help cutting grass at the cemetery when he ran past the Atlee family plot. The soil was settling around the Judge, but Ray did not stop or even slow down to inspect it. The men who'd dug the grave were digging another. There was a death and a birth every day in Clanton. Things changed little.

It was not yet eight o'clock and the sun was hot and the air heavy. The humidity didn't bother him because he'd grown up with it, but he certainly didn't miss it either.

He found the shaded streets and worked his way back to Maple Run. Forrest's Jeep was there, and his brother was slouched in the swing on the porch. 'Kinda early for you, isn't it?' Ray said.

'How far did you run? You're covered in sweat.'

'That happens when you jog in the heat. Five miles. You look good.'

And he did. Clear, unswollen eyes, a shave, a shower, clean white painter's pants.

'I'm on the wagon, Bro.'

'Wonderful.' Ray sat in a rocker, still sweating, still breathing heavily. He would not ask how long Forrest had been sober. Couldn't have been more than twenty-four hours.

Forrest bounced from the swing and pulled the other rocker near Ray. 'I need some help, Bro,' he said, sitting on the edge of the chair.

Here we go again, Ray said to himself. 'I'm listening.'

'I need some help,' he blurted again, rubbing his hands fiercely as if the words were painful.

Ray had seen it before and had no patience. 'Let's go, Forrest, what is it?' It was money, first of all. After that, there were several possibilities.

'There's a place I want to go, about an hour from here. It's way out in the woods, close to nothing, very pretty, a nice little lake in the center, comfortable rooms.' He pulled a wrinkled business card from his pocket and handed it to Ray.

Alcorn Village. Drug and Alcohol Treatment Facility. A Ministry of the Methodist Church.

'Who's Oscar Meave?' Ray asked, looking at the card.

'A guy I met a few years ago. He helped me, now he's at that place.'

'It's a detox center.'

238

'Detox, rehab, drug unit, dry-out tank, spa, ranch, village, jail, prison, mental ward, call it whatever you want. I don't care. I need help, Ray. Now.' He covered his face with his hands and began crying.

'Okay, okay.' Ray said. 'Give me the details.'

Forrest wiped his eyes and his nose and sucked in a heavy load of air. 'Call the guy and see if they have a room,' he said, his voice quivering.

'How long will you stay?'

'Four weeks, I think, but Oscar can tell you.'

'And what's the cost?'

'Somewhere around three hundred bucks a day. I was thinking maybe I could borrow against my share of this place, get Harry Rex to ask the judge if there's a way to get some money now.' Tears were dripping from the corners of his eyes.

Ray had seen the tears before. He'd heard the pleas and the promises, and no matter how hard and cynical he tried to be at that moment, he melted. 'We'll do something,' he said. 'I'll call this guy now.'

'Please, Ray, I want to go right now.'

'Today?'

'Yes, I, uh, well, I can't go back to Memphis.' He lowered his head and ran his fingers through his long hair.

'Somebody looking for you?'

'Yeah,' he nodded. 'Bad guys.'

'Not cops?'

239

'No, they're a helluva lot worse than cops.'

'Do they know you're here?' Ray asked, glancing around. He could almost see heavily armed drug dealers hiding behind the bushes.

'No, they have no idea where I am.'

Ray stood and went into the house.

Like most folks, Oscar Meave remembered Forrest well. They had worked together in a federal detox program in Memphis, and while he was sad to hear that Forrest was in need of help, he was nonetheless delighted to talk to Ray about him. Ray tried his best to explain the urgency of the matter, though he had no details and was not likely to get any. Their father had died three weeks earlier, Ray said, already making excuses.

'Bring him on,' Meave said. 'We'll find a place.'

They left town thirty minutes later, in Ray's rental car. Forrest's Jeep was parked behind the house, for good measure.

'Are you sure these guys won't be snooping around here?' Ray said.

'They have no idea where I'm from,' Forrest replied. His head was back on the headrest, his eyes hidden behind funky sunshades.

'Who are they, exactly?'

'Some really nice guys from south Memphis. You'd like them.'

'And you owe them money?'

'Yes.'

'How much?'

'Four thousand dollars.'

'And where did this four thousand bucks go?'

Forrest gently tapped his nose. Ray shook his head in frustration and anger and bit his tongue to hold back another bitter lecture. Let some miles pass, he told himself. They were in the country now, farmland on both sides.

Forrest began snoring.

This would be another Forrest tale, the third time Ray actually loaded him up and hauled him away for detox. The last time had been almost twelve years earlier – the Judge was still presiding, Claudia still at his side, Forrest doing more drugs than anyone in the state. Things had been normal. The narcs had cast a wide net around him, and through blind luck Forrest had sneaked through it. They suspected he was dealing, which was true, and had they caught him he would still be in prison. Ray had driven him to a state hospital near the coast, one the Judge had pulled strings to get him into. There, he slept for a month then walked away.

The first brotherly journey to rehab had been during Ray's law school years at Tulane. Forrest had overdosed on some vile combination of pills. They pumped his stomach and almost pronounced him dead. The Judge sent them to a compound near Knoxville with locked gates and razor wire. Forrest stayed a week before escaping.

He'd been to jail twice, once as a juvenile, once as an adult, though he was only nineteen.

241

His first arrest was just before a high school football game, Friday night, the playoffs, in Clanton with the entire town waiting for kickoff. He was sixteen, a junior, an all-conference quarterback and safety, a kamikaze who loved to hit late and spear with his helmet. The narcs plucked him from the dressing room and led him away in handcuffs. The backup was an untested freshman, and when Clanton got slaughtered the town never forgave Forrest Atlee.

Ray had been sitting in the stands with the Judge, anxious as everyone else about the game. 'Where's Forrest?' folks began asking during pregame. When the coin was tossed he was in the city jail getting fingerprinted and photographed. They found fourteen ounces of marijuana in his car.

He spent two years in a juvenile facility and was released on his eighteenth birthday.

How does the sixteen-year-old son of a prominent judge become a dope pusher in a small Southern town with no history of drugs? Ray and his father had asked each other that question a thousand times. Only Forrest knew the answer, and long ago he had made the decision to keep it to himself. Ray was thankful that he buried most of his secrets.

After a nice nap, Forrest jolted himself awake and announced he needed something to drink.

'No,' Ray said.

'A soft drink, I swear.'

They stopped at a country store and bought sodas. For breakfast Forrest had a bag of peanuts.

'Some of these places have good food,' he said when they were moving again. Forrest the tour guide for detox centers. Forrest the Michelin critic for rehab units. 'I usually lose a few pounds,' he said, chomping.

'Do they have gyms and such?' Ray asked, aiding the conversation. He really didn't want to discuss the perks of various drug tanks.

'Some do,' Forrest said smugly. 'Ellie sent me to this place in Florida near a beach, lots of sand and water, lots of sad rich folks. Three days of brainwashing, then they worked our asses off. Hikes, bikes, power walks, weights if we wanted. I got a great tan and dropped fifteen pounds. Stayed clean for eight months.'

In his sad little life, everything was measured by stints of sobriety.

'Ellie sent you?' Ray asked.

'Yeah, it was years ago. She had a little dough at one point, not much. I'd hit the bottom, and it was back when she cared. It was a nice place, though, and some of the counselors were those Florida chicks with short skirts and long legs.'

'I'll have to check it out.'

'Kiss my ass.'

'Just kidding.'

'There's this place out West where all the stars go, the Hacienda, and it's the Ritz. Plush rooms, spas, daily massages, chefs who can fix

243

great meals at one thousand calories a day. And the counselors are the best in the world. That's what I need, Bro, six months at the Hacienda.'

'Why six months?'

'Because I need six months. I've tried two months, one month, three weeks, two weeks, it's not enough. For me, it's six months of total lockdown, total brainwashing, total therapy, plus my own masseuse.'

'What's the cost?'

Forrest whistled and rolled his eyes. 'Pick a number. I don't know. You gotta have a zillion bucks and two recommendations to get in. Imagine that, a letter of recommendation. "To the Fine Folks at the Hacienda: I hereby heartily recommend my friend Doofus Smith as a patient in your wonderful facility. Doofus drinks vodka for breakfast, snorts coke for lunch, snacks on heroin, and is usually comatose by dinner. His brain is fried, his veins are lacerated, his liver is shot to hell. Doofus is your kind of person and his old man owns Idaho." '

'Do they keep people for six months?'

'You're clueless, aren't you?'

'I guess.'

'A lot of cokeheads need a year. Even more for heroin addicts.'

And which is your current poison? Ray wanted to ask. But then he didn't want to. 'A year?' he said.

'Yep, total lockdown. And then the addict has to do it himself. I know guys who've been to prison for three years with no coke, no crack, no drugs at all, and when they were released they called a dealer before they called their wives or girlfriends.'

'What happens to them?'

'It's not pretty.' He threw the last of the peanuts into his mouth, slapped his hands together, and sent salt flying.

There were no signs directing traffic to Alcorn Village. They followed Oscar's directions until they were certain they were lost deep in the hills, then saw a gate in the distance. Down a tree-lined drive, a complex spread before them. It was peaceful and secluded, and Forrest gave it good marks for first impressions.

Oscar Meave arrived in the lobby of the administration building and guided them to an intake office, where he handled the initial paper-work himself. He was a counselor, an adminis-trator, a psychologist, an ex-addict who'd cleaned himself up years ago and received two Ph.D.s. He wore jeans, a sweatshirt, sneakers, a goatee, and two earrings, and had the wrinkles and chipped tooth of a rough prior life. But his voice was soft and friendly. He exuded the tough compassion of one who'd been where Forrest was now.

The cost was $325 a day and Oscar was recommending a minimum of four weeks. 'After that, we'll see where he is. I'll need to ask some pretty rough questions about what Forrest has been doing.'

'I don't want to hear that conversation,' Ray said.

'You won't,' Forrest said. He was resigned to the flogging that was coming.

'And we require half the money up front,' Oscar said. 'The other half before his treatment is complete.'

Ray flinched and tried to remember the balance in his checking account back in Virginia. He had plenty of cash, but this was not the time to use it.

'The money is coming out of my father's estate,' Forrest said. 'It might take a few days.'

Oscar was shaking his head. 'No exceptions. Our policy is half now.'

'No problem,' said Ray. 'I'll write a check for it.'

'I want it to come out of the estate,' Forrest said. 'You're not paying for it.'

'The estate can reimburse me. It'll work.' Ray wasn't sure how it would work, but he'd let Harry Rex worry about that. He signed the forms as guarantor of payment. Forrest signed at the bottom of a page listing all the do's and don'ts.

'You can't leave for twenty-eight days,' Oscar said. 'If you do, you forfeit all monies paid and you're never welcome back. Understand?'

'I understand,' Forrest said. How many times had he been through this?

'You're here because you want to be here, right?'

'Right.'

'And no one is forcing you?'

'No one.'

Now that the flogging was on, it was time for Ray to leave. He thanked Oscar and hugged Forrest and sped away much faster than he'd arrived.

Chapter 25

Ray was now certain that the cash had been collected since 1991, the year the Judge was voted out of office. Claudia was around until the year before, and she knew nothing of the money. It had not come from graft and it had not come gambling.

Nor had it come from skillful investing on the sly, because Ray found not a single record of the Judge ever buying or selling a stock or a bond. The accountant hired by Harry Rex to reconstruct the records and put together the final tax return had found nothing either. He said that the Judge's trail was easy to follow because everything had been run through the First National Bank of Clanton.

That's what you think, Ray thought to himself.

There were almost forty boxes of old, useless files scattered throughout the house. The cleaning service had gathered and stacked them in the Judge's study and in the dining room. It took a few hours but he finally found what he was looking for. Two of the boxes held the notes and research – the 'trial files' as the Judge had always referred to them – of the cases he'd heard as a special chancellor since his defeat in 1991.

During a trial the Judge wrote nonstop on yellow legal pads. He noted dates, times, relevant facts, anything that would aid him in reaching a final opinion in the case. Often he would interject a question to a witness and he frequently used his notes to correct the attorneys. Ray had heard him quip more than once, in chambers of course, that the notetaking helped him stay awake. During a lengthy trial, he would fill twenty legal pads with his notes.

Because he was a lawyer before he was a judge, he had acquired the lifelong habit of filing and keeping everything. A trial file consisted of his notes, copies of cases the attorneys relied on, copies of code sections, statutes, even pleadings that were not put with the official court file. As the years passed, the trial files became even more useless, and now they filled forty boxes.

According to his tax returns, since 1993, he had picked up income trying cases as a special chancellor, cases no one else wanted to hear. It was not uncommon in the rural areas to have a dispute too hot for an elected judge. One side would file a motion asking the judge to recuse himself, and he would go through the routine of grappling with the issue while proclaiming his ability to be fair and impartial regardless of the facts or litigants, then reluctantly step down and hand it off to an old pal from another part of the state. The special chancellor would ride in without the baggage of any prior knowledge and without one eye on reelection and hear the case.

In some jurisdictions, special chancellors were used to relieve crowded dockets. Occasionally, they would sit in for an ailing judge. Almost all were retired themselves. The state paid them fifty dollars an hour, plus expenses.

In 1992, the year after his defeat, Judge Atlee had earned nothing extra. In 1993, he'd been paid $5,800. The busiest year – 1996 – he'd reported $16,300. Last year, 1999, he was paid $8,760, but he'd been ill most of the time.

The grand total in earnings as a special chancellor was $56,590, over a six-year period, and all earnings had been reported on his tax returns.

Ray wanted to know what kinds of cases Judge Atlee had heard in his last years. Harry Rex had mentioned one – the sensational divorce trial of a sitting governor. That trial file was three inches thick and included clippings from the Jackson newspaper with photos of the governor, his soon to be ex-wife, and a woman thought to be his current flame. The trial lasted two weeks, and Judge Atlee, according to his notes, seemed to enjoy it tremendously.

There was an annexation case near Hatties-burg that lasted for two weeks and had irritated everyone involved. The city was growing west-ward and eyeing some prime industrial sites. Lawsuits got filed and two years later Judge Atlee gathered everyone together for a trial. There were also newspaper articles, but after an hour of review Ray was bored with the whole mess. He couldn't imagine presiding over it for a month.

But at least there was money involved in it.

Judge Atlee spent eight days in 1995 holding court in the small town of Kosciusko, two hours away, but from his files it looked as though nothing of consequence went to trial.

There was a horrendous tanker truck collision in Tishomingo County in 1994. Five teenagers were trapped in a car and burned to death. Since they were minors, Chancery Court had jurisdiction. One sitting chancellor was related to one of the victims. The other chancellor was dying of brain cancer. Judge Atlee got the call and presided over a trial that lasted two days before it was settled for $7,400,000. One third went to the attorneys for the teenagers, the rest to their families.

Ray set the file on the Judge's sofa, next to the annexation case. He was sitting on the floor of the study, the newly polished floor, under the vigilant gaze of General Forrest. He had a vague idea of what he was doing, but no real plan on how to proceed. Go through the files, pick out the ones that involved money, see where the trail might lead.

The cash he'd found hidden less than ten feet away had come from somewhere.

His cell phone rang. It was a Charlottesville alarm company with a recorded message that a break-in was in progress at his apartment. He jumped to his feet and talked to himself while the message finished. The same call would simultaneously go to the police and to Corey Crawford. Seconds later, Crawford called him. 'I'm on the way there,' he said, and sounded like he was running. It was almost nine-thirty, CST. Ten-thirty in Charlottesville.

Ray paced through the house, thoroughly helpless. Fifteen minutes passed before Crawford called him again. 'I'm here,' he said. 'With the police. Somebody jammed the door downstairs, then jammed the one to the den. That set off the alarm. They didn't have much time. Where do we check?'

'There's nothing particularly valuable there,' Ray said, trying to guess what a thief might want. No cash, jewelry, art, hunting rifles, gold, or silver.

'TV, stereo, microwave, everything's here,' Crawford said. 'They scattered books and magazines, knocked over the table by the kitchen phone, but they were in a hurry. Anything in particular?'

'No, nothing I can think of.' Ray could hear a police radio squawking in the background.

'How many bedrooms?' Crawford asked as he moved through the apartment.

'Two, mine is on the right.'

'All the closet doors are open. They were looking for something. Any idea what?'

'No,' Ray answered.

'No sign of entry in the other bedroom,' Crawford reported, then began talking with two cops. 'Hang on,' he told Ray, who was standing in the front door, looking through the screen, motionless and trying to think of the fastest way home.

The cops and Crawford decided it was a quick strike by a pretty good thief who got surprised by the alarm. He jammed the two doors with minimal damage, realized there was an alarm, raced through the place looking for something in particular, and when he didn't find it he kicked a few things for the hell of it and fled. He or they – could've been more than one.

'You need to be here to tell the police if anything is missing and to do a report,' Crawford said.

'I'll be there tomorrow,' Ray said. 'Can you secure the place tonight?'

'Yeah, we'll think of something.'

'Call me after the cops leave.'

He sat on the front steps and listened to the crickets while yearning to be at Chaney's Self-Storage, sitting in the dark with one of the Judge's guns, ready to blast away at anyone who came near him. Fifteen hours away by car. Three and a half by private plane. He called Fog Newton and there was no answer.

253

His phone startled him again. 'I'm still in the apartment,' Crawford said.

'I don't think this is random,' Ray said.

'You mentioned some valuables, some family stuff, at Chaney's Self-Storage.'

'Yeah. Any chance you could watch the place tonight?'

'They got security out there, guards and cameras, not a bad outfit.' Crawford sounded tired and not enthusiastic about napping in a car all night.

'Can you do it?'

'I can't get in the place. You have to be a customer.'

'Watch the entrance.'

Crawford grunted and breathed deeply. 'Yeah, I'll check on it, maybe call a guy in to watch it.'

'Thanks. I'll call you when I get to town tomorrow.'

He called Chaney's and there was no answer. He waited five minutes, called again, counted fourteen rings then heard a voice.

'Chancey's, security, Murray speaking.'

He very politely explained who he was and what he wanted. He was leasing three units and there was a bit of concern because someone had vandalized his downtown apartment, and could Mr. Murray please pay special attention to 14B, 37F, and 18R. No problem, said Mr. Murray, who sounded as if he was yawning into the phone.

254

Just a little jumpy, Ray explained.

'No problem,' mumbled Mr. Murray.

It took one hour and two drinks for the edginess to relent. He was no closer to Charlottesville. There was the urge to hop in the rental car and race through the night, but it passed. He preferred to sleep and try to find an airplane in the morning. Sleep, though, was impossible, so he returned to the trial files.

The Judge had once said he knew little about zoning law because there was so little zoning in Mississippi, and virtually none in the six counties of the 25th Chancery District. But somehow someone had cajoled him into hearing a bitterly fought zoning case in the city of Columbus. The trial lasted for six days, and when it was over an anonymous phone caller threatened to shoot the Judge, according to his notes.

Threats were not uncommon, and he'd been known to carry a pistol in his briefcase over the years. It was rumored that Claudia carried one too. You'd rather have the Judge shooting at you than his court reporter, ran the conventional wisdom.

The zoning case almost put Ray to sleep. But then he found a gap, the black hole he'd been digging for, and he forgot about sleep.

According to his tax records, the Judge was paid $8,110 in January 1999 to hear a case in the 27th Chancery District. The 27th comprised two counties on the Gulf Coast, a part of the state the Judge cared little for. The fact that he would voluntarily go there for a period of days struck Ray as quite odd.

Odder still was the absence of a trial file. He searched the two boxes and found nothing related to a case on the coast, and with his curiosity barely under control he plowed through the other thirty-eight or so. He forgot about his apartment and the self-storage and whether or not Mr. Murray was awake or even alive, and he almost forgot about the money.

A trial file was missing.

Chapter 26

The US Air flight left Memphis at six-forty in the morning, which meant Ray had to leave Clanton no later than five, which meant he slept about three hours, the usual at Maple Run. On the first flight, he dozed off en route, again in the Pittsburgh airport, and again on the commuter flight to Charlottesville. He inspected his apartment, then fell asleep on the sofa.

The money hadn't been touched. No unauthorized entries into any of his little storage units at Chaney's. Nothing was out of the ordinary. He locked himself inside 18R, opened the five fireproof and waterproof boxes, and counted fifty-three freezer bags.

Sitting on the concrete floor with three million dollars strewn around him, Ray Atlee finally admitted how important the money had become. The real horror of last night had been the chance of losing it. Now he was afraid to leave it.

In the past few weeks, he had become more

curious about how much things cost, about what the money could buy, about how it could grow if invested conservatively, or aggressively. At times he thought of himself as wealthy, and then he would dismiss those thoughts. But they were always there, just under the surface and popping up with greater frequency. The questions were slowly being answered – no it was not counterfeit, no it was not traceable, no it had not been won at the casinos, no it had not been filched from the lawyers and litigants of the 25th Chancery District.

And, no, the money should not be shared with Forrest because he would kill himself with it. No, it should not be included in the estate for several excellent reasons.

One by one the options were being eliminated. He might be forced to keep it himself.

There was a loud knock on the metal door, and he almost screamed. He scrambled to his feet and yelled, 'Who is it?'

'Security,' came the reply, and the voice was vaguely familiar. Ray stepped over the cash and reached for the door, which he cracked no more than four inches. Mr. Murray was grinning at him.

'Everything okay in there?' he asked, more of a janitor than an armed guard.

'Fine, thanks,' Ray said, his heart still frozen.

'Need anything, let me know.'

'Thanks for last night.'

'Just doing my job.'

Ray repacked the money, relocked the doors,

and drove across town with one eye on the rearview mirror.

The owner of his apartment sent a crew of Mexican carpenters around to repair the two damaged doors. They hammered and sawed throughout the late afternoon, then said yes to a cold beer when they were finished. Ray chatted with them as he tried to ease them out of his den. There was a pile of mail on the kitchen table, and, after ignoring it for most of the day, he sat down to deal with it. Bills had to be paid. Catalogs and junk mail. Three notes of sympathy.

A letter from the Internal Revenue Service, addressed to Mr. Ray Atlee, Executor of the Estate of Reuben V. Atlee, and postmarked in Atlanta two days earlier. He studied it carefully before opening it slowly. A single sheet of official stationery, from one Martin Gage, Office of Criminal Investigations, in the Atlanta office. It read:

Dear Mr. Atlee:

As executor of your father's estate, you are required by law to include all assets for valuation and taxation purposes. Concealment of assets may constitute tax fraud. The unauthorized disbursement of assets is a violation of the laws of Mississippi and possible federal laws as well.

Martin Gage
Criminal Investigator

His first instinct was to call Harry Rex to see what notice had been given to the IRS. As executor, he had a year from the date of death to file the final return, and, according to the accountant, extensions were liberally granted.

The letter was postmarked the day after he and Harry Rex went to court to open the estate. Why would the IRS be so quick to respond? How would they even know about the death of Reuben Atlee?

Instead, he called the office number on the letterhead. The recorded message welcomed him to the world of the IRS, Atlanta office, but he would have to call back later because it was a Saturday. He went online and in the Atlanta directory found three Martin Gages. The first one he called was out of town, but his wife said he did not work for the IRS, thank heavens. The second call went unanswered. The third found a Mr. Gage eating dinner.

'Do you work for the IRS?' Ray asked, after cordially introducing himself as a professor of law and apologizing for the intrusion.

'Yes, I do.'

'Criminal Investigations?'

'Yep, that's me. Fourteen years now.'

Ray described the letter, then read it verbatim.

'I didn't write that,' Gage said.

'Then who did?' Ray snapped, and immediately wished he had not.

'How am I supposed to know? Can you fax it to me?'

Ray stared at his fax machine, and, thinking quickly, said, 'Sure, but my machine is at the office. I can do it Monday.'

'Scan it and e-mail it,' Gage said.

'Uh, my scanner's broke right now. I'll just fax it to you Monday.'

'Okay, but somebody's pulling your leg, pal. That's not my letter.'

Ray was suddenly anxious to rid himself of the IRS, but Gage was now fully involved. 'I'll tell you something else,' he continued. 'Impersonating an IRS agent is a federal offense, and we prosecute vigorously. Any idea who it is?'

'I have no idea.'

'Probably got my name from our online directory, worst thing we ever did. Freedom of Information and all that crap.'

'Probably so.'

'When was the estate opened?'

'Three days ago.'

'Three days ago! The return's not due for a year.'

'I know.'

'What's in the estate?'

'Nothing. An old house.'

'Just some crackpot. Fax it Monday and I'll give you a call.'

'Thanks.'

Ray put the phone on the coffee table and

asked himself why, exactly, had he called the IRS?

To verify the letter.

Gage would never get a copy of it. And in a month or so he would forget about it. And in a year he wouldn't recall it if anyone mentioned it.

Perhaps not the smartest move so far.

Forrest had settled into the routine of Alcorn Village. He was allowed two calls a day and they were subject to being recorded, he explained. 'They don't want us calling our dealers.'

'Not funny,' Ray said. It was the sober Forrest, with the soft drawl and clear mind.

'Why are you in Virginia?' he asked.

'It's my home.'

'Thought you were visiting some friends around here, old buddies from law school.'

'I'll be back shortly. How's the food?'

'Like a nursing home, Jell-O three times a day but always a different color. Really lousy stuff. For three hundred bucks plus a day it's a rip-off.'

'Any cute girls?'

'One, but she's fourteen, daughter of a judge, if you can believe that. Really some sad people. We have these group bitch meetings once a day where everyone lashes out at whoever got them started on drugs. We talk through our problems. We help one another. Hell, I know more than the counselors. This is my eighth detox, Bro, can you believe it?'

262

'Seems like more than that,' Ray said.

'Thanks for helping me. You know what's sick?'

'What?'

'I'm happiest when I'm clean. I feel great, I feel smart, I can do anything. Then I hate myself when I'm on the streets doing all that stupid stuff like the other scumbags. I don't know why I do it.'

'You sound great, Forrest.'

'I like this place, aside from the food.'

'Good, I'm proud of you.'

'Can you come see me?'

'Of course I will. Give me a couple of days.'

He checked in with Harry Rex, who was at the office, where he usually spent the weekends. With four wives under his belt, there were good reasons he wasn't home much.

'Do you recall the Judge hearing a case on the coast, early last year?' Ray asked.

Harry Rex was eating something and smacking into the phone. 'The coast?' He hated the coast, thought they were all a bunch of redneck mafia types.

'He was paid for a trial down there, January of last year.'

'He was sick last year,' Harry Rex said, then swallowed something liquid.

'His cancer was diagnosed last July.'

'I don't remember any case on the coast,' he said, and bit into something else. 'That surprises me.'

'Me too.'

'Why are you going through his files?'

'I'm just checking his payroll records against his trial files.'

'Why?'

'Because I'm the executor.'

'Forgive me. When are you coming back?'

'Couple of days.'

'Hey, I bumped into Claudia today, hadn't seen her in months, and she gets to town early, parks a brand-new black Cadillac near the Coffee Shop so everybody can see it, then spends half the morning piddling around town. Whatta piece of work.'

Ray couldn't help but smile at the thought of Claudia racing down to the car dealership with a pocket full of cash. The Judge would be proud.

Sleep came in short naps on the sofa. The walls cracked louder, the vents and ducts seemed more active. Things moved, then they didn't. The night after the break-in, the entire apartment was poised for another one.

Chapter 27

Trying hard to be normal, Ray took a long jog on a favorite trail, along the downtown mall, down Main Street to the campus, up Observatory Hill and back, six miles in all. He had lunch with Carl Mirk at Bizou, a popular bistro three blocks from his apartment, and he drank coffee afterward at a sidewalk café. Fog had the Bonanza reserved for a 3 P.M. training session, but the mail came and everything normal went out the window.

The envelope was addressed to him by hand, nothing on the return, with a postmark in Charlottesville the day before. A stick of dynamite would not have looked more suspicious lying there on the table. Inside was a letter-size sheet of paper, trifolded, and when he spread it open all systems shut down. For a moment, he couldn't think, breathe, feel, hear.

It was a color digital photo of the front of 14B at Chaney's, printed off a computer on regular copier paper. No words, no warnings, no threats. None were needed.

When he could breathe again he also started sweating, and the numbness wore off enough for a sharp pain to knife through his stomach. He was dizzy so he closed his eyes, and when he opened them and looked at the picture again, it was shaking.

His first thought, the first he could remember, was that there was nothing in the apartment he could not do without. He could leave everything. But he filled a small bag anyway.

Three hours later he stopped for gas in Roanoke, and three hours after that he pulled into a busy truck stop just east of Knoxville. He sat in the parking lot for a long time, low in his TT roadster, watching the truckers come and go, watching the movements in and out of the crowded café. There was a table he wanted in the window, and when it was available he locked the Audi and went inside. From the table, he guarded his car, fifty feet away and stuffed with three million in cash.

Because of the aroma, he guessed that grease was the café's specialty. He ordered a burger and on a napkin began scribbling his options.

The safest place for the money was in a bank, in a large lock box behind thick walls, cameras, etc. He could divide the money, scatter it among several banks in several towns between Charlottesville and Clanton, and leave a complicated trail. The money could be discreetly hauled in by briefcase. Once locked away, it would be safe forever.

The trail, though, would be extensive. Lease forms, proper ID, home address, phones, here meet our new vice president, in business with strangers, video cameras, lock box registers, and who knew what else because Ray had never hidden stuff in a bank before.

He had passed several self-storage places along the interstate. They were everywhere these days and for some reason wedged as close to the main roads as possible. Why not pick one at random, pull over, pay cash, and keep the paperwork to a minimum? He could hang around in Podunktown for a day or two, find some more fireproof boxes at a local supply house, secure his money, then sneak away. It was a brilliant idea because his tormentor would not expect it.

And it was a stupid idea because he would leave the money.

He could take it home to Maple Run and bury it in the basement. Harry Rex could alert the sheriff and the police to watch for suspicious outsiders lurking around the town. If an agent showed up to follow him, he'd get nailed in Clanton, and Dell at the Coffee Shop would have the details by sunrise. You couldn't cough there without three people catching your cold.

The truckers came in waves, most of them talking loudly as they entered, anxious to mix it up after miles of solitary confinement. They all looked the same, jeans and pointed-toe boots. A pair of sneakers walked by and caught Ray's attention. Khakis, not jeans. The man was alone and took a seat at the counter. In the mirror Ray saw his face, and it was one he'd seen before. Wide through the eyes, narrow at the chin, long flat nose, flaxen hair, thirty-five years old give or take. Somewhere around Charlottesville but impossible to place.

Or was everyone now a suspect?

Run with your loot, like a murderer with his victim in the trunk, and plenty of faces look familiar and ominous.

The burger arrived, hot and steaming, covered with fries, but he'd lost his appetite. He started on his third napkin. The first two had taken him nowhere.

His options at the moment were limited. Since he was unwilling to let the money out of his sight, he would drive all night, stopping for coffee, perhaps pulling over for a nap, and arrive at Clanton early in the morning. Once he was on his turf again, things would become clearer.

Hiding the money in the basement was a bad idea. An electrical short, a bolt of lightning, a stray match, and the house was gone. It was hardly more than kindling anyway.

The man at the counter had yet to look at Ray, and the more Ray looked at him the more convinced he was that he was wrong. It was a generic face, the kind you see every day and seldom remember. He was eating chocolate pie and drinking coffee. Odd, at eleven o'clock at night.

He rolled into Clanton just after 7 A.M. He was red-eyed, ragged with exhaustion, in need of a shower and two days' rest. Through the night, while he wasn't watching every set of headlights behind him and slapping himself to stay awake, he'd dreamed of the solitude of Maple Run. A large, empty house, all to himself. He could sleep upstairs, downstairs, on the porch. No ringing phones, no one to bother him.

But the roofers had other plans. They were hard at work when he arrived, their trucks and ladders and tools covering the front lawn and blocking the driveway. He found Harry Rex at the Coffee Shop, eating poached eggs and reading two newspapers at once.

'What are you doing here?' he said, barely looking up. He wasn't finished with his eggs or his papers, and didn't appear too excited to see Ray.

'Maybe I'm hungry.'

'You look like hell.'

'Thanks. I couldn't sleep there, so I drove here.'

'You're cracking up.'

'Yes, I am.'

He finally lowered the newspaper and stabbed an egg that appeared to be covered with hot sauce. 'You drove all night from Charlottesville?'

'It's only fifteen hours.'

A waitress brought him coffee. 'How long are those roofers planning on working?'

'They're there?'

'Oh yes. At least a dozen of them. I wanted to sleep for the next two days.'

'It's those Atkins boys. They're fast unless they start drinking and fighting. Had one fall off a ladder last year, broke his neck. Got him thirty thousand in workers' comp.'

'Anyway, why, then, did you hire them?'

'They're cheap, same as you, Mr. Executor. Go sleep in my office. I got a hideaway on the third floor.'

'With a bed?'

Harry Rex glanced around as if the gossip-mongers of Clanton were closing in. 'Remember Rosetta Rhines?'

'No.'

'She was my fifth secretary and third wife. That was where it all started.'

'Are the sheets clean?'

'What sheets? Take it or leave it. It's very quiet, but the floor shakes. That's how we got caught.'

'Sorry I asked.' Ray took a long swig of coffee. He was hungry, but not ready for a feast. He wanted a bowl of flakes with skim milk and fruit, something sensible, but he'd be ridiculed for ordering such light fare in the Coffee Shop.

'You gonna eat?' Harry Rex growled at him.

'No. We need to store some stuff. All those boxes and furniture. You know a place?'

'We?'

'Okay, I need a place.'

'It's nothing but crap.' A bite of a biscuit, one loaded with sausage, Cheddar, and what appeared to be mustard. 'Burn it.'

'I can't burn it, at least not now.'

'Then do what all good executors do. Store for two years, then give it to the Salvation Army and burn what they don't want.'

'Yes or no. Is there a storage place in town?'

'Didn't you go to school with that crazy Cantrell boy?'

'There were two of them.'

'No, there were three of them. One got hit by that Greyhound out near Tobytown.' A long pull of coffee, then more eggs.

'A storage place, Harry Rex.'

'Testy, aren't we?'

'No, sleep-deprived.'

'I've offered my love nest.'

'No thanks. I'll try my luck with the roofers.'

'Their uncle is Virgil Cantrell, I handled his first wife's second divorce, and he's converted the old depot into a storage warehouse.'

'Is that the only place in town?"

'No, Lundy Staggs put in some of those ministorage units west of town, but they got flooded. I wouldn't go there.'

'What's the name of this depot?' Ray asked, tired of the Coffee Shop.

'The Depot.' Another bite of biscuit.

'By the railroad tracks?'

'That's it.' He began shaking a bottle of Tabasco sauce over the remaining pile of eggs. 'He's usually got some space, even put in a block room for fire protection. Don't go in the basement, though.'

Ray hesitated, knowing he should ignore the bait. He glanced at his car parked in front of the courthouse and finally said, 'Why not?'

'He keeps his boy down there.'

'His boy?'

'Yeah, he's crazy too. Virgil couldn't get him in Whitfield and couldn't afford a private joint, so he figured he'd just lock him up in the basement.'

'You're serious?'

'Hell yes, I'm serious. I told him it wasn't against the law. Boy's got everythang – bed-room, bathroom, television. Helluva lot cheaper than paying rent in a nuthouse.'

'What's his name?' Ray asked, digging the hole deeper.

'Little Virgil.'

'Little Virgil?'

'Little Virgil.'

'How old is Little Virgil?'

'I don't know, forty-five, fifty.'

To Ray's great relief, no Virgil was present when he walked into the Depot. A stocky woman in overalls said Mr. Cantrell was out running errands and wouldn't be back for two hours. Ray inquired about storage space, and she offered to show him around.

Years before, a remote uncle from Texas had come to visit. Ray's mother scrubbed and polished him to the point of misery. With great anticipation they drove to the depot to fetch the uncle. Forrest was an infant and they left him at home with the nanny. Ray clearly remembered waiting on the platform, hearing the train's whistle, seeing it approach, feeling the excitement as the crowd waited. The depot back then was a busy place. When he was in high school they boarded it up, and the hoodlums used it as a hangout. It was almost razed before the town stepped in with an ill-advised renovation.

Now it was a collection of chopped-up rooms flung over two floors, with worthless junk piled to the ceiling. Lumber and wallboard were stacked throughout, evidence of endless repairs. Sawdust covered the floors. A quick walk-through convinced Ray that the place was more flammable than Maple Run.

'We got more space in the basement,' the woman said.

'No thanks.'

He stepped outside to leave, and flying by on Taylor Street was a brand-new black Cadillac, glistening in the early sun, not a speck of dirt anywhere, Claudia behind the wheel with Jackie O sunglasses.

Standing there in the early morning heat, watching the car race down the street, Ray felt the town of Clanton collapse on top of him. Claudia, the Virgils, Harry Rex and his wives and secretaries, the Atkins boys roofing and drinking and fighting.

Is everybody crazy, or is it just me?

He got in his car and left the Depot, slinging gravel behind. At the edge of town the road stopped. To the north was Forrest, to the south was the coast. Life would get no simpler by visiting his brother, but he had promised.

Chapter 28

Two days later, Ray arrived on the Gulf Coast of Mississippi. There were friends from his law school days at Tulane he wanted to see, and he gave serious thought to spending time in his old haunts. He craved an oyster po'boy from Franky & Johnny's by the levee, a muffaletta from Maspero's on Decatur in the Quarter, a Dixie Beer at the Chart Room on Bourbon Street, and chicory coffee and beignets at Café du Monde, all of his old haunts from twenty years ago.

But crime was rampant in New Orleans, and his handsome little sports car could be a target. Lucky the thief who stole it and yanked open the trunk. Thieves would not catch him, nor would state troopers because he kept precisely at the posted limits. He was a perfect driver – obeying all the laws, closely eyeing every other car.

The traffic slowed him on Highway 90, and for an hour he crept eastward through Long Beach, Gulfport, and Biloxi, hugging the beach, past the shiny new casinos sitting at the water, past new hotels and restaurants. Gambling had hit the coast as fast as it had arrived in the farmlands around Tunica.

He crossed the Bay of Biloxi and entered Jackson County. Near Pascagoula, he saw a flashing rented sign beckoning travelers to stop in for All-You-Can-Eat-Cajun, just $13.99. It was a dive but the parking lot was well lit. He cased it first and realized he could sit at a table in the window and keep an eye on his car. This had become his habit.

There were three counties along the Gulf. Jackson on the east and bordering Alabama, Harrison in the middle, and Hancock on the west next to Louisiana. A local politician had succeeded nicely in Washington and kept the pork flowing back to the shipyards in Jackson County. Gambling was paying the bills and building the schools in Harrison County. And it was Hancock, the least developed and populated, that Judge Atlee had visited in January 1999 for a case that no one back home knew about.

After a slow dinner of crawfish étoufée and shrimp rémoulade, with some raw oysters thrown in, he drifted back across the bay, back through Biloxi and Gulfport. In the town of Pass Christian he found what he was searching for – a new, flat motel with doors that opened to the outside. The surroundings looked safe, the parking lot was half-full. He paid sixty dollars cash for one night and backed the car as close to

276

his door as possible. He'd changed his mind about being without a weapon. One strange sound during the night, and he'd be outside in a flash with the Judge's .38, loaded now. He was perfectly prepared to sleep in the car, if necessary.

Hancock county was named for John, he of the bold signature on the Declaration of Independence. Its courthouse was built in 1911 in the center of Bay St. Louis, and was practically blown away by Hurricane Camille in August 1969. The eye ran right through Pass Christian and Bay St. Louis, and no building escaped severe damage. More than a hundred people died and many were never found.

Ray stopped to read a historical marker on the courthouse lawn, then turned once more to look at his little Audi. Though court records were usually open, he was nervous anyway. The clerks in Clanton guarded their records and monitored who came and went. He wasn't sure what he was looking for or where to begin. The biggest fear, however, was what he might find.

In the Chancery Clerk's office, he loitered just long enough to catch the eye of a pretty young lady with a pencil in her hair. 'May I help you?' she drawled. He was holding a legal pad, as if that would somehow qualify him and open all the right doors.

'Do y'all keep records of trials?' he asked,

trying hard to string out the 'y'all' and overemphasizing it in the process.

She frowned and looked at him as if he had committed a misdemeanor.

'We have minutes from each term of court,' she said slowly, because he obviously was not very bright. 'And we have the actual court files.' Ray was scribbling this down.

'And,' she said after a pause, 'there are the trial transcripts taken down by the court reporter, but we don't keep those here.'

'Can I see the minutes?' he asked, grasping at the first item she'd mentioned.

'Sure. Which term?'

'January of last year.'

She took two steps to her right and began pecking on a keyboard. Ray looked around the large office where several ladies were at their desks, some typing, some filing, some on the phone. The last time he'd seen the Chancery Clerk's office in Clanton there had been only one computer. Hancock County was ten years ahead.

In a corner two lawyers sipped coffee from paper cups and whispered low about important matters. Before them were the property deed books that dated back two hundred years. Both had reading glasses perched on their noses and scuffed wing tips and ties with thick knots. They were checking land titles for a hundred bucks a pop, one of a dozen dreary chores handled by legions of small-town lawyers. One of them noticed Ray and eyed him suspiciously.

That could be me, Ray thought to himself.

The young lady ducked and pulled out a large ledger filled with computer printouts. She flipped pages, then stopped and spun it around on the counter. 'Here,' she said, pointing. 'January '99, two weeks of court. Here's the docket, which goes on for several pages. This column lists the final disposition. As you'll see, most cases were continued to the March term.'

Ray was looking and listening.

'Any case in particular?' she asked.

'Do you remember a case that was heard by Judge Atlee, from Ford County? I think he was here as a special chancellor?' he asked casually. She glared at him as if he'd asked to see her own divorce file.

'Are you a reporter?' she asked, and Ray almost took a step backward.

'Do I need to be?' he asked. Two of the other deputy clerks had stopped whatever they were doing and were frowning at him.

She forced a smile. 'No, but that case was pretty big. It's right here,' she said, pointing again. On the docket it was listed simply as *Gibson v. Miyer-Brack*. Ray nodded approvingly as if he'd found exactly what he wanted. 'And where would the file be located?' he asked.

'It's thick,' she said.

He followed her into a room filled with black metal cabinets that held thousands of files. She

279

knew exactly where to go. 'Sign here,' she said, handing over a clipboard with a ledger on it. 'Just your name, the date. I'll do the rest.'

'What kind of case was it?' he asked as he filled in the blanks.

'Wrongful death.' She opened a long drawer and pointed from one end to the other. 'All this,' she said. 'The pleadings start here, then discovery, then the trial transcript. You can take it to that table over there, but it cannot leave the room. Judge's orders.'

'Which judge?'

'Judge Atlee.'

'He died, you know.'

Walking away, she said, 'That's not such a bad thing.'

The air in the room went with her, and it took a few seconds for Ray to think again. The file was four feet thick, but he didn't care. He had the rest of the summer.

Clete Gibson died in 1997 at the age of sixty-one. Cause of death, kidney failure. Cause of kidney failure, a drug called Ryax, manufactured by Miyer-Brack, according to the allegations of the lawsuit, and found to be true by the Honorable Reuben V. Atlee, sitting as special chancellor.

Mr. Gibson had taken Ryax for eight years to battle high cholesterol. The drug was prescribed by his doctor and sold by his pharmacist, both of whom were also sued by his widow and children. After taking the drug for about five years, he began having kidney problems, which were treated by a different set of doctors. At the time, Ryax, a relatively new drug, had no known side effects. When Gibson's kidneys quit completely, he somehow came to know a Mr. Patton French, attorney-at-law. This happened shortly before his death.

Patton French was with French & French, over in Biloxi. A firm letterhead listed six other lawyers. In addition to the manufacturer, physician, and pharmacist, the defendants also included a local drug salesman and his brokerage company out of New Orleans. Every defendant had a big firm engaged, including some heavyweights from New York. The litigation was contentious, complicated, even fierce at times, and Mr. Patton French and his little firm from Biloxi waged an impressive war against the giants on the other side.

Miyer-Brack was a Swiss pharmaceutical giant, privately owned, with interests in sixty countries, according to the deposition of its American representative. In 1998, its profits were $635 million on revenues of $9.1 billion. That one deposition took an hour to read.

For some reason, Patton French decided to file a wrongful death suit in Chancery Court, the court of equity, instead of Circuit Court, where most trials were by jury. By statute, the only jury trials in Chancery were for will contests. Ray had sat through several of those miserable affairs while clerking for the Judge.

Chancery Court had jurisdiction for two reasons. First, Gibson was dead and his estate was a Chancery matter. Second, he had a child under the age of eighteen. The legal business of minors belonged in Chancery Court.

Gibson also had three children who were not minors. The lawsuit could've been filed in either Circuit or Chancery, one of a hundred great quirks in Mississippi law. Ray had once asked the Judge to explain this enigma, and as usual the answer was simply, 'We have the greatest court system in the country.' Every old chancellor believed this.

Giving lawyers the choice of where to sue was not peculiar to any state. Forum shopping was a game played on the national map. But when a lawsuit by a widow living in rural Mississippi against a mammoth Swiss company that created a drug produced in Uruguay was filed in the Chancery Court of Hancock County, a red flag was raised. The federal courts were in place to deal with such far-flung disputes, and Miyer-Brack and its phalanx of lawyers tried gallantly to remove the case. Judge Atlee held firm, as did the federal judge. Local defendants were included, thus removal to federal court could be denied.

Reuben Atlee was in charge of the case, and as he pushed the matter to trial, his patience with the defense lawyers wore thin. Ray had to smile at some of his father's rulings. They were terse, brutally to the point, and designed to light a fire under the hordes of lawyers scrambling around the defendants. The modern-day rules about speedy trials had never been necessary in Judge Atlee's courtroom.

It became evident that Ryax was a bad product. Patton French found two experts who blasted the drug, and the experts defending it were nothing but mouthpieces for the company. Ryax lowered cholesterol to amazing levels. It had been rushed through the approvals, then dumped into the marketplace, where it became extremely popular. Tens of thousands of kidneys had now been ruined, and Mr. Patton French had Miyer-Brack pinned to the mat.

The trial lasted for eight days. Against the objections of the defense, the proceedings began each morning precisely at eight-fifteen. And they often ran until eight at night, prompting more objections, which Judge Atlee ignored. Ray had seen this many times. The Judge believed in hard work, and, with no jury to pamper, he was brutal.

His final decision was dated two days after the last witness testified, a shocking blow for judicial promptness. Evidently, he had remained in Bay St. Louis and dictated a four-page ruling to the court reporter. This, too, did not surprise Ray. The Judge loathed procrastination in deciding cases.

Plus, he had his notes to rely on. For eight

days of nonstop testimony, the Judge must have filled thirty legal pads. His ruling had enough detail to impress the experts.

The family of Clete Gibson was award $1.1 million in actual damages, the value of his life, according to an economist. And to punish Miyer-Brack for pushing such a bad product, the Judge awarded $10 million in punitive damages. The opinion was a scathing indictment of corporate recklessness and greed, and it was quite obvious that Judge Atlee had become deeply troubled by the practices of Miyer-Brack.

Even so, Ray had never known his father to resort to punitive damages.

There was the usual flurry of post-trial motions, all of which the Judge dismissed with brusque paragraphs. Miyer-Brack wanted the punitive damages taken out. Patton French wanted them increased. Both sides received a written tongue-lashing.

Oddly, there was no appeal. Ray kept waiting for one. He flipped through the post-trial section twice, then dug through the entire drawer again. It was possible the case had been settled afterward, and he made a note to ask the clerk.

A nasty little fight erupted over the fees. Patton French had a contract signed by the Gibson family that gave him fifty percent of any recovery. The Judge, as always, felt that was excessive. In Chancery, the fees were within the sole discretion of the Judge. Thirty-three percent had always been his limit. The math was easy to do, and Mr. French fought hard to collect his well-earned money. His Honor didn't budge.

The Gibson trial was Judge Atlee at his finest, and Ray felt both proud and sentimental. It was difficult to believe it had taken place almost a year and a half earlier, when the Judge was suffering from diabetes, heart disease, and probably cancer, though the latter was six months from being discovered.

He admired the old warrior.

With the exception of one lady who was eating a melon at her desk and doing something else online, the clerks were off at lunch. Ray left the place and went to find a library.

Chapter 29

From a burger joint in Biloxi, he checked his voice mail in Charlottesville and found three messages. Kaley called to say she'd like to have dinner. A quick discard took care of her, forever. Fog Newton called to say the Bonanza was clear for the next week and they needed to go fly. And Martin Gage with the IRS in Atlanta checked in, still looking for the fax of the bogus letter. Keep looking, Ray thought to himself.

He was eating a prepackaged salad at a bright orange plastic table, across the highway from the beach. He could not remember the last time he'd sat alone in a fast-food joint, and he was doing so now only because he could eat with his car close by and in plain sight. Plus the place was crawling with young mothers and their children, usually a low-crime group. He finally gave up on the salad and called Fog.

The Biloxi Public Library was on Lameuse Street. Using a new map he'd purchased at a convenience store, he found it and parked in

286

a row of cars near the main entrance. As was his habit now, he stopped and observed his car and all the elements around it before entering the building.

The computers were on the first floor, in a room encased in glass but with no windows to the outside, to his disappointment. The leading newspaper on the coast was the *Sun Herald*, and through a news-library service its archives could be searched back to 1994. He went to January 24, 1999, the day after Judge Atlee had issued his ruling in the trial. Not surprisingly, there was a story on the front page of the metro section about the $11.1 million verdict over in Bay St. Louis. And it was certainly no surprise to see that Mr. Patton French had a lot to say. Judge Atlee refused comment. The defense lawyers claimed to be shocked and promised to appeal.

There was a photo of Patton French, a man in his mid-fifties with a round face and waves of graying hair. As the story ran on it became obvious that he had called up the paper with the breaking news and had been delighted to chat. It was a 'grueling trial.' The actions of the defendants were 'reckless and greedy.' The decision by the court was 'courageous and fair.' Any appeal would be 'just another attempt to delay justice.'

He'd won many trials, he boasted, but this was his biggest verdict. Quizzed about the recent spate of high awards, he downplayed any suggestion that the ruling was a bit outrageous. 'A jury in Hinds County handed out five hundred million dollars two years ago,' he said. And in other parts of the state, enlightened juries were hitting greedy corporate defendants for ten million here and twenty million there. 'This award is legally defensible on every front,' he declared.

His specialty, he said as the story wound down, was pharmaceutical liability. He had four hundred Ryax cases alone and was adding more each day.

Ray did a word search for Ryax within the *Sun Herald*. Five days after the story, on January 29, there was a bold, full-page ad that began with the ominous question: Have You Taken Ryax? Under it were two paragraphs of dire warnings about the dangers of the drug, then a paragraph detailing the recent victory of Patton French, expert trial attorney, specializing in Ryax and other problematic drugs. A victims' screening session would take place at a Gulfport hotel for the following ten days with qualified medical experts conducting the tests. The screening was at no cost to those who responded. No strings attached, or at least none were mentioned. In clear letters across the bottom of the page was the information that the ad was paid for by the law firm of French & French, with addresses and phone numbers of their offices in Gulfport, Biloxi, and Pascagoula.

The word search produced an almost identical ad dated March 1, 1999. The only difference was the time and place of the screening. Another ad ran in the Sunday edition of the *Sun Herald* on May 2, 1999.

For almost an hour, Ray ventured out from the coast, and found the same ads in the *Clarion-Ledger* in Jackson, the *Times-Picayune* in New Orleans, the *Hattiesburg American,* the *Mobile Register,* the *Commercial Appeal* in Memphis, and *The Advocate* in Baton Rouge. Patton French had launched a massive frontal assault on Ryax and Miyer-Brack.

Convinced that the newspaper ads could spread to all fifty states, Ray grew weary of it. On a guess, he did a Web search for Mr. French, and was welcomed to the firm's own site, a very impressive piece of propaganda.

There were now fourteen lawyers in the firm, with offices in six cities and expanding by the hour. Patton French had a flattering one-page biography that would have embarrassed those with thinner skins. His father, the elder French, looked to be eighty if a day, and had taken senior status, whatever that meant.

The firm's thrust was its rabid representation of folks injured by bad drugs and bad doctors. It had brilliantly negotiated the largest Ryax settlement to date – $900 million for 7,200 clients. Now it was hammering Shyne Medical, makers of Minitrin, the widely used and obscenely profitable hypertension drug that the FDA had pulled because of its side effects. The firm had almost two thousand Minitrin clients and was screening more each week.

Patton French had hit Clark Pharmaceuticals for an eight-million-dollar jury verdict in New Orleans. The drug at war there was Kobril, an antidepressant that had been loosely linked to hearing loss. The firm had settled its first batch of Kobril cases, fourteen hundred of them, for fifty-two million.

Little was said about the other members of the firm, giving the clear impression that it was a one-man show with a squad of minions in the backrooms grappling with thousands of clients who'd been gathered up on the street. There was a page with Mr. French's speaking engagements, one with his extensive trial calendar, and two pages of screening schedules, covering no less than eight drugs, including Skinny Bens, the fat pill Forrest had mentioned earlier.

To better serve its clients, the French firm had purchased a Gulfstream IV, and there was a large color photo of it on the ramp somewhere, with, of course, Patton French posed near the nose in a dark designer suit, with a fierce smile, ready to hop on board and go fight for justice somewhere. Ray knew that such a plane probably cost about thirty million, with two full-time pilots and a list of maintenance expenses that would terrify an accountant.

Patton French was a shameless ego pit.

The airplane was the final straw, and Ray left the library. Leaning on his car, he dialed the number for French & French and worked his way through the recorded menu – client, lawyer, judge, other, screening information, paralegals, the first four letters of your lawyer's last name. Three secretaries working diligently for Mr. French passed him along until he came to the one in charge of scheduling.

Exhausted, Ray said, 'I really would like to see Mr. French.'

'He's out of town,' she said, surprisingly polite.

Of course he was out of town. 'Okay, listen,' Ray said rudely. 'I'm only doing this one time. My name is Ray Atlee. My father was Judge Reuben Atlee. I'm here in Biloxi, and I'd like to see Patton French.'

He gave her his cell phone number and drove away. He went to the Acropolis, a tacky Vegas-style casino with a Greek theme, badly done but absolutely no one cared. The parking lot was busy and there were security guards on duty. Whether they were watching anything was uncertain. He found a bar with a view of the floor, and was sipping a soda when his cell phone beeped. 'Mr. Ray Atlee,' said the voice.

'That's me,' Ray said, pressing the phone closer.

'Patton French here. Delighted you called. Sorry I wasn't in.'

'I'm sure you're a busy man.'

'Indeed I am. You're on the coast?'

'Right now I'm sitting in the Acropolis, a wonderful place.'

'Well, I'm headed back, been down to Naples

291

for a plaintiff's counsel meeting with some big Florida lawyers.'

Here we go, thought Ray.

'Very sorry about your father,' French said, and the signal cracked just a little. Probably at forty thousand feet, streaking home.

'Thank you,' Ray said.

'I was at the funeral, saw you there, but didn't get a chance to speak. A lovely man, the Judge.'

'Thank you,' Ray said again.

'How's Forrest?'

'How do you know Forrest?'

'I know almost everything, Ray. My pretrial preparation is meticulous. We gather information by the truckload. That's how we win. Anyway, is he clean these days?'

'As far as I know,' Ray said, irritated that a private matter would be brought up as casually as the weather. But he knew from the Web site that the man had no finesse.

'Good, look, I'll be in sometime tomorrow. I'm on my yacht, so the pace is a bit slower. Can we do lunch or dinner?'

Didn't see a yacht on the Web page, Mr. French. Must've been an oversight. Ray preferred one hour over coffee, as opposed to a two-hour lunch or an even longer dinner, but he was the guest. 'Either one.'

'Keep them both open, if you don't mind. We're hitting some wind here in the Gulf and I'm not sure when I'll be in. Can I have my girl call you tomorrow?'

'Sure.'

'Are we discussing the Gibson trial?'

'Yes, unless there's something else.'

'No, it all started with Gibson.'

Back at the Easy Sleep Inn, Ray half-watched a muted baseball game and tried to read while waiting for the sun to disappear. He needed sleep but was unwilling to tuck in before dark. He got Forrest on the second try, and they were discussing the joys of rehab when the cell phone erupted. 'I'll call you back,' Ray said and hung up.

An intruder was in his apartment again. A burglary in progress, said the robotic voice from the alarm company. When the recording went dead, Ray opened the door and stared at his car, less than twenty feet away. He held the cell phone and waited.

The alarm company also called Corey Crawford, who called fifteen minutes later with the same report. Crowbar through the door on the street, crowbar through the door to the apartment, a table knocked over, lights on, all appliances accounted for. The same policeman filing the same report.

'There's nothing valuable there,' Ray said.

'Then why do they keep breaking in?' Corey asked.

'I don't know.'

Crawford called the landlord, who promised to find a carpenter and patch up the doors. After the cop left, Corey waited in the apartment and called Ray again. 'This is not a coincidence,' he said.

'Why not?' Ray asked.

'They're not trying to steal anything. It's intimidation, that's all. What's going on?'

'I don't know.'

'I think you do.'

'I swear.'

'I think you're not telling me everything.'

You're certainly right about that, Ray thought, but he held his ground. 'It's random, Corey, relax. Just some of those downtown kids with pink hair and spikes through their jaws. They're druggies looking for a quick buck.'

'I know the area. These aren't kids.'

'A pro wouldn't return if he knew about the alarm. It's two different people.'

'I disagree.'

They agreed to disagree, though both knew the truth.

He rolled in the darkness for two hours, unable even to close his eyes. Around eleven, he went for a drive and found himself back at the Acropolis, where he played roulette and drank bad wine until two in the morning.

He asked for a room overlooking the parking lot, not the beach, and from a third-floor window he guarded his car until he fell asleep.

Chapter 30

He slept until housekeeping got tired of waiting. Checkout was noon, no exceptions, and when the maid banged on the door at eleven forty-five he yelled something through the door and jumped in the shower.

His car looked fine, no pry marks or dents or scrapes around the rear. He unlocked the trunk and quickly peered inside: three black plastic garbage bags stuffed with money. All was normal until he got behind the wheel and saw an envelope tucked under the windshield wiper in front of him. He froze and stared at it, and it seemed to stare back at him from thirty inches away. Plain white, legal size, no visible markings, at least on the side touching the glass.

Whatever it was, it couldn't be good. It wasn't a flyer for a pizza delivery or some clown running for office. It wasn't a ticket for expired parking because parking was free at the Acropolis casino.

It was an envelope with something in it.

He slowly crawled out of the car and looked around on the chance he'd spot someone out there. He lifted the wiper, took the envelope, and examined it as if it might be crucial evidence in a murder trial. Then he got back in the car because he figured someone was watching.

Inside was another trifold, another color digital picture printed off the computer, this one of unit 37F at Chaney's Self-Storage in Charlottesville, Virginia, 930 miles and at least eighteen hours away by car. Same camera, same printer, no doubt the same photographer who no doubt knew that 37F was not the last unit Ray had used to hide the money.

Though he was too numb to move, Ray drove away in a hurry. He sped along Highway 90 watching everything behind him, then suddenly veered to the left and turned onto a street that he followed north for a mile until he abruptly pulled into the parking lot of a Laundromat. No one was following. For an hour he watched every car and saw nothing suspicious. For comfort, his pistol was next to his seat, ready for action. And even more comforting was the money sitting just inches away. He had everything he needed.

The call from Mr. French's scheduling secretary came at eleven-fifteen. Crucial matters had conspired to make lunch impossible, but an early dinner would be his pleasure. She asked if Ray would come to the great man's office

296

around 4 P.M., and the evening would proceed from there.

The office, a flattering photo of which appeared on the Web site, was a stately Georgian home overlooking the Gulf, on a long lot shaded with oaks and Spanish moss. Its neighbors were of similar architecture and age.

The rear had recently been converted into a parking lot with tall brick walls around it and security cameras scanning back and forth. A metal gate was opened for Ray and closed behind him by a guard dressed like a Secret Service agent. He parked in a reserved place, and another guard escorted him up to the rear of the building, where a crew was busy laying tile while another planted shrubs. A major renovation of the office and premises was rapidly winding down.

'The governor's coming in three days,' the guard whispered.

'Wow,' Ray said.

French's personal office was on the second floor, but he was not in it. He was still on his yacht, out in the Gulf, explained a comely young brunette in a tight, expensive dress. She led him into Mr. French's office anyway and asked him to wait in a sitting area by the windows. The room was paneled in blond oak and held enough heavy leather sofas, chairs, and ottomans to furnish a hunting lodge. The desk was the size of a swimming pool and covered with scale models of great yachts.

'He likes boats, huh?' Ray said, looking around. He was expected to be impressed.

'Yes, he does.' With a remote she opened a cabinet and a large flat screen slid out. 'He's in a meeting,' she said, 'but he'll be on in just a moment. Would you like a drink?'

'Thanks, black coffee.'

There was a tiny camera in the top right corner of the screen, and Ray assumed he and Mr. French were about to chat via satellite. His irritation at waiting was slowly building. Normally, it would've been boiling by now, but he was captivated by the show that was unfolding around him. He was a character in it. Relax and enjoy it, he told himself. You have plenty of time.

She returned with the coffee, which, of course, was served in fine china, F&F engraved on the side of the cup.

'Can I step outside?' Ray asked.

'Certainly.' She smiled and returned to her desk.

There was a long balcony through a set of doors. Ray sipped his coffee at the railing and admired the view. The wide front lawn ended at the highway, and beyond it was the beach and the water. No casinos were visible, not much in the way of development. Below him, on the front porch, some painters were chattering back and forth as they moved their ladders. Everything about the place looked and felt new. Patton French had just won the lottery.

'Mr. Atlee,' she called, and Ray stepped inside the office. On the screen was the face of Patton French, hair slightly disheveled, reading glasses perched on his nose, eyes frowning above them. 'There you are,' he barked. 'Sorry for the delay. Have a seat there, if you will, Ray, so I can see you.'

She pointed and Ray sat.

'How are you?' French asked.

'Fine. You?'

'Great, look, sorry for the mix-up, all my fault, but I've been on one of these damned conference calls all afternoon, just couldn't get away. I was thinking it would be a lot quieter here on the boat for dinner, whatta you think? My chef's a damned sight better than anything you'll find on land. I'm only thirty minutes out. We'll have a drink, just the two of us, then a long dinner and we'll talk about your father. It'll be enjoyable, I promise.'

When he finally shut up, Ray said, 'Will my car be secure here?'

'Of course. Hell, it's in a compound. I'll tell the guards to sit on the damned thing if you want.'

'Okay. Do I swim out?'

'No, I've got boats. Dickie'll bring you.'

Dickie was the same thick young man who'd escorted Ray into the building. Now he escorted him out, where a very long silver Mercedes was waiting. Dickie drove it like a tank through the traffic to the Point Cadet Marina, where a

299

hundred small vessels were docked. One of the larger ones just happened to be owned by Patton French. Its name was the *Lady of Justice.*

'The water's smooth, take about twenty-five minutes,' Dickie said as they climbed on board. The engines were running. A steward with a thick accent asked Ray if he'd like a drink. 'Diet soda,' he said. They cast off and puttered through the rows of slips and past the marina until they were away from the pier. Ray climbed to the upper deck and watched the shoreline fade into the distance.

Anchored ten miles from Biloxi was the *King of Torts,* a hundred-forty-foot luxury yacht with a crew of five and plush quarters for a dozen friends. The only passenger was Mr. French, and he was waiting to greet his dinner guest. 'A real pleasure, Ray,' he said as he pumped his hand and then squeezed his shoulder.

'A pleasure for me as well,' Ray said, holding his ground because French liked close contact. He was an inch or two taller, with a nicely tanned face, fierce blue eyes that squinted and did not blink.

'I'm so glad you came,' French said, squeezing Ray's hand. Fraternity brothers couldn't have pawed each other with more affection.

'Stay here, Dickie,' he barked to the deck below. 'Follow me, Ray,' he said, and they were off, up one short flight to the main deck, where a steward in a white jacket was waiting with a starched F&F towel folded perfectly over his arm. 'What'll you have?' he demanded of Ray.

Suspecting that French was not a man who toyed with light booze, Ray said, 'What's the specialty of the house?'

'Iced vodka, with a twist of lime.'

'I'll try it,' Ray said.

'It's a great new vodka from Norway. You'll love it.' The man knew his vodkas.

He was wearing a black linen shirt, buttoned at the neck, and tan linen shorts, perfectly pressed and hanging nicely on his frame. There was a slight belly, but he was thick through the chest and his forearms were twice the normal size. He liked his hair because he couldn't keep his hands out of it.

'How about the boat?' he asked, waving his hands from stern to bow. 'It was built by a Saudi prince, one of the lesser ones, a coupla years ago. Dumb-ass put a fireplace in it, can you believe that? Cost him twenty million or so, and after a year he traded it in for a two-hundred-footer.'

'It's amazing,' Ray said, trying to sound sufficiently awed. The world of yachting was one he had never been near, and he suspected that after this episode he would forever keep his distance.

'Built by the Italians,' French said, tapping a railing made of some terribly expensive wood.

'Why do you stay out here, in the Gulf?' Ray asked.

'I'm an offshore kind of guy, ha, ha. If you know what I mean. Sit.' French pointed, and they lowered themselves into two long deck chairs. When they were nestled in, French nodded to the shore. 'You can barely see Biloxi, and this is close enough. I can do more work out here in one day than in a week at the office. Plus I'm transitioning from one house to the next. A divorce is in the works. This is where I hide.'

'Sorry.'

'This is the biggest yacht in Biloxi now, and most folks can spot it. The current wife thinks I've sold it, and if I get too close to the shore then her slimy little lawyer might swim out and take a picture of it. Ten miles is close enough.'

The iced vodkas arrived, in tall narrow glasses, F&F engraved on the sides. Ray took a sip and the concoction burned all the way to his toes. French took a long pull and smacked his lips. 'Whatta you think?' he asked proudly.

'Nice vodka,' Ray said. He couldn't remember the last time he'd had one.

'Dickie brought fresh swordfish out for dinner. Sound okay?'

'Great.'

'And the oysters are good now.'

'I went to law school at Tulane. I had three years of fresh oysters.'

'I know,' French said and pulled a small radio from his shirt pocket and passed along their dinner selections to someone below. He glanced at his watch and decided they would eat in two hours.

'You went to school with Hassel Mangrum,' French said.

'Yes, he was a year ahead of me.'

'We share the same trainer. Hassel has done well here on the coast. Got in early with the asbestos boys.'

'I haven't heard from Hassel in twenty years.'

'You haven't missed much. He's a jerk now, I suspect he was a jerk in law school.'

'He was. How'd you know I went to school with Mangrum?'

'Research, Ray, extensive research.' He swigged the vodka again. Ray's third sip went straight to his brain.

'We spent a bunch of dough investigating Judge Atlee, and his family, and his background, his rulings, his finances, everything we could find. Nothing illegal or intrusive, mind you, but old-fashioned detective work. We knew about your divorce, what's his name, Lew the Liquidator?'

Ray just nodded. He wanted to say something derogatory about Lew Rodowski and he wanted to rebuke French for digging through his past, but for a second the vodka was blocking signals. So he nodded.

'We knew your salary as a law professor, it's public record in Virginia, you know.'

'Yes it is.'

303

'Not a bad salary, Ray, but then it's a great law school.'

'It is indeed.'

'Digging through your brother's past was quite an adventure.'

'I'm sure it was. It's been an adventure for the family.'

'We read every ruling your father issued in damage suits and wrongful death cases. There weren't many, but we picked up clues. He was conservative with his awards, but he also favored the little guy, the working man. We knew he would follow the law, but we also knew that old chancellors often mold the law to fit their notion of fairness. I had clerks doing the grunt work, but I read every one of his important decisions. He was a brilliant man, Ray, and always fair. I never disagreed with one of his opinions.'

'You picked my father for the Gibson case?'

'Yes. When we made the decision to file the case in Chancery Court and try it without a jury, we also decided we did not want a local chancellor to hear it. We have three. One is related to the Gibson family. One refuses to hear any matter other than divorces. One is eighty-four, senile, and hasn't left the house in three years. So we looked around the state and found three potential fill-ins. Fortunately, my father and your father go back sixty years, to Sewanee and then law school at Ole Miss. They weren't close friends over the years, but they kept in touch.'

304

'Your father is still active?'

'No, he's in Florida now, retired, playing golf every day. I'm the sole owner of the firm. But my old man drove to Clanton, sat on the front porch with Judge Atlee, talked about the Civil War and Nathan Bedford Forrest. They even drove to Shiloh, walked around for two days – the hornet's nest, the bloody pond. Judge Atlee got all choked up when he stood where General Johnston fell.'

'I've been there a dozen times,' Ray said with a smile.

'You don't lobby a man like Judge Atlee. Earwigging is the ancient term.'

'He put a lawyer in jail once for that,' Ray said. 'The guy came in before court began and tried to plead his case. The Judge threw him in jail for half a day.'

'That was that Chadwick fella over in Oxford, wasn't it?' French said smugly, and Ray was speechless.

'Anyway, we had to impress upon Judge Atlee the importance of the Ryax litigation. We knew he wouldn't want to come to the coast and try the case, but he'd do it if he believed in the cause.'

'He hated the coast.'

'We knew that, believe me, it was a huge concern. But he was a man of great principle. After refighting the war up there for two days, Judge Atlee reluctantly agreed to hear the case.'

'Doesn't the Supreme Court assign the special chancellors?' Ray asked. The fourth sip sort of slid down, without burning, and the vodka was tasting better.

French shrugged it off. 'Sure, but there are ways. We have friends.'

In Patton French's world, anyone could be bought.

The steward was back with fresh drinks. Not that they were needed, but they were taken anyway. French was too hyper to sit still for long. 'Lemme show you the boat,' he said, and bounced out of his chair with no effort. Ray climbed out carefully, balancing his glass.

Chapter 31

Dinner was in the captain's galley, a mahogany-paneled dining room with walls adorned with models of ancient clippers and gunboats and maps of the New World and the Far East and even a collection of antique muskets thrown in to give the impression that the *King of Torts* had been around for centuries. It was on the main deck behind the bridge, just down a narrow hallway from the kitchen, where a Vietnamese chef was hard at work. The formal dining area was around an oval marble table that seated a dozen and weighed at least a ton and made Ray ask himself how, exactly, the *King of Torts* stayed afloat.

The captain's table sat only two this evening, and above it was a small chandelier that rocked with the sea. Ray was at one end, French at the other. The first wine of the night was a white burgundy that, following the scalding by two iced vodkas, was tasteless to Ray. Not to his host. French had knocked back three of the vodkas, had in fact drained all three glasses, and his tongue was beginning to thicken slightly. But he tasted every hint of fruit in the wine, even got a whiff of the oak barrels, and, as all wine snobs do, had to pass this useful information along to Ray.

'Here's to Ryax,' French said, reaching forward with his glass in a delayed toast. Ray touched his glass but said nothing. It was not a night for him to say much, and he knew it. He would just listen. His host would get drunk and say enough.

'Ryax saved me, Ray,' French said as he swirled his wine and admired it.

'In what way?'

'In every way. It saved my soul. I worship money, and Ryax has made me rich.' A small sip, followed by the requisite smacking of the lips, a rolling of the eyes. 'I missed the asbestos wave twenty years ago. Those shipyards over in Pascagoula used asbestos for years, and tens of thousands of men became ill. And I missed it. I was too busy suing doctors and insurance companies, and I was making good money but I just didn't see the potential in mass torts. You ready for some oysters?'

'Yes.'

French pushed a button; the steward popped in with two trays of raw oysters on the half shell. Ray mixed horseradish into the cocktail sauce and prepared for the feast. Patton was swirling wine and too busy talking.

308

'Then came tobacco,' he said sadly. 'Many of the same lawyers, from right here. I thought they were crazy, hell, everybody did, but they sued the big tobacco companies in almost every state. I had the chance to jump into the pit with them, but I was too scared. It's hard to admit that, Ray. I was just too damned scared to roll the dice.'

'What did they want?' Ray asked, then shoved the first oyster and saltine into his mouth.

'A million bucks to help finance the litigation. And I had a million bucks at the time.'

'How much was the settlement?' Ray asked, chewing.

'More than three hundred billion. The biggest financial and legal scam in history. The tobacco companies basically bought off the lawyers, who sold out. One huge bribe, and I missed it.' He appeared to be ready to cry because he'd missed a bribe, but he rallied quickly with a long pull on the wine.

'Good oysters,' Ray said, with a mouthful.

'Twenty-four hours ago, they were fifteen feet down.' French poured more wine and settled over his platter.

'What would've been the return on your one million dollars?' Ray asked.

'Two hundred to one.'

'Two hundred million bucks?'

'Yep. I was sick for a year, lots of lawyers around here were sick. We knew the players and we had chickened out.'

309

'Then along came Ryax.'

'Yes indeed.'

'How'd you find it?' Ray asked, knowing the question would require another windy answer, and he'd be free to eat.

'I was at a trial lawyers' seminar in St. Louis. Missouri is a nice place and all, but miles behind us when it comes to tort litigation. I mean, hell, we've had the asbestos and tobacco boys running around here for years, burning money, showing everybody else how it's done. I had a drink with this old lawyer from a small town in the Ozarks. His son teaches medicine at the university in Columbia, and the son was on to Ryax. His research was showing some horrible results. The damned drug just eats up the kidneys, and because it was so new there was not a history of litigation. I found an expert in Chicago, and he found Clete Gibson through a doctor in New Orleans. Then we started screening, and the thing snowballed. All we needed was a big verdict.'

'Why didn't you want a jury trial?'

'I love juries. I love to pick them, talk to them, sway them, manipulate them, even buy them, but they're unpredictable. I wanted a lock, a guarantee. And I wanted a speedy trial. Ryax rumors were spreading like crazy, you can imagine a bunch of hungry tort lawyers with the gossip that a new drug had gone bad. We were signing up cases by the dozens. The guy with the first big verdict would be in the driver's seat,

310

especially if it came from the Biloxi area. Miyer-Brack is a Swiss company –'

'I've read the file.'

'All of it?'

'Yes, yesterday in the Hancock County Court-house.'

'Well, these Europeans are terrified of our tort system.'

'Shouldn't they be?'

'Yes, but in a good way. Keeps 'em honest. What should terrify them is the possibility that one of their damned drugs is defective and might harm people, but that's not a concern when billions are at stake. It takes people like me to keep 'em honest.'

'And they knew Ryax was bad?'

French choked down another oyster, swallowed hard, gulped a half pint of wine, and finally said, 'Early on. The drug was so effective at lowering cholesterol that Miyer-Brack, along with the FDA, rushed it to the market. It was another miracle drug, and it worked great for a few years with no side effects. Then, bam! The tissue of the nephrons – do you understand how the kidneys work?'

'For the sake of this discussion, let's say I don't.'

'Each kidney has about a million little filtering units called nephrons, and Ryax contained a synthetic chemical that basically melted them. Not everybody dies, like poor Mr. Gibson, and there are varying degrees of damage. It's all

311

permanent, though. The kidney is an amazing organ that can often heal itself, but not after a five-year bout with Ryax.'

'When did Miyer-Brack know it had a problem?'

'Hard to say exactly, but we showed Judge Atlee some internal documents from their lab people to their suits urging caution and more research. After Ryax had been on the market for about four years, with spectacular results, the company's scientists were worried. Then folks started getting real sick, even dying, and by then it was too late. From my standpoint, we had to find the perfect client, which we did, the perfect forum, which we did, and we had to do it quick before some other lawyer got a big verdict. That's where your father came in.'

The steward cleared the oyster shells and presented a crabmeat salad. Another white burgundy had been selected from the onboard cellar by Mr. French himself.

'What happened after the Gibson trial?' Ray asked.

'I could not have scripted it better. Miyer-Brack absolutely crumbled. Arrogant shitheads were reduced to tears. They had a zillion bucks in cash and couldn't wait to buy off the plaintiffs' lawyers. Before the trial I had four hundred cases and no clout. Afterward, I had five thousand cases and an eleven-million-dollar verdict. Hundreds of lawyers called me. I spent a month flying around the country, in a Learjet, signing co-rep agreements with other lawyers. A guy in Kentucky had a hundred cases. One in St. Paul had eighty. On and on. Then, about four months after the trial, we flew to New York for the big settlement conference. In less than three hours we settled six thousand cases for seven hundred million bucks. A month later we settled another twelve hundred for two hundred million.'

'What was your cut?' Ray asked. It would've been a rude question if posed to a normal person, but French couldn't wait to talk about his fees.

'Fifty percent off the top for the lawyers, then expenses, the rest went to the clients. That's the bad part of a contingency contract – you have to give half to the client. Anyway, I had other lawyers to deal with, but I walked away with three hundred million and some change. That's the beauty of mass torts, Ray. Sign 'em up by the truckload, settle 'em by the trainload, take half off the top.'

They weren't eating. There was too much money in the air.

'Three hundred million in fees?' Ray said in disbelief.

French was gargling with wine. 'Ain't it sweet? It's coming so fast I can't spend it all.'

'Looks like you're giving it a good shot.'

'This is the tip of the iceberg. Ever hear of a drug called Minitrin?'

'I checked your Web site.'

313

'Really? What'd you think?'

'Pretty slick. Two thousand Minitrin cases.'

'Three thousand now. It's a hypertension drug that has dangerous side effects. Made by Shyne Medical. They've offered fifty thousand a case and I said no. Fourteen hundred Kobril cases, antidepressant that causes hearing loss, we think. Ever hear of Skinny Bens?'

'Yes.'

'We have three thousand Skinny Ben cases. And fifteen hundred –'

'I saw the list. I assume the Web site is updated.'

'Of course. I'm the new King of Torts in this country, Ray. Everybody's calling me. I have thirteen other lawyers in my firm and I need forty.'

The steward was back to collect their latest leftovers. He placed the swordfish in front of them and brought the next wine, though the last bottle was half full. French went through the tasting ritual and finally, almost reluctantly, nodded his approval. To Ray it tasted very similar to the first two.

'I owe it all to Judge Atlee,' French said.

'How?'

'He had the guts to make the right call, to keep Miyer-Brack in Hancock County instead of allowing them to escape to federal court. He understood the issues, and he was unafraid to punish them. Timing is everything, Ray. Less than six months after he handed down his

314

ruling, I had three hundred million bucks in my hands.'

'Did you keep all of it?'

French had a bite on a fork close to his mouth. He hesitated for a second, then took the fish, chewed for a while, then said, 'I don't understand the question.'

'I think you do. Did you give any of the money to Judge Atlee?'

'Yes.'

'How much?'

'One percent.'

'Three million bucks?'

'And change. This fish is delicious, don't you think?'

'It is. Why?'

French put down his knife and fork and stroked his locks again with both hands. Then he wiped them on his napkin and swirled his wine. 'I suppose there are a lot of questions. Why, when, how, who.'

'You're good at stories, let's hear it.'

Another swirl, then a satisfied sip. 'It's not what you think, though I would've bribed your father or any judge for that ruling. I've done it before, and I'll happily do it again. It's just part of the overhead. Frankly, though, I was so intimidated by him and his reputation that I just couldn't approach him with a deal. He would've thrown me in jail.'

'He would've buried you in jail.'

'Yes, I know, and my father convinced me of

this. So we played it straight. The trial was an all-out war, but truth was on my side. I won, then I won big, now I'm winning even bigger. Late last summer, after we settled and the money was wired in, I wanted to give him a gift. I take care of those who help me, Ray. A new car here, a condo there, a sack full of cash for a favor. I play the game hard and I protect my friends.'

'He wasn't your friend.'

'We weren't amigos, or fraternity brothers, but in my world I've never had a greater friend. It all started with him. Do you realize how much money I'll make in the next five years?'

'Shock me again.'

'Half a billion. And I owe it all to your old man.'

'When will you have enough?'

'There's a tobacco lawyer here who made a billion. I need to catch him first.'

Ray needed a drink. He examined the wine as if he knew what to look for, then sucked it down. French was into the fish.

'I don't think you're lying,' Ray said.

'I don't lie. I cheat and bribe, but I don't lie. About six months ago, while I was shopping for airplanes and boats and beach homes and mountain cabins and new offices, I heard that your father had been diagnosed with cancer, and that it was serious. I wanted to do something nice for him. I knew he didn't have much

316

money, and what he did have he seemed hell-bent on giving away.'

'So you sent him three million in cash?'

'Yes.'

'Just like that?'

'Just like that. I called him and told him a package was on the way. Four packages as it turned out, four large cardboard boxes. One of my boys drove them up in a van, left them on the front porch. Judge Atlee wasn't home.'

'Unmarked bills?'

'Why would I mark them?'

'What did he say?' Ray asked.

'I never heard a word, and I didn't want to.'

'What did he do?'

'You tell me. You're his son, you know him better than me. You tell me what he did with the money.'

Ray pushed back from the table, and holding his wineglass, he crossed his legs and tried to relax. 'He found the money on the porch, and when he realized what it was, I'm sure he gave you a thorough cursing.'

'God, I hope so.'

'He moved it into the foyer, where the boxes joined dozens of others. He planned to load it up and haul it back to Biloxi, but a day or two passed. He was sick and weak, and not driving too well. He knew he was dying, and I'm sure that burden changed his outlook on a lot of things. After a few days he decided to hide the money, which he did, and all the while he

317

planned to get it back down here and flog your corrupt ass in the process. Time passed, and he got sicker.'

'Who found the money?'

'I did.'

'Where is it?'

'In the trunk of my car, at your office.'

French laughed long and hard. 'Back where it started from,' he said between breaths.

'It's had quite a tour. I found it in his study just after I found him dead. Someone tried to break in and get it. I took it to Virginia, now it's back, and that someone is following me.'

The laughter stopped immediately. He wiped his mouth with a napkin. 'How much did you find?'

'Three million, one hundred and eighteen thousand.'

'Damn! He didn't spend a dime.'

'And he didn't mention it in his will. He just left it, hidden in stationer's boxes in a cabinet beneath his bookshelves.'

'Who tried to break in?'

'I was hoping you might know.'

'I have a pretty good idea.'

'Please tell me.'

'It's another long story.'

Chapter 32

The steward brought a selection of single malts to the top deck where French had settled them in for a nightcap and another story, with a view of Biloxi flickering in the distance. Ray did not drink whiskey and certainly knew nothing about single malts, but he went along with the ritual because he knew French would get even drunker. The truth was flowing in torrents now, and Ray wanted all of it.

They settled on Lagavulin because of its smokiness, whatever that meant. There were four others, lined like proud old sentries in distinctive regalia, and Ray vowed he'd had enough to drink. He'd sip and spit and if he got the chance he'd toss it overboard. To his relief, the steward poured tiny servings in short thick glasses heavy enough to crack floors.

It was almost ten but felt much later. The Gulf was dark, no other boats were visible. A gentle wind blew from the south and rocked the *King of Torts* just slightly.

'Who knows about the money?' French asked, smacking his lips.

'Me, you, whoever hauled it up there.'

'That's your man.'

'Who is he?'

A long sip, more smacking. Ray brought the whiskey to his lips and wished he hadn't. Numb as they were, they burned all over again.

'Gordie Priest. He worked for me for eight or so years, first as a gofer, then a runner, then a bagman. His family has been on the coast forever, always on the edges. His father and uncles ran numbers, whores, moonshine, honky-tonks, nothing legal. They were part of what was once known as the coast mafia, a bunch of thugs who disdained honest work. Twenty years ago they controlled some things around here, now they're history. Most of them went to jail. Gordie's father, a man I knew very well, got shot outside a bar near Mobile. A pretty miserable lot, really. My family has known them for years.'

He was implying that his family had been part of the same bunch of crooks, but he couldn't say it. They'd been the front guys, the lawyers who smiled for the cameras and cut the backroom deals.

'Gordie went to jail when he was about twenty, a stolen car ring that covered a dozen states. I hired him when he got out, and over time he became one of the best runners on the coast. He was particularly good at the offshore

320

cases. He knew the guys on the rigs, and when there was a death or injury he'd get the case. I'd give him a nice percentage. Gotta take care of your runners. One year I paid him almost eighty thousand, all of it in cash. He blew it, of course, casinos and women. Loved to go to Vegas and stay drunk for a week, throw money around like a big shot. He acted like an idiot but he wasn't stupid. He was always up and down. When he was broke he'd scramble and make some money. When he had money, he'd manage to lose it.'

'I'm sure this is all headed my way,' Ray said.

'Hang on,' French said. 'After the Gibson case early last year, the money hit like a tidal wave. I had favors to repay. Lots of cash got hauled around. Cash to lawyers who were sending me their cases. Cash to doctors who were screening thousands of new clients. Not all of it was illegal, mind you, but a lot of folks didn't want records. I made the mistake of using Gordie as the delivery boy. I thought I could trust him. I thought he would be loyal. I was wrong.'

French had finished one sample and was ready for another. Ray declined and pretended to work on the Lagavulin.

'And he drove the money up to Clanton and left it on the front porch?' Ray said.

'He did, and three months after that he stole a million dollars from me, in cash, and disappeared. He has two brothers, and at any given

321

time during the past ten years one of the three
has been in prison. Except for now. Now they're
all on parole, and they're trying to extort big
money out of me. Extortion is a serious crime,
you know, but I can't exactly go to the FBI.'

'What makes you think he's after the three
million bucks?'

'Wiretaps. We picked it up a few months ago.
I've hired some pretty serious characters to find
Gordie.'

'What will you do if you find him?'

'Oh, there's a price on his head.'

'You mean, like a contract?'

'Yes.'

And with that, Ray reached for another single
malt.

He slept on the boat, in a large room somewhere
under the water, and when he found his way to
the main deck the sun was high in the east and
the air was already hot and sticky. The captain
said good morning and pointed forward, where
he found French yelling into a phone.

The faithful steward materialized out of thin
air and presented a coffee. Breakfast was up on
the top deck at the scene of the single malts,
now under a canopy for shade.

'I love to eat outdoors,' French announced as
he joined Ray. 'You slept for ten hours.'

'Did I really?' Ray asked, looking again at his
watch, which was still on Eastern time. He was
on a yacht in the Gulf of Mexico, unsure of the

day or time, a million miles from home, and now burdened with the knowledge that some very nasty people were chasing him.

The table was spread with breads and cereals. 'Tin Lu down there can fix anything you want,' French was saying. 'Bacon, eggs, waffles, grits.'

'This is fine, thanks.'

French was fresh and hyper, already tackling another grueling day with the energy that could only come from the prospect of a half a billion or so in fees. He was wearing a white linen shirt, buttoned at the top like the black one last night, shorts, loafers. His eyes were clear and dancing around. 'Just picked up another three hundred Minitrin cases,' he said as he dumped a generous portion of flakes into a large bowl. Every dish had the obligatory F&F monogram splashed on it.

Ray had had enough of mass torts. 'Good, but I'm more interested in Gordie Priest.'

'We'll find him. I'm already making calls.'

'He's probably in town.' Ray pulled a folded sheet of paper from his rear pocket. It was the photo of 37F he'd found yesterday morning on his windshield. French looked at it and stopped eating.

'And this is up in Virginia?' he asked.

'Yep, the second of three units I rented. They've found the first two, I'm sure they know about the third. And they knew exactly where I was yesterday morning.'

'But they obviously don't know where the

money is. Otherwise, they would have simply taken it from the trunk of your car while you were asleep. Or they would've pulled you over somewhere between here and Clanton and put a bullet in your ear.'

'You don't know what they're thinking.'

'Sure I do. Think like a crook, Ray. Think like a thug.'

'It may come easy for you, but it's harder for some folks.'

'If Gordie and his brothers knew you had three million bucks in the trunk of your car, they would take it. Simple as that.' He put the photo down and attacked his flakes.

'Nothing is simple,' Ray said.

'What do you wanna do? Leave the money with me?'

'Yes.'

'Don't be stupid, Ray. Three million tax-free dollars.'

'Useless if I get the ole bullet in the ear. I have a very nice salary.'

'The money is safe. Keep it where it is. Give me some time to find these boys, and they'll be neutralized.'

The neutralization sapped any appetite Ray had.

'Eat, man!' French barked when Ray grew still.

'I don't have the stomach for this. Dirty money, bad guys breaking into my apartment,

324

chasing me all over the Southeast, wiretaps, contract killers. What the hell am I doing here?'

French never stopped chewing. His intestines were lined with brass. 'Keep cool,' he said. 'And the money'll be yours.'

'I don't want the money.'

'Of course you do.'

'No I don't.'

'Then give it to Forrest.'

'What a disaster.'

'Give it to charity. Give it your law school. Give it to something that makes you feel good.'

'Why don't I just give it to Gordie so he won't shoot me?'

French gave his spoon a rest and looked around as if others were lurking. 'All right, we spotted Gordie last night over in Pascagoula,' he said, an octave lower. 'We're hot on his trail, okay? I think we'll have him within twenty-four hours.'

'And he'll be neutralized?'

'He'll be iced.'

'Iced?'

'Gordie'll be history. Your money'll be safe. Just hang on, okay.'

'I'd like to leave now.'

French wiped skim milk off his bottom lip, then picked up his mini radio and told Dickie to get the boat ready. Minutes later, they were ready to board.

'Take a look at these,' French said, handing over an eight-by-twelve manila envelope.

'What is it?'

'Photos of the Priest boys. Just in case you bump into them.'

Ray ignored the envelope until he stopped in Hattiesburg, ninety minutes north of the coast. He bought gas and a dreadful shrink-wrapped sandwich, then was off again, in a hurry to get to Clanton, where Harry Rex knew the sheriff and all his deputies.

Gordie had a particularly menacing sneer, one that had been captured by a police photographer in 1991. His brothers, Slatt and Alvin, were certainly no prettier. Ray couldn't tell the oldest from the youngest, not that it mattered. None of the three resembled the others. Bad breeding. Same mother, no doubt different fathers.

They could have a million each, he didn't care. Just leave me alone.

Chapter 33

The hills began between Jackson and Memphis, and the coast seemed time zones away. He had often wondered at how a state so small could be so diverse: the Delta region along the river with the wealth of its cotton and rice farms and the poverty that still astonished outsiders; the coast with its blend of immigrants and laidback, New Orleans casualness; and the hills where most counties were still dry and most folks still went to church on Sundays. A person from the hills would never understand the coast and never be accepted in the Delta. Ray was just happy he lived in Virginia.

Patton French was a dream, he kept telling himself. A cartoonish character from another world. A pompous jerk being eaten alive by his own ego. A liar, a briber, a shameless crook.

Then he would glance over at the passenger's seat and see the sinister face of Gordie Priest. One glance and there was no doubt this brute and his brothers would do anything for the money Ray was still hauling around the country.

An hour from Clanton, and again within range of a tower, his cell phone rang. It was Fog Newton and he was quite agitated. 'Where the hell have you been?' he demanded.

'You wouldn't believe me.'

'I've been calling all morning.'

'What is it, Fog?'

'We've had a little excitement around here. Last night, after general aviation closed, somebody sneaked onto the ramp and put an incendiary device on the left wing of the Bonanza. Boom. A janitor in the main terminal just happened to see the blaze, and they got the fire truck out pretty fast.'

Ray had pulled onto the shoulder of Interstate 55 and stopped. He grunted something into the phone and Fog kept going. 'Severe damage though. No doubt it was an act of arson. You there?'

'Just listening,' Ray said. 'How much damage?'

'Left wing, the engine, and most of the fuselage, probably a total loss for insurance purposes. The arson investigator is already here. Insurance guy's here too. If the tanks had been full it would've been a bomb.'

'The other owners know about it?'

'Yes, everyone's been out. Of course they're first on the suspect list. Lucky you were out of town. When are you coming back?'

'Soon.'

He made it to an exit and pulled into the gravel lot of a truck stop, where he sat in the heat for a long time and occasionally glanced down at Gordie. The Priest gang moved fast – Biloxi yesterday morning, Charlottesville last night. Where are they now?

Inside, he drank coffee and listened to the chatter of the truckers. To change the subject, he called Alcorn Village to check on Forrest. He was in his room, sleeping the sleep of the righteous, as he described it. It was always amazing, he said, how much he slept in rehab. He'd complained about the food, and things had improved slightly. Either that or he had developed a taste for pink Jell-O. He asked how long he could stay, like a kid at Disney World. Ray said he wasn't sure. The money that had once seemed endless was now very much in jeopardy.

'Don't let me out, Bro,' he pleaded. 'I want to stay in rehab for the remainder of my life.'

The Atkins boys had finished the roof at Maple Run without incident. The place was deserted when Ray arrived. He called Harry Rex and checked in. 'Let's drink some beer on the porch tonight,' Ray suggested.

Harry Rex had never said no to such an invitation.

There was a level spot of thick grass just beyond the front sidewalk, directly in front of the house,

329

and after careful deliberation Ray decided it was the place for a washing. He parked the little Audi there, facing the street, its rear and its trunk just a step from the porch. He found an old tin bucket in the basement and a leaky water hose in the back shed. Shirtless and shoeless, he sloshed around for two hours in the hot afternoon sun, scrubbing the roadster. Then he waxed and polished it for an hour. At 5 P.M., he opened a cold bottle of beer and sat on the steps, admiring his work.

He called the private cell phone number given to him by Patton French, but of course the great man was too busy. Ray wanted to thank him for his hospitality, but what he really wanted was to see if they had made any progress down there icing the Priest gang. He would never ask that question directly, but a blowhard like French would happily deliver the news if he had it.

French had probably forgotten about him. He didn't really care if the Priest boys nailed Ray or the next guy. He needed to make a half a billion or so in mass tort schemes, and that took all his energies. Indict a guy like French, for payoffs or contract killings, and he'd hire fifty lawyers and buy every clerk, judge, prosecutor, and juror.

He called Corey Crawford and got the news that the landlord had once again repaired the doors. The police had promised to keep an eye on the place for the next few days, until he returned.

The van pulled into the driveway shortly after

330

6 P.M. A smiling face jumped out with a thin overnight envelope, which Ray stared at long after it had been delivered. The airbill was a preprinted form from the University of Virginia School of Law, hand-addressed to Mr. Ray Atlee, Maple Run, 816 Fourth Street, Clanton, MS, dated June 2, the day before. Everything about it was suspicious.

No one at the law school had been given the address in Clanton. Nothing from there would be so urgent as to require an overnight delivery. And he could think of no reason whatsoever that the school would be sending him anything. He opened another beer and returned to the front steps, where he grabbed the damned thing and ripped it open.

Plain white legal-size envelope, with the word 'Ray' hand-scrawled on the outside. And on the inside, another of the now familiar color photos of Chaney's Self-Storage, this time the front of unit 18R. At the bottom, in a wacky font of mismatched letters, was the message: 'You don't need an airplane. Stop spending the money.'

These guys were very, very good. It was tough enough to track down the three units at Chaney's and take pictures of them. It was gutsy and also stupid to burn up the Bonanza. Oddly, though, what was most impressive at the moment was their ability to swipe an airbill from the business office at the law school.

After a prolonged moment of shock, he

realized something that should have been immediately obvious. Since they'd found 18R, then they knew the money wasn't there. It wasn't at Chaney's, nor at his apartment. They'd followed him from Virginia to Clanton, and if he'd stopped somewhere along the way to hide the money, they would know it. They'd probably rummaged through Maple Run again, while he was on the coast.

Their net was tightening by the hour. All clues were being linked, all dots connected. The money had to be with him, and Ray had no place to run.

He had a very comfortable salary as a professor of law, with benefits. His lifestyle was not expensive, and he decided right there on the porch, still shirtless and shoeless, sipping a beer in the early evening humidity of a long hot June day, that he preferred to continue that lifestyle. Leave the violence for the likes of Gordie Priest and hit men hired by Patton French. Ray was out of his element.

The cash was dirty anyway.

'Why'd you park in the front yard?' Harry Rex grumbled as he lumbered up the steps.

'I washed it and left it there,' Ray said. He had showered and was wearing shorts and a tee shirt.

'You just can't get the redneck outta some people. Gimme a beer.'

Harry Rex had been brawling in court all day, a nasty divorce where the weighty issues were which spouse had smoked the most dope ten years ago and which one had slept with the most people. The custody of four children was at stake, and neither parent was fit.

'I'm too old for this,' he said, very tired. By the second beer he was nodding off.

Harry Rex controlled the divorce docket in Ford County and had for twenty-five years. Feuding couples often raced to hire him first. One farmer over at Karraway kept him on retainer so he would be available for the next split. He was very bright, but could also be vile and vicious. This had wide appeal in the heat of divorce wars.

But the work was taking its toll. Like all small-town lawyers, Harry Rex longed for the big kill. The big damage suit with a forty percent contingency fee, something to retire on.

The night before, Ray had been sipping expensive wines on a twenty-million-dollar yacht built by a Saudi prince and owned by a member of the Mississippi bar who was plotting billion-dollar schemes against multinationals. Now he was sipping Bud in a rusted swing with a member of the Mississippi bar who'd spent the day bickering over custody and alimony.

. 'The Realtor showed the house this morning,' Harry Rex said. 'He called me during lunch, woke me up.'

'Who's the prospect?'

'Remember those Kapshaw boys up near Rail Springs?'

'No.'

'Good boys. They started buildin' chairs in an old barn ten years ago, maybe twelve. One thang led to another, and they sold out to some big furniture outfit up in the Carolinas. Each of 'em walked away with a million bucks. Junkie and his wife are lookin' for houses.'

'Junkie Kapshaw?'

'Yeah, but he's tight as Dick's hatband and he ain't payin' four hundred thousand for this place.'

'I don't blame him.'

'His wife's crazy as hell and thinks she wants an old house. The Realtor is pretty sure they'll make an offer, but it'll be low, probably about a hundred seventy-five thousand.' Harry Rex was yawning.

They talked about Forrest for a spell, then things were silent. 'Guess I'd better go,' he said. After three beers, Harry Rex began his exit.

'When are you going back to Virginia?' he asked, struggling to his feet and stretching his back.

'Maybe tomorrow.'

'Gimme a call,' he said, yawning again, and walked down the steps.

Ray watched the lights of his car disappear down the street, and he was suddenly and completely alone again. The first noise was a rustling in the shrubbery near the property line, probably an old dog or cat on the prowl, but regardless of how harmless it was it spooked Ray and he ran inside.

Chapter 34

The attack began shortly after 2 A.M., at the darkest hour of the night, when sleep is heaviest and reactions slowest. Ray was dead to the world, though the world had weighed heavily on his weary mind. He was on a mattress in the foyer, pistol by his side, the three garbage bags of cash next to his makeshift bed.

It began with a brick through the window, a blast that rattled the old house and rained glass and debris across the dining room table and the newly polished wooden floors. It was a well-placed and well-timed throw from someone who meant business and had probably done it before. Ray clawed his way upright like a wounded alley cat and was lucky not to shoot himself as he groped for his gun. He darted low across the foyer, hit a light switch, and saw the brick resting ominously next to a baseboard near the china cabinet.

Using a quilt, he swept away the debris and carefully picked up the brick, a new red one with sharp edges. Attached was a note held in place by two thick rubber bands. He removed them while looking at the remains of the window. His hands were shaking to the point of not being able to read the note. He swallowed hard, tried to breathe, tried to focus on the handwritten warning.

It read simply: 'Put the money back where you found it, then leave the house immediately.'

His hand was bleeding, a small nick from a piece of glass. It was his shooting hand, if in fact he had such a thing, and in the horror of the moment he wondered how he could protect himself. He crouched in the shadows of the dining room, telling himself to breathe, to think clearly.

Suddenly, the phone rang, and he jumped out of his skin again. A second ring, and he scrambled into the kitchen where a dim light above the stove helped him grapple for the phone. 'Hello!' he barked into the receiver.

'Put the money back, and leave the house,' said a calm but rigid voice, one he'd never heard, one he thought, in the blur of the moment, carried a slight trace of a coast accent. 'Now! Before you get hurt.'

He wanted to scream, 'No,' or 'Stop it,' or 'Who are you?' But his indecision caused him to hesitate, and the line went dead. He sat on the floor, and with his back to the refrigerator he quickly ran through his options, slim as they were.

He could call the police – hustle and hide the money, stuff the bags under a bed, move the mattress, conceal the note but not the brick, and carry on as if some delinquents were vandalizing an old house just for the hell of it. The cop would walk around with a flashlight and linger for an hour or two, but he would leave at some point.

The Priest boys were not leaving. They had stuck to him like glue. They might duck for a moment, but they were not leaving. And they were far more nimble than the Clanton night-watchman. And far more inspired.

He could call Harry Rex – wake him up, tell him it was urgent, get him back over to the house and unload the entire story. Ray yearned for someone to talk to. How many times had he wanted to come clean with Harry Rex? They could split the money, or include it in the estate, or take it to Tunica and roll dice for a year.

But why endanger him too? Three million was enough to provoke more than one killing.

Ray had a gun. Why couldn't he protect himself? He could fend off the attackers. When they came through the door, he'd light the place up. The gunfire would alert the neighbors, the whole town would be there.

It just took one bullet, though, one well-aimed, pointed little missile that he would never see and probably feel only for a moment, or two. And he was outnumbered by some fellas who'd fired a helluva lot more of them than Professor

338

Ray Atlee. He had already decided that he was not willing to die. Life back home was too good.

Just as his heart rate peaked and he felt his pulse start to decline, another brick came crashing through the small window above the kitchen sink. He jerked and yelled and dropped his gun, then kicked it as he scrambled toward the foyer. On hands and knees he dragged the three bags of cash into the Judge's study. He yanked the sofa away from the bookshelves and began throwing the stacks of bills back into the cabinet where he'd found the wretched loot in the first place. He was sweating and cursing and expecting another brick or maybe the first round of ammo. When all of it had been crammed back into its hiding place, he picked up the pistol and unlocked the front door. He darted to his car, cranked it, spun ruts down the front lawn, and finished his escape.

He was unharmed, and at the moment that was his only concern.

North of Clanton, the land dipped in the backwaters of Lake Chatoula, and for a two-mile stretch the road was straight and flat. Known simply as The Bottoms, it had long been the turf of late-night drag racers, boozers, ruffians, and hell-raisers in general. His nearest brush with death, prior to that moment, had been in high school when he found himself in the backseat of a packed Pontiac Firebird driven by a drunken Bobby Lee West and drag racing a Camaro driven by an even drunker Doug Terring, both cars flying at a hundred miles an hour through The Bottoms. He had walked away from it, but Bobby Lee had been killed a year later when his Firebird left the road and met a tree.

When he hit the flat stretch of The Bottoms, he pressed the accelerator of his TT and let it unwind. It was two-thirty in the morning, surely everyone else was asleep.

Elmer Conway had indeed been asleep, but a fat mosquito had taken blood from his forehead and awakened him in the process. He saw lights, a car was approaching rapidly, he turned on his radar. It took almost four miles to get the funny little foreign job pulled over, and by then Elmer was angry.

Ray made the mistake of opening his door and getting out, and that was not what Elmer had in mind.

'Freeze, asshole!' Elmer shouted, over the barrel of his service revolver, which, as Ray quickly realized, was aimed at his head.

'Relax, relax,' he said, throwing up his hands in complete surrender.

'Get away from the car,' Elmer growled, and with the gun pointed to a spot somewhere around the center line.

'No problem, sir, just relax,' Ray said, shuffling sideways.

'What's your name?'

'Ray Atlee, Judge Atlee's son. Could you put that gun down, please?'

340

Elmer lowered the gun a few inches, enough so that a discharge would hit Ray in the stomach, but not the head. 'You got Virginia plates,' Elmer said.

'That's because I live in Virginia.'

'Is that where you're headed?'

'Yes sir.'

'What's the big hurry?'

'I don't know, I just –'

'I clocked you doing ninety-eight.'

'I'm very sorry.'

'Sorry's ass. That's reckless driving.' Elmer took a step closer. Ray had forgotten about the cut on his hand and he was not aware of the one on his knee. Elmer removed a flashlight and did a body scan from ten feet away. 'Why are you bleedin'?'

It was a very good question, and, at that moment, standing in the middle of the dark highway with a light flashed in his face, Ray could not think of an adequate response. The truth would take an hour and fall on unbelieving ears. A lie would only make matters worse. 'I don't know,' he mumbled.

'What's in the car?' Elmer asked.

'Nothing.'

'Sure.'

He handcuffed Ray and put him in the backseat of his Ford County patrol car, a brown Impala with dust on the fenders, no hubcaps, a collection of antennae mounted on the rear bumper. Ray watched as he walked around the

TT and looked inside. When Elmer was finished he crawled into the front seat, and without turning around said, 'What's the gun for?'

Ray had tried to slide the pistol under the passenger's seat. Evidently it was visible from the outside.

'Protection.'

'You got a permit?'

'No.'

Elmer called the dispatcher and made a lengthy report of his latest stop. He concluded with, 'I'm bringin' him in,' as if he had just collared one of the ten most wanted.

'What about my car?' Ray asked, as they turned around.

'I'll send a wrecker out.'

Elmer turned on the red and blue lights and pushed the speedometer to eighty.

'Can I call my lawyer?' Ray asked.

'No.'

'Come on. It's just a traffic offense. My lawyer can meet me at the jail, post bond, and in an hour I'm back on the road.'

'Who's your lawyer?'

'Harry Rex Vonner.'

Elmer grunted and his neck grew thicker. 'Sumbitch cleaned me out in my divorce.'

And with that Ray sat back and closed his eyes.

Ray had actually seen the inside of the Ford County jail on two occasions, he recalled as

Elmer led him up the front sidewalk. Both times he had taken papers to deadbeat fathers who'd been years behind in child support, and Judge Atlee had locked them up. Haney Moak, the slightly retarded jailer in an oversized uniform, was still there at the front desk, reading detective magazines. He also served as the dispatcher for the graveyard shift, so he knew of Ray's transgressions.

'Judge Atlee's boy, huh?' Haney said with a crooked grin. His head was lopsided and his eyes were uneven, and whenever Haney spoke it was a challenge to maintain a visual.

'Yes sir,' Ray said politely, looking for friends.

'He was a fine man,' he said as he moved behind Ray and unlocked the cuffs.

Ray rubbed his wrists and looked at Deputy Conway, who was busy filling in forms and being very officious. 'Reckless, and no gun permit.'

'You ain't lockin' him up, are you?' Haney said to Elmer, quite rudely as if Haney were in charge of the case now, and not the deputy.

'Damned right,' Elmer shot back, and the situation was immediately tense.

'Can I call Harry Rex Vonner?' Ray pleaded.

Haney nodded toward a wall-mounted phone as if he could not care less. He was glaring at Elmer. The two obviously had a history that was not pretty. 'My jail's full now,' Haney said.

'That's what you always say.'

Ray quickly punched Harry Rex's home number. It was after 3 A.M., and he knew the interruption would not be appreciated. The current Mrs. Vonner answered after the third ring. Ray apologized for the call and asked for Harry Rex.

'He's not here,' she said.

He's not out of town, Ray thought. He was on the front porch six hours ago. 'May I ask where he is?'

Haney and Elmer were practically yelling at each other in the background.

'He's over at the Atlee place,' she said slowly.

'No, he left there hours ago. I was with him.'

'No, they just called. The house is burning.'

With Haney in the backseat, they flew around the square, lights and sirens fully engaged. From two blocks away, they could see the blaze. 'Lord have mercy,' Haney said from the back.

Few events excited Clanton like a good fire. The town's two pumpers were there. Dozens of volunteers were darting about, all seemed to be yelling. The neighbors were gathering on the sidewalks across the street.

Flames were already shooting through the roof. As Ray stepped over a water line and eased onto the front lawn, he breathed the unmistakable odor of gasoline.

Chapter 35

The love nest wasn't a bad place for a nap after all. It was a long narrow room with dust and spiderwebs and one light hanging in the center of the vaulted ceiling. The lone window had been painted sometime in the last century and overlooked the square. The bed was an iron antique with no sheets or blankets, and he tried not to think about Harry Rex and his misadventures on that very mattress. Instead, he thought of the old house at Maple Run and the glorious way it went into history. By the time the roof collapsed, half of Clanton was there. Ray had sat alone, on the low limb of a sycamore across the street, hidden from all, trying in vain to pull cherished memories from a wonderful childhood that simply had not happened. When the flames were shooting from every window, he had not thought of the cash or the Judge's desk or his mother's dining room table, but only of old General Forrest glaring down with those fierce eyes.

Three hours of sleep, and he was awake by eight. The temperature was rising rapidly in the den of iniquity, and heavy steps were coming his way.

Harry Rex swung the door open and turned on the light. 'Wake up, felon,' he growled. 'They want you down at the jail.'

Ray swung his feet to the floor. 'My escape was fair and square.' He had lost Elmer and Haney in the crowd and simply left with Harry Rex.

'Did you tell them they could search your car?'

'I did.'

'That was a dumb-ass thing to do. What kinda lawyer are you?' He pulled a wooden folding chair from the wall and sat down near the bed.

'There was nothing to hide.'

'You're stupid, you know that? They searched the car and found nothing.'

'That's what I expected.'

'No clothes, no overnight bag, no luggage, no toothbrush, no evidence whatsoever that you were simply leaving town and going home, per your official story.'

'I did not burn the house down, Harry Rex.'

'Well, you're an excellent suspect. You flee in the middle of the night, no clothes, no nothing, you drive away like a bat outta hell. Old lady Larrimore down the street sees you in your funny little car go flyin' by, then about ten minutes later here come the fire trucks. You're

346

caught by the dumbest deputy in the state doin'
ninety-eight, drivin' like hell to get away from
here. Defend yourself.'

'I didn't torch it.'

'Why did you leave at two-thirty?'

'Someone threw a rock through the dining
room window. I got scared.'

'You had a gun.'

'I didn't want to use it. I'd rather run away
than shoot somebody.'

'You've been up North too long.'

'I don't live up North.'

'How'd you get cut up like that?'

'The brick broke the window, you see, and
when I checked it out, I got cut.'

'Why didn't you call the police?'

'I panicked. I wanted to go home, so I left.'

'And ten minutes later somebody soaks the
place with gasoline and throws a match.'

'I don't know what they did.'

'I'd convict you.'

'No, you're my lawyer.'

'No, I'm the lawyer for the estate, which by
the way just lost its only asset.'

'There's fire insurance.'

'Yeah, but you can't get it.'

'Why not?'

'Because if you file a claim, then they'll
investigate you for arson. If you say you didn't
do it, then I believe you. But I'm not sure
anybody else will. If you go after the insurance,

then those boys will come after you with a vengeance.'

'I didn't torch it.'

'Great, then who did?'

'Whoever threw the brick.'

'And who might that be?'

'I have no idea. Maybe some guy who got the bad end of a divorce.'

'Brilliant. And he waits nine years to get revenge on the Judge, who, by the way, is dead. I will not be in the courtroom when you offer that to the jury.'

'I don't know, Harry Rex. I swear I didn't do it. Forget the insurance money.'

'It's not that easy. Only half is yours, the other half belongs to Forrest. He can file a claim for the insurance coverage.'

Ray breathed deeply and scratched his stubble. 'Help me here, okay?'

'The sheriff's downstairs, with one of his investigators. They'll ask some questions. Answer slowly, tell the truth, blah, blah. I'll be there, so let's go slow.'

'He's here?'

'In my conference room. I asked him to come over so we can do this now. I really think you need to get out of town.'

'I was trying.'

'The reckless driving and the gun charge will be put off for a few months. Give me some time to work the docket. You got bigger problems right now.'

348

'I did not torch the house, Harry Rex.'

'Of course you didn't.'

They left the room and started down the unsteady steps to the second floor. 'Who's the sheriff?' Ray asked, over his shoulder.

'Guy named Sawyer.'

'Good guy?'

'It doesn't matter.'

'You close to him?'

'I did his son's divorce.'

The conference room was a wonderful mess of thick law books thrown about on shelves and credenzas and the long table itself. The impression was given that Harry Rex spent hours in tedious research. He did not.

Sawyer was not the least bit polite, nor was his assistant, a nervous little Italian named Sandroni. Italians were rare in northeast Mississippi, and during the tense introductions Ray detected a Delta accent. The two were all business, with Sandroni taking careful notes while Sawyer sipped steaming coffee from a paper cup and watched every move Ray made.

The fire call was made by Mrs. Larrimore at two thirty-four, approximately ten to fifteen minutes after she'd seen Ray's car leave Fourth Street in a hurry. Elmer Conway radioed at two thirty-six that he was in pursuit of some idiot doing a hundred miles an hour down in The Bottoms. Since it was established that Ray was driving very fast, Sandroni spent a long time nailing down his route, his estimated speeds,

349

traffic lights, anything to slow him down at that hour of the morning.

Once Ray's exit route was determined, Sawyer radioed a deputy, who was sitting in front of the rubble at Maple Run, and told him to drive the exact course at the same estimated speeds and to stop out in The Bottoms where Elmer was once again waiting.

Twelve minutes later, the deputy called back and said he was with Elmer.

'So in less than twelve minutes,' Sandroni said as he began his recap, 'Someone – and we're assuming this someone was not already in the house, aren't we, Mr. Atlee? – entered with what evidently was a large supply of gasoline and soaked the place thoroughly, so thoroughly that the fire captain said he'd never smelled such a strong odor of gas, then threw a match or maybe two, because the fire captain was almost certain the fire had more than one point of origin, and once the matches were thrown this unknown arsonist fled into the night. Right, Mr. Atlee?'

'I don't know what the arsonist did,' Ray said.

'But the times are accurate?'

'If you say so.'

'I say so.'

'Move along,' Harry Rex growled from the end of the table.

Motive was next. The house was insured for $380,000, including contents. According to the Realtor, who'd already been consulted, he'd been writing up an offer to purchase it for $175,000.

'That's a nice gap, isn't it, Mr. Atlee?' Sandroni inquired.

'It is.'

'Have you notified your insurance company?' Sandroni asked.

'No, I thought I'd wait until their offices open,' Ray responded. 'Believe it or not, some folks don't work on Saturday.'

'Hell, the fire truck's still there,' Harry Rex added helpfully. 'We got six months to file a claim.'

Sandroni's cheeks turned crimson but he held his tongue. Moving right along, he studied his notes and said, 'Let's talk about other suspects.'

Ray didn't like the use of the word 'other.' He told the story about the brick through the window, or at least most of the story. And the phone call, warning him to leave immediately. 'Check the phone records,' he challenged them. And for good measure, he threw in the earlier adventures with some demented soul rattling windows the night the Judge died.

'Y'all had enough,' Harry Rex said after thirty minutes. In other words, my client will answer no more questions.

'When are you leaving town?' asked Sawyer.

'I've been trying to leave for the past six hours,' Ray replied.

'Real soon,' said Harry Rex.

'We may have some more questions.'

'I'll come back whenever I'm needed,' Ray said.

Harry Rex shoved them out the front door, and when he returned to the conference room he said, 'I think you're a lyin' sonofabitch.'

Chapter 36

The old fire truck was gone, the same one Ray and his friends had followed when they were teenagers and bored on summer nights. A lone volunteer in a dirty tee shirt was folding fire hoses. The street was a mess with mud strewn everywhere.

Maple Run was deserted by midmorning. The chimney on the east end was still standing, as was a short section of charred wall beside it. Everything else had collapsed into a pile of debris. Ray and Harry Rex walked around the rubble and went to the backyard, where a row of ancient pecan trees protected the rear boundary of the property. They sat in the shade, in metal lawn chairs that Ray had once painted red, and ate tamales.

'I didn't burn this place,' Ray finally said.

'Do you know who did?' Harry Rex asked.

'I have a suspect.'

'Tell me, dammit.'

'His name is Gordie Priest.'

'Oh him!'

'It's a long story.'

Ray began with the Judge, dead on the sofa, and the accidental discovery of the money, or was it an accident after all? He gave as many facts and details as he could remember, and he raised all the questions that had been dogging him for weeks. Both stopped eating. They stared at the smoldering debris but were too mesmerized to see it. Harry Rex was stunned by the narrative. Ray was relieved to be telling it. From Clanton to Charlottesville and back. From the casinos in Tunica to Atlantic City, then back to Tunica. To the coast and Patton French and his quest for a billion dollars, all to be credited to Judge Reuben Atlee, humble servant of the law.

Ray held back nothing, and he tried to remember everything. The ransacking of his apartment in Charlottesville, for intimidation only, he thought. The ill-advised purchase of a share in a Bonanza. On and on he went, while Harry Rex said nothing.

When he finished, his appetite was gone and he was sweating. Harry Rex had a million questions, but he began with, 'Why would he burn the house?'

'Cover his tracks, maybe, I don't know.'

'This guy didn't leave tracks.'

'Maybe it was the final act of intimidation.'

They mulled this over. Harry Rex finished a tamale and said, 'You should've told me.'

'I wanted to keep the money, okay? I had

354

three million bucks in cash in my sticky little hands, and it felt wonderful. It was better than sex, better than anything I'd ever felt. Three million bucks, Harry Rex, all mine. I was rich. I was greedy. I was corrupt. I didn't want you or Forrest or the government or anyone in the world to know that I had the money.'

'What were you gonna do with it?'

'Ease it into banks, a dozen of them, nine thousand dollars at a time, no paperwork that would alert the government, let it pile up over eighteen months, then invest it with a pro. I'm forty-three; in two years the money would be laundered and hard at work. It would double every five years. At the age of fifty, it would be six million. Fifty-five, twelve million. At the age of sixty, I'd have twenty-four million bucks. I had it all planned, Harry Rex. I could see the future.'

'Don't beat yourself up. What you did was normal.'

'It doesn't feel normal.'

'You're a lousy crook.'

'I felt lousy, and I was already changing. I could see myself in an airplane and a fancier sports car and a nicer place to live. There's a lot of money around Charlottesville, and I was thinking about making a splash. Country clubs, fox hunting –'

'Fox hunting?'

'Yep.'

'With those little britches and the hat?'

'Flying over fences on a wild horse, chasing a pack of hounds that are in hot pursuit of a thirty-pound fox that you'll never see.'

'Why would you wanna do that?'

'Why would anyone?'

'I'll stick to huntin' birds.'

'Anyway, it was a burden, literally. I mean, I've been hauling the cash around for weeks.'

'You could've left some at my office.'

Ray finished a tamale and sipped a cola. 'You think I'm stupid?'

'No, lucky. This guy plays for keeps.'

'Every time I closed my eyes, I could see a bullet coming at my forehead.'

'Look, Ray, you've done nothing wrong. The Judge didn't want the money included in his estate. You took it because you thought you were protectin' it, and also guardin' his reputation. You had a crazy man who wanted it more than you. Lookin' back, you're lucky you didn't get hurt in the whole episode. Forget it.'

'Thanks, Harry Rex.' Ray leaned forward and watched the volunteer fireman walk away. 'What about the arson?'

'We'll work it out. I'll file a claim, and the insurance company will investigate. They'll suspect arson and thangs'll get ugly. Let a few months pass. If they don't pay, then we'll sue, in Ford County. They won't risk a jury trial against the estate of Reuben Atlee right here in his own courthouse. I think they'll settle before trial. We may have to compromise some, but we'll get a nice settlement.'

Ray was on his feet. 'I really want to go home,' he said.

The air was thick with heat and smoke as they walked around the house. 'I've had enough,' Ray said, and headed for the street.

He drove a perfect fifty-five through The Bottoms. Elmer Conway was nowhere to be seen. The Audi seemed lighter with the trunk empty. Indeed, life itself was shedding burdens. Ray longed for the normalcy of home.

He dreaded the meeting with Forrest. Their father's estate had just been wiped out, and the arson issue would be difficult to explain. Perhaps he should wait. Rehab was going so smoothly, and Ray knew from experience that the slightest complication could derail Forrest. Let a month go by. Then another.

Forrest would not be going back to Clanton, and in his murky world he might never hear of the fire. It might be best if Harry Rex broke the news to him.

The receptionist at Alcorn Village gave him a curious look when he signed in. He read magazines for a long time in the dark lounge where the visitors waited. When Oscar Meave eased in with a gloomy look, Ray knew exactly what had happened.

'He walked away late yesterday afternoon,' Meave began as he crouched on the coffee table in front of Ray. 'I've tried to reach you all morning.'

'I lost my cell phone last night,' Ray said. Of all the things he'd left behind when the rocks were falling, he couldn't believe he'd forgotten his cell phone.

'He signed in for the ridge walk, a five-mile nature trail he's been doing every day. It's around the back of the property, no fencing, but then Forrest was not a security risk. We didn't think so, anyway. I can't believe this.'

Ray certainly could. His brother had been walking away from detox units for almost twenty years.

'This is not really a lockdown facility,' Meave continued. 'Our patients want to stay here, or it doesn't work.'

'I understand,' Ray said softly.

'He was doing so well,' Meave went on, obviously more troubled than Ray. 'Completely clean and very proud of it. He had sort of adopted two teenagers, both in rehab for the first time. Forrest worked with them every morning. I just don't understand this one.'

'I thought you are an ex-addict.'

Meave was shaking his head. 'I know, I know. The addict quits when the addict wants to, and not before.'

'Have you ever seen one who just couldn't quit?' Ray asked.

'We can't admit that.'

'I know you can't. But, off the record, you

and I both know that there are addicts who will never kick it.'

Meave shrugged, with reluctance.

'Forrest is one of those, Oscar. We've lived this for twenty years.'

'I take it as a personal failure.'

'Don't.'

They walked outside and talked for a moment under a veranda. Meave could not stop apologizing. For Ray, it was nothing unexpected.

Along the winding road back to the main highway, Ray wondered how his brother could simply walk away from a facility eight miles from the nearest town. But then, he had fled more secluded places.

He would go back to Memphis, back to his room in Ellie's basement, back to the streets where pushers were waiting for him. The next phone call might be the last, but then Ray had been half-expecting it for many years. As sick as he was, Forrest had shown an amazing ability to survive.

Ray was in Tennessee now. Virginia was next, seven hours away. With a clear sky and no wind, he thought of how nice it would be at five thousand feet, buzzing around in his favorite rented Cessna.

Chapter 37

Both doors were new, unpainted, and much heavier than the old ones. Ray silently thanked his landlord for the extra expense, though he knew that there would be no more break-ins. The pursuit had ended. No more quick looks over the shoulder. No more sneaking to Chaney's to play hide-and-seek. No more hushed conversations with Corey Crawford. And no more illicit money to fret over, and dream about, and haul around, literally. The lifting of that burden made him smile and walk a bit faster.

Life would become normal again. Long runs in the heat. Long solo flights over the Piedmont. He even looked forward to his neglected research for the monopolies treatise he'd promised to deliver by either this Christmas or the one after. He had softened on the Kaley issue and was ready for one last attempt at dinner. She was legal now, a graduate, and she simply looked too fine to write off without a decent effort.

His apartment was the same, its usual condition since no one else lived there. Other than the door, there was no evidence of a forced entry. He now knew that his burglar had not really been a thief after all, just a tormentor, an intimidator. Either Gordie or one of his brothers. He wasn't sure how they had divided their labors, nor did he care.

It was almost 11 A.M. He made some strong coffee and began shuffling through the mail. No more anonymous letters. Nothing now but the usual bills and solicitations.

There were two faxes in the tray. The first was a note from a former student. The second was from Patton French. He'd been trying to call, but Ray's cell phone wasn't working. It was handwritten on the stationery from the *King of Torts*, no doubt faxed from the gray waters of the Gulf where French was still hiding his boat from his wife's divorce lawyer.

Good news on the security front! Not long after Ray had left the coast, Gordie Priest had been 'located,' along with both of his brothers. Could Ray please give him a call? His assistant would find him.

Ray worked the phone for two hours, until French called from a hotel in Fort Worth, where he was meeting with some Ryax and Kobril lawyers. 'I'll probably get a thousand cases up here,' he said, unable to control himself.

361

'Wonderful,' said Ray. He was determined not to listen to any more crowing about mass torts and zillion-dollar settlements.

'Is your phone secure?' French asked.

'Yes.'

'Okay, listen. Priest is no longer a threat. We found him shortly after you left, laid up drunk with an old gal he's been seeing for a long time. Found both brothers too. Your money is safe.'

'Exactly when did you find them?' Ray asked. He was hovering over the kitchen table with a large calendar spread before him. Time was crucial here. He'd made notes in the margins as he'd waited for the call.

French thought for a second. 'Uh, let's see. What's today?'

'Monday, June the fifth.'

'Monday. When did you leave the coast?'

'Ten o'clock Friday morning.'

'Then it was just after lunch on Friday.'

'You're sure?'

'Of course I'm sure. Why do you ask?'

'And once you found him, there was no way they left the coast?'

'Trust me, Ray, they'll never leave the coast again. They've, uh, found a permanent home there.'

'I don't want those details.' Ray sat at the table and stared at the calendar.

'What's the matter?' French asked. 'Something wrong?'

362

'Yeah, you could say that.'

'What is it?'

'Somebody burned the house down.'

'Judge Atlee's?'

'Yes.'

'When?'

'After midnight, Saturday morning.'

A pause as French absorbed this, then, 'Well, it wasn't the Priest boys, I can promise you that.'

When Ray said nothing, French asked, 'Where's the money?'

'I don't know,' he mumbled.

A five-mile run did nothing to ease his tension. Though, as always, he was able to plot things, to rearrange his thoughts. The temperature was above ninety, and he was soaked with sweat when he returned to his apartment.

Now that Harry Rex had been told everything, it was comforting to have someone with whom to share the latest. He called his office in Clanton and was informed that he was in court over in Tupelo and wouldn't be back until late. He called Ellie's house in Memphis and no one bothered to answer. He called Oscar Meave at Alcorn Village, and, expecting to hear no news of his brother's whereabouts, got exactly what he expected.

So much for the normal life.

After a tense morning of back-and-forth negotiations in the hallways of the Lee County Courthouse, bickering over such issues as who'd get the ski boat and who'd get the cabin on the lake, and how much he would pay in a lump-sum cash settlement, the divorce was settled an hour after lunch. Harry Rex had the husband, an overheated cowboy on wife number three who thought he knew more divorce law than his lawyer. Wife number three was an aging bimbo in her late twenties who'd caught him with her best friend. It was the typical, sordid tale, and Harry Rex was sick of the whole mess when he walked to the bench and presented a hard-fought property settlement agreement.

The chancellor was a veteran who'd divorced thousands. 'Very sorry about Judge Atlee,' he said softly as he began to review the papers. Harry Rex just nodded. He was tired and thirsty and already contemplating a cold one as he drove the backroad to Clanton. His favorite beer store in the Tupelo area was at the county line.

'We served together for twenty-two years,' the chancellor was saying.

'A fine man,' Harry Rex said.

'Are you doing the estate?'

'Yes sir.'

'Give my regards to Judge Farr over there.'

'I will.'

The paperwork was signed, the marriage mercifully terminated, the warring spouses sent to their neutral homes. Harry Rex was out of the courthouse and halfway to his car when a lawyer chased him down and stopped him on the sidewalk. He introduced himself as Jacob Spain,

Attorney-at-Law, one of a thousand in Tupelo. He'd been in the courtroom and overheard the chancellor mention Judge Atlee.

'He has a son, right, Forrest?' Spain asked.

'Two sons, Ray and Forrest.' Harry Rex took a breath and settled in for a quick visit.

'I played high school football against Forrest; in fact he broke my collarbone with a late hit.'

'That sounds like Forrest.'

'I played at New Albany. Forrest was a junior when I was a senior. Did you see him play?'

'Yes, many times.'

'You remember the game over there against us when he threw for three hundred yards in the first half? Four or five touchdowns, I think.'

'I do,' Harry Rex said, and started to fidget. How long was this going to take?

'I was playing safety that night, and he was firing passes all over the place. I picked one off right before half-time, ran it out of bounds, and he speared me while I was on the ground.'

'That was one of his favorite plays.' Hit 'em hard and hit 'em late had been Forrest's motto, especially those defensive backs unlucky enough to intercept one of his passes.

'I think he was arrested the next week,' Spain was saying. 'What a waste. Anyway, I saw him just a few weeks ago, here in Tupelo, with Judge Atlee.'

The fidgeting stopped. Harry Rex forgot about a cold one, at least for the moment. 'When was this?' he asked.

'Right before the Judge died. It was a strange scene.'

They took a few steps and found shade under a tree. 'I'm listening,' Harry Rex said, loosening his tie. His wrinkled navy blazer was already off.

'My wife's mother is being treated for breast cancer at the Taft Clinic. One Monday afternoon back in the spring I drove her over there for another round of chemo.'

'Judge Atlee went to Taft,' Harry Rex said. 'I've seen the bills.'

'Yes, that's where I saw him. I checked her in, there was a wait, so I went to my car to make a bunch of calls. While I was sitting there, I watched as Judge Atlee pulled up in a long black Lincoln driven by someone I didn't recognize. They got the thing parked, just two cars down, and they got out. His driver then looked familiar – big guy, big frame, long hair, kind of a cocky swagger that I've seen before. It hit me that it was Forrest. I could tell by the way he walked and moved. He was wearing sunglasses and a cap pulled low. They went inside, and within seconds Forrest came back out.'

'What kinda cap?'

'Faded blue, Cubs, I think.'

'I've seen that one.'

'He was real nervous, like he didn't want anyone to see him. He disappeared into some trees next to the clinic, except I could barely see his outline. He just hid there. I thought at first he might be relieving himself, but no, he was just

366

hiding. After an hour or so, I went in, waited, finally got my mother-in-law, and left. He was still out in the trees.'

Harry Rex had pulled out his pocket planner. 'What day was this?' Spain removed his, and as all busy lawyers do, they compared their recent movements. 'Monday, May the first,' Spain decided.

'That was six days before the Judge died,' Harry Rex said.

'I'm sure that's the date. It was just a strange scene.'

'Well, he's a pretty strange guy.'

'He's not running from the law or anything, is he?'

'Not at the present,' Harry Rex said, and they both managed a nervous laugh.

Spain suddenly needed to go. 'Anyway, when you see him again, tell him I'm still mad about the late hit.'

'I'll do that,' Harry Rex said, then watched him walk away.

Chapter 38

Mr. and Mrs. Vonner left Clanton on a cloudy June morning in a new sports utility four-wheel drive that promised twelve miles to the gallon and was loaded with enough luggage for a month in Europe. The District of Columbia was the destination, however, since Mrs. Vonner had a sister there whom Harry Rex had never met. They spent the first night in Gatlinburg and the second night at White Sulphur Springs in West Virginia. They arrived in Charlottesville around noon, did the obligatory tour of Jefferson's Monticello, walked the grounds at the university, and had an unusual dinner at a college dive called the White Spot, the house specialty being a fried egg on a hamburger. It was Harry Rex's kind of food.

The next morning, while she slept, he went for a stroll on the downtown mall. He found the address and waited.

A few minutes after 8 A.M., Ray double-tied the laces of his rather expensive running shoes, stretched in the den, and walked downstairs for the daily five-miler. Outside, the air was warm. July was not far away and summer had already arrived.

He turned a corner and heard a familiar voice call, 'Hey, boy.'

Harry Rex was sitting on a bench, a cup of coffee in hand, an unread newspaper next to him. Ray froze and took a few seconds to collect himself. Things were out of place here.

When he could move, he walked over and said, 'What, exactly, are you doing here?'

'Cute outfit,' Harry Rex said, taking in the shorts, old tee shirt, red runner's cap, the latest in athletic eye glasses. 'Me and the wife are passing through, headed for D.C. She has a sister up there she thinks I want to meet. Sit down.'

'Why didn't you call?'

'Didn't want to bother you.'

'But you should've called, Harry Rex. We could do dinner, I'll show you around.'

'It's not that kind of trip. Sit down.'

Smelling trouble, Ray sat next to Harry Rex. 'I can't believe this,' he mumbled.

'Shut up and listen.'

Ray removed his running glasses and looked at Harry Rex. 'Is it bad?'

'Let's say it's curious.' He told Jacob Spain's story about Forrest hiding in the trees at the oncology clinic, six days before the Judge passed away. Ray listened in disbelief and slid lower on the bench. He finally leaned forward with his elbows on his knees, his head hung low.

'According to the medical records,' Harry Rex was saying, 'he got a morphine pack that day, May the first. Don't know if it was the first pack or a refill, the records are not that clear. Looks like Forrest took him to get the good stuff.'

A long pause as a pretty young woman walked by, obviously in a hurry, her tight skirt swaying wonderfully as she sped along. A sip of coffee, then, 'I've always been suspicious of that will you found in his study. The Judge and I talked about his will for the last six months of his life. I don't think he simply cranked out one more right before he died. I've studied the signatures at length, and it's my untrained opinion that the last one is a forgery.'

Ray cleared his voice and said, 'If Forrest drove him to Tupelo, then it's safe to assume Forrest was in the house.'

'All over the house.'

Harry Rex had hired an investigator in Memphis to find Forrest, but there was no trail, no trace. From somewhere within the newspaper, he pulled out an envelope. 'Then, this came three days ago.'

Ray pulled out a sheet of paper and unfolded it. It was from Oscar Meave at Alcorn Village, and it read: 'Dear Mr. Vonner: I have been unable to reach Ray Atlee. I know the whereabouts of Forrest, if by chance the family does not. Call if you would like to talk. Everything is confidential. Best wishes, Oscar Meave.'

'So I called him right away,' Harry Rex said, eyeing another young woman. 'He has a former patient who's now a counselor at a rehab ranch out West. Forrest checked in there a week ago, and was adamant about his privacy, said he did not want his family to know where he was. Evidently this happens from time to time, and the clinics are always caught in a bind. They have to respect the wishes of their patient, but on the other hand, the family is crucial to the overall rehabilitation. So these counselors whisper among themselves. Meave made the decision to pass along the information to you.'

'Where out West?'

'Montana. A place called Morningstar Ranch. Meave said it's what the boy needs – very nice, very remote, a lockdown facility for the hard cases, said he'll be there for a year.'

Ray sat up and began rubbing his forehead as if he'd finally been shot there.

'And of course the place is pricey,' Harry Rex added.

'Of course,' Ray mumbled.

There was no more talk, not about Forrest anyway. After a few minutes, Harry Rex said he was leaving. He had delivered his message, he had nothing more to say, not then. His wife was anxious to see her sister. Perhaps next time they could stay longer, have dinner, whatever. He patted Ray on the shoulder, and left him there. 'See you in Clanton' were his last words.

Too weak and too winded for a run, Ray sat on the bench in the middle of the downtown mall, his apartment above him, lost in a world of rapidly moving pieces. The foot traffic picked up as the merchants and bankers and lawyers hustled to work, but Ray did not see them.

Carl Mirk taught two sections of insurance law each semester, and he was a member of the Virginia bar, as was Ray. They discussed the interview over lunch, and both came to the conclusion that it was just part of a routine inquiry, nothing to worry about. Mirk would tag along and pretend to be Ray's lawyer.

The insurance investigator's name was Ratterfield. They welcomed him into the conference room at the law school. He removed his jacket as if they might be there for hours. Ray was wearing jeans and a golf shirt. Mirk was just as casual.

'I usually record these,' Ratterfield said, all business as he pulled out a tape recorder and placed it between him and Ray. 'Any objections?' he asked, once the recorder was in place.

'I guess not,' Ray said.

He punched a button, looked at his notes, then began an introduction, for the benefit of the tape. He was an independent insurance examiner, hired by Aviation Underwriters, to investigate a claim filed by Ray Atlee and three

372

other owners for damages to a 1994 Beech Bonanza on June 2. According to the state arson examiner, the airplane was deliberately burned.

Initially, he needed Ray's flying history. Ray had his logbook and Ratterfield pored through it, finding nothing remotely interesting. 'No instrument rating,' he said at one point.

'I'm working on it,' Ray replied.

'Fourteen hours in the Bonanza?'

'Yep.'

He then moved to the consortium of owners, and asked questions about the deal that brought it together. He'd already interviewed the other owners, and they had produced the contracts and documentation. Ray acknowledged the paperwork.

Changing gears, Ratterfield asked, 'Where were you on June the first?'

'Biloxi, Mississippi,' Ray answered, certain that Ratterfield had no idea where that was.

'How long had you been there?'

'A few days.'

'May I ask why you were there?'

'Sure,' Ray said, then launched into an abbreviated version of his recent visits home. His official reason for going to the coast was to visit friends, old buddies from his days at Tulane.

'I'm sure there are people who can verify that you were there on June the first,' Ratterfield said.

'Several people. Plus I have hotel receipts.'

He seemed convinced that Ray had been in

Mississippi. 'The other owners were all at home when the plane burned,' he said, flipping a page to a list of typed notes. 'All have alibis. If we're assuming it's arson, then we have to first find a motive, then whoever torched it. Any ideas?'

'I have no idea who did this,' Ray said quickly, and with conviction.

'How about motive?'

'We had just bought the plane. Why would any of us want to destroy it?'

'To collect the insurance, maybe. Happens occasionally. Perhaps one partner decided he was in over his head. The note is not small – almost two hundred grand over six years, close to nine hundred bucks a month per partner.'

'We knew that two weeks earlier when we signed on,' Ray said.

They shadowboxed for a while around the delicate issue of Ray's personal finances – salary, expenses, obligations. When Ratterfield seemed convinced that Ray could swing his end of the deal, he changed subjects. 'This fire in Mississippi,' he said, scanning a report of some type. 'Tell me about it.'

'What do you want to know?'

'Are you under investigation for arson down there?'

'No.'

'Are you sure?'

'Yes, I'm sure. You can call my attorney if you'd like.'

374

'I already have. And your apartment has been burglarized twice in the past six weeks?'

'Nothing was taken. Both were just break-ins.'

'You're having an exciting summer.'

'Is that a question?'

'Sounds like someone's after you.'

'Again, is that a question?'

It was the only flare-up of the interview, and both Ray and Ratterfield took a breath.

'Any other arson investigations in your past?'

Ray smiled and said, 'No.'

When Ratterfield flipped another page, and there was nothing typed on it, he lost interest in a hurry and went through the motions of wrapping things up. 'I'm sure our attorneys will be in touch,' he said as he turned off the recorder.

'I can't wait,' Ray said.

Ratterfield collected his jacket and his briefcase and made his exit.

After he left, Carl said, 'I think you know more than you're telling.'

'Maybe,' Ray said. 'But I had nothing to do with the arson here, or the arson there.'

'I've heard enough.'

Chapter 39

For almost a week, a string of turbulent summer fronts kept the ceilings low and the winds too dangerous for small planes. When the extended forecasts showed nothing but calm dry air for everywhere but South Texas, Ray left Charlottesville in a Cessna and began the longest cross-country of his brief flying career. Avoiding busy airspace and looking for easy landmarks below, he flew west across the Shenandoah Valley into West Virginia and into Kentucky, where he picked up fuel at a four-thousand-foot strip not far from Lexington. The Cessna could stay aloft for about three and a half hours before the indicator dipped below a quarter of a tank. He landed again in Terre Haute, crossed the Mississippi River at Hannibal, and stopped for the evening in Kirksville, Missouri, where he checked into a motel.

It was his first motel since the odyssey with the cash, and it was precisely because of the cash that he was back in a motel. He was also in

Missouri, and as he flipped through muted channels in his room, he remembered Patton French's story of stumbling upon Ryax at a tort seminar in St. Louis. An old lawyer from a small town in the Ozarks had a son who taught at the university in Columbia, and the son knew the drug was bad. And because of Patton French and his insatiable greed and corruption, he, Ray Atlee, was now in another motel in a town where he knew absolutely no one.

A front was developing over Utah. Ray lifted off just after sunrise and climbed to above five thousand feet. He trimmed his controls and opened a large cup of steaming black coffee. He flew more north than west for the first leg and was soon over the cornfields of Iowa.

Alone a mile above the earth, in the cool quiet air of the early morning, and with not a single pilot chattering on the airwaves, Ray tried to focus on the task before him. It was easier though, to loaf, to enjoy the solitude and the views, and the coffee, and the solitary act of leaving the world down there. And it was quite pleasant to put off thoughts of his brother.

After a stop in Sioux Falls, he turned west again and followed Interstate 90 across the entire state of South Dakota before skirting the restricted space around Mount Rushmore. He landed in Rapid City, rented a car, and took a long drive through Badlands National Park.

Morningstar Ranch was somewhere in the hills south of Kalispell, though its Web site was purposefully vague. Oscar Meave had tried but had been unsuccessful in pinpointing its exact location. At the end of the third day of his journey, Ray landed after dark in Kalispell. He rented a car, found dinner then a motel, and spent hours with aerial and road maps.

It took another day of low-altitude flying around Kalispell and the towns of Woods Bay, Polison, Bigfork, and Elmo. He crossed Flathead Lake a half-dozen times and was ready to surrender the air war and send in the ground troops when he caught a glimpse of a compound of some sort near the town of Somers on the north side of the lake. From fifteen hundred feet, he circled the place until he saw a substantial fence of green chain link almost hidden in the woods and practically invisible from the air. There were small buildings that appeared to be housing units, a larger one for administration perhaps, a pool, tennis courts, a barn with horses grazing nearby. He circled long enough for a few folks within the complex to stop whatever they were doing and look up with shielded eyes.

Finding it on the ground was as challenging as from the air, but by noon the next day Ray was parked outside the unmarked gate, glaring at an armed guard who was glaring back at him. After a few tense questions, the guard finally admitted that, yes, he had in fact found the place he was looking for. 'We don't allow visitors,' he said smugly.

378

Ray created a tale of a family in crisis and stressed the urgency of finding his brother. The procedure, as the guard grudgingly laid out, was to leave a name and a phone number, and there was a slight chance someone from within would contact him. The next day, he was trout fishing on the Flathead River when his cell phone rang. An unfriendly voice belonging to an Allison with Morningstar asked for Ray Atlee.

Who was she expecting?

He confessed to being Ray Atlee, and she proceeded to ask what was it he wanted from their facility. 'I have a brother there,' he said as politely as possible. 'His name is Forrest Atlee, and I'd like to see him.'

'What makes you think he's here?' she demanded.

'He's there. You know he's there. I know he's there, so can we please stop the games?'

'I'll look into it, but don't expect a return call.' She hung up before he could say anything. The next unfriendly voice belonged to Darrel, an administrator of something or other. It came late in the afternoon while Ray was hiking a trail in the Swan Range near the Hungry Horse Reservoir. Darrel was as abrupt as Allison. 'Half an hour only. Thirty minutes,' he informed Ray. 'At ten in the morning.'

A maximum security prison would have been more agreeable. The same guard frisked him at the gate and inspected his car. 'Follow him,' the

guard said. Another guard in a golf cart was
waiting on the narrow drive, and Ray followed
him to a small parking lot near the front
building. When he got out of his car Allison was
waiting, unarmed. She was tall and rather
masculine, and when she offered the obligatory
handshake Ray had never felt so physically
overmatched. She marched him inside, where
cameras monitored every move with no effort at
concealment. She led him to a windowless room
and passed him off to a snarling officer of an
unknown variety who, with the deft touch of a
baggage handler, poked and prodded every
bend and crevice except the groin, where, for
one awful moment, Ray thought he might just
take a jab there too.

'I'm just seeing my brother,' Ray finally
protested, and in doing so came close to getting
backhanded.

When he was thoroughly searched and sanitized, Allison gathered him up again and led him
down a short hallway to a stark square room that
felt as though it should have had padded walls.
The only door to it had the only window, and,
pointing to it, Allison said gravely, 'We will be
watching.'

'Watching what?' Ray asked.

She scowled at him and seemed ready to
knock him to the floor.

There was a square table in the center of the
room, with two chairs on opposite sides. 'Sit

here,' she demanded, and Ray took his designated seat. For ten minutes he looked at the walls, his back to the door.

Finally, it opened, and Forrest entered alone, unchained, no handcuffs, no burly guards prodding him along. Without a word he sat across from Ray and folded his hands together on the table as if it was time to meditate. The hair was gone. A buzz cut had removed everything but a thin stand of no more than an eighth of an inch, and above the ears the shearing had gone to the scalp. He was clean-shaven and looked twenty pounds lighter. His baggy shirt was a dark olive button-down with a small collar and two large pockets, almost military-like. It prompted Ray to offer the first words: 'This place is a boot camp.'

'It's tough,' Forrest replied very slowly and softly.

'Do they brainwash you?'

'That's exactly what they do.'

Ray was there because of money, and he decided to confront it head-on. 'So what do you get for seven hundred bucks a day?' he began.

'A new life.'

Ray nodded his approval at the answer. Forrest was staring at him, no blinking, no expression, just gazing almost forlornly at his brother as if he were a stranger.

'And you're here for twelve months?'

'At least.'

'That's a quarter of a million dollars.'

He gave a little shrug, as if money was not a

problem, as if he just might stay for three years, or five.

'Are you sedated?' Ray asked, trying to provoke him.

'No.'

'You act as if you're sedated.'

'I'm not. They don't use drugs here. Can't imagine why not, can you?' His voice picked up a little steam.

Ray was mindful of the ticking clock. Allison would be back at precisely the thirtieth minute to break up things and escort Ray out of the building and out of the compound forever. He needed much more time to cover their issues, but efficiency was required here. Get to the point, he told himself. See how much he's going to admit.

'I took the old man's last will,' Ray said. 'And I took the summons he sent, the one calling us home on May the seventh, and I studied his signatures on both. I think they're forgeries.'

'Good for you.'

'Don't know who did the forging, but I suspect it was you.'

'Sue me.'

'No denial?'

'What difference does it make?'

Ray repeated those words, half-aloud and in disgust as if repeating them made him angry. A long pause while the clock ticked. 'I received my summons on a Thursday. It was postmarked in Clanton on Monday, the same day you drove

382

him to the Taft Clinic in Tupelo to get a morphine pack. Question – how did you manage to type the summons on his old Underwood manual?'

'I don't have to answer your questions.'

'Sure you do. You put together this fraud, Forrest. The least you can do is tell me how it happened. You've won. The old man's dead. The house is gone. You have the money. No one's chasing you but me, and I'll be gone soon. Tell me how it happened.'

'He already had a morphine pack.'

'Okay, so you took him to get another one, or a refill, whatever. That's not the question.'

'But it's important.'

'Why?'

'Because he was stoned.' There was a slight break in the brainwashed facade as he took his hands off the table and glanced away.

'So he was suffering,' Ray said, trying to provoke some emotions here.

'Yes,' Forrest said without a trace of emotion.

'And if you kept the morphine cranked up, then you had the house to yourself?'

'Something like that.'

'When did you first go back there?'

'I'm not too good with dates. Never have been.'

'Don't play stupid with me, Forrest. He died on a Sunday.'

'I went there on a Saturday.'

'So eight days before he died?'

'Yes, I guess.'

'And why did you go back?'

He folded his arms across his chest and lowered his chin and his eyes. And his voice. 'He called me,' he began, 'and asked me to come see him. I went the next day. I couldn't believe how old and sick he was, and how lonely.' A deep breath, a glance up at his brother. 'The pain was terrible. Even with the painkillers, he was in bad shape. We sat on the porch and talked about the war and how things would've been different if Jackson hadn't been killed at Chancellorsville, the same old battles he's been refighting forever. He shifted constantly, trying to fight off the pain. At times it took his breath away. But he just wanted to talk. We never buried the hatchet or tried to make things right. We didn't feel the need to. The fact that I was there was all he wanted. I slept on the sofa in his study, and during the night I woke up to hear him scream- ing. He was on the floor of his room, his knees up to his chin, shivering from the pain. I got him back in his bed, helped him hit the morphine, finally got him still. It was about three in the morning. I was wild-eyed. I started roaming.'

The narrative fizzled, but the clock didn't.

'And that's when you found the money,' Ray said.

'What money?'

'The money that's paying seven hundred dollars a day here.'

'Oh, that money.'

384

'That money.'

'Yeah, that's when I found it, same place as you. Twenty-seven boxes. The first one had a hundred thousand bucks in it, so I did some calculations. I had no idea what to do. I just sat there for hours, staring at the boxes all stacked innocently in the cabinets. I thought he might get out of bed, walk down the hall, and catch me looking at all his little boxes, and I was hoping he would. Then he could explain things.' He put his hands back on the table and stared at Ray again. 'By sunrise, though, I thought I had a plan. I decided I'd let you handle the money. You're the firstborn, the favorite son, the big brother, the golden boy, the honor student, the law professor, the executor, the one he trusted the most. I'll just watch Ray, I said to myself, see what he does with the money, because whatever he does must be right. So I closed the cabinets, slid the sofa over, and tried to act as though I'd never found it. I came close to asking the old man about it, but I figured that if he wanted me to know, then he would tell me.'

'When did you type my summons?'

'Later that day. He was passed out under the pecan trees in the backyard, in his hammock. He was feeling a lot better, but by then he was addicted to the morphine. He didn't remember much of that last week.'

'And Monday you took him to Tupelo?'

'Yes. He'd been driving himself, but since I was around he asked me to take him over.'

385

'And you hid in the trees outside the clinic so no one would see you.'

'That's pretty good. What else do you know?'

'Nothing. All I have is questions. You called me the night I got the summons in the mail, said you had received one too. You asked me if I was going to call the old man. I said no. What would've happened if I had called him?'

'Phones weren't working.'

'Why not?'

'The phone line runs into the basement. There's a loose connecting switch down there.'

Ray nodded as another little mystery was solved.

'Plus, he didn't answer it half the time,' Forrest added.

'When did you redo his will?'

'The day before he died. I found the old one, didn't like it much, so I thought I'd do the right thing and equally divide his estate between the two of us. What a ridiculous idea – an equal split. What a fool I was. I just didn't understand the law in these situations. I thought that since we are the only heirs, that we should divide everything equally. I wasn't aware that lawyers are trained to keep whatever they find, to steal from their brothers, to hide assets that they are sworn to protect, to ignore their oaths. No one told me this. I was trying to be fair. How stupid.'

'When did he die?'

'Two hours before you got there.'

'Did you kill him?'

A snort, a sneer. No response.

'Did you kill him?' Ray asked again.

'No, cancer did.'

'Let me get this straight,' Ray said, leaning forward, the cross-examiner moving in for a strike. 'You hung around for eight days, and the entire time he was stoned. Then he conveniently dies two hours before I get there.'

'That's right.'

'You're lying.'

'I assisted him with the morphine, okay? Feel better? He was crying because of the pain. He couldn't walk, eat, drink, sleep, urinate, defecate, or sit up in a chair. You were not there, okay? I was. He got all dressed up for you. I shaved his face. I helped him to the sofa. He was too weak to press the button on the morphine pack. I pressed it for him. He went to sleep. I left the house. You came home, you found him, you found the money, then you began your lying.'

'Do you know where it came from?'

'No. Somewhere on the coast, I presume. I don't really care.'

'Who burned my airplane?'

'That's a criminal act, so I know nothing.'

'Is it the same person who followed me for a month?'

'Yes, two of them, guys I know from prison, old friends. They're very good, and you were very easy. They put a bug under the fender of your cute little car. They tracked you with a GPS. Every move. Piece of cake.'

'Why did you burn the house?'

'I deny any wrongdoing.'

'For the insurance? Or perhaps to completely shut me out of the estate?'

Forrest was shaking his head, denying everything. The door opened and Allison stuck her long, angular face in. 'Everything okay in here?' she demanded.

Fine, yes, we're swell.

'Seven more minutes,' she said, then closed it. They sat there forever, both staring blankly at different spots on the floor. Not a sound from the outside.

'I only wanted half, Ray,' Forrest finally said.

'Take half now.'

'Now's too late. Now I know what I'm supposed to do with the money. You showed me.'

'I was afraid to give you the money, Forrest.'

'Afraid of what?'

'Afraid you'd kill yourself with it.'

'Well, here I am,' Forrest said, waving his right arm at the room, at the ranch, at the entire state of Montana. 'This is what I'm doing with the money. Not exactly killing myself. Not quite as crazy as everybody thought.'

'I was wrong.'

'Oh, that means so much. Wrong because you got caught? Wrong because I'm not such an idiot after all? Or wrong because you want half of the money?'

'All of the above.'

'I'm afraid to share it, Ray, same as you were.

388

Afraid the money will go to your head. Afraid you'll blow it all on airplanes and casinos. Afraid you'll become an even bigger asshole than you are. I have to protect you here, Ray.'

Ray kept his cool. He couldn't win a fistfight with his brother, and even if he could, what would he gain by it? He'd love to take a bat and beat him around the head, but why bother? If he shot him he wouldn't find the money.

'So what's next for you?' he asked with as much unconcern as he could show.

'Oh, I don't know. Nothing definite. When you're in rehab, you dream a lot, then when you get out all the dreams seem silly. I'll never go back to Memphis, though, too many old friends. And I'll never go back to Clanton. I'll find a new home somewhere. What about you? What will you do now that you've blown your big chance?'

'I had a life, Forrest, and I still do.'

'That's right. You make a hundred and sixty thousand bucks a year, I checked it online, and I doubt if you work real hard. No family, not much overhead, plenty of money to do whatever you want. You got it made. Greed is a strange animal, isn't it, Ray? You found three million bucks and decided you needed all of it. Not one dime for your screwed-up little brother. Not one red cent for me. You took the money, and you tried to run away with it.'

'I wasn't sure what to do with the money. Same as you.'

'But you took it, all of it. And you lied to me about it.'

'That's not true. I was holding the money.'

'And you were spending it – casinos, airplanes.'

'No, dammit! I don't gamble and I've been renting airplanes for three years. I was holding the money, Forrest, trying to figure it out. Hell, it was barely five weeks ago.'

The words were louder and bouncing off the walls. Allison took a look in, ready to break up the meeting if her patient was getting stressed.

'Give me a break here,' Ray said. 'You didn't know what to do with the money, neither did I. As soon as I found it, someone, and I guess that someone was either you or your buddies, started scaring the hell out of me. You can't blame me for running with the money.'

'You lied to me.'

'And you lied to me. You said you hadn't talked to the old man, that you hadn't set foot in the house in nine years. All lies, Forrest. All part of a hoax. Why did you do it? Why didn't you just tell me about the money?'

'Why didn't you tell me?'

'Maybe I was going to, okay? I'm not sure what I had planned. It's kinda hard to think clearly when you find your father dead, then you find three million bucks in cash, then you realize somebody else knows about the money and will gladly kill you for it. These things don't happen every day, so forgive me if I'm a little inexperi-enced.'

The room went silent. Forrest tapped his fingertips together and watched the ceiling. Ray had said all he planned to say. Allison rattled the doorknob, but did not enter.

Forrest leaned forward and said, 'Those two fires – the house and the airplane – you got any new suspects?'

Ray shook his head no. 'I won't tell a soul,' he said.

Another pause as time expired. Forrest slowly stood and looked down at Ray. 'Give me a year. When I get out of here, then we'll talk.'

The door opened, and as Forrest walked by, he let his hand graze Ray's shoulder, just a light touch, not an affectionate pat by any means, but a touch nonetheless. 'See you in a year, Bro,' he said, then he was gone.